THE ETHOS EFFECT

L. E. Modesitt, Jr.

TOR®

A TOM DOHERTY ASSOCIATES BOOK
NEW YORK

This is a work of fiction. All the characters and events portrayed in this book are either products of the author's imagination or are used fictitiously.

THE ETHOS EFFECT

Copyright © 2003 by L. E. Modesitt, Jr.

Edited by David G. Hartwell

A Tor Book
Published by Tom Doherty Associates, LLC
175 Fifth Avenue
New York, NY 10010

www.tor.com

Tor® is a registered trademark of Tom Doherty Associates, LLC.

ISBN-13: 978-0-7653-4712-1
ISBN-10: 0-7653-4712-1

First Edition: October 2003
First Mass Market Edition: December 2004

Printed in the United States of America

0 9 8 7 6 5 4

In memoriam

For Eric Maier, who always understood the eternal
nature of the struggle shown in life and in this
story, with both heart and mind

COMMANDER

Chapter 1

Two officers sat side by side in the cramped command couches of the RSFS *Fergus* as the light cruiser accelerated away from the Galway system. The younger officer, a dark-haired woman with blue eyes and pale white skin, wore the double silver bars of a first lieutenant on the collar of her green shipsuit and the embroidered antique silver wings of a junior pilot on its chest. The older officer, a green-eyed, black-haired, sharp-featured man with skin the color of aged fine oak, wore the silver leaves of a commander, with the command star, and the wings of a senior pilot. Below the wings were the faded characters of his name—Van C. Albert.

"Dust density?" asked Van.

"Point three and steady,
Commander."

"What does that mean, Lieutenant Moran?" Van's implant continued to show minute fluctuations in the density readings, fluctuations that came from the ship systems, not the dust beyond the hull and shields. While the gravs could theoretically handle accelerations as high as eight while maintaining a steady one gee within the ship, Van kept the acceleration at three solid gees. Anything more created unnecessary strain on the systems for a vessel as old as the *Fergus*. Then, the RSFS *Fergus* should have been retired or rebuilt decades earlier, he reflected, not that she hadn't been a good cruiser for her time, but the newer Argenti cruisers wouldn't take that long to turn her shields to shreds, and even some of the recently commissioned Revenant cruisers were getting to that point. The Eco-Tech ships were roughly equivalent to those of the Argentis, but no one wanted to fight an Eco-Tech pilot, not the way they were modified, trained, and linked to their ships.

"We could fold nets and jump, ser. The coordinates for Leynstyr are set."

"Would you recommend that, now?"

"No, ser."

"Why not?"

"If we wait until the density drops below three, we can make the jump with twenty percent less power."

"How do you know it will drop that far?" pursued Van.

"It does in most systems, ser."

"How long would you wait to see?"

"That would depend, ser. If we needed to jump, I wouldn't wait. Now . . . the collectors are running in the green . . . another ten minutes."

Standing wave message for you, ser. The words burned across the shipnet to Van from the comm officer, Sub-major Parnell.

I'll take it, now. While still monitoring the *Fergus*'s telltales, Van shifted his concentration to focus on the incoming message. It was short. Given the enormous power requirements, even with compressions, all standing wave messages were short—and urgent. Nothing short of urgency could justify their use and cost.

Proceed soonest to Gotland, Scandya system, to replace RSFS *Collyns*, FFA. Orders arriving Gotland via courier . . .

The authentication codes indicated that the message had come directly from the Chief of Space Operations at Republic Space Force headquarters on Tara. Van had no idea why the CSO was rerouting the *Fergus* to Gotland, right in the middle of transit from Galway to their assigned picket station off Leynstyr. The *Muir* had already been on station off Leynstyr for all too long.

"Lieutenant . . ." Van shifted his attention back to the junior pilot. "What are the accumulator reserves right now? What will they be in ten and fifteen minutes, assuming a standard density drop-off?"

"Ser . . . let me check."

Van waited, still trying to figure out the reasons for the change in orders, then flashing back to Parnell. *Did you double-check the authentications?*

Yes, ser. They were red over green priority, ser.

Van tightened his lips. Red over green meant trouble. At least, it always had. But why send the *Fergus*, old and creaky as she was?

"Ser . . . I see what you mean," offered Moran from the second pilot's couch.

"Tell me. Don't just tell me that you understand."

Moran stiffened, then spoke. "The accumulators aren't fully charged. It will take about eight minutes from now. We'd come out of jump with less than full power for shields or acceleration. In a combat situation—"

"Good!" Van forced a smile. "You've got it. The way things are now, you don't ever want to come out of a jump underpowered—not if you can help it. I'd like to spend more time on that, but we've got to make some adjustments, Lieutenant. We've had a change in orders. Reconfigure for a jump transit to the Scandya system. Then, let me check the setup and coordinates."

"Ah . . . yes, ser."

"We just received a standing wave message from the CSO, ordering us to Gotland with all due haste."

"Yes, ser." Moran paused. "Gotland, ser? Scandya system?"

"That's affirm."

While Lieutenant Moran calculated, Van called up what

background the shipnet had on Scandya, skimming through the data as quickly as he could.

Scandya system . . . orange five, plus six, trailing arm [O11145 Rel Galactic Center] . . . two planets with significant population: Gotland @ .93 Tellurian norm, 1.02 G at sea level . . . atmospherics within acceptability for nonmods . . . Malmot @ .72 Tellurian norm, .65 G . . . atmospherics at limit of acceptability [basic terraforming completed 1104 N.E.] . . .

Government . . . modified rep. republic, universal adult suffrage. Nonstandard meritocracy overrides . . . continent-based, single-house, parliamentary assembly, planetary executive with veto power, all executive functions operated and executed at planetary level, limited bureaucracy . . . two principal political parties, the Liberal Commons (LC) and the Conservative Democrats (CD) . . . considerable unrest, with local riots, for the past half century, until the election of the present premier [Erik Gustofsen (CD)] . . . skilled at mediating conflicts . . .

What in Moll Magee was a "nonstandard meritocracy override"? Van had never seen that terminology in a background section. And what had been the sources of the past unrest? Most planetary systems were well beyond that kind of dissent.

Economic . . . postextractive, belt-mining, and low nanoformulation technology . . . also large natural food sector . . .

Military . . . universal military service [unisex] . . . ground and planetary defense rated superior . . . in-system space defense limited capability . . . ten corvettes [equiv. *Robartes* class] and two cruisers [equiv. *Gregory* class]. No dreadnoughts or battle cruisers. No outspace fixed emplacements . . .

Van paused and rescanned the military data. Effectively, the Scandyans had no real defenses against out-system attacks. The universal military service meant that Gotland and Malmot could be destroyed, or, rather life on both planets could be, but that neither could be conquered—*if* the Scandyans maintained their resolve.

Political . . . Scandya system is the closest nonaligned inhabited system to Tymuri [orange five point five, plus six, trailing arm (O11157 Rel Galactic Center)] . . . Revenant "missionary" training base . . .

Van called up the multidimensional image of Orange sector, then zeroed in on Scandya system, as depicted in the shipnet representation. As he had suspected, Gotland and Malmot were the last nonaligned planets between the "outer" inspin systems affiliated with the Taran Republic and the Revenant systems. "Below" and "inward" of both lay the far larger Argenti Commonocracy, although the Argentis were really oligarchs of the old style.

. . . at present, during the government headed by Gustofsen, Scandyans are maintaining open trade and have requested that other systems respect their neutrality by maintaining no military presence in the Scandya system. "No military presence" has been defined as one military vessel and one courier . . .

The *Collyns* was a full battle cruiser, the first of the latest class. So why was the *Fergus*, antiquated by comparison, being sent to Scandya? Had something happened to the *Collyns*? Or had the *Collyns* been ordered out into some action against the Revenants, and the RSF needed a presence off Gotland?

The standing wave hadn't said, for the obvious reason that standing wave was open to anyone, and, even with encryption, there was the possibility of the message being decoded. That meant that one Commander Van Albert had to read between the words of the message.

"Calculations complete and on the net, ser," reported Lieutenant Moran.

"Thank you, Lieutenant." Van scanned, then checked her work. "Good. As soon as the accumulators are fully charged, you may begin the countdown for jump."

"Yes, ser."

The *Fergus* replacing a full battle cruiser in a pivot system at a time of increasing interstellar tensions? Van kept his frown to himself. While a full battle cruiser carried a crew of fifteen, the *Fergus* carried but ten—the commander, two other pilots, the comm officer, the engineer, two system techs, the weapons officer, and two weapons techs—and all were loaded down with auxiliary duties, most of which revolved around some aspect of maintenance on the aging *Fergus*.

"All hands, stow all loose items. Batten down all equipment. One minute to zero gee. One minute to zero gee. Three minutes to jump." Lieutenant Moran's voice filled both the shipnet and the ship's speakers.

After scanning the prejump checklist, and the shipnet reports from each station, the lieutenant glanced at the commander. "All stations secure for zero gee, ser. Ready to collapse photon nets."

"Commence zero gee. Collapse photon nets."

Eeeeeee! The piercing wail of the zero-gee alarm filled the *Fergus*, then cut off.

"Entering zero gee," Moran announced. "All hands remain secured. Two minutes to jump. I say again. Two minutes to jump."

Van checked the screens, extending himself into the webs that drew in all the Energy Distortion Indications from the entire Galway system, trying to see if he could detect any EDI sources. There should not have been any, except for the single orbit station around Galway three, the one conducting and monitoring the terraforming project that, in a few hundred years, might yield another habitable water world for the Taran Republic. Even with the detectors set at full gain, he could find nothing, and closed them down.

"All detectors null, Lieutenant."

"Detectors null, ser. Photon nets null."

"Proceed to countdown, Lieutenant."

"All hands. One minute to jump. I say again. One minute to jump." Moran's voice echoed through the *Fergus*.

Van watched as she shut down every operating system, one right after the other. Gravity had already gone. Ventilators and purifiers shut down.

At ten seconds before translation, Moran made the final announcement. "All hands. Ten seconds to jump." Then she cut off the remaining systems, including the shipnet, except for the jump generator and the accumulators.

"Ready to jump, ser."

"Proceed, Lieutenant."

Moran pressed the large red stud—the one operation that was *always* manual.

Everything turned inside out. The blackness of the control area turned white. Van felt as though he'd been twisted inside out, or at least into some strange dimension, for that instant that seemed endless, yet remained unmeasurable by any device ever invented.

A searing flash of light and darkness, darkness and light, flared through the *Fergus*, and the jump was complete.

"Powering up, ser." Moran's fingers brought up the shipnet, and then her net commands brought all the systems back on-line, beginning with shields and nets.

The moment the detectors were back on-line, and the comparators verified that they were indeed on the fringes of Scandya system, with less than two hours of translation error, Van began to search the detector screens, wondering what he might find.

One scan and Van stiffened. Less than fifty emkay—out-system and "behind" them—was the EDI track of something bearing down on the *Fergus*.

"I have the conn!" Van triggered the emergency siren and diverted power from all nonvital systems into the photon nets, the drives, and shields, immediately turning the *Fergus* into the oncoming ship—a heavy cruiser of some sort with distorted EDI tracks. Or an EDI of some type he'd never seen.

Torps inbound! came from Weapons.

Van caught four on the net monitors and put full power into the shields, letting the photon nets fade. Standard shields were supposed to hold against three. Not against four, and certainly not the old shields of the *Fergus*.

"Desensitizing."

All the screens and detectors went blank.

Even so, Van could feel the wash of energy against the shipnet. As it subsided, he opened the detectors, shifted power to the nets, and continued to build acceleration toward the unknown cruiser.

More torps!

Got them! There were two.

Van shifted power to the shields, but left enough for nets and screens to keep building speed and collecting hydrogen and dust—or before long he wouldn't have any mass for the fusactor at the rate of power he was using.

Again, he waited until milliseconds before the expected impact before desensitizing, then shifted full power to the nets for a long moment. What he planned was a gamble, but the *Fergus* couldn't stand too many more torp impacts against its weaker screens—certainly what the attacker was counting on.

The courses weren't collision-based, but close enough for Van's purposes, especially against a newer vessel, and the *Fergus* continued to accelerate outward, the photon nets growing and gathering hydrogen and other various bits of dust that would become reaction mass for the fusactor.

Any ID on bogey?

No, ser.

With less than a minute before CPA, Van watched and waited, feeling the sweat pouring from his forehead despite the chill in the cockpit.

Then, even as Weapons announced, *Torps!*, Van diverted full power to the nets, squeezing them forward and hurling dust and hydrogen at the oncoming cruiser. Nearly simultaneously, he released two torps, and then a second set of two, even as he slewed the *Fergus* across the path of the attacker, and then cut all power to everything and diverted all power to the shields, desensitizing the ship as well.

Eeeeeeee! The EMP bled in over the damped equipment, and the *Fergus* actually rocked for an instant.

Van smiled, coldly.

After another five hundred milliseconds, he extended the screens and detectors.

They revealed a hot and rapidly expanding ball of gas, and several irregular fragments of metal.

Comm . . . any indications of who that was?

No, ser. Didn't match any profile. EDI could have been off-tuned rev. Shields were close to Keltyr . . .

Van opened the photon nets to let them rebuild mass, then swung the *Fergus* back in-system, slowly and sluggishly on what power and mass remained to the *Fergus*.

He scanned what lay inward. The EDI traces from in-system—well in-system—indicated a battle cruiser orbiting Gotland, next to a large orbital station, and the colors suggested strongly that the vessel was Revenant. A smaller EDI came in shortly, a Taran courier, probably the one with detailed orders from the CSO for the *Fergus*. There were two other light cruisers stationed where they could open fire on the Revenant cruiser, and the EDI traces suggested they were the Scandyan cruisers. The only other non-Scandyan vessel was a frigate—Argenti from what Van could tell—also orbiting Gotland.

There was no sign of the *Collyns*.

Van blotted his forehead and turned to Moran. "You have the conn, Lieutenant. Take her for now. Maintain half shields."

"Yes, ser. I have it. Maintaining half shields."

Van cleared his throat, then began to speak, also forming the message for the shipnet, for those linked there. "All hands. This is the commander. We just fought off an attack by an unknown cruiser, and we are entering the Scandyan system. Just before jump we received urgent orders to divert here, then proceed to Gotland, the fourth planet, where we are to receive more detailed orders. We are replacing the battle cruiser *Collyns*. Right now, that's all I know, but we'll keep you informed as we can. That is all."

Weapons status? Van snapped across the shipnet to Lieutenant Mitchel.

Twenty-one torps left, ser.

Thanks, Weapons. Engineer?

Fusactor's close to the heat limit, ser. Port rear quadrant shield is almost amber. Starboard converter is running at eighty.

Thanks.

"Ser?" asked Moran. "Who . . . was that a Rev ship? Or Argenti? And why did they come after us? It's not like we're trying to take over anyone else's systems."

"I don't know, Lieutenant. None of the IDs match. The drive EDIs were altered—or they belong to a system we've never heard of, and the torp traces were so standard that it could have been anyone. And they didn't bother to tell us who they were."

"Ser . . . I'd heard of . . . what you did . . ."

"But how did I know how to do it?" Van laughed, harshly. "That's what commanders are for. You learn your ship, what she can do, what she can't. The *Fergus* doesn't have shields like the newer cruisers, but the photon nets and the collectors were overengineered. That was because of the inefficiency of converters when she was built. They didn't bother to change the nets when she was refitted ten years back. That's why there's an intake governor."

"I've never seen anyone squeeze the nets that way."

"Except for something like that, you don't want to. We lost close to twenty percent of one converter and nearly overheated the fusactor. I'll probably have to answer for that as well. But it was the only way . . . what I did was use all the matter in the nets to overload their shields. Shields don't care whether what's coming at them is gas and dust or a torp. The total mass load is what matters. Mass times velocity. I accelerated the mass in the nets, then let the torps punch through." Van paused. "It won't work in a fight against more than one, maybe two ships, because you're basically limited to the power in the accumulators and mass tanks until you can deploy the nets again, and your shields are likely to fail before you can."

"Oh . . ."

Commander Van Cassius Albert leaned back in the command couch. In less than an elapsed standard hour, he and the *Fergus* had gone from heading to a routine picket station in the quietest part of the Taran Republic into a battle in a pivot system. They'd been attacked by an unknown heavy cruiser, almost as if they'd been expected. The *Fergus* was headed inward to a system that its commander didn't know for a purpose he also didn't know, and orders he could only guess at. Van studied the detectors once more, then ran a check on all the ship systems once more, although he doubted he'd find more than the engineer and weapons officer had found.

Still . . . he'd have to draft a battle report and dispatch it by message torp back to RSF headquarters. He could do that in the twenty-odd hours it would take them to reach Gotland.

His lips curled into an ironic smile. After all the years in service, he still found it amusing that ships could jump between systems near-instantaneously, and yet getting to the jump corridors took hours, if not days. Then, jumps avoided the light-speed limits, which even the most powerful photon drive systems could not.

He took a slow and deep breath before beginning to use the shipnet to draft his report.

Chapter 2

While much has been written about so-called crises of faith in the life cycle of individuals, what is seldom recognized, and even when so recognized, usually dismissed, is that societies also undergo crises of faith.

A societal crisis of faith occurs when the values that produced a particular incarnation of a society no longer correspond to the values held by the individuals and organizations holding economic, political, and social power in that society. Paradoxically, these value changes *seem* to occur first on a social level. In reality the changes are already far advanced by the time they appear, because in most societies social standing and mobility lag behind economic and political power. Those with economic power seldom wish to flaunt values at variance with social norms, and those in the political arena prefer a protective coloration that in fact straddles the perceived range of values, while ostensibly preferring the most popular of values. . . .

Although all stable societies rest firmly on a consensus of values, invariably the individuals in those societies prefer not to discuss those values, except in glittering generalities, not because they are unimportant, but because they are so important that to discuss them seriously might open them to question and reinterpretation. Thus, the very protections of a society's values preclude any wide-scale and public reevaluation of those values and any recognition of a potential crisis of values.

Since "morality" is the sum total of those values, the first public symptom of a crisis of values is usually a series of comments about the growing immorality of society—almost always directed at the young of a society who have absorbed what their elders are in fact doing, rather than professing. . . .

Values, Ethics, and Society
Exton Land
New Oisin, Tara
1117 S.E.

Chapter 3

The messroom was an oblong box, barely four meters in length and three in width, the bulkheads covered with a permaplast finish that was supposed to resemble walnut, with a table and benches that, in a pinch, might seat all of the crew. The overhead was an off-white that imitated plaster poorly and gave an impression of dinginess, no matter how often it was cleaned. The deck was covered with a permaplast supposed to resemble gray ceramic tile in a diamond pattern. All the furnishings were anchored firmly to the deck.

Van sat at the head of the table, in the sole chair, sipping the strong black café he favored from a dull black mug. On his right was Sub-commander Forgael, the executive officer and chief pilot, dark circles under her eyes. On Van's left was Sub-major Driscoll, the engineer.

Driscoll had just finished reading the hard copy draft of the battle report, and he slid it back across the table. "It's accurate, Commander."

"But too blunt?"

"No, it's not," replied Forgael. "Everything in there is factual. HQ won't like the fact that an unknown battle cruiser attacked a Taran ship, and they'll send a raft of queries that will suggest that it can't be unknown and that either you aren't interpreting the systems data correctly, or that you've neglected updating the recognition parameters."

"So I need to point out that I.S. updated both just before we left Sligo Station?" Van laughed. "Then they'll find some other way to suggest I screwed up."

"You did, ser," Driscoll replied dryly. "The only thing worse than losing a ship to an attack is to destroy the attacker, especially with an older cruiser that shouldn't win. It's worse if we need repairs, because they'll have to fund them."

Forgael winced.

Van took another swallow of café and nodded. "The Home party will claim that it shows we don't need more and newer ships, and the Liberals will insist that it demonstrates that RSF officers are bloodthirsty rock apes who torp innocents on sight. And the Marshal's Council won't be happy either way." Especially not with Commander Van Cassius Albert.

"I don't see who had anything to gain." Forgael smiled. "I didn't express that quite correctly. Who didn't have something to gain, I meant."

The three officers nodded, almost simultaneously, although none spoke.

Everyone would have gained something with the loss of the *Fergus*—except the commander and crew. The Taran Republic would have gotten rid of a near-obsolete ship and a difficult commander, as well as have obtained a demonstration of why newer and better ships were needed. Both the Argentis and the Revenants could have blamed each other for escalating border tensions, and gained political and popular support. The Eco-Tech Coalition could have breathed a sigh of relief that they wouldn't have to fight another war against the Revenants. Scandya could have played everyone off against each other.

But . . . with the success of the *Fergus*, the whole situation merely degenerated into a problem and embarrassment for everyone. The RSF would be blamed for having a torp-happy commander going off uncontrolled, and all the others risked either embarrassment for incompetence or for lack of knowledge about the situation. Even the Scandyans wouldn't be happy, not when an obsolete cruiser potted an intruder outside their own system, suggesting that one antique cruiser was more effective than the entire Scandyan space force.

Van rose. "Thank you both. I'll need to make some changes before I send this off." He took the cup to the adjoining galley, where he emptied it, racked it in its place, turned and left the galley, then the mess. As he eased into the main passageway fore and aft, behind him, he could just catch the whispers.

"You don't think it was an accident . . ."

"With the commander . . . after the *Regneri* incident? . . . planned as potted palms . . ."

That was what Van thought as well, but he said nothing as he walked the few meters forward to the cubicle he rated as commander. There he revised the battle report, then fed it into the message torp.

He accessed the shipnet, linking to Lieutenant Moran. *Lieutenant?*

Yes, Commander?

I'm about to release a message torp to RSF Depot. Report on our encounter entering the system. Just wanted you to know.

Yes, ser. I'll log it.

Van keyed the release, then monitored the torp from the shipnet until it jumped and translated back toward the depot off Sligo Station.

Then he stretched out on the narrow bunk. He hoped he could sleep before he had to relieve Lieutenant Moran on the controls.

They had another eighteen hours before they reached Gotland. By then, the message torp would have reached the RSF Depot, and the marshal and his council would begin to decide what to do with the *Fergus* and her commander.

Chapter 4

In the darkness of the damped cockpit, Van continued to scan the passive inputs from the detectors, waiting, watching. The lieutenant in the couch beside him said nothing.

A line of light, merely a representation of a lase-search, swept across the virtual repscreen toward Van and the ship.

Detection probable. Detection probable.

"I know that," muttered Van to himself. "It's what they think we are that counts, not that we're here."

Detection probability at unity.

Van ignored the shipnet warning. His shields were down. Playing like an inert hunk of metallic asteroid was far safer than broadcasting his presence with their energy field. The converted terraforming vessel—a ship that amounted to a heavy cruiser—could crush his shields as if they didn't exist with its particle beams and torps. He still had no idea what the renegade *Vetachi* was doing where it was—or why. But he had to do something because it was bearing down on the colony ship that lay in-system of Van.

Detection probability at unity.

Waiting in the darkened and damped cockpit, sweating, Van took in all the data as the larger vessel swept toward him.

Then, in the moment when his ship was between the inner and outer shields of the attacker, he triggered off his torps, in sets of two, as fast as he could—then lifted shields and accelerated.

The huge ship, seemingly looming over the corvette in the out-system darkness, shuddered as the third and fourth torps actually penetrated the hull.

Then . . . torps and debris flared everywhere.

Van watched, openmouthed, as an errant torp flared toward the *Regneri*, and as the colony ship split into fragments . . .

"NOOO!!!"

Van bolted upright in his bunk, almost cracking his head against the low overhead. His heart was racing, and his body was covered with sweat.

Ten years, and he still had nightmares about it. The Board of Inquiry had exonerated him, even recommended him for a commendation in taking out the raider, probably a Revenant "black" ship, but the commendation hadn't happened. No one wanted to commend a corvette jockey whose actions had cost the lives of three hundred highly trained colonists—even if it had been a freak accident that couldn't have been duplicated if the situation had been replicated a hundred times.

From then on he'd received one difficult assignment after another. After the Inquiry, it had been the *Gortforge*, the last of the *Niamh* class, with an entirely new and green crew because the former officers and crew had been court-martialed for refusing to fire on the Keltyr merchanter carrying the escaping rebels of Coole. After reading the report, Van had sympathized with the crew, since more than three-quarters of those on board the *Bonnie Prince* had been women and children. The Marshal's Council doubtless hadn't seen it that way, because the rebels had been Keltyr sympathizers who had destabilized Coole so much that riots still occasionally broke out.

After he'd completed two tours on the old *Gort*, and after RSF had decided to retire the ultralight cruiser, he'd been given command of the *Fergus*, yet another ship plagued with problems. Except there hadn't been any in the two years he'd been commander.

Sitting in his bunk, still sweating, Van blotted himself dry, then stretched back out, hoping he could sleep. After a while he did doze off, without nightmares, but with disturbing dreams he couldn't quite remember when he woke.

He climbed back up into the cockpit, after a small meal—breakfast, he supposed—bolstered with the evil-tasting Sustain.

Forgael slipped out of the command couch with a grace that Van had always admired and envied. Her smile was as ironic as ever, but then, given that she was a good ten years older than Van, with a solid record that had never been adequately rewarded, the irony was more than understandable to him.

"Nothing new, Commander. The Rev cruiser hasn't moved. EDI suggests stand-down. The Argentis are headed out-system, but not along our corridor. They're pushing it, looks like a solid two-gee acceleration."

"You think they had something to do with that cruiser?" Van eased into the command couch and took over the screens and net.

"No. I'd bet either Rev or Keltyr. Kelts would still like to make us pay, and the Revs want Scandya system."

"The Argentis are heading home to spread the word? Or bailing out before they get embroiled?"

"Both," she replied.

Van nodded.

"I'd estimate another thirty minutes to switchover. Not enough to get any sleep."

"No. Not much."

Thirty-seven minutes passed before the *Fergus* neared the restricted area off Gotland. By then, Lieutenant Moran had taken her place in the second couch, since two pilots were required prior to and after translation and when nearing restricted spaces.

"Switchover checklist," Van ordered.

"Nets and collectors to ten percent," Moran stated.

"Stet."

"Detectors to full sensitivity . . ."

Once the checklist was complete, Van swept the area in-system before the *Fergus*, one last time, because once the *Fergus* shut down her nets in so close to Scandya's sun, he'd be limited to the power in the accumulators. He was also limited to the fractional gee power of the unaugmented ionjets. The detectors only showed the Scandyan ships, the Rev battle cruiser, still in stand-down, and the RSF courier.

Van checked the ship systems again. The starboard converter was still only at eighty-five, a trace better than after the encounter out-system, but not good enough for another fight or sustained high-speed in-system operations. The port rear quadrant shield was out of the amber, but by so little that it might as well have been amber. Any significant strain—even a small chunk of space debris—would probably blow the shield.

"Switching over," Van announced.

The *Fergus* continued to creep—or so it seemed—toward Gotland orbit control.

"Gotland orbit control, this is RSFS *Fergus*, inbound from Galway. Request orbit clearance."

"Stet, *Fergus*. Request duration of orbit."

Van thought for a moment. That was hard to say, but he'd never been parked anywhere for more than a standard week. On the other hand, he didn't know how long it would take Sub-major Driscoll to repair the damaged converter and shield generator—if he and his techs even could.

"Orbit control, estimate three weeks. Maintenance required."

"*Fergus*, request purpose of visit, and payment method for services."

"Orbit control, purpose is maintenance, port call, and message pickup. Payment method is intersystem credit transfer, Taran military subset."

"Stet, *Fergus*." The slightest pause followed. "Interrogative excessive EMP in outer system."

"Orbit control . . . source of excessive EMP noted, but *Fergus* was unable to determine source." That much was true.

"*Fergus* . . . Scandyan System Defense Force requests any additional data you have on source. At your convenience."

"Stet, orbit control. If we have any data, will send." He wasn't about to give the Scandyans the data and report he'd dispatched to RSF HQ. "Request lock assignment."

"*Fergus*, your lock is Orange three."

"Orbit control, understand Orange three. We have the beacon."

It was almost an hour later when the *Fergus* slipped into the dampers.

"Orbit control, *Fergus* is secure. Request power changeover."

"Lock crew has it, *Fergus*. Welcome to Gotland."

"Orbit control, thank you." Van wasn't so certain he'd be welcome. He took the fusactors off-line. The cockpit lights dimmed, then brightened as station power—and full one-gee gravity—filled the *Fergus*. Van eased out of the command couch. The back of his shipsuit was damp, as it always was. And now, he'd have to deny having any data. The Scandyans couldn't force it from him, and RSF certainly didn't want him to provide it to anyone.

Chapter 5

After the *Fergus* had locked in to Gotland orbit station, Van had undertaken a thorough postflight and systems check. That had taken hours. After that, he'd approved the crew rotation for both maintenance duties and release time aboard the orbit control station. Then, back in his cabin, he'd written up his notes on maintenance requirements.

With those in hand, he and Major Driscoll had met and decided on what actually could be done—such as repairing the converter and the ailing shield generator—while they were at Gotland orbit control, and as they waited for whatever orders might be headed their way. No such orders had arrived during the next day, but it had taken them almost the entire day to track down the contract maintenance chief of the orbit station, and another half day to work out the arrangements.

Then, once those details had been settled, he and Driscoll had returned to the *Fergus*, and Van had begun writing the maintenance request report that he was required to dispatch back to RSF HQ. HQ would be less than pleased with the projected costs of the repairs, but they'd have no choice but to approve them, since, if anything happened to the *Fergus*, no one would want to explain that maintenance had been denied.

He'd worked on that less than an hour when he was interrupted again.

Commander, there's a Commander Baile here to see you, ser. RSF commander, I mean, ser, came from Shennen, the female head comm tech, standing quarterdeck watch.

I'll be right there. Van closed off the small console in the corner of the cubicle that served as cabin and office and stood, moving toward the midships lock.

I'll tell him, ser. Shennen's net presence seemed melodic, unlike that of Parnell, who always seemed nasal, or Driscoll, who rumbled.

Thanks. What did the commander want? Van wasn't even aware that there was an RSF commander in Scandya system, unless he happened to be the military attaché to the Taran embassy. He certainly couldn't be the commanding officer of the RSFS *Aherne*—the courier that had just locked at the station, presumably with orders for the *Fergus*. Courier pilots were always either senior lieutenants or sub-majors, usually women, because couriers were two-person ships, pilot and tech, with cramped space for no more than two passengers. They were ships built around beefed-up propulsion systems for high acceleration in-system and precision jump translations. Compact female pilots generally handled the acceleration and the cramped quarters better than men.

Van slipped from his cabin and dropped back along the ten meters of the main fore and aft passageway past the mess and galley to the two-meter-square quarterdeck—essentially the space inboard of the crew docking lock.

The commander who waited with Shennen was trim, half a head shorter than Van, and with lustrous gray hair. While his face was thin, he bore no wrinkles, and his eyes looked almost youthful.

"Commander," offered Van.

"Commander James Baile." He inclined his head to Van. "We need to talk."

"My cabin."

Baile nodded. "That would be fine."

As they walked forward, Baile added, "I just arrived on the *Aherne*."

A cold feeling settled in Van's gut. "Then you know what happened here?"

"I read your battle report on the way out. The marshal thought I should be fully briefed."

Van liked the sound of that even less, and said nothing until he closed the hatch to his cabin. He didn't bother to offer a chair, since there was only one. "What can I do for you?"

"I'm the one CSO tasked to deliver your orders."

"Orders?" Van had orders being delivered personally? Why? Because he'd destroyed the unknown cruiser? How could anyone have even known about that at RSF headquarters before his torp arrived? How could they have even found a replacement in something like forty-eight standard hours?

Baile extended a dark gray envelope. "You ought to read them before we talk."

Van took the envelope, eased open the seal, and began to read. Then he read them again, finally focusing in on the key words.

> . . . temporary duty as RSF liaison to ambassador of Tara to Scandya on Gotland . . . detached immediately . . . estimated duration of duty not to exceed twelve standard months . . .

Van finally looked up at the older commander. "Do you have any idea—"

"Why the CSO is sending a junior commander as a military liaison to the ambassador while a senior commander takes over his command?" Baile laughed ruefully. "It ought to be the other way around. Right?"

"I don't know what to think." Van had thought a great deal, and quickly, but none of it was anything he wanted to express. "Can you give me any idea what this is all about?"

"I also have a briefing cube for you. I don't know its contents. What I think is only an educated guess . . ." Baile quirked his lips. "Tensions have been high in this sector. The *Fergus* was attacked. We can't afford to station a squadron near Scandya, and the Scandyans won't let us base one here. Because there wasn't any evidence, except through the detector screens of the *Fergus* and the torp message you sent, what happens if the Revs or the Argentis or the Kelts claim that you attacked them?"

The whole idea of the antiquated *Fergus* attacking anything seemed ludicrous to Van, but what seemed absurd in the cockpit wasn't always seen as such by the various Arm governments.

"They could claim that you attacked a merchanter or a corvette on a peaceful approach."

"So I've been relieved by a more experienced officer?"

"Actually, my presence sends two messages, Commander. First, it's a way of saying, between the words, that New Oisin thinks you were right, and second, by putting a more senior officer in charge of the *Fergus*, that the RSF has no intention of backing down."

"And the marshal can also claim that the RSF certainly doesn't want to escalate matters, and that's why a more senior commander has taken over command of the *Fergus*."

"Exactly."

"Why am I being detached as a liaison officer here?"

"Again, I would have to guess . . ."

Van doubted that there was any guessing at all, but "guessing" allowed deniability.

"First, because you come from Sulyn, you speak Old Anglo, and Revenant and Kelt are both variants of Old Anglo. You also speak Hispyn fluently. Second, you're not known outside of the RSF. Both the Revs and the Argentis keep dossiers on officers likely to command capital ships or be posted to diplomatic assignments. Third, you look younger than you are. Fourth, you're black Taran."

Outside of the first reason, Van couldn't see that any of the others made sense, and that bothered him even more. "And you? You don't speak Old Anglo?" That was a rhetorical question, because all RSF officers did, as did most of the Republic. The question was more to express Van's irritation.

"Oh, I do. I'm from Weathe, and you can't get more Old Anglo than that." Baile's words were matter-of-fact.

"I assume they sent you with operating orders, Commander?" asked Van.

"I have those orders. They're sealed. I won't know what they are until after I relieve you."

Van nodded slowly, trying to conceal his surprise. Usually, an officer taking command was fully briefed.

"I was fully briefed on the tactical, technical, and strategic considerations of operating in and around Scandya system,"

Baile explained, "but I was told that my orders are included in the command cube."

"I see," Van replied. What that meant was that the CSO didn't want the orders known to anyone until Baile took command—even to Baile.

Baile cleared his throat.

"Yes, Commander?" asked Van.

"There is a down-shuttle to Valborg, leaving in four standard hours."

Detached immediately meant exactly that. Van nodded. "I'll be ready."

"I'll be back in about two hours. You can brief me on anything urgent then."

"Yes, ser."

After Commander Baile left the cabin, Van began to gather his gear. He still needed to tell Forgael and the rest of the crew.

Chapter 6

In less than twenty minutes, Van had changed into a set of travel greens and packed up his gear—two duffels' worth, plus a shoulder bag. Then he slipped the briefing cube into the console on the small desk that would shortly no longer be his, placing his hand in the authenticator until the console stated, "Accepted."

The holo image that appeared in the middle of the small cabin was that of a commodore whom Van did not recognize.

"Commander Van, I'm Commodore Wadding, senior advisor to the Chief of Space operations. I'm sure that you're puzzled at the suddenness of your reassignment to the embassy of the Republic in Valborg. I'd like to assure you that the marshal is not displeased with your actions. A quick analysis of the data you enclosed with your battle report suggests that the vessel was of Revenant construction, but that is all that can be said at present. Your assignment to the embassy in Valborg should not be regarded as a demotion. Successful completion of that duty will put you in line for a major command . . ."

Van frowned. A major command meant at least a battle cruiser, certainly a step up from the *Fergus*. But how could one measure successful completion of duty as a military liaison?

". . . Commander Cruachan was the previous military attaché in Valborg. He was missing for several weeks, and his body was found just a short time ago. The official report was that he had been knocked overboard while sailing alone just outside the Valborg harbor and drowned . . . You are junior for such a post, admittedly, but you are known to be quick-thinking and physically well endowed . . ."

Van tried not to bristle at the words "physically well endowed," knowing them as a code phrase.

"Normally, attachés have already had some diplomatic exposure, but we need an immediate replacement to assist Ambassador Rogh. As you may have noted from the briefing materials in the *Fergus*'s netsystem, Scandya is volatile politically, and has been held on a moderate course by the extraordinary political talents of Premier Gustofsen. It would seem that we now need an officer such as you in this post, and since you are already there in Scandya . . . Your task is both simple and difficult. You are to supervise what few intelligence activities we already have in place, and you are to report any information that might be of use to the CSO, particularly information concerning the intentions, capabilities, and actions of the Revenants, the Argentis, and especially the Keltyr . . ."

Van continued to listen to the commodore's specific charges to him, stiffening after more than several minutes of redundancies.

"You are to commit to personal internal netlink the following codes, authentications, and contacts. They will be fed only from a commander's console, so, if you are using another, please stop here, and only continue at the command console of an RSF vessel."

Van swallowed and stepped closer to the console, putting on the headset that mirrored those in the cockpit.

The data flowed into and through him, as he routed it into personal storage—as ordered.

The image of the commodore reappeared.

"If you did not commit the data, please reset and do so immediately. You have exactly twenty seconds."

Van checked the data. So far as he could tell, he had committed everything, not that he knew what it all meant.

The twenty seconds passed.

"The cube is now blank," said the holo image. "The CSO and I wish you well."

After the image faded, Van tried the cube again.

"The cube has failed," the console announced. "No information can be obtained."

Van linked into the speakers and the shipnet. "All hands. This is the commander. There will be a briefing in ten minutes in the mess. All officers and techs are requested to be personally present. During the briefing, the quarterdeck watch will secure the lock door to orbit station."

By the time he entered the mess, the nine other members of the *Fergus*'s crew had all gathered there.

"Please be seated." Van took the chair at the head of the mess table, knowing it was for the last time. Before he began his speech, he ran his eyes over each of the nine, starting with Driscoll and ending with Forgael. "Some of you have probably guessed what I'm going to tell you, but I'd prefer to make it official. I've been transferred—immediately—to become the military attaché to the Taran embassy on Gotland. Commander Baile will be arriving in a few minutes to assume command. Neither he nor I know all the details, but apparently the previous RSF attaché in Valborg died unexpectedly in a boating accident, and the CSO needed an officer with command experience." Van shrugged. "I had the fortune or misfortune to be convenient."

"This wouldn't have anything to do with the 'incident' out-system, would it, ser?" asked Sub-major Driscoll.

"Commander Cruachan died sometime back," Van pointed out. "The CSO only found out a week ago. I suspect that when we were diverted here to take over for the *Collyns*, they decided that the simplest solution was to transfer me ahead of schedule." That was partly true, at least.

"Do you know what we'll be doing, ser?" asked Forgael.

"No. Commander Baile has sealed operating orders for the *Fergus*."

"Starscut . . ." muttered someone at the end of the table.

Shennen's lips tightened, but she said nothing.

A Commander Baile is at the lock, announced the shipnet. *Someone will be right there,* Van link-replied.

"The commander is here," Van said. "Any last questions?"

The mess was silent.

Van rose and left them, leaving the mess and reaching the quarterdeck in a few strides. There, he opened the lock.

Baile stood there with one slim duffel and a shoulder bag.

"Welcome aboard, Commander. I was briefing everyone on the change of command."

"You finished that?"

"Just as you arrived." Through the net, Van could sense Forgael, and he half turned. "Commander Baile, this is Sub-commander Forgael."

"Pleased to meet you, ser," replied Forgael pleasantly.

"I'm looking forward to working with all of you." Baile's words and smile were both warm and youthful-sounding.

Van envied the warmth, for he'd never had that quality. After a moment, he said, "We'd better get on with the change in command."

"Lead on, Commander," Baile said.

Van did, turning left off the quarterdeck and making his way forward to his cabin.

The two stepped inside, and Baile set down the duffel, looking to Van. Van stepped to the console and placed his hand in the authenticator. *Change of command.*

Insert new CO's cube.

Commander Baile inserted his cube into the commander's console.

Accepted, subject to approval of Commander Van, the shipnet announced.

Van linked with the net, running down the protocols, the codes, and the command accession protocol. All was in order.

Approved, Van stated, keying in his approval as well.

Command transferred.

Van felt suddenly isolated, as his access to the command protocols dropped away, and he could only access the shipnet in a general sense, not even so much as the most junior tech aboard the *Fergus.* "She's all yours, Commander."

"Thank you, Commander. I wish you well in Valborg." Baile smiled, professionally.

"We'll do what we can." Van slipped the shoulder bag in place, then lifted both duffels and stepped from the cabin that had been what home he had for the last two years.

The new commander of the *Fergus* followed him.

As Van neared the small quarterdeck, Forgael stepped forward. Her smile was sad. "We'll miss you, ser."

Ser—no longer commander. Despite the vague assurances of Commodore Wadding, he wondered if he would ever command another ship.

"I'll miss all of you." And he would, Forgael especially.

Then, with a salute, he stepped from the quarterdeck out into Gotland orbit station.

He had not taken three steps away from the lock when the station system intercepted him.

Inquiry? Name, destination? The stationnet "sounded" officious and obnoxious.

Van supposed that was necessary to get attention, but he politely replied with his identity, and immediate destination—shuttleport two to Valborg. He kept walking along the main corridor.

Purpose of trip to Valborg?

Take up duties at Taran embassy.

The feel of the net changed. *Commander Van . . . would you please explain?*

The previous military attaché died in a boating accident several weeks ago. I'm being transferred to take his place.

For several minutes, as Van walked by two empty lock ports, the stationnet was silent.

Please report to the out-system personnel office opposite shuttleport lock one before embarking on the Valborg shuttle. It should only take a moment, Commander.

Stet, station.

There was no response from the stationnet, not that Van had expected one.

The corridor—or thoroughfare—that linked all the lock ports was a good ten meters wide and five high. The corridor bulkheads provided planetside vistas that changed in real time, presumably scenes from Gotland, although Van did not know that. He walked down a projected street that ran between gray stone buildings, with rust-colored tile roofs. The lighting suggested early morning, with long shadows.

He passed a replica of a café of some sort, but only two women in uniforms he did not recognize were seated at a table under a holo umbrella. By the time Van had walked another two hundred meters along the gently curving corridor, less than a twentieth the circumference of the station, the scene had changed. Ahead, on the bulkhead to his right, was a vista that looked seaward across a small fishing harbor. To his left were warehouses set back from piers.

When he left the locking areas, the scenes vanished, replaced by arches containing various establishments—a cantina whose flashing holo sign advertised every legal beverage in the Galaxy, a bookseller whose far more discreet sign claimed the ability to load any published work into any reader used in the tech worlds, a clothing shop that suggested the traveler stop and obtain the proper wear for the culture ahead.

Van smiled. Military shipsuits and uniforms were standard enough anywhere, and accepted as such.

Another three hundred meters finally brought him to the section of the station devoted to the planetary shuttles—just three locks, as opposed to the number available at an orbit station for a larger system such as Tara, where there were eight locks, half busy at once.

His destination was clearly marked by the flashing red banner above the inboard archway opposite shuttle lock one: EMPLOYMENT CLEARANCE—OUT-SYSTEM ORIGIN. With a smile in place, Van stepped through the archway. His implants easily picked up the scan from the concealed detectors. To his right, a burly man was gesturing at the gray-clad Scandyan entry control officer. "I tell you, I *do* have an exim permit!"

"Just come this way, ser. If you please. We'll straighten this out in no time." The Scandyan entry control officer smiled pleasantly.

"You're not putting me away in some back room to rot! I know your kind." The man started to turn, then, abruptly, sagged where he stood.

The control officer smiled sadly. Within moments, another gray-uniformed woman appeared from somewhere inboard with a pallet-sled, and the two Scandyans loaded the inert form on the pallet. The woman eased the pallet toward the back of the entry control office.

Even without complete access to the station's protocol's and systems, Van could sense the nanite barrier that held in the sleep gas. He wanted to shake his head. Some people never understood that invisible controls were no less effective than obvious armed guards and weapons. In fact, for most people they were more effective, because when they operated people got the impression that such controls were everywhere—and that was a physical impossibility.

Van stepped to the empty console from where a tall blonde beckoned. He set down the duffels.

"Yes, ser?"

"Commander Van Albert. You requested I stop by here before taking the shuttle to Valborg." Van extended the thin datacard that doubled as his RSF ID, and also held all his public clearances and qualifications. "It's in GalStan format."

The woman took it. "Thank you, ser." She inserted the datacard in the reader, then handed it back to Van. "It should only be a moment, Commander."

Less than a minute later, she looked up, then extended a thin green card. "You're cleared. Give this to the control officer at the shuttle. You might not need it, but we never know if they always remember to update their systems when they lock in. You shouldn't need to check with us after this. I hope you enjoy your tour in Valborg." She smiled warmly. "Most officers do."

"Thank you." Van picked up his gear, turned, and left the entry control office, turning left and walking another hundred meters to shuttleport two. There, a handful of men and women sat in the synthwood straight-backed chairs in the bay outside the lock.

Van walked up to the slender man standing behind a chest-high console. "Is this where I check in for the Valborg shuttle?"

"Yes, ser. You've been through personnel?"

Van showed both datacard and the thin green card.

"I'll need those for a moment, and also an authorization of some sort for the shuttle charge."

"I can code that in," Van said, handing over the two cards.

"Right there." The shuttle clerk nodded toward the miniature console to Van's left.

Van touched the pad, then used his implant to input the authorization codes from his orders.

"You're cleared and paid for, ser. We'll be boarding in about half an hour."

"Thank you." Van nodded and picked up his gear once more, heading for one of the straight-backed chairs. There he sat down and studied those waiting, one after another, picking out several Argentis, a Kelt trader, a good dozen Scandyans of both genders and varied occupations, and four male Revenant missionaries.

After the Eco-Tech-Revenant War, and the settlement reached only because the Revenants had been visited by another prophet, most of the tech worlds had followed the Eco-Tech Coalition's example and allowed a handful of Revenant missionaries. Van had his doubts about prophets, either Taran or Revenant, but it didn't make much sense to express those doubts. He'd heard that the Revs had actually had some success in the Argenti and Keltyr systems. They'd been less successful in the Taran systems.

Finally, he settled back to wait for the boarding call.

Chapter 7

After turning his duffels and shoulder bag over to the shuttle cargo clerk, Van stepped into the windowless passenger cabin of the Valborg shuttle, taking in the center aisle, the two-by-two seating, and the relatively compact couches. Those all indicated a magshuttle, and that Gotland had a relatively strong magnetic field, meaning that it had not been terraformed—or not extensively. He checked his seat number and slipped into the couch in the third row, the one against the wall, fastening his harness and restraints.

Shortly, a junior officer in shimmering whites appeared. He paused, studied the assignments, and finally took the aisle seat beside Van.

As he took in the Revenant lieutenant, Van repressed a smile, then waited for a time.

The Rev officer did not look toward Van.

"They do put us in close together," Van offered in Old Anglo.

"It happens on magshuttles," replied the Rev.

"You on planetside leave?" Van asked politely.

"No. Duty."

Van studied the white uniform, then nodded. "Guard detachment at the embassy? Or are you a courier?"

The Rev frowned. "If you don't mind . . ."

"It doesn't matter," Van said. "I was only making conversation. I've never been planetside here. Have you?"

"Yes."

"Anything of particular note you'd recommend seeing?"

The Rev forced a smile. "The coastline north of Valborg is spectacular, especially from the crater rim of Haakon. Also, everyone says that the purple surf of Eschen is not to be believed, but I have not seen it." The Rev paused, then added, "If you will excuse me, ser, I am not much in the mood for conversation."

Van didn't push the issue. He'd made enough of a point.

"Please check your harnesses. The shuttle is separating from orbit station at this time."

The shuttle ride down from orbit station was smooth and uneventful—and quiet.

The Rev officer did not even look at Van, but kept his eyes closed all the way down until the shuttle was down and gliding toward the terminal. Then he flashed a brief smile. "I wish you well in Valborg, ser."

Before Van could reply, the Rev had turned and was hurrying off the shuttle.

"Please do not forget your baggage." The voice from the hidden speakers was female. "You will be scanned as you disembark. If there are any questions, you will be met by a port official. At times, the scanners are not as accurate as we would like. At other times, passengers may have misunderstood what is allowed onto Gotland . . ."

Van reclaimed his baggage, neither hurrying nor dawdling, and left the shuttle. He walked through the disembarkation tube, carrying his gear. After twenty meters, his implants registered scanning activity. He kept walking. He couldn't imagine that what he carried would be considered a problem. The disembarkation tube opened onto a windowless corridor ten meters wide, but less than ten meters ahead it widened into a space a good twenty meters wide, but only ten deep, fronting the automatic exit gates. The walls were of a blue-tinted marble, without carvings, pillars, or adornment of any kind.

In the last few meters before the corridor widened, a single Scandyan port official stepped forward out of the booth on the left side and beckoned to the stocky and mustached man in front of Van. "Ser, one moment, please."

"Might I ask why?" inquired the man, who wore a dark blue singlesuit, the kind favored for intersystem travel by both functionaries and the few commercial tech-travelers.

"Disembarkation scanning revealed what might be contraband in your bag, ser. We'd like to check."

"The only things I have are professional samples, and I declared those at the orbit station."

"That may be, ser. If they're on the approved list, you'll be on your way in a moment."

"I was told they were." The stocky man sighed as he offered the shoulder bag.

Neither man looked at Van as the Taran officer slipped to the left and around the pair, and then up to one of the automatic exit gates, which scanned Van, then opened.

Outside, under a covered portico supported by square pillars of the same bluish marble, a line of groundcars waited, each bearing a single silvery triangle on the roof directly above the windscreen. Each one sported a shimmering metallic finish of a different shade. The midday sunlight beyond the portico was so bright that even in the shade of the portico, the groundcars glimmered as though they had been lit from within.

Van stepped forward, behind a lithe woman in a dark gray business singlesuit. She stepped toward the first groundcar, and Van moved to the second, one with a metallic green sheen. A side bin door opened, and Van set the duffels inside, but kept the shoulder bag when he slid into the rear seat.

"Where to, ser?" asked the woman driver, not turning to look at Van.

"The embassy of the Republic of Tara. On Knutt Boulevard."

"Taran embassy, it is." The groundcar swept away from the shuttleport.

Within minutes, the vehicle was gliding noiselessly along the guideway downhill from the shuttleport toward Valborg, spread out to the east of the green hills and against the blue bay. The city itself seemed a patchwork of green areas and white stone buildings, except for the harbor, which looked to be entirely of white stone—warehouses, buildings, and piers. Even the oceangoing vessels appeared white in the brilliant sunlight.

"This is my first time in Valborg. What should I know that no one will think to tell me?"

The driver laughed. "You don't have enough time for that."

"You could start," Van suggested.

The driver nodded. After a moment, she spoke. "First thing . . . there's no place that serves authentic Scandyan food . . . and if there is, you don't want to try it. Most authentic Scandyan fare was fish bleached with chlorine, then slathered with salt and a paste that tastes like bad plaster."

"Is there any good seafood?"

"The ice crabs are good, and some places fix the giant clams pretty well. Otherwise, stick with fowl or meat. The hill quail are good."

"Anything specially worth seeing?"

"The purple surf up at Eschen, but it's best at dawn. I personally think the Cliff Spire at Kiruna is more impressive."

"Is that . . . ?" Van let the words trail off.

"That was the personal residence of Baron Byrnedot—he was the last commissioner before Scandya declared its independence from the Argentis. It's been kept exactly the way he left it on the morning that the Argenti snipers assassinated him." The driver didn't speak for a moment.

With his implants, Van could sense the incoming transmission, but not the content—just the energy flow. He glanced out of the groundcar. Immediately beyond the guideway—on each side—was a landscaped park, with winding stone walks, tall evergreens, and sculpted junipers and pfitzers. Van did not see any deciduous trees, nor any bushes. He saw only a handful of people, at widely separated intervals.

"Sorry," the driver apologized. "Just got routing for after I drop you off."

"I understand." Van paused. "I hadn't known about the assassination. Is that something that is still a problem . . . with the Argentis, I mean?"

"Not for most people. That was nearly two hundred fifty years back. Most folks worry more about the Revs these days. Not that there's been any problem, but with the Argentis in-Arm, and the Revenants out-Arm, and the two not caring for each other that much . . . well . . . you'd have to be blind and deaf not to worry some."

"There's always someone," Van temporized.

"It's been said that you Tarans don't care much for the Revs, either."

"We worry, too," Van admitted. "It's not as bad as the war years between the Eco-Techs and the Revs . . . but . . . you never know."

The driver eased the groundcar off the guideway and through a scanning gate, then onto a wide boulevard. "This is Knutt Boulevard, but the embassy is another two klicks north."

"Are there other embassies along here?"

"All of them are within a klick of the boulevard, except the Rev embassy. Theirs is at the front of their enclave to the south." She gestured at a gold-and-green building with extravagant and sweeping curves. "That's the Keltyr embassy and consulate there."

The structure certainly reflected the Kelt flamboyance, Van thought.

"Is it true?" asked the driver.

"Is what true?"

"You're a pretty senior officer, aren't you?"

"I'm a commander."

"There was another Taran commander here. He was an ocean sailor. The newstabs said he was a good one. But he drowned, didn't he?"

"That was what was reported."

"Funny that a man drowned on the calmest day of the spring."

"That wasn't reported," Van replied.

The driver shrugged. "I only know what I hear."

"What else have you heard?"

"Well . . . the Hulsfred Blues are going to win the korfball title . . ."

Van could sense a smile in her voice. "Who will come in second?" he asked.

"Who knows? Does anyone care? That's like coming in second in a war, and no one really likes that."

"No. That's true."

"Here we are." The groundcar came to a stop before a long and low white stone structure that reminded Van of the regional parliament building in Kerry. "That'll be fifteen, ser."

Van mentally fumbled with the local net access for a moment before transferring the funds.

"Thank you." The door opened.

Van stepped onto the smooth permacrete sidewalk beside the groundcar, extracting his duffels from the side bin behind the passenger section.

As he lifted his gear, the driver's window slid down. She smiled pleasantly.

"Have a good day, Commander Albert."

Van managed to smile as he stepped back. "Thank you. I appreciated the information about Valborg."

"It was nothing. You keep your eyes open, and you'll learn more in a day. There's a lot happening if you look closely." The driver closed the window and slipped away from the entry to the embassy.

"Ser?" asked the guard in the uniform of the Taran Marines.

"Commander Albert, reporting for duty." Van looked at the long structure.

"Second archway, ser," the corporal suggested.

"Thank you." Van didn't look back as he entered the

embassy. He hoped that the groundcar driver worked for Scandyan intelligence. Whoever she worked for, he'd gotten the messages. Before Van had even taken his second step into the main foyer of what was clearly the consular section of the embassy, a fresh-faced and red-haired younger man, wearing a dark gray singlesuit with narrow green pinstripes, appeared.

"Commander Albert, ser?"

"That's me."

"Sean Bulben, ser. I'm fourth secretary here." He grinned. "That means I run errands and handle grunt work for everyone. Dr. Hannigan sent me to escort you."

"Lead on, Sean." Van laughed.

"This way, ser."

Van followed Bulben past another pair of Marines and down a corridor to a ramp leading upward to a landing, where it reversed its way back to the second level. Halfway up, Van could feel the security screens, but Bulben pulsed a code, and the screens let them pass.

At the top, Bulben stopped, gesturing to his left. "All the offices of important people are up here. Yours is, too. The ambassador's is on the south end, and yours and the first secretary's are on each side. You're on the west, and he's on the east." The young diplomat turned and walked along the corridor until they reached the next-to-last doorway on the left.

Bulben opened the door, holding it as if he expected Van to enter first.

Van did, stepping into a sitting room with a couch and several armchairs.

"You can leave your things here for the moment." Bulben rapped on the inner door. "Dr. Hannigan? Commander Albert is here."

"Have him come in. You can head back down to your duties, Sean."

Bulben looked to Van, then nodded and slipped away.

In turn, Van left the duffels in the outer office, but kept the shoulder bag as he opened the inner door and stepped through the dark wooden doorway. The office beyond was no more than four meters square. The innermost wall was entirely filled with shelves containing antique printed books. The outer wall held a window more than three meters wide and two high. The wall away from the door was paneled in the same dark oak as the doorframe, the bookshelves, and the window casements, but held only a single picture—a holo of the main parliament building in New Oisin.

The bronze nameplate on the old-style table desk read— Ian Hannigan. The man who stood behind the desk was a good six centimeters shorter than Van's hundred and ninety, with black hair, a long and narrow nose between two bright blue eyes incongruously alive and cheerful in an otherwise sad and thin face.

Van closed the door, leaving his gear behind in the outer office.

"Commander Albert . . . welcome." Hannigan gestured to the chairs across from him, then sat down exactly as Van did. "Ambassador Rogh wanted to see you as soon as you arrived and after I gave you a quick briefing on the situation here." Hannigan leaned forward, resting his forearms on the polished cherry of the desk, steepling his fingers. "How much do you know about what's happening here in Scandya system?"

"Only bits and pieces," Van replied. "I was ordered to bring the *Fergus* here, and I assumed that was because the *Collyns* was dispatched elsewhere. I'd heard that the previous military attaché drowned while sailing."

"That was the official story and report. I have my doubts it was true," Hannigan said. "I don't think he ever understood how dangerous Gotland can be."

"Do you have any reason for those doubts?" asked Van.

Hannigan leaned back slightly. A wry smile appeared, then vanished. "Not a one. The commander was most cautious. It seemed unlikely, but sometimes the unlikely happens."

"If it was not an accident, who might have wanted to kill him . . . and why?"

"There's no shortage of possible perpetrators. The Revs don't like our presence here. Neither do the Keltyr. The local isolationists don't want any inside or outside military presence, and the Conservative Democrats want to arm Scandya to at least parity with us, and there's a demonstration by the partisans of one party or the other practically every month. The Argentis still believe that Scandya ought to be theirs, and that's after over two hundred years of Scandyan independence. The Eco-Tech Coalition looks down its collective nose at anyone who doesn't practice strict conservation and population control." Hannigan paused. "That's just the briefest of summaries. I have a set of datablocs for you with more detailed information."

"Are any of them angry or determined enough to assassinate a military attaché?"

"They all are. Whether they would, that's another question. Except for the Keltyr—and, of course, Scandya system itself—we're the weakest of those affected by what happens here. I've suggested to the ambassador that Commander Cruachan's death was a message."

"Or an attempt to raise tensions so that someone makes a mistake?" asked Van.

"That's another unfortunate possibility." Hannigan frowned. "I have to say that your posting here worries me. The marshal understands the ministry's concerns about an officer . . . of your inclination . . ."

Van managed to smile, hard as it was. "My reputed inclination, perhaps?"

"Unfortunately, Commander, your reputation is why you are here, and your reputation may be far more critical than your actual and present inclinations."

"Should I ask who you want destroyed?" Van let an edge creep into his voice.

Hannigan laughed, warmly. "We don't want anyone destroyed. Also, the senior military attaché ranks as a first secretary. So I couldn't order you to do anything, especially anything like that, and that would be the last thing Ambassador Rogh would want. He believes that any problem can and should be solved diplomatically."

Van nodded. Hannigan had delivered another very clear message.

"You won't have much time to get abreast of the situation, because the summer social season is about to begin."

"Summer social season?"

"In most systems, things get social in the winter. Here, the winters were so brutal that the opposite social customs evolved. Summers are most pleasant here, you'll find, if warmer than one would think from the winter."

Van nodded.

"We don't have an intelligence network here, as such, except for you, and the rest of the professional staff, but there's an in-net where those who are inclined can post data and observations."

That didn't match the background information Van had studied, but he did not say anything.

"Let's go see the ambassador." Hannigan rose.

So did Van.

"Once he's seen you, I'll have your briefing materials, and have Sean show you to your quarters in the north wing. They're quite nice."

"And yours are where?"

"In the north wing on the opposite end." Hannigan laughed, then opened the door. Van picked up his gear once more and followed.

The ambassador had an actual assistant in his outer office, an older blonde who smiled as the two men entered.

"You must be Commander Albert. I'm Meg MacDonagh, the ambassador's personal assistant."

"Ah . . . that means you're the one who runs every-thing?" Van replied with a smile. "I'm pleased to meet you."

"She runs everything except the ambassador," Hannigan added.

"Just this little office," she demurred. "The ambassador is waiting for you, Commander. He said he'd see you at fifteen hundred, Doctor."

Hannigan nodded, then slipped out, closing the door behind him.

Once more, Van set aside his duffels and followed Mac-

Donagh, who opened the inner door without even knocking. "Commander Albert, Ambassador."

The ambassador's office was far larger than that of the first secretary—a space a good ten meters from side to side and eight in depth. The desk was faced out from the east wall, so that the ambassador could look to the door on the north wall or the wide window overlooking the formal garden below. Closer to the door, on the west wall, was a replica hearth with two armchairs, upholstered in green leather, facing it, a low table between them.

"I'm very glad to see you, Commander." Ambassador Rogh had faded red hair, a cheerful smile, green eyes, and a deep and reassuring voice, the kind that suggested that he was eminently trustworthy.

Van distrusted the voice and the man, but that wasn't new. After the *Regneri* incident, he'd come to realize that trusting any politician, civilian or military, was foolhardy and dangerous, if not usually occupationally fatal. "I'm here, Ambassador Rogh. Dr. Hannigan has indicated that we may be in for most interesting times."

As Meg MacDonagh stepped back, slipping out and closing the door, Ambassador Rogh nodded to the chairs before the hearth, with its replicated fire. "We need to chat, Commander."

Van waited until the older man eased into the chair facing the closed door before he seated himself.

"Your ultimate superior—the marshal," the ambassador began, "he believes that the best remedy for the uncertain situation here in the Scandya system would be a full RSF squadron orbiting Gotland and another orbiting Malmot. He doesn't have one squadron to send. So he sent you." A wintry smile crossed Rogh's face. "Just by arriving here, you delivered a message. The only problem is that we don't know who the recipient is."

"Message, ser?" asked Van politely.

"I know all about the unidentified cruiser you took out. Doubtless every embassy in Valborg knows, and certainly Marshal Kenaal does. Kenaal won't be displeased, because you did what he'd like to have done but doesn't have the resources for. Making you the senior military attaché sends a second message, but it's one we can't back up. That leaves you—and me—in a very exposed position, Commander."

"Can you tell me what happened to the *Collyns*, ser?"

Rogh frowned, an expression of considerable annoyance.

Van continued to smile, politely, waiting.

"I would . . . if I could. The marshal has not seen fit to inform me. Not so far. I had thought you might know."

"The *Fergus* was ordered here to replace the *Collyns*, but we received no information beyond that."

"We're in the same ship, then, Commander." Rogh laughed again, but the laugh faded quickly. After an interval of silence, he spoke again. "I'm sure that Ian told you about my preference for diplomatic solutions, or solutions that involve methods other than military might."

"He did."

"Part of that reflects Ian's own preferences. I feel we must avoid a military approach, not because I am philosophically opposed, but because a military solution is impractical for two reasons. First, it could only destablize an already polarized local government. Second, we cannot raise forces anywhere close to the size of the Revenant and Argenti forces that could be brought to bear here—or against us. That means we must tread with care, using your expertise . . . and reputation . . . as an implied statement of position, and not as a direct threat or confrontation . . ."

Van nodded.

"You will be working more closely with Cordelia Gregory than with the other secretaries. She is the second secretary, and she is an expert in trade and economics. Unlike poor Ian, she understands both the military capabilities and limitations. I will warn you, however, that she is not the greatest supporter of the RSF."

"Oh? Why would that be?"

"It would be better if she told you." Rogh stood. "It's good that you're here. We'll need to chat in more detail, in a day or so, once you've struggled through all the briefing materials and have a better understanding of the situation. But I did want to see you as soon as you arrived."

Sean Bulben was once more waiting for Van in the outer office, although Van had not sensed any messages being sent to the fourth secretary.

"I'll show you your office . . . then we'll set up your security codes and passes . . . and do the same for your quarters. . . . Once you're settled, of course, you'll take control of the embassy security systems and codes. I had to do it, because . . . well . . . no one else wanted to." Sean smiled apologetically.

Van had no doubts that the afternoon would be very long, as would the days that followed.

Chapter 8

By the end of eightday, four days after his arrival in Valborg, Van's head was splitting. Learning the procedures and systems on a new ship was simple compared to all the economic, local military, and related cultural and political information he'd been expected to assimilate. He'd reset the embassy security systems and made some changes to the operating parameters. Those changes had been met with amused tolerance by the professional staff—and he hadn't told anyone about the overrides that only he could use. The worst part was that so much of what he'd had to study contained equivocations and qualifications that made him cringe.

He also doubted that anyone truly understood the conflicts and the seesaw balance of power between the two political parties of Gotland—except perhaps Premier Gustofsen.

He glanced around his office—almost a mirror duplicate of Hannigan's, even to the placement of the table desk and chairs and the built-in wall bookcase, although there were far fewer volumes, and some shelves were totally bare. After taking a momentary break, he looked back at the words on his office console screen. . . .

>   . . . while ostensibly an open society, the Scandya system planets have consistently denied access to alien species. Most puzzling was the immediate and adamant denial of relations with the Farhkan Colloquy following independence, since the Farhkans have had a long history of disinterested study and noninvolvement in human societies . . . later analyses suggested that Scandyan leaders were concerned that the observational program agreed to by the Eco-Tech Coalition during the war between the Coalition and the Community of the Revealed had resulted in fundamental and undesirable impacts upon Eco-Tech culture and that Scandya did not wish to suffer a similar fate. This tentative conclusion remains unproven, but whether unproven or not, the position of Scandya with regard to nonhuman aliens remains unchanged, although the Farhkans have not made any effort to reopen the question . . .

Van rubbed his forehead. Could the ship that had attacked the *Fergus* been Farhkan? No . . . the observed characteristics had been human. Also, no human ship had ever successfully survived an armed confrontation with a Farhkan vessel. While every one of those confrontations had been far earlier and begun by a human vessel, human arms technology still did not appear to have attained the same level as that of the Farhkans.

So . . . who had been directing the attacking cruiser? And why?

In some ways, the "why" was simpler. Whoever controlled the Scandya system gained a strategic staging point and leverage. If the Revs controlled it, they nearly encircled the "lower" systems in the Argenti sphere. If the Argentis did, they had a straight jumpshot at two of the major Rev military missionary/staging bases. If the Keltyr gained control of Scandya, they'd have enough of a technological base to challenge Tara. The RSF was in a position where whatever it did in Scandya, it couldn't gain—only lose. And that didn't help.

Van continued reading for another half hour, when there was a discreet tap on his door.

"Yes?"

Sean Bulben opened the door and peered in. "Commander? You asked me to let you know when Dr. Gregory returned. She's in her office now. It's the one right off the ramp."

"Thank you, Sean."

As Hannigan had intimated, Cordelia Gregory had made a point of avoiding Van, and for several days, he had let her. Enough was enough, however. Van used his implant to flick off the console, then stood, making his way out through his empty outer office and into the main corridor. The second and third secretaries did not have outer offices or sitting rooms. So Van knocked on the door.

"Come in." The woman's voice was firm, resonant with only the slightest hint of the melodic.

He opened the door and stepped inside, bowing slightly as he did.

Dr. Cordelia Gregory was dark-haired, with pale white skin and deep, dark green eyes. Her lips and eyebrows were thin. She rose from behind her desk.

"Dr. Gregory, I'm Van Albert. Dr. Hannigan had indicated that it was likely we'd be working together, and I thought I should introduce myself. I'd left several messages, but it seemed as though we were always missing each other."

"It is most likely that we will be working together." Her words were polite, even, and without the slightest hint of warmth. "There is often a correlation between economic and military data and their implications."

"I fear that you have far more experience in such correlations than do I."

"That is to be expected. The RSF usually considers economic and social concerns as of far less import than military ones."

"And the diplomatic corps is often known for the reverse," Van pointed out. "Which might be why it would be advantageous to work together." He wondered why she was clearly so hostile to him. He'd never even met the woman before.

"I'm certain that is what is expected, and I'll offer any professional assistance you may find necessary, Commander."

Van didn't know what to say. He'd effectively been dismissed by someone subordinate to him, but he wasn't in a military situation, and a quiet reminder or reprimand wasn't appropriate. Yet, accepting such an attitude from the doctor wasn't wise, either. "Without more than your passive assistance, Doctor, I doubt that we will meet anyone's expectations, and that would not be advantageous for you, for me, or for the Republic."

"I stand corrected, Commander." Gregory's tone was even more chill.

Van offered a smile, rueful and as warm as he could make it. "I wasn't offering a correction, just an observation." He paused. "I'm not a diplomat, trained in the observation of human nature to read entire motivations from subtle gestures. It's clear even to me that either who or what I am displeases you. Yet, unless I'm hopelessly mistaken, we've never met."

"You're correct, Commander. We have not met." Gregory offered a tight smile. "And I'm sorry to say that who and what you are is hard for me."

"A commander in the RSF?"

"Not just a commander."

"Then what?" Van could sense the tension in both her posture and her words.

"My older sister was on the *Regneri*."

"I'm sorry."

"I am most certain you are. At least, as sorry as any officer devoted to violence could be."

What could he say to that? After a moment, he bowed his head slightly. "I also stopped eating babies a good twenty years ago, Doctor."

Her face paled, and she stiffened.

Before she could speak, he added, softly. "I am sorry for your loss. I'm also sorry for all those who lost loved ones on the *Regneri*. No one could have predicted what happened, and nine hundred and ninety-nine times out of a thousand, such a freakish event would not have occurred. That doesn't make it any less painful for you, or your family. I am not sorry for those who died aboard the *Vetachi*, and, faced with that situation again, I would still have to try to stop the *Vetachi*. The renegades who commanded that ship had already killed over a thousand innocents on Freya and on Culain. They would have killed more, had I let them escape."

"You've obviously rehearsed that answer."

"No. I've thought about it, and for what it's worth, I still have nightmares about it, Doctor. But you might recall that the *Vetachi* was effectively a cruiser, and I had a corvette, far smaller, with shields easily crushed by such a large ship in any protracted fight. Either way, the situation was far from optimal. I knew there was a good chance that my corvette might not survive, but I had to take that chance. That was what we were there for, although none of us on the *Eochaid* was undertaking a suicide mission. No one ever could have anticipated that a successful attack would release a torp that would home in on the *Regneri*. The Board of Inquiry established that such an event could and did happen only because of improper weapons control on the renegade, and even so, the odds of something like that happening were infinitesimal."

"That's the problem with force and violence, Commander."

"I agree, Doctor. It is a problem. It has always been a problem. The concomitant problem is that sometimes the other answers are worse. Letting the *Vetachi* escape would only have condemned more innocents to die, perhaps many more."

"I *know* that my sister died. You don't know that letting the *Vetachi* go would have led to more deaths."

"No. I don't." Van refrained from noting that the doctor didn't know the opposite, either. "Not with absolute certainty. But ships from three separate Arm governments had been looking for the *Vetachi* for two years. During that time, they plundered a colony ship and three orbital outposts and killed over four hundred people."

"Commander . . . I don't think that you will ever convince me, and it's probably even less likely that I'll convince you. You have convinced me of one thing, and that I can live with."

Van waited.

"You're not entirely the monster I envisioned. I think you were wrong. I always will, but it's clear you made a reasoned decision under stress and tried to do the best you could. It's also clear from every word you've said, and in the way that you've said it, that it will always remain with you. I'm glad for that. It's not something that should be forgotten."

"No. And I won't." Not with nightmares for ten years.

"I sincerely hope that is so, and I hope that you still have occasional nightmares. I do."

Van wasn't quite certain what to say to that.

"I will work with you, Commander. I cannot say I will ever be more than cordial. I loved my sister."

"That . . . would be helpful."

"Did you have something in mind?" she asked.

"Not yet. No . . . there is something. Could you do a rough analysis of the cost and resource commitment of maintaining a cruiser on station in the Scandya system for a month without access to any local orbit facilities?"

"Such as the unknown cruiser that attacked the *Fergus*? I can do that." Gregory nodded, a curt movement.

Van hadn't told anyone, but Gregory knew. "The ambassador told you?"

"Just me and the first secretary."

"The ship didn't match any profile in the RSF databanks. I just wondered if there might be any sort of social or economic analysis that might help with identification."

She pursed her lips. "Just in a general sense. Building and operating that large a deep-space vessel would show in the stats of any of the smaller systems, even in the Republic's

stats, and in the Keltyr stats. But the economies of the major
Arm governments—the Argenti, the Revenants, the Coalition—are large enough that even a multilateral could build or
convert such a ship without its showing up."

"And piracy from farther away is also a possibility,"
mused Van.

"You don't think so."

"No. Someone had to have a reason to attack the *Fergus*.
You don't attack an armed vessel except for a very good reason. The *Fergus* would show up on any EDI detector as a
warship. I'm inclined to doubt the attack was because they
mistook the *Fergus* for another ship."

"I'm not military, but I would agree."

"You have any problems where my expertise might help?"
asked Van.

"Actually . . . yes." Gregory lifted a databloc. "I've laid
them out here."

As he took the databloc, Van wondered if everywhere he
went people would recall his past and act as suspiciously.
Still . . . by confronting the issue with the doctor, he'd turned
open and cold anger into something less, and anything less
was better than where they had started.

"I'll look into them. I might have to check back with you."

"That's fine, Commander. I'm not going anywhere this
week."

Van bowed slightly as he left.

Chapter 9

At ten minutes past noon on twoday, Van sat in the embassy's
senior staff dining room at a table for four. Across from him
was Ian Hannigan. To his right was Cordelia Gregory, and to
his left Emily Clifton, the embassy's third secretary. The
other three tables were vacant.

Before seating himself, Hannigan had moved the purple-and-white orchid centerpiece to an adjoining table. "Better to have a senior staff meeting over lunch." Hannigan looked at Van.

"Double duty," Van agreed.

"And it's easier to swallow your words with food," added Emily Clifton, with a twinkle in the gray eyes that seemed at variance with the severe face and pulled-back blond hair.

The hint of a frown crossed Hannigan's face, then vanished.

Van made a note to spend more time with Clifton, swamped as he felt in trying to learn a position for which he'd had neither training nor experience.

A squarish middle-aged servingwoman appeared with a tray from which she took four salads. Van used only the red vinegar on his greenery, skipping the oil. With the rich food provided by the embassy, he felt he should be skipping even more, much as his internal nanites balanced his metabolism. He took a sip of the café—hot enough, but weak and brownish.

"The first order of business," began Hannigan, "is house-keeping. The ministry auditors have requested that we keep better track of personal use of embassy vehicles." Once more, he looked to Van. "You probably won't have much personal usage, but, because your personal reimbursements come from the RSF diplomatic account, and they're always late, it's very important that you log your personal usage immediately."

"I can see that," Van replied.

"The second item is the upcoming Scandyan independence celebration . . . the two hundred and fiftieth anniversary. I've posted the details on the master schedule, with notes to each of you."

"How will that affect us directly?" asked Van, not wanting to access the net in the middle of a conversation and also wanting to see what Hannigan had to say.

"The ambassador will have to be present at the ceremony. You'll need to coordinate with the SDF to ensure security precautions are adequate. We'll also be hosting several functions . . ."

"Over several weeks?"

"It's a two-week celebration. We'll have an opening night reception—that's always been rotated, and this year it's our turn. Then there will be the luncheon that the ambassador's wife will host the following week, and the Boating Day Festival . . . and the final reception . . ."

The servingwoman appeared with four plates. Van's held the Circassian Beef with noodles. He took a bite, enjoying the taste of real food.

"The festivities the night before end with fireworks and a holo-laser display," added Emily Clifton. "It's quite spectacular—especially the first two or three times you see it."

"Now . . . it is very important to the Scandyans," said Hannigan.

"How do the Argentis feel about it?" asked Van.

"They participate, as do all the embassies. It *was* two hundred and fifty years ago, and times have changed."

From what Van recalled, the Argentis never forgot anything, and he doubted that they'd forget a rebellion that had cost them both pride and strategic position—even after two hundred and fifty years.

"There's also the embassy fund drive for the Byrnedot Home." Hannigan looked to Clifton.

"Sean's in charge of that, and he reported that all embassy staffers have contributed."

Van had been cornered by the fourth secretary on the third day, and, discretion besting valor, had also agreed to a modest contribution.

"Then . . . there's the education initiative . . .

Van repressed a yawn, listening and finishing off the remainder of his lunch.

". . . and last, I'd like you all to think about your sections of the annual report. Those will be due in draft at the end of Septem, and both Commander Albert and I will be reviewing them, then circulating the drafts, including our own sections, for your comments." Hannigan smiled broadly, then asked, perfunctorily, "Do any of you have any questions or comments?"

"Yes . . . actually," Van said quickly. "Was there any investigation of Commander Cruachan's death? I can't find any references to it on the netsystem."

"Oh . . . there were two RSF security officers. There wasn't really much to investigate about the commander's death. They just went over the Scandyan constabulary's reports, then checked his body to make sure that the reports were accurate. They also did a security check of the embassy netsystem. That's standard anytime a senior staffer dies on duty, whatever the cause. They reported that the commander had drowned, as the Scandyan investigation had shown, and that there was no breach of security in the netsystem." Hannigan shrugged. "That report would only have been on Cruachan's access, mine, and the ambassador's, but it wasn't put on Cruachan's, since he was dead. I'll put a copy on yours, and you can read it yourself. Very dry."

"Thank you." Van nodded.

"Is there anything else? Good. We'll meet on fiveday next week." Hannigan smiled and pushed his chair back.

When Van returned to his office, he glanced out the window at the hills to the west, golden green in the early summer sun. He checked the netsystem. The report on Cruachan's death wasn't there yet. So he slipped out of his office and down the corridor to the doorway to the third secretary's office—slightly ajar.

"You can come in, Commander," Emily Clifton called. "Close the door after you."

Van closed the door and settled into the single chair across the standard desk from the third secretary. "I got your message."

"Message?"

Van let his face remain expressionless.

Abruptly, Clifton's severe face screwed up into laughter. Finally, she shook her head. "It's hard . . . to remember . . . that all uniforms aren't the same. Even after . . ."

"Commander Cruachan . . . would he have sent a message of a most discreetly polite nature?"

"How did you know? Did you know him?"

"No. But I've read his reports, and you do get a feel for people by the way they write."

"You've been having a hard time with Cordelia, haven't you?"

"Let's say that we've established a working relationship. I doubt it will ever be more."

"I'd guess not. That was all Commander Cruachan managed, with all his gallant manners."

"I'm afraid I'm more direct than he was."

"I noticed." Clifton's voice was dryly ironic, but not cold.

"Since I am . . . what should I be doing that I haven't been—that affects you, that is?"

"You are direct."

"I learned a long time ago that I got into trouble trying to be subtle." He laughed softly. "Then I got into more trouble being direct."

"Sometimes, it's that way." After a moment, she went on. "I can't say that I need any help with anything at this moment."

"I might," Van offered.

The thin blond eyebrows lifted, and the gray eyes fixed on him.

"You deal with the other embassies, right? And with the local media?"

She nodded. "The media here are *very* local. That's why we put out the summaries of the Arm news, the burst transmissions that come in on standing wave. The locals get it, but you won't see much of it in the local casts or holos."

"Have you seen any shift in reporting in the last two months, or anything different in the attitudes or appearances of the other embassies?"

Clifton shook her head again. "That's one of the things I'm tasked with, and I can say I haven't seen any changes at all. After the commander's death, I wondered, and I went back and ran a whole series of analyses. The newscasts, the localnet content, everything. We got exactly the same results as the year before, and the year before that—going back almost a decade." Her face turned severe once more. "The commander's death bothers you. You wanted a reaction, didn't you? Otherwise, you would have asked Dr. Hannigan privately. Why?"

"Because it led to my being posted here, and I'm not that qualified for the post, if you haven't noticed already."

"You *are* direct."

"Better to be direct, and acknowledge the obvious, and get on with learning the job, than pretending you know more than you do."

That got another laugh before Clifton said, "You're acting as if you think that Commander Cruachan's death wasn't an accident."

"I don't know that." Van wasn't about to admit that was the only explanation that felt right and that he had absolutely no evidence, except the unlikelihood that a senior officer who had great experience sailing would drown on a calm day.

"Let me think about it," offered the third secretary.

"Thank you." Van smiled and rose. "And I will stop by more frequently."

For a moment, her smile erased the severity of her face.

Chapter 10

By fiveday, Van was pacing back and forth in his office. Virtually all he had done for an eightday was read reports and papers, all necessary because he'd effectively known nothing about Scandya and even less about being a military attaché. He'd seen almost nothing of Valborg.

Abruptly, he walked out of his office and down the corridor. He paused outside Emily Clifton's door, then knocked.

"Come in."

Van slipped inside her office. "I have a favor to ask, if you're not terribly busy."

"I'm not that busy, not until tomorrow. After I turn in the

revisions to the media plan for the Scandyan independence celebration, Ian will decide on all sorts of changes. Why? What is this favor?"

"A short guided tour of Valborg, especially the sights I should see."

"Sean could—"

"But Sean doesn't know as much as you do, and I'd really appreciate it if you'd guide me."

A faint smile crossed Emily's face. "I imagine Dr. Hannigan would not complain if you knew more about Valborg from the embassy's perspective." The smile broadened slightly. "And I would not mind a few hours away from the revised, revised, and rerevised media plan."

"Are you sure?"

"Let me see if we can get a car and driver."

Van stood and waited while Emily made the arrangements, and then the two of them walked out of her office and down the ramp to the main level.

A groundcar stood waiting outside the side staff door to the embassy. Emily walked ahead of Van and stopped by the open driver's window. "Sonya . . . we're going to give Commander Albert a tour, starting with the Government Square, and then the harbor, and the multi district."

"Yes, ser," replied the woman. "Up Knutt to Independence and into the square off that?"

"That would be fine."

Van held the groundcar door for the third secretary.

"You don't have to do that, Commander."

"Old courtesies die hard," he replied, shutting her door and walking around to the other side, where he slipped into the rear seat beside her.

"Valborg was built on a plantation scale," Emily began, as the groundcar eased out of the gates and crossed the southbound lane of Knutt to turn north. "That's why the main streets are all divided boulevards, and why, except in the newer sections southwest of the city, all the houses are relatively far apart, even the small ones. They had this illusion of equality, and that anyone could live anywhere, because the prices of the initial parcels were fixed, with the requirement that they not be subdivided. That's why you'll find small houses beside mansions in many places." She laughed. "The fixed prices didn't last, of course, but the size requirements did. Now this part of the city is one of the more exclusive ones."

Van took in the dwellings on each side. Immediately to the north of the embassy was a private residence half the size of the embassy—enormous for a single-family dwelling—with a gated groundcar entry, and beyond that was a much smaller house, perhaps half the size of the one in which Van had grown up. Both dwellings were stone-walled, with blackish green slate roofs. They passed several more smaller houses, on either side of Knutt, also of stone and slate, before Sonya guided the groundcar onto a curving ramp that led into an even wider boulevard heading eastward, in what Van knew to be the general direction of the harbor and government center.

"We're on Independence now," Emily explained.

Van glanced from one side of the boulevard to the other. On both sides were white permastone walks. "I don't see many people out."

"You won't, except on the enddays, and then you'll see a lot more, mostly running and jogging. Things are so spread out—except in the true center of Valborg or the southwest—that it's hard to get anywhere except by groundcar or guideway tram."

"Doesn't seem that efficient . . ."

"That wasn't the goal of the original settlers—On your side, there, that's the old Kleborg mansion. It's a museum now, and it's been kept in its original state, except restored, of course."

Van looked, but behind the white stone walls could see only the upper stories of another sprawling stone-walled structure. "Everything's stone . . ."

"It took a while to get trees here. Most of them are less than a century old, something about a native root worm . . . A lot of the older places are stone and synthwood."

"Not many groundcars for these boulevards," Van observed.

"Same problem . . . they built big and wide, and far apart. So, except in the morning or late afternoon, they look almost deserted."

"That's expensive . . ."

"The original settlers had the credits . . . brought in twice as much planoforming equipment as they needed. What they didn't bring in was much military capability. That's how the Argentis could take over so easily. On your left, across the median park there, that's the original opera house. It's still used today—only in the winter, and with the winters here, even you'll be going."

With his own background, Van would have gone anyway.

As they neared the gleaming buildings to the east, Emily continued to point out various landmarks. ". . . music conservatory . . . post-Argenti . . . botanical institute . . . Up ahead, on the hill overlooking the lower city and the harbor, that rectangle of buildings is Government Square . . ."

Sonya turned right, off Independence Boulevard and into the first crowded street or avenue that Van had seen. They drove up a gentle incline, past an area of greenery set in ascending terraces. The park was surrounded by low white stone walls, and held more than a few people either walking or seated on white stone benches.

"That's the public garden, or rather the northern part. Beyond that is the square, and the Parliamentary Assembly Hall—the long, flat-walled building."

The groundcar slowed almost to a crawl in the heavier traffic.

The Assembly Hall was the most unpretentious government building Van had ever seen—literally a long white stone box with rectangular windows at irregular intervals, with a set of wide and low stone steps in the middle, leading to a squared entryway. The Scandyan flag flew on a single staff above the entryway, but there were no domes, cupolas, minarets—nothing rising above the level roof of the building. People actually walked across the square, and several groups were standing on the steps.

"The Liberal Commons party controlled the government

when it was built, and they felt that government buildings in other systems were too grandiose . . ."

The Assembly Hall could never have been charged with that, Van reflected.

"The lawns that circle the building are considered part of the square . . . and it overlooks the harbor . . . can see if you look left how it slopes down to the lower city and the harbor . . . Any questions?" asked Emily.

"No, not about Government Square," Van replied. He did wonder why she did not seem to have any admirers—at least, not from what he could see. He knew that the first and second secretaries were married, but he hadn't seen their significant others.

But Emily had a subdued directness that attracted Van, although he wasn't quite sure why. That, he had to admit, even as he pushed away the thoughts of anything serious. Not when he had so much yet to learn and so many unresolved questions.

Chapter 11

What is "ethical" or moral? A general definition is that actions that conform to a "right set of principles" are ethical. Such a definition begs the question. Whose principles? On what are those principles based? Do those principles arise from reasoned development by rational scholars? Or from "divine" inspiration? Does it matter, so long as they inspire moral and ethical behavior?

For some, it does matter, as it did for the ancient author who claimed that without a deity, every action is permitted. In practice, with or without a deity, every action is permitted unless human social structures preclude it. Yet, on what principles are those social structures based? Ethics and morality?

Such questioning can quickly run in circles, especially

since most individuals wish to think well of themselves, and it is difficult to think well of oneself if one defines one's own activities as immoral or unethical. For example, genocide can be rationalized as an ethical means to racial purity, or as a means for societal survival, and both purity and survival can easily be rationalized, and have been throughout history, as ethical.

Are values and behaviors that perpetuate a given society ethical *per se*? Are values handed down by prophets and religious figures as the word of a deity necessarily more ethical than those developed by ethicists and scholars?

Theocracies and other societies using religious motives, or pretexts, have undertaken genocide, torture, and war. Ideologues without the backing of formal religious doctrine or established theocratic organizations have done the same.

The obvious conclusion is that "moral" values must be ethical in and of themselves, and not through religious or secular authority or rationalized logic. This leads to the critical questions. How can one define what is ethical without resorting to authority, religious doctrine, or societal expediency? And whom will any society trust to make such a judgment, particularly one not based on authority, doctrine, or expediency?

> *Values, Ethics, and Society*
> Exton Land
> New Oisin, Tara
> 1117 S.E.

Chapter 12

By twoday of his second week in Valborg, Van had learned as much as he could, without more context, from the records left by Commander Cruachan and from Doctors Hannigan and Gregory. The RSF Security report on Cruachan's death was both detailed and dry, and concluded that the commander had drowned after being struck from behind by the boom of his catamaran and that there had been no breach of embassy security. Emily Clifton had confirmed that media patterns of other embassies and local media had not varied after the commander's death.

Outside of a few inquiries from Hannigan and the ambassador and one briefing paper that the ambassador had requested on Keltyr military forces, Van had been left largely to his own devices. He had found the small exercise facility, and resumed his fitness program, something he hated almost as much as being reminded of the *Regneri*.

Dr. Gregory's reaction to the *Regneri* tragedy still bothered Van, almost as much as his own nightmares. Cordelia Gregory was an intelligent woman, and yet her entire focus had been on her sister. There had been little real understanding or compassion for the hundreds of others killed by the renegades—or for the additional deaths that would have followed if the *Vetachi* had escaped. Her reaction had also convinced Van that there would be little he could ever say in that regard, and that further discussions on the subject would only be fruitless.

On the strictly professional front, Van hadn't wanted to take on the Keltyr or the Revenant military attachés immediately, and he especially hadn't wanted to meet the Argenti attaché until he knew more about the local Scandyan situation. He was also surprised to find that the Eco-Tech Coalition did not have a full embassy, but only a liaison and consulate office.

As he'd worked through the files, Van had studied Cruachan's reports in greater detail. He could sense he was missing something, but he wasn't sure what. So he kept searching and discovered that the commander had often met with a Commodore Petrov of the Scandyan System Defense Force. There were no notes on the substance of the meetings. Van had decided to meet with Petrov.

Getting an appointment had been easy enough, and nine hundred on fourday found him in an embassy groundcar, headed northward toward the headquarters complex of the Scandyan SDF. Clouds loomed over the hills to the west, hinting at a late afternoon rain, and the air smelled faintly of dust and a scent somewhere between a sweet weedgrass and swamp roses.

Van's driver was a slender Scandyan named Stefan.

"Do you recall how often Commander Cruachan came out here?" Van asked.

"He used to come out here almost every eightday."

"I've gotten the impression that he was a very straightforward man."

Stefan cocked his head, as if thinking. "Honest . . . that he was. And honorable. He talked, once, about how much simpler life was as a ship commander."

"I've already discovered that. Did he say why?"

"I can't say that he did, ser. He didn't talk much, except about sailing and the weather, and sometimes about not understanding women."

Had Cruachan also had a run-in with Cordelia Gregory? "He liked sailing, didn't he?"

"He did, ser. He liked to sail by himself. He said it was a way to clear his thoughts."

"We can all use that at times."

"Yes, ser."

The Scandyan SDF headquarters was housed in a six-sided, two-level building constructed of the same bluish marble as the shuttle terminal. Stefan guided the groundcar up to the receiving gatehouse set forward of the eastern wing, where Van stepped out of the car and up to the booth before the single gate. The Scandyan tech in summer whites seated behind the nanite screen looked at him. "Yes, ser?"

"Commander Van Albert, Taran embassy. I have an appointment at nine-thirty with Commodore Petrov." Van slid across his military datacard, and waited.

The sentry ran the datacard under the scanner, then handed it back, along with a thin white wand. "You're cleared to Commodore Petrov's office. It's on the first level in section three. The wand will guide you. If you go past the office, it turns red. If you go too far, it whistles. Then you'll find security all around you. Just keep the end of the wand green, and you'll get there."

"Thank you."

"That's what we're here for, ser." The young man smiled.

The gate opened as Van walked toward it. The building wings were larger inside than they had seemed from outside. His boots echoed in the stone corridors, and he passed but a handful of rankers and officers—no civilians—as he let the wand guide him. All in all, it was a good ten minutes before he reached the outer office of the commodore, with a small sign proclaiming, EXTERNAL AFFAIRS: COMMODORE RAFEL PETROV. The wand had remained green, and Van had not seen any sign of security, but his implant had registered more than four scans from various units.

As he entered, Van could sense another scan, triggered by the senior ranker stationed behind a console and screen just inside the doorway.

"Commander Albert, Commodore Petrov is expecting you. The center archway, if you please, ser."

Van nodded and headed for the center archway, another scanning station. As he passed through, the door at the other end opened, and he stepped into a spacious office. The wide southern windows looked out upon a paved courtyard. Standing beside a conference table was Commodore Petrov—who could have passed for either Scandyan or Revenant—blue-eyed, blond, tall, and impressive in immaculate summer white uniform.

"Greetings, Commander Albert." The older officer gestured toward the empty seats at the table, even as he reseated himself.

"I'm glad that we could get together," Van replied.

"So am I. When did you arrive in Valborg?"

"A little more than an eightday ago." Van offered what he hoped was a rueful smile. "My transfer was unexpected, and it's taken a little while to get caught up on what was waiting."

"I imagine. I'd heard that Ambassador Rogh had finally gotten a replacement for Commander Cruachan. Fine officer. One of the most honest officers I've met."

"I didn't know him, but everyone reported that he was most accomplished. And honest." Van laughed. "It's always a challenge replacing someone like that."

"What is life without challenges?" countered Petrov. "Would you care for something to drink?"

"Café . . . strong, if you have it."

"Your predecessor liked it that way as well." Petrov's face blanked for just a fraction of a second as he accessed his net.

Through his own implant, Van could feel the quick pulse, but could not decipher either the protocol or the message. "Could be a deepspace habit."

"It might well be." An amused smile followed Petrov's words. "I had hoped that you would follow the example of your predecessor. He was most diligent in informing me of the concerns of your RSF, and in turn, I was equally diligent in conveying our interests and concerns."

Van had to concentrate to follow Petrov's accented Old Anglo, although he hadn't had quite so much difficulty with the embassy service staff recruited from Scandya. "That could be mutually beneficial in these times."

"Information is useful in all times," Petrov replied. "You are correct that it is even more so in these times. We do share certain common interests . . ."

"I would think so."

Petrov did not speak for a moment, and Van wondered if he had said something wrong. Then a side door slid open, and a ranker stepped though with a tray on which were two cups filled with steaming liquid. The ranker set the tray on the conference table midway between the two officers, then departed as silently as he had come.

"The café is closest to you," said Petrov. "The pitcher is heavy cream, a specialty here if you care to try it."

"And you?"

"Tea. I inherited the taste from my grandfather. It's an old Russe custom, and I found I liked tea far better than café or other beverages."

Van sipped the café. It was strong, but good, not oily or

with the faintly burned taste that came from overroasted beans. "Good café."

"Commander Cruachan thought so." Petrov took a sip of his tea before continuing. "The interest most common to us both is the desire not to be perceived as a threat to the three major powers that surround Scandya. The next common interest is to maintain a stable government."

"I know that *is* a problem," Van said, "but not why."

"Simply put, Commander, for hundreds of years, Scandya has had an internal cultural conflict. The first settlers fled well ahead of the Old Earth diaspora, and they wanted nothing to do with anyone else. We were the first system settled in this region of the Arm. Then, about four hundred years ago, the Argentis arrived, with their fleets. We had none. As conquerors, their rein was comparatively light, and they upgraded and modernized our industry and technology. They were sensitive to our feelings about . . . our culture . . . and most of those they resettled here came from similar cultural and racial heritages."

"Such as your family?" Van guessed.

"Exactly. Except those of us from that heritage knew that we could not remain free, even after the rebellion, unless we developed and maintained an armed force. The recidivists, who persist in calling themselves Liberals, have opposed that. In the few times when they have controlled the assembly, they have tried to reduce or eliminate the SDF."

Van nodded.

"So now we find ourselves between conflicting powers, and we have little interest in being allied to any of those. Your government is one of the least objectionable, but even your RSF wishes to enhance its position here and throughout the Arm so that the Taran Republic is considered close to an equal of the Coalition or the Revenant theocracy."

"Theocracy?"

Petrov shrugged. "That is what they are. It has been less than a year since they annexed Samarra, and already there are tales of what has happened. . . ."

"Tales?" Van said, wondering how Petrov might respond.

"What one would expect from a theocracy. Those who protest excessively either have no jobs or exceedingly low-paid jobs for long hours. Professionals who do not convert find themselves slowly isolated. But . . . as I was saying, too often those in our line of work are forced to use political terms of little meaning. In private, I prefer to be more accurate."

Van laughed. "How would you describe the Taran Republic . . . accurately?"

"Do you wish to know?"

Van wasn't sure he wanted to. "It would be best if I did."

"Ah . . . an honest man. You do not particularly wish to know, but know you must. Very well . . . the Taran Republic is a system moving from controlled democratic anarchy to bureaucratic democracy, on its way to greater power and Byzantine complexity and ethical degeneration. There will be more unrest, and a possible military coup if the government does not seem to respond to the events perceived to threaten the Republic."

A coup? "Don't all governments risk ethical degeneration as the territory they control increases?"

"They do indeed. That is one reason why Scandya never sought more systems. The other was that by the time we regained an adequate technological basis to expand, all the systems around us were already controlled by others with larger fleets. We like to claim ethical reasons for our comparative weakness." Petrov laughed.

Van smiled. Petrov's directness was both refreshing and disarming, as it was certainly intended to be. "Don't we all like to claim we're acting ethically?"

Petrov did not answer that question, remaining silent for a moment before speaking again. "I understand you were commanding the *Fergus*, and that you ran into some . . . difficulty . . . after you came out of jump. Our EDI records suggest it might even have been some sort of conflict. With a much larger vessel. You have more skill than your RSF will admit."

Van shrugged. "We noted some strange EMP activity. I'm sure you understand. You seem to have very competent personnel, and I imagine that they're usually quite accurate in their analyses of these sorts of things."

Petrov nodded. "They are indeed, and, I'm most glad to know that you feel that way as well. The EDI patterns could not have matched an Argenti or a Revenant ship, and it would have been highly unlikely that it could have been a Coalition vessel."

Van smiled. "You mean, if there had been a conflict, any Eco-Tech vessel of that size would have prevailed because it would have been worth twice its size in combat?"

"Sometimes three times. Coalition corvettes have destroyed battle cruisers." Petrov sipped his tea. "How are you finding Valborg?"

"I've seen very little, so far."

"You should see the Cliff Spire—the real home of Scandyan independence, you know, although you won't find it listed as such in the histories. And the purple surf at Eschen, and in the winter, the ice caves of Maloa."

"I'll see what I can do after I dig my way clear of all the reports." Van took another sip of the café. "Do you have any other suggestions?"

Petrov rested his forefinger against his temple for a moment. "I will have to think about that. I like to suggest things that appeal to each individual, and I fear I do not know you well enough to make further suggestions." He leaned back and lifted a datacube, which he extended to Van. "This contains all the public releases the SDF has made since the death of your predecessor. There is a great amount of information there, and I thought that you would find it helpful in this form. That way, when we meet again, we may be able to discuss any of those items about which you may have questions."

Van took the cube, slipping it into his jacket pocket. "I appreciate your thoughtfulness."

"Not at all. You need to know what we are doing, and I need to know how your government feels. That I cannot know unless you are well informed." Petrov pushed back his chair and stood. "Next time, we will have more to discuss, but it has been a pleasure."

"For me as well."

As Van rose, Petrov added. "You know that Commander Cruachan was not only a fine sailor, but he had once been an underwater operative? A most accomplished and amazing man, and I do miss him. It is a pleasure to see that you share some of his traits, and I do hope that we will have many more meetings where we can exchange information."

"So do I, Commodore. So do I."

Petrov remained standing and smiling as Van left the office.

As Van let the wand guide him back toward the front of the headquarters building, he considered Petrov's parting words. Cruachan had once been an underwater operative? That meant subconscious-level nanite breathing capacity. The man couldn't have drowned—not accidentally. How would Petrov have known? What did Petrov have to gain, either by revealing the truth, if that were what he did, or lying?

As he hurried toward the waiting groundcar, Van had the feeling that Petrov had told the truth. That in itself was chilling. And why had he offered Van a datacube rather than shooting a straight transmission to Van at the embassy? Until he studied the contents of the cube, Van couldn't even guess at that.

After reaching the embassy, on the way back to his office, he stopped at Emily Clifton's door, paused, then knocked.

"Come in, Commander."

"Thank you." Van closed the old-fashioned wooden door behind him, but did not sit down.

Clifton had stood as he entered. "How can I help you?"

"It's an odd question, but . . . Have you ever been to Cliff Spire?"

Her expression turned quizzical. "No. Should I have been?"

"I don't know. Several people have recommended that I go see it."

"That's the historical site—the house of the last Argenti planetary governor, isn't it? I always wondered why the Scandyans made it a memorial."

"Perhaps we should go out there on one of the enddays and see why?"

"If that is an invitation, Commander, I will accept." Again, the smile smoothed out the severity of the third secretary's face.

"If you're accepting, it's an invitation."

They both laughed.

"How are things going?" she asked.

"More slowly and in a more complex fashion than I'd hoped, but about as I had expected."

"You're a realist. I imagine you've had to be."

"Yes. One learns."

She nodded.

Van cleared his throat. "That's all I had, but . . . thank you, and we'll work out the time for sevenday—if that's all right with you?"

"Sevenday will be good."

With a nod, Van ducked out of the third secretary's door.

Back in his own office, Van realized what had bothered him. Commander Cruachan had been on leave for a week before the "accident," and Van could have sworn that some of the reports were dated during that period. He used his implant to set up another netsystem search.

Search complete, announced the net after several moments.

Before reviewing those search results, Van checked the netsystem for any background on Commander Cruachan. As Van had suspected, all personnel details on the commander had been removed after his death, and there was no way to get to them, except through the headquarters personnel system at RSF HQ.

Van went through the commander's reports. Four of the reports, although dated before Cruachan's death, indicated that they had been changed more than a week after his reported death date. One had been dated "officially" six days before the commander's death, and there was no way to access the more secure levels of the embassy from outside the embassy—not unless Cruachan had been more than a mere attaché, and that raised even more questions.

Van called up the first of the reports with the altered dates, reading through it carefully.

> . . . Local news sources have reported increased high-tech info-trades between Scandya and the Coalition and between Scandya and the Argentis. The Scandyan Trade Ministry has declined to provide details, citing the information as privileged . . .

The report went on to provide data on Scandyan microtronics production. Why would the commander have even bothered with a report dealing with standard microtronics? That area was Cordelia Gregory's.

Van called up the second report with the anomalous date. It was about local shellfish production. He'd wondered about it when he had first skimmed through Cruachan's reports. With a smile, he tried another inquiry against the complete planetary database.

Match found, the net announced.

The match was a local business story in an economic report, and the text was identical to that of Cruachan's report.

Van leaned back in his chair. Someone had replaced the original reports. But who? What had been in those reports? Was there any way to discover who had done so, and from where?

Van went back to work.

Two hours later, he was little wiser, if hungrier, having worked through the lunch. There was no record of who had made the changes, not even a link to an individual, a console, nothing but the change date. While it would have been easy to disguise or falsify the date on a personal console, trying that on a unified system would have left more traces than leaving the date alone—unless the falsifier were extremely skilled and had a great deal of access and time on the system.

That told Van that whoever had altered them had known the system better than most, but that whoever did hadn't had much time.

Commander? came the Meg MacDonagh's inquiry on the netsystem. *The ambassador would like to see you and Dr. Hannigan. Are you free at the moment?*

I'll be right there. Did he say what the meeting was about?

No, ser, and you'd best make it five minutes.

Van leaned back in his chair. What did the ambassador want?

He waited four minutes, then walked to the ambassador's outer office. Meg MacDonagh smiled, but it was a professional smile. Van smiled back. Hannigan appeared, and they both walked into the ambassador's office.

Rogh didn't say a word, but Van could sense the pulse from his implant. Then, after the privacy cone swirled into place around the three men, the ambassador looked at Van, then at Hannigan. "I've received a report from ministry headquarters that suggests something may take place during the Scandyan independence week celebration. The ministry doesn't offer any specific details, except to note that both the Revenant and Argenti fleets are in an increased state of readiness, and that the Coalition has dispatched three heavy cruisers to Mara—that's the closest Coalition system to Scandya."

"The same thing happened last year," Hannigan said mildly. "Nothing occurred."

Rogh looked at Van. "Have you come across anything that might shed light on this?"

"I just met with Commodore Petrov at the SDF. I was still going over things when you called the meeting."

"What did he have to say?"

"He was very pleasant. He said he was dispatching all the material he would have given to Commander Cruachan. I haven't had a chance to go through it. He did suggest that the ship that attacked the *Fergus* could not have been Argenti, according to the Scandyan SDF." Van studied Hannigan as he spoke, but the first secretary didn't seem at all surprised.

"Did you bring that up?" Rogh's voice sharpened ever so slightly.

"No, ser. But he knew. He said, fairly clearly, that the *Fergus* had apparently encountered a much larger vessel. I told him that we had encountered some excessive EMP activity, as I'd reported to orbit control when they asked, but that I hadn't been able to identify the source."

Rogh nodded. "All you could say, I imagine."

"I'd rather not lie outright at this point, not when they clearly know what happened." Van still wanted to know why the RSF had told the ambassador about the attack.

"That's interesting," mused Rogh. "The vessel couldn't have been Coalition or Farhkan. So they believe it was probably Revenant, but they don't want to say that, even in confidence. Of course, they could just be telling you that to see how we react."

"That's very possible," Van admitted. "He didn't seem terribly fond of the Revenants. He mentioned that there was already repression in Samarra. I don't know why he did. Perhaps to feel me out. It's the first time I've met with the commodore. He seems open, but some officers are very good at seeming that way."

Rogh raised his eyebrows, then, as if thinking the better of it, nodded. "That is true. What else did he say?"

"Very little beyond pleasantries. He said that Commander Cruachan had been a good officer and attaché and that he'd been sorry to learn of his drowning."

"No offense to you, Commander, but we all were." Rogh cleared his throat. "I'd like you to meet with all the other major attachés as soon as you can, and see what you can learn."

"Yes, ser."

Rogh turned to Hannigan. "Is there any way you and the second secretary can speed up that economic analysis of the changes in Scandyan defense capabilities?"

"I don't see how, ser, but we're close to the end."

Rogh shook his head. "That's all, then."

The grayish mist of the privacy cone vanished, and Van and Hannigan stood.

Chapter 13

Early on eightday morning, wearing a casual gray singlesuit, one of the few nonuniform garments he had, Van stepped out of the embassy for a walk. All he had done, with the exception of his sight-seeing tour with Emily Clifton, had been to work, see people in his office or in theirs, and write or research.

Once out into the low sunshine and the still-cool morning air, Van inhaled deeply, enjoying the mixed fragrances from the flower beds along the walks to the embassy—closed on the enddays, of course. Then, with a smile, he stretched and walked out to the wide stone path that flanked Knutt Boulevard. He turned south.

The property next to the embassy was a modest-sized dwelling, surrounded by a low stone wall, less than a meter high, but on the top of the stone wall was an ornate iron-grill fence that rose another three meters. Still, through the grillwork Van could appreciate the manicured lawn and the formal gardens on the north side of the house—which resembled an oversize stone cottage, except for the black-green slate roof. He saw no one outside.

Only a handful of groundcars glided down Knutt Boulevard, most of them on the far side of the parklike median, headed northward.

A couple jogged toward him. Both were fair-skinned and blond. Van nodded politely, but neither looked at him as they passed. Then, from behind him, he heard a bell.

"On your left."

With that, another couple rode past on bicycles, the first Van had seen in years. They were older, but both man and woman were also blond. Ahead, perhaps a hundred meters, Van saw three figures—man, woman, and child. They were walking in the same direction as he was, but more slowly.

Across the boulevard rose another imposing mansion, one with two long wings, a grape arbor, a stone gazebo overlooking a pond on which swam a pair of swans—a setting that might have belonged to one of the ascendancy on Old Earth. Van thought he saw a group being served a meal within the gazebo. While his parents would have appreciated the grounds and the setting, they certainly wouldn't have approved of the massive concentration of wealth required to obtain and maintain the estate, but then his home world of Sulyn had always been less traditional and less enamored of concentrations of either wealth or power.

His eyes drifted back to the central parkway—or median—dividing Knutt Boulevard. The squared-off box-wood hedges formed a waist-high border, and, roughly every ten meters, the hedge had been allowed to grow higher, then trimmed into some form of topiary. The one closest to Van was that of a peacock with a fanned tail. The next one appeared to be an eagle with outstretched wings.

As he neared the three walking toward him, he nodded. "Good morning."

There was no reply from the man, perhaps five years younger than Van, slightly taller, and with sandy blond hair, just the curtest of nods. The woman did not bother to nod at all. After they had passed Van, they spoke in low voices.

". . . looks like he belongs in the southwest . . ."

". . . too well dressed . . . diplomat . . . Argenti, Hyndji . . . maybe . . . lots of embassies here . . ."

The voices faded behind Van as he increased his speed. Belongs in the southwest? Was that where those who weren't fair-skinned lived?

He picked up the speed of his walk. He did need more exercise.

Chapter 14

Van read the fiveday news summary carefully, trying to ensure that he understood not just what he read, but the implications behind the words before him. The lead item was clear enough.

Fifteen individuals were detained briefly after fourday's demonstration in Government Square, but were released later . . .

The Assembly must understand that technology transfer, no matter how noble the purpose, is a Trojan horse that can only lead to the subjugation of Scandya and all we hold dear," said Temra Piersen, speaking for the Activist Committee of the Liberal Commons.

"The Liberal Commons continue to behave like the extinct ostriches of Old Earth, unable to lift their heads out of the sand to see what exists in the Galaxy today," countered Alexi Bunaev . . .

In a brief speech to the Assembly, Premier Gustofsen urged "a meeting not only of minds, but of the emotions and passions behind those minds, passions that have served Scandya well in its quarter millennium of freedom . . ." Gustofsen later met in a closed meeting with both party leaders . . .

Although not so obvious, the third item on the projected holo screen stood out for Van.

Bishop Dane of the Community of the Revealed—more familiarly known as the Revenant ambassador to Scandya—offered the blessing for the public ceremony opening the new Tabernacle, a replica of the main Tabernacle in Wystuh on Orum . . .

The holo screen displayed a gleaming white octagonal structure, with another building in the background—one with eight glistening white stone towers soaring into a grayish blue sky under a brilliant sun. A caption appeared at the bottom—"Tabernacle and Temple—Wystuh, Orum." Then the image switched to a single structure, a smaller replica of the main Revenant Tabernacle.

Although the Gotland Tabernacle was constructed adjacent to the Revenant embassy, "our services and our way are open to all," according to the ambassador. He went on to say that the Tabernacle represented the vision of the prophet, and that all good people needed to look beyond the morality of convenience to live by the commandments of God and not the convenience of man . . .

Van wondered about how open the Samarrans felt the Revenant way might be.

Construction on the Tabernacle began last year, after Premier Gustofsen signed the bilateral technical trade agreement with the Revenant systems. Gustofsen had undertaken a long campaign to win over both the isolationist partisans within his own Conservative Democratic party, as well as the leftist greens of the Liberal Commons . . . Negotiations after the agreement led to the establishment of Trans-Scandyan Microtronics. The terms of the agreement were virtually identical to those of the earlier agreement with the Argenti Commonocracy that established SNI [Scandyan Nanitic Industries], which turned its first significant profit last year . . .

An ironic smile crossed Van's lips. Both the Revs and the Argentis were doing missionary work. The Revenants were more obvious, but most people, he'd discovered, found solid creds a better basis for faith than promises in the hereafter. Then . . . were those just the people he knew?

He frowned, recalling that his background briefing materials had mentioned riots and great unrest before Gustofsen had become premier. The article seemed to imply that those divisions still existed, and that Gustofsen remained adept at bridging them.

He switched to the in-net briefings sent to him from RSF HQ in New Oisin.

RSF commissions RSFS *Mangan* . . . third in the new *Addams* class . . .

After repeated RSF requests, Keltyr authorities remove "scientific" expedition from nebula watch post near Corotake . . .

RSF officers return from exchange duties with Revealed Community units . . . operational duties mutually beneficial . . .

Third fleet discovers abandoned installation near Sulyn . . .

The last item had personal interest for Van, and he focused on it.

. . . the installation, concealed within a nickel-iron asteroid with an extremely eccentric orbit, had been recently abandoned . . . contained ion traces consistent with military propulsion systems and weapons . . . RSF experts are investigating . . .

Van frowned. Every asteroid capable of holding an installation of the size reported in the dispatch had long since been tracked, since Sulyn's iron deposits were generally deep and hard to mine. At least, he thought such asteroids had been well tracked.

He shut down the holo display and stood. He'd have to hurry not to be late for his meeting with the Argenti attaché. Fortunately, the Argenti embassy was only three klicks farther northward on Knutt Boulevard and half a klick to the west. Had it been less than two klicks, Van would have considered walking it, but he had a tendency to walk quickly and sweat heavily, and arriving soaked wouldn't have helped his personal presentation.

Again, Stefan was the one who drove him.

As the groundcar hummed northward, on near-empty streets, Van reviewed what he knew. Cruachan had left several reports on Colonel Marti, and those reports suggested a cool and calculating senior Argenti officer—one who revealed little, yet subtly pressed for every advantage and bit of information that he could extract.

Van had gone over all the material in the datacube from Commodore Petrov, and had been more than a little surprised to find that it had included the annual budget requests from the SDF to the Scandyan parliament, along with a narrative summary of the status of all the Scandyan armed forces, including the space forces, and the general budgetary and procurement plans for the next five years—all very modest.

Those figures Van had turned over to Cordelia Gregory, with a request for her to analyze them to see how accurate and possible they were.

"Ser, we're almost there," Stefan announced.

Van looked up. The footprint of the Argenti embassy complex was scarcely larger than that of the Taran embassy, but the building was three stories in height—a silvery metallic structure, rising on the north side of a courtyard that enclosed a garden of some sort. The building was taller and more angular than those they had passed so far.

Stefan guided the groundcar toward a gated entryway. The guard in the black-trimmed silvers of the Argenti forces recognized the Taran codes and waved Stefan onward as the gate swung open. Van still had to present his datacard at the main entry. He was not issued wand or guard, but merely told that Colonel Marti's office was on the second level in the north wing.

The embassy was not unguarded. As he walked the corridors that held but a mere handful of people, every ten meters, or less, Van could sense another pulse of energy from the security systems, and, with the aid of his implant, identified at least a dozen concealed autoweapons emplacements set high in the blue marble walls of the main corridors. While the

Taran embassy also had such emplacements, they were far fewer and contained far less power.

Van found the office without difficulty. Colonel José Marie Marti—that was the holo banner outside the archway.

Inside, a young woman smiled warmly. "Commander Albert? Colonel Marti is expecting you. The open door." Her Anglo was but slightly accented, and her friendliness obvious.

"Thank you," Van replied in Hispyn.

Marti was brown-eyed, black-haired, olive-skinned, and a centimeter or two taller than Van. He was standing. Both his eyes and smile were warm as he half bowed. "Commander Albert, a pleasure to meet you." The colonel's Hispyn was eloquent and flowing—and also very clear.

"The pleasure is truly mine," Van replied, in Hispyn, "and I appreciate your kindness in seeing me with so little notice."

"You speak Hispyn with almost no accent, Commander, and that is most rare for a fighting officer." Marti smiled. "They all say that you are an accomplished battle commander."

"I am better described as competent and fortunate, and can only hope that the Lady Fortune continues to smile upon me."

Marti smiled broadly. "You know Cameros?"

"You have unmasked me. His words are better than mine," Van confessed.

The Argenti officer laughed. "You are indeed unlike your predecessor. He was a man of few words, and those were brief."

"He may have been wiser than I," Van suggested. "We Tarans have the weakness of loving words more than silence."

"Learning is sharing, and one cannot learn if one offers nothing to share, and words are the manner in which one must share knowledge." Marti stepped toward the doorway that opened onto a small terrace, more of a miniature garden. "I had thought we might enjoy the morning. In another few weeks, it will be too hot."

Van followed the colonel. The two settled into the chairs on each side of a white-enameled wrought-iron table in the shade of the wall. Even before they had fully seated themselves, the aide who had greeted Van appeared with a tray, on which were two steaming cups of café.

"Commodore Petrov had mentioned that you were a café drinker, like me, and so I took the liberty . . ." Marti offered, raising his own cup.

"Thank you." Van sipped. The café was good, with a slightly nutty taste. "This is good. Is it Argenti? It tastes close to what I have had . . ."

"Alas . . . no." Marti tilted his head slightly. "I should say it is not directly Argenti. It comes from a plantation begun by Baron Byrnedot. He was a most amazing man. He was actually Scandyan, but he became a member of the Argenti diplomatic corps. That was common then. Before his assassination he had established the café plantation near the old governor's residence. It is still there, and after matters settled down, we purchased the land back. The Scandyans were happy to receive cold credits for what they saw as close to worthless hillside land."

"It must have been sometime later."

"A mere hundred years."

Van laughed at the dry tone.

"The baron had also established an agreement with the Farhkans to trade observational details for certain technologies to be established on Gotland. After his assassination, the rebels repudiated the agreement." Marti smiled ironically and took a sip of café.

"He had set up an agreement with the Farhkans?" Van took another sip of café.

"I can assure you that it is accurate. The baron was not killed by Argenti agents, either. That would not have been in our interests."

"The Scandyans claim he suggested the rebellion. That was in your interests?"

"What is claimed and what occurred may not always be the same," Marti said. "You may be aware of this from your own experience." The hint of a twinkle appeared in his dark eyes.

"It has come to my attention that this happens," Van admitted. "So . . . why did you not attempt an agreement with the Farhkans directly after that?"

"The Farhkans were not interested. That is what the diplomatic archives say. We also know that the Farhkans have rebuffed all attempts since then. So far as we can determine, they have agreements only with the Coalition. Although those have become most limited in recent years, they have been a matter of long-standing concern." Marti shrugged. "Were those agreements with the Revenants, the concerns would have been far greater, you understand."

"That I do." The very thought of the Revenants with any advanced alien technology left Van feeling very cold. "Who were the rebels, then? You're suggesting that neither the Argenti government nor thoughtful Scandyans wanted a revolt."

"You wonder why I bring up history to an officer who has just become a military liaison?"

"I think I understand," Van replied, "but it might be better to hear it in your words."

"And wiser, no doubt. Very well . . . Three hundred years ago, the Taran Republic was struggling to survive. The Keltyr had scarcely colonized four systems. The Coalition and the Revenants were locked in a fight to the death. In part, because we were aware that the raciogenetic background of the Scandyan colonists was somewhat different—"

"Is that a polite way of saying that they had lighter skins?" Van asked with a laugh.

"That, and a different cultural outlook," Marti admitted. "We made concession after concession here in Gotland. We even wrote off the planoforming costs of Malmot. Taxes were lower here than in the central Argenti systems." Marti looked blandly at the Taran commander.

"It would certainly seem that the Scandyans had no real reason for a revolt, and the Argentis were clearly trying to avoid provoking one," Van concluded.

"Exactly my thoughts. They have been the thoughts of many over the years. Yet there was a revolt, and it was in someone's interests, and those perhaps only looked like they were Scandyan."

Van knew all too well what culture looked like the Scandyans—the Revenants.

"Ah . . . but we should not dwell in too much detail upon the past," Marti said, his point made. "How are you finding Valborg?"

"Cooler than home. Sulyn. It's one of the warmer Taran planets."

"You prefer the warm?"

"I prefer reasonable cool, whenever possible."

"Gotland will be to your liking in the winter, but you will care little for the months ahead."

"So I have heard. How long have you been stationed here?"

"Three years. I arrived several months after Commander Cruachan. Did you know him?"

"I'd never met him. Had you run across him before?"

"No. We met for the first time here on Gotland. He was a most polite and courteous officer. Reserved, but most correct. We had little in common except our profession and our assignments. He liked to sail, and I have always preferred the heights. He was little interested in women—he said he had never married—and I brought my wife here at my own expense."

Van was impressed. That alone must have cost the colonel tens of thousands of credits. "That could not have been inexpensive."

"It was not, but life . . . it is fragile, and how could one not appreciate it to the fullest when one realizes that? One cannot hoard life. It still slips through the fingers."

"It does." Van smiled. "But hoarding is an old Taran habit, and one that dies hard."

"Even for one . . . such as you?"

"You mean . . . black Tarans? Our skins may be a bit darker or more bronzed, but we can be as bad as the others that way." Van finished the last of his café and set the cup down.

"I think not. A man who borrows the words of Cameros cannot hoard all of his life."

From there, the conversation slipped into generalities, and various promises to keep each other informed, and, precisely fifty minutes after he arrived, Van stepped back out of the colonel's office and made his way back to the waiting groundcar.

He settled into the rear seat, still thinking over what the colonel had implied. The Scandyan revolt actually created by Revenant agents? It made sense, in an obverse way, since it weakened the Argenti presence on the edge of Revenant territory, but, if that were so, why was there no mention of the possibility in the histories and political analyses?

"Ser . . . something up ahead," Stefan said.

Van looked up. An electrolorry was angled across the road, blocking the right-hand side, not that it probably would tie up too much traffic, since, as usual, there wasn't much. From what he read and watched, the only traffic was in the center of Valborg and in the southwest.

As Stefan slowed to a stop a good five meters back, abruptly the side gate of the lorry—the one turned toward the embassy groundcar—gave way, and lengths of pipe rolled down and crashed onto the street. Some continued rolling toward the embassy vehicle, but Stefan could not move back, not with the large gray groundcar that had stopped less than a meter behind them, the only other groundcar in sight.

Van had a very chill feeling. Even before the last pipe rolled against the rough pile that built up against the front of the groundcar, he was out and moving, his implant and system tuned up to combat-ready.

The first man—blocky and young—had a vibroknife. Van slammed that aside and twisted the heel of his boot through the would-be attacker's knee. The *crunch* was sickening. Van twisted the man's wrist and upper arm, with another snap, and the vibroknife dropped to the stone walk.

Van dropped flat, even before the wicked *thwip!* of a slash-disc flew through the space where he had been standing. His implant located the second man—no more than four meters to his left.

Van grasped one of the shorter lengths of pipe, then launched himself. The shorter pipe thudded into the bearded man's chest, and the hand holding the disc-gun flew back. Before the second attacker could bring it back forward, Van followed the pipe with a flurry of well-placed elbows and knees. The second man collapsed.

Van turned, and a line of fire slashed at his left shoulder. He moved toward the pain, quickly, and smashed his good arm and elbow into the third man's throat, following with a knee. The man dropped his disc-gun and sagged to the ground, trying to gasp for air. Van might have crushed his larynx enough for him to suffocate, although he didn't think so. He really didn't care.

Van surveyed the area, but could see no one else nearby. The gray groundcar behind the embassy vehicle was empty, presumably having been driven by one of the attackers, and several other groundcars were approaching from the west.

"Ser?" Stefan said, holding a dressing. "You are bleeding."

Van had noted the pain, but not the bleeding, and he looked almost stupidly at the slash in his left arm. "Yes . . . you'd better use that, and then notify the local authorities."

"I already called the constabulary, ser. They are on the way." Stefan ripped open the jacket sleeve more and applied the pressure dressing to the slash in Van's left arm.

"Good."

"The newsies have been saying that violence is up here in Valborg, but I've never seen anything like this." Stefan tightened the dressing. "That should do for now."

"I haven't either," Van admitted. He looked over the three fallen men. The one whose knee and arm he had broken was trying to crawl away. Van stepped toward the struggling man. "If you move another centimeter, I'll snap your other leg."

"Frig you . . ." The man fumbled toward his jacket with his good arm.

Van slammed a snap kick into the other's chin. A small stunner clanked onto the pavement, and the attacker collapsed forward. Van swept the stunner away with his foot. "If you wouldn't mind picking that up, Stefan . . . with a cloth or something."

"Ah . . . yes, sir."

The second man groaned, trying to stagger to his feet. *Thrummm* . . . Stefan had triggered the stunner.

Van glanced at the driver.

"It seemed wiser, ser."

Van held in a laugh. It had been wiser. In his present state of mind, Van might have done far worse, and Stefan had sensed that.

The groundcars that had been nearing stopped. One turned around. The other waited. Then, from overhead, came the sound of a flitter roaring down. The downwash from the ducted airflow whipped Van's uniform around him, but only for a moment, as the shimmering white craft settled into the open space in front of the angled electrolorry.

Two constables rushed out. One watched the three fallen attackers. The other hurried over to Van and Stefan.

"What happened, ser?" asked the fresh-faced constable.

"I don't know. The lorry stopped, and then pipes flew off it. I got out to see what was happening, and one of them lunged at me with a vibroknife. I kicked at him, and I guess I was lucky. He fell down. The second fellow . . . the last pipe rolled down and smashed into him. The third one . . . his disc-gun slashed me in the arm, and we struggled." Van shrugged, and wished he hadn't, as an arrow of fire slashed up his left arm. He winced.

"Lot of blood there, ser."

"It took a moment for me to find the dressing, Officer," Stefan volunteered. "I've contacted the embassy, and they have a doctor waiting."

"The embassy?"

Van extended his datacard. "I'm Commander Albert, military attaché to the Taran embassy. I'd had a meeting with my counterpart at the Argenti embassy, and we were headed back when this happened."

Despite his earlier concern about Van's injury, the young constable was most thorough in his questions, asking and reasking about the same details.

". . . you say a pipe hit him. How hard might that have been?"

". . . and you just kicked him?"

". . . about that stunner once more. You say that the one with the shattered knee had that?"

Van kept his answers short and the same, and after what seemed a good hour, the two constables finally let Stefan and Van leave the scene—long after the three attackers had been carted away by a groundwagon.

As Stefan drove back toward the Republic embassy, Van thought over the attack.

Why would anyone attack him? Since he'd arrived on Gotland, he'd done almost nothing, except meet a few people and write reports and analyses for the ambassador. He'd probed into nothing except Commander Cruachan's reports. Could the attack have been mistaken identity?

It clearly hadn't been for theft. The three had wanted him, and no one else.

He'd have to think more, because at the moment he couldn't think of a single reason why anyone on Gotland would want him dead—or captured.

Then, too, the meeting with Colonel Marti had bothered him, not because it hadn't gone well, but because it had. From what Van could tell, Colonel Marti didn't at all fit the profile conveyed by Cruachan's reports, except in physical terms. Was that because Cruachan had not been that fluent in Hispyn? Or because Cruachan had seen more than Van had?

Van honestly couldn't tell. He just hoped that it wouldn't be too long before he could. And before he had some idea about why he'd been attacked.

Stefan's report to the embassy must have been circulated, because a number of people were waiting in the hallway on the upper level as Van came up the ramp after the doctor—whom he didn't know—checked the wound, sprayed it with nanites, and re-dressed it. Van carried the bloody outer jacket over his right arm.

Cordelia Gregory's mouth opened as she saw Van and the dark bloodstains across his lower sleeve. "Stefan said . . . what did they do . . . to you?"

"Three young fellows tried to rob us. They didn't much care if I survived the attempt." Van offered a twisted smile. "But they got a little too close."

"You didn't hurt them, did you?" asked the second secretary. Her eyes narrowed.

"Not too much. The local authorities have them in custody." Van wasn't about to explain.

Sean Bulben said nothing. Nor did either of the aides Van didn't know.

Van made his way to his office. He could have gone to his quarters, but all he would have done there was pace. He laid the uniform jacket on the corner of the table desk, thinking that he'd need a replacement, and settled into the chair behind the desk. Trying to ignore the muted throbbing in his arm, he considered about how to get the information he needed from the netsystem.

There was a knock on Van's door. He could sense a feminine presence. "Yes?"

"Commander . . . I heard . . ."

"You can come in, Emily."

Clifton eased into the inner office. Her eyes went to the bloody jacket on the corner of the desk, then to the dressing on Van's arm. "Are you all right?" She shook her head. "That's a stupid question. How badly are you hurt?"

"It's a glancing gash from a disc-gun—deep enough and long enough for a lot of blood. Almost no muscle damage."

"Stefan said you took on three toughs and disabled them all." She paused. "He said you almost killed two with your bare hands."

Van almost shrugged, but didn't, offering a sheepish

expression. "I have a temper. I get angry when people I don't know try to ambush me."

"What if that's the point?" Emily asked wryly.

"To get me angry enough to commit murder?" Van took a deep breath. "I hadn't thought of that. It's possible . . . but I don't have any idea who would want to."

"Maybe it's not you. Did you ever think of that?"

"I'd thought about mistaken identity, but you think that it's more to discredit the embassy."

"Tarans have a reputation for being hotheaded. Things are tense in this part of the Arm right now. What if the Revs or the Kelts wanted to discredit us?"

"The Kelts are as hotheaded—"

"Even better," she suggested.

Van nodded. "It's possible." And it was a better explanation than he had. That was certain. He smiled. "What time tomorrow?"

"Do you still want to go . . . tomorrow?"

"I don't see why not. Walking around and looking at an old governor's palace isn't going to do much harm. The wound is more bloody and painful than really damaging. A long fairly shallow cut. It'll bother me more if all I do is sit around and think about it."

"You're certain?"

"Absolutely. The place doesn't open until ten hundred. What if we leave the embassy at nine-thirty? Or is that too early?"

"Hardly. I'm a morning person."

"Then I'll see you then." Van offered a smile. He was actually looking forward to seeing Cliff Spire.

"I'll be ready."

After Emily had left, Van eased back in his chair. She'd had a good point about his not being a target personally . . . and perhaps she was right. Yet . . . if she were, and he'd just happened to be in the wrong position at the wrong time, what was really going on in the Arm that had created tensions that high? They'd been high for a century. What was different now?

Chapter 15

Van did not sleep well, even with the pain-suppressants in the wound dressing. Nightmares about the *Regneri* combined with the attack by the unknown cruiser and assault by the three men, until his dreams were a pastiche of violence, underscored with puzzlement. At six hundred he finally got up, showered, and dressed in a casual dark green jumpsuit, since he certainly wasn't going anywhere on embassy business. He fixed himself café in his own quarters, along with a simple omelet—simple because he'd neglected to stock his larder with more than a few basics.

Then he settled into the one comfortable armchair in his compact sitting room, and tried to sort out what he knew. There were blatant hints that Cruachan's death had been murder, and Commodore Petrov had nearly stated as much. Someone had used the embassy system to alter some of Cruachan's reports after his death. Van would have bet on the RSF security experts investigating Cruachan's death. Whether they had altered those reports for security reasons or for more sinister ones was something that Van couldn't have proved one way or another.

Then, there was Cruachan himself. Everyone had thought him honorable and intelligent. He had worked well with Petrov, but he had not liked Colonel Marti. Yet Marti had been complimentary about the commander. Marti had also provided more insight in some areas than had all the RSF and Republic briefing documents. Add to that an unstable Scandyan political situation, so unstable that there were regular protests in front of the Parliament building. Finally, most important personally, someone seemed to have taken a dislike to Van.

Since his thoughts weren't providing much in the way of

insight, Van used his implant to route his inquiry to the local constabulary, calling up a holo image before him.

"Constable Ebbers."

"Constable, this is Commander Albert from the Taran embassy. Yesterday, you may recall, I was attacked by three men . . ."

"Yes, ser."

"Constable, have you found out anything from those young fellows who attacked me?"

The Scandyan officer's face blanked for a moment. "I regret . . . No . . . we have not."

"Are they still in custody?"

"Just a moment, ser."

Van found himself looking at a blank projection screen for several minutes, until the image of an older officer appeared. "Commander Albert?"

"Yes? I was just asking if you had found out anything—"

"We did find out one thing, ser."

"Yes?" Van didn't like the officer's tone, as if the man were probing. "Could you tell me what that might be—if it's possible?"

"We aren't likely to get much information from them."

"Why not?"

"All three died last night."

"What?" Van certainly hadn't expected that. "In custody? They weren't that badly hurt."

"No, ser. You aren't leaving Gotland anytime soon, are you?"

"I just was posted here."

"We'll be sending someone out to see you, probably on oneday. That's all I can say, ser."

"That's all?"

"Yes, ser. We'll be in touch."

Van was looking at a blank screen once more. He collapsed it, looking out the window, but scarcely seeing the puffy white clouds over the hills to the northwest. Finally, he triggered his implant. Even through the embassy netsystem, even though he'd reserved the embassy groundcar the day before, it took almost half an hour to go through the forms required to check out the car for the day. He walked down to the vehicle area, and it took another quarter hour to locate the white groundcar and get the duty supervisor to release it.

Emily Clifton was waiting by the main entrance, even though he was ten minutes early. She wore a turquoise green blouse and matching trousers, with a small black belt pack on her left side. Her short blonde hair was swept back above her ears.

"You really want to get away from the embassy, don't you?" he asked, as she slid into the passenger side of the front seat.

"Just be careful, Commander . . . or I'll sit in the back and make you into a hired driver."

"Bad morning?"

"Bad evening. I spent three hours with Madame Rogh going over the protocol and arrangements for her independence week luncheon."

"I've never met the lady, but the subject sounds hard on everyone." Van eased the groundcar out through the embassy gate, past the duty Marine, and onto Knutt Boulevard.

"It is. It was so much easier when Mary Gonne was ambassador. Her partner was much more easygoing. Of course, the fact that her partner was female made the Revenants extraordinarily uncomfortable." Emily's laugh was almost a giggle of joy.

"I can imagine," Van said dryly.

"You don't approve?"

Van laughed. "I had two fathers."

"You?" After a moment, she added, "You're serious, aren't you?"

"Mostly. My mother lived next door with her partner. But she was killed in a climbing accident after I joined the RSF. Her partner moved, didn't want to stay in the house."

"I never would have guessed . . ." Emily shook her head. "And you?" She added quickly. "I'm sorry. That's terribly rude. You certainly don't—"

Van brushed off her demurral. "That's all right. Although

my fathers hoped, they never pressed, and, no, I don't take after them that way. I only hope I do in others, though."

Emily didn't say anything, but nodded encouragingly.

"Dad Cicero is one of the most honest men I know. He's also an exceedingly good advocate. Dad Almaviva is a singer . . . he can sing anything, and he's the head of the opera company associated with Sulyn University."

"They must be something."

"Why do you say that?" Van asked.

"They let you do what you wanted, not what they wanted."

"They did. There were a few cautions and hard questions. They pointed out that most of the Republic was far more conventional than Sulyn, and not terribly supportive of officers from a heritage of single-sex partners and darker skins, but, in the end, they let me chart my own course. Both of them still send me cubes, especially when they're worried about me."

"I can't say I hear from my family that much, not anymore."

"Oh?" Van didn't know what else to say.

"I left home early. Was an RSF tech for one tour. Liked the ships, but not . . . that doesn't matter. Got out and made my way through the university. My mother was killed in a flitter crash ten years ago, and my father had left years before. The only thing he left me, my mother said, was my middle name. Sometimes I hear from my brothers, but not often."

"That could be hard. I know I still have my family." Van paused. "Your middle name?"

"Senta, from some ancient opera. He said that there weren't enough good women in the Galaxy, but he never explained it. I finally looked it up, almost decided to have it changed, but then what would I have?"

Van nodded sympathetically.

"You know?"

"Yes. *Der Fliegende Holländer*. Dad Almaviva sang the captain's role." Van wanted to say something about how her middle name fit, because she did seem the good and faithful type, never fully understood . . . but he scarcely knew her.

After a silence, Emily asked, cheerfully, "I should have asked earlier, but . . . do you know where we're going?"

"I did check the maps and directions. We're taking Knutt Boulevard north to the west guideway, and follow that to the Ridgeline Road exit. Then we go north for two klicks until we see the signs."

The sign was so small Van almost missed it—just a golden oak oblong affixed to a wooden post with darker letters reading CLIFF SPIRE carved into the wood. An arrow pointed down the lane barely wide enough for two groundcars to pass. The paving was ancient synthstone, flanked by a pfitzer hedge higher than the roof of the groundcar.

Slightly more than a half klick northward, the lane turned east, and then, twenty yards later, the hedge and lane both ended. On the right was a carpark, with space for a good thirty vehicles. There were but three there.

"It's not exactly thronged," observed Emily.

"No." Van eased the embassy vehicle into one of the empty spaces, then got out and stretched. The hillside air was cooler, fresher, and the breeze was welcome.

To the north stood the former governor's mansion, a single-story structure of a dark green stone that seemed to blend into the walled terraces—also constructed of the same green stone—that rose up the hillside to meet it.

"Look," Emily said.

Van turned. He hadn't really been looking, but Cliff Spire had not been a fanciful name. The grounds to the east, overlooking the northern part of Valborg and the bay and ocean beyond, were literally peninsula-like—a good fifteen hectares of low gardens and flowers. The ground was flat, as if it had been cut out of the hillside. The gardens were in flower, and each section seemed to carry out a different color scheme. For a time, Van just stood at the beginning of the gray flagstone path that wound along the gardens on the southern side of the estate.

Emily stepped up beside him. "If this is what he created . . ."

"It's a spectacular view and setting."

They walked slowly along the path, stopping at the first flower bed. The borders were sculpted in scalloped curves, the curves outlined by a pale green permanite edging. Just inside the edging was a border of a low ground cover with pale blue flowers, each not much bigger than the tip of a stylus, but there were thousands, tiny blue starbursts against the dark bluish green leaves. Behind the ground cover were bushes roughly thirty centimeters high. Each bush had been grown and trimmed into the shape of a seven-pointed star.

Van counted several to make sure. All had seven points. He wasn't sure he'd ever seen a seven-pointed star before. He looked to Emily. "Have you ever seen a seven-pointed star before?"

"Seven-pointed star?"

"The bushes." He pointed, then watched as she counted.

"You're right. Seven points. I haven't seen that before."

Van took another deep breath, taking in the perfume of the flowers, a mixture of scents that seemed to change with the light, swirling breeze. One moment, the odor was predominantly cinnamon mint, the next a lavender rose, and then a pungent marigold-like musk.

"Was that obvious to you?" she asked, as they walked through the cool midmorning hill breeze to the second flower bed along the flagstone path.

"The star pattern? It stood out."

Emily nodded.

They stopped before the second assemblage of plants and flowers—clearly based on pinks, but the shapes, to Van, at least, were ovals that looked most like spiral galaxies. He did not say so, and they moved to the next flower bed.

It took more than two hours, even for a cursory look at the flower beds, the turf maze, and the topiary arrangements in the gardens, before they climbed the wide green stone staircase that ran up the center of the terraces and reached the covered veranda—and a guide who stood there.

"The governor often sat here after his evening meal," offered the young man, who wore a uniform with which Van was unfamiliar. "He built Cliff Spire with his own funds.

That was why he could place it so far from the colonial assembly building. He'd planned to retire here, after his diplomatic service."

"Did he have any family?" asked Emily.

"He had both a daughter and a son. After his death, the daughter emigrated to Perdya—"

"She went Eco-Tech?"

"That's right. His son was already in the Argenti space forces, and he never returned to Gotland. His wife lived here another thirty years, then gifted Cliff Spire to the Spire Foundation and left Gotland."

"How sad," murmured Emily.

Van agreed, but didn't say so.

"You can get the best idea of what Cliff Spire is like if you go to the left after you enter," the young guide continued, "and move from the front sitting room to the formal dining area, and then along the front rooms. Just make a long oval, and you'll end up in the study on the right side of the foyer."

"Thank you."

The front sitting room appeared strangely modern, with a long couch, flanked by two dark wood end tables, facing the east windows. The only object obviously from the past was in the northeast corner of the sitting room—a concert-sized acoustical piano, cordoned off with green velvet ropes.

From the sitting room they entered the formal dining room, twenty-five meters long and ten in width, with a polished cherrywood table that stretched fifteen meters. Van counted fifteen matching chairs on each side, and two at the end, but another eight were set around the room, flanking the china cabinets and the two sideboards. The table was set as if for a formal dinner.

"Madame Rogh would love this," said Emily quietly.

"I'm sure."

From there they followed the hallway to the pantries, the kitchen, and the staff wing. It took another hour before they reached the last room of their tour—the study opposite the foyer where they had entered. A table desk faced the wide windows. The entire wall behind the desk was composed of

built-in wooden bookcases, and every shelf was filled with
the antique books. A book lay open on the desk.

"I don't think I've ever seen so many books in one place,
not even in the museum in New Oisin," murmured Emily.

"It is a museum, and it looks as though they've re-created
the way it was just before Byrnedot was killed."

"That's right. It's just as he left it when he went down to
speak to the assembly," offered the guide from the doorway
into the foyer. "His wife closed the room and never disturbed
a thing." He turned away to greet another group that had
entered the mansion from the front veranda. "You can get the
best idea of what Cliff Spire is like if . . ."

Van walked over behind the desk, leaning forward over the
velvet ropes, and straining to see the last entries in what had
to be a diary or journal.

> . . . 15 Sextus . . . there is nothing to be done, but to try once
> more to persuade them to look to the future, and not to the
> past. We must all live in the same Galaxy, no matter what our
> background and what our appearance. In the end, none will
> rule over those who do not wish it so. I have tried to make Got-
> land a world where there is less oppression and more justice
> than anywhere in the Argenti sphere . . . and my success may
> be my undoing. We shall see.

The writing ended.

Van straightened, nodding to himself. He could see how
what Byrnedot had written could have been interpreted to
favor the cause of Scandyan secession, but, based on what
Colonel Marti had said, the alternative made even more
sense. Once more he was reminded how people saw what
they wished to see.

Was *he* seeing what he wished to see? He didn't think so,
because he really didn't have a bias about the past history of
Gotland. His bias was just trying to make sense out of it all,
but then, maybe that was an even greater prejudice than ide-
ology.

"What are you thinking?" Emily's voice was quiet.

"About history. About how even the best and most able have difficulty in combating shortsightedness and greed . . . and how it never changes."

"That's . . . depressing."

"I'm sorry. I'll have to make it up to you somehow."

"That's a proposition. Is it decent or indecent?"

"It has to be decent," Van replied, as they stepped back into the entry foyer, momentarily empty. "We don't know each other well enough for it to be otherwise."

That brought a smile to Emily's eyes and mouth.

They began to walk down the green stone staircase toward the lower level path that would take them back to the carpark.

"What now, Commander?"

"A good meal. Do you have any suggestions?"

"One or two." A twinkle flashed in her gray eyes.

Van laughed. "I'll drive. You navigate."

"I'll accept that bargain."

For the first time in days, Van was enjoying himself.

Chapter 16

On oneday, after a thankfully quiet eightday, not much past midmorning, Van found himself with two Scandyan constables in his embassy office—Constable Lieutenant Rolfes and Constable Sergeant Bentssen. Technically, Van could have refused to have met with them, especially since he'd been the assaulted party, and diplomatic precedent was more than clear on the right of a diplomat to self-defense, a precedent hammered out over millennia of bad examples.

After almost an hour of questions from the lieutenant, Van was beginning to believe he should have refused to meet with the pair.

". . . and you cannot think of any reason why these men of

good background would have decided to behave as they did?" Rolfes asked.

"I haven't the faintest idea. I'd never met any of them. I've only been in Valborg for two weeks, and most of that time has been spent here at the embassy trying to catch up on what wasn't done after my predecessor's death. I was wondering . . . have you discovered anything new about the three?"

"So far there's been little progress on that front," Rolfes replied. "Now . . . about the third man . . . was it necessary to use the degree of force you employed on the third man?"

"I think I've answered that question about three times, Lieutenant," Van replied tiredly. "I was unarmed. They all had weapons. I was just trying to survive. I did not use lethal force." He paused, and then added, "It took your incarceration to kill them. I certainly had nothing to do with that. What I wanted to know, and what I still want to know, is any information about why those three had set up an attack on me. I've also asked that question at least three times, and you, unlike me, have given no information at all."

"We really don't know, ser," Rolfes replied politely.

"I think that translates into something along the lines of your having some information, not knowing what it means, and keeping it to yourselves until you can make sense of it."

Rolfes stiffened.

"I'm a military man, Lieutenant. I'm not a diplomat. I've been patient. I've answered all your questions to the best of my ability. I've answered all of them at least twice, sometimes even four times. You've answered almost none of mine. I'd like to point out, once again, that I was the one attacked. You have witnesses to that. You even have some street surveillance images that bear that out. Yet you seem to be acting as if I were the guilty party, as if it were my fault that I was attacked."

"Ser . . . I don't believe—"

"It's not what you said, Lieutenant. It's the way you've proceeded. Might it just possibly be because my skin is a few shades more to the bronze? Or is it because the Taran Republic cannot bring as many cruisers into your section of the Arm?" Van could see the lieutenant begin to flush, and he laughed. "You see. You're getting upset because I even suggested you're proceeding in a biased fashion. Think about how I feel . . ."

"This is a most unusual situation, ser," Rolfes protested. "The last time a diplomat was assaulted was over a hundred years ago. This is not at all normal. We're just trying to discover why it happened."

"I suggest that you look into the background of the three men. You might talk to their families, their friends and associates."

"We have, ser. We've spent almost three days intensively questioning them, and there's nothing there."

Van forced a polite smile. "And what about their deaths?"

"The medical examiners can find no reason for their deaths. Their hearts just . . . stopped."

"That's an interesting datum in itself, I'd think."

For the first time, Rolfes looked both puzzled and interested.

"There are only three Arm powers with those kinds of abilities, and Scandya, the Keltyr, and the Taran Republic aren't among them."

"That's a serious charge—"

Van laughed again. "It's not a charge. It's an observation, and it doesn't mean that those three had anything to do with it directly. It does mean that the three had to have had contact—if indirectly—with someone with access to those technologies. It also means that someone didn't want you to discover what they're doing, and, if I were you . . . I'd think about the implications of that a lot more than whether I may have used slightly excessive vigor in defending myself against men who were obviously a far greater danger to Scandya than am I." Van stood. "I wish you the best in your investigation."

"But . . ." began Constable Sergeant Bentssen.

Rolfes rose smoothly. "The commander is right, Bentssen. There's not much that questioning him further will establish." He bowed to Van, excessively.

"You're right, Lieutenant. But *I* didn't say it." Van refrained from suggesting that the lieutenant focus on the problem, rather than upon Van himself.

After the two had left, and after he'd spent a good ten minutes trying to cool down, he left his office and headed for the third secretary's spaces.

"Come on in, Commander." Emily studied Van as he stood there. "You're angry."

"It shows that much?"

"You don't hide strong feelings well."

"I'm not angry with you." Van shook his head. "I just spent the last hour with two very polite Scandyan constables . . . two very polite and obtuse constables . . ." He went on to summarize the meeting. ". . . so, as the embassy's media expert, I thought you should know. I'll also have to send a memo to the ambassador, but I wanted you to know before I told him, because he'll probably come to you immediately."

"So will Ian."

"Rogh will tell him?"

"As soon as you walk out of his door—or as soon as he can fire off an implant message without giving it away." Emily frowned. "I still . . . that's disturbing . . . I'd heard . . . but . . ."

Rather than ask, Van waited.

"Like you, I try to maintain contacts around Scandya. There's a Hyndji consulate, not even an embassy, because they don't have a presence in the Arm. Sanji is a friend, and he was telling me that he'd noticed people were getting cooler and cooler toward him. He insisted it wasn't imagination. There have been a few stories in the media, too. And then there was the Liberal Commons demonstration last week against allowing Argenti and Hyndji scientists into Scandya. I'm beginning to wonder."

"Wonder what?"

"Bias . . . prejudice." Emily frowned. "It doesn't make any sense."

"Prejudice never does. But I see what you mean. Unless . . ."

"Unless what?"

"The Argentis . . . some of them are darker-skinned than I am."

"But Scandya is already independent," she pointed out. "The locals don't need to exploit prejudice for a revolution. They haven't for centuries."

"But Scandya needs allies to remain independent. Who benefits from fanning prejudice?"

"You think the Revenants would stoop that low?"

Van laughed. "People have always stooped that low, even when we were all crammed into one planet."

"I suppose so." Emily sighed. "I'll run another search—after I finish the latest follow-ups for Madame Rogh's luncheon." Her smile was both rueful and warm. "I'll let you know."

"Thank you." Van stepped out of her office and walked back toward his own. He'd have to tell both the ambassador and Hannigan, but he needed just a few more minutes to prepare himself. He needed to be dispassionate, and he also wanted to think out the best way to ensure that the two drew the same conclusion that Emily had.

Still . . . it bothered him. He wasn't sure whether the Scandyan blindness or the apparent easy acceptance of prejudice bothered him more. Then, that choice was simply between one form of stupidity and another.

He opened his own office door and stepped inside.

Even though the Coalition did not have a full embassy, Van thought he ought to pay a call on the Eco-Tech military liaison—if there was one. Before he contacted the Coalition office, he decided to try once more to make contact with Submarshal Brigham Taylor, the Revenant military attaché. He'd put in a call almost a week earlier and heard nothing. He'd try to reach the Revenant sub-marshal first, and then see about the Eco-Tech office before he told the ambassador about the morning's inquisition. By then, he might be calmer.

Chapter 17

The Revenant sub-marshal had again failed to get back to Van—but Van did get a return call from the Coalition liaison office later on oneday, asking if a meeting with a Major Murikami on threeday would be suitable. Van had confirmed it immediately. After he'd accepted the meeting, he had gone back to puzzling over the matter-of-fact attitude taken by the Ambassador Rogh about Van's treatment by the Scandyan constabulary.

"It's their planet," Rogh had said. "You just have to do the best you can.'

Van doubted that Rogh would have been so philosophical if he'd been the one being questioned by the Scandyan constabulary, but he'd just nodded.

Two more mornings had passed without event. By threeday morning, along with everything else, Van found himself still fretting about the *Fergus*, since he'd seen nothing on the embassy infoservice or anywhere else. Finally, by late morning, he used the embassy net to connect to Gotland orbit control, and then to connect to the *Fergus*.

The image that appeared was that of Shennen, the head comm tech. "Republic ship *Fergus*, Tech Shennen. How might I help you, ser . . . Ser? Commander?"

"It's me, Shennen. Is Commander Baile available?"

"Let me check, ser."

The image of the trim, graying, but youthful-faced commander appeared almost instantly. "Commander Albert, what can I do for you?"

"I just thought I'd check back with you, to see if there was anything I might have overlooked, and also, out of interest, to see how the repairs were coming."

Baile's face offered a warm smile. "It's kind of you to

check, but you were most effective, and left everything in good order. We've had some delays because we've had to get replacement shield generators from Tara, and a systems check indicated we probably should also replace one of the jump generators, just to be safe. But it won't be long now."

"That's good to hear." Van paused. He couldn't really ask where the *Fergus* was headed or whether the ship was going to stay in Scandya system. "Have you heard anything about the previous stationkeeper?"

"You know I can't . . ." Baile shrugged.

"I know." Even if Baile knew about the fate of the *Collyns*, he couldn't have said, but his expression as much as told Van that he didn't know.

"Is there anything else, Commander?" asked Baile.

"No, you've been most kind. Tell the crew I've been thinking of them."

"That I will."

The screen blanked. Van didn't know much more than before, but he had checked.

At thirteen forty-five, after reading more reports that said little, and a meal Van didn't recall even right after he'd eaten it, Van was in the back of the embassy groundcar being driven by Stefan southward on Knutt Boulevard. The Eco-Tech liaison office was a small building less than a third the size of the first floor of the Taran embassy. There were no guards in front—just a carpark set amid a gardenlike space. Stefan parked the car, and Van walked to the front entrance and into the entry foyer, where he studied the holo screen projected there. Major Murikami's office was to the left.

The first doorway on the right—open—was labeled IIS, with no explanation of the initials. As Van walked by, he glanced inside, taking in the compact room where a tall and trim blond man was talking to a younger man. Although the older man wore a simple black shipsuit without insignia, his bearing was military. Van wondered if he happened to be a former Coalition officer.

The next office on the left was the one he wanted: SERVICE LIAISON—MAJOR M. MURIKAMI. He'd always pondered why the Eco-Techs called their military forces the Service, but he'd never gotten a real answer from the few Coalition officers he'd encountered.

He stepped inside, catching the security screening, the autoweapons focused on the entryway, and the pulsed *Welcome* that his implant picked up. The space inside was small, no more than three meters by four, and held four armchairs and a low table.

"You must be Commander Albert," said the officer in the olive green shipsuit standing in the doorway to an office off the reception area. On his chest were the wings of a deep-space pilot, and the shoulder insignia were the triple bars of a Coalition major.

"Major Murikami?"

"Come on in." Major Murikami was trim and muscular, and a good ten centimeters shorter than Van. He led the way into the inner office. A series of narrow windows overlooked a garden containing a pond set among rocks and trees. The setting radiated peacefulness.

Van paused and studied the setting.

"It's very restful. Too restful at times." Murikami smiled wryly and sat down at the desk.

Van took one of the two armless chairs across from the major. "I was a little surprised to find that the Coalition didn't have a full embassy here in Scandya."

"We don't have full embassies anywhere, Commander," returned Murikami. "It reduces problems and costs. Our consular operations are designed for practicality. We gather and disseminate information and decide on the suitability of potential immigrants. We provide local analysis of economic and political conditions, but we don't get involved in local or Arm politics, and we leave actual military decisions to the High Command." The boyish-looking major added, "In short, we do everything an embassy does, except with a lower profile and a much lower cost."

Van laughed. "And you avoid the entanglements of local politics."

"The Coalition's found that for us it works better that way."

Van wondered if the Coalition were as open as Murikami made it seem. Or did the Coalition handle its political and covert operations totally outside any obvious channels?

"Well . . ." Van began, "is there any information that I can provide?"

"We'll take anything you'd like to send us, but we're under strict orders not to press, snoop, or spy." Murikami offered the boyish smile once more.

"This is my first liaison assignment," Van said. "I'm probably revealing my ignorance, but is that a standing policy for all Coalition liaison officers?"

"Absolutely. It has been for more than two hundred years."

"Since the end of the Eco-Tech-Revenant conflict?"

"Approximately. I don't know the exact date the policy was implemented."

"What else goes on here? I noticed an office as I came in . . . it doesn't seem to fit . . ."

"Oh . . . IIS. They're a private foundation that gathers information on economic and social structures throughout the Arm. We had extra space and leased it to them—just for the next year. Generally, they spend a year on a planet, doing an in-depth survey, provide a copy to the government gratis, then move on, but leave a smaller office behind."

"They must have a considerable endowment." Either that, or they were the covert operation Van was looking for—except they were right out in the open.

"I don't think so. They sell their data to a wide range of multilaterals and businesses. The free copy to the government is to allow some local check on the use of the data."

"Then," asked Van, intrigued in spite of himself, "what's to keep the various multis from getting the data from the government?"

"It isn't packaged specifically for the multis, and they'd have to spend a great deal of time massaging the data to get what they wanted. By the time they did, their competitors who bought market-specific data and recommendations would have the jump on them. That's what the local director told me, anyway." Murikami smiled once more. "There must be something to it. IIS has been around for close to a hundred and fifty years, I've been told."

"You ever work with them?"

Murikami laughed, not totally humorously. "We stay as far away as we can. They're very friendly, and they don't say anything. On most planets, they lease space well away from us, but they had some trouble when they showed up to take possession of an office they'd leased."

"Their tans were too dark?"

"It is a problem here," Murikami admitted. "No one wants to offend the Coalition government . . . but one of our foundations, not associated with the government, that's another story, and Scandyan civil rights laws don't apply to out-system aliens."

Van nodded. The more he looked at Scandya, the less he liked the system. "Do you get many applicants for immigration to the Coalition?"

"Not anymore. There aren't many non-Scandyan-looking individuals left here, and most of those who are won't pass our screening."

"What's involved with that?"

"It's just basic character," Murikami said. "We don't take most troublemakers. We don't take the lazy. We use a standard nanite employment screen, nothing fancy, plus an interview."

"There can't be many who can afford it."

"We offer a reduced fare on a Service transport, and a long-term, low-interest loan. Not many take it, but it amounts to a hundred or so individuals a year."

In effect, reflected Van, the Coalition underwrote a troopship transit to Scandya once a year. For humanitarian reasons? Or bottom-line business, because anyone who would take those terms was intelligent and determined? "Is this a Coalition policy with all Arm systems?"

"No one seems to mind," Murikami pointed out.

"Do you get access to the SDF?" Van asked bluntly.

"Enough. They'd prefer not to meet with me, but they don't want to offend the Coalition. So they smile politely in front of clenched teeth—except for Commodore Petrov. He's always been helpful." Murikami looked at Van, the smile fading. "You know that the RSF has cut off all of the top-level military feeds to your embassy, don't you?"

"I can't say I'm surprised. What do you think might be the reason?"

"Normally, that means military action, and a desire to make sure that the local embassy can't give away anything."

Van shrugged. "I can't imagine what sort of action we'd even be talking about. We can't match the Coalition, the Revs, or the Argentis. If we did anything against the Keltyr or Scandya itself, I can't imagine any of you would stand by."

"I'm just a liaison officer. I can't speak for the Service, but it does seem that there might be something that's happening that you or the ambassador might understand too well if you had full information. That's always been the past pattern of the RSF."

Past pattern of the RSF? Van was getting a good firsthand example of why no one wanted to be on the wrong side of the Coalition. "I can honestly say that I don't know about anything along those lines." Van paused. "I suppose that doesn't help. Even if I did, I'd have to say that I didn't. But it may just be because I'm new."

"That is possible."

Murikami didn't believe that, Van could tell.

"It also may be," the major went on, "that you were posted here from an assignment where you would not know anything that might come to pass."

"Possible," Van agreed. "Since you have much more experience in this than I do, what should I be looking for?"

Murikami smiled. "Anything that would benefit the RSF. It might not be to the advantage of the Taran Republic or its people. That's the problem with military forces that are too independent of civilian control."

"The other side of the problem," Van countered, "is that in systems where there's too much civilian control, like Scandya, the very independence of the system is threatened."

"That's also true, which makes life very interesting."

"Interesting" was another word for dangerous. "Yes, it does. What else should I know?"

"Beyond what I suggested, I can't say." Murikami paused. "Since we're trading information, what should I know?"

Van fingered his chin. "You probably know everything that I'd say. Xenophobia is rising here in Scandya. The Revs are fanning it and profiting from it, but I couldn't offer a shred of hard proof. The Argentis don't want to occupy the system, but they might to stop a Rev takeover."

"What about the Republic?"

"We'd like Scandya to remain independent."

Murikami nodded. Again, Van felt that the major disagreed, but wasn't about to dispute Van.

"We certainly don't want the Revs in control of the system," Van added.

"I doubt anyone does—except the Revenants themselves. That hasn't stopped them in the past. Every year, they take another system, if not more."

"You stopped them."

"We did. The cost was incredible. The war almost destroyed both societies. We'd rather not see anything on that scale ever again."

Again, Murikami was saying more than what his words conveyed.

"I don't think anyone would," Van replied.

Murikami smiled politely. "If you don't have any more questions, Commander . . ."

Van rose. "I appreciate your time, and your information. Thank you."

"My thanks to you for your courtesy. I wish you the best." Murikami also stood, as if following Van's lead.

Once outside the Coalition major's office, Van walked toward the foyer. The door to the IIS office was closed. Van could sense that it was empty. He had to wonder about the foundation. As he left the building and headed toward the groundcar, Van couldn't help but frown. Murikami didn't at all fit the profile of an Eco-Tech officer. He was far too direct and forthright, but did that mean that he was unusual, or that the Coalition trained the liaison officers to step outside their cultural profiles? Either way, that bothered Van. The man had wanted something from Van, and he'd gotten it. What? That Van was ignorant of something about to happen? That also worried Van.

The other, and even larger worry was what Murikami had suggested about the RSF. The Coalition was worried about the RSF. The RSF was worried about the Revs, and so were the Argentis. The Scandyans were worried about everyone, and who knew what the Revs were worried about?

And Van didn't really have the faintest idea what was about to happen, only that something was, and that he'd probably be blamed in some way or another.

He squared his shoulders as he neared the groundcar.

Chapter 18

Another long week came and went, and before Van knew it, it was sixday night once more, and the opening diplomatic reception for the Scandyan independence celebration was at hand. The lower south level of the Taran embassy was decorated and open to hundreds from the diplomatic community and from the ministries of the Scandyan government. Van had checked the security systems three times, after the staff had set and adjusted them, and hoped that he hadn't overlooked anything, especially considering what Major Murikami had suggested.

Van wore formal greens and the handful of medals he'd been awarded—the ones all officers got for surviving. Holding a nearly untouched pale ale, he stood in the second drawing room, his chosen unofficial station, since he didn't like the crowded larger main reception room.

Emily Clifton appeared at his elbow, wearing a matching pink jacket and trousers. "You look very distinguished, Commander."

"You look far better than that, Emily. In fact, you look very beautiful." After he said them, Van worried that his words were too personal, but he still wouldn't have taken them back.

"I should make certain that you wear that formal uniform more often." She glanced toward the archway to the main reception room. "I need to keep close to the ambassador."

"Good luck."

With a smile and a nod, she slipped back into the crowd. Van watched until she disappeared into the main room.

From among the swirl of unfamiliar and half-familiar faces emerged another that Van recognized—Rafel Petrov.

"Commander Albert."

"Commodore." Van inclined his head. "How are matters? I saw that the Liberal Greens are insisting the Scandyan Space Defense Forces are too large. They were almost rioting."

Petrov smiled tightly. "The premier called it an overexuberant display of feelings."

"The SDF isn't exactly a massive force, and all the analyses indicate it's efficient. Why are they so against it?"

"They believe that the funds would be better spent here on Gotland. On what, they cannot agree, but they all feel strongly that they should be."

Van laughed sympathetically. "I'm sorry. We don't live in that kind of a Galaxy."

"No, my friend, we do not." Petrov paused. "You have not met the Revenant military attaché, have you? Sub-marshal Brigham Taylor?"

"The sub-marshal has been otherwise occupied," Van said dryly. "For weeks now."

"A pity." Petrov grinned, an almost maniacal expression. "Then you must meet his ambassador. Come with me."

His ale still in hand, Van followed the commodore into the main reception room and to the southeast corner, beside the shelves that held Ambassador Rogh's collection of ancient manuscripts, some dating back to prehistory on Old Earth.

The commodore eased up in front of a slender man in a brilliant white dinner jacket, with matching trousers having a gold stripe on the outer seam. He had striking white hair, watery blue eyes, and a slightly rounded face.

"Commander," offered Commodore Petrov, "I'd like you to meet Ambassador Jared Dane of the Revenants of the Prophet, the Community of the Revealed."

The ambassador nodded slightly.

"Ambassador Dane, this is Commander Van Albert, the new military attaché for the Taran Republic. He is the former commander of the cruiser *Fergus* and former commander of the corvette *Eochaid*. Since he has had some difficulty in reaching Sub-marshal Taylor, I thought you should meet him."

"Most kind of you, Commodore Petrov," replied Dane. "Good to meet you, Commander."

"And you, ser." Van took in the smiling visage of the bearded diplomat, offering his own smile in return, one he scarcely meant.

Petrov slipped away into the crowd, but Van could see Hannigan moving closer to them.

"Great tan you've got, Commander." The ambassador guffawed.

"It comes with the genes, Ambassador. All of us black Tarans have good tans."

"You good with your fists? That come with the genes, too?" asked the ambassador, his tone open and genial, as if asking about a pleasant day.

Van smiled, if coolly. "All RSF officers can take care of themselves. That's true of officers in all forces, I'm sure." Van had been forced to learn that a long time ago, as had his ancestors, ages back when the Deseretists—one of the precursor faiths of the Revenants—had stamped the mark of Cain on them. "I'm sure your officers can." He paused briefly. "I met one of them coming down on the shuttle. Impressive-looking young officer. Very conscious of his heritage and duties, too."

He could sense the wince from Hannigan, standing to his left.

"He must have been. You Tarans aren't easily impressed." Ambassador Dane smiled.

Van returned the smile once more, adding calmly, "No, we're not. Some call it Taran humor. We tell things as they are, and everyone laughs because they can't believe anyone can be so direct." Then Van laughed gently, even as he noticed the woman with white-blonde hair slipping up to the ambassador's shoulder. Her green eyes and pale white skin confirmed her Revenant background. She did not look at Van.

"Pleased to meet you, Commander." Dane gave a last smile. "I see that I'm being summoned." With a nod, he turned and eased away.

As the Revenant departed, Hannigan stepped up beside Van. "You were . . . rather direct with Ambassador Dane," he murmured.

"Only truthful, Ian. I suppose that's too direct for senior diplomats."

"I suppose so."

Van could sense the unease behind Hannigan's humorous tone. "That's why there's only one military attaché. Two would be too many."

Hannigan shook his head, then abruptly turned. "The ambassador wants something." With his words, he was gone.

Van looked out over the faces, none familiar except for those of the Republic embassy staffers.

"Greetings, Commander."

Van turned to see Colonel Marti holding a wineglass, almost full.

"Greetings. I didn't see you come in." Van answered in Hispyn.

"I was late. I noticed you had only recently appeared yourself."

"I was in the second room," Van explained. "How are matters going for you?"

"Less eventfully than for you, from what I have learned." Marti smiled sympathetically.

"The local constabulary wanted to find me at fault for defending myself."

"Always . . . that is the way of it. The victim is at fault, and the Lord help him if he actually turns matters the other way."

"Like poor Byrnedot and the Argentis?" asked Van lightly.

"There is a . . . rough similarity." Marti pursed his lips, then moved closer and lowered his voice. "You should be among the first to know. I'm being ordered back to Silvium for assignment to the general staff."

"That sounds like quite an honor. Congratulations."

"I'll be leaving the day after tomorrow. I had to send my wife yesterday. There aren't that many commercial vessels, you know." Marti's smile turned ironic, as he extended his hand. "I did want you to know."

Automatically, Van took it, and found a datacard pressed into his own hand. He managed to palm it and slip it up his sleeve. He hoped he wasn't too awkward. "I wish you the best."

"And you, also." Marti inclined his head, then drifted away.

"Commander?"

Van turned to find another figure in uniform—a black-haired, black-eyed woman commander in the formal blue-green of the Keltyr. Her skin was milk white. Only the fine lines radiating from the corners of her eyes—and the rank insignia—betrayed her age.

"Yes?" he replied.

"Ayrllis Salucar, Commander, KSF—and defense attaché to our embassy here."

"I'm pleased to meet you, Commander," Van replied with a smile. "I would have been in touch with you sooner, except . . ." He gestured around the room. "And the fact that there were huge numbers of reports to catch up on."

Commander Salucar nodded. "I'd hoped to meet you. For professional and personal reasons."

"You have me at a loss," Van confessed, finally taking another sip from his glass of very warm pale ale.

Salucar smiled faintly. "You wouldn't know. My oldest brother was commander of the Aixenpax research station."

No matter where he went, the *Regneri* affair followed him. Aixenpax had been the planoforming operation that the *Vetachi* had raided—killing all the military personnel and half the scientists—immediately before Van had destroyed the renegade vessel. He inclined his head to Salucar. "I am sorry, Commander."

"You couldn't do anything about Aixenpax," she replied. "You did stop the *Vetachi*, and I don't see what else you could have done. If you hadn't, who knows how many others would have died or suffered?"

Van glanced sideways, briefly, to see Cordelia Gregory and Emily Clifton easing away. He wondered what Gregory had heard, before he answered. "I've told myself that for years. Sometimes, it even helps for a few minutes."

Salucar glanced after the departing pair, raising her eyebrows.

"The dark-haired woman's sister was on the *Regneri*. She thinks I was wrong."

"She's never seen the carnage, then."

"No."

"It's the same with some of ours. Unfortunately." Salucar tilted her head, not flirtatiously. "You're cautious, aren't you?"

"In my position, wouldn't you be?"

Rather than laughing, as Van might have done in her position, she nodded. "I would be very cautious."

"We should have that meeting before long," Van suggested.

"Call me on oneday," Salucar suggested.

"I will," Van promised.

Then the Kelt commander was gone, and Van went to find a fresh pale ale, although he had drunk less than half of the first one.

The reception dragged on. It was near midnight when Van retreated to his office. Not once had he seen either the Eco-Tech major or anyone who had looked to be from the Coalition liaison office. Nor had he seen anyone from the Hyndji consulate. Had he just missed them?

Back in his office, he slumped into his chair and looked at the card he'd gotten from Marti. Finally, he disconnected the netsystem line, put his console on local, and inserted the card. No face, no image appeared, just text, lines and lines of text, and the text was in Old Anglo. It could have come from anywhere, and that was doubtless what Marti had intended. Van read carefully and slowly. Certain phrases jumped out at him, although they were in no way highlighted.

. . . continued inability of Premier Gustofsen to create an infrastructure bridging the differences between the militant Conservative Democrats and the isolationist Liberal Commons . . . Without Gustofsen, the return of civil unrest is highly likely, but the Conservative Democrats (CDs) would retain power in the Scandyan parliamentary assembly, and the militant isolationist faction would dominate . . . compromise with the isolationist LCs would ensure no outside alliances . . .

CD ministry heads have been holding meetings with Trans-Scandyan Microtronics on a continuing basis . . . far more often than with SNI . . . also a number of the purported TSM "officials" arrived at Gotland orbit station in Revenant couriers. The official explanation was that no commercial transport was available and that the Revenant space forces made space available to facilitate more open trade arrangements, which would reduce the possibility of conflict in the mid-Arm region . . .

The independent system of Aluyson has accepted through a plebescite "a closer union" with the Community of the Revealed. The plebescite reflects the near-total control of the Aluyson economy by Revenant institutions. The process began over two decades ago with the assassination of then-dictator Charleston Browne and the ensuing collapse of an already-shaky economy . . . Through an earlier military agreement, Aluyson has already been a basing point for Revenant fleets, and moral reeducation institutes have been established for close to five years on all major continents . . .

"Moral reeducation institutes?" That was a term Van hadn't heard before, but it certainly squared with what he did know about the Revenants.

. . . plebescite was monitored by military officials from several systems, including General Diego Salazar of the Argenti
Space Forces, Sub-marshal Jon D. Vickry of the Taran RSF,
and Overmarshal Prasad Ghandi . . . Vickry was the officer in
charge of liaison with the Revenant military, quoted as saying,
"The Revenants have been quite professional and
impartial . . ."

Van frowned. Why would Marti have included an item
about the Revenant takeover of yet another independent system—and quoted an RSF sub-marshal? He read on, but the
rest of the article shed no light on why, and from what he'd
seen of Colonel Marti, what Van had received was all that
Marti was prepared to offer.

. . . the location of the RSFS *Collyns* remains unknown, and
the Taran Republic has repeatedly stated that the *Collyns* is
"engaged in sensitive operations" and that the RSF is unable
to comment further at present . . . sources indicate that the
RSFS *Fergus* will be replaced on station in Scandya by a
cruiser of the *Addams* class . . . vessel close to dreadnought
capabilities . . .

Van nodded slowly. Marti had known, and probably Major
Murikami had known about the pending transfer of the *Fergus*, yet there was nothing in the embassy system that had
told Van. He could only speculate on what else he didn't
know, and he didn't have enough information to speculate
accurately.

While there was not a single item in the text reports that by
itself made a definitive prediction on what might happen in
Gotland, the assemblage was chilling to Van. And he couldn't
see that there was much that he could do—except watch. He
could have reported the information on the *Fergus*, but his gut
told him that would be counterproductive—and most unwise.

Chapter 19

Van did not sleep well sevenday or eightday night, and was up early on oneday, scanning the news summaries, the RSF briefing items, and following what he thought was the least biased Scandyan all-news stream: UpNews.

> ... timed for Independence Week celebrations, yesterday's demonstration in Government Square sent thirty people to the medcenters, including an eight-year-old girl who had been playing in Independence Park. She was struck by a rock thrown by one of the demonstrators when it was caught by a constable's malfunctioning shield unit ... broken arm, but expected to recover ... Whether the Conservative Democrats will recover from the public outcry against the demonstration is another question. The CDs had staged the event to protest the effort on the part of Liberal Commons members to extend debate on space defense funding ...

> Floor Leader Haarlan had this to say. "Less than a month ago, there was a space battle at the fringe of our system. No one reported it, not even the commander of the victorious vessel, who was promptly transferred—to a diplomatic post right here in Valborg. This transfer also concealed, or at least no one had the courtesy to inform us, a certain sign of lack of respect. Without an adequate defense force, how can we maintain our independence, let alone hold the respect of other Arm governments ..." Rebutting this was Liberal Commons line whip Svensen. "The space force being pushed by the CDs is well beyond the economic and financial capabilities of Scandya. Long before those ships were ready, we would be bankrupt and once more purchased hectare by hectare, manufactory by manufactory, by the Argentis, who have already purchased

thousands of enterprises driven to the wall by excessive CD taxation . . ."

Absently, Van lowered the volume. The problem seemed insoluble everywhere. Prosperity and social stability rested on high levels of education and research, and high levels of spending on those resulted in innovation and progress—making a system attractive for takeover, either economic or military—unless it maintained a solid defense force. But . . . for a system to maintain enough power to protect itself, it had to levy higher taxes. That meant lowering levels of social and medical services, and increasing social unrest. And with lower levels of educational and research expenditures, the defense forces tended to lag behind others in capabilities, and that led to less ability to hold on to economic and military advantages.

A larger government—such as the Argentis or the Revenants—could funnel funds from many systems into concentrated research, and since, once discovered, knowledge was easily transferable within a political structure, it was far easier to maintain both an increasing technological and knowledge base and a military structure. Scandya—and to a lesser degree, the Keltyr and the Republic—had a much harder time balancing that. With system or planetary governments largely controlling interstellar travel, it was far easier to restrict technology transfer than in the ancient days when all humankind had lived on one planet.

He turned to the holo projection, now beaming a commercial message.

    . . . and marriage is a sacred covenant between a man and a woman, an old and cherished covenant that has stood behind the faith and values that mankind has always cherished . . . see what marriage truly is . . . read the *Book of the Prophet*, free from the Community of the Revealed . . .

Van flipped off the holo and checked the time. Nine hundred. Using his implant, he accessed the embassy netsystem and made the contact with the Keltyr embassy. "Commander Ayrllis Salucar, please. This is Commander Van Albert of the Republic of Tara's embassy."

"One moment, Commander," replied the AI taking the call—the image of a pleasant-looking and friendly woman.

Van waited.

The AI image smiled. "Commander Salucar is free at fourteen hundred. Would that be satisfactory?"

"I'll be there at fourteen hundred."

Van broke the connection and went back to the embassy-generated news summary. There was no mention of any out-system news, military or otherwise. After a month, he still had seen no RSF or Republic reports on the *Collyns*—even on the internal data circulated on the secure net—and no references to the *Fergus*, although the update summary listed the *Fergus* as still under repair off Gotland orbit control.

Van went on to the other items in his routine, from writing comments on the costs of refitting a dreadnought for Cordelia Gregory to continuing his analysis of the Scandyan SDF and reviewing critically all the information that Commodore Petrov had dropped on him. He'd read through it all once, but he had the feeling that he'd missed too much. So he was going back through each of the items more carefully—as he had time.

At fourteen hundred on oneday afternoon, Van walked into an office in the Keltyr embassy smaller than his, but on the second floor, overlooking a fountained garden, whose ancient brick walls were covered with ivy, and very bucolically contrasting to the brilliant green-and-gold outer walls of the embassy.

"You do follow up," offered Commander Salucar, motioning to the small round table set almost beside the wide window. Four chairs circled the table.

"I do my best." Van settled into a chair that did not offer a view of the garden below.

"Why, might I ask, did you take so long getting in touch?" asked Salucar. "Because—"

"You're Keltyr?" Van laughed.

"Or a woman?"

"No. I can assure you that neither had anything at all to do with my slowness. I started with the Scandyans."

"Is that all?"

"Almost," Van admitted.

She frowned, then nodded slowly. "You worried about the potential Keltyr-Taran conflict?"

"I'm worried about all conflicts, but I can't pretend that I understand Scandya, and I thought it best to start there." He glanced at the dark-haired commander. "You've been here longer than I have. What do you think about yesterday's demonstration?"

"The demonstrations are a way of allowing expression of deeply held and contrasting views without paralyzing the political system. Premier Gustofsen has to allow them, or he risks losing control of the assembly."

"They seem rather violent . . ."

"They are. The Scandyans can be a violent people. They don't have outlets for aggression in their social structure, and historically they engaged in some form or another of military action, often among themselves. Civil war would be a disaster, now, and they know it. They remember the civil war all too well and don't wish to repeat that, either—"

"Civil war?" Van didn't recall anything like that.

"They call it the war for independence, but it was probably more of a civil conflict than a true rebellion against outside control. Byrnedot was trying to work out a peaceful separation, and the Argentis were willing. The secessionists didn't want a peaceful separation. They wanted to use the separation as an excuse to seize the assets of those with close ties to Silvium. The backlash was so great that the settled Argentis remaining on Scandya managed to create a power base through the Conservative Democrats. At first, they were the minority party, but in the last century, they've gained more and more power, because, frankly, they make more sense. The Liberal Commons have been looking for other allies."

"The Revenant tie?" suggested Van.

"That's the strongest, but I doubt that it's the only one."

Salucar paused. "If I might ask . . . why are you here? Beyond the obvious that you were ordered here."

"With Commander Cruachan's death, they needed someone here quickly, and I was close to being ready for a transfer to other duty. I think they also wanted a military man without a diplomatic outlook here." The truth—or partial truth—was better than an evasive answer, and Van had the feeling that Salucar would know instantly if he were lying.

She smiled. "You like to use the truth, don't you?"

"I've never had much choice," Van replied. "Most people can tell when I lie."

"A man who knows his limits is the most dangerous of all."

"That's a Lederman-Maier quote," Van noted.

"It's a good one, don't you think?"

"I don't know." Van chuckled. "I've known some very effective liars. That just isn't one of my skills."

"I'm sure you have others." Salucar's voice was dry. "What do you intend to do as attaché? Go to receptions? Write analyses? Or are you here to further the RSF expansion?"

"I'm already doing the first two. I've certainly not been instructed on the third, and, even if I were, I doubt that I'd be very good at it, not in diplomatic means. And I no longer have a cruiser at my command. So I don't have a great deal of firepower." Van smiled. "What about you? Are you here to foil anything that the Republic might attempt?"

"But . . . of course!" Salucar laughed heartily. "And I'll do so with the ships I don't have, the diplomatic access denied to Kelt women, especially by the Revenants, and with the feminine deviousness that I never inherited."

"We seem to have similar problems," mused Van. "How soon before the Revs and the Argentis come to blows over Scandya?"

"They have been for twenty years. The blows are mostly economic—except for the concealed confrontations on the fringes of border systems. They both want to control the politics and the economy while allowing Scandya to appear independent for the moment. The Argentis know they can't take actual control, but the Revs aren't under that constraint.

They took over Samarra last year and Aluyson this year. Probably, by next year, they'll take another, and be working on subverting three or four others, either by outright economic takeover, or by fomenting an internal civil war, or by supporting whatever local political party will weaken the system the most. It could even have been here, except the Scandyans seem to understand that for now. At least, they keep electing Gustofsen. In the interim, he's trying hard to keep both the Keltyr and the Republic from slowly being squeezed out by the Argentis and the Revs, but we're still being played off against each other."

"Do you have a solution for that?" asked Van.

"No more than you do," she replied.

"Then . . . why did you almost insist on this meeting?"

"Why not? You seemed bright. I don't see any point in conflict between our governments. That will only cost us and strengthen the Coalition, the Revs, and the Argentis. Even if they conflict, there's little point in our doing so personally."

"You think that the RSF will listen to me?"

"No. But sooner or later, you'll be able to act. You're the kind that does. That's why the RSF doesn't know what to do with you. They figure that they *might* need you sometime, and so they keep moving you around so that you don't do too much damage in the meantime."

"You're very flattering." Van managed a heavy dose of irony.

"You prefer deviousness, you wonderful man?" Salucar opened her eyes wide, batting her eyelashes excessively. She only maintained the caricatured image of a seductress for a few seconds. "You see? I can't even do it in jest."

Van laughed.

She offered an exaggerated shrug, one that asked what else Van would have expected.

"You didn't say why you wanted to meet," Van finally said.

"To suggest that everyone wants to weaken Scandya, but each in a different way."

"What do you get out of telling me this?" Van asked.

"The hope that you'll report it to both the RSF and your ambassador. If the Republic and the Keltyr work against those efforts, we might be able to stabilize this place. Stable and stronger, Scandya will keep the Argentis and Revs off-balance."

"What about the Coalition?"

"They're lasers tuned to the invisible light. We know that, and maybe you do. Anyone who's messed with them in the last two centuries has ended up dead or worse. Individuals, I mean. That's the level they operate on. People who hatch plans against them die, vanish, explode, burst into flames—the list is pretty long. But they'll do anything to avoid an out-and-out war. They'd even let half the Arm go up in flames, in a Rev-Argenti war, so long as their half wasn't touched."

"And only you—Kelts—know that?"

Salucar laughed harshly. "Your RSF knows it. So does Argenti SS. The Revs have known it longer than anyone—since the reappearance of their prophet. That was a miracle no one expected. It probably has something to do with what the Coalition has gotten by cooperating with the Farhkans, but neither the Eco-Techs nor the Farhkans are saying, and they haven't for almost three centuries."

Van fingered his chin. He didn't think Salucar was lying. His implant, and his instincts, told him that she believed totally what she was telling him. But, like him, she could use the truth, and she was probably better than he was at it. She'd had more practice.

"Are you saying that the Coalition could be an ally, then?" he finally asked.

"No. They're just not our enemy—or yours. They've got a different agenda, and what it is . . . that's anyone's guess. Has been for years."

Van tried again. "The Argentis want Scandya militarily weak, but independent. The Revs want an economic collapse so that they can offer aid and rebuild the system their way. The Scandyans have this . . . myth that the Argentis were monsters. They weren't, but it doesn't matter. Argenti occupation or annexation would trigger a true revolt and rebellion, and the Argentis aren't stupid. The Revs can't bring enough military force to bear, not right now, but . . . if they can undermine the economy and political systems . . . who else would be politically acceptable who has the resources to rebuild Scandya? The Coalition is predominantly Shinto genetically; they're not acceptable. Neither are the Argentis. We don't have that kind of resources. Nor do you." Van shrugged. "Does that end the examination?"

"Pretty much." Commander Salucar stood. "I'll see you at our reception on Independence Night, won't I?"

Van also stood. "I'll be here."

"Good."

"Thank you." After bowing slightly to Salucar, Van walked out of her office, down the circular ramp, and out to the groundcar, where Stefan waited.

As he sat in the rear seat on the short ride back to the Taran embassy, Van wanted to massage his head. It wasn't aching, but he felt like it should be. He had all too much more research and analysis to do. While he generally believed what Salucar had said—with a few important exceptions and omissions— he also wanted to see for himself if he could corroborate some of what she had said, preferably through information to which she had no access. She'd made no real secret of trying to guide his thoughts, and that also bothered him. Was he that stupid? Or naive? Or didn't anyone care what he thought?

The last was the most probable.

He took a deep breath. Space battles were so much easier—and they were of far shorter duration.

Chapter 20

At ten hundred on twoday, Van sat in Cordelia Gregory's office. The summer sun filled the room with a bright indirect light that showed the spartan professionalism of an office empty of anything personal—without holos of family, without mementos of any sort.

The second secretary waited for Van to speak.

"I was wondering," Van began. "Do we have any decent information on how much capital investment the Revenants are directing into Scandya, Gotland in particular? And where?"

"We have some indications," she replied. "The analysis I did late last year is accurate within ten to fifteen percent. The current quarterly economic figures don't show any major swings in investment, and that would indicate matters have not changed significantly."

Van hadn't seen any such analysis on the embassy netsystem. "Could you make a copy of that available to me?"

"Of course." Cordelia Gregory offered a quizzical look. "Might I ask why?"

"I don't want to reinvent fire, so to speak. I feel we're seeing two kinds of warfare being waged—one of them clearly economic, and your analysis will help confirm or deny that. I'd also like to compare sector flows to military technology-related industries, on the secondary level, of course." That was because direct out-system investment in primary-level military multilaterals was forbidden under Scandyan law.

"Both the Revs and the Argentis are trying to gain a greater economic foothold here. That's been obvious for years." Cordelia Gregory lifted her left eyebrow to emphasize the point.

"The analyses also address specific industries and patterns of investment?"

"Naturally. But—"

"You've obviously thought this out in great detail, and it might be better if I studied your work first," Van interjected. "That way, I won't be asking you about matters you've already addressed. It may be that you've already answered most of my questions, and"—he managed a sheepish smile—"that way I won't ask too many repetitious and stupid ones."

Gregory actually smiled, if faintly. "I'll copy the entire archive to your access."

Van inclined his head. "Thank you very much."

"Will you let me know . . . when . . . you finish . . . whatever?"

"I certainly will, although I suspect I'll have at least one or two follow-up questions before I write anything. Before I send anything to the ambassador, I'll send you a draft for comment. That way, you can make sure that I haven't inadvertently done violence to your work."

"I do appreciate that consideration, Commander."

Van stood. "I'm doing my best to get on the jumpline, and I'm the one who appreciates being able to tap your expertise."

That got him a nod, and Van slipped from her office while matters remained on a pleasant and professional level.

True to her word, Gregory had an archive waiting for Van under his own codes by the time he'd returned to his office. He scanned the titles quickly, then concentrated on the large report—the one he hoped held what he was seeking. It took him all afternoon, and more than a few calculations, before he had a rough analysis set up and written out. He scanned the charts, figures, and explanations, then the conclusions he had drawn.

Over the past twenty years total investment from Argenti and Revenant sources has been virtually identical [less than 2% difference between the amounts from Argenti sources and Revenant sources]. The pattern of investment has been markedly different. With a few high-profile exceptions, the majority of capital from Revenant sources has flowed into three areas: information technology; media-related industries; and food and natural resources.

A survey of Scandyan communication and information systems reveals a 70% correlation with Revenant systems, both in component utilization and system configuration.

Van's quick survey was based on what he'd been able to find, and upon his own past briefings on Revenant technology. He'd actually come up with a higher figure, but dropped the percentage because of the thinness of his sample.

Revenant investment has been even more concentrated in the public comm sector. In fact, Revenant ownership of the three major commercial Scandyan netsystems is at the maximum out-system ownership permitted under Scandyan law [33%].

Whether through plan or coincidence, this concentration of investment in media multilaterals is also matched by a high correlation of professional staff and managers with semantic markers suggesting Revenant origin [as many as 40% of key personnel could have Revenant affiliations of some type].

That was also a somewhat subjective conclusion, but Van wanted the point to hit hard.

Argenti investment is more diverse and what concentration there is falls in the areas of microtechnology, medical and bio-pharmacology, basic nanetic formulation.

As expected, given Scandyan law, neither Scandyan nor Argenti investors have positions in industries or multilaterals with significant military contracts. Argenti investment exists in publicly held companies below the foreign investment prohibition, but there is virtually no Revenant investment in such entities . . .

Did he want to spell out the obvious? Van decided against it, finished with an innocuous closing paragraph, and sent copies to the first, second, and third secretaries, requesting comments.

He leaned back in his chair. Given what Gregory and he had discovered, the inflammatory impartiality of media stories made perfect sense. That part was easy enough to see. What worried Van was the knowledge that, in a situation as complex as Scandya, he'd missed more than he'd discovered.

He was also more than a little worried by the latitude he'd been given by the ambassador and the lack of input from Hannigan—and by the continued lack of detailed military information from either the Foreign Ministry or the RSF.

Chapter 21

Threeday and fourday passed, and Van spent his time responding to inquiries from various secretaries and the ambassador, and in trying to formulate a strategy for Taran military posture vis-à-vis Scandya that he could recommend. Van had received absolutely no comment on his analysis of the military-economic situation in the Scandyan system. He'd had no response from yet another call to Sub-marshal Brigham Taylor of the Revenant embassy, but he had received numerous requests for scattered bits of information from both Hannigan and the ambassador, ranging from the rank structure of the Scandyan SDF to the size of the largest class of Coalition warship. By fiveday afternoon, he had just received a detailed commentary over the net from Cordelia Gregory and was wondering if he would get any other comments. Then there was a knock on the door.

Van looked up, used his implant, and said, "You can come in, Emily."

Emily Clifton slipped into the chair across the desk from Van. "It's about your report."

"What do you think?"

"I'm sorry. With all the arrangements for the past week, I was swamped. But I finally read your report." She looked at him. "If I'm right about where you're headed, it's frightening."

"Do you think I'm wrong?" he asked.

She frowned, and the expression made her face look more severe than usual. "I'd worry that it makes too much sense.

People usually do what they feel like doing, and then rationalize what they've done afterward. They think they're logical, but they're not. You're suggesting a logical pattern on the part of both the Argentis and the Revenants."

It was Van's turn to frown. "No. Just on the part of the Revenants. The Argentis seem to be following a long-held cultural pattern, almost instinctive. That's the way they've approached most of their colonies and former colonies."

"Do you think the Revenants are that logical—logical enough to plot this kind of takeover?"

"I don't know. I do know that they have a superiority complex of some sort. Commander Cruachan didn't have any problem meeting with their military attaché, but the same attaché won't even return my calls. Their ambassador practically called me a lower-class citizen at our reception, and their junior officers avoid talking to me, almost to the point of rudeness. Colonel Marti suggested, indirectly, that the Argentis are mostly the wrong color for dealing with the Revenants. Commander Salucar also noted that the Revenants tend to minimize or deny access to women. I got a similar set of observations from the Coalition consulate."

"With all that ideological prejudice, you think that the Revs can be logical?" Emily smiled.

"If they're not being logical," Van returned, "we've got a pattern that's been in place for decades, if not centuries, and we've got even bigger problems, because it controls everyone."

"Could they have two patterns—one for dealing with outsiders and one inside?"

"They could, but that would cause other problems."

"Such as?" asked the third secretary.

Van shrugged, helplessly. "I can't answer that. It's just a feeling on my part."

Emily smiled slowly. "I'd trust your feelings more than your analysis."

Van was still amazed at how much the smile transformed her, and it took him a moment before he replied. "That may be, but the ambassador, Dr. Hannigan, and Dr. Gregory won't."

"What did Cordelia say?" asked Emily.

"She has problems with my methodology, and with the lack of statistical rigor in my samples. She thinks that I can't prove conclusively that the investment patterns are actually planned, rather than a coincidental random walk created by two separate and disinterested classes of investors." Van smiled sardonically. "She did applaud my comparatively open-ended conclusions."

"And Dr. Hannigan?"

"I haven't gotten back anything from him," Van replied. "I'm not certain that I will."

"What will you do?"

"Incorporate your observations and Dr. Gregory's and send it to the ambassador—and everyone else. What else can I do?" He paused. "Oh, and make sure my full dress uniform is ready for the big Keltyr reception to celebrate Scandyan Independence Day." Van stood.

"You are more cynical than I am," replied Emily, also standing.

"We make a good pair that way."

She looked down, ever so slightly, not quite meeting his eyes. "I'd hate to be paired up merely for my cynicism."

"So would I . . . but . . . sometimes cynicism is the last refuge of the idealist."

She looked up, almost abruptly. "You mean that, don't you?"

Van shrugged helplessly, and then they both laughed.

It was the best moment of the day for Van.

Chapter 22

On sevenday evening, at nineteen-forty, Van waited in the Taran embassy's front foyer. In front of him was Cordelia Gregory, standing with a tall redheaded man whom Van felt he should know. To his left was Sean Bulben, and to his right was Ian Hannigan with a woman who looked to be his wife.

Ambassador Rogh stood before the small group. For several moments, he said nothing, waiting for silence. The murmurs died away, and the ambassador shifted his weight from one foot to the other, cleared his throat, then spoke. "I know you've all seen my memo about this evening, but I wanted to make it very clear. We will all leave in the embassy cars together after this. When the fireworks are over, sometime around ten-thirty, Madame Rogh and I will return. You may stay later, as you choose, and there will be an embassy car shuttling back and forth until somewhat after midnight.

"I must remind you that no weapons, not even dress daggers, or bootknives . . . anything at all, are to be worn for the function at the Keltyr embassy." Ambassador's Rogh's eyes were chill as he surveyed Van, then each of the embassy secretaries in turn. Only Sean Bulben fidgeted. "This is an important function, and you are to represent Tara as I know you can. Premier Gustofsen will even be there briefly, sometime before and during the fireworks and flareshow. I would request that you not approach him, and if approached by him, keep the conversation on light matters or good wishes for another celebration of his system's independence . . . As always, your behavior reflects on Tara."

Van wondered about the ambassador's cautions. Did the man know something Van should, or was he just fussy about ceremonial occasions?

As the ambassador turned and was joined by his wife on the way from the foyer toward the cars outside, Sean murmured, "Every time there's a big function, he gives us *the* talk."

"His predecessor did, too," added Emily from behind them. "It must be in the ambassadorial how-to manual that they don't show us."

Van couldn't help but smile at the dryness of her tone.

"Roger," Cordelia Gregory said firmly to the redheaded man, "the second groundcar."

Van lagged behind Dr. Hannigan and his wife, and Dr. Gregory and her escort, and ended up—by choice—in the rear seat of the third and last embassy groundcar with Sean

Bulben and Emily. He glanced at Sean. "Who was that with Dr. Gregory?"

"Oh . . . that was her husband. Roger Cromwell."

"The tech staff manager?"

"The same one. She ranks him, and that's the way she likes it."

Emily—sitting in the middle—glanced to her right at Sean, but did not speak.

Sean flushed and looked out the window as the groundcar turned out onto Knutt Boulevard and left the embassy. "Well . . . it is. She orders him around just like she does me."

Van couldn't help but smile faintly. "How many people will be at this function?" He looked sideways at Emily, taking in her profile and noting the high cheekbones and the clean lines of her nose, perfectly in harmony with her face, neither small and pert nor large and dominating.

She did not turn. "Over a hundred from the diplomatic community, another hundred or so from the Scandyan political and military communities, and probably a scattering of others. Some Scandyan media types will find a way to inveigle invitations, also, trying to see if they can get anything on the premier. They don't care much for him."

"And half of them look down on you, and the other half don't bother," Sean added. "Least, that's always how it is if you're a fourth secretary."

"It's not that bad," Emily said.

"Almost." Sean's tone was morose. "You're not a fourth secretary."

Both Emily and Van laughed. A long moment passed before Sean also laughed.

When the groundcar pulled to a stop a good ten minutes later, the moment Van stepped from the embassy car, sliding out and holding the door for Emily, he could sense the sweep of a surveillance system—and then another.

Van and Emily followed Dr. and Mrs. Hannigan and Dr. Gregory and her husband into the Keltyr embassy, past the four Kelt guards—in dress blue-green uniforms, but with long-barreled, high-charge stunners at hand.

Once inside, Emily smiled and slipped away, and Van decided to pay his respects to Commander Salucar first. He began to make his way through the crowd in the main reception room, looking from side to side as he did. Although the Taran contingent had arrived punctually, the foyer and the first reception room of the Keltyr embassy were already half-filled with people.

Van started to ease past the older blond officer in resplendent whites adorned with braid and metals, who was talking to a willowy woman—also blonde, with skin almost as white as the officer's uniform. Then Van stopped, smothering a cynical smile. "Sub-marshal Taylor. It's good to see you."

The sub-marshal looked up from his tête-à-tête with the woman, a fleeting expression of annoyance crossing his face. "Yes? I don't believe—"

"Of course not. You wouldn't. Commander Van Albert, Taran RSF. I'm Commander Cruachan's replacement at the embassy." Van raised his voice to carry, but only to the point where it would seem that he was trying to make himself heard over the crowd. "I've attempted to set up a courtesy call several times, but you've obviously been more than a little occupied." Van emphasized the last phrase slightly, then inclined his head politely toward the woman before turning back to face the sub-marshal, and lowering his voice a trace. "I won't trouble you further this evening, but I do hope we can get together before too long."

"Ah . . . yes . . . we should do that, Commander."

"I'll be in touch, Sub-marshal." Van nodded once more, and then slipped along the wall.

"That was nasty."

Van turned to see Emily Clifton standing beside an ornate and polished antique acoustical piano that was so spotless that Van wondered if it had been played in the last century. Beside her was a slender man in a white formal jacket.

"You caught me." Van shrugged helplessly.

"The marshal wasn't too happy. His look at your back was like a laser," she said, before gesturing to the man. "Raoul, this is Commander Van Albert, our RSF attaché. Commander, this is Raoul deLevain, my counterpart here at the Keltyr embassy."

Van bowed slightly. "I'm pleased to meet you, Raoul."

Raoul smiled humorously. "After what you did to the marshal, I'm glad that you are pleased to meet me."

"I *am* pleased to meet you," Van replied. He detected an accent in the man's old Anglo, but couldn't place it. It certainly wasn't anything like that of Commander Salucar. "As for the sub-marshal, I occasionally forgive, but I never forget." He smiled as he finished the words.

"They do neither," Raoul observed.

"So I understand."

Emily raised her eyebrows. "This *is* supposed to be a friendly reception, not the starting locale of the next interstellar war."

Van bowed slightly. "I understand. I'll attempt to remember that all is serene and peaceful here in the Galactic Arm."

"Commander . . ." Emily shook her head in mock-despair.

Raoul bent toward Emily, whispered a few words, then bowed to Van. "I must go, but it has been a pleasure meeting you, Commander. A pleasure indeed."

Once the Kelt had moved away, Van eased closer to Emily, respectfully closer. "What was the parting comment, if I might ask?"

Emily smiled, then leaned and whispered into his ear. "He said you are a refreshingly honest change from your predecessor."

Van couldn't help but feel her momentary warmth close to him, but that feeling was gone almost as soon as she moved back after her words died away. "I suspect that means that I'm hopelessly direct, and doomed to failure."

"Only in the reception and drawing rooms, Commander." Emily stiffened.

Van could sense the comm pulse, since it was embassy-linked, but not the content, directed as it was to her.

"Dr. Hannigan needs something for the ambassador." Emily offered a crooked smile and slipped away.

Van continued onward, eventually finding Ayrllis Salucar

in the drawing room off the second reception area, talking to an older man in a formal white jacket. Easing back and waiting, Van studied the DeVelle print on the wall—a scene of ancient warriors in leather and bronze caught by the first light of the rising sun. Van could admire the artistry, but had to question whether an ancient warrior leader would have bothered with a formal dawn consultation with lesser chieftains right before a battle.

When the older man stepped away, Van moved toward Salucar. "Commander . . . I just wanted to pay my respects. I wouldn't want to be accused of neglecting you."

A smile crossed the dark-haired Kelt officer's face. "Unlike some, you do listen."

"I do try." Van half turned and gestured toward the crowd. "This is quite a gathering."

She nodded. "That's why all the embassies are happy to rotate it. We've had to bring in some serving help, and screening them was another chore."

"You've got extra surveillance in place, don't you? And some of those servers are probably reporting to you?"

"Now . . . we shouldn't get too professional at the moment, Commander."

"Then I won't. How long have you been with the embassy? I trust that's not too professional?"

"Close, but acceptable. Two years and three months. I had the *Martel* before that."

"Cruiser?"

"Old and very light cruiser," Salucar replied.

"And they decommissioned the *Martel* after your tour?"

"They did. It doesn't surprise you at all."

"I wrote a book similar to that, once," Van said dryly.

The barest hint of a quizzical look flashed across her face, then vanished. "Some patterns repeat themselves, I suppose."

"Always. The trick is to discover which pattern and who benefits. I've always figured out the pattern, just too late to be as effective as I'd have liked to be."

"You weren't late in the *Regneri* affair," she pointed out.

"I was in what came later," he said.

Salucar nodded. "Those kinds of patterns." She stiffened ever so slightly. "I must excuse myself. There are a few things to check before Premier Gustofsen arrives."

After Salucar moved away, Van made his way toward one of the buffet tables, where he took one of the small blue-green china plates, edged in silver, and filled it with miniature sandwiches of various sorts, not one of which was more than a mouthful, two thin slices of melon topped with prosciutto, and a few anachad nuts. Then he waited at the table serving as a bar, until the tall blond bartender got to him.

"Ser?"

"Pale ale."

"Aurelian or Edauer?"

"Edauer."

Van took the ale and, with his plate, eased into a corner behind the antique piano, where he took a sip of the Edauer, a brew with a decidedly hopped edge, but an edge that was welcome after all the talking. Then he began on the sandwiches.

"Commander?"

Van turned to see an Argenti colonel standing almost beside him. He didn't know the man, but replied in Hispyn. "Colonel? I am afraid we have not met."

"No, we have not," the officer replied. "I'm Colonel Ferdinando Casteneda, Colonel Marti's replacement."

"I'm pleased to meet you." Van inclined his head.

"And I, you." The colonel smiled.

"When did you arrive in Valborg?"

"Yesterday." Casteneda shrugged. "It was a most sudden transfer."

"From where, might I ask?"

"You could, and I would be obliged to answer only generally. I was working in a certain information . . . capacity."

Van laughed. "That is either bureaucracy, senior command staff, or intelligence, but I won't press the matter." He'd already assessed the other's reaction to each possibility and decided that Casteneda had been in intelligence—and he wanted Van to know it, but without saying so directly. That was another troubling factor about the Scandyan situation—a high concentration of intelligence and potential scapegoats in the same place. "When did Colonel Marti leave?"

"The day before I arrived, I was told."

"Is your ambassador due to be replaced soon?"

The colonel smiled faintly. "I would not be among the first to know that. Is yours?"

"Not that I know."

"You see?"

"I appreciate your letting me know of your arrival. We should meet more formally once the Scandyan independence celebrations are over."

"I would concur." Colonel Casteneda bowed slightly. "I look forward to that. I will be contacting you once I am more settled."

"The best of fortune in that," Van replied.

"Thank you." With a last bow, the Argenti colonel slipped away, as if he were almost relieved not to have spent too much time with Van.

Van finished the small sandwiches, then went back for seconds. As he ate what passed for his dinner, he noted that he had not seen Major Murikami, not that he had expected to find anyone from the Coalition consulate. He passed off the empty plate to a server, tall and blond, and, pale ale in hand, drifted through one room, then another.

Perhaps an hour passed before he returned to the bar, where he traded his half-drunk and warm pale ale for another. He had also observed some individuals he had not met, but who appeared to be from more distant systems, including one woman in traditional Hyndji garb. He wondered how many others there were, and whether they might play any role in the developing struggle over Scandya.

"You look deep in thought." Emily Clifton reappeared, trailed by Sean Bulben.

"Appearances can be deceiving," Van replied after a quick swallow of the Edauer pale ale. "I was just thinking that I ought to be thinking."

"About what?"

"That was what I was thinking about."

Emily shook her head, but Sean just looked bewildered.

A flurry of energy pulses—comm pulses—seemed to flash around Van, although the sense of flashing was more of an illusion created by his RSF implant to provide a semivisible signal to him. "Isn't the Scandyan premier due to arrive at any time?"

"I think he just did," Emily replied. "I can see some more Scandyan security by the doors to the main reception area."

"It won't be long before they start the fireworks and flareshow," Sean said, glancing from Emily to Van. "We should go out into the side garden. The ambassadors are going out there. They've got places on that stand. We'll have to peer over everyone . . ."

"I suppose we should," replied Emily, a hint of resignation in her voice. "The ambassador always asks how their show compares to our last one."

The three moved slowly, with the sluggish flow of bodies toward the doors that had been opened out onto the south lawn. It took almost fifteen minutes before they were out into the cooler night air.

The sky had finally darkened into the deep green-tinged purple close to black that was full night on Scandya. In the west, halfway between the horizon and the zenith, Van picked out the unwinking disc-point that had to be Malmot. Despite the growing crowd on the stretch of lawn just to the south of the embassy building, Van could smell the fragrance of lilacs and roses, two of the more durable remnants of the flora of Old Earth. Farther from the embassy, stretches of grass and garden were still without more than isolated clumps of functiongoers, as if most wished to remain close to the embassy.

Van turned and looked across the dais where the ambassadors and, in some cases, their spouses, had settled in. Then, he realized something. The comm pulses he'd felt on and off all evening had faded almost entirely away. That bothered him, although he couldn't say why.

At one end of the dais, a server was offering various drinks upon a tray.

Van could sense something . . . something about the tall blond server, and he eased away from Emily and toward the server. Despite his garb and demeanor, the young man looked and felt more like a Marine—and yet he didn't.

Van looked toward the other end of the platform where the ambassadors were seated, and then back to the middle, where the premier sat. Two security types in white and green stood behind him, and another pair were stationed on the ground behind the dais. The Scandyan security guards— three men and a woman—were carrying sidearms in throw-holsters, but Van couldn't tell what the sidearms might be—wide-angle stunners, slug throwers, or tanglers. On the far end of the dais was another server, also tallish and blond.

Van began to feel very uneasy, and began to work his way through the crowds to a point closer to the dais, through diplomatic staff in groups, closely bunched, but not jammed in tight. "Excuse me . . . please . . . excuse me . . ."

He got more than a few glares, but the uniform helped—he thought.

A single green beam of light flared upward, corruscatingly brilliant, the green a perfect match with the green of the Scandyan flag, and the green in the uniforms of the Scandyan security guards. Two more lines of light crossed the first two. Then a blazing image of the Scandyan banner—an evergreen set between two irregular halves of a golden globe— appeared as a projection on the point where the three beams of green light appeared.

From somewhere, came the sounds of a band playing a stirring melody Van had not heard, but which he presumed was either the Scandyan anthem or a well-loved piece with ties to the revolution and Scandya. He shook his head, trying to concentrate on the dais.

The two servers had moved closer to the center of the dais,

still carrying their trays with several drinks remaining on them. The server on the left end straightened, and, before moving to the next diplomat, glanced out across the lawn, if but for an instant.

Van followed the glance, seeing another server offering a tray to a couple beside a small fountain—the only pair in that entire section of the lawn. He swept the lawn, noting a fourth server well to the west, where there were but three people, who had to have been unable to truly see the lights because they were directly under them. The three were moving back toward the main area, glancing upward, but the server did not move.

But Van did, even before the positioning of the four truly registered. He wasn't quite running, when he leapt onto the dais, moving toward the nearest server.

The man turned, took in Van's uniform, and threw the entire tray at the Taran commander.

Van ducked and kept moving, ignoring the exclamations and curses.

The two Scandyan security guards stepped in front of the premier, and the other two on the ground vaulted onto the dais. Lines of light flashed from everywhere—that was the way it seemed to Van—and the server who had thrown the tray pitched forward across the dais. So did two of the premier's guards.

More lines of light flashed around Van, and then a series of *cracks* from a slug-throwing rifle echoed across the lawn and the stunned diplomats. Several of the ambassadors had scrambled off the dais, and chairs were scattered everywhere.

Van kicked one out of the way as he saw the server on the other end take a shot, with blood welling across the arm of his white jacket. That didn't stop the man, who staggered, then drew a pistol of some sort.

Another of the Scandyan guards went down, and Van lost sight of the premier, who had dropped behind the dais with a cover of Kelt security. But the single server kept moving toward Van. He was less than three meters away and turning the pistol toward Van.

Van bent and picked up one of the overturned chairs by its back, then charged.

Crack! The first shot missed. At least, Van didn't feel it, and he rammed the chair into the server.

Crack!

Green light flared around Van, and it felt as though lines of fire were flaying him.

Black and green flared around him, and then he saw nothing.

After a time—how long he didn't know—he looked up from where he lay on his back. There were people, medtechs, around him, but the sky was still dark.

A face swam into view—Commander Salucar's face. She looked down at him.

Van tried to speak, but all that came out was a mumble.

Salucar looked down at him. "Who did it? How did you know? How?"

Van blinked, holding back the darkness by sheer force of will. ". . . too . . . many . . . scapegoats . . ."

The darkness rolled over him, submerging him, carrying away the rest of the words he might have said.

Chapter 23

Over the past three millennia, social scientists, historians, and ethicists have all debated the history, purpose, and reason for the development and subsequent failure of ethical systems in society after society. From these endless studies, several facts appear obvious, yet ignored.

First, the ancient Judeo-Christian concept of "original sin" as defined in basic prediaspora Catholic/Christian theology was and remains an extremely useful tool for social indoctrination, because (1) it provides a reason for evil while also allowing people to accept that evil is not the fault of the given individual; (2) supplies a rationale for why people need to be taught ethics and manners; and (3) still requires that people adhere to an acceptable moral code.

Second, genetic studies have since revealed that only a small minority of human beings have a strong genetic predilection toward either "morality" or "immorality." This has historically posed a problem for any civil society based on purely secular rule because (1) society in the end is based on some form of self-restraint; and (2) the impetus to require self-discipline and to learn greater awareness of what is evil and unacceptable lacks the religious underpinnings present in a theocracy or a society with a strong theocratic presence. Likewise, history has also demonstrated most clearly that the majority of individuals are uncomfortable in accepting a moral code that is not based on the "revelation" of a divine being, because in matters of personal ethics, each believes his or her ethics are superior to any not of "divine" origin.

As transparently fallacious as this widely accepted personal belief may be, equally transparent and fallacious—and even more widely accepted—are the ethical and moral systems accepted as created by divinities—and merely revealed to the prophets of each deity for dissemination to the "faithful." Throughout history, this has been a useful but transparent fiction because the "divine" origin of moral codes obviates the need for deciding between various human codes. Humans being humans, however, the conflict then escalates into a struggle over whose god or whose interpretation of god is superior, rather than focusing on the values of the codes themselves . . .

> *Values, Ethics, and Society*
> Exton Land
> New Oisin, Tara
> 1117 S.E.

Chapter 24

Van wasn't certain, but he thought he was being carried on a stasis stretcher to a flitter. Then the darkness came in over him like the blackness of space between galaxies, dark and cold and empty, with the occasional pinlight of something that didn't belong there in the deeps, like a rogue star.

Every time that the darkness lifted, waves of heat and pain surged over him, burning his arm and his leg once more, seemingly in even greater fire and agony. In the brief intervals between darkness and pain, Van caught a vision of lines of energy around and through him, and sheets of light that he could only have called translucent flowing down on both sides of wherever he lay.

He tried to concentrate, to bring the images into greater focus, but each time he attempted such intensity, the misty cool darkness surged back over him, and he dropped into the endless blackness.

Then . . . he woke. For the first time, he could feel specific pain—not a wash of agony, but areas of pain. His left arm was on fire, and so was his right leg. His lower rib cage throbbed, even as shallowly as he was breathing, and his lower abdomen felt as if it had been cut into small pieces with an ancient sword, then sewed back together with a large and dull needle.

A thin medtech or doctor stood beside the medcradle. "Commander? Can you hear me?"

"Yes." Van had to struggle to croak out the word.

"Good." The woman nodded. "I'm Dr. Calyen. I've been working with you for some time now, not that you've been fully aware of it. We need to run some tests on you. These are of the kind that require you to be awake. It's likely to get somewhat painful before it's over, but the longer you can remain alert, the more we can do for you."

"Go . . . ahead." Van's throat was so dry, or so unused to talking, that he half gagged on the second word. He could hear a low rumbling, then saw another tech pushing a cart toward the medcrib.

"Once the equipment is set up, I'm going to ask you some questions. Some you can answer with a simple 'yes' or 'no.' Others may take a short sentence. I may also ask you to think about something—or to try to visualize an object or a color." The doctor's tone became sharper with her next words. "This is important. The harder you work on this test, the better your recovery will be." There was a pause. "Do you understand that?"

"Yes . . . going to be . . . a struggle. If I don't . . . work hard . . . I'll be hurting more . . . later . . ."

"Exactly."

"Doctor . . . how long . . . have I . . . been here?" Van struggled to get the words out.

"You've been in the crib for almost six months."

"Six . . . months . . . ?" Van couldn't keep the amazement from his rusty voice.

"You're fortunate to be alive. You had severe injuries and systemic trauma. You took laser wounds, disc-gun slashes, and a heavy explosive slug through one shoulder, another through the side of your abdomen, and a third through your leg. Even so, we could have dealt with all that in a few weeks, no more than three months. But you also were shot with what we believe was an outlawed biotech slug. It contained a number of SAD nanites . . ."

"Sad nanites?" Van had never heard of nanites being sad—or happy.

"Acronym," Dr. Calyen explained. "Search and destroy nanites. The RSF believes that they were intended for the Scandyan premier, not for you. You were fortunate that we had just received and installed some advanced equipment from a Coalition manufacturer." She smiled. "We were all fortunate. You were the test case, and the results were so good that we've been able to save a number of others with what we've learned."

"How long before I'm up . . . around?"

"That may be a while yet."

"Permanent injuries?" Van had to wonder with all the areas of pain.

"It doesn't look that way," Dr. Calyen said cheerfully, "but your muscle tone is almost nonexistent, and you'll need patterning to integrate your new arm and leg . . . possibly some biofeedback for your right ear. We need some baselines . . . that's what these tests are for . . ."

There was a period of silence while the equipment, whatever it might have been, was positioned beside Van's medcrib.

"Say your full name," the doctor requested.

"Van . . . Cassius . . . Albert."

"When were you born?"

"Seventeen Novem, 1094 New Era."

"Where were you born?"

"Bannon, Sulyn . . ."

"Would you try to picture a blue box?"

". . . a yellow sphere?"

The questions and requests seemed to go on and on. Then they stopped. Van had no idea what sort of baseline the doctor had been trying to establish, and he was so tired that he wasn't certain he cared.

"Commander . . ."

Van blinked his eyes open.

"Thank you. You did very well."

Van hadn't done much, but then, he wasn't certain he could have done more, either.

"There are messages on the console beside the crib, and some handwritten missives as well. We've saved them until you were well enough to appreciate them."

"Thank you." Van could see the doctor's smile, but her words seemed to fade in and out.

". . . you're too tired now. Just rest. They'll be there when you wake . . ."

The next time he woke, the pain was less—but it was still there, in the arm and shoulder, the leg, the ribs, the abdomen—and in his right ear and his "good" hand. He still didn't recall all the wounds that Dr. Calyen had enumerated, but that could have been because he'd been in shock. Anyone with those wounds should have been in shock. Still . . . he wondered. He shivered. For some reason, he felt cold.

Even as he shivered, he could feel heat radiating into him from beneath and from above.

"That should help."

Van turned his head slowly, his eyes focusing on a medtech, a man who looked too young to be either tech or doctor.

The young man consulted a screen before him. "Good. You're doing very well. You'll be on a regular schedule from now on. Your midday meal will be here in about a half hour. Dr. Calyen thought this would be a good time of day to bring you out."

"Out? Out of . . . what?" Van realized his bed/crib had been inclined so that he was resting in almost a sitting position.

"You've been in a low-temp coma. You had some severe brain swelling . . . those bioweps, you know. But you don't need to worry. Everything worked. Dr. Calyen said that she even cleaned up some other problems. Once you're fully recovered, you'll probably be just a touch sharper than before." The tech consulted the small handscreen, then smiled, pointing to the hand console attached to the side of the crib. "A lot of people worried about you. You've got a batch of messages there. The handwritten ones are on the table." With a last smile, he slipped out of the room.

For a moment, Van studied the medcenter room. Nothing special, just a space perhaps four meters wide and not quite four deep with smooth walls. The window to his left revealed a view of the hills to the west of Valborg, deep in snow, but from where he half lay, half sat, Van could not see much of the grounds around the medcenter, just the upper portions of evergreens, also covered in deep and powdery snow. The scene outside the window brought a different kind of chill. The last time he'd been truly awake, it had been midsummer.

His fingers felt simultaneously weak and stiff, but he fumbled with the handscreen, letting it project a holo image before him, one large enough that he didn't have to strain eyes that still seemed to blur small objects and details.

The first few messages were from the ambassador and the embassy staff, all wishing him well. Those from Rogh and Hannigan were slightly warmer than perfunctory, but not much.

The third one was from Cordelia Gregory, and it was short. He read and reread the key words.

> . . . your actions at the Keltyr embassy showed great courage, and that did not surprise me, for it has always been clear that you have never lacked courage. What warmed and surprised me was the way in which you drew fire and tried to save others. From your effort and example, I think that I can finally put the *Regneri* tragedy in perspective, and for that I thank you . . . I regret that I cannot tell you that personally, because I am being sent to Keshmar as second secretary . . .

Drawing fire? Van certainly hadn't intended to draw fire. He'd just wanted to make sure that none of the ambassadors or the premier had been shot. He smiled bemusedly. Whatever.

Then, much farther down the queue, were the messages from his fathers. Dad Cicero had wished him well, said he was praying for Van's full recovery and hoping he could come home before he was posted somewhere else, and concluded:

> . . . As always, we love you, and worry for and about you. Also, as always, you have gone beyond duty, and that is an example that impresses your brother and sister, but I would hope that you have done so for reasons deeper than mere duty . . . we look forward with great joy to your next visit, whenever that may be . . .

Dad Almaviva had been more verbose.

> . . . all the Sulyn media nets have scanned stories about your heroism in saving the ambassadors and the premier of Scandya, and about your career as one of the shining lights in the RSF from Sulyn. That's probably partly because of your friend Ashley, but even he couldn't make bricks without straw. There's even a scholarship that's been started in your name at the Shennon Academy . . . We're all so proud of you, but we have worried, and were so relieved to hear that you are expected to make a full, if lengthy recovery . . . Your cousin Aeron has done a portrait of you in your uniform. He used old-style oils. He claims that is the proper medium for an old-style hero in a time when ethics and duty are falling by the way . . . I fear that in a larger sense he may be right. The arts are receiving less support, and what support there is goes into those venues where the presentation overwhelms the content, just as the media has emphasized the results and vision of your actions without showing or explaining the reasons behind them. We know your reasons, but who else will know? . . . Still, we all love you, and miss you, and look forward to seeing you . . .

Van wasn't sure he truly knew the reasons for his actions. He had just known that he had to act.

When he finished reading the screen messages, he picked up the topmost of the old-fashioned envelopes on the table beside his bed/crib, opening it and reading over the words from Ayrllis Salucar.

> . . . now been posted as commanding officer of Research Station Epsilon, out in the middle of nowhere. I'm still not sure whether to damn you or thank you. If you hadn't stopped the last assassin, I'd have been court-martialled or retired. Since you did, the Review Board decided that anything that looked overtly punitive was best avoided. So I'll finish out my shortened career at Epsilon . . . but I will have a career, and after retirement, no one will care or remember . . .

Van smiled sadly. Salucar had been set up almost as badly as he had, if not worse. The Keltyr high command had clearly figured that something bad was going to happen in Scandya, something that they could do nothing about, and had posted a scapegoat as military attaché. Had the RSF thought the same? Van wouldn't have been surprised. In fact, he would have been surprised if they hadn't, after the way matters had developed.

He yawned, but still picked up the next envelope. It was from Emily Clifton. He frowned. Why the envelope, rather than a screen message?

Commander,

I truly hope this finds you well and recovering. Although we only worked together for a short time, it was memorable and rewarding.

When you read this, I will be on Meroe in the Kush system, once more as the third secretary. I'm certain that someone will have briefed you, but after the Independence Day incident, everyone was detached. Dr. Hannigan took an early retirement. The ambassador returned to Tara to collect his pension as a former senator. Cordelia Gregory was posted to Keshmar, and Sean to Dhyli on Nuindya. You'll be sent somewhere else also, I'd bet.

There were hundreds of people in that garden when the assassins began to fire. You, the Keltyr commander, and four security people were the only ones who acted. Two of the security types died, and the rest of you were wounded. It happened so fast, yet you managed to get to the dais almost as fast as security. I just stood and watched. We media types are good at watching, I guess, but I did manage to get off a report to both the ministry and RSF about how you managed to thwart the assassins. I also made sure that the local and interstellar nets got a copy. That was the least I could do.

If you ever do get to Kush—while I'm there—I can assure you of a warm reception. I'd like to see you again.

The signature was just her first name.

Behind the note was the hard copy of a press release. Van didn't read it. He would, later.

He couldn't help smiling, if sadly. He'd not only liked Emily Clifton, more than a little, but he'd felt the stirrings of a kind of affection and love he'd never experienced for long, and he wished he'd been able to see her again. He slipped the note back into its envelope, then sat back to rest—and to think—while he waited for his meal.

Chapter 25

In the winter gray light just before dawn, Van woke abruptly. He could hear two voices outside his door echoing in the quiet of the medcenter.

". . . another week before the regrowth is solid enough for full-scale therapy . . ."

". . . compare to his previous physical abilities?"

". . . should be every bit as good. He's responded well, and he could even be somewhat better . . ."

"But it will take time?"

"It's not something you can hurry, not in a case like this."

Van waited as the two figures—Dr. Calyen and an RSF commodore—stepped into his room and toward the medcrib, although most of the equipment that had surrounded Van had been removed days earlier—except for nonintrusive monitors.

Dr. Calyen said nothing, standing back from the short, trim, and dark-haired commodore.

The commodore cleared his throat, in the way that small men often did, before beginning. "Commodore, I'm Brion Guffree. Since I was concluding the RSF report on the incident, and since Dr. Calyen said that you were now fully aware and well on the road to recovery . . ."

Van was being addressed as commodore? He managed not

to frown or look curious as he waited for whatever would be revealed by the words of the other officer.

". . . I just wanted to let you know that you've been awarded the Republic Cross by the council for your exemplary efforts in saving the premier of Scandya. You've also been promoted to commodore, effective the first of Septem . . ."

Awarded the second highest decoration—for what amounted to stupidity in facing an armed squad of assassins? Or dumb courage at best? And promoted? "Ah . . ." Van found himself stammering. He concentrated and forced out the words. "I did what I could."

"You did it very well, Commodore."

"What happened? You said you were part of the inquiry. What can you tell me?" asked Van.

"There were eight assassins in and around the light display. Your actions allowed Kelt security—and the premier's bodyguards—to stop them."

"Who were they?"

"We still don't know. I don't think anyone does or that anyone ever will. All eight were advanced-stage clones, and they all dropped over dead, some even before being taken into custody, the rest before they could be interrogated. Some sort of reactive nerve poison, triggered by programming. There was no way to revive any of them, and it appears that no one knows for whom they worked. The clones did have Revenant gene patterns, but that's not conclusive."

"Because anyone could have used a pattern from another culture?"

"Exactly. They could have worked for anyone. Each government knows what it knows, but the guilty party isn't about to admit it. It could have been a local group as well. We may never know. Premier Gustofsen was unhurt, and he even managed to win the fall elections. Scandya has stepped up its security screening of visitors and immigrants, and has requested that no out-system ships larger than standard cruisers enter Scandyan system spaces. The Revenant government has charged that the attack was Argenti-backed, and the Argentis have suggested that only the Revs had anything to gain by the death of the premier . . ." The commodore shrugged. "Nothing has really changed."

Van doubted that, but he just nodded, before asking, "Do you know where I'm likely to be posted? Or is it too early in my recovery to say."

Guffree did not quite meet Van's eyes. "The doctors say that it could be another six months to a year before you'd be in the same physical condition that you were before the attack . . . and could return to duty in that status . . ."

"Could?" Van didn't like the sound of that.

"Oh, Dr. Calyen has assured me that your health will be perfect when you leave here. That's not quite the question." Guffree spoke quickly, as if he wished to get through the next words. "Because you were so severely injured, the Review Board also recommended that, once your rehabilitation is completed, you be granted a full retirement stipend as a commodore."

"But if I'm not permanently injured . . . ?"

"Commodore, you lost both an arm and a leg. You suffered severe internal injuries. The doctors say that, after rehab, you'll be as good as new, perhaps better. But full rehab is likely to take as long as a year, and in cases where such lengthy medical care is required for a senior officer, it's been found that retirement is more appropriate . . . and in your case, a full career retirement is certainly deserved."

Van didn't know what to say. He knew he never would have been promoted to commodore had he not been wounded, yet . . . "I see. I don't know quite what to say."

Guffree laughed warmly. "You don't have to. The Republic rewards its heroes, and we like for them to be able to receive those honors personally, because so often they can't."

Van understood that. He'd seen too many officers and techs die already. A thought came to his mind. "The *Collyns*? Do you know anything?"

Guffree frowned. "I shouldn't speak much about that. Let us just say those on board were among those we cannot reward in any meaningful way."

"I understand." That didn't surprise Van at all. It would have had to have been something like that to have required the *Fergus*'s immediate transfer to Scandya. But it still nagged at him. He wondered if it always would.

"I'm certain you do, Commodore." Guffree smiled again. "It's good to know that you'll recover completely, and I'm happy to have been able to tell you about your commendation and promotion."

"Thank you," Van replied, as warmly as he could. "It . . . takes some getting used to."

"You'll manage, Commodore. I'm sure you will." Guffree paused, then extended a large envelope. "I took the liberty of collecting some of the media stories about you. I thought you might like to show them to friends and family. There's also a copy of the summary of my report."

"I appreciate that," Van replied.

"It was something we could do, and I'm happy I could." Guffree bowed his head. "I'd like to stay and chat, but there's a shuttle to catch."

"You don't want to miss that."

"The ship would wait, but I'd rather not be known as a commodore who pulls that kind of rank." With a last smile, Guffree turned and left.

Van looked at Dr. Calyen. "I will recover fully?"

Calyen glanced toward the door, then stepped toward the medcrib, and spoke quietly. "You should be fully recovered, the way you're progressing, in three months. It might be a little less or a little more, but I'd bet on less."

Van nodded slowly. The RSF would claim that Van would have been out of touch for a year and a half—not nine months—and now they finally had an honorable way to slip one Van Cassius Albert out of the RSF—with a medal, a promotion, and full retirement. And there wasn't anything he could do about it.

He looked blankly at the unopened envelope. How long he did, he wasn't sure, but when he looked up, Dr. Calyen was no longer in the room.

After another pause, he opened the envelope that Guffree had handed him. He started with the news stories.

(Valborg, Scandya) Eight high-level clones attacked Premier Erik Gustofsen in the middle of a light show at the Keltyr embassy on Independence Day night. Lasers, disc-guns, and even slug throwers were leveled at the controversial premier. When it was all over, Gustofsen was untouched. But two security guards were dead, and four others were wounded. The military attaché of the Taran embassy was so severely injured that doctors are still struggling to keep him alive, and the military attaché of the Keltyr embassy was wounded and released.

The eight attackers all died immediately following the unsuccessful assault. The Valborg constabulary has refused comment on whether they were all programmed clones, but sources close to the investigation have indicated that the clones followed a basic Revenant genetic pattern. That pattern does not necessarily indicate who planned and implemented the attack because a number of organizations and governments have the capability of using such a gene pattern.

"If the attackers were clones," commented Revenant Ambassador Jared Dane, "and if the gene pattern were similar to some of our citizens, that would almost certainly prove that we were not involved, but set up as scapegoats." Similar views were expressed by others in the diplomatic community. Temra Piersen of the Liberal Commons denounced the suggested Revenant tie as "little more than a smear campaign" by those wishing Argenti annexation.

Premier Gustofsen called for calm, and tendered his public appreciation to the Taran military attaché for his "foresight and bravery . . ." He also indicated that a letter of commendation and appreciation would be forthcoming.

Van smiled wanly. There hadn't been any private messages from the premier, nor any public ones that he'd seen. But perhaps a communiqué had gone to New Oisin. That might have been the reason for the Taran commendation and promotion. He went back to reading.

The Taran commander, Van Albert, apparently recognized the attackers before they were in position and sounded a warning. Albert vaulted onto the dais with the ambassadors and the premier, keeping the attackers from getting clear shots at the premier until security guards shielded Gustofsen with their own bodies. Albert was hit with multiple weapons. He is in critical condition at Valborg Medcenter. Doctors would not comment on his condition.

Most of the other transcripts of media stories were along the same lines as the first—except for the one from Taran Media.

(New Oisin, Tara) Last week in Valborg, the capital of the Scandyan System, eight well-armed clones attacked the Scandyan premier. The aim of the attack was foiled by the quick thinking of the Taran embassy's military attaché. Commander Van Albert was severely wounded and may not even survive, let alone recover fully. Yet his actions prevented what might have led to a civil war in Scandya, since by all accounts, the premier is the only figure presently capable of maintaining Scandyan neutrality.

Although we appreciate and applaud the commander's heroism, as should every citizen, neither the Republic nor its peoples should have to rely on uncommon individual heroism in other systems to protect us and our children. While the RSF has taken pains to deny the story, it is fairly certain that the RSFS *Collyns* has been lost in space, most probably another hidden casualty of an indirect and undeclared conflict that threatens to engulf the entire Arm. Another cruiser is also missing and presumed lost. In this time of growing tension between the Revenants and the Argenti systems, the RSF must have more and better ships and technology if we are not to find ourselves in the same predicament as do the Scandyans . . .

Van set down the stories and reached for Emily Clifton's envelope, taking out her press release, and comparing it to what had been aired and printed in various media. He nodded slowly. From what she had written, Van felt Emily was probably largely responsible for his commendation and promotion, rather than his appearance before another Review Board.

He looked down at the unread summary report. He'd have to read that as well. But not yet. He shook his head slowly, then looked outside, where the skies had darkened and even more snow had begun to fall.

Chapter 26

Intermittent fat flakes of late spring snow drifted down from dark gray clouds as the groundcar came to a stop outside the Taran embassy. A stocky commander, with streaks of gray in his hair, stood just outside, waiting as Van stepped from the embassy groundcar that had brought him from the rehab facility where he had spent the last two months. Van's breath steamed in the chill, and he could feel the unseasonable cold knifing through him, despite the officers' heavy winter coat.

"Commodore, welcome back. I'm Bert Maine." The commander offered a warm smile. "Do you have any gear?"

Van held up the small duffel he carried. "Just a few personal items."

After a moment, the older but junior officer asked, "How long will you be staying here?"

"Just a few days. I'm scheduled on a courier on sixday. The *Morraha*, I think." Van knew the question was a formality, designed to confirm what Commander Maine already knew, that Van would only be at the embassy for five days.

"The ambassador wanted a few words with you as soon as you came in, and, after that, I'll be giving you the general staff codes so that you don't have to have an escort around the embassy. They were all changed after the Independence Day . . . incident." He turned and gestured for Van to enter the embassy.

"I can imagine."

The Taran Marine corporal on guard duty stiffened as the two officers neared.

"Carry on," Van said quietly.

Once inside the embassy, Van followed Maine toward the stairs to the upper level.

"Shame to hear about your old ship, Commodore," offered the commander.

His old ship? Which one? "The *Fergus*?" Van stopped.

Maine looked curiously at Van.

"You have to remember that for six months I was in an induced coma," Van said gently. "I still haven't caught up on everything."

"Ah . . ." Maine nodded understandingly. "They didn't tell me that."

"The *Fergus*?" Van prompted.

"Yes. Sad thing it was. Must have happened not long after you were injured. Vanished in jump transit from here to Tara. RSF tried to keep that quiet, coming so soon as it did after the *Collyns* going missing, but word did get out to some of us, and then everyone knew." Maine shook his squarish head. "At least now they can all see we need more and better ships, but it's been a heavy price to pay." He started up the steps.

Van stood at the bottom of the stairs. The *Fergus* . . . missing like the *Collyns*? How? The old cruiser had been checked over thoroughly, or should have been. Ships did occasionally vanish in midjump, but there had been only a handful in hundreds of years. Had the cruiser just been too old to repair properly? Or had the Revenants managed some hidden attack?

Van glanced up the steps, then followed Maine. He was breathing harder than he would have liked when he reached the top of the stairs in the office wing of the embassy. Rehab

hadn't gotten him back in the shape he'd been in, not by even
a short jumpshift. He did sense the stronger screens, and the
pulse of Commander Maine's access codes.

Maine turned left. "The ambassador is anxious to see you,
ser."

Suddenly warm, Van slipped out of the winter coat and
folded it over his arm, then followed the other along the corridor to the door at the south end.

Even the ambassador's personal assistant was new, a
round-faced younger woman who stood immediately as Van
stepped into the outer office. "Commodore Albert. We had so
hoped you would come back before you left for Tara."

Van wasn't aware that he'd had much choice. He smiled.
"I'm very glad to be here." That was true, especially given
the alternatives.

"Ambassador George is waiting for you." The assistant
hurried to the door to the inner office and opened it.

"I'll be back shortly," added Commander Maine.

"Thank you." Van set his small duffel on the floor and laid
his coat across the back of one of the chairs before turning to
follow the woman.

The ambassador—a lanky man with black hair and piercing hazel eyes—strode forward to meet Van. "William
George, Commodore. You're a very famous man, and I
couldn't overlook the opportunity to greet you on your return
to the embassy." The ambassador gestured to the leather armchair on one side of the low table before the replica hearth.
Unlike his predecessor, he waited until Van had seated himself, then sat down. George leaned forward with a pleased
smile. "I'd like to hear your side of the story, from you in person, but I do have a slightly official function to perform first."

Wondering what that might be, Van just nodded and waited.

"You may not realize it," the ambassador went on, "but
your actions improved our standing immensely with the
Scandyans." He gestured to a simple pasteboard box on the
table, measuring slightly less than a half meter on a side and
roughly twenty centimeters high. "That's a token from Premier Gustofsen. Personally. He said that he wished it could

be more, but understood the limitations on gifts to RSF personnel." When Van did not reach for the box, George lifted it and handed it to Van.

Van took it, then slipped off the top. Inside, surrounded by padding, was a second box, one of a dark wood, with two seals inlaid side by side on the hinged top, and connected by a chain that appeared to be solid gold inlaid into the wood. One seal was that of the RSF, the other, Van assumed, of Scandya. Under the seals were two lines of writing in Old Anglo script, again inlaid in solid gold.

With greatest appreciation to Commodore Van Cassius Albert, RSF
From Erik Gustofsen, Premier, Scandyan Confederation

Van studied the box, then carefully unlatched the catch and lifted the top. Inside was a medal, one he did not recognize.

"It's the Star of Dedication. That's the highest award they can give to a non-Scandyan. The box is a personal token from the premier, and RSF officers, I am assured, can accept personal tokens that carry no overt commercial value."

While the wooden box carried no overt commercial value, Van had already seen that all the colors and shapes of the two seals had been cut and set in gemstones and gold, and the stones and artistry made the box far more than a mere token. "It's beautiful."

The ambassador extended an envelope, sealed with green wax and a gold ribbon. "This comes with it."

Van had to fumble with his belt kit to get out his knife, and he carefully opened the envelope without breaking the seal. Then he read the words inside, handwritten.

This is a mere token of thanks from me and from my family. We cannot express how much your selfless action has meant, both to us and to the people of Scandya. We hope that both the Star and the box will remind you in good times and bad that there are those of us who can appreciate honor and selflessness, especially when purchased so dearly.

Beneath was a simple signature—Erik Gustofsen.

Ambassador George slipped another large and flat envelope on the table. "That has the official proclamation from the Scandyan Assembly."

"I can't say that I anticipated any of this." Van had really expected that the promises he had read about more than two months earlier would have been conveniently forgotten by everyone.

"You made a great impression, Commodore. A great impression."

Van replaced the "token" box inside its container. He would read the proclamation later. He glanced toward the window. Outside, the snow had begun to fall more heavily.

"How did you know what was going to happen?" asked George. "I read the RSF inquiry, the one they submitted to the ministry. But it never said anything about how you knew."

Neither had the summary report that Van had read, and no one had talked to him—at least not that he recalled, although he had no idea whether he might have been interrogated under sedation, but there was no mention of that in the summary.

"I didn't know," Van replied, "except for three things. A number of the servers at the Keltyr embassy looked like they were former military. The Kelt military attaché had told me that they had all been screened thoroughly, and then I saw servers on the lawn where there were very few people, but in places where they had a clear field of fire. The only real target had to be the premier. He was the only one that wasn't replaceable." Van shrugged.

"Why did the screening tip you off?"

"Because the Kelt commander was a professional, and the only way that they could have passed screening was through duplication, and that meant clones."

"You mean . . . whoever did it had duplicate clones of each assassin, one programmed to pass screening, and one . . ."

Van nodded. "It's the only way it would work. Programmable clones are blank slates. That means they take their programming hard. You can't deprogram without destroying them." Even as he spoke, he wished he'd kept that conclusion to himself and decided against revealing anything else—not that there was much at that point.

"Who . . ."

Van shrugged. "That, I couldn't even guess. You can create a motive for just about anyone. I'd be skeptical that it was the Revenants because I'd think they'd use another genetic pattern. But then, they could have figured that everyone would think that. I just don't know."

Ambassador George smiled. "That's something—to figure that out as it was happening."

"I was lucky. Or maybe I wasn't."

"I doubt it was luck." The ambassador rose. "I'd like to talk longer, but I hope we'll see you at dinner or lunch one of these days before you go."

Van rose, careful to gather the box and envelope.

Outside, Commander Maine was waiting, holding Van's duffel. Van made no move to take it as he reclaimed his coat.

"If you'd link to the netsystem, Commodore?"

Van did, and picked up the general access codes for the embassy, but not those that required special clearances. He could also sense that his codes were trace-linked. He couldn't do much about that, either. He locked them into his memory. "I've got them."

"Good. We'll head to your quarters."

Once they were back in the main corridor, Maine added, "We did move all your records and personal effects to your personal quarters. I hope that we got everything, but . . . well . . . we don't have that much office space . . ."

"I understand. No one knew when I'd be back, and you had to get on with the tasks at hand." Van didn't worry about funds. Once his personal account reached a certain level, the excess was transferred automatically to an account on Sulyn—code-named VCA. Dad Cicero also had access to that account. Van had done that to allow his father to continue his prudent and effective investing on Van's behalf, something an officer moving from system to system certainly couldn't do.

Neither officer spoke much on the walk to Van's quarters. Nor did they say much there.

Van didn't feel like talking, and it was clear that Maine was ready to return to his duties.

After the commander left, Van surveyed his quarters. He could tell that neat as everything looked, his rooms had been searched, and probably more than once. That was certainly to be expected under the circumstances.

He glanced to the window, but the snow continued to fall. After taking a deep breath, he settled into the armchair in the sitting room. He'd need to step up his conditioning. That he could tell. Other than that, and his orders to report to New Oisin for debriefing and mustering out into full retirement, he hadn't the faintest idea what lay ahead. He'd just never thought that he'd be retired so quickly and so young. Even after three months, he hadn't really accepted that, and he hadn't felt like trying to figure out the future during rehab— not when every day had left him exhausted.

Everything that had happened to him seemed almost surreal, and he wasn't quite sure why, except that he didn't think it was just his own personal reaction, or that it was the result of his injuries. Whether he'd ever discover what really had happened at the Keltyr embassy was also another question. And what had happened to the *Collyns* and the *Fergus* were also unanswered questions. He wanted answers, needed answers; but needing to know and being able to discover that knowledge were two separate issues.

He looked at the late spring snow once more, then shivered involuntarily.

Chapter 27

Just before noon on threeday, for at least the tenth time in the previous hour, Van looked out the window of the sitting room in his embassy quarters. Snow—wet fat flakes—had continued to fall intermittently. If he hadn't been following his exercise program rigorously, he probably would have been even more restless, with so little to do.

Van looked up from the holo projection of the complete RSF report on the Independence Day incident. He'd had to insist that Maine make it available to him, suggesting that, despite his current status without diplomatic clearances, it would be viewed as less than proper for a hero of the Taran Republic not to be able to read the report of his own actions. Maine had concurred, reluctantly, but with the limitation that Van could only read it on the embassy netsystem and could not print out any hard copy.

For all his efforts, the RSF report shed no more illumination on the event. There were more facts—such as the discovery of an abandoned cloning facility in a warehouse in the commercial district of Valborg and records of materials and common biologicals going to the business front there—Valborg Biologicals. But, according to the RSF investigators and the materials cited from the Valborg constabulary, none of the tracks went anywhere. The company had been set up five years earlier by a Dartigan Dumas, a citizen of Keshmar, and the bonding had been in Galactic Arm securities. Officials of Galactic Arm indicated that the funds had come from a Keshmaran Commercial Credit clearinghouse, and without traveling half the Arm to Keshmara there was no way to trace the originator.

Even then, Van suspected there would be no trace. The operation had been conducted in a way that indicated vast resources—governmental resources—but that had been a foregone conclusion. Of course, the report made no mention of either the *Collyns* or the *Fergus*.

Incoming from Integrated Information Systems, the netsystem announced.

The name was familiar, but Van couldn't place it. He debated, then said, "Accept."

The image on the screen was that of a man who appeared, at least in comparison to the spartan furniture behind him, tall and broad-shouldered. His short-cut, almost military-styled hair was blond, with faint streaks of silver. His eyes might once have been bright blue, but now bore the washed-out faded intensity of a deep-space pilot, probably a former Revenant military pilot, Van judged.

The tall man smiled politely and spoke. "Commodore, I'm Trystin Desoll with IIS."

"IIS? I can't say I've ever heard of it."

"Integrated Information Systems. We're a foundation out of Cambria—on Perdya."

Van nodded. Now he remembered—they had an office in the Coalition Consulate because they'd run into problems leasing space in Valborg, but that was about all he knew, except that Cambria was the capital of the Eco-Tech Coalition. He frowned. The man didn't look like an Eco-Tech.

Desoll laughed, warmly and with understanding. "I know. I don't look like I'm Eco-Tech. It's a family curse. I look like a Revenant, but I can assure you that I come from a long-standing Eco-Tech heritage."

"I'm not much in the mood to buy whatever you're selling," Van said politely.

"I'm not selling. I'm looking to buy, and I'd very much like to talk to you in person. I'd be happy to stop by your quarters or meet you anywhere you might wish."

"I'm leaving Scandya on sixday."

"I'll make time for you whenever it's convenient," Desoll replied.

Van smiled wryly. In a way, anytime was convenient, and he might as well get it over with. Besides, what did he have to lose besides time? He already was finding that he had more than he wanted of that. "In an hour—at your office. You're still in the Coalition consulate?"

There was the slightest flicker of surprise on Desoll's face, followed by a smile. "We are. Thirteen-fifteen?"

"I'll be there." Van broke the link. He wondered about the Eco-Tech's smile. The man had almost seemed pleased. He also wondered why he'd agreed to meet Desoll. Curiosity? Or a dawning recognition that he was going to have to do something else with his life? The idea of an idle retirement, even a comfortable one, was totally unacceptable to Van.

He'd never been able to sit and do nothing, or busy himself with meaningless hobbies.

Van linked into the embassy netsystem to request a driver and a car, and was immediately assured that one would be waiting for him at twelve-forty.

Then he reread the RSF report, but he didn't find much new. The only other new bit of information that he found wasn't in the report itself, but buried in the notes at the rear. That was the observation that the Revenant ambassador, Jared Dane, had been recalled to Orum, where he'd been elevated to the Quorum, whatever that was. What it also meant was that Dane had not been disgraced or reprimanded, but apparently rewarded.

At twelve-thirty, Van donned his winter dress coat over his winter greens and walked down to the embassy's front portals. As promised, the groundcar was waiting. Van didn't know the embassy driver—Stefan had also apparently been dismissed or left in the time Van had been in rehab—but the woman knew her craft and, despite the continuing snow, had him at the Coalition consulate at thirteen hundred. For a moment, Van thought about making Desoll wait, but dismissed that thought immediately. What was the point?

He looked at the driver. "I won't be long."

"That's not a problem, Commodore. Take as much time as you need. I'll be here." She smiled warmly.

"Thank you." As he walked through the slush that even the nanitic deicers couldn't melt and remove fast enough, Van asked himself how long the respect and semi–hero worship would last. Not all that long, he decided.

There was no one in the corridors of the Coalition consulate, and, as had been the case when he had visited the Coalition consulate before, the door to the IIS office was open. Van walked inside, and toward the inner office with the open door.

Trystin Desoll had already sensed Van and stood in the doorway before Van reached it. The Eco-Tech wasn't all that much taller than Van, but he was broader, and, in person, exuded a quiet sense of power and authority. Clearly, the man had been a commander of some sort.

"I appreciate your coming to see me, Commodore." Desoll closed the door behind Van.

"I have the feeling you might have been a commodore or more yourself," Van suggested.

Desoll laughed. The sound was warm, appreciative, and rueful, all at once. "No . . . the highest I ever got was senior commander."

That surprised Van, although he couldn't say why. He settled into one of the wooden armchairs, which, despite its lack of upholstery and padding, was shaped in such a way that it was surprisingly comfortable. "You said you were buying. What are you buying?"

Desoll sat in the other wooden armchair, both in front of the desk. He looked directly at the younger man. "I'm looking for a very senior officer and pilot to help us here at IIS. I thought you might be interested."

"I'm not looking for a console job." Not unless he couldn't find anything else.

"I guess I wasn't clear. I'm looking for an officer to command an IIS ship. It's not as big as the kind of commands you've had—it's about the size of a corvette—but with automated systems so that you and one tech can operate everything."

"You can afford ships like that?"

"We have two. The third, the one we'd hope you'd consider, is almost completed. It's scheduled for delivery in six weeks." A smile followed. "That means seven or eight, but not longer than that because there are penalties for a later completion."

Van nodded slowly. IIS was clearly more than it seemed. Very few multilaterals could afford to own and operate one interstellar ship, let alone three. And he'd never heard of a foundation with interstellar vessels. "I have to say that what you say intrigues me. I've never heard of a foundation with jumpships. I don't want to seem too . . . presumptuous . . . but it would almost seem that there would have to be a . . . governmental link."

Desoll nodded in return. "I can see where you would think

that. Any reasonable and intelligent individual would consider that as the most logical possibility. I can assure you that
the IIS is not funded, either directly or indirectly, by any government, or by any entity affiliated with any human government or bureaucracy anywhere."

"That's easy to say . . ."

"That's true. As a condition of your employment, if you
are still interested after I describe the duties and compensation, we will allow you access to all IIS records and systems.
Furthermore, we will place a bond equivalent to one year's
compensation at any financial institution you choose, anywhere, and in your name. If you feel that you have been
deceived in any way, all you have to do is request that bond
be turned over to you, and that will be done."

That was surprising. Van had never heard of any black
operation willing to offer such conditions, nor one relying
solely on the views of the would-be employee. After a
moment, he asked, "Could you tell me more about the duties
and responsibilities involved with . . . such trust?"

"Some of it's very basic," Desoll replied. "We develop
proprietary information of all sorts and package it for clients
across the Arm. It's too detailed for economic transmission
by standing wave, and not something we'd like to broadcast
across the Galaxy. We also have developed some extremely
sophisticated information handling and analysis systems
which we prefer, for obvious reasons, to manage ourselves.
We've grown to the point that two ships are no longer suffi-
cient. In addition, because we have a reputation for scrupu-
lous honesty and punctuality, we also take consignments of
similar technology and information for large multilaterals
and deliver them in the course of our own operations. We
charge dearly for that service, but not so dearly as would be
the case if they had to send couriers and buy commercial
space without guarantees of security." Desoll took a sip from
the glass of water on the desk, then continued. "In addition,
we want someone with the experience and stature to deal
with the senior executives of both governments and multilaterals. We can find pilots, and we can find executives and

politicians, but finding someone who combines both sets of skills—and who has a demonstrated record of accomplishment and unblemished integrity . . . That is very difficult."

"I'm not a good politician. You should have discovered that by now."

"I'd have to disagree, Commodore. You've survived three incredibly difficult situations in the RSF. Not only survived, but gained reluctant admiration."

Van almost laughed. Instead, he asked, "Putting all that aside . . . why me?"

"You're black Taran, right?"

"No secret about that."

"What do you know about Eco-Tech culture—the racial aspect?"

Van stopped and looked at the other man—tall, blond, fair—a perfect Rev or Scandyan. Except, if he'd been born and raised in Cambria, he wouldn't have been perfect, not when all the Eco-Techs Van had met were smaller, dark-eyed, with darker skins, and dark brown or black hair, and faint slants to their eyes. "I never thought about it that way."

"We're interested in educated, decisive, and highly qualified pilots who aren't bound by traditional cultural constraints. We're also interested in officers who have gained an understanding of how multilateral, military, and governmental organizations operate, and who have gained that experience the hard way."

Van had to admit his experience hadn't been gained in the easiest way.

"Now . . . there is one other aspect of the job."

Van waited for the catch.

"We're one of the few foundations or multis who deal with the Farhkans. They prefer not to bring their ships into certain systems. On occasion, we will transport a Farhkan or go into their systems and pick up or deliver various items. Would dealing with them bother you?"

Desoll watched Van closely.

Van didn't even have to think about that, although he'd only seen a single Farhkan in his life, and only from a distance. "No. I can't see why it would." In another way, that also made sense. IIS was handling something else profitable that others wouldn't think about. Van did wonder how IIS had established the relationship, but it wasn't the time to ask.

"That's good." Desoll waited. "Do you think you'd be interested in IIS?"

"I'll still have to think about it," Van demurred.

"Take all the time you want." Desoll smiled, and somehow the expression was both sad and understanding. "The offer's open. We'll leave the ship preserved for a year, if we have to, before we pick someone who's not right."

"I'm going back to Tara on sixday, and then home to Sulyn." Van shrugged. "I hadn't planned on this."

"I understand. I really do. When I was retired, it came as a shock also. We share some similarities there, because I'd just finished a . . . an assignment where I'd been badly injured, and it took more than a year before I was well enough to return home. And then I was retired."

Van was certain that Desoll had almost said "a mission." Had the man been an intelligence operative? Yet what he said about his own medical experiences and retirement rang true—almost too true. "I take it that was a while ago?"

"Quite a while ago." Desoll smiled. "Eventually, I got tired of gardening, and then my wife died. That was when I decided to work with IIS. While I've made mistakes, I've never regretted working here."

"What's the structure? I mean, who do you work for?"

"The board, I suppose. I'm the managing director."

"You're the head of IIS?"

An embarrassed smile crossed the older man's face. "We're a very lean organization. With our overhead, we have to be. You'd be a senior director, say the equivalent of a senior vice president or vice director general or something like that. Oh . . . the pay is complete health protection, and I mean complete, anywhere in the Arm, and an annual stipend of a quarter million Coalition credits—that works out to about four hundred thousand Argenti creds. I don't have the current

Taran equivalent, but it's around three hundred fifty thousand. And all expenses."

Van did swallow. There might have been a hundred individuals on all of Sulyn who made that kind of income.

"We pay a great deal, but we ask a great deal, Commodore. Particularly absolute integrity."

"It's impressive," Van conceded, then asked, "Just what does this job entail? For that amount of credits, you must want a lot more than a pilot. Even with impeccable integrity."

"It all centers on being a pilot. As you know, much as the Arm governments would like to pretend otherwise, piracy and raiding still exist, if on a limited scale. Our ships all have far larger drives and shields than would otherwise be the case. We also carry, as I mentioned, extraordinarily valuable goods upon occasion. You would also be expected to learn more about the foundation and take over some of the duties I now have. As we've expanded, I find myself stretched far too thin."

"But you don't need a pilot for that, do you?"

"Given our structure and operations, it makes much more sense. That's another reason why we're interested in a tested and more senior officer. One who understands how important trust is for an organization."

Van cocked his head. "That would seem obvious, but you don't think many people recognize that?"

"Outside of the military, no. That's been my experience, at least. But like all disillusioned idealists, I tend to be cynical."

Van couldn't help but chuckle at the ironic self-mockery. "What else does a disillusioned idealist believe?"

"Don't rescue anyone unless you want to be responsible for them for life."

"That's an old belief."

"It's also true." Desoll smiled. "After all this, are you still willing to consider IIS?"

"I'll consider it, but I still have to think about it, unless you need an answer now."

"No. We have some leeway." Desoll smiled, again almost sadly. "It may be that I can arrange to stop by Sulyn in several months. If you come to a decision before that . . ." He extended a plastic oblong. "That will cover a standing wave message to reach me wherever I am. Just indicate yes or no, and, if yes, where we can reach you."

Van took the oblong. He doubted he'd accept the job offer from an unknown Eco-Tech foundation, but it would have been foolish to decline before he had explored the alternatives. "Thank you, Director Desoll." He rose.

"Trystin, please. I hope we'll hear from you." Again . . . there was sadness behind the warm smile.

Van had the feeling that Trystin was even older than he looked to be, perhaps a good decade older. "It might be a while. I don't know what will happen in New Oisin."

"I understand. But do take care of yourself. Whatever you decide, you have much to offer. Just make sure you do what fits who you are."

Van was still puzzling over Desoll's last words as he walked toward the waiting groundcar. Doing what fitted him? While it was certainly good advice, it seemed strange that Desoll would offer it to a man he hardly knew.

Chapter 28

By sixday morning, as he rode in the groundcar to the Valborg shuttle terminal, Van still knew little more than he had when he had returned to the embassy. The embassy records showed nothing beyond what he had already learned from the RSF report and his own experience, and since no one remained from the previous diplomatic staff, his personal inquiries revealed little else, even those he had hurriedly made to Commodore Petrov and the military attachés he had known so briefly before being wounded. He had managed five more days of fairly vigorous reconditioning exercise, not so strenuous as he would have liked, but what he could do.

Everyone had been polite, deferential, even awed, but that hadn't led to any more information. Nor had his searches of events on Scandya revealed anything—and he'd been using the public nets for that line of inquiry ever since he'd entered rehab. The fact that there was so little information and so little time before he was being sent back to Tara was troubling. But then, everything from the time the *Fergus* had entered the Scandyan system had been troubling. And neither the Scandyan databases nor the embassy records revealed anything new about either the *Fergus* or the *Collyns*. Nor had he discovered anything more about the mysterious death of Commander Cruachan.

He'd also learned little about IIS, except that what he had found seemed to confirm what Desoll had said. Yet he still couldn't understand why the man was so interested in him, and that bothered Van. For all the lip service given to retiring officers, once the flowery language ended, no one paid that much for broken-down commanders—commodores.

When the embassy groundcar pulled up to the terminal, the driver smiled. "We all wish you well, Commodore."

"Thank you." Van returned the smile, then reclaimed his two duffels and his carry bag, walking through the portals toward embarkation control.

"Ser? Over here." A gray-haired control officer in the gray uniform worn by all Scandyan transport controllers beckoned from a console to Van's right.

Van tendered his datacard.

The official took the card. Then his eyes widened. "Ser? You're the man who saved the premier?"

"I don't know that I saved him. I tried, and it worked out."

"I knew you looked familiar. I'm so glad to see you up and around, ser. For a while they were saying you might not make it."

"It took a while," Van admitted. "Longer than I would have liked."

"You're cleared, Commodore. Out-gate three. Have a good trip. And thank you."

"I did what I could, but thank you."

The port controller must have coded something, because, as Van left the screening portals, two more controllers stepped forward, tipping their hats.

"Have a good flight, Commodore," said the woman.

Van found that he had the front left row in the magshuttle to himself, the seat beside him empty—the only empty seat in the shuttle.

As he waited, his implant and enhanced hearing picked up fragments of conversations.

"Who is he . . . ?"

". . . Taran officer . . . senior type . . . commodore or sub-marshal . . ."

". . . don't know, but overheard one of them saying something about owing him . . ."

". . . owing a Taran officer?"

". . . what they said . . ."

"Wish they owed me like that."

Van smiled. He doubted any of them would have knowingly paid the price that had gained him his small bit of comfort and privacy on the shuttle.

Less than two hours later, he was gathering his gear and stepping out of the shuttle and through orbit control screening. He'd let the other passengers disembark first, then followed them out into the grayness of orbit control, where the air smelled faintly of oil and metal, as did all orbit control stations, in spite of all the air purification equipment and systems.

"Commodore Albert!" Standing beyond the debarkation area was a young Scandyan port controller—with a ground-cart. "Ser."

Van carried his gear toward the controller.

"Ser. We checked, and your courier is all the way on the other side of the station. Thought you wouldn't mind if we . . ."

Van grinned. "I wouldn't mind at all. I've been out of rehab less than a week, and the muscles aren't back to what I'd like."

"We thought something like that."

Van set the duffels in the bin then sat down beside the driver. "I do appreciate this."

"It's the least we can do, ser."

Van caught the absolute conviction in the young man's voice, the same sort of conviction that had been in the ground personnel's words as well. Why had his actions been that important to them? Because they knew that Premier Gustofsen was so vital to the future of Scandya? Because everyone knew? That was definitely a frightening prospect.

"We all do what we can," Van replied, as the groundcart lifted off the deck and eased along the center of the corridor. He admitted to himself that he was very happy not to have to lug all his gear halfway around the orbit station.

Even so, he felt uneasy, as if someone were following him. Yet, even with his implant, he couldn't pick up any signals. Still, he was certain that someone was watching him, but the corridors of the orbit station were just crowded enough that he couldn't pick anyone out, especially with the speed of the groundcart. Was that another reason why he'd been met? Did Scandyan intelligence think he'd been targeted and want to make sure he left Scandyan territory safely?

How could he tell? After all, he reminded himself, he'd never been trained for intelligence or espionage. He was just a ship driver, and one about to be retired.

"We're about there, ser. It's EM-three." The cart slowed and came to a stop.

Van stepped down to the deck and turned to the controller. "Thank you." He hoisted his gear.

"Our pleasure, ser. Have a good jump."

"I certainly hope to." The lock was closed, not that Van expected less from a courier, which basically carried a pilot and a tech. He triggered his implant.

Morraha, *this is Commodore Van Albert, for transport to Tara.*

We've been waiting for you, ser. The lock door swung open, and almost immediately a slender RSF captain stood there.

"Captain Nialla, Commodore." She reached forward to take one of the duffels. "Let me give you a hand here."

"A pleasure to see you, Captain. And I'll accept that hand. I wouldn't have once, but for now, I appreciate it."

As he entered the courier, Van noted that the port controller had not moved the groundcart, at least not while the lock was open.

Chapter 29

Following his orders, two days later, after a long one-jump trip on the *Morraha*, a crowded down-shuttle ride to New Oisin, and an expensive commercial groundcar ride, Van reached RSF headquarters. There, he was escorted impartially to the visiting senior officers' quarters, where he waited two days for another physical, which took a full day. He was grateful that he had arrived in Oisin's fall, rather than full winter.

On fourday morning, he was sitting, waiting in the outer office of Sub-marshal Vickry, deputy chief of RSF Intelligence and Strategy, for his scheduled debriefing. He knew he'd run across the name before, and not just on the RSF organizational chart, but he couldn't remember where.

"Commodore Albert, Sub-marshal Vickry will see you," said the senior tech at the console.

Van rose and stepped through the archway that held more screening equipment and then into the office that stretched a good ten meters by eight, overlooking the Yeats Green.

Vickry was redheaded, with age-faded freckles, and rail-thin. Intensity radiated from him. He did not rise from his desk console, simply gesturing to the chairs facing him. "Commodore Albert. I'm glad to see you back in health."

"Thank you, ser," Van replied, after easing himself into the chair directly facing Vickry.

"I've been assured that, if you take care, you'll enjoy a long and healthy retirement." The sub-marshal's smile was professionally warm, the kind of forced emotion that Van distrusted.

Van waited.

"Commodore, Marshal Connolly and I have reviewed the available information on the Scandyan incident, and there are several aspects of the event where we thought your personal observations might be useful. You are known to have been an impartial and highly ethical officer, and that reputation makes your observations that much more important."

"I'd be happy to share those with you, ser. I don't know that I saw that much more . . ."

Vickry waved off the demurral. "Commodore, you clearly saw more than anyone else because you were the first to react, and certainly the first correctly to assess the danger. No false modesty, if you please. I'd like you to explain in your own words why you reacted."

"It was almost an accident," Van began. "I noted that some of the servers were tall, almost like Rev troopers. That was just an idle thought at first, but I saw several like that. Then, when we left the embassy building and went out on the lawn for the flareshow, I saw two of them on the dais, and one glanced out across the lawn. I looked where he looked, and there was another server there, with a tray, and only one person anywhere near . . ." Van went through the entire incident again, word by word, action by action.

After Van finished, Vickry nodded slowly. "Coincidence, in a way, that you happened to be in the right position to see all that, but what appeared to be unconnected events to others, you saw with a trained and observant eye." He paused before speaking. "I understand that, after your release, you visited the Coalition consulate again. What was your rationale for that?"

Van forced a smile. "I'd read the summary report that Commodore Guffree provided me. As you may know, I contacted all attachés remaining in Valborg whom I knew and who remained, not that there were that many. I hoped to find out if I'd missed something."

"Did you?"

"Nothing that seemed to add to the RSF report," Van said. "There were a few more facts and some confirmation of what I'd seen."

"You had mentioned to Ambassador George that you thought that there were other clones involved. Did you have any hard evidence for that conclusion?"

Once more, Van wished he had not made that admission. "No, ser. That was circumstantial, as I told the ambassador. The Keltyr military attaché had told me that they had put all the temporary help through intensive screening. The Kelt commander seemed most professional, and duplicate clones seemed the only way possible." Van shrugged. "That was my surmise. I don't have any idea if that was how it was done, but it could have been done that way, and I certainly couldn't think of any other."

"What about simply gimmicking the Kelt embassy screens?"

Van paused, then replied carefully, "That might have been possible. I'm not into espionage. My implant registered that they had screens, and I'm certain that any overt malfunction would have been detected. But, if someone had a way to pass just the assassins . . . how would anyone know? Except the Kelts, and they certainly wouldn't admit that kind of failure."

"No. They wouldn't," Vickry agreed.

"You could probably discover that, though," Van mused. "It ought to be possible to find out if the Kelts did any extensive changes in the embassy's structure or equipment after the incident to rectify any shortcomings that they had discovered."

"That certainly would be possible."

That response confirmed to Van that Vickry had already looked into that possibility—with no success, making Van's hypothesis even more likely.

"Tell me, Commodore. Did you ever have any contact with the Revenant embassy?"

Van shook his head. "Not except in passing. I was introduced to the Revenant ambassador at one function, then introduced myself to their attaché at the Kelt reception. I'd made a number of calls to the attaché, but none of them were ever returned, and he didn't even recognize my name when I introduced myself."

"Yet Commander Cruachan had no difficulty there."

"That may be. Perhaps he was more skilled at making contacts with the Revenants. He doubtless had more experience before taking his post."

"Ah . . . yes. There is that. Now . . . did you gain any new insights from the Coalition attaché? Major Murikami, was it?"

"Some. He noted that the Sandyans and the Revenants both had exhibited a growing prejudice against the Argentis and the Coalition—or their peoples."

For the first time, Vickry looked truly interested. "What did he say, more exactly?"

"I don't recall his exact words, but they were to the effect that both avoided doing business with darker-skinned peoples, such as the Coalition, the Hyndjis, and the Argentis."

"Most interesting. Did he offer any examples?"

"He said that he knew of some businesses that had had trouble obtaining leases for the use of property, and that the consulate had tried to help." Before Vickry could ask another question, Van asked one that had been bothering him. "You know I was the commander of the *Fergus*, and I'd heard that—"

"That was a terrible thing, Commodore. Very regrettable. It's always a great loss whenever the RSF loses a ship, especially when we can't determine how."

"You never found out what happened?"

"The *Fergus* entered jumpspace, but never emerged. The Scandyans were kind enough to let us check their records, and they show a clean drop."

"And there's nothing else?"

"The best judgment is that the *Fergus* had strained something in the jump generator. It could have been building for some time, just below the detection threshold. Or it could

have been your . . . encounter with that unknown cruiser."
Vickry smiled sympathetically, almost as if to suggest that
he wasn't holding Van responsible. "We don't know. It's
even possible that the *Fergus* encountered a . . . an
unfriendly battle cruiser when she emerged . . . wherever
that might have been. There aren't any records of an energy
disturbance in the system where the ship was scheduled to
arrive."

Van kept his face in an expression of polite concern as he
realized that Vickry either was lying about the jump generator or didn't know that it had been replaced. "Where?"

"I really can't say, Commodore. I'm sure you understand
that. Now . . . about the Keltyr commander . . . how thorough
do you think her personnel screening was?"

The questioning, gentle yet unyielding, continued, touching on every event affecting Van, then turning back again and
again to subjects Van thought had been covered already.

". . . how many times did you actually visit with the Keltyr
attaché?"

"Why did you visit the Coalition in the first place?"

"What was your impression of Kelt military preparedness
from your talks with the commander?"

"Did Major Murikami provide any other insights . . ."

When Van left the office, well after noon, for the first time
he almost felt ready to retire from the RSF. He also felt, once
more, for the first time since he had returned to Tara, that he
was being watched.

Chapter 30

In the end, there was no ceremony for Van's retirement, nor
one for the awarding of his medal, the Star of the Republic.
Nor did he meet with anyone of higher rank except the sub-
marshal, or indeed, any other officers except the doctors for

his retirement physical and other officers in passing and at meals in senior officers' mess.

Sub-marshal Vickry met once more with Van and presented him with his retirement papers—including a hard copy sheet that indicated Van's personal account had been credited seventy-eight hundred credits for unused leave and another two thousand for back pay as a commodore—and the medal in a case. The sub-marshal didn't even offer to pin the medal on Van.

Now that Van was officially retired, his priority on transport had dropped, and he couldn't get a space on an RSF ship headed for Sulyn for more than two weeks. While that wasn't exactly unexpected, since transport of a retired officer to his home of record was of far lower priority than the needs of the RSF for transporting active duty officers, and since the RSF was still quartering him, it was nonetheless unsettling to go from having couriers immediately transporting him to going space available.

Also unsettling was the deactivation of the RSF access to his implant. There was no sense in removing the implant itself, on the off chance that a retired officer might be recalled, not when access could simply be blocked by a simpler procedure during a retirement physical. Although Van could still send and receive standard comm signals, the comparative narrowness of what he sensed was as if he'd lost part of his hearing—and in a way, he had.

In the time remaining on Tara, Van stepped up his exercise program and began to investigate the possibilities for employment and positions open to young retired RSF commodores. He started with the Taran flag line—Quasar—and asked for and received an appointment with one Eron Harvey, senior director for personnel—if four days later. None of the other spacegoing concerns had even returned his calls.

Harvey's office was a third again larger than that of Sub-marshal Vickry and filled with handcrafted walnut and mahogany furnishings. It also was on the third level of the sprawling Quasar complex just to the west of the New Oisin shuttle terminal and overlooked a replica Taran country garden, complete with shamrocks. Van didn't see any small statues of leprechauns when he glanced out the window before sitting down before the replica Gregory desk from behind which Director Harvey studied him.

"Commendations, promotions, citations . . . I must say that you have an impressive record . . . Commodore, is it?" Harvey frowned.

"Not anymore," Van replied with a smile.

"I suppose not." Harvey cleared his throat. "I have to ask why you're interested in a junior pilot's position with Quasar."

"I'm a pilot," Van replied. "That's what I do best. I'd like to keep doing it. In the RSF, once you get to be a commodore, you don't stay as a pilot." Especially if they retire you.

"With all that service and rank, I would imagine you have a considerable retirement . . ."

"It's comfortable," Van replied. "That leaves me free not to worry about compensation."

"I'm sure of that. It's a good position to be in. Still . . . why would someone who's commanded the largest vessels of the RSF want to start all over under someone who doesn't know as much as you do?"

"As I said, I'm a pilot. I know that part of the job well. I can't say I know the commercial side."

Harvey nodded, then squared his shoulders. He did not look directly at Van. "Well . . . I can understand your feelings about wanting to keep doing what you do well, and there's no doubt that your talents and skills are considerable. But . . . I have to be frank. We hire only former military pilots. We've made it a policy not to hire pilots with only one tour or those who've made a career of the military. The first category don't know enough, and they're generally looking for a comfortable position. Those in the second category have more than enough experience, but, frankly, they tend to be less . . . flexible. We've found that a balance between youth and experience works better for us . . ."

In short, Van concluded, Quasar wanted someone else to pay for the costs of training pilots, and then to get them young enough to mold them into the desired Quasar mold, doubtless diplomatic and deferential and oh-so-glad to be working for Quasar.

He wondered if that was the way the other transport outfits felt.

Chapter 31

Van looked across to the command couch, where the older commander reached forward, his index finger poised over the large red jump button.

"Don't!" Van exclaimed.

"It's a perfectly normal jump, commander," explained the gray-haired senior officer. "We're just headed back to Leynstyr." His eyebrows lifted, and for a moment his face shifted, looking more like that of a far younger officer—fair, blond, and oh-so-infallible—before returning to the image of a youthful but still gray commander.

Van wanted to explain that the jump wasn't normal, that it couldn't be normal. Instead, in slow motion, he watched as Commander Baile depressed the jump button.

"No!" Van exclaimed—too late.

Black became white, and white black—and then brilliant red, pain red, swirled through the cockpit, sheer agonizing pain.

Van sat up with a jolt, sweat pouring down his face, his heart pounding. Of course it had been a nightmare. He'd never been on the *Fergus* with Commander Baile, and two commanders would almost never be before the control board at the same time. But it had seemed so real . . . once more.

He wiped his forehead.

Then, the nightmares about the *Regneri* always seemed real. He blotted his forehead again, and checked the time. It was almost time to get up, and he doubted he could get back to sleep in any case. He took a long deep breath and swung his feet over the side of the bed in the visiting senior officers' quarters.

Why the nightmare about the *Fergus*? He hadn't done anything. Unless, somehow, his last battle with the unidentified cruiser had overstrained something. But the jump generators weren't linked to any combat functions—not to shields, or nets, or fire control—and one of them had been replaced.

Somehow, he harbored guilt . . . but why? He hadn't even been near the *Fergus*.

Slowly, he rose and walked toward the fresher and the shower he needed to wash away the sleep and the stench of fear, fear that he had somehow been responsible, and fear that festered within. Maybe . . . more exercise would help.

Chapter 32

As another ten days passed, as his exercise and conditioning efforts continued, Van discovered that all the other concerns in the Taran system that were in the market for space pilots were also looking for younger men and women. He also searched all the news archives that were open-access, but could find no new information that might have shed light on what had happened to the *Fergus*. He was alternating between quietly seething about Sub-marshal Vickry's quiet hint that the *Fergus* might have been lost because of Van's actions in dealing with the renegade cruiser and trying to decide why Vickry had thrown that at him.

Then, too, he was bothered, because he continued to feel that he was being watched, but by whom or why, he still had not been able to confirm.

One of the cometary mining firms—SpaceRec—did make an offer—but for an operations director. Van turned it down, wondering as he did if he were making a mistake. But he hadn't felt all that comfortable as a military attaché, and being an ops director would have required more desk and political skills.

So on oneday, he presented himself at the New Oisin terminal, took the orbital shuttle, and once on Tara orbit control two, made his way through the crowded corridors to lock EM-ten, where the RSFS *Sligo* was docked.

The tech on lock duty—third class at that—saluted Van. "Welcome aboard, Commodore. Commander says we'll be unlocking as soon as Major Dolan arrives. You have the first couch in the passenger cabin. Lockers are aft of the cabin."

"Thank you."

"You're welcome, ser."

With that, Van lugged his two duffels aft and stowed them in the second locker. Then he made his way forward and settled into the first couch of the four. Its gray thermafoam was clean, but worn.

He leaned back and closed his eyes, trying to plan what he might do once he was home on Sulyn. He'd certainly try to see what pilots' positions might be available, but after his experiences in New Oisin, he wasn't too hopeful. He could contact Trystin Desoll at IIS, but the idea of working for a Coalition organization continued to bother him. Much as Desoll had insisted IIS wasn't a black or off-budget agency for the Eco-Techs, Van still had his doubts. But it was a piloting job. Of course, his family would want him to stay near Sulyn, particularly his sister Sappho. He hoped that he'd find something on Sulyn.

At the sound of steps, he opened his eyes.

Major Dolan was a tall and round-faced redhead with a thin body beneath her long neck. As she carried a single duffel past Van, he judged that she was probably only thirty-five, and with the collar insignia of logistics, and her age and service branch suggested a recent promotion.

She paused, then smiled and spoke. "Greetings, Commodore."

"Greetings, Major. Go ahead and stow your gear."

"Yes, ser."

She returned quickly and settled into the couch across from Van's. "I have to say I'm surprised to see you here, ser."

"I was just retired," Van said. "Once that happens . . ." He shrugged.

Her gray eyes studied him for a moment. "Medical? I hope I'm not prying. I suppose that's why I'm in logistics. No tact. But you look too young to be retired, especially as a commodore."

"It happens." Van didn't feel like explaining. "You're being transferred to Sulyn?"

"Actually, I'm headed to the research station off Aeylen. Someone has to keep track of all the widgets and supplies, and if the RSF supply type isn't at least a major, no one really listens. That's what the detailer told me."

"I wasn't aware that Aeylen was an RSF project."

"Oh . . . it's not, but they've run into some interesting developments, and the RSF research arm has been operating the station for almost twenty years. It's really a converted biostation."

The only research the RSF supported was weapons research. Why would there be an RSF station off a world being planoformed? What possible type of weapons research could there be?

"That's been going on for centuries—the planoforming, that is."

"So I was told." Dolan smiled faintly. "Is Sulyn your home?"

"That's where my family is and where I was raised." As he spoke, Van realized that he really didn't think of Sulyn as home. He wanted to see his family, but did he really want to settle down in Bannon—or anywhere else on Sulyn?

"They'll be glad to see you."

"I'll be glad to see them."

There was a cough from the passageway at the front of the cabin. Both officers looked up to see the tech standing there.

"Sers . . . we'll be delocking in a moment. If you would secure your harnesses . . ."

Van had already secured his, but he checked it again.

When he looked up, the tech was gone, and the hatch between the passageway and the cabin had been closed.

Van just hoped that the short standing wave message he had sent had reached his fathers. They'd welcome him, no matter what; but he hated surprising people, even family, because it usually meant that someone or something got slighted.

Chapter 33

Once Van reached Sulyn orbit control, he had to wait almost eight hours for the shuttle down to Bannon, which only ran twice a day, as opposed to the more frequent runs to the planetary capital of Domigua. He spent most of the time and close to a hundred credits accessing news reports and other information, both about the Republic and the transportation and out-system resource extraction situation so that he would have a better grasp of the job possibilities. When he had exhausted that, he ran a search of Sulyn's news files, but there was nothing new there on the *Fergus*. Then he paced, for a time, before finding an eatery where he had a sandwich that tasted only slightly better than flavored sawdust.

The inbound clearance at orbit control was perfunctory, and the down-shuttle almost as worn and tired as the *Sligo* had seemed, but Van couldn't help but smile as he stepped from the terminal in Bannon and out into the late afternoon sunlight. He walked as quickly as he could with his three bags, moving toward the groundcar lane, when he heard cheers from somewhere.

"There he is!" someone announced.

Van wondered what celebrity had been on the shuttle. Some rez-songster? He glanced around, but no one seemed to be near him.

Beyond the groundcar lane, someone was waving a banner,

on which were written the words "Welcome home, Van! Bannon's own hero!"

Him? A hero? Before he could react, a group of media types moved toward him from his left. He hadn't seen them at first, concentrating as he'd been on seeing whether any of his family had come to meet him.

"Van? Or should I say Commodore?"

Van turned, half-squinting into the afternoon light, taking in the long-faced but still-youthful-looking—and familiar—commentator. "Is that you, Ashley?" At that moment, Van thought he saw Sappho and her children in the crowd, but he didn't see Arturo or Margaret—or his fathers, either.

The commentator laughed. "The first words from a returning hero. Yes, it's me. Now . . . how about a few words for the people of Sulyn. You're the first recipient of the Star of the Republic in years. How do you feel?"

"I'm glad to be here." That was mostly true. "I'm looking forward to seeing my family. It's been several years."

"Spoken like a true son of Sulyn. For those of you just tuning in, this is Commodore Van Albert, the RSF officer who single-handedly and without weapons prevented the assassination of the premier of Scandya. Why did you do it, Commodore?"

"It had to be done. No one else was in a position to act."

"As simple as that? Didn't you think about the danger of eight armed assassins?"

"Not until I was in the medcrib recovering." Van managed a rueful laugh, still wondering what all the media hype was about. "Then I had a lot of time to think."

"We understand you were retired after the incident. Would you care to comment on that?"

"That was a decision by the RSF. According to the doctors, I'm fully recovered, and able to do anything I ever could."

"What do you think you'll do?"

"Spend some time with my family first. Then . . . we'll see."

"Thank you very much, Commodore. We wish you well. And that's it from the Bannon shuttle terminal, where one of

Sulyn's sons has returned home a hero in three systems." The professionally bright tone vanished from Ashley's voice as he stepped forward, and said, far more personally, "It's good to see you. Mairee and I worried when we'd heard you'd been wounded."

Van glanced from his former classmate toward the crowd on the other side of the groundcar approach lane, smaller than it had first appeared, but still waving banners and signs for the media. "This . . . this was a little surprising."

"You don't think we'd let a real hero slip into town without notice, do you?"

Van smiled.

"Or that your family would?"

"Don't tell me . . . ?" Van began.

"There they are." Ashley pointed to Van's left.

A long charter-type pale green groundcar eased up. Two familiar faces appeared—those of his fathers—the narrow and serious latte face of Dad Cicero and the broader and smiling darker face of Dad Almaviva.

"Are you going to stand there and gawk?" called Almaviva, his booming bass voice riding over the dying cheers. "You're going to miss the curtain."

That had always been Dad Almaviva's favorite expression with his three children. Whenever they threatened to be late, they were going to miss the curtain. Dad Cicero had preferred to suggest that he'd haul them up before the bar. For years, Van had pictured being dragged up before a huge iron bar, until he'd finally understood what his advocate father had meant. Somehow, not knowing had been more frightening.

Dad Almaviva bounded out of the groundcar and threw his arms around his son. "Van!" His voice rumbled as he hugged Van.

Dad Cicero stood back, more reserved as always, waiting for Van to survive Almaviva's crushing embrace. Then he stepped forward and gave Van a much lighter and quicker hug, but it was as demonstrative as Van had ever seen his advocate father in public.

"I'll get your stuff," Almaviva said. "Everyone's going to meet us back at the house."

Van ended up in the rear-facing but lushly upholstered seat, looking at his fathers.

Dad Almaviva was smiling broadly. "You didn't expect that, I'd wager a full stage."

Van had never understood how one could wager a full stage, but the familiar words were more than welcome.

Dad Cicero was smiling faintly, almost as if relieved when the groundcar eased away from the terminal.

Van had barely settled back when Dad Almaviva asked the first question.

"How long did the trip from Tara take . . . ?"

"Did you have a chance to get to the opera in New Oisin?"

". . . heard that Alygnia was doing *The Fall of Denv* . . . Have you heard him?"

Dad Cicero offered an amused smile, then leaned back and listened.

The drive back to the villa took nearly half an hour, but then, with all the answers Van provided, he scarcely noted the time. The villa was on the north side of Bannon, in the low hills separating the city from the badlands.

When the chartered groundcar pulled away from the circular drive, Van realized he'd never even seen the driver. He lifted a duffel and the carry bag and started for the portico shielding the front foyer, but Cicero had slipped ahead and had the door open.

Van glanced at the stone ledge on the right wall of the entry foyer, catching sight of a bonsai cedar. "That's new."

"I suppose so," replied Cicero. "I've been working with it for almost thirty years, but it's only been here for the past two. It gets the morning sun from the skylights and seems to like it there. So I never moved it. The Silysia didn't like it there."

"Let's get your stuff back to the guest suite," boomed the stocky Almaviva. "Sappho and Arturo and their children will be here any moment."

Bemusedly, Van followed Dad Almaviva, carrying one duffel and his smaller bag. Cicero followed with the other duffel. After depositing all his gear, Van washed up quickly and hurried back to the great room.

The villa was little changed from what Van remembered. He thought the tan of the exterior stucco was a shade lighter, and the reddish roof tiles slightly more faded, but the great room, with the huge hearth that was seldom ever used except as an open space in which to place Dad Almaviva's latest floral creations, looked almost the same. The greenhouse was doubtless still unchanged, although he hadn't looked, and certainly Dad Cicero's study and Dad Almaviva's studio were the same.

Sappho was the first to come bursting through the door— tall like Cicero, but even lighter-skinned than Van, with flaming golden red hair. She practically launched herself at her older brother, giving him the kind of hug that Dad Almaviva always bestowed. "I'm glad you're back—and safe."

She released him and turned to the two girls who stood back shyly, one reaching to Van's chest, the other barely to his waist. She looked to the taller. "You remember Lesnym . . . and this is Farah."

Van bowed slightly. "Lesnym . . . Farah."

"Aelsya will be here as soon as she can. She was on call, and, of course, some idiot working on a groundcar put his leg and foot in the wrong place." Sappho snorted. "When you teach, you hope students grow up, but some never do." She grinned. "You look good, really good for someone they thought wouldn't make it."

"I need to work on the conditioning," Van admitted.

Sappho began to usher Lesnym and Farah toward the great room, murmuring, "Your granddad Almaviva will have some special treats, I know . . ."

Van was about to follow her and the girls when the front door opened again, and three more figures stepped inside. "Arturo!"

"Van." While Arturo looked like Almaviva, and hugged like him as well, if with a hint of Cicero's reticence, he had

Cicero's logical and legal mind and worked as one of Cicero's associates. "I'm sorry we couldn't get to the welcoming ceremony . . ."

"It's enough that you're here," Van replied, wondering why Arturo had even brought up the matter. It wasn't as though Van kept score. When he stepped back, he looked to Arturo's wife. "Margaret. It's so good to see you . . . and Despina."

"It's good to see you. Everyone was so worried when we heard about the trouble in Scandya. But you look good." Margaret was small and petite, with a golden olive tinge to her skin.

Standing beside her mother, Despina clearly took after her father's side, almost as tall as Arturo, but her hair was a lustrous wavy brown and her eyes a brilliant green. She smiled shyly.

"You have grown, young lady," Van announced. "And uncles always say embarrassing things like that."

"Always," the teenager affirmed.

Van gestured for the three to precede him into the great room.

No sooner had he stepped onto the green tiles of the floor there than Almaviva appeared, wearing his splattered cook's apron. "Everyone must be famished!"

"Is that a command, Dad?" asked Arturo. "Be thou famished and empty the board?"

"Just about," replied Sappho.

For that moment, Van was glad to be back in Bannon.

Chapter 34

Much later, after Van's brother and sister and their offspring and spouses had departed, and the villa had quieted under the night sky of fall, Van looked from the worn leather armchair where he sprawled across the great room toward Dad Cicero.

"Now that everyone's gone, what was that welcoming demonstration about?"

Cicero gestured to the more slender Almaviva. "It was that dad's idea."

"You always say that when you two agree," Van pointed out. "What were you two up to?"

Dad Cicero looked at his eldest son. "There was a lot more to what happened on Scandya, wasn't there?"

"Yes." There wasn't much point in evading Dad Cicero, as all too many opposing advocates had discovered over the years. "There were hints everywhere, but I never could find out anything, except by circumstantial evidence and by what wasn't there." Van looked at his advocate father. "How did you know?"

"Something I heard from Al Lingoneer."

"Is he still the director general of Sulyn TransMedia?"

"For another few years." Cicero offered his cool and logical smile. "He'd received a message sometime back, and then a follow-up last week. From the RSF media office. They usually like to offer all sorts of publicity about RSF accomplishments. You know, the hometown girl or boy makes good. This was different. He was told that you'd been through a great deal, and that the RSF really thought that your privacy ought to be respected. Al wasn't told not to run stories or get interviews—just a request to respect your privacy. He asked me. We agreed that it would be up to you, and then the two of us here decided for you. We thought you needed the biggest story you could get when you got here. Dad Almaviva figured out how to put it together. He even made sure there were some pros there."

"You two." Van shook his head.

"We did what we could for our boy," Almaviva said. "Whether the RSF wanted it or not. Things haven't been . . . well, let's just say that New Oisin has once again begun to regard Sulyn as a trouble spot."

"Do you think we were wrong?" asked Cicero almost simultaneously.

"Probably not. I've had the sense I've been followed ever since I left Scandya. I haven't been able to see who it was."

"You want to tell us what you can?" Cicero pressed.

Van nodded. "It all started when the *Fergus* was suddenly ordered to Scandya . . ." Once more, he went through the entire story, trying to not forget or skip anything. Neither father said a word, just letting him talk.

When he had finished, Dad Almaviva looked at Cicero. "You were right."

"So were you."

They nodded almost in unison.

"Why did you say that bit about New Oisin?" Van asked. "What's happening?"

"Nothing yet," Almaviva answered, "but the university just got 'guidance' from the Ministry of Education on the need for more accurate information on students and faculty. They want even more demographic information—in the guise of being better able to tailor programs. That usually isn't the reason for that sort of thing." He shrugged. "Just a feeling."

Van nodded.

"What are you going to do now?" asked Cicero, his eyes catching Van's.

"Work more on getting back in condition and trying to find a job as a pilot. I miss it."

"Do you think you can?" asked Dad Almaviva.

Van shrugged. "I won't know if I don't try. Do either of you have any ideas?"

"Sulyn Trans-Arm . . . but they don't care much for me. Not after I won that judgment against them for the fabricators."

"What you did was right. Even the Justiciary wrote an opinion that supported you all the way." Then Van laughed, ruefully. "What's right doesn't matter. It's only what's expedient."

"And profitable," added Dad Cicero. "That's the problem today. It's the modern ethos effect."

"The ethos effect?" asked Van.

"I've heard this before," commented Dad Almaviva, "but you haven't, Van. It's the subject of his latest article for the *Legal Review*."

Van waited.

"It's an outgrowth of the commodification of law. I won't cite the legal opinions and the more recent laws passed by the Republic's parliament, and our assembly, but, simply put, it's what happens to ethics and morality in a civil society when economics reigns unchecked."

"I thought you believed in the market economy." Van held back a grin. "You were always telling me that any other system was doomed to painful failure."

Cicero did grin, showing even white teeth against his flawless latte complexion. "I'm talking now about when economics reigns unchecked, and that means when the negative externalities of not following an ethical course are not included in the marketplace. That was the problem in the case against STA." He shook his head. "I'm digressing, and I'll never finish. Old time laissez-faire economic systems simply assumed that everything had a price, and that, if left alone, supply and demand would balance at an optimum price. As a general rule, it works fairly well. Or it does so long as there's an independent moral system underlying it."

Van was tired, and he knew he looked dazed.

"Let's try it another way," Cicero said. "Assume everything has a price."

"Everything does—eventually," Van pointed out.

"Does that mean that ethical behavior also has a price? And that, if it is scarce, it becomes harder and harder for the average citizen to purchase?"

"I don't know about that."

"Look at history. How many societies were there where ethical behavior in trade and government were not the norm, but where bribery was necessary merely to ensure that both merchants and functionaries did their jobs? Then, in the worst cases, whether or not the job was done depended not on ethics, but on market power, on who could pay the highest price. In some societies that was obvious. In others, like the

Noram Commonocracy, that aspect of the market economy was far from obvious. They had an elected government, and everyone could vote. And they had a seemingly open legal system. But that system was based on the assumption that an adversarial system would provide the truth and justice. At times, it did, but only when both advocates were of close to equal ability and when the issues were relatively simple. Most times, the court ended up deciding for the party with the most resources, unless the case happened to be one that was truly egregious. The same thing began to happen with the legislative bodies, because once large nation-states developed and semimodern communications emerged, the number of citizens represented by each legislator grew so large that only those candidates with the resources to purchase those communication services could reach the citizens. So, in the end, both the laws and their interpretation became commodities purchased by the highest bidders. This still would not have been a problem, except that the so-called common people opted for what was called 'bread and circuses' and voted for those legislators who levied higher taxes on the richer segments of society in order to pay for public services first for the poor, then for even the middle classes. Just before the Commonocracy collapsed, only ten percent of the population owned something like three-quarters of the assets and resources, and those few were paying ninety percent of the taxes."

Van frowned. He understood the history, but not where his father was going. "I'm missing something."

"I'm getting there, Van. It's complex, and that's why it's happening again, because no one really wants to understand complicated structures. We always look for simple answers, and they're usually wrong." Cicero took a sip from the tall beaker of water beside his chair. "Because the rich controlled the wealth, the legislators really only looked to them. So those who were wealthy had effectively bought the government and the legal system. Both became economic tools. The system lasted for a long time because these people weren't stupid. They factored in the negative externalities of environmental problems, and those of the worst social and economic problems. In a sense, the economic system worked. What eventually brought the system down was the perception that, for all the appearances, there was no ethical basis to the system, the feeling that ethics were relative to wealth, and that the wealthy had no ethics and bought their way out of being ethical." Cicero laughed. "What's ironic is that they had it totally backward."

Van was definitely lost. He just shook his head. "I can't say I understand at all."

"The loss of ethics by the wealthy was a symptom, not a cause. What brought down the system was the unwillingness of the everyday citizens to live up to their own responsibilities. They allowed themselves—in fact, they pushed—to be corrupted. They insisted that public benefits—education, public safety, transportation systems—all be paid for by the rich. That doesn't work economically unless you allow the rich more income. Once, the head of a business might have made between ten and a hundred times what one of the workers might. At the end of the Commonocracy, some heads of multilaterals made thirty thousand times what their workers did. At the same time that these so-called common people deplored the excesses of the rich, they filed hundreds of thousands of frivolous or semifrivolous claims against businesses and governments for millions or hundreds of millions of credits, often for trivial injuries. Most of them did not even bother to vote for their legislators, then complained when the elected officials—"

"What does this have to do with your article?" Van interrupted as gently as he could.

"It should be obvious. We're seeing the beginning of the same thing here. The law becomes more and more of a tool for influencing economic and political events, rather than an arbitrator between conflicting parties. The more it becomes a tool, the less people want to take personal responsibility, and the more power is concentrated in the hands of the few . . . and that leads to more problems . . . like the rise of old-time simplistic and intolerant faiths . . . and an emphasis on simple answers that create even more injustice . . ."

"Cicero's always been a crusader at heart," suggested Almaviva. "You know that, Van."

Van smiled. "Crusading won't get me a job, though."

"Do you need one, really?" asked Almaviva. "Retiring as a full commodore? You always had a good voice and presence. You could get involved in theater here, like you did in school . . ."

"I don't think I'm ready for that," Van replied.

"You could still try STA," said Dad Almaviva. "You might not be that happy with them, but they're the only possibility for transstellar pilots. In-system, there are a couple of others." He looked to Cicero.

"CCA is usually looking for pilots," Dad Cicero added. "That's all in-system, but they go all the way out. Do a lot of work steering ice comets."

"Have they made any real progress with the Aeylen project?"

Both older men laughed, almost simultaneously, and once again, Van felt the warmth that had surrounded him for the years of his youth.

Chapter 35

For the first week in Bannon, Van concentrated on his family, rest, and his fitness program. He enjoyed the quiet dinners especially, and Dad Almaviva's tales of his voice students and current opera production. But he also enjoyed Dad Cicero's succinct observations about law and life.

Van had already begun to see some results from his early workouts in New Oisin and the continuing efforts on the hill trails around the villa, and found his stamina improving rapidly. When he ran the trails, he still wondered if someone were watching, not that he could tell, either from listening, or from the limited functions left to his implant.

After ten days of family and exercise, he returned to investigating piloting possibilities. As Dad Cicero had prophesied, Van never even talked to anyone beyond the netsystem at STA, but after another week, shortly after eleven hundred, Van was sitting in the office of Farris Macks, assistant director of personnel for CCA. Van felt a little strange in the new gray business singlesuit, but since he was no longer on active duty, the uniform wouldn't have been appropriate.

Macks was a thin man younger than Arturo, and Arturo was ten years younger than Van. Macks never quite looked at Van as he ushered him into his office and settled behind a desk that was little more than an overgrown console. The office itself was a windowless cube, with a flickering holo of the hills to the north of Bannon, a poor substitute for a window.

"You have an impressive service record . . . Commodore Albert. Most impressive. It is not that often that someone from Bannon is both a flag officer and a hero." Macks chuckled dryly. "And returns to tell of it."

"CCA has an open invitation for experienced pilots," Van offered. "I think I qualify on the experience."

"That you do. That you do. You know we only work in-system. Not one of our ships has a jumpdrive in it. Not one."

"I know. Before I became an RSF officer, I'd looked into becoming a commercial pilot." Van smiled. "Back then, CCA was one of the multis that told me I needed military experience."

"Oh, we like that experience. We still do." Macks smiled wanly. "I've never met a commodore before. What is it like? Being a commodore, I mean, with all those people ready to obey your every order?"

Van laughed gently. "It's not like that, at all. It's much more like being an executive in a multi. All officers have to do what their superiors want. A commodore just has a little more freedom in accomplishing those objectives. Of course, you've also got more responsibility and accountability." Van felt as though he were fudging over the issue, true as he knew his response to be, because he'd never been a real commodore.

"Yes, yes . . . that must be so. It's just . . . I think this is the first time we've ever seen so senior an officer seeking a piloting position."

"A good pilot is a good pilot," Van suggested.

"A good pilot is a good pilot. I'll have to remember that. It's a good way of putting it."

"CCA has a good reputation for the ability of its pilots," Van added. "I'd like to think I could add to that reputation."

"I'm sure you could, Commodore. I'm sure you could."

Van decided not to press, but to wait.

Macks finally cleared his throat and managed to look at Van. "Ah . . . actually, Commodore . . . how can I put this . . . properly?" He glanced down, then back at Van. "I guess . . . really . . . there isn't an easy way to put it. You're too good and too experienced for us. It . . . well, it hasn't happened this way before, but . . . you see, if we paid you what you're worth . . . and then there's the problem of who could train you to our methods, and . . . no . . . I'm so sorry, but it just wouldn't work out. I really am . . . so sorry, I mean."

Van almost felt sorry for Macks. The job of refusing Van had clearly been delegated, and for that alone, Van had a much lower opinion of CCA and its management. Quasar had at least handled him with a certain amount of class. Macks was doing his best, but his best wasn't reflecting well on the multilateral.

"I think I understand." Van stood. "I appreciate your honesty and forthrightness, Director Macks." Hard as it was, he smiled. "The best of luck to you."

Before the younger man could react, Van turned and left the office, making his way out and down the ramps to the walkway.

The CCA building was on the west side of Bannon Park. Van walked to one of the benches set opposite a flower bed filled with carmine and yellow sunflowers, almost ready to fade, but not quite. He looked back toward the CCA building, then accessed his personal link account. The only message was from Sappho, reminding him that he was having dinner with Aelsya and her on sevenday.

After a time of looking at the flowers, he again linked into the pubcomm and found TransMedia. *Ashley Marson, please.*

Surprisingly, after all his efforts without results, there was a response.

Marson, here.

Ashley? Van Albert. Are you free for a bite to eat shortly?

Van? Hold one . . . I'll see what I can do.

Van waited.

I can do it. Café Metropole in fifteen?

See you there.

Café Metropole was actually set inside the old Twin Winters Hotel, long the staple for luxurious accommodations for travelers, and the last place where he and Ashley had eaten, nearly twenty years before. Trust Ashley to have remembered. The Twin Winters was on the east side of Bannon Park, only a short walk. Van rose and started off.

He reached the café first, and asked if Ashley had a table. The table was ready, and Van took it, but didn't even have a chance to order something to drink before the newsie appeared.

"Same old punctual Van. It's good to see you in less official clothes." Ashley dropped into the chair across the table with a sigh. "I begged off a luncheon seminar on the need for a bottom-line approach to media success."

Van winced. "I thought most of the media nets were fairly profitable."

"They want us to stay that way." Ashley looked up to the server—a human server was one of the amenities of the antique café. "Red Bandito Stout."

"Whatever's the best pale ale," added Van, before turning back to Ashley. "You were saying?"

"Oh, I read the annual reports. TransMedia was only running a thirty percent profit last year. *Only.* You get the feeling that nothing is ever enough. I'm still an idealistic kid at heart."

"If you're so idealistic," asked Van, grinning, "why did you go along with the returning hero story, anyway?"

"Still the same direct Van, aren't you?"

"Sometimes."

"First, because I am idealistic. Second, because Al asked me to. Third, because you damned well deserved it. And fourth, because you and your family never asked for anything." Ashley shrugged. "Good enough?"

Van laughed.

"We ran it for three straight casts. That ought to help. You want to tell me about it?" Ashley paused as the server set the drinks on the polished teak surface. "Just a moment."

Both Van and Ashley glanced over the discreetly projected holo menus.

"I'll have the quail special, with the house salad."

"The same, but with the small fruit plate," Van added.

Ashley looked at Van. "What exactly did you do to upset the RSF enough to get you honored and retired almost on a pretext?"

"The injuries were real. Very real."

"So it was a real pretext." Ashley's words curled with irony.

"I think they've always wanted to get rid of me, but with the commendations, and the way the Board of Inquiry on the *Regneri* affair backfired . . . they couldn't ever find a reason that would pass the laugh test. Not until this came along. Then, they could get me out on a medical, and by promoting and commending me, how could anyone say it was unfair?"

"Makes sense. As far as it goes. You want to talk about that?"

"There's not much to say. I've been looking for piloting jobs . . ."

"You won't get one. The RSF has contracts with most of the outfits. Those who aren't under contract have major clients or suppliers who do."

"What have you heard?"

"Nothing." The newsie took another swallow of the stout. "That's the problem. When you see things happen, and no one knows anything, when you don't hear things, and you can't find out why, that's when there's a problem."

"Can you tell me what's really happening here?" asked Van.

"Outside of a resurgence of the Christos Revivos? Or the new Temple of the Community of the Revealed?"

"They've built a temple here in Bannon?"

"Out to the southwest. On a hill where you can see it for klicks. They're getting converts, too. I guess it's the times. Everyone wants certainty, and the old faiths provide it. God sets the only rules. Men run things, and women follow. Marriage is only between man and woman . . ."

Van winced.

Ashley laughed, the sound deep with irony. "You see. Everything's the same as it's always been, except more so. Thought that was why you left." He paused. "And the worst of it is that it's better here than on Tara or in most of the other Taran systems. We've still got some local perquisites. Of course, that puts us on the bottom of the list for any sort of support from the Taran Parliament."

Van sipped the pale ale. It tasted flat, but he wasn't sure it was the ale. "That was one of the reasons. Also, I'm not logical enough to be an advocate, and not gifted enough for singing or the arts, and not tactful enough for business or anything else. I'm not exactly a multi man. That doesn't leave much."

"Yet you came back."

"My family's here."

Ashley just looked at Van.

Finally, Van shrugged. "I guess I had to see if things had changed."

"Have they?"

"I appreciate my fathers more, and the family, but I'm not sure anything else has changed."

"I always liked your fathers. Still do. Heard your Dad Almaviva in the BOP production of *Cesare*. Last year he did Daland in *Der Fliegende Holländer* again. He was incredible. In a way, he reminded me of you."

"Because I'm always back on a ship? Because in three

times seven years, I've never found the right woman?" Van shook his head. "I don't know. Getting to stay a pilot doesn't look that promising. My dads have been more successful in pursuing their careers to the end."

"You'll do fine," Ashley said. "Does Almaviva still cook those fantastic meals?"

Van laughed. "He does. That's another reason why I've had to keep working out." After a moment, he asked, "How about Mairee and your kids?"

"Mairee . . . she has her own dance studio now. She hung up the slippers about five years ago. Likes being her own boss. There's a healthy waiting list. Marina is a junior at the Academy . . ."

As Ashley talked, Van listened, appreciating the moment . . . and still wondering why all that his friend mentioned seemed so distant. He took a long sip of the pale ale. It wasn't flat, he decided, but it didn't taste the way he recalled.

Was that the danger of trying to revisit the past? Was it ever as remembered?

Chapter 36

After the dinner, Aelsya had volunteered to do the dishes. Sappho and Van sat on the rear terrace of the couple's hillside house, looking to the north at the badlands and feeling the swirling twilight breeze that mixed the hot air of the rocky wasteland with the cooler air sweeping down from the higher hills to the west.

"That was a good dinner," Van said.

"Thank Aelsya," Sappho replied. "I'm just the *sous*-chef when it comes to cooking. Our kids know that. Lesnym's nice enough not to say anything. Farah complains if I'm cooking."

"You're better than you let on. You just don't want to cook that much."

"That just might be." Sappho laughed softly. "Aelsya's always said as much, but she likes to cook. So it works out—except those nights when she's at the medcenter."

The silence grew, punctuated by the squealing chirps of the badlands crickets that weren't really crickets, but mutated miniature land arthropods that filled that niche.

"You still look like you're somewhere deep in space, Van," Sappho finally said.

"In a way, I am." Van looked toward the apple trees, whose upper branches rose over the stone wall that separated the garden on the north side from the small orchard beyond. "I always knew what I wanted to be, and I'd never thought beyond that."

"Can't you still be a pilot? I know there aren't many positions, but . . . with your record . . . ?"

"That's the problem. They all know my record. They don't want heroes, or people who look into problems. They want an interstellar shuttle driver, one who gets passengers and cargo from orbit control alpha off planet beta to orbit control delta off planet gamma exactly on schedule with the minimum use of energy and the minimum deviation from schedule. Or they want someone to push rocks and water comets around with the least use of energy and no complaints."

"There must be someone . . ."

Van didn't reply.

"There is, isn't there?"

"There is . . . but . . . I just don't know."

"They're not renegades, are they?"

Van shook his head. "No. They're a Coalition outfit, something called IIS—Integrated Information Systems. I ran a track on them—as well as I could. Ashley's also looking into it for me, but I haven't heard back from him." Van had also asked Ashley for stories or background about the *Fergus*, claiming that he hadn't seen anything because he'd been in the medcenter. "From what I could dig up, it's an old operation, but it's never been very big."

"Old? How old?"

"A hundred and fifty years old. Could be older."

"It must be a large multilateral to have interstellar ships. It does, doesn't it?"

"Three. But it's a foundation."

"A foundation with interstellar ships? I never heard of one that had ships."

"I think there are a few. Not many."

"What's the problem?"

"They're Coalition-based."

"Do they have offices in the Republic?"

"Supposedly."

"Would you get home more often than you did in the RSF?"

"Probably not."

"What about pay? You don't need the money, do you, not with a commodore's pension?"

"The compensation is considerable," Van admitted.

"You don't think they're reputable?"

"Anything that's lasted more than a century has to be fairly reputable. There's not a hint of anything wrong with them. Some odd things . . ."

"Odd . . . wrong?"

"Not exactly. The managing director made an odd comment, though, one about being careful whom you rescue because you'll be responsible for whatever happens."

Sappho laughed. "It's true, isn't it?"

"True enough, but why would he tell me that?"

"To see your reaction, of course. People are always asking weird things in interviews."

"I suppose so. I liked him . . . no . . . I don't know that I liked him, but I felt he was solid."

"Then . . . ?" Sappho left the word hanging. "You say you want to keep being a pilot . . ."

"I don't know."

"You do, too. You sound like you did when you were accepted for RSF training."

"I do?" he asked, almost involuntarily.

"You get that way when you feel you ought to do something, but you can't explain why. Especially if it takes you away from the family." She laughed gently. "I think we all do. Dad Cicero always wanted us to be able to explain why we wanted to do things. But sometimes, there are things you just have to feel. That's always been Arturo's problem. He won't let himself really feel. He's always looking for approval, particularly for public approval."

"That never mattered to you. Dad Cicero worried that you wanted to flout convention too much, just for the sake of it."

"I wasn't that bad. I saw things. I still see things, and when you see things, and you're young, you want to make a statement. Sometimes, Cicero told me, you shouldn't." Sappho laughed. "Sometimes, he was right. Sometimes, he wasn't. He wasn't that thrilled with Aelsya, you know?"

"You've been together for more than fifteen years."

"Sixteen next month. I've never regretted it. But I couldn't have explained it then, and I'd still have a hard time."

Van nodded.

"In the end, big brother, you're going to have to do what you feel. And you won't have the comfort of cold logic."

Van was afraid she was right.

Chapter 37

Van sat in the ancient leather-covered chair in Dad Cicero's home study, looking out the side window at the bonsai garden. He had continued to think over what Sappho had said the night before. Why was he so concerned? After a moment, Van forced his thoughts back to IIS. The foundation was no newcomer. In fact, it was older than some of the outfits he'd already approached for a job. Was it just the Coalition tie? Or a feeling? Why did he feel that way?

Incoming from Ashley Marson, the home net announced.

Accept. Van let the full projection fill Dad Cicero's home study.

Ashley's face filled the projection, the boyish grin still as engaging as it had been when they'd both been at Shennon Academy. "Van, you asked me to see what we had on the IIS outfit. It's not much. It's a private foundation, headquartered in the Coalition. It's an old operation, more than a century, but our records don't go back any farther. They do info studies. Last one here in the Republic . . . well . . . they did it for Salyrien, about thirty years back. Whatever it was, it must have worked. Salyrien was number three formulator on Sulyn, and about to go under. Within five years they were number two, and you know where they are today. Not much went public, except that at one annual meeting—that's what our files show—the director general was attacked for the fee, and he pointed out that, based on the IIS recommendations and findings, Salyrien's profits, revenues, and market share were way up. . . ."

Van nodded for Ashley to continue.

"They have a small office in Domigua, and they publish a confidential data report for client subscribers only, but we don't know of anything else . . . Never been a complaint or legal action against them . . ."

An office in Domigua, but Desoll had given him codes for a standing wave reply? Was that so the response wouldn't have to be forwarded? Or because Desoll wanted to bypass the local office? If so, why?

"There's an old note in the files, but I can't verify it. It just said something to the effect that IIS delivers . . . but they're not a multi to mess with."

"I thought they were a foundation."

"They are. I'm just telling you what I found." Ashley smiled. "They look a lot better than STA for you, but don't tell anyone I said so."

"What about the *Fergus*?"

"There were a couple of stories, one on a relay from New Oisin. Not much more than you told me. Hold on. I'm sending it."

"Thanks. It's just . . . well, I was the commander, and I didn't find out until months later."

"I understand. Sometimes it helps to see it holoed out." Ashley's smile was understanding. Then he stiffened. "I've got to run. Someone's claiming that Councilwoman Styrns has channeled district business to her niece's firm, and it's coming up at the council meeting."

"Thanks, Ashley."

"Let me know."

"I will."

Van sat forward at the console setup, then called up the story on the *Fergus*. As Ashley had said, there was nothing he didn't know. The story didn't even mention any of the officers or techs, or what the ship had been doing, just a vague reference to its disappearance, and the statement that the RSF had concluded that the ship had been lost to unknown causes.

He read it twice. Finally, he called up the results of his previous inquiry and printed out two hard copies. He looked at the first copy, scanning through the results once again, his eyes catching the key sentences and phrases.

Integrated Information Systems . . . Proprietary Foundation, HQ, Cambria, Perdya, Eco-Tech Coalition . . . Managing Director T. Desoll . . . approx. 150 planetary offices in the Arm . . . total employees, unknown, estimated @ 400–700. Primary focus is information acquisition, process, and analysis. Secondary focus, secure interstellar transport . . . Total assets, estimated @ 4 b. credits [Taran Republic equiv.] . . .

A listing of known clients followed.

Van read through it again. He'd probably end up calling IIS, but he'd still run it by his fathers to see if he'd missed anything. Van thought about trying to make dinner, then shook his head. Instead, he donned an old singlesuit and went out and weeded the herb garden, then pruned the lemon-and-lime tree, collecting the too-fragrant fallen and rotting lemons.

By the time he had finished, and cleaned up, Dad Almaviva had returned and was already puttering in the kitchen. Van slipped in and acted as *sous*-chef. Before Almaviva had the chicken iscalantia on the table, Cicero arrived and settled on one of the stools to watch, commenting, "Always good to have a son who knows his place when he gets home, even if he is a commodore . . . He's neat. You have to give him that, Almaviva. Would have made a great advocate . . ."

Van laughed and shot back. "You would have made a great critic."

"Except he confuses pitch with timbre and everything else," charged Almaviva.

Eventually, they ate.

Afterward, as he took a last bite of the chicken, Van glanced to the dining room sideboard and the printouts there.

Dad Cicero lifted his glass of water. "You've been holding back something. What is it?"

"I have." Van stood and reclaimed the printouts from the sideboard. He handed one to each man. "I'd like your opinions. I have an idea, but I'd like to see if I've missed anything."

Cicero read through his printout quickly, then read it again. The third time, he took out a stylus and jotted down some notes. Almaviva read more slowly, and just once.

Van waited.

"I take it that they've offered you a position," began Cicero.

"Senior director and chief pilot of a new interstellar ship."

The advocate's eyebrows rose. "You're being more cautious than when you joined the RSF. You told us after you'd done it." He lifted the printout. "They seem reputable enough. Why are you so concerned? Or are you being diplomatic and letting us see all this before you actually do it?"

"He's a few years older and more cautious," suggested Almaviva. "That's not always better. Sometimes, it's best just to take a healthy bite out of life."

"Ah, yes," returned Cicero, "the healthy bite. A wonderful metaphor, you know. Except . . . that's truer than Almaviva would like. The problem is that human beings are creatures of appetite, and the tools we have to conquer that appetite are all flawed. Gluttony sates one, but only momentarily, and abstinence reduces consumption, but not appetite. One of the tools most employed is logic. But the great fault of logic is that it seems so reasonable, even when it is not, and thus, unless used wisely, logic becomes the master and the individual the slave."

"I can't believe you, the advocate, are saying that," Van managed.

"When my son, the hero and commodore asks for my opinion, all logic is confounded." Cicero laughed. "Besides, there are times, believe it or not, when too much logic is wrong. Almaviva always reminds me when I take logic too far."

"It's not that often anymore," added the singer. "At first . . . well, I'd sing some ridiculous soprano aria, like a countertenor, rather than argue. Then he'd laugh, and we'd talk it out. It works well when you can combine feeling and logic."

"And if they conflict?" asked Van, dryly. "Can you sing or reason your way clear?"

Cicero shrugged. "You have to make a choice, and refusing to make one is also a choice."

"Oh, it's simple enough," commented Almaviva. "Van, you gave your best for the RSF, and you feel that you were never appreciated fully. That was even with the decorations and the promotions. You don't want to be disappointed again. So you've been talking to second-rate outfits, knowing that they can't disappoint you because you don't expect anything. That's no way to approach life. We all get disappointed. That's not the point. You have to be what you are and let the disappointments fall where they will. That's poor Arturo's problem. He's never discovered what he is—only what his talents are, and he's been letting them define him."

Cicero nodded slowly. "People are more than the sum of their talents."

"Is Arturo unhappy, then?"

"Let's just say that he's less happy than he could be. He tries too hard to fit in. I've warned him about where that can lead, but . . ."

"He knows better," said Almaviva with a laugh. "Trying to

fit in can make a man a slave to whoever's in power, but he won't see that. Not yet."

"It's hard for anyone," mused Cicero, as if he did not want to continue with the subject of Arturo.

Van didn't press.

Later, after his fathers went to bed, Van took out the plastic card, and used the data to send a standing wave message to IIS. He might have been making a mistake, but he was certain that remaining on Sulyn—or anywhere within the Republic— was a bigger one, and he couldn't afford to keep looking back.

Chapter 38

Three days had passed since he'd sent off the standing wave message, and Van had heard nothing. Not that he'd expected an immediate response, not given interstellar distances, but he had finally made his decision, and he wanted to get on with it.

Vehicle in drive, the house system announced.

Van walked from the study where he'd been using Cicero's accesses to see if he could find out more information on the interstellar information market. If he were going to join IIS, he might as well see what he could find. He stopped beside the door and looked out through the long window. An electrolorry had pulled up into the circular drive, and a tall, dark-haired man hopped out, carrying a small package in his left hand. He marched to the door of the house. The logo on the side of the lorry was a winged emblem with the initials SFD inside, and Van belatedly recognized the personal courier service.

He opened the door, assuming that the package was for one of his fathers.

Thrummm.

The deliveryman sprawled across the tiles of the portico, the package bouncing lightly away from the door. A weapon-

shaped device followed, clattering dully. Instinctively, Van
ducked and simultaneously swept the weapon away from the
fallen figure, glancing toward the lorry.

From behind the Norfolk pine bordering the neighbor's
wall—the house where his biological mother had once
lived—emerged a figure in a nondescript tannish singlesuit.

Van frowned, but there was something about the newcomer. He smiled ruefully as he recognized Trystin Desoll.

A second figure appeared from the garden on the right,
wearing a sight-blurring camouflage suit, and carrying a long-
barreled stunner. It was an effort for Van to look at that figure.

"You're all right, aren't you?" asked Desoll, as he neared
Van.

"Surprised."

"I thought they might try something like that."

"You actually waited for them," Van said. "You just
waited."

"We wouldn't have waited much longer," Desoll replied.
"But I thought it might be better if you saw for yourself,
rather than relying on my word. You've already taken a great
deal on faith." Desoll laughed. "Of course, we could have set
this up, too, but I hope you can see why that wouldn't exactly
be to our benefit."

In the press of what had just happened, Van hadn't even
thought of that. He frowned. In bringing it up, Desoll had
made another point. "You think I'm that skeptical?"

The older man just raised his eyebrows.

Van almost laughed. Instead, he nodded.

Without a word, the figure in camouflage scooped up the
weapon lying on the tiles, a miniature stunner of some sort,
then dragged the limp figure of the courier back into the electrolorry. Even as Van watched, the electrolorry moved away,
nearly silently.

"What will happen?"

"Nothing much. He'll be out for a day or so, and he won't
remember much of what happened. People get excited about
murders, but when no one's injured, and nothing's stolen,
except a small chunk of someone's memory, they can't say

too much publicly. Someone will find the lorry, and the unconscious man who isn't a courier, but is dressed like one, and that will keep the RSF from saying too much. The RSF won't like it, but they won't find out for a few hours."

"You knew. Back on Scandya, you knew," Van stated.

Desoll shook his head. "I knew you wouldn't fit in. You're the type that can't go home, even when you do. Whether you'd admit it . . . that I didn't know. And whether you'd signal in time was another question."

"In time?"

"You know you've been watched, I'm sure."

"Your people?"

Desoll smiled faintly. "No. I've had several local operatives—we have a list of people we can hire on most planets—watching the RSF agents who've been watching you."

"Why?"

"I hate to lose good people. These days, they're too hard to find."

"In all of the Arm? I find that hard to believe."

"You can believe it or not. Let's try a little elementary mathematics. How many really good deep-space pilots are there in the RSF?"

"I'd say there might be five hundred pilots, all told, a thousand if you count former pilots."

"How many are as good as you are? Be honest."

"Twenty that I know."

"I'd guess half that, but let's say that works out to a hundred in the entire RSF. First, how many would consider leaving the RSF? Second, out of those, how many would you trust totally with your life—and an interstellar ship carrying millions in cargo value?"

Van hadn't thought of those aspects.

"And how many of those have the intelligence and the ability to react in nonpiloting situations the way you did on Scandya? Then add in a few other characteristics, like maturity, a basic sense of fairness . . ." Desoll laughed. "There aren't many of you."

Van still wasn't so sure.

"You'll see," Desoll promised.

That bothered Van even more, but he pushed the thought aside. "You said you had another ship? Who pilots that one?"

"I have to confess to a bit of nepotism there. It's one of my younger relatives, much younger—Nynca. You'll meet her sooner or later. That just depends on projects and schedules."

"Am I the only nonrelative in IIS?"

"Hardly. We have a staff of almost five hundred in various posts. Nynca's my only relative. It just happens that she happened to have the talents we needed. No one else in the family did—not when I got involved with IIS."

Van caught the faintest trace of emotion, but Desoll smiled. "By the way, that little device that looks like a stunner wasn't. It projects a different wave structure. Very effective at creating heart fillibration. You were retired for medical reasons, weren't you?"

"Yes."

"You see? Retired commodore suffers fatal heart seizure. No one happened to be around to get you care. So sad."

Van shuddered.

"We need to be going. They will miss that operative before long. Can you pack and get out of here? I'd really recommend not using the net to tell your family, not until you're on Sulyn orbit station. IIS will pay for the calls from there."

"Traces, again?"

"We don't know, but it's likely that the nets of all your family are shadowed." Desoll looked at Van. "I really would suggest that you pack quickly and leave a handwritten message for your family here. Tell them you'll call them direct within a few hours. If you wait too long, it might be more difficult to leave."

"Won't they stop me? If this . . ."

"They still have to operate within limits. For now, anyway. I'll bring up a groundcar and wait in the drive here. I would suggest that you wear your full dress uniform, miniature medals and all. We'll be with you, but they've wanted to keep this quiet."

"They?"

"The RSF. Who else?"

Who else indeed?

Van nodded. "I'll only be a few minutes."

Chapter 39

Van packed only one duffel and his carry bag. The duffel wasn't even full, but most of what he'd brought back from Scandya with him had been RSF uniforms, and he wouldn't need those. The only uniforms he put in the duffel were ship-suits, because the insignia peeled off. He also kept his ship-boots, and added the newer gray and black singlesuits. Then he scrawled out a quick note, saying that he'd followed up on the discussion that they had had several nights before and that he'd be calling shortly.

The beige groundcar was waiting in the drive, with a driver whom Van didn't recognize. The groundcar's boot was open, and Van put his gear there, then slipped into the back seat beside Desoll. The driver, a man of indeterminate age, eased the vehicle out of the circular drive. The electrolorry was nowhere in sight.

"I'm still puzzled as to why you're so interested in me," Van finally said, after he had ridden in silence for a good ten minutes.

"Think about it. IIS is taking delivery of a ship worth close to a billion credits. I shouldn't be trying to get the very best commander for it?"

"That's flattering, but . . . I don't know that I'd fit that description."

"Part of what you're saying is false modesty. You are good, and you know it. That's why you were upset at being retired. You were punished for being good, both as an officer and as a ship commander." Desoll paused. "And part of what you're saying is because you've been isolated. Overall, the commanders in the Keltyr and Taran space services have been among the best in recent years—although that's changing quickly. You haven't dealt with the commanders of Argenti, Hyndji, or Revenant warships."

"What about Coalition commanders?"

"They're also among the best, but most aren't suited temperamentally to IIS."

"Temperamentally?"

"My homeland has, shall we say, the tendency to believe in *The Truth*. So do the Revenants. That was part of what caused the Great War of the past. Now, we've decided to mind our own gardens and hope that everyone else fights."

"It seems to be working," Van said dryly.

"It might, for a time," Desoll pointed out. "Until the Revenants and the Argentis swallow up or annex all the smaller systems."

The driver turned onto the Southway and clicked the groundcar into automatic tracking, but did not turn his attention from the guideway.

"Because of the urgency of our departure," Desoll went on, "there are some matters that we'll have to handle along the way, once we leave Sulyn. While we're outbound, prior to jump, you can decide about the bonding account—"

"Outbound? On one of your vessels?"

"My ship, actually. The *Elsin*—registered as a commercial Coalition vessel, although it's also registered with the Argenti and Hyndji systems as well. That combination allows us open access to most systems. You'll learn which systems respond best to which, and that will be in your shipnet as well."

His ship? Van was still having trouble believing that.

"As for the bond . . . let me finish. Where you have it placed is certainly up to you, but I'd recommend that it be in either an Argenti, Hyndji, or Coalition institution. If you want a smaller system, Kush would be all right, and so would Keshmara, although I'd give the edge to Kush."

"Any of those systems?"

Desoll smiled. "You pick the system, and that will be the first training hop for you, to get you used to our systems. Actually, we have one stop first. We'll be making a hop to where we can reactivate and upgrade your implant. Before that, you won't be able to link to the ship."

Van had wondered, but he could also see that trying to reactivate his implant on Sulyn wouldn't have been wise. He still wondered why people were trying to kill him, whether on Scandya or on his home planet. He hadn't been involved in politics. He hadn't done anything except his duty, not so far as he could tell.

Desoll slipped a plastic card to Van. "That's your shuttle passage. It's a little deceptive. It lists a return down-shuttle to Domigua tomorrow afternoon, and there's a reservation in the quarters section of the station. I've triggered a delay message to your parents' home that confirms our meeting tomorrow on the orbit station to discuss possible employment, and suggested that we tour the Domigua office afterward."

"You think that they'll accept that?"

"If they don't, they don't. Generally, most organizations expect people to move deliberately, and what I said in the message is what they'll expect. We aren't counting on that, of course. The *Elsin* is ready to break orbit the moment we delock. We'll do a relay so that you can contact your family after we've actually cleared the station."

"How do I get through outbound clearance?"

Desoll grinned. "You don't have to. Your passage says that you're coming up for a meeting and leaving tomorrow."

"What?"

"You're crew on the *Elsin*. All I certify is that I'm not carrying any outbound passengers. I declare the cargo. That's the responsibility for outbound clearance that rests with the outbound ship. No one questions crew, especially pilots. After all, just how many pilots are there that aren't either military or those with regulated commercial enterprises?"

"Three?" asked Van, forcing a laugh.

"I know of ten in the entire Arm. Not even the RSF is going to force double clearances for ten people. And, once you're on board, you're effectively out of Republic territory—unless there's a declared war, which there's not."

This time Van's laugh wasn't forced—before he said, "I do have to get on the shuttle."

"That's why the uniform."

Before long the driver swept into the lane for departing shuttle passengers.

Feeling a little foolish in his full dress greens, Van got out of the groundcar, reclaimed his small carry bag, in keeping with an overnight stay on the orbit station, and walked from the groundcar toward the Bannon shuttle terminal. Half a pace back, in a gray shipsuit, Trystin Desoll carried the large duffel.

Once inside, Van tendered the passcard Desoll had given him, as well as his own datacard.

"Commodore . . . you're leaving so soon. Hoped you'd stay."

"I'm just going up to the station for a meeting," Van replied ambiguously.

"You going back to duty?"

"I'm looking at a special assignment."

"Good for you." The terminal controller handed Van both cards with a smile.

Van did not look back, nor at Desoll. They ended up seated beside each other, on what was clearly a newer shuttle.

"Newer shuttle," Van finally said, as the craft lifted off.

"Newest I've seen here," Desoll replied. "Usually the newer ones are used on the Domigua lifts and drops."

"That makes sense, I'd guess."

Neither man said more than small talk, and little enough of that, until they had disembarked and were walking away from the shuttle exit along the gray corridors of orbit control.

"We're headed to C-four."

"That's a low number."

"It's the last commercial lock," Desoll pointed out.

Last was a relative term, since the station was effectively a disc, and the military locks began—or ended—just past the lock affording access to the *Elsin*.

Desoll seemed to be walking casually, but Van could sense that the older man was taking in everything.

Van himself could sense no one directly following them, but his chest was still tight as they neared the lock.

Desoll pulsed something, and, suddenly, the lock door irised open. A figure in a gray shipsuit stood there. She was slender and only came to Van's shoulder, but he could see the stunner in her hand.

"Inside," Desoll said.

Van stepped into the ship lock, and the other two followed. First the station lock door closed, and then, once they cleared the ship lock, it did also.

"Halfway there." Desoll gestured to the tech.

"Eri, this is Commander Albert. Commander, this is Eri, my one and only tech, chief crew, and indispensable super-cargo and troubleshooter." Desoll turned. "Eri . . . would you throw the commander's bags somewhere, and then strap in. The quicker we're clear, the happier I'll be."

Once the tech had left, Van looked at Desoll. "Commander?"

"Well, you're going to be commanding. That's what all our pilots are called." He grinned, and for a moment, looked far younger. "All three of us, now." He paused. "And there is one semiretired backup we can call on in emergencies, but he'd really rather we didn't. Now . . . into the cockpit. You take the right seat. Eri usually keeps me company, but she understands."

Van followed Desoll, strapping into the second seat.

Even as he settled in, Desoll was on the comm. He looked at Van. "I'll talk through the clearances and put them on speaker. Usually, it's all netlink."

Van realized that, without his implant, he wouldn't have heard a thing. "Thank you."

"Sulyn control, this is Coalition commercial ship *Elsin*. Ready to delock and depart."

"Wait one, *Elsin*."

"They always say that," Desoll said dryly. "The clearance was filed hours ago."

"Coalition ship *Elsin*, reduce ship grav to nil."

"Affirm, Sulyn control. Ship grav is nil."

Van could feel the weightlessness as the artificial grav field died, and then the blink of the internal ship lights as the ship's fusactor took on the load.

"Delocking under way. Do not initiate power on thrusters or jets."

"Understand delocking. Holding power."

A muffled *clunk* echoed through the ship. Van felt the slight sway as the mag-grapplers reversed their fields and thrust the *Elsin* clear of the station dampers. Then the ship's gravs came on—at a full gee, or close enough that it made little difference.

"Coalition ship *Elsin*, cleared for low-power maneuvering."

"Stet, control. Low-power maneuvering. Lifting for exit corridor this time."

"Cleared for exit corridor."

Desoll fed in power on the fusactors, as smoothly as Van had ever seen or felt. "Sulyn control, Coalition ship *Elsin*, outbound this time."

"Stet, *Elsin*. Happy jumps."

"Eri . . . would you set up a comm relay to orbit control for Commander Albert."

"Yes, ser. It's almost ready. Commander Albert, the controls are on the panel to your right. You'll be superimposed on an office background. It's actually Commander Desoll's office on Cambria. That seemed appropriate."

"Thank you." Van smiled as his fingers touched the comm studs, since his implant was useless on the *Elsin*.

A blank screen appeared, followed by the simple spoken words, "Please state the party you wish to contact."

Van thumbed in the bypass codes.

"Cicero Albert or Almaviva Albert?" asked the homenet.

"Cicero."

A swirl of color followed, then Cicero appeared—in a white singlesuit—in his office. "Van. Might I ask where you are?"

"I've taken that position we talked about," Van replied,

choosing his words carefully. "It appears as though I didn't have many other options. I'm headed off for some more training. I know it's short notice, but the alternatives were worse. I had an unplanned visitor this morning, and that convinced me that this position was where I should be."

"You won't be back soon, then?"

"I wouldn't guess so. I'll have to see."

"The best of fortune, son."

"Thanks, Dad."

"You take care. I'll transfer you to Almaviva. He's at the company studio."

The screen swirled again, longer, before Almaviva appeared. He was wearing half of a Clethian period costume. "You're off, Cicero tells me."

"I am. I don't think I was meant to stay in Bannon."

Almaviva laughed, a sound of sadness of humor twisted together. "You never were, son. You never were. Your stage is grander than that. Just take care of yourself . . ."

Van swallowed hard when he finally broke the links. He turned to Desoll. "Thank you for the relays. I'm sure it was costly . . ."

"Not nearly as costly as it would have been if you hadn't decided as soon as you did." The older pilot smiled, but did not offer an explanation.

Desoll did not turn his attention back to Van for nearly an hour. All the time, Van monitored what the older pilot did—and that was little, for two reasons. Desoll's initial course and power settings had been close to flawless, and Van's implant was completely useless in tracking the pilot-ship interactions.

Van also studied what he could of the ship. When he had entered the *Elsin*, Desoll had been moving so quickly that Van had only gotten a hasty impression, and he had no real idea of the size of the vessel. From what Van had been able to see on the board before him, the *Elsin* was far bigger than Van had realized, larger than a Republic corvette, perhaps almost the size of an old-style light cruiser like the *Gortforge*. Only the bare minimum of manual controls were set before

Desoll, and that was an acknowledgment that the ship was so sophisticated that those controls were only useful for emergencies or basic operations in-system.

Abruptly, the *Elsin*'s commander turned to Van. "There's one aspect of this position that I did not fully reveal to you."

Van stiffened.

"You recall that I mentioned that we dealt with the Farhkans, and also that our first jump was to rebuild your implant so that you could handle the *Elsin*, then your own ship?"

"They're going to do that?" Van felt cold at that thought.

"They're far better than any human doctors. I know. Personally."

"You?"

"I was badly injured on my last Service assignment. I ended up at a Farhkan base. They saved my life. Later, I found out that I would have died anywhere else." Desoll shrugged. "You worry about it too much, and I can arrange for the implant to be reactivated on Perdya. It won't be as good, but I understand."

Van considered. There was a time to be skeptical and a time to trust. He knew very little about IIS. Or about the mysterious Trystin Desoll. He did know one thing. So far, Desoll had been truthful and kept his word, and he hadn't been able to say that about the RSF lately.

"I'll go with the Farhkans."

Trystin Desoll nodded, and Van felt as though he had crossed an invisible bridge to another land. Or was it another Galaxy, or the underside of the one where he had lived?

Chapter 40

The jumpshift from Sulyn system to whichever Farhkan system Desoll had selected was the same as any other jump— white turned black, and blackness became incredibly white, and both seemed to last forever within an instant that was

over almost before it registered—all the impossible contra-
dictions that the human body felt during a jump transition.

Without a functioning implant, not only did Van not know
their destination, but he felt lost even in the cockpit, because
the *Elsin* had almost no physical visual instruments on the
board before them—just basic EDI, thrust, velocity, and closure indicators, and the emergency use manual levers and
stick for thrust and drives to the left of the command seat—
that and a screen view projected before him that could have
been almost any star system in the Arm.

Once Desoll had the *Elsin* steady on an inbound course, he
stood. "Let's go back to the mess—it's really just an oversize
galley, but it sounds better to call it the mess."

"You don't have much in the way of manual instruments
here." Van followed the other down the narrow passageway.

"No. It's better that way, and once your implant's up,
you'll see why." The older man stopped in front on the compact bank of formulators and what looked like the modern
version of an ancient stove. "Electronics just doesn't boil
water right. I take tea," the older man said, extracting one kettle from a cabinet. "You?"

"Café, if you have it. If not, tea will be fine."

Desoll swung out another device, set in its own recessed
space. "We carry both, even the right kind of cafémaker. Eri
and I generally take tea, but there's plenty of café." His hands
were deft, and soon both kettle and cafémaker were beginning to steam.

"Have you given any thought to where you want that bond
set up?"

"I have a question. Can I have a beneficiary to that, so that
if anything happens to me in the first year . . . ?"

Desoll smiled. "I should have mentioned that. The bond
also doubles as accident indemnity. Doing what we do, no
one will insure us, even though we've never lost anyone."

"In how many years?"

"From the beginning—more than a hundred. We still
could. We're moving into a dangerous time in history. It
could be more dangerous than the Eco-Tech-Revenant War."

"You think so?"

"Yes. We'll talk about that after you tell me where you want your bond."

"What about Kush?"

"We can do that. I'd recommend either the Candace Bank or the Nabatan Trust, but you could choose branches of the Argenti Arm Fiduciary Trust or Cambrian Holdings."

"Do you know every financial institution in this part of the Arm?"

"Most of them. In our business, you have to know whom you can trust, and they have to know that they can trust us." Desoll filled a large mug with café and handed it to Van. For a moment, his eyes seemed to glaze, and then he focused on Van. "Space debris. Just checking."

Van still was getting used to the idea that Desoll was running the ship from wherever he was. In the RSF, command was in the cockpit, but Van could see that would be impractical in a vessel with such a small crew.

"Tea, Eri," Desoll added, pouring a mug of that and handing it to the tech, who had appeared from somewhere aft of the mess. Desoll gestured to the narrow table beyond the galley. "We could sit down." He poured himself a mug and slid onto the anchored bench on one side.

Eri sat on the other side, farther aft, allowing Van to sit across from Desoll.

"Is there any real difference between the Candace Bank and the Nabatan Trust?"

"They're both solid. We've done business with both. I'd give the edge to the Nabatan, but you couldn't go wrong with either."

"Why would you favor the one?" Van knew he was being difficult, in a way, but he was as much feeling out Desoll as obtaining information.

Eri smiled knowingly.

Van looked at her. "Why does he favor the one?"

"He has a friend there. She is a good banker, but she is also a very nice lady."

Van sensed the absolute truth and laughed, heartily. Somehow, that single sentence, said truthfully and yet shyly, made Trystin Desoll seem far more human.

Desoll actually flushed for a moment.

"We might as well give your lady friend the business," Van replied.

"There's another thing we need to take care of, as well, and for that I'd really recommend one of the Coalition banks."

"Oh?"

"Your pay. You'll be paid automatically to whatever account you designate, but since we're a Coalition-registered organization, I'd recommend a Coalition bank. That's where it's going now. You could then have automatic transfer to another institution. I'd actually recommend that for part of your pay . . ."

Van nodded. He'd never had to worry about the details, not in the RSF.

All told, they spent almost two hours dealing with the various aspects of Van's new employment. Eri left after a few minutes.

When they finished, Desoll showed Van to one of the two spare staterooms. It was more like a flag cabin on an RSF ship, with a closet and drawers for other clothes, a small built-in console, a double bunk, and a separate if compact fresher. Van hung up his gear, changed from his uniform into one of the green shipsuits, after removing the insignia, then returned to the cockpit. The older pilot was absorbed in something through the shipnet, and Van just slipped into the right seat and waited.

Finally, Desoll turned to Van. "We'll be calling in, in a while. I'll also do the comm verbally, although what the Farhkans will get is through the implant, and I'll have the shipnet translate their replies verbally. Once we've got your implant back in shape, on the outbound, you'll pick it all up. They don't communicate aurally, the way we do. So they either have to talk to people with implants or use mechanical devices. They don't like the mechanical speaking devices and avoid them whenever they can."

"You seem to know a great deal about them."

"I had to learn. It took a long time." Desoll fell silent.

"Where are we?"

"A Farhkan system they call Dharel—that's as close as I can come to their pronunciation. It's the one nearest to the Coalition-Revenant-Argenti axis."

Another half hour passed, then Van sensed . . . something, a *hissing* over the shipnet was the closest way of describing it.

"That's them." Desoll cleared his throat. "Farhka Station Two, this is Coalition ship *Elsin*, code name Negative Absolute, pilot Desoll, patron Rhule Ghere, inbound for scheduled resupply, cargo pickup, and medical procedures."

Van could sense that Desoll was doing something, but his implant could only trace a vague sense of the energy flows. Then Desoll turned to Van. "You have to name a patron to dock here. Rhule Ghere is the patron of IIS. So he's your patron." Desoll smiled. "He died a century ago, but he's still our patron. Remember that, Rhule Ghere."

"Rhule Ghere," Van repeated, concentrating on the name.

The same faint hissing filled the cockpit area when the response came back. "Ship *Elsin*, Pilot Desoll, you are cleared for approach and locking. Do you have the beacon?"

"Farhka Station Two, affirmative. We have the beacon. Proceeding as cleared."

Desoll's approach and docking were as smooth as his undocking and departure from Sulyn orbit control had been. Except for the shutdown and power transfer procedures, Van could hardly tell when the *Elsin* was docked.

"Smooth approach," he offered.

"Thank you. At our ages, though," Desoll said with a smile, "they ought to be." He paused. "They're waiting for us."

"Ser?" Eri stood in the passageway behind the cockpit.

Desoll turned to the petite tech. "Eri, they should be here with the dispatches, and the cargo, in fifteen minutes. After you've got that and onloaded the gear for Commander

Albert, you can button up and rest, so long as you're on the shipnet. We've got a few chores to take care of."

"Yes, ser."

Desoll nodded to Van. "We might as well get on with it."

The lock opened as they neared, and there was a puff and a rush of air as the pressures equalized. Van had the feeling that the Farhkans were used to a slightly higher air pressure, and probably meant a higher gee field on their home planet. The sensation that hit Van as they stepped through the lock and into the station corridor beyond was the smell—or scent—a bewildering combination of musk and cleanliness.

Less than five meters down a gray-green corridor stood a Farhkan—the first one Van had ever seen face-to-face, and face-to-face was definitely not the same as a holo view. Holo views didn't convey either the smell or the *strangeness*.

The bipedal alien had two arms, and he wore the equivalent of shimmering gray fatigues. Iron gray hair that was more like fur topped the square head, and the red eyes showed no differential between pupil and iris. The flexible nose flapped with every breath, and only had a single nostril. Blunt crystal-like teeth, not quite fangs, but that long, extended beyond the almost lipless mouth.

Van could sense the communications between the Farhkan and Desoll, but only as the faintest *hissing* through his obviously inadequate comm implant.

"They have the equipment set up," Desoll said. "This is Dr. Fhale. Again, that's an approximation."

Van inclined his head to the alien, who was only slightly taller than he was, but broader. The alien did not seem particularly menacing, but how could one tell?

The alien nodded in return, then turned, as if he expected them to follow.

Van and Desoll did.

"They are a very peaceful species," Desoll added. "Their last interspecies conflict was before we left Old Earth."

"Carefully phrased, there," Van said dryly.

Ahead of them, the alien snorted.

"He's laughing. They came into contact with the Revenants about four hundred years ago. They suggested to the Revenants that Farhkan systems were not open to Revenant colonization. The Revs disagreed. The Farhkans suggested more strongly. The Revs still disagreed. Before it was all over, they had to destroy a number of Revenant ships before the Revs got the idea. The Farhkans were not happy about it. One told me that it set them back thousands of years."

What seemed to be a solid wall split into a trapezoidal entry. The two humans followed the Farhkan into a room that was completely empty except for what looked like an operating table tilted at a forty-five-degree angle and shaped into the form of a chair.

"You just sit down there." Desoll stepped back several paces, watching.

Van eased himself into the chair.

Desoll frowned. "Ah . . . before we proceed . . . Dr. Fhale wants to talk with you. This room is set up so that you'll hear him over the speakers."

"Talk with me?"

"We are providing you a favor," came a voice from above Van. "In return, we would like a few minutes of conversation and thought from you. It will help us in improving our understanding of you and of your species."

"I'll offer what I can." As he spoke, Van noted that Desoll seemed both surprised, and yet not surprised.

"You have killed other humans, have you not?"

"In combat situations . . ."

"Is not a death a death?"

"It is," Van admitted.

"Then why do you offer an explanation?"

Van thought for a moment. "Because . . . I mean . . . there's no difference to those who died, but there is a difference to me. There is a difference . . . between killing someone because you feel like it and to prevent that person from killing others."

"Can you see what will happen in the future? Do you know that with certainty?"

Van had been over that ground before. "With absolute certainty? No? But when you are facing a ship that has already killed hundreds of innocent civilians time after time, the probability of those actions continuing is high enough to justify the assumption that they will kill again."

The Farhkan said nothing for a time.

Van wondered if the conversation were finished, but he waited.

"Is any person innocent—other than a newborn or one recently born?"

"Probably not. But there are degrees of innocence, and there are those who have done no harm to others—or no great harm. And there are those who have done great harm."

"You would decide that?"

"When I must," Van admitted. What exactly did the Farhkan have in mind?

"Do all humans believe the same values are correct?"

"No."

"Are your values more ethical?"

"I would like to think so."

"Do you know that?"

"No."

"Yet you have killed when it is possible that the values of those who killed were more ethical than yours. Is that ethical?"

"I don't know about their values, Doctor. I know that their actions, which presumably reflected those values, were less ethical."

"How do you know that?"

Van reflected. "There's no good answer to that question."

The Farhkan barked, a sound Van hoped was laughter, then asked, "Is any value that preserves a society ethical?"

"No. Not necessarily."

"Then what is the basis for ethics? Do you believe in a deity that determines what is correct and moral?"

"No."

"On what do you base your values?"

"On what I must," Van replied. "Upon what I have seen and what I have learned."

"Are they adequate when you are making decisions that will kill some beings and spare others?"

"I can only hope so."

The Farhkan barked his laugh again, then nodded to Desoll. "We should proceed." He stepped closer to the chair, adjusting a cablelike protrusion that had lowered itself from the ceiling until it was just above Van's head.

"You'll probably notice some disorientation, and you may lose some memory of what happens here," Desoll said, "but you won't feel it, except that you won't recall what happened in the chair."

Van frowned. "It didn't take that to deactivate—"

"No. But didn't it take a full operation to put in the implant? This isn't like that, but it's more complicated to undo what they did than merely turning off your functions. Also, we have to add a little capacity so that you can link with the Farhkans and some of the other out-systems that don't use Arm-standard freqs."

That made sense, especially after the *Elsin*'s approach to the Farhkan station.

Van blinked.

There was a moment of blackness, and then he was still sitting in the chair.

Except his buttocks were sore—and there were some sore patches in his skull, needlelike points. "I lost more than a few moments," Van protested.

You did. The response came from the Farhkan, with a slight hissing overtone, but far clearer than most direct implant communications. *There was some damage. It was intentional. We repaired it.*

"The RSF?"

Dr. Fhale couldn't say, only that it was there, Desoll replied. His link was crystal clear.

Van's lips tightened. *I'm all right now?*

You are operating at maximum normal human capacity, the Farhkan replied.

They're very literal, Desoll commented.

How else can one be ethical if not with maximum accuracy? Yet there was a trace of what Van would have called humor in the response.

"Ethical?" *Ethical?* Van's implant echoed his words.

All life is a struggle with ethics. Those who fail to understand that are doomed to extinction. You should have gathered that from our conversation. The barking snort followed the Farhkan's unspoken communication. *You will learn. If you are fortunate.*

The last seemed more command than observation.

You should move. Slowly at first, added the Farhkan.

Van eased his way out of the chair. All around him swirled pulses of energy, various nets or systems he had been unaware of before. "Is this . . ." *Is this normal?*

It is an enhanced implant, very similar to, but better than, the standard Coalition implant.

Van stopped walking for a moment, just short of the reopened trapezoidal opening. He glanced back. The Farhkan had vanished.

"Is that all?" Van hoped it was.

"You'll have to get used to using it. We'll be working on that over the next week or so."

"Was that a threat . . . the business about not understanding ethics leading to extinction?"

"The Farhkans certainly have that kind of power, but they don't believe in using it that way. They believe it would lead to an internal conflict that would destroy them."

"That kind of power?" Van replied, stifling a yawn as he walked.

"More than that kind of power." Desoll nodded toward the

lock ahead. "We need to get back to the ship. You're going to need some food and some sleep," Desoll said.

Van found he was yawning again as he walked beside the older pilot. "How long was I out? That was more than a few minutes. Much more. But I can't tell how much. My implant clocks were frozen."

"About three hours. Someone had set a few more traps in you, probably when you were in the medcrib."

"Traps?"

"Locator, remote trigger transmitter." Desoll lifted a bag. "You can see for yourself later."

"What?" Van was stunned, then outraged. Absently, he noted that he seemed more able to sense overtones in Desoll's words and gestures. "But why?"

"I could guess, but it would only be that. My best judgment is that the gadgets weren't RSF at all. That either the Scandyans or the Revenants had a hand in it. That might also be why the RSF wanted you out of the way. They may have thought you'd been compromised."

"That doesn't make sense," Van said. "None of it does. There's no reason for you to invent it, but there's no reason why—" He paused.

"There isn't?" asked Desoll. "Didn't there have to be a reason why the *Fergus* was attacked? And a reason why the Scandyan premier was targeted? In both cases, you stopped something."

"How did you know about the *Fergus*?"

"Major Murikami told me. Most of the military in Scandya knew."

Van nodded slowly. That was true enough. Commodore Petrov had made that clear from the beginning. "Do you have any ideas about that? And what happened later?"

"We'll talk about it later. You need to get back to the ship and get some rest."

Van yawned again. He felt as if he'd run a dozen klicks. He did need food and sleep. That was also clear.

Chapter 41

Van slept a good ten hours, but woke feeling more rested than he had in weeks. Even the pinpoints of soreness on his skull were gone. The hot water of his shower felt good—and it didn't feel or smell recycled, although it had to have been. After he dressed, he looked over the miniature implants that Desoll had handed him the night before, but he could make no sense of them and slipped them into a locker. Desoll and Eri were at the mess table eating when he joined them, but a third plate was set out for him, as was a cup of café.

"Thank you."

"Thank Eri," Desoll replied. "She heard you. I was working on schedules."

"What sort of schedules?"

"The Farhkans are kind enough to let us send message torps here. There were several waiting. First, we need to work out a jump route to Keshmara via Kush. We've got a deliverable in Keshmara. We'll have to work in what we can, because I've been served with a judicial inquiry order to appear before the Transport Commission in Cambria in three weeks. There's an anonymous claim that IIS has violated its foundation charter by engaging in transportation of persons as primary carriage trade . . ."

"They're claiming we run a passenger line?"

"We don't. We don't even fit the definition. A ship has to have conveyance space for more than ten passengers outside of crew quarters. It's an old harassing trick. If the managing director or a prime official doesn't appear, then our charter is suspended until I do."

"They want something?"

"The Service wants information on Revenant ship movements, according to IIS Cambria, but they can't just ask. They have to pressure us to prove that the information was good."

"Are you sure that's what they want?"

"No." Desoll took a long swallow of tea. "But it's my best guess. Either that or they want information we can't give them, and then I'll have to make a stink about how they're abusing their power. They know I would. So I doubt it's that."

"You'd threaten to make a stink, and they back off?"

"Information cuts two ways. It would be expensive, but we could."

Van didn't want to pursue that, not on an empty stomach. After sipping the café, better than any shipboard café he'd ever had, he began on the mushroom and cheese omelet, also good. He took several bites. "Good food."

"It has to be. We spend too much time on board for it to be bad." Desoll's tone was dry. After a time, he observed, "You come from a very ethics-oriented background. Hasn't your father published a great deal on ethics and the law?"

"Some."

"And what is he saying now?" asked Desoll, after refilling his mug of tea. He sat back down in front of an empty platter.

Van debated before answering. "My father said that the Republic was facing an ethical crisis." He smiled. "He always used to say to beware of the person who trumpets his ethics."

"Cicero's published works are impressive, and they suggest an even deeper consciousness."

"Do you know *everything* about my background?" asked Van ruefully.

"As much as I could find out. We're going to be trusting you with close to a billion credits worth of ship. Don't you think that we would investigate thoroughly?" From the other side of the mess table, Desoll laughed. The laugh died away as the older man went on. "Your father is too modest and too conservative in his assessments, I fear. Those traits are the mark of a good and careful advocate, but like most ethical men of judgment, he still wishes to believe better of human foibles and frailty than he should."

"You think he's right?"

"The situation is far worse than he believes, and it's something that has affected human societies throughout the entire Arm. He finds it hard to understand that some societies and some belief systems are fundamentally flawed, inherently dishonest, if you will."

"Such as?"

"The Revenants, for one. They operate from the basic assumption that anything they do is correct. It was perfectly correct to replace the government on Nraymar, then annex it and turn all the Dzinists into day laborers if they didn't convert. Ten years later, it was clearly their deity's wish that Samarra become part of the Revenant theocratic realm, and that once more, those not of the faith be relegated to second-class citizenship or worse. They've already started the same process on Aluyson. Anything that they do is sanctioned by their theocratic authorities. When it can't be sanctioned, or they get caught out, they deny it happened. Once, in a great while, when they can neither sanction nor deny, they will change, and pretend that they didn't. I've only . . . known that to happen once, and it stopped their expansion cold—for about one generation."

"What are the Revs really like? Do you know what Orum is like?"

"You can meet Revs anywhere these days, and they all act in similar patterns." Desoll shrugged. "The Jerush system is closed to outsiders. You have to be a believer, and pass a gene scan in order to set foot on Orum."

"Oh . . . I didn't . . ."

"They try to keep that quiet. It's not unprecedented. Other faiths throughout history have imposed similar restrictions."

"What can you tell me about Orum? Isn't that where they have their grand temple."

Desoll laughed. "I'm surprised you haven't seen holos . . . they broadcast them everywhere, with the eight towers soaring into the sky, gleaming white symbols of purity and faith."

"You don't sound terribly impressed."

"I'm not. I'm Eco-Tech, remember, and we lost millions of

people fighting off their military missions. A gleaming symbol of purity and faith built on millions of bodies over centuries . . . that doesn't exactly impress me."

"I assume they didn't literally build . . ."

"Oh, no. Wystuh is a very clean and beautiful city, with white stone walls, and well-dressed and polite people." Desoll stopped. "At least, that's what those who've been there say, and what the holos show."

For a moment, Van had been convinced that Trystin had spoken from personal experience.

"Just the sort of symbol and city for a people convinced that God has appointed them stewards of the Galaxy, righteous in their beliefs of such."

"Don't we all like to think we're right?" Van pointed out.

"You're correct about that. The Coalition, just to illustrate your point, is trying to convince itself that the problem of the Revenants will go away—or that it's someone else's problem. So far, thankfully, most people don't believe that as an article of faith, but I do worry that will happen. There's a significant difference between thinking we're right, or trying to rationalize what we do as right, and *believing* without hesitation or question that what we do is right."

Van thought about that. Here he was discussing ethics with a man who was piloting an expensive ship, who personally ran a foundation larger than many multis, and who seemed to know more about his background than did the RSF. And the man had had Van's implant repaired and upgraded by an alien who also had wanted to discuss ethics. There was a clear connection, but Van didn't see where it led. "Both you and Dr. Fhale seem quite into ethics."

"It's very important to the Farhkans. It ought to be important to humans, but it's something observed more in the breaking than in the supporting."

"Why do you think so?"

"Because, in the long run, there's nothing more important than understanding ethics. Can you think of anything else?"

Van stopped to think. Anything more important than ethics?

Desoll stood. "When you're finished, we'll delock and head out for Kush. We could have left earlier, but I wanted you to feel the departure, because the next time you come back here will be in your own ship."

Van hurried through the omelet, a biscuit, and another cup of café. He figured out the sanitary setup in the galley, did his own dishes, then washed up before heading forward.

Desoll's stateroom door was open, and Van glanced inside, then stopped, taking in the space. The commander's cabin was more than twice the size of Van's, with an even wider bed, a double closet, and bookshelves over the couch—with restrainers for the antique volumes. Through another door was a large bathroom-fresher. One corner of the main stateroom was an office with comm and console equipment that would have been appropriate to either a flag officer or a managing director of one of the largest multilaterals—but then, Van realized, Desoll was the managing director of what amounted to a good-sized multi.

He just looked for a moment before moving ahead to the cockpit and strapping himself in.

Here are the protocols for the Elsin, Desoll offered, across the link. *They can only be used by me or you or Nynca. There's a limited key for Eri and the techs, in case of an emergency, but under all but those circumstances, the IIS ships are totally implant-controlled.*

Van locked in the keys, both through his improved implant, and into his memory the hard and concentrated way.

Desoll leaned back in the left seat. *Go ahead. Spend some time exploring the systems before we notify control.*

Thank you. Van did. First he traced all the command lines, then the power system. That was the first surprise. The *Elsin*'s had photon nets with more projection than the *Fergus* had, not that much greater, but considering that the IIS ship massed considerably less . . . Then Van discovered that the converters and accumulators were oversize, and that the fusactors were as well. That was nothing compared to the shock when he discovered that the *Elsin* was armed—with twin torp bays.

How many torps?

Desoll grinned. *Don't have weapons on this vessel, Commander. We have enhanced message torps.*

How many enhanced message torps?

Just twenty.

Twenty torps—as many as a corvette carried.

Van studied the screens as well, then turned to Desoll. "Effectively, you've got a light cruiser here. Does anyone know?"

"Outside of the IIS crews, and the builder, there's not a living soul who does. The torp bays are standard message torp bays. Most ships only have one, but two wouldn't be considered that strange for what we do, since we could need a backup bay. Our torps do fit message torp configurations. They come from an armaments' outfit in Keshmara who thinks that we're a black Coalition outfit," Desoll added. "The screens are equivalent to a battle cruiser's for about ten minutes. Then, they'll shred at that intensity."

"You have three ships like this?"

"The *Salya*'s not quite as powerful. Your ship has slightly larger fusactors and more powerful drives."

"What's it called?"

Desoll looked at him. "I thought I'd leave the name to you. We can't register until we take possession."

Van remained half-dazed. He was being handed command of a vessel that almost could have taken over the entire system of Scandya by a man he scarcely knew.

"You scarcely know me," Desoll said softly. "I know you somewhat better."

Van stiffened.

"Coalition implant," Desoll said. "You've already guessed. I was in intelligence at the end of my time in Service. Enhanced hearing. I can pick up some subvocalization. It's too tiring to do for long. You could, too, if you work at it."

What have I gotten myself into? Van looked blankly ahead, at the holo projection of the stars, presumably as seen from where they were docked to the Farhkan station.

Ready?

I'm ready, Van affirmed. As ready as he'd ever be.

Eri, strap in and stand by for departure.

"Yes, ser. Ready for departure."

The ship grav dropped to nil, and the fusactors went from standby into power-up mode. Van could sense all that, now, as the commander ran through the checklist.

Farhka Station Two, Coalition ship **Elsin,** *standing by for departure.*

Ship **Elsin,** *we are releasing locking. You are clear for departure.*

Desoll offered just the faintest touch to the steering thrusters, and the *Elsin* eased away from the Farhkan station.

Through his implant, Van used the scanners and monitors to study the alien station—a creation that hung in orbit around the moon of a gas giant, well away from the star's habitable zone. The station was trapezoidal—effectively a four-sided truncated pyramid—whose surface blended into the visual background and which radiated no energy. By the time the *Elsin* was only a handful of klicks away, even the ship's instruments were having a hard time discerning the station.

Are their ships like that? Nonradiating?

Yes. You can't find them unless they're using projected screens or drives. I understand they have internal screens inside the outer hull as well.

Van watched until they were well clear of the station.

You have the conn, Commander, Desoll said. *You need a little practice. Just move her up to full nets and full acceleration. You need to have a feel for full power . . .*

I have the conn, ser.

As he linked more deeply with the *Elsin,* Van felt the shock drop away as he began to enjoy the responsiveness and the sheer power of the ship, a vessel with the grace and maneuverability of a corvette, but with the power of a light cruiser, if not more.

Even though Desoll had used piracy as a rationale, the *Elsin* had far more than it needed to escape renegades. Van did not want to ask why the *Elsin*—or the ship that would be his—would need such power. Not yet.

But, sooner or later, he would have to. That he also knew.

Chapter 42

Van and Desoll stepped through the golden exit doors of the shuttle terminal and out into blazing white light. Van squinted. The midsummer sun of Sulyn was bright, but the light falling across Kurti, capital of Meroe, was even more brilliant—and it was only midmorning, and they were under a roofed portico of pale greenish white stone.

"Bright," Van murmured, realizing the inanity of the comment as he spoke.

"At midday, it's hard to see anything without bioadjustment or dark goggles," Desoll said.

As they walked, Van looked ahead for groundcars or shuttles or some form of transport. He could feel the slightly heavier gravity of Meroe, and the thicker and more humid atmosphere. He wondered how Emily was taking the heavier gravity. He hoped he'd have time to stop and see her, perhaps after they took care of the financial necessities.

"No groundcars?"

"They don't use them in the cities. There's a guideway induction rail plaza ahead."

A series of small domed cars, each able to take ten people, waited through an archway.

Desoll flashed a card past the scanner—twice. "I've paid for you as well. We'll get you a card account here, and then you can add systems to it as you go. I'd have preferred to do that first, but Miryam is meeting with a potential client this afternoon, and I did want you to meet her."

"You're the managing director." As he entered the lead car behind the older man, Van glanced around, but no one was near them. When the door closed and the guideway car began to move, he asked, "How many systems are on your card?"

"Over a hundred. The cards are linked to your implant. I have yours, but it's not activated. They just look like a standard datacard, but the advantage is that no one else can use it. Your ship will have the records of your card, and you can create a duplicate if yours gets lost."

"I see." Van was half-stunned by the thought that IIS datacards were casually accepted in hundreds of systems. He glanced out the windows of the small car. Even with the polarized shielding, everything was bright. The guideway was flanked with neatly shaped bushes with needlelike leaves. Beyond the bushes was a space of grass, and then a park on either side of the guideway, with winding walks composed of white stones. Beyond the guideway park were buildings, structures set in clusters. Both the number of buildings in each cluster and their spacing, height, and size varied greatly, although none looked to be more than ten stories in height. A number, here and there, resembled step pyramids, but others were just featureless shapes. None had projections. From what he saw, Kurti was certainly unlike any other city Van had visited.

The guideway car curved off the main guideway and along a much narrower strip of parkway, westward toward a set of three step pyramids, one of a pale golden stone, another of a deep green, and the third of green-tinged white. The car stopped, and the doors opened. Van followed Desoll along a walkway bordered by low spiny plants with blazing yellow flowers. The walkway led to a square arch at the base of the greenish white step pyramid. As he walked closer, Van could see that the building did have windows, but they were disguised by holo projections that created the image of solid stone walls.

The shade of the entry was a relief to Van. Beyond the vaulted entry was an inside colonnade, flanked with greenery. Desoll followed the bricked walkway for another twenty meters before turning left and approaching a trapezoidal door that slid open into a recess as the two approached.

A dark-skinned, muscular woman almost as tall as Van turned as the two men entered. Her broad and welcoming smile showed brilliant white teeth. "Trystin, as punctual as ever." Her eyes went to Van. "You must be Commodore Albert."

"Retired," Van replied.

"I'm Miryam Adullah." She continued to study Van.

"Miryam is one of the best planetary directors in IIS," Desoll said. "And the most imposing."

"You're always filled with compliments," Miryam responded. "I love it when you show up." Her laugh was deep and rich and full.

"She tells me what I need to know, whether I want to hear it or not." Desoll smiled.

"That's what planetary directors are supposed to do." Miryam gestured toward another trapezoidal doorway, beyond which was a circular conference table with five chairs.

After the three had seated themselves, Desoll spoke. "We won't be here long, and I wanted you to meet Commodore Albert because I don't know when he'll be back here. He'll probably be covering the more spinward planetary offices."

"Making him take the long jumps?"

"Not all of them."

Miryam turned to Van. "Trystin is very serious. I always tell him that it wouldn't hurt him to laugh more." She paused. "You're the serious type, too. I can tell."

Van grinned. "Sometimes. I have a sister like you."

"Was she in the RSF, too?"

"Hardly. She's a university professor. Her partner's a doctor."

"Partner? You look like you came from a regular orbit."

Van shook his head. "That's me. My fathers . . . one's an advocate, and the other's a singer and opera director."

Miryam looked to Desoll. "I see why you wanted me to

meet him. First time you've brought in anyone that has real blood in their veins."

Desoll lifted his hands in a helpless shrug before grinning. "It wouldn't matter who I brought in. You'd still find a way to abuse me."

"I have to. No one else will." But Miryam was smiling as broadly as Trystin.

Desoll's smile faded. "Is there anything I need to know or you need me to do?"

"Not this time. You know I'm meeting with Serangao in an hour—less than an hour. They like the idea of outside resources behind the office, but they want those resources well behind and out of sight. They play on the idea of using local sources and talent."

"That's fine," Trystin replied. "Play it the way you think best."

Miryam looked to Van, then Desoll. "How long will you be here?"

"We're leaving late this afternoon. We've got an urgent deliverable on Keshmara."

"Too bad." Miryam smiled at Van. "If I could take the commodore to G'zai's, it wouldn't hurt IIS at all."

"Next time," Desoll said.

Miryam looked to Van. "You heard it. That's a promise."

"She never forgets," Desoll said with a laugh.

"And aren't you glad?" Miryam rose from the table. "I'm sorry about the timing."

"Things happen that way," Desoll acknowledged, also standing.

"She's rather impressive," Van said, once they were out of the office and walking back along the colonnade.

"Formidable," Desoll corrected. "She's personally responsible for bringing in every major client we have here. Meroe is one of our most successful and profitable operations, and that's despite the fact that the Kushite systems need our services less than most independent systems do."

"What . . ." Van didn't complete the sentence.

"IIS supplied the capital she couldn't have gotten otherwise. She was from the Pharsi clan, and historically they've been looked down on as poor risks. I didn't think so. She was a skinny little girl, but she always had that drive. She's never forgotten." Desoll stopped at the guideway gate, which opened shortly.

"Now where?" asked Van, as they boarded the small car.

"The Nabatan Trust, to take care of those financial matters."

The guideway car ride was but a few minutes, and the car came to a halt at a covered concourse outside another of the white step pyramid structures.

Van followed Desoll along a covered but open portico that led to the main entrance of the building. Once inside, Desoll turned to his left, away from an open lobby with various public consoles, and down a narrower corridor to a console that stood before the closed gate blocking the ramp beyond. He entered a code and spoke. "Trystin Desoll for Daidae Mubarca. Accompanied by Commander Van Albert."

After a moment, the gate opened, and Van followed Desoll past the single guard, who stood behind a second screen and nodded politely at the pair. The two men walked up the stone ramp, a surface that looked perfectly smooth, yet provided traction for their dress boots. At the top of the ramp, they turned right, passing through an unseen security screen.

The woman who stepped from the arched doorway at the end of the corridor had dark smooth skin, short shimmering silver hair, deep gray eyes, and a welcoming smile.

"Trystin! I hadn't expected to see you so soon again." She gestured toward the expansive office beyond the archway, one filled with carved wooden furniture, none of it upholstered, but curved in a way that reminded Van of the Eco-Tech style, yet was clearly different.

Once inside the office, Desoll inclined his head to the woman. "Van, this is Daidae Mubarca, Nabatan Trust's managing partner for investments." He nodded to Van. "Daidae, this is Van Albert. He's our new senior director, and he'll be taking command of our newest ship."

"A pleasure to meet you, Commander." The silver-haired woman spoke with great warmth.

"And you." Van bowed slightly. "I've heard only good of you."

"He's as charming as you are, Trystin."

"I fear not, Director," Van replied. "I've much to learn from the commander."

"He's wise, too." She nodded, then turned to Desoll. "You wanted . . . ?"

"I'd like to transfer . . ." Desoll seemed to make a mental calculation, "four hundred twenty thousand Ks from the IIS operations account to a personal account for Commander Albert. He'll also need it tied to his draw card." Desoll handed over an ordinary-looking datacard. "The same normal limits as mine."

"Your standard limit? Ten thousand per draw?" asked Mubarca.

"That's right, and also a transfer link from his personal account in Cambrian Holdings." Desoll nodded. "And a beneficiary arrangement. He'll give you those details." Desoll smiled, then stepped back. "I'll be outside."

Mubarca smiled, her eyes on the commander as he stepped away. "He is one in millions. You will see." Her gray eyes fixed on Van as though he were the only one in the Galaxy, and Van understood immediately Desoll's attraction to the woman. "Your beneficiary?"

"Can I name joint beneficiaries? I'd like to name my brother and sister."

"We can certainly do that . . ."

As she linked the data into the Trust's systems, Van had a feeling similar to the one that had come over him when he'd first received the orders for the *Fergus* to relieve the *Collyns* off Scandya. He was jumping blind into a future that was more uncertain than anything he'd ever faced.

Chapter 43

After they finished at Nabatan Trust, Desoll guided Van to a nearby restaurant, where Van ate dishes that he'd never tasted, much less seen, but which would have delighted Dad Almaviva.

Near the end of the meal, the older man looked at Van. "I've got a few items to follow up on. You might as well look around, and I'll meet you at the shuttle terminal at sixteen hundred."

Once Desoll was on his way, Van used a pubcomm to call the Republic embassy and ask for directions. It took two different guideways to get to the embassy, a truncated pyramid of a pale greenish white stone that still seemed blinding in the early afternoon sun.

He stepped through the shaded outer archway, then through a nanite-based climate barrier into the cooler air of the public area. There, he found a vacant console, where he put through a call to the third secretary.

An image appeared against the wall behind the console, and Van couldn't tell if it were Emily or a simmie. "Ah . . . this is Van Albert . . ."

"Commander?" The surprised expression clearly indicated that the respondent was Emily, and not a simmie. "Where are you?"

"Down in the public area of the embassy. I just got here, and I was hoping you might have a few minutes."

"I'll make them. I'll be right down." The image vanished.

Van walked away from the console and toward the archway his implant indicated security devices, then stopped to wait.

He'd been standing there for several minutes when a Taran

Republic Marine appeared. "That area's off-limits, fellow." The tone was polite, but clearly unwelcoming.

Van turned and forced a smile. "I know." He produced the card with his commodore's ID. "And it's commodore to you, Corporal. I'm waiting for the third secretary."

"Ser, I don't care . . ."

"Corporal!"

Van was actually pleased to see Emily's look of disapproval, and he was certainly not the only one to recognize its force, because the Marine stepped back.

"Commodore Van is one of the most decorated officers in the RSF," Emily went on. "He was also the military attaché at the Scandyan embassy who saved the prime minister there."

Emily was wearing a slightly mussed tan singlesuit that tended to wash her out, along with a darker brown jacket, but to Van she looked marvelous, even with her stern expression.

The corporal took another step back. "Yes, ser." He nodded to Van. "I'm most sorry, ser."

"You were doing your duty," Van said politely, although he could tell that the Marine didn't seem all that sorry. "Carry on." He turned his back on the corporal and faced Emily. "I won't be in Kurti long, but I'd hoped I could catch you."

Emily brushed back a strand of disarrayed hair, then smiled. "We're in the middle of various projects, but . . . I can . . . I mean, I'm so glad you could . . ."

"So am I. I won't take much of your time, because I have to catch a shuttle a bit after sixteen hundred."

"My office would be best." She gestured toward the archway.

Van followed her, noting, as he passed through the security scanning, how simple the protocols seemed with his new implant. As in Valborg, the senior staff offices were on the second level, up a long ramp that doubled back on itself once.

Emily closed the door to her small office—again a single room—and sat down in one of the two chairs opposite the console. "I can't believe you're here, Commander, I mean, Commodore."

Van took the other chair. "Just Van. The rank doesn't mean much when you're retired."

"For a moment downstairs, I almost didn't recognize you without the uniform."

Van grinned. "I do fit in around here a bit more."

Emily flushed. "I didn't mean that."

Van could sense she hadn't, and wondered why he was so sensitive. Had it been the Marine? Then, he had been sensitive all his life. He just hadn't dared to make any comments. "I'm sorry. I know you didn't."

"How did you ever get to Kush, Commodore? Or should I ask?"

"Van," he reminded her again. "And you can ask. I'll even answer. I'm now in training to be a command pilot for an Eco-Tech outfit . . ." As briefly as he could, and omitting the actions on Sulyn to murder him, he summarized his hiring by IIS.

"You must be going to do more than pilot a ship from point to point. I can't imagine you being happy doing that, and you don't look miserable."

Van offered an exaggerated expression of misery. "Is that better?"

"You look like you're in pain, not misery."

Van laughed, and then they both did. "I'm supposed to be handling a bunch of other duties as well, but the training for that will be in Perdya, I understand." He paused, not sure of what else to say, before asking, "How are things going here?"

"As well as at any embassy, and better than at some. The ambassador's good, and so is the first secretary. The second secretary's more like a male version of Cordelia, but not quite as sharp . . ."

"There aren't many that sharp," Van said, before adding quickly, "She's so sharp that I came out of meetings looking for wounds."

Emily smiled, but Van could sense the tiredness behind her smile.

"You've had a hard week, I take it?" he asked.

"Enough to wish I didn't have six years for minimum

immediate retirement. Yes. There's a dissident group here . . . refugees from Sulyn . . ." Emily looked down. "I mean . . ."

"You don't have to soften it. Sulyn's always been independent-minded."

"They're claiming that the Republic has been forcing certain black Taran businesses to sell to larger multis, using regulatory policies . . . as inducements . . ."

"I wouldn't be surprised," Van said. "On and off, that's been a problem for years on Sulyn. I'd thought that it had gotten better—until I was retired, and one of the mediacasters I grew up with suggested that things had recently taken a turn back." After a moment, he asked, "You're being asked to deny it? Come up with statistics and reports, and it's getting hard to do?"

Emily nodded. "There are all sorts of statements, but Alaster—he's the second secretary—can't find any real numbers that support them, and we're getting hit with charges that claim we can't. The numbers we're getting from New Oisin don't track with the older series, and that's giving us both headaches."

Van nodded. "That makes it tough."

"And I'm supposed to have the text of another release ready by four o'clock for the ambassador to review this evening."

"Maybe I'd better go . . . I wouldn't want to have you thinking of me as the reason something didn't get done." Van didn't want to leave, not since it had been so long since he'd seen her, but he also didn't want to leave her blaming him for any trouble she might get into for missing a deadline. He just looked at her for a long minute, slightly disheveled. He was glad he'd come. He could always sightsee before he met Desoll.

"I can take a few more minutes. It's mostly done." She grinned. "Besides, you're from Sulyn, and I can always say that I was getting a historical perspective." The grin vanished. "How did it happen? Sulyn becoming part of the Republic, that is?"

"All the alternatives were worse, and the Republic made a

lot of concessions in the early days. I think the politicians on Tara have regretted it ever since, and it's been a cause of friction for generations."

"What sort of concessions?"

"There's an outright prohibition on media censorship. Local multi tax levels are capped, and the rates are lower, which means that there are smaller revenues per capita from Sulyn. Same-gender unions have equal legal preference and status, and that kind of discrimination is subject to stiff penalties. Independent justiciary . . . Those sorts of things."

Emily was frowning. "With that background, it's hard to make a case for martial law."

"Martial law?"

"The RSF sent in a domestic peacekeeping unit, but there aren't any reports of trouble. Not yet."

"I'm glad to hear that." Van frowned. "I don't see why the RSF would be involved. Historically, all the protests in Sulyn have been of the peaceful, civil-disobedience type, not armed riots or that sort of thing . . ."

"I don't know why the RSF is there." A rueful smile appeared. "I do know that you just made my job harder."

"That seems to be something I've been good at." Van decided not to press for more information, since it was clear Emily had told him close to all she knew.

"Oh . . . you sound like Sean."

"Sean had something . . ."

From there, the conversation drifted into summaries of what had happened to the senior staffers from Scandya.

Abruptly, Emily looked up.

"I can tell I'd better leave," Van said, "or you'll be facing the ambassador's wrath, or that of the first secretary."

"Can't you . . . couldn't we have dinner?"

"I wish we could," Van said, "but by dinnertime, we'll be headed out-system. Like you, I'm not the one in charge." He stood.

So did Emily, almost reluctantly, it seemed to Van.

"I'm so glad you did come."

"So am I." He grinned. "But you'd better get back to that release, or you won't be."

Emily made a gesture as if to brush off his words, even as she nodded.

When Van left the embassy, he was well aware that the same Marine was watching him closely, although the corporal made no move toward him.

Van barely made it to the shuttle terminal by sixteen hundred, but he was there five minutes before Desoll. That just gave him more time to worry about what was happening on Sulyn, but he could find nothing on the pubcomm channels, not beyond what Emily had told him.

By eighteen hundred local, they were back in the *Elsin*, preparing to delock from Meroe orbit station. Desoll seemed so rushed that Van didn't bring up the matter of seeing Emily, not under the circumstances. He wished he'd had more time to talk with her.

"Normally, we'd spend more time here," Desoll explained, "but we do have an urgent deliverable on Keshmara, and the urgent ones are what keep IIS going financially."

"Do we know what?" probed Van from the cockpit's second couch.

"No. I'll tell you more once we're clear." *You have the conn.*

I have the conn, ser.

Meroe orbit control, Coalition ship **Elsin,** *ready for delocking and departure.*

Wait one, **Elsin.** *Maintenance tug at your two-twenty. Clear to break power links, but hold at lock.*

Holding at lock, control. Have tug on screens. Van pulsed Eri on the shipnet. *Eri, we're going to null gee.*

Thank you, ser, came back over the shipnet.

After cutting the power link to the station and dropping the ship grav to nil, Van checked the screens, and the fusactor run-up again, still half-amazed at both the ship and the control provided by his enhanced implant. No wonder no one wanted to fight the Coalition Service pilots.

Coalition ship Elsin, cleared for delocking. Incoming traffic, red zone, approximately one emkay.

Elsin clearing lock charlie two this time. Have traffic on screens. Will stay green until clear. Van used just a touch on the side steering thrusters, then another touch on the main thrusters.

Elsin, cleared for low-power departure.

Stet, control. Departing this time.

As he eased the *Elsin* away from the orbit control station, Van checked the systemwide EDI, noting the various drive emissions. A Revenant courier was decelerating toward Meroe orbit control, while three Kushite light cruisers were patrolling beyond the comet belt, each patrol sector looking to be roughly a third of the system. There were two Coalition fast couriers, one locked on the other side of orbit control from where the *Elsin* had been, and the other seemingly taking station on the larger moon Omdhurman.

"Does Kush have some sort of agreement with the Coalition?" Van asked.

"Several, as I recall."

"Including military assistance?"

"There is one like that." The older pilot's eyes twinkled. "Why do you ask?"

"The two Coalition couriers on station, and the fact that there only seem to be a handful of ships in the Kush defense force."

"Warships are expensive, and Kush is not that well off. They're still paying down the planoforming debt to the Argentis."

"But their alliance is with the Eco-Techs?"

"They share borders with the Coalition, Keshmara, and the Revenants, as much as you can call borders those regions claimed by those systems. Each, including Kush, has claimed a number of uninhabitable systems without planets that could be planoformed."

"I'll bet Kush doesn't patrol those it has claimed."

"The Kushite SDF does not."

Van nodded, as he spread the photon nets to twenty percent, and the *Elsin* began to angle up out of the plane of the ecliptic toward the low-dust regions where jumpshifts were possible.

Chapter 44

A tall man in shifting robes and a matching white turban ushered the two commanders into the fifth-floor waiting area. Van walked to the expanse of armaglass that overlooked the River Plaza through which they had entered the governmental complex. On the far side of the River Khorl was a matching plaza or park, with tall spreading trees and miniature buildings that resembled ancient temples. The river itself was a wide expanse of shimmering blue-gray in the afternoon sunlight, somehow appropriate for the city of Keshmar, planetary capital of Keshmara.

From the door to the left, there was a cough.

Van turned.

A slender man, also in white robes, but with short dark hair, and without any headgear, stood in the doorway. "The minister will see you."

Van let Desoll take the lead as they entered the office, which held a circle of padded and backed, but armless, stools set around a low table.

Standing before the chairs and table was a small man, with the lines in his face that signified the great age that not even advanced medical treatments could erase. His smile was somehow both professional and personal. "Director Desoll . . . a pleasure to see you again."

"And you, too, Minister Sahid." Desoll bowed.

So did Van.

"I took the liberty of bringing Senior Director Van Albert

with me. I thought you should meet, because at times in the future he may be the one carrying out IIS responsibilities."

"Ah . . . You are not departing?"

"Not for many, many years. Not until the white stars turn red . . ." Desoll smiled. "But the Arm has more people and more systems, and as it expands, so must we, or we will not be able to continue to provide the services you deserve."

"And for which we pay."

"You do indeed." Desoll grinned. "But far less than if you were required to provide them yourselves."

"Please be seated." The minister took a stool, seemingly at random, but as soon as he sat, a young man appeared with a tray.

Van could smell the café, strong, black . . . and sweet.

Following the minister's example, Van drank, throwing the tiny cup's contents back in a single swallow.

Sahid turned to Van. "You are also a pilot and commander?"

"Yes, Minister Sahid."

"He is a commodore," Desoll added. "Not a mere commander as was I."

"You were never a 'mere commander,' my friend." Sahid looked straight at the older commander. "I would that we did not need your services."

"I understand."

"Alas, we do. We have begun to implement an integrated infrastructure control system on Behai. Most of the components have been fabricated there. The controllers themselves, they cannot be. They are not terribly delicate. In fact, they are most sturdy. But it does not matter how tough they are if they do not arrive."

"I see."

"I am most certain you do. The Coalition monitors the Keshmara system, but not a more . . . isolated system such as Behai."

"We will undertake delivery," Desoll affirmed. "Assuming the specifications and mass figures are as your dispatch indicated."

"They are correct." Sahid smiled, sadly. "We appreciate your willingness to transport our new systems to Behai. As you will discover, for some reason, the KMFS *Aleysn* was . . . unsuccessful."

Desoll nodded. "And you cannot afford any more delays? Or duplicate systems and missing ships?"

"No. For many reasons, which you also know. We also may require other services, to assure ourselves of its continued successful operation, with periodic updates."

"I understand, Minister Sahid. You realize, of course, that such service on this short notice requires a great deal of readjustment in our schedules."

"We understand that it will trigger the special services provision. Upon delivery confirmation, the special services bonus will be paid."

"When will the equipment be ready?"

"It will take three days."

Desoll nodded. "We will remain at orbit station for delivery. There is some other business that we can attend, and we will not charge for the waiting time."

"You have always been most considerate in that fashion." The minister extended a datableoc. "The complementary bloc will be delivered with your cargo."

"It will need to be packed most securely."

"That is why it will take at least two days." Sahid stood. "I thank you, Director. Would that I could trust all as I do you. The Arm would be a better place."

"We all do what we can." Desoll stood, as did Van.

"Ah . . . but some do it so much better." The minister flashed a smile. "I look forward to hearing of your success."

Desoll and Van offered slight bows.

Neither spoke until they were walking along the river. Desoll thumbed his belt, and Van could sense the privacy field.

"Special services bonus?" Van asked.

"You know what lies in-Arm from Keshmara?"

Van called up his memory. "It's all Revenant systems, most uninhabitable, but maybe a dozen being planoformed."

"How likely is it that a Keshmaran transport courier would

just vanish without a trace on a regular jumpshift to its own colony system?"

"The Revs took it out?"

"We'll go on that assumption."

"Why did they call on us? We're not a private fleet." Except, Van reflected, as he finished, the *Elsin* was the equivalent of a light cruiser, and with more speed and stronger shields.

"The Keshmarans don't have that much of a space force, and they can't afford to lose couriers, and they can't be everywhere. There's probably a Revcorvette out there with orders to blast down anything commercial. It's a way of isolating a system. Since they agreed not to send any more troids—asteroid ships—and since they can't send anything toward the Coalition, and since the Argentis are up-Arm, what does that leave?"

"Kush, Keshmara, and Jeavan, and a bunch of bootstrap systems, all out by themselves," Van replied. "I hope this is worth it."

"In credit terms for this transit alone, probably not. The special bonus is three hundred million Argenti creds, and the annual retainer is only one hundred fifty million."

Van still had trouble with the figures. Only four hundred million, and not enough? Then, the *Elsin* was worth a billion creds, according to Desoll.

"Minister Sahid figures that if the Revs take on a Coalition ship, first, he doesn't risk anything, and second, the Coalition might get more than a little upset. He can also claim that the Revs are breaking their nonaggression agreement, and this time, he has proof."

"Will they be there and come after us?"

"Who knows?" The cold smile told Van that Desoll knew very well what was going to happen.

Van kept his frown to himself. "What are we going to do for the next several days?"

"As I told the minister, I do have some loose ends to tie up with the local IIS office here. I can start now, but it will take most of tomorrow. If you don't mind, I'd like you to be on board, just in case they deliver early or in case something comes up. If I get finished with everything tomorrow, then the day after I'll sit the ship, and you can have that time to explore Keshmar. I'll also open a credit line here on Cambrian Holdings for you, keyed to your payroll. If you want to transfer your personal account to another Eco-Tech banking institution when we get to Cambria, of course, you can, but that's where your pay has been going for now."

"When did I start getting paid?"

"The day the RSF retired you. I thought that was only fair. You've got two months pay. One month for a bonus."

Van had to admit that Desoll had been very open about everything, if sometimes belatedly, from Farhkans to compensation—and the risks. He'd mentioned piracy from the start. Van just hadn't expected that the Revs would be the pirates—or that IIS would be acting as a part-time interstellar mercenary or private fleet.

But from the compensation . . . he should have.

Chapter 45

On fourday, Van arrived at the embassy of the Republic of Tara on the west side of the River Khorl at slightly before eleven hundred. He had no trouble entering the business section of the embassy, and immediately headed toward one of the Marine guards, hoping to head off a confrontation like the one that had occurred on Meroe.

"Yes, ser." The ranker was polite, but not deferential.

"I'm Van Albert. Commodore Van Albert." Van fished out the retired officer's datacard and presented it. "I used to work with the second secretary, Cordelia Gregory. We were stationed on Scandya together. I'd appreciate it if you'd tell her I'm here."

The guard took the card, verified it, and handed it back.

Then he stepped away and touched the wall console. He waited some time before speaking. "Dr. Gregory. There's a Commodore Albert here to see you. I checked his ID . . . tall officer . . . Yes . . . yes, ser. Right away." He inclined his head to Van. "I'm to escort you up, ser."

"I appreciate that, Corporal." He followed the Marine through the screened gate to the side of the business lobby. As Van passed through the screens, he almost paused. His new implant picked up the codes and protocols, and he had the feeling that he could have actually twisted them enough to gain entry himself. What had the Farhkan doctor done? Or was that another Coalition ability that added to the mystique? But with such abilities, why were they avoiding any direct conflicts with the Revs? Desoll had said they were, but Van hadn't been that satisfied with the answer. Because of a war over two hundred years before?

At the top of the ramp, the corporal turned left.

Cordelia Gregory was actually standing outside her door, waiting. "Thank you, Corporal."

"My pleasure, Doctor." The Marine slipped away.

"Commander . . . I mean, Commodore . . . to what do I owe . . . ?"

Van could tell that, behind the formality, Cordelia Gregory was flustered, bewildered, and even slightly pleased. "I was here on Keshmara, and I had some free time. Since you'd been transferred here before I recovered, I thought I only ought to stop by."

"I'm so glad you did. Please come into the office. It's a little disarrayed."

Van followed her in, closing the door and sitting down in front of the desk console.

After a moment, she seated herself. "I wrote you . . ."

"I know, and I very much appreciated the words and the thoughts."

"How long . . . you were severely injured."

"Six months in the medcrib, and two months rehab." Van gestured to the documents scattered on the flat surface beside the console. "You look . . . quite involved . . . What . . . ?" He let his words trail off."

"Mostly economic analysis—until last week. Then we had to deal with the Sulyn problems. You're from there, as I recall."

"I heard that the RSF had sent in a domestic peacekeeping team. From what I'd heard, and from what I know, it seemed . . . excessive. Sulyn has always been an independent place, but one where the protests were always civil."

"That's been a real problem in explaining it to the Keshmaran government," Gregory admitted. "We did send back a communiqué suggesting that reaction here was less than favorable." She shook her head. "And then yesterday . . . well . . . it's already all over the mediacasts."

Van waited, puzzled.

"The Keshmaran government announced this morning that they had discovered the identity of a Dartigan Dumas."

"That name is familiar . . ." Van tried to recall why he knew the name.

"According to the Scandyans, he was the one who put together that front—"

"Oh . . . that Scandyan Biologics place?"

"Valborg Biologics," Gregory corrected him. "But Dumas never existed. It was a Revenant front. They funneled the credits into a blind account here, and then to Scandya. The Keshmaran government is furious—not at us—but they expelled the Revenant ambassador and the first secretary, and demanded a formal apology and indemnification. The Scandyans are also demanding indemnification and an apology. That's all the Scandyans can ask for. I wouldn't be surprised if this almost destroys the Liberal Commons Party on Scandya. . . ." She shook her head. "Anyway . . . that's what I've been up to . . ."

"How did this come to light? It's been months . . ."

She shrugged, turning her hands up. "The Keshmarans aren't saying, except that they have documentary records, and the incontrovertible evidence that it was orchestrated by the first secretary of the Revenant embassy here. It happened practically overnight."

"Overnight?"

"The Keshmar First party is demanding the confiscation of all Revenant assets."

"That seems . . ."

"That's because they're a religious party, offshoots of the original Mahmetists, the ones who didn't become Revenants. They feel the Revenants lost the Word of God and are totally depraved."

"Don't all true believers feel that way about those who don't embrace their view?"

"Most of them," Gregory admitted. "Now . . . what are you doing? And why are you here?"

Van ignored the abrupt change of subject, understanding that she had said all she wanted to. "I've landed a piloting position with an Eco-Tech outfit, and I'm effectively in training until my ship is ready."

"An Eco-Tech multilateral?" Gregory's eyebrows rose.

"I interviewed with all the Republic multis, and they all said I was either overqualified or too senior. I don't know much beyond piloting, as you know. I was offered this job, and I took it." Van smiled.

"Good for you!" Gregory actually sounded pleased for him. "How do you like it so far?"

"It's very different. The outfit is a combination of high-end information and analysis, organizational consulting, high-priced delivery service, and specialized troubleshooting." Van felt the description wasn't shading the truth too much, at least as he saw IIS. "So far, I haven't seen the troubleshooting part, and I'm learning about the others."

"What sort of information analysis?"

"They have planetary offices on something like a hundred planets, and they collect all sorts of data, then analyze it for trends and seek out clients or serve existing clients. As a pilot, I'm supposed to be more in the line of delivering the results. They're too complex for cost-effective standing wave transmission, not to mention too proprietary."

"The clients are mostly multis?"

"They also have some governments, smaller systems, as clients."

"They have an office here?" She shook her head. "They must, or you wouldn't be here."

"They do, and I met one of the clients yesterday. It's proving a different kind of education." That was certainly true enough.

She smiled. "Is it so hush-hush that you can't tell me?"

"IIS—Integrated Information Systems."

She nodded thoughtfully. "I've heard of them. Very sophisticated and old operation. Very low profile. Privately held, so that there's not much of a public record. Has a good reputation for serving its clients."

"That's the impression I've been getting, but I've only been on board for a few weeks."

"You didn't take much time for retirement."

"I had plenty of time to think during rehab. Also, this was one of those opportunities that I had to take." Not for the normal reasons, but Van didn't have to explain why.

"No. I imagine there aren't that many openings for experienced pilots."

"There aren't, but I hadn't realized that until I started looking."

"The multis all want two-tour military pilots who are good drivers and little more. You're doubtless a good driver, but there's more there."

"I'd like to think so," Van admitted.

"There is." Cordelia Gregory smiled, then stiffened, listening to the netsystem.

Van made an effort with his own implant, seemingly slowly sifting through the protocols, recognizing a certain similarity, then being able to catch the last of the link he was not supposed to be able to receive—and would not have been able to receive even had he codes as the embassy's current military attaché.

. . . *soon as you can . . . ambassador was insistent about you briefing him on the economic implications of the Revenant mess . . . you know, what they're likely to do. Could they pull out of the multis they've invested in here, and what would that do? . . .*

Van tried to keep his face politely blank.

I have someone here . . . I'll be there as soon as I can.

No more than five minutes.

I'll be there, Dr. O'Hara.

Gregory offered a resigned expression to Van.

"Trouble?" Van asked.

"This Revenant thing. Now the ambassador wants an economic briefing."

"Economics? You mean . . . if the Revevants could pull out economically? I wouldn't think they provide any financial aid, do they? Keshmara seems independent that way."

"The Revenants have the third largest financial institution here—the Bank of Orum. If they closed it . . ."

"But that would hurt them as much as anyone."

"You don't think they'd take a loss to hurt someone else worse?" asked Gregory. "When it turns out that they apparently didn't have any problems shooting you and a bunch of other innocents?" She rose. "I'm sorry, but the first secretary was very insistent."

Van was glad she finally viewed him, if not totally accurately, as an innocent. He stood as well. "It does seem that the Revenants don't care too much for those that don't embrace their view of the Galaxy." He smiled, ruefully and self-deprecatingly. "But then, I've always had to struggle with that problem."

She returned the smile as she opened the door. "You and most civilized people realize they have that problem. We struggle with it. They don't even recognize it." With a last smile, she said, "It was wonderful to see you, but I must go. Will you be around long enough to have a lunch or something?"

Van shook his head. "We leave tomorrow, and I have to get back to the ship."

"Do stop the next time you're here."

Van nodded. As he hurried down the ramp, with Cordelia Gregory watching, he wondered what had happened to make her so much more friendly. Or was it that he had not been so defensive? Or both? Or had she learned something about the

Revs that he should know? Or did she feel sorry for him because of the Sulyn situation. That nagged at Van. He just hoped that reaction throughout the Arm would pressure the Taran government and the RSF to back off.

All he could do was hope.

Chapter 46

Van returned to the *Elsin* on the late afternoon shuttle up from Keshmar.

Desoll met him just inside the lock. "I'm glad you're back early. The minister must have pushed. They finished loading in the systems less than an hour ago."

"I'm sorry. I didn't know."

"It's not your fault. It's been a while since I've brought on anyone, and I just forgot that we need to link you into the local IIS net. That way, you can check in periodically."

That made perfect sense, but Van wouldn't have thought of it, either.

"How do you feel?"

"I'm not tired."

"You can take a nap for the out-system travel."

Van had an idea that wasn't exactly a suggestion. "I'll try it."

To his own surprise, he actually slept, to be awakened by a shipnet pulse. *Commander Albert . . . Commander Desoll would appreciate you in the cockpit in a few minutes.*

Eri?

Who else?

Van laughed to himself. *I'll be there.*

Because he was groggier than he'd realized, he took a quick shower.

Eri handed him a mug of café as he passed the galley door. "You can take a moment to have it. I asked."

Van took the cup gratefully, wondering why he'd been so

tired. Was it that he was having a harder time than he'd realized readjusting to shipboard life? When he finished the café—more quickly than he would have liked, but he hadn't wanted to keep Desoll waiting—he washed the cup and racked it, then hurried forward and into the second seat.

"We're fifteen minutes out from the jump point," Desoll said. "And you're about to get another lesson in IIS ships."

"Which lesson is this?" Van bantered back.

"The drive lesson. Our drives are tuned to Coalition military standard. That's no patriotism, but efficiency. But we'll sacrifice a percent or two for camouflage. We can retune automatically to any standard in the Arm. The farther we go from our baseline, of course, the greater the power loss, but the retuning is fairly quick. It takes only about three minutes. Coming into Behai, we'll tune to Coalition commercial."

"I assume that's because—commercial standard—is the same as the Keshmaran standards. And the lower baseline tuning is easier on the accumulators and drives?"

"Right. Keshmaran ships tune to Coalition commercial. Even their military does. If anyone's watching, they'll think we're Keshmaran, because the Coalition doesn't send commercial traffic here, and we won't match a military profile."

"Because the oversize shields keep our EDI emissions to a lower profile?"

Desoll nodded. *Now . . . follow me on the control net.*

Van did, noting the protocol, and also noting that it was hidden under the "housekeeping" functions, and innocuously labeled as DT MONITOR. *Well hidden.*

There's always the possibility that we might need outside maintenance or repairs. No sense in making things obvious.

Within two minutes, Van could see the change in the *Elsin's* EDI signature. Had he seen the new signature, he certainly would have considered the ship—at least, initially—as a commercial vessel.

You have the conn. See if you can sense the difference in responsiveness.

I have the conn. Van tried upping the acceleration slightly.

Desoll was right. There was a difference, subtle but measurable.

Then he concentrated just on *being* the ship, sensing all of the systems, in a way that hadn't been possible with his "old" implant.

I'll take the conn and jump, Commander, Desoll said.

Van hadn't realized how much time had passed. *You have the conn.* He had already assumed that Desoll would take over either before the jump to Behai—or immediately after.

Eri, Commander, strap in tightly. We're going to null gee, and we might have some high-gee maneuvers. I hope not. But we could.

Van frowned to himself as ship gravity dropped to nil. With artificial gravs and shields? High gee meant more than a little stress on both vessel and crew.

Stand by for jump.

Standing by.

Everything went black, inverted into white, and time stretched and compressed—and then they were on the outskirts of a system with a G-5 star, and a planetary system more compact than most inhabited systems, angling down toward the fourth planet.

EDI track at our zero two zero, plus fifteen, one thousand emkay.

The EDI was Revenant—Van caught that immediately—and about the size of a large corvette—what the Revs termed a frigate, big enough to take everyone else's corvettes, but without quite the shields and power of a true light cruiser.

Coming for us. Not a question in the world.

Van noted that Desoll had left the shields on standard, and had not increased acceleration, but instead had the photon nets at full extension, sucking in mass and diverting power to the oversize accumulators. They were still too far away for standard comm. As the time passed, Van checked the closure rates. The Rev was continuing to accelerate outbound.

Eight minutes to closure. Desoll retuned the drives, and within minutes, Van could feel the additional power. *He won't even notice, think it's a desperate trick by a Keshmaran courier.*

True to Desoll's prediction, the Rev frigate continued to accelerate toward the *Elsin*.

Four minutes to closure.

Two minutes.

Abruptly, a pair of torps flared from the Rev frigate, orange-dashed lines on the netplot, arrowing toward the *Elsin*, and then the Rev began a steep full-power turn, accelerating enough that Van could see the overtone freqs that indicated the Rev was on the edge.

Didn't like what he saw. Desoll poured full accel into the *Elsin*, turning it to chase the Rev, even as the Rev torps screamed toward the *Elsin*.

At the last moment, Desoll diverted all power, everywhere, into the shields.

Van's mouth opened. That degree of power cross-connection and flexibility was unheard of in any ship he knew.

Both torps flared into energy, and the shield indicators never left the center of the green. Desoll returned the forward shields to normal, cut the trailing shields to minimum. The acceleration jammed Van back into his couch as the *Elsin* seemed to leap across the netplot toward the Rev.

The Rev had no more power to spare, but another set of torps flared outward, circling toward the *Elsin*. Once more, the shields handled the flood of energy, and although the Rev had momentarily gained some, it was less than a fraction of an emkay.

In another two minutes, more torps flared toward the *Elsin*, and they too were shrugged aside.

Van wondered why Desoll didn't use his own torps, but he had the feeling that the older commander knew very well what he was doing. Van just wished he understood what.

Another set of torps, followed immediately by two more, flashed toward the *Elsin*. This time, on the second set of detonations, the shields' integrity indicators dipped slightly, but only slightly. Then the overtones of the Rev frigate's drives became even more ragged, and the *Elsin* began to close more rapidly.

Van watched as Desoll began to flex the photon nets, much the way Van had in dealing with the unknown cruiser off Scandya.

Suddenly, Desoll contracted the nets and cut them momentarily, effectively launching the accumulated mass still in the nets and not fed to the fusactors straight at the faltering Rev.

Torp one away.

Van watched through the shipnet monitors, understanding exactly what was coming, knowing it would happen even as Desoll turned the *Elsin* away from the Rev frigate.

First, the compacted and charged gas and interstellar dust slammed into the Rev's shields, with enough force that the shields went amber, almost red. Then the single torp struck.

Full shields, desensitizing.

The outer monitors all went blank, cut off by the damped shields.

After two minutes, Desoll released the shields.

Van blotted his steaming forehead with the back of his arm. He studied the EDI and the monitors. Outside of a slight rise in the ambient temperature, one that was almost undetectable, and certainly would be so in hours, if not minutes, there was no sign of the Revenant frigate.

Desoll blotted his own damp face. *Do you understand?*

Van did. *We're torp-limited, with the territory we cover. Each torp has to count. I've used something like the net trick myself. Not quite that way.* He still wondered if the Rev's destruction had been necessary, with the frigate's screens and drives going.

"You're wondering, aren't you?" Desoll asked out loud. "Or you should be. Why I just didn't avoid them?"

"I was," Van admitted.

"What happens if they report that there's a ship like the *Elsin*? Within weeks, they'll start plotting where we're headed. We might stand off a cruiser, and we've got the speed to escape a full battle cruiser or a dreadnought . . . but then what? Also, there's the ethical problem. They destroyed one essentially unarmed courier that we know of, and possibly a number of other ships, to try to isolate Behai. And they would have kept doing it. A frigate carries about thirty torps. How many did they have left?"

"I counted ten." Even Van didn't like those implications.

"This way, the frigate vanishes. No one knows for sure what happened. The EDI records, if they even keep them at Behai orbit control, will show three different drive signatures in that area of the out-system, and they're not that precise from their baseline."

"So Rev intelligence, if there is any, will think that Keshmara sent a cruiser?"

"That's the general idea. Either that, or they won't know what actually happened, which would be even better."

"Don't they suspect . . . or won't they?"

"Just how is an unarmed commercial ship going to take on and destroy a full Revenant frigate?" asked Desoll.

Van nodded slowly.

"Now, we can deliver the goods to Behai . . ."

"With all that accel, they're all right?"

"They were packed to handle twenty gees. Minister Sahid knew there was a possibility of evasive maneuvers."

Evasive maneuvers? Van choked back laughter, inappropriate as it was. Then he checked the systemwide EDI. There was no sign of any other warships, and only a few in-system vessels, clearly involving in belt mining or resource transportation. Behai was definitely a developing colony world.

"And this pays for IIS?" Van asked.

"It also helps keep the peace for the smaller systems, and we do it in several ways. This was just one way."

"How does destroying a Rev corvette keep the peace? Couldn't it just make things worse?"

"The destruction is only part of the effort. First, we don't tell anyone. That means that the Revs can't say much, because the corvette wasn't supposed to be there. They have a reputation for that sort of thing, have had for centuries. Second, it creates uncertainty, because they don't know how they lost the ship. Not for sure. Third, it helps the weaker systems remain independent, and the more diversity there is in the Arm, eventually, the better that is. Fourth, over time, it weakens the warlike systems. They have to account, one way or another, for ships and training costs and crews."

"Wait . . . why is diversity important? Every time I've seen diversity conflicts in a culture, it leads to unrest and warfare."

Desoll smiled. "You're making an assumption that diverse systems and diversity within a culture are the same. Even so, do you think it's a good idea that everyone be culturally pressed into the same mold?"

After his worries about Sulyn, Van had an answer, but he didn't feel like voicing it. "But . . . how does IIS stay in business? Who pays for the torps and weapons. You can't very well invoice Keshmara for those."

"We just submit an invoice for transport costs—even so, our services are cost-effective. We also get a large portion of our revenues from retainers. No one retainer is that large, but spread over a hundred systems and more than a hundred years, they do add up, enough to support the small planetary offices and the two main offices. There's the one in Cambria and a smaller one in Santonio. They come up with the business and information strategies. What we do is simple in theory. In practice, it gets harder. On any given world with an indigenous or local culture, we seek out organizations and businesses rooted in that culture, but especially those that are competing against—and losing to—larger institutions funded outside the culture. We provide information, technology transfer, and strategies. Sometimes it works; sometimes it doesn't. Our records show that we're very successful about twenty percent of the time, and moderately successful around fifteen percent. Five percent of the time, the business survives when it wouldn't have. We take a large equity position in return, plus a long-term retainer. Either party can break the agreement without cause at any time. They usually don't, because that would free us to go to a competitor. We usually don't because, if it's worked, why should we invest all those resources again? But, if a client sells out our ideals, we won't hesitate to break them. And we have."

Van shivered. "And . . . you think this is . . . ethical?"

"No one is ever forced to take our services." There was a pause. "Do you think the alternative is more ethical? The military or commercial takeover of system after system by out-system entities with greater resources."

"Are you—is IIS the principal backer of the Nabatan Trust?"

Desoll grinned, almost sheepishly. "We ended up in a strange position there. We hold large minority positions in both the Candace Bank and the Nabatan Trust. That's unusual. It's only happened a handful of times, usually due to the local regulatory structure."

Van shook his head.

Enough. We need to get to Behai, then to Perdya. You have the conn.

I have the conn. Van checked the fusactors, then the accumulators. *Unless there's something I've missed, I'll bring the gravs on-line.*

That's fine.

Van brought up the artificial gee to ship-normal, a full gee for the *Elsin*. He continued to monitor the entire system as the *Elsin* proceeded in-system.

Again, he couldn't dispute that Desoll was right about dealing with the Rev ship, which had been acting like a true pirate or renegade. Desoll was making the Revs pay for their actions. That was clear enough, and it was effective. Was it right?

What was right? Merely telling the Keshmarans and the rest of the Arm wouldn't have stopped the Revs, and doing nothing and turning a blind eye avoided making a real choice. Still . . . Van couldn't help wondering what he had gotten into and where it would lead.

Chapter 47

Perdya—the world that directed the Eco-Tech Coalition—
had three orbit stations. One was strictly military. One was
Eco-Tech commercial, and one was non-Eco-Tech. Non-
Eco-Tech military vessels were allowed at the military orbit
station—provided they were corvette-sized or smaller.
Larger foreign military vessels were simply prohibited.

The *Elsin* locked in at orbit control two—the commercial
station. An IIS maintenance crew was waiting, and a tug-
tender was easing up to the IIS ship even as the crew of three
left, with enough clothing for a week.

"Does this happen every time you dock here?" asked Van,
as they walked the corridor of the station toward the down-
shuttle terminal.

"Every time." Desoll grinned, then explained. "It's been
almost a year. Nine months before that. Heavier work, that
has to be handled at Aerolis."

Van understood the torp strategy even better.

"We'll have to stop at immigration control," Desoll added.
"Everything's been taken care of, but they'll need a parametric scan to put with the file."

"Parametric scan?"

"Everyone who enters an Eco-Tech world gets scanned. If
you're not in the files, you're detained until your situation is
resolved."

Immigration control was just after the end of the ship
locks, before the shuttleports. Van glanced farther along the
corridor.

"That's right," Desoll said. "There's another control point
on the other side of the station. Two-thirds for docking ships,
one-third for shuttles, and you can't get to the shuttleports

without passing immigration. No one makes you stop, not until you get stopped at the lock screens and sent back."

Van nodded as he followed Desoll to the first console—the one labeled SECURED EMPLOYMENT.

The older man extended a datacard. "I'm Trystin Desoll of IIS. Director Albert is our new senior director. The information is in here, and it should be on file."

"Thank you, ser. I'll need his datacard as well."

Van stepped up and handed the woman his card.

She scanned both cards and waited. Then she nodded. "The employee bond is in order, Director Desoll." She turned to Van. "Director Albert, you've been granted residence status in the Coalition for so long as you are an employee of Integrated Information Systems. If you remain an employee continuously for five years, you will be granted permanent residence status. If you terminate your employment before then, unless you find other approved employment, you must leave Coalition territory within six months, or be approved for some class of immigrant status."

Van nodded.

"If you would step over here, to the scanner, please? Stand right in the blue box."

Van followed her instructions. He didn't see any equipment, but assumed it was in the overhead. His implant sensed the scanning. He tried not to frown, because, again, he thought that the protocols were almost elementary.

The woman placed his datacard in a reader of some sort, then waited. After a moment, she retrieved the card. "That should do it." She handed Van back the datacard. "Your information is in the Coalition system. If the card is damaged or lost, you can go to almost any financial institution and have a replacement issued." A pleasant smile followed. "Enjoy your stay on Perdya."

"Thank you."

"Oh . . . and you are in luck. The down-shuttle to Cambria will be loading in forty-three minutes."

"Very organized," Van said, as the three moved toward the shuttle.

"Organization doesn't always solve the problems," Desoll observed. "Sometimes, it just makes things worse because people equate it with understanding."

"They think they understand, and feel they can deal with the problems because they're organized."

"Something like that."

They only waited about twenty minutes before boarding began for the down-shuttle. Van sensed the scanning and comparison, and understood what Desoll had said. With only a little effort, he felt he could have used his improved implant to bypass the system and pass him through as green. The shuttle was only half-full, and the three of them had a row to themselves, Van and Desoll on one side and Eri on the other.

Once the shuttle delocked, Desoll added, "You and Eri have penthouse quarters in the IIS office."

"You have a home here, I assume?" asked Van.

"My family home is out beyond Eastbreak. I don't see it that often these days. But we'll get you settled."

"Eri?" Van turned to the tech, looking across the aisle.

"I have family here, but my sister's house is small, and my mother lives in Sytka. That's one of the southern continents. My mother's research took her there, and they liked it so much that they stayed."

Less than an hour later, the shuttle landed without announcements, and they carried their bags off. There were no officials waiting, although Van did sense the screening as they walked through the corridor from the shuttle to the terminal foyer.

Once they stepped through the last set of portals, and into the late afternoon sunlight, and a warm and fragrant breeze, Desoll turned to Van. "We will have to carry our own gear. Groundcars are frowned upon, and most transit is by the sub-trans—or walking."

"You don't have a groundcar?"

Desoll laughed. "I have one small one. It's at the house. The annual usage taxes are almost what it cost."

Van winced.

"The Coalition uses the market system to ensure the environment remains protected. You can own anything you want, but, for some things, the environmental taxes will bankrupt you."

"Do they tax foundations and multis the same way?"

"Mostly. We do have a multiperson groundcar at the office. If we have more than four people going somewhere we can use it." Desoll walked briskly toward a low portal, with ramps and steps downward.

They waited ten minutes for the induction tube train. Although it was mostly full, there were seats. As the subtrans approached a station announced as Westbreak, Desoll stood up and motioned. The three took the ramp up from the underground station, coming out in a gardenlike plaza.

Desoll pointed northwest, along a tree-lined boulevard, to a ridge rising out of trees a good half klick away. "There's the office." He began to walk toward the ridge. "To build it, we also had to build the park. The park is about thirty hectares."

Van couldn't believe that. The "ridge" was a structure that angled up from the parklike setting to the west until it loomed over the forest below. But the ridgelike office structure looked to be six or seven floors, and no more than a hundred fifty meters by forty, and for that, IIS had been required to create a park that was a hundred times the footprint of the building?

"Of course, it makes a pleasant setting, and everyone who works there enjoys it. So do all the neighbors," Desoll added dryly. "Getting the architecture and the terrain to blend was a challenge, but the designers worked it out, I'm told."

"How old is it?"

"About eighty years old."

That explained the maturity of the trees and the serenity of the setting as the three walked down the tree-lined promenade from the station to the IIS structure. When he neared the building, Van could see that the irregular exterior was a greenish bronze composite that looked neither metallic nor stone, but somewhere in between, almost like someone had polished an irregular ridge jutting from the ground, then left

it. There were no visible windows, and only a simple archway, leading to a closed portal.

Desoll pulsed the portal open. The foyer beyond was modest, but well lighted, and empty.

On the rear wall of the foyer were lifts. To the right were
ramps.

"Eri . . . you can go on up. We'll go to the offices first."
Another smile crossed Desoll's face, and he looked to Van.
"You have one." He stepped into the lift, and the others fol-
lowed.

The two men stepped out on the fifth floor, into a wide corridor, leaving Eri to continue up. Desoll turned to his left and
walked quickly westward.

Natural light flooded in from clerestory windows set in
nooks between offices, although the windows had not been
visible from outside. The doors to the offices the two passed
were generally open. Each office seemed to be the same size,
five meters by five, with a window wall overlooking the park.
Several of those working looked up from their consoles as
the two passed, but most did not. A few smiled politely.

A stocky black-haired man stood waiting near the end of
the corridor, inclining his head slightly. "Director Desoll,
Director Albert."

"Van, this is Joseph Sasaki. Joe is the Cambrian director of
IIS, the one who really runs the operation. Generally, I do
what he recommends."

Sasaki laughed gently. "Except for the twenty percent of
the time when I'm wrong."

Beyond Sasaki, Van could see three open doors—old-
fashioned wooden doors, like all those they had passed. The
center door showed a conference room with a long table,
flanked with wooden chairs, without upholstery. The doors to
the left and right opened onto corner offices that looked to be
six or seven meters square—about two-thirds the size of the
conference room. Each corner office had slanted wraparound
windows, an old-style table desk with two consoles, a single
desk chair, three chairs facing the desk, and two low book-

cases. The only difference that Van could see in the offices was that the bookcases of the office on the right had antique books in it, while the shelves of the one on the left were empty.

"I've noticed already that he doesn't make many mistakes," Van observed.

Now.

Van caught the subvocalization as if Desoll had dropped it onto an open link and almost said something before he realized that Joe Sasaki hadn't even noticed.

"No, he doesn't." Sasaki gestured to the office on the left, the one with a southwest exposure. "This is yours, Director Albert. You can certainly change the furniture arrangements, and I imagine that over time, you'll add the touches you want. We just wanted to make sure that it was ready for you when you got here."

"Thank you." Van wasn't sure that he could have said anything else. The more deeply he was getting involved with IIS, the less he understood what Trystin Desoll had in mind. It certainly wasn't for him to be just a pilot, even the pilot of what amounted to an overpowered light cruiser with an open license on pirates and Revenants.

Chapter 48

Van walked to the wide sitting room window of his penthouse quarters and looked northward across Cambria—a city of greenery, of trees, of spacious parks, and of low buildings. At six floors, the IIS building was not the tallest in or around the city, but there were few above ten stories, with the exception of the single tower just to the west of the shuttle terminal.

A mug of café in his hand, Van slowly walked back and

forth, absently taking in the news, looking out but not really seeing the city.

... Technology Party elected Alan Fujimari ... Fujimari campaigned on the issue of ethic community ... advocated turning the planet of Mara over to those who cannot accept the founding ideals of Eco-Technology ...

... Constituent Assembly has approved a measure requiring that all large out-system funds transfers by non-Coalition organizations or individuals be accompanied by verification of identity and be available for public inspection on the planetary net ... in reaction to the Revenant funding of the attempted assassination of the Scandyan premier ...

... all Revenant missionaries in Coalition ... presence provided for under the so-called Treaty of the Prophet ... have been recalled by the Revelator of the Revealed ...

Was that a threat of sorts by the Revenants? Van didn't know enough about that culture to be sure. He was just glad that, from what the IIS research staff had been able to tell him, the RSF had backed off on actually landing the domestic peacekeeping team on Sulyn, and that the Taran government had reaffirmed Sulyn's local rights. The downside to that was that there had been protests in New Oisin about special treatment for Sulyn. One way or another, no one seemed happy.

Van checked the time. It was only seven-fifteen, and he wasn't supposed to meet Desoll—Trystin—until nine hundred. He really didn't want to pace around the office, and by the time he'd been briefed on all the codes, met a few key people, then had dinner the night before, and gotten settled in the quarters, Van hadn't seen much of Cambria.

He nodded, deciding to take a walk before he went to his office. He could stand to stretch his legs and get a feel for things. He washed out the café mug in the sink of the small kitchen, then headed out through the small foyer and to the upper lobby serving the four penthouse quarters.

He saw no one in the lift, nor in the main lobby. Outside, he headed eastward, away from the IIS structure and the park. Less than a hundred yards from the building, he walked past a group of youngsters, wearing school uniforms and headed the other way, shepherded by two teachers, both male, and both a good head shorter than Van.

While none of the students looked at him directly, he could still hear several comments.

". . . tall . . . outlander . . . Argenti maybe . . ."

". . . least he's not a Rev . . ."

Van walked almost a klick, past well-tended houses, set in clusters with garden settings around them, before he began to circle back westward. Before long, he reached the northern edge of the IIS park. There, he sat down on a curved wooden bench in the cool morning sunlight, taking in the peacefulness of the well-landscaped park. Dad Almaviva would have liked it, he decided, with the bushes in proportion and in harmony with the winding stone walks, the low grass, and the low flowers.

A young mother passed, holding the hand of a boy who couldn't have been more than four.

". . . Tajo . . . don't stare . . . it's not polite . . ."

". . . he has funny eyes . . ."

Funny eyes? Because they weren't slightly slanted? Van shook his head slightly.

He stood and headed back to the IIS building. Once there, he made his way up to his office, where he looked blankly at the console. He knew there was all too much he didn't know, but he wasn't even sure where to begin.

"Hello, there. You must be Van."

Van turned. The dark-haired and sharp-featured woman who stood in the doorway looked to be close to Van's age, but Van had always found it hard to guess ages, particularly women's, because there were so few visual clues. People didn't lose hair and gain massive wrinkles until close to ends of their lives, and skin tone stayed good.

"I'm Nynca Desoll."

"The commander of the *Salya*, and another senior director.

Trystin . . ." Van almost stumbled over the director's first name, so little had he used it. "He told me a little about you. Very little."

"Actually, I'm not a senior director. I'm not suited for that. I'm director of long-term planning. What else did he say?"

"He said you were a relation of his. That's all he said. I hope you can explain."

"Not very well. It's complicated," Nynca said. "Too complicated to explain, but when I want to get him riled a bit, I call him 'Gramps.'" She laughed. "It gets him every time."

Van respected her desire for him not to pry. Nynca could have been the daughter of a child Desoll had not known about—or worse—and Van had no desire to get into that sort of inquiry. "He doesn't look that old."

"He is older than he looks, but don't let that fool you."

"I won't. I've seen him in action."

"That's right. He mentioned that you ran into a little trouble off Behai."

"He handled it with very little fuss or difficulty," Van said.

"He usually does." Her voice was matter-of-fact. "He has for a long time."

"What do you do as director of planning?"

She smiled. "Everything, but two things primarily. I look for commercial opportunities, and I design implementation strategies."

"Nynca!" Desoll stood in the open doorway of Van's office. "When did you get in?"

"Last night. Late shuttle. I got your message."

Desoll looked to Van. "Have you been trying to weasel information from Nynca?"

"She's as open and forthright as you are," Van replied. "She's told me no lies, and not deceived me, but I haven't learned much. You've taught her well."

"I've said nothing along those lines to her," the older man protested.

"By example, then," Van countered.

Both Desolls smiled before Trystin looked to Van. "I've been checking on the new ship. Aerolis affirms that they've met the terms, and we'll take possession a week from tomorrow. You'll be ready for that after what you'll be learning in the next week. As much as you can be." After the briefest of pauses, he added. "I may not be ready. The director of finance for Outsystem Affairs has asked for an informal meeting next threeday."

"Why?" asked Nynca. "Do you know?"

"Not for certain. Her assistant suggested that it might be wise for me to be prepared to address why our use of multiple financial institutions was not a way of avoiding taxation. I've asked Laren and her staff to prepare a short report on that— one that we could put on any pubnet."

"They won't believe you," Nynca said.

"They may not. We don't pay profits taxes, because we don't have any, but still have to pay usage and service taxes, and employee support taxes. I asked Laren to put together a chart comparing us to their politically favored charities and multis. That will be in the report as well."

Nynca smiled. "Blackmail."

"Just public disclosure . . . or the threat of it. If they get sticky, we could also publicize which ministers got support from which of them."

Van just listened.

"But," Desoll said abruptly, "I can't do much yet, not until she gets the information to me, and Van and I have a lot to cover." He looked to Van.

"You are going to be *very* busy," Nynca said to Van before she looked to the older Desoll. "I'll be in my office when you finish with Van. I have the initial strategy for Aldyst."

"It won't be until after lunch," replied Trystin.

The way Nynca nodded left Van with a vague sense of dread.

"I need to get something from my office," the managing director said. "I'll be right back."

Van walked to the window, looking southeast toward the shuttleport. The senior director returned almost immediately, closing the outer door to Van's office, but leaving the door to the conference room open. Van turned.

"I thought this was interesting." Desoll handed Van four sheets of paper, clearly reproduced from an older document. "And extremely perceptive."

Van glanced down at the top sheet and read the title: *Dynamics of Information Handling in a Closed Environment.* It was his graduation thesis—or rather the title page and introductory summary. The original thesis had run something like three hundred standard pages, not including the supporting data and citations. "Where . . . ?"

"It's part of what IIS does." Desoll made a sweeping gesture that took in the building around them. "We gather information and find ways to make it uniquely usable to our clients. And profitable."

"That sounds like what many people have claimed for thousands of years. Obviously, IIS does more than that. Why has it been more successful?"

"Because most people truly don't understand information, what it represents, and what can be done with it. Even those who know what can be done are bound by their own preconceptions. You have to realize that the vast majority of people can only accept and use information that fits their perception of reality. There is a small minority that will see information objectively, but generally cannot find a way to use it profitably. There is a minuscule percentage that can see information objectively and use it, and a somewhat larger group that, if threatened, will accept the assistance of someone who can use information. The last group forms most of our client base."

"For the sake of discussion," Van said, "I'll accept that without question, if you can explain just how you can make information profitable enough to support an Arm-wide multi or foundation with the assets and scope of IIS."

"Fair enough. How about case studies?" Without waiting for Van's agreement, Desoll linked to the console and pulsed a set of names and codes. Immediately, the holo projection appeared, displaying the name Aergis Industries, nothing more. "This is an Argenti multi—it is now, but it wasn't when they first became our client. They designed holo display inserts—pop-ups, side-slides, that sort of thing—for the medianets. They were a glorified artistic job shop, and what they created was based on the market perception of either the companies whose products and services they advertised or of the nets themselves. Those perceptions were generally roughly accurate, but only in a general sense. So . . . we offered a proposition. Follow our creative lead for a year, and we get half the increase in revenues, plus the right to buy twenty percent of the company, and if they didn't increase by at least twenty percent, IIS would buy the business at a price that would guarantee a solid profit for the family that owned it." Desoll shrugged. "They were almost bankrupt. They're now the dominant creative advertiser in a three-system, four-world market."

"That says what you did. It doesn't say how."

"We started out examining what they were doing, why they were doing it, and identified every single assumption, stated or unstated. Then we checked the assumptions against our databases, and against our psychological model—"

"Psychological model?"

"Yes. That was one of the first aspects of IIS. It started out as a foundation devoted to the study of human behavior."

"There have been hundreds of—thousands of years' worth of studies—and no one . . ." Van shook his head. "What was unique about this model?"

"One unique aspect was that we persuaded the Farhkans to part with some of their data. More than two centuries back, during the Eco-Tech-Revenant War, they'd undertaken a study of human psychology, which they made available to the Coalition in exchange for certain technological refinements." Desoll smiled. "An outside perspective always adds a dimension that self-study lacks. Then, after restructuring and codifying the Farhkan data, IIS made an effort to collect as many 'outside' human studies as possible. For example, a Coalition study of Revenant culture or behavior, and Argenti study of Hyndji attitudes, etc. Then, we did cross-comparisons of the inside studies with the outside studies . . ."

Van still didn't see where Desoll was going, but he nodded.

"All human cultures have an economic component, and how that component operates is tied to psychology. So far as we know, no one else ever attempted to consolidate and correlate such a massive effort. IIS also enlisted several Farhkans to analyze the preliminary results. That added years to the project, but resulted in more useful insights. So, in the case of Aergis Industries, the case at hand, we looked at the products they were pushing, who they thought was buying them, who really bought them, then redesigned the approach." Desoll laughed. "We also lied."

"Lied?"

"We told everyone what they wanted to hear—that we were using the same techniques others had used for years and that we were managing the business better. The form of what we were doing was similar, and what we did worked. So no one really looked that much further."

To Van, it was still theoretical.

"All right. Take groundcars. In non-Coalition cultures, they're theoretically a transportation device. But, in point of fact, depending on the culture, they can either be a functional necessity, a display of male power, a display of sexual independence, a status symbol, or about a dozen other factors. To sell groundcars, you have to know what the product will do in that culture, what role the product plays, and why a particular type or model will or will not fit in the desired niche. Historically, these kinds of sales have been handled most effectively one-on-one, after what one could call mass display of the product, with a range of messages in different media incarnations, had made potential consumers aware of the product, thus allowing the end salesperson to make the final appeal based on his or her intuitive psychology. But . . . if you know in advance the role of the product, the psychological and practical appeal by ethnic, economic, gender, and social background, you can segment the market much more effectively. Our psychological model has proven very effective in refining that approach . . ." Desoll called up a table. "Here is the history of initial account promotions . . ."

Van watched and listened for the next hour as Trystin Desoll dissected thirty years of success with Aergis Industries. His head was aching when the older man powered down the holo display.

"Do you have a better idea now?" asked Desoll.

"I'm getting it," Van replied cautiously. "I'm still not sure where I fit it. I can understand how all this works, but I certainly couldn't create a plan like the one you showed me. I could monitor it, and make sure it got implemented . . . but surely you have others who could do that."

"What's the biggest barrier to effective organization of a multisystem organization?"

"Time and distance."

"And the inability of those running it to understand the individual dynamics involved in how organizations need to adapt to different cultures," Desoll added. "What I do, and what you're going to learn to do, is to provide coordination, control, understanding, direction—and glue."

"Glue?"

"There are two kinds of organizations—those held together by bureaucratic systems and traditions, and those held together by a shared vision. The first are extremely good at surviving, but seldom accomplish much more. The second can change a planet or a corner of the Galaxy, but only so long as the vision remains shared and vital—and that requires people at the top who embody that vision. You have that potential. You've been given second-rate crews and ships for years—and yet outperformed those considered first-rate." Desoll pointed to the sheets of paper on the corner of the desk. "You've also got a first-rate mind, and vision—"

"They barely passed that thesis," Van protested.

"That was their problem. I had it submitted to the University of Cambria, anonymously. I asked for an objective opinion from various thesis committees. Half wanted to fail it. The other half claimed it was brilliant. For the record, I agree with the latter."

"Why do you need me?" That was really the bottom-line

question. "Or were you trying to get a pilot and do a rescue job at the same time?"

Trystin's face tightened, the first hint of anger Van had seen. "I can't afford rescues." His voice was cold.

Van thought he could almost hear, *One was enough.* "I'm sorry. I just find it hard to believe—"

"Believe it. Ambitious, intelligent, and ethical commanders who can manage are almost impossible to find these days. I'm not doing you any favors. By the time two years have passed, you'll have earned every credit." Desoll's face cleared. "IIS has gotten too big for one director to handle it all, because it requires someone whose ethics have been so deeply instilled that they're instinctual, not merely easy rules of behavior, and because IIS needs to continue to project an image of power."

Van still was doubtful.

"And because I don't have time to do everything that needs to be done, including some work on a new power transmission technology project that's taking far more effort than I'd ever thought. I can't do that, which is vital for our future, and the future of the Arm, and still continue to present an image of presence and power. I need you to help with that."

Why an image of power?

Van must have subvocalized that, he realized, as Desoll nodded.

"That is the question, isn't it? I'll give you part of the answer. Actually, I've already given you part—that was what we did off Behai."

"To keep the peace?"

Desoll shook his head. "No. No one can ever keep the peace, not among humans, no matter what the Farhkans believe. To keep the bureaucracies honest, because bureaucracies are only interested in self-perpetuation, and the best of ideals are the first casualty of expediency. Organizations that go beyond survival are both the economic and pragmatic hope for the future. By offering alternatives to the established powers—as we did with Aergis—we make a goodly profit while keeping societies more open and flexible. By doing the occasional dirty job off a Behai, we also help keep greater economic and cultural diversity in the Arm—and make money doing it. What we do is far from easy, and learning all you'll need to know won't be easy, either.

You'll have to learn the general outline of the human model and the details of every major project in your sector— that's about half of the IIS projects. I'll keep the other half. But you'll have time, because you'll pick them up one by one over the next few years."

Van wondered if he'd ever learn half as much as Desoll already knew, but the man did say he had a few years. Van would need them. Of that, he was certain. He was also more certain, even if he had risked Desoll's anger, that the man had a definite need for him that went beyond what had been explained. He just wished he knew what it might be.

Chapter 49

On threeday, a week and two days after Van had arrived in Cambria, the *Elsin* approached the Aerolis complex—built within and around a nickel-iron asteroid in the outer belt of the Perdyan system.

*Aerolis prime, Coalition ship **Elsin**, requesting clearance and docking instructions.*

***Elsin**, welcome to A-prime, cleared to beacon.*

Understand cleared to beacon this time.

Desoll used delicate puffs on the thrusters to ease the *Elsin* toward the beacon, set on a spindly tower rising from the asteroid. Van scanned the net and monitors to study the ship that was locked to a second tower, the ship that was to be his to command. The fusactors were down, because there were no EDI emissions, but even without an energy corona Van could tell that the other ship was powerful, just from the design, and from the size. Desoll's docking was smooth, as if he'd docked to asteroid towers so often it was second nature.

*A-Prime, **Elsin** locked and powered down to station-keeping.*

*Thanks, **Elsin**. Jynko's at your lock.*

Stet.

Desoll slipped from the command couch, looking aft toward Eri and Alya, the other tech who had appeared with Eri when she had joined them at Perdya orbit station two. "We'll be doing the inspection. Don't know how long it will take."

Eri just nodded. So did Alya.

Both Van and Desoll wore space armor, but carried their helmets. They were met just outside the *Elsin*'s lock by an angular Belter wearing a vacsuit, with its collapsible helmet clipped to his equipment belt.

"Director Desoll. Said it would be you."

"Who else?" Desoll gestured to Van. "This is Commander Albert. It will be his ship."

"Mason Jynko, Commander." The angular Belter nodded. "You two ready for the inspection?"

"We're ready."

"Have to use the main lock at the base of tower two." Jynko turned and hand-over-handed his way down the tower corridor.

Van and Desoll followed.

The exterior inspection was, in a sense, perfunctory, although the three inspected the elongated spheroid carefully, using suit lamps and a handscanner that Desoll had produced. All the exterior inspection proved was that everything was there.

Then they returned to the lower main lock, took off their helmets, and went up the tower and into the ship. Once inside, they began with the mech spaces. Van noted that Desoll paid particular attention to the accumulators and the supercon lines linking the fusactors to the accumulators and the jumpshift generators. The lower interior was spotless.

The living spaces were on the same pattern as those of the

Elsin, with two crew cabins, and two spare cabins—except that the wooden veneer in the commander's spacious cabin was a light blond wood, and all the trim was an off-white, making the new ship even lighter in feel than the *Elsin*. That was something that Van appreciated greatly.

Finally, and last, they entered the cockpit.

"Now . . . the board's the way you specified . . . minimum of manual controls, and we installed the link systems you provided, according to the specs. Your other director's been out here more'n a few times, checking on things. Signed off on the shipnet."

"Yes, Nynca's very good on detail," Desoll said with a smile.

Van settled into the command couch and began the powering-up, using the full maintenance checklist, taking his time, and going over every single item, checking all the links, all the routines and subroutines. All the links were clear, clearer than he had felt in any other ship.

All in all, it took almost two hours. Neither Desoll nor Jynko said a word, although Desoll clearly followed Van through everything.

Finally, Van looked across the cockpit. "Maintenance check complete. Everything checks."

"What do you think?" Desoll smiled.

Van could only shake his head. "She's . . . beautiful. She's more than that . . ."

A faint grin appeared on Jynko's face.

"What are you going to name her?" asked Desoll. "We'll need to know."

Van had thought about it. He'd thought about naming it after his sister, but that wouldn't have been quite right. He'd finally decided. "*Joyau*. It's an ancient word for 'jewel.' I think that fits."

Desoll nodded. "Short and appropriate. I've always disliked commercial ships with names like *Starflight Hope* or *Princess Regina* . . . You understand what I mean?"

Van did.

"We'll put *Joyau* on the acceptance form, then," Jynko said.

"After Commander Albert completes the power trials out-system," Desoll added.

"Of course. Only one jump and back." Jynko rose. "You going, Director Desoll."

"I'll ride second seat, and we'll call over one of the techs."

"Fine." Jynko nodded. "I'll have everything ready when you return." He grinned. "Don't be too long."

Once Jynko left, Desoll looked to Van. "Your tech."

"You have one in mind?" Van lifted his eyebrows.

"Would you mind if I assigned Eri as your tech, at least for a time?"

That surprised Van, although he hadn't seen any overt affection between the two. "No . . . if that's all right with you."

Desoll laughed. "Eri's been a friend, never more than that, and she's already raised one family. She's told me that she's not about to raise another, or train another husband. She will consent to training another commander."

This time Van laughed. "I trust I'm trainable."

"She thinks so. So do I."

"I'm sure she knows things that I don't."

"She should, and that's the idea."

Van was sure of that.

As Desoll linked to call Eri, Van ran through the links again. For a time, he'd thought he'd never have another ship, and to have one like the *Joyau*—that was even more unbelievable.

DIRECTOR

Van triggered the lock closed behind him as he stepped into the *Joyau*, docked at C-two of Winokur orbit control.

Eri appeared before Van got another step farther toward either the galley or his stateroom.

"Were you successful?"

"They agreed, and the retainer is in the local branch of Cambrian Holdings. It's not that much." Van shrugged. "Winokur isn't that well-off, but the planetary assembly had delegated authority to the bonding agency. They really want to strengthen local multis. If . . . *if* Krecor follows the plan, and *if* Bonifils and Chabre can keep their management on track, it ought to work." Van eased into the galley, where he turned on the cafémaker.

Eri followed, clearly wanting more details.

Van didn't blame her, since she'd been sitting the ship. "I promised the first set of formulator templates within a week of deposit. That we can do. Those are the ones we brought. They get the second set in two months, and I'll have to torp that request off to IIS Cambria. We'll have to pick those up somewhere—either meet Trystin or make a long jump to Perdya—in six weeks. But we'll need to swing back by here about then anyway to see what Trans-Win Microtronics is up to . . ." He poured himself a mug of café. "Seems like every Rev front multi is Trans something or other."

Eri nodded politely.

Van grinned. "There's a down-shuttle to Wypres in an hour. I've got to catch up on some things. You want a day to look around, and whatever?"

"I could do that."

"Would you *like* to?" Van countered.

"Would you like me to?" Eri replied politely.

Van sighed. "Go! I'll see you tomorrow, no later than sixteen hundred ship time."

"Yes, ser, Commander." Eri spoiled the subservient words with an impish smile, before she slipped toward her cabin.

Van still didn't quite understand how a woman ten years older than he was could look impish, but there were many things he still didn't understand, even after working with Eri for more than two years, and that wasn't one he was going to attempt.

He took the café and the small case he'd carried down to Wypres and back up, slightly lighter, into his stateroom, sliding the case behind a restrainer in the top bookshelf. Then he pulsed on the holo display, requesting the latest news update from the orbit control net.

After another sip of café, Van settled into the chair and looked at the first lines of the news summaries holo-stacked in the air above the flat surface before his stateroom console, representing page after page from the IIS office in Cambria. He still had to read the analyses that had come with them on the message torp. Even after passing two years in command of the *Joyau*, he was at times astounded at the volume and accuracy of the information that poured into the ship.

He glanced across the lead lines projected up in front of him, then scanned them quickly.

Keshmaran assembly accepts Coalition basing plan . . .

Revenant Quorum denies planned annexation of Kushite border system . . .

Eco-Tech Service accepts three new battle cruisers . . .

Keltyr executive claims missing cruiser destroyed by Revenant battle group . . .

Argenti Montaje debates out-system base expansion . . .

For the past several years, slowly, almost inexorably, the news had gotten worse and worse, although IIS business had improved. But then, it could be that it had improved because other matters were degenerating.

From the number of times Trystin had been summoned before some Coalition commission, board, committee, or government official, it was clear enough to Van that IIS wasn't a Coalition black operation. At the same time, Van had the definite feeling that the Coalition wasn't so much concerned about what IIS was doing as worried about not knowing.

Van took another sip of the already-too-cool café.

The reason behind that Coalition attitude seemed to be exactly what Trystin had said a year earlier. While the Eco-Techs worried about Rev expansion, they'd do almost anything to avoid another war with the Revs, including turning a blind eye on IIS activities, provided they enhanced or did not harm the Coalition.

The Revs also didn't want an all-out armed conflict, but they didn't seem averse to using any and all kinds of force and persuasion against anyone except the Coalition and the Argentis—and it was working. Still . . . there was little enough IIS could do, except offer its services to strengthen local multilaterals against outside onslaught. In attempting that there were always problems, more than he'd had a chance to look into. He took another sip of café and called up the message that had been forwarded from the IIS office in Cambria—just text, because full video and audio were still expensive over interstellar distances. He smiled as he read.

. . . enjoyed your last message. While many of our acquaintances find it hard to believe that you are senior director of an influential foundation and commander of a private interstellar ship, I cannot say that you do not deserve it, for you more than most have earned what you have gained. Nonetheless, because of your heritage, there will always be questions about ability, especially now in the Republic, and you must always comport yourself with dignity and caution.

Dad Cicero was as much as saying that matters were also continuing to degenerate in Bannon and on Tara, and that, if he did come home, he needed to watch his back and then some. The fact that Cicero had not mentioned that after the abortive RSF peacekeeping ploy also bothered Van, because that meant things were not at all good.

Sappho and Aelsya have discussed following your example, but, until that can be resolved, for the moment have decided to devote themselves to their work and children. Lesnym and Farah are indeed bright girls—and a joy to their grandfathers. Arturo continues in his pursuit of the law along the ancient traditions that have been making a resurgence in Sulyn and throughout the Republic, but he has been a great support to this aging advocate and a true son of Sulyn . . .

Van winced. What Cicero was saying was that Arturo couldn't—or wouldn't—see what was happening and was accepting or even buying into it.

Margaret remains as sensitive as always, but is supportive of Arturo and Despina in all they do. Despina has become a truly beautiful young woman, and shares Almaviva's love of music. Her voice is developing well, and he says she is naturally unforced and open . . .

After Van read the missive—twice—he leaned back and closed his eyes, thinking about Bannon and the new Revenant temple there, and the growth of converts to the Christos Revivos, and he wondered what would happen next.

Finally, he pulled up his analyses and the scheduling requests that had come with the latest message torp. The newly opened IIS office on Korvel had requested a visit by a director—for advice—and Trystin had passed that on to Van, since Korvel system was a much shorter jump from Winokur than from wherever Trystin was—he hadn't said, as he usually didn't, only that he was working on the power transmission technology project.

The IIS planetary director on Islyn had requested a director to help him interview and select his potential replacement. Van checked the files. Camryn Rezi—the IIS PD on Islyn—was only sixty. Islyn was an affiliate Hyndji system, meaning that Islyn was independent but tied to the Hyndji financial and trade structure and procured its space defense vessels and support equipment from the same sources as did the Hyndji Defense Force.

Van called up a colored dimensional holo projection, trying to refresh his memory of where exactly Islyn was. The position confirmed it. While Islyn was closer to Hyndji systems, it nestled in an almost empty area of the Arm, and the area between it and Pyshwan, the nearest Hyndji system, was a turbulent area with paradimensional tensions that precluded direct jumps. The closest direct jump was actually from Colsiti, one of the more recently planoformed Revenant systems. The other system power that was close was Keltyr.

Knowing where Islyn was, he turned to the next item. There had been no reports from the one-person IIS office on Beldora for almost six months. Nor had there been any fund transfers for three. Beldora was even more isolated than Islyn, another independent system farther out-Arm from the Revenants and Keltyr, where direct access was blocked by the same unique configuration of turbulence and paradimensional tensions as Islyn, except that they were on opposite sides.

He decided to make the courtesy call on Korvel first, because it was almost on the way to the two problem systems. Both jumps would require more power than he liked; but he didn't like the feel of either situation, and, left to themselves, matters that felt bad always got worse.

Chapter 51

At 13:28 Van walked into the Korvel Mercantile Tower, then took the lift to the third floor. From there, he made his way along the southern corridor to the open door beside the IIS spelled out in silvered letters on the taupe plaster wall. He stepped inside.

A young man looked up from the console. "Ser?"

"I'm Director Van Albert. I had a—"

"Oh, ser, you caught me off guard." The young man rose quickly. "Director Myller told me to expect you. She's waiting for you." He took three steps to his left and peered into the office. "Director Myller, Director Albert is here."

"Thank you." Van smiled stepped through the open door, closing it behind him.

Tall and thin, not quite angular, Sherren Myller glanced at Van from where she stood beside her console. "It's good of you to respond so quickly. I hadn't expected . . ."

"You'd thought that Director Desoll would be here, I imagine," Van replied. "Under many circumstances he would be. But Korvel was closer for me, and it might have been a while before Director Desoll could have made it."

She gestured to the two upholstered chairs before the console.

Van took one, setting the small case he carried on the floor beside the chair and waiting for Myller to seat herself.

"How was your trip?" she asked.

"Long. They all are." Van smiled. "Korvel seems to be a pleasant place. Very friendly."

"We think so. The few out-system travelers I've met all agree with you." Myller offered a rueful expression. "I don't have the experience to make a comparison."

"According to the news and what I could pick up on business indicators, matters seem to be going fairly well." Van had noticed that price indices had increased more than expected for the past year, but hadn't had the time to look into that. "Your message was carefully worded, but it suggested that you have a problem."

Myller's lips twisted into an ironic smile. "We do. It's not one that any of us anticipated, and it's not something that's a major problem. Not yet, anyway . . . but Director Desoll suggested that I should let IIS headquarters know if something came up that seemed out of the ordinary. This isn't . . . but it is."

Van waited. He wanted to hear the problem in her own words.

"It's . . . excessive liquidity. Interest rates here are effectively at less than one percent. That's down from three percent a year ago, and five percent two years ago. Most times, when you see that kind of drop in interest rates, it means an economic slowdown of some sort, but all the indices are up, everything, especially the price indices. Classically, that means an influx of capital . . . but so far as we can determine, there's been no increase in the personal savings rate. There's been no increase in reported multilateral profits. There's been no reduction in taxes, and we can't track any kind of other windfall—except total deposits in financial institutions."

"That means a transfer of credits from somewhere outside the system, a fairly large flow of funds," Van speculated, "if it's had that kind of impact on the system economies. Do you know the source?"

"Not officially," Myller replied.

"Unofficially?"

"Almost all the fund transfers have come in through Argenti and Hyndji institutions, although some have immediately been transferred to Korvelian institutions."

"No Revenant or Coalition institutions?"

"No significant change from previous years," replied Myller.

"Do you have any idea where those transfers are coming from?"

"We can't link them absolutely, but according to immigration figures, there's been a significant increase in immigrants from Denaria, Kylera, Islyn, Drakka, and Constantia. The absolute numbers aren't that large, of course."

Van understood that. Only the truly affluent could afford interstellar transport, when personal passage for a single individual generally ran the equivalent of the average worker's annual income—and that didn't include the inbound bond that most systems required for immigrants. "And what would you do if you were one of those affluent immigrants?"

"I'd use those credits to buy whatever I thought would be a producing asset. If you buy annuities or pure financial instruments, the returns will be down. Probably, I'd go for those with a higher ROI."

Van nodded. "You don't really need me here for that. You know what to do."

"In economic and investment strategy, that's probably true. But Korvel's never seen this kind of credit inflow."

"It will probably create social changes," Van hazarded. "I'd guess that local crime will increase, in some areas, anyway. Borderline businesses will stay afloat longer than they would otherwise. Government social programs will be increased for as long as five years, and then tax revenues will drop off. There will be political unrest when that happens. I couldn't say that for sure, but I'd look at the formulator sectors that would be most affected in one way or another . . ."

Van and Myller talked for another hour, before spending the rest of the afternoon laying out a more detailed strategy outline and a series of progress reports that Myller would send to IIS Cambria.

When Van left Korvel on the magshuttle back up to orbit control, he just hoped he'd caught everything and that he'd pointed Myller and the Korvelian IIS office in the right direction. He also needed to check out the systems that had been the source of the immigrants and, presumably, the flow of funds. Since he had planned to go to Islyn in any case, he'd also look to see what might be causing a fund outflow. He had the feeling that either he'd have trouble pinpointing the problem or that it would be so obvious that he'd almost wish he hadn't found out.

Chapter 52

Van checked the coordinates with the Islyn system comparator once he had the *Joyau* headed in-system. He had improved considerably at getting the ship closer to the edge of destination systems. That was a technique that hadn't mattered as much with a warship, but did much more with the *Joyau*, since jump exits closer to the system reduced both costs and transit times.

Inbound, he sat in the command seat and called up the records on the IIS office on Islyn. Principal clients were AdVer, the local and second-line creative advertising multi; MT, a microtronics formulator; and Xcil, the energy generation and distribution system on the second most populous continent. The local office also had developed a good dozen smaller clients. There was nothing to suggest trouble in the IIS client and operating files. That didn't mean trouble hadn't developed, only that it hadn't been visible before.

Van had an idea that the problem was Revenant-based. After he'd finished with Sherren Myller and returned to the *Joyau*, he'd checked over the systems she had mentioned. Like Islyn, Denaria, Kyleria, and Constantia were all systems reachable by relatively short direct jumps from either Colsiti or Riks—both Revenant systems. But until he got to Islyn, that was just speculation.

Next came the files on Islyn, files far better than the RSF data files. Trystin either knew, or had ways of finding out,

matters that the RSF didn't suspect. Or that they didn't want
their commanders to know, which was also likely.

Islyn system, single inhabited planet [Sandurst]. Tellurian
type. 1.03 gee. Stand-atmos. pressure at SL, 1.2 T; O_2 content
.18; four continents . . .

Space defense system is rudimentary . . . three corvettes
[equiv. Coalition *Moore* class] and four in-system
patrollers . . . one orbit control station and one out-system
base . . .

Political system—unified multiparty proportional representation in a unicameral assembly [Quorum] without staggered
terms . . .

Cultural—polyglot agglutination, no strong religious or political dominance in colonization and early development, planet
originally discovered and used as Tellurian-style base for
long-line observations of Nebula 6AXV-2001, neutron
star/black hole interactions, space-time dimensional twists . . .
later colonization by Prime-One group . . . colonizer failed . . .
Hyndji emergency support, in return for colonization by Dzin
dissidents . . .

Although Van wasn't the political expert Trystin was,
Van could already see the structural problems with the Islyn
system.

. . . domestic unrest resulted in Wars of Assimilation
[1040–1093 S.E.] . . . final political restructuring under
Rehmad Dersai and Islyn First [IF] party. Principal opposition
Social Equality [SE] party. IF has maintained an open trade
and tech-transfer policy, resulting in competing efforts by the
Hyndji Commonality, the Revenants, and the Argentis . . . IF
has recently exhibited a stronger preference for Revenant-
compatible technology and systems in government procurement . . .

Van continued to study the information on Islyn, periodically checking the net, the EDIs, and the far-screen monitors—which showed no ships except for the Islyn defense forces and two commercial vessels in stand-down off Sandurst, presumably locked in at orbit control.

When he could study no more, he left Eri in the cockpit, set the alarms, and tried to take a nap. He was restless, and somehow, before long, he was back in the cockpit, but not the same cockpit.

Van glanced toward the older commander as Baile reached forward, his index finger poised over the large red jump button.

"Don't!" Van exclaimed.

"It's perfectly normal." For a moment Baile's face was that of a far younger officer—fair, blond, and oh-so-infallible.

Van opened his mouth to explain that the jump wasn't normal. Instead, Baile looked away and depressed the jump button.

"No!" Van exclaimed—too late.

Black became white, and white black—and then brilliant red, pain red, swirled through the cockpit, sheer agonizing pain.

Van jolted upright in his bunk. Sweat poured down his face, and his heart was pounding.

After a moment, he wiped his forehead.

Once more, it had seemed so real. Then, the nightmares about the *Regneri* and the *Fergus* always seemed real. After three years, he still harbored guilt—the repetition of the same nightmare indicated as much. But why?

He blotted his forehead again and checked the time. Then he took a long deep breath and swung his feet over the side of the wide bunk—too wide for just one person, but no one except him had ever slept there. Slowly, he rose and walked toward the fresher and the shower he always needed after the nightmares.

When he returned to the cockpit, the *Joyau* was still more than an hour out from Sandurst. Once settled back into the command couch, he checked the EDI and the system plot, but there were no new ships around Islyn—not unless they had totally shut down all energy sources. Then he went over the summary reports about the IIS office once more. There wasn't anything to indicate why a successful PD would want a successor. Van hoped it was for personal reasons, but he had his doubts. Those would have to wait until after he contacted Rezi.

He squared himself in the command couch, not that he had to, but old habits died hard. *Sandurst Orbit Control, Coalition Ship Joyau, requesting approach clearance.*

Ship Joyau, please beam ID. Interrogative purpose.

Van didn't like that at all. The orbit controller sounded exceedingly military. He glanced across the cockpit. "Eri . . . full harness."

"Yes, sir."

"Don't know, but . . ." Van pulsed the standard Coalition ID, waited a moment, and replied, *Orbit control, Coalition ship Joyau, purpose of visit is foundation business. Joyau is registered IIS ship. Visiting IIS office.*

Ship Joyau, wait one, under advisement. Continue approach this time.

Van studied the EDI detectors, but could see no energy buildups, and no ships besides those already plotted, and only one patroller standing off orbit control.

Cleared to lock charlie two. Request Galstan payment authorization.

Understand cleared to charlie two. Authorization follows.

Van had to wonder if ships had refused to pay or if Islyn was desperate for Arm credits.

The *Joyau* was almost opposite lock charlie two when control replied, *Authorization accepted. Welcome to orbit control, ship Joyau.*

Thank you, control. Commencing docking this time.

Once the *Joyau* was linked in to orbit control, using station power, Van put the fusactors on standby—but not complete stand-down.

After checking the orbit station, and the unnatural levels of energy concentrations opposite the three commercial locks, Van also left the ship's secondary shields in place.

Eri looked from the second couch. "You look concerned, Commander."

"They're a bit touchy. I think we'll stay aboard until I make contact with Rezi."

Van used the shipnet to access the planetary commnet—and the local office.

The image he got was that of a simmie receptionist. "This is IIS, Kahla. We're not immediately available. Please leave a message."

Van checked the codes, then bypassed the regular messages to link directly to the PD's net. *Director Rezi, this is IIS Senior Director Van Albert. I'd appreciate your getting back to me as soon as possible . . .* Van left the routing codes.

Then he turned to Eri. "We'll fix something to eat, and then I'm going to take a nap until he returns the call. You probably should, too."

Van didn't get the sleep.

As he was finishing what was dinner, a formulated stir-fry that Eri had programmed into the galley equipment, the net alerted him.

Incoming from Camryn Rezi.

Accept, project.

The image that appeared in the space over the mess table was that of a man with skin midway between Van's and that of a typical Revenant, with hair so black it held a shade of blue, and deep brown eyes. He was neither young nor old and wore a light gray singlesuit.

"Director Albert. I'm so glad you're here. I had hoped, but not expected, such a prompt response."

"We're on orbit station, Director Rezi. We just arrived a short time ago." Van didn't offer to meet Rezi. He wanted to see the man's response.

"I know you're on a tight schedule. It might be best if I took a shuttle up there. I should be able to make the next one, and that would put me up there in a little over four hours. Would that be satisfactory?"

"That would be satisfactory," Van replied. "I look forward to seeing you, and I trust you will have a listing of the possible candidates and their backgrounds."

"I certainly will. I'd best hurry."

The screen blanked.

Van leaned back slightly on the mess table bench.

"He does not want you to go planetside," Eri observed. "Do you think that he fears what you will find at the office?"

"He's bright, according to Trystin's notes. If there were something wrong with the office, he wouldn't have asked for us to come." Van shook his head. "I should have thought of this earlier. Can you arrange for us to get topped off before he gets here?"

"If the connections are standard, I can have it done in fifteen minutes."

"They should be Hyndji." He paused. "You'd better wear a full-nanite shield. They've got something focused on the outer lock. If you keep the station lock closed, you ought to be fine."

"I had already thought the personal shield might be wise," replied the older tech. "You think the whole system is leaning Revenant?"

"It's leaning somewhere, if it hasn't already gone." Van frowned. "I can't say I understand. The cultural background doesn't look like it's slanted right for the Revenants, but I can't believe that it's Hyndji. They don't operate that way. I'll link into the station's newsdata while I'm waiting."

"I will make certain that our mass tanks are full." Eri stood and left the mess.

Van retreated to his stateroom and began with the current Islyn political news, scanning through the more recent headlines.

Earthquake Rocks Ghaiphar . . .
Court Bans MaidenAct Concert . . .

Van swept into the details, more curious than anything.

... West Continent Appeal Judiciary rejected the appeal of MaidenAct, dismissing the claim of the singing group that the Public Decency Act applies only to apparel in performance and not to speech, so long as that speech is not blasphemous ...

He was getting the impression that it was going to take all the time he had and more to get a feel for Islyn, as well as the feeling that he wasn't going to like what he found. But he went back to his scanning.

SE Whip Dies in Groundcar Malfunction ...
Thousands Flee Cairen Volcano ...
Guard Mobilized for Cairen ...
Christos Revivos vies with Revealed ...

Van called up that one, but it was a short article noting that among deists the two fastest growing religions were the Community of the Revealed and Christos Revivos. Van stiffened at the last line: "... overall, the percentage of deists on Islyn has increased from 29% to 55% over the past five years, with only a moderate slowing in growth ..."

Why, suddenly, was there an increase in old-style religion? The uncertainty of the times? Its simplistic appeal? Van couldn't say he knew. Finally, he went back to scanning headlines.

Miniature Steeds Woo Crowds ...
Sermons Exempt from Anti-Hate Laws ...

That one was predictable, and depressing.

"Deep Ocean Catch Down ...
"Santorinae Nova No Threat ...

Van went through almost a hundred headlines before another one caught his eye.

"IF Praises Equalization Act . . .

What was the equalization act? Van kept searching until he came to a paragraph that made some sense.

> . . . rationale for the Economic Equalization Act. Out-system multilaterals have come to control all the major avenues of commerce on Sandurst, skimming off profits and weakening Islyn. By requiring local divestiture, the Quorum has returned control of our economic destiny to our own people . . .

But what was local divestiture? He was afraid he had a good idea, and keyed in a search on the Equalization Act. There were twenty stories about the act—and not a single one said more than what he'd already found. The IF supported it, and the SE opposed it, and there was a great debate on what the effect would be, whether it would isolate Islyn or whether it would revitalize the planetary economy, but there wasn't a single story that explained the terms of the act.

Feeling short on time, Van abandoned the Equalization Act and pressed on through the headlines and associated stories. Normally, he would have gone to the local IIS office, where he would have received a meaningful synopsis and analyses, but the Islyn office had been open less than ten years. The last report was over a year old—and that indicated none of the problems that were appearing in the more recent media reports.

"Commander?" Eri appeared in the stateroom doorway.

Van checked the time. Had three hours already passed? "Is Director Rezi here?"

"He is at the lock. He keeps looking over his shoulder."

Van pulsed the lock open even before he left the stateroom.

Rezi was still looking at the lock when Van stood there on the ship side.

"Director Rezi . . . I'm sorry. I was tied up in some research, and the time got away from me. Do come aboard."

Rezi looked at Van, as if comparing his presence to a mental image, then smiled. "I am certain you are busy, and I appreciate your making time for me."

"That's what we're here for." Van stepped back and let Rezi board the *Joyau*, immediately closing the ship lock behind the Islyn. "We'll have to use my stateroom. We don't have a conference room *per se*."

Rezi glanced toward the cockpit, then toward Eri, who had donned a holstered stunner, Van noted. "You are like . . . Director Desoll? Your own pilot?"

"That's correct. All senior directors are." Van motioned for Rezi to enter the stateroom.

"You were a Coalition officer?"

"No. I was a Taran RSF commodore. Please sit down." Van took the console chair, facing Rezi in the anchored easy chair.

"I assume your ship is screened, Director Van?"

"Very tightly. Are things that bad?"

"Not yet, but they will be."

"Why? How?"

"I apologize, Director Van. I do apologize." Rezi produced two datacards from the narrow pack at his belt, half-standing to lean forward and set them on the flat space beside the console. "The first card has the authorizations and the transaction codes. I've transferred all IIS assets and arranged for all retainers, so long as possible, to be paid to and routed through the Bank of Raipur. That's because the IF is about to push through a freeze on all funds transfers out of Islyn through Coalition or Argenti institutions. They already prohibited transfers from institutions associated with nonmajor systems—"

"Only Hyndji and Revenant institutions will be able to make those transfers?"

"That is correct."

Van nodded. "And what about candidates for your position? That was a blind?"

"Exactly. Under the Economic Equalization Act, the majority interests of all out-system enterprises will have to be sold to Islynan citizens by the end of the calendar year. The local employees or directors automatically assume control of such entities unless other arrangements are made by that time. I arranged to purchase fifty-five percent of the local IIS office, rather than assuming control, because that way I can transfer funds for that purchase, and I can still rebate a proportionate share of earnings after expenses. The IF will not allow that to continue for too long, a year, two at the most." Rezi shrugged. "I am only returning what is yours, and I will send the retainers and royalties as I can for as long as I can. That is the best that I can do. You will be able to verify that."

"Who's behind this? Really?" Van snapped out the question, hoping to catch Rezi off-guard enough to get a subvocalized response.

Revenants "The IF Party. They have spent five years working to pass the Equalization Act. I believe they are receiving funds and technical support from several Revenant multilaterals. You know AdVer; it has been an IIS client. They have served notice that they are severing the agreement with IIS because they have been purchased, and the new ownership feels that such an arrangement will no longer be beneficial."

"The new ownership?"

"KLS. It is a Revenant multilateral headquartered in Braha."

"What about MT?"

"Nothing so far. We are still providing services."

"Xcil?"

Rezi shrugged.

Van nodded slowly. "The other datacard?"

"It contains information that may be of use to IIS."

Van continued to press Rezi for almost two hours, but the man continued to impress him as generally honest. It would have been far easier for Rezi simply to wait and take all of the IIS local assets and future retainers—assuming the Equalization Act did in fact allow that.

In the end, he just thanked Rezi and saw him out the ship lock.

Then he made sure the *Joyau* was ready for emergency delocking before he began a second search, this one heading straight for the public law sections of the Quorum's public access section. Public Law 24-21 contained all the provisions Rezi had cited. It also contained a provision stating that out-system ownership by entities with legal status in either the Rev or Hyndji systems would not be covered by PL 24-21 until two years after the initial effective date of the law.

Another hour later, Van walked out of his stateroom.

Eri was in the mess. "Now?"

"Let's hope they'll let us depart peacefully. But we'll strap in in case they don't."

Van did so, then brought both fusactors on line, throwing more power to the ship's secondary shields—the ones that ran under the thin outer ablative layer of the hull. He dropped the ship grav to nil and unlinked from station power.

*Sandurst Orbit Control, this is Coalition ship **Joyau**. Preparing for departure. Request departure clearance this time.*

***Joyau**, control, wait one.*

Van prepared to use full power on the thrusters if the station didn't depower the lock magholds and dampers.

***Joyau**. Reduce ship grav to nil and report.*

Ship grav at nil.

Depowering dampers. You are cleared for separation and low-power departure this time.

Van did not leave the cockpit until they were a good two hours outbound from Islyn.

Then, he went back to his stateroom to check over the cards Rezi had left. Van did not insert the cards he had received from Rezi into the ship system, nor into the separate IIS system in his stateroom, but into a third reader. The third reader was isolated physically and electronically from all other systems in order to determine data compatibility and to ensure that any datacard read contained no VDAs or the equivalent.

Van transferred the data on the first card to another card, running all the information through an assembly-disassembly and vetting process that separated the data from the structure beneath it before making the transfer. He did the same for the second and third cards.

The first card seemed to be exactly what Rezi had claimed. The second card contained information on every major business and multilateral on Islyn, including the share of out-system ownership and the name and home system of the owner. Even with a brief survey, Van could see that most of the key formulation, energy distribution, and communications multis had significant Revenant ownership.

For a time, he just looked blankly at the bookshelves.

Then he returned to the cockpit and began to set up the jump coordinates for Beldora.

Chapter 53

At the edge of the Islyn system, Van checked everything—accumulators, fusactors, and all the internal systems one last time, and then the jump coordinates for Beldora once more. Recalling his last nightmare, he ran a separate diagnostic on the jump generators before looking across the cockpit to the second seat where Eri sat. "Make sure you're fully strapped in for high gee."

"You sound more and more like Commander Desoll," she observed, tightening her harness.

Did years of jumping into unfamiliar or semifamiliar systems do that? Van squared himself in the command couch and actuated the jump generator—implant/net driven on the *Joyau*, rather than manual as on an RSF ship. The cockpit turned inside out, black becoming white, white black, and grays and colors some inverted shades that were not colors at all for the endless instant that was a jumpshift.

Once back in normspace, even before checking the comparator inputs and coordinates, Van was checking the monitors, scanning all the EDIs as they registered—one frigate, and two corvettes, all with Revenant drive signatures. There were no other interstellar ships, but Van could make out fusactor drive in-system ships, ships that looked like mining tugs, but the tugs were well in-system, well inside the belt, and well away from normal system mining areas.

Why would so many mining tugs be that far in-system?

Van's guts tightened. He could only think of one reason—using the tugs to gather system debris to bombard Beldora itself. Dealing with the tugs would have to wait because one of the corvettes was less than a thousand emkay away, turning from a parallel course toward the *Joyau*.

He glanced across the cockpit. "Eri . . . Rev ships all over the place. Prepare for high gee."

"Yes, ser." A faint smile crossed her face.

Van turned the *Joyau* toward the corvette, keeping his screens at standard, but accelerating toward the Revenant and widening the photon nets to full intake.

Five minutes passed, the two ships moving inexorably toward each other, before the corvette fired a single torp at the *Joyau*.

Van continued to accelerate toward the smaller Revenant ship, shifting power to the shields only as the torp neared the *Joyau*. The shields didn't flicker with the explosion, and there was no strain on the accumulators as they picked up the mass and energy caught by the nets and funneled to them. At less than a quarter emkay the Revenant loosed two more torps, and shifted course slightly, off a head-to-head course.

Van turned the *Joyau* back onto a collision course.

The corvette swept into a tight turn away from the *Joyau*, angling on a cross-orbital course in-system, but more directly toward the Revenant frigate.

Both torps flared harmlessly against the *Joyau*'s shields.

Van eased the *Joyau* directly onto a stern chase, diverting more power into the drives and cutting out the *Joyau*'s artificial gravs, but the acceleration was only two gees, since that

was enough to overtake the corvette long before the other
Revenant ships could reach them. While the *Joyau* could hold
her own against any single Revenant ship currently in the
Beldora system, Van certainly didn't want to take on two at
once.

Yet another set of torps flared from the Revenant as the
Joyau continued to cut the distance between the two ships.

Van could see the acceleration from both the frigate and
the other corvette as they began to move toward the *Joyau*
and the corvette, but it would take hours for either to reach
them.

The corvette fired another set of torps.

The first set of torps detonated on the shields, as did the
second set, several minutes later.

By then Van was almost on top of the Revenant corvette,
and he was carrying more than a little mass in the photon
nets. He began to condense the photon nets, concentrating
the mass as much as he could, then contracted them, before
squeezing and accelerating the mass into the corvette's
screens—he followed with a single torp.

Under the mass/velocity impact, the corvette's screens
oscillated between amber and red, then flashed red and collapsed. The single torp was enough to turn the corvette into
dust.

Van rebuilt the photon nets to collect as much energy and
as mass as possible, and watched as the accumulators fed the
mass to the fusactors. Then he studied the system, checking
the plot, particularly of the cometary belt and the outer gas
giants.

After a time, he adjusted the ship's course, so that the
Joyau angled both in-system and above the ecliptic. Again,
he checked the positions of the mining tugs, but they were
not that much closer to Beldora. That was both good and
bad—good because he might have time, and bad because the
slowness of their approach meant they were pushing all too
many tonnes of mass.

Finally, he turned to Eri. "We'll have about an hour before
we meet the next Revenant."

"How many are there?"

"Two more. A frigate and a corvette. They'll probably try to coordinate an attack on us." Van loosened his harness, then released it and stood. As usual, the back of his shipsuit was damp.

"Would you like some café, Commander? And something to eat?" Eri also unstrapped and stood, stretching.

"Yes, please." He almost felt guilty. Almost.

The curried fish that Eri created with the compact formulator in the galley was tasty. That might have also been because he was hungrier than usual.

"We're likely to see more combat-type situations in the next year," Van said quietly. "Do you still want to stay on as tech?"

"Why would I not?"

"It's going to get more dangerous."

"Life is dangerous." Eri sipped from her mug of green tea. "You do not move away from danger. Should I?"

Van laughed. "I had to ask. You told me how you became a tech for Commander Desoll, but never why."

"I had been a Coalition tech before I had children. They grew up. My husband wanted me to raise him as well after they left the house. I did not want another child. So I left." She shrugged. "IIS is better than the Service. You and Commander Desoll use your tools to make the Arm a better place. The Service only worked to make it a safer place for those who were Eco-Techs." The impish grin appeared. "And I make far more credits than anywhere else."

Van wondered what Eri did with the credits. He'd certainly never seen her spend much.

He concentrated on the shipnet. The Revenants were less than a half hour away. "We'd better button up. I need to get back forward. Thank you. I was hungry."

"You're welcome." She motioned for him to go forward. "Don't be too long."

"With you or Commander Desoll at the conn, that would not be wise."

"I hope you're not saying that we're hard on techs."

"You're both hard on the unprepared."

Van was afraid he understood. Even before he was fully strapped into the command couch, he was checking and calculating. The Revenant corvette and frigate had closed up, almost to the point where their shields overlapped. That alone told Van that their strategy was very basic—get close enough to fire enough torps to overload the *Joyau*'s shields.

While the *Joyau* could take the impact of three or four torps close to simultaneously, the frigate might be able to get off as many as four at once, and the corvette two. Van had no thought of allowing that to happen. He studied the system's cosmography and density plot, then made a few more calculations, easing the *Joyau* ten degrees to starboard, still on close to a head-to-head intercept, but knowing that the Revenants would adjust their course.

He smiled as they did.

Eri slipped into the second seat and fastened her harness.

Van edged the *Joyau* another ten degrees starboard, watching the Revenant ships as they readjusted their course accordingly. The frigate was to the left of the corvette. That was why Van was edging the *Joyau* to starboard. Ten minutes passed in silence.

Unidentified Coalition vessel, you are intruding. Drop your shields immediately or be destroyed.

"I think not," Van murmured under his breath. "I think not."

He cut all power to the drives momentarily, used the steering thrusters to turn the *Joyau* ninety degrees to her course line, then pushed full power to the drives once more, watching as the separation between the Revenants and the *Joyau* widened. With both the recognition and response lag, Van opened up enough distance that the *Joyau* was beyond practical torp range. The Revenant frigate had responded first, not surprisingly, since the frigates were a newer class and probably had better monitors and EDIs than the corvette, which was something Van had factored into his plans.

The back sensors from the photon nets flashed amber, signifying greater density ahead, and isolated chunks of mass.

Van had to back off the power, recalculating the distance to the areas of increased dust and ice density and the Revenant frigate.

He found another corridor and angled the *Joyau* along it.

The Revenant abruptly slowed, then altered course to follow the *Joyau*.

While most of the cosmic debris was dust-size or perhaps pebble-size, Van knew that there would be an ice fragment somewhere, large enough for his purposes. The question was not whether there was one there, but whether he could find one soon in the hundred-klick diameter of the photon screens at full extension. If he didn't, he'd have to go to his alternate tactics.

Because Van was having to feel his way through the dust and debris, the frigate was gaining, and would be back in torp range within minutes. He eased more power to the drives, trying to stretch the time before he'd have to go into combat mode, whether he wanted to or not.

Another series of warnings flashed amber from the monitors. Van grinned as he located the debris and one chunk of ice. He shifted the nets, reinforcing the area around the irregular mass of dust and ice, while easing the *Joyau* around his catch, then using the photon nets to hold the chunk of ice just before the *Joyau*. The Revenant's EDI detectors would not register a nonradiating mass, and even closer in, laser imaging would not show something the size of a groundcar as separate from the *Joyau* itself.

Van turned the *Joyau* head-to-head with the frigate. With the added mass of the ice, his acceleration wasn't what it would have been, but the closure rate was great enough in any case.

As the Revenant frigate had slowed, the corvette had crept forward so that the pair were again overlapping screens.

Van continued to accelerate.

The moment he was within torp range, he fired the first of his torps head-on at the frigate. After a moment, he fired a second.

The frigate responded with a pair of torps, followed by two from the corvette.

Van waited, watching, calculating. Then he cut all power to everything except shields. "Desensitizing."

He could sense the wash of energy, and the *Joyau*'s shield indicators flickered, but stayed in the green.

Immediately, Van unshuttered and checked the monitors.

Four more torps were headed toward them, and they still weren't close enough for what he needed. He watched as the two ships launched another set of four.

"Desensitizing."

He kept the *Joyau* shuttered through two sheets of energy from the torps, and this time the secondary shield generator dropped into the amber and stayed there. He couldn't afford to wait any longer. He pulsed the nets, then reversed the drives for a good minute to decelerate, the joint effect launching the ice comet fragment toward the shields of the frigate. Then he began launching his own torps, two at a time, until he had six running toward the two Rev ships. He hoped that the generally nonreflecting ice mass would not show on the Revenants' monitors until just before it impacted their shields. It shouldn't, but . . .

In the meantime, four torps flashed toward the *Joyau*.

Van desensitized the ship, boosted all the power he could into the shields, sent out another round of torps, and waited.

When he unshuttered, he had only one shield generator— but there were expanding rings of debris and energy where the two Revenant ships had been.

He took a deep breath, then turned to Eri. "Time for you to go to work. Number two shield generator's gone." He returned ship gravity to one gee.

"What did you do?" she asked.

"Used the photon nets to scoop up some ice cometary fragments. Then we went head-to-head with the frigate, and I used the nets to throw all the fragments at him—and I added six torps as well, fired as quickly as possible. They'd overlapped screens. So when the frigate had to contract his screens to deal with the ice and torps, I sent a double volley at the corvette. Screens couldn't take that, and just before they went to amber, I fired more torps at the Rev."

"Before they went to amber?"

"There's a moment of instability when shields are overlapped if one fails. I was trying to take advantage of that. It worked." This time, anyway, he added to himself.

"At the cost of one shield generator. If you had to fix it . . . you wouldn't be so cavalier about it." The impish smile negated the words.

"I wouldn't know where to start."

"How much time do I have?" Eri unstrapped.

Van checked the monitors once more, but there were still no other Revenant ships in the system. In fact, there were no other interstellar ships in the system—unless the Beldorans had one in total standby and shut down. "Until someone else comes out of jump. That could be ten minutes or ten days."

"When I tell you, you'll have to depower the entire shield section."

"Let me know," Van replied. He concentrated on watching and studying the plots and EDI indicators. The mining tugs continued their deliberate progress toward Beldora itself.

All told, Eri spent almost two hours aft and below before she returned.

Van looked at her. "Yes . . . no?"

"Yes. In a way. You really stressed the shields. The main shield generator won't last fifteen minutes under attack. The secondary will manage five—if we're lucky."

"Then we'll have to be prepared to run and jump. But we need to finish up here."

"Finish up? There are other ships?"

"No. Not armed interstellar ships. Mining tugs. The Revs are into destruction on the cheap. Take an isolated system, wipe out its small defense force, then drop rocks from beyond orbit on the most inhabited areas. When the steam and dust have settled, the planet's ready for Rev recolonization. No unnatural radiation. No survivors who could claim it was much besides a strike by a fragmented asteroid."

Eri winced.

"We've got some torps left, enough to take out the tugs." She nodded.

Van turned the *Joyau* in-system.

Hours later, the *Joyau* swept down toward the first mining tug. Van captured a few images, verifying that the captured tug was using its shields and screens to herd debris inward toward the single inhabited planet—Beldora. Then he fired a single torp.

Four hours, and eight torps, later, the *Joyau* was outbound on a supraecliptic course. There were no operating mining tugs, not that Van could determine, and still no other Revenant ships. That was just as well.

Van studied the empty screens. He'd stopped the invasion—for the moment, but he couldn't exactly patrol the system. He'd cost the Revs three ships, and that wasn't bad, but he had the feeling that whatever they sent back to Beldora would be more than the *Joyau* could handle.

Incoming standing wave message.

Accept.

Unknown warship. The people of Beldora thank you. We would appreciate it if you would please convey the attached to the nearest Hyndji embassy or consulate.

Van frowned. Why couldn't the Beldorans send such a message themselves? He called up the system coordinates and checked the notes.

Both Beldora and Islyn were in blank zones—areas where, because of transdimensional tensions, standing wave could not be sent or received over interstellar distances.

After a moment, he checked the attachment. It was encrypted, as he had expected, but there were standing wave address coordinates.

He replied. *Will forward attachment.*

Our thanks.

Van had the feeling that he'd just involved the Coalition in brinksmanship with the Revenant Community of the Revealed, but it would come out sooner or later that a warship with Coalition signature drives had wiped out a small Revenant force in Beldora system. He hoped it was later.

As he turned the *Joyau* out-system, he began to prepare a message torp that requested a rendezvous with Trystin at one of the prearranged points—the uninhabited Hyksos system. On the way, he could also stop at Neuquen, the regional capital of the spinwardmost section of the Argenti Commonocracy. Coalition ships were still welcome there, and they might be able to pick up replacement shield generators there.

And . . . just after he reentered normspace outside Neuquen, he would forward the encrypted message, both to the Hyndji embassy there, and to Dhyli itself. He'd also keep a copy. While he couldn't decode it, it was possible that Trystin or someone in IIS could.

Chapter 54

The *Joyau* was locked into M-2, a maintenance lock of Neuquen orbit station two. Van was sitting before the console in his stateroom, going over the local news feeds, scanning through the political happenings.

Montaje Increases Out-Space Defense Budget . . .
Keltyr Executive Denies Cruiser Lost in Syrenae . . .
Director Defends Rising SocSer Costs . . .
High Court Denies Revealed Community Appeal . . .

He caught sight of Eri in the open doorway and looked up.

"The shield generators are in and hooked up. The maintenance supervisor asked three times about them," Eri said. "I told them we blew them on debris in an uncharted system, and that sort of problem was why we needed such heavy generators."

"How are they?"

"They're good generators. Too good."

"Too good?"

"They're military-issue. Designed for small cruisers. They don't call them light cruisers here."

"How do they mesh with our systems?"

"You'll have about five percent greater holding, and six percent greater power draw. That's within parameters. It might even be a better trade-off, considering what you've been doing with the shields." The last line was delivered deadpan, with but the faintest glint in the tech's eyes.

"Thank you, most honored senior technician." Van couldn't help grinning. "I will try to destroy attackers with less strain on the systems." The grin dropped. "Unless we get more torps, we won't be doing much of anything that way."

"You haven't heard anything?"

"Just a confirmation of the rendezvous. No details. I did say that we were very low on message torps. On an open wave, I didn't want to say more."

"He will understand that."

Van hoped so. "How long before we can depart?"

"At least six hours. That's if all the reprogramming takes and if the systems checks don't reveal something else."

"The way things are going, they will."

"It's possible."

Incoming from Captain-General José Marie Marti, Argenti Space Forces.

From Colonel—General Marti? Van wondered. Marti had supposedly gone off to intelligence, but that had been almost three years earlier. *Accept.*

Eri slipped away as the holo image shimmered into being in the space beside the console. The holo image was definitely that of Marti, if in a far more impressive uniform.

"Commodore Albert."

"General Marti." Van smiled, answering in Hispyn. "I'm merely a retired commodore, while you are a rising general. What can I do for you?"

"I had hoped you might visit Neuquen at some time. I just returned on the *Garcie*. It's one of our newest class dreadnoughts. You might be able to pick it up on your screens. It's too large to dock at the station . . ."

Van linked to the monitors. There was definitely a dreadnought holding station off Neuquen orbit station two. "I see. It is very impressive."

"If it would not delay you unduly, would you mind being my guest for a meal here on orbit station? There is a private dining area that is quite good—The View. I could meet you in half a standard hour."

"I would be pleased to have dinner with you." Van wasn't about to go anywhere that Marti didn't want him to go—not with a dreadnought that close and able to follow him anywhere in-system. He could devise an exit strategy that would probably work . . . but that was high risk, and the *Joyau* was not going anywhere soon. He might as well see what the general wanted.

"A half hour, then."

Van spent fifteen minutes getting cleaned up and donning his best gray shipsuit. Then he told Eri and left the *Joyau*, using his implant to seal the ship's lock behind him.

The View was halfway around Neuquen orbit station two, and down a corridor paneled in dark cherry with actual carpeting. A single attendant stood by an old-style wooden podium.

"Ser?"

"Commodore Van. I'm supposed to be meeting General Marti." Van spoke in Hispyn.

"Ah . . . he is here and expecting you. If you would . . ."

Van followed him toward a large booth against the wall on one side. The View was aptly named, with a full-screen holo view on all walls above head height, displaying the view from the orbit station, with Neuquen below. Van could even make out the bulk of the *Garcie*.

Marti stepped out of the booth and waited as Van approached the booth and its shimmering white linen cloths, silver cutlery, and deep leather seats.

"Commodore!"

"General."

The functionary slipped away.

"I took the liberty of ordering you a pale ale. I hope you do not mind," Marti offered after he reseated himself.

"That is what I would have chosen. But then, you have always been observant." After seating himself, Van took a sip of the ale. "This is good."

Marti lifted his own drink, an amber wine. "To friends and good acquaintances."

Van lifted the ale, and they both drank.

"I am so pleased that you are here," Marti said. "I had read the reports on the . . . incident at the Keltyr embassy on Scandya, and when I learned that you had been decorated and retired . . . I had feared that you might have suffered some permanent injuries."

"No. It was a long recovery, but there was no lasting damage."

"That is good."

"You're the local military commander?"

"Ah, no. I am far too young and inexperienced for that."

"The deputy commander?"

"One of two, the junior assistant commandant of the Spinward Region." Marti looked up as a waiter in a white jacket and deep green trousers appeared, proffering two menus.

Van nodded. The View was very expensive. Printed menus, liveried waiters, tables and booths spaced widely, and very subdued music, so low he hadn't noticed it at first, but just loud enough and projected in such a fashion that each table sat in its own island of privacy. Apparent privacy. Van suspected that the arrangement allowed most effective recording of what was said. He studied the menu, then waited.

"I will have the greens, the wild mushroom soup, and the broiled shrimpsters." Marti handed the menu back. "And the Puilossa with the main course."

"The greens, the mushroom soup, but I'd like the marinated pringhorn, medium."

"Thank you, seniors."

Van took another sip of the ale.

"You are the commander of a private vessel. It is a rather impressive ship, especially for one privately owned," the general observed.

"I was fortunate enough to obtain a position as commander and senior director for a Coalition foundation."

Marti tilted his head to the side. "There is quite a dossier on IIS and its managing director. Everything is always absolutely legal, done impeccably. Its clients always prosper, and they do so without large fund transfers into their accounts. In fact, they actually pay IIS for services rendered. You know . . . that is most amazing for a black operation."

Van smiled. "I'd thought they were, also, when they first approached me. In fact, I initially refused for that reason."

Marti nodded. "You would have to take that position."

Belatedly, Van recalled that an Argenti nod was almost a negative. "It's an easy position to take when it happens to be the truth."

"Yet there is a certain . . . impression . . ."

"I'm certain that the Coalition is not opposed to a foundation whose work enhances the image and commerce of Coalition multis and citizens."

"Nor one that diminishes the effectiveness of a theocracy's efforts, no doubt."

All Van could do was shrug.

Marti laughed. "You are less than fond of organizations that are not as they seem. Or religions that seek empires."

"That is a fair statement."

The salads arrived, and the waiter slipped away silently.

"Why would you then insist . . . the resources in your ship alone . . ."

"IIS has over a hundred planetary offices, with paying clients for all of them."

"And you have seen all of these offices?"

"I've been in over forty in the last two years, and I've seen transactions and clients for most of the others."

Marti fingered his chin. "You almost convince me."

"I can only tell you what I know and see."

"And this Trystin Desoll? He is a most elusive soul."

"He's very real."

"Oh . . . there is no doubt of that. Did you know that he has been the managing director for at least fifty years?"

Van looked hard at Marti. "I knew he was older, but fifty years?"

"There are rumors of a longer link, but we can find no records before that. There has been a T. Desoll who owns a dwelling in Cambria for over eighty years."

"He's probably named after one of his ancestors with the same initial. One of my fathers and I share the same initials, except he goes by his middle name, and I go by the first name."

Marti shrugged. "It is possible."

"You know a great deal about IIS." Especially for a military officer.

"One discovers that one must know something about everything." Marti smiled. "I did take the liberty of checking on your maintenance work. I suggested an upgrade on the generators you requested, and the station maintenance personnel agreed."

"I appreciate that." Van finished his salad, and it was whisked away and replaced with a delicate gold-rimmed porcelain bowl with the wild mushroom soup.

"I did wonder how you managed to strain them so badly."

"We ran into some unexpected ice and debris," Van said. "IIS does a lot of work in less charted systems." He tried the soup, tangy and yet with a rich but not heavy creaminess.

"Such as?" Marti smiled broadly.

Van grinned in return. "Our last business was on Islyn."

Marti raised his eyebrows. "Do you have any business left there?"

"Forty-five percent, until they figure out a way to take that. How did you know?"

"The Commerce Committee of the Montaje requested our assessment of possible military action to protect Argenti investments there." Marti frowned. "It's too far out for us to support properly . . . but we thought about it. We did send some . . . information to . . . some others."

"Your Hyndji counterparts?"

"They are somewhat closer, and I do not believe that they would appreciate a Revenant buildup in that part of the Arm. We are limited in what we can do, no matter what others think." He smiled again. "That is another reason why I was glad to see that you have taken over IIS operations in this part of the Arm."

"A retired RSF commodore?" Van took a last spoonful of the soup.

"I would judge that as a retired black Taran RSF commodore you are probably in a far better position with IIS than you would be remaining in the Republic."

"You think that . . . the acceptance of diversity . . . within the Republic . . . ?" Van left the question open-ended on purpose.

"The Republic has pushed a great deal of resources into expanding the RSF, and that has taken a toll on the economy. Economic unrest translates into social unrest—" Marti stopped as the server appeared and removed the soups, replacing them with the main course—and a new wineglass filled with an almost colorless vintage for Marti and a fresh pale ale for Van, although he had drunk less than half of the first glass.

Neither man spoke for several minutes, and Van did enjoy the pringhorn, a taste similar to veal, but delicately smokier, with hints of scores of other flavors, perhaps because of the marinade.

"What do you know of Director Desoll?" asked Marti.

"He looks like, acts like, and admits that he was a former Coalition commander. He has kept his word scrupulously in any dealing I've observed, and that has been reinforced by observations, records, and by the statements of dozens of others."

"His honesty is unquestioned. He is also an excellent pilot, perhaps better than any living pilot in the Arm."

"That is saying a great deal," Van pointed out.

"It is." Marti frowned. "His honesty troubles me greatly—that is, the degree of his honesty. Only saints or madmen are so honest, and I cannot believe he is a saint. That is perhaps because there have been a number of unexplained disappearances of Revenant vessels, almost always when his ship has been in that quadrant." The general shrugged. "Sheer coincidence, I must say."

"What else could one say?" Van agreed. "But he certainly doesn't act like a madman."

"Such ones do not." Marti paused. "There is another problem. The Coalition retirement records go back over a century—those that are open to the public. There is no record of a Trystin Desoll. Yet he is clearly a military pilot. One cannot mistake it."

Van could see where Marti was going. "So . . . if he is telling the truth, he wasn't a Coalition pilot, or he was a pilot more than a hundred years ago? Or he's not telling the truth?"

"I fear he is telling the truth."

"You think he's one of the handful of immortals?" Van had always thought that tales of such individuals were rumors, or wild speculation.

"Who knows?" Marti shrugged, then laughed. "If I said that, who would believe it? Besides, you must make your own judgments, and you, my friend, have very good judgment."

Van wasn't so sure of that.

"You must try the flan. There is nothing like it anywhere else."

Van did try the flan, and it was excellent. He wasn't sure it was that unique. .

Marti offered more witty sayings, good wishes, and observations about Neuquen, but nothing more about Trystin Desoll or IIS. Or the RSF.

After leaving the general outside The View, as Van walked back to the maintenance lock that held the *Joyau*, Van had the definite impression that the general had conveyed what he had intended. What Van didn't know was why. Marti had not seemed to think that Desoll posed a threat to the Argenti, and his actions seemed to convey a tacit support for IIS.

Still, Van would ask Eri to double-check the shield generators once again—and everything around them. And he had to write a report for Trystin on everything he'd observed in the various systems. He wouldn't mention what happened—just the Revenant presence and military and economic actions.

Chapter 55

The *Elsin* was waiting beyond the orbit of Dhannar—the eighth planet of the Kush system—when the *Joyau* flashed out of jump. It was a good hour later before the two locked together, and Trystin joined Van in the commander's stateroom of the *Joyau*.

Recalling Marti's speculations, Van couldn't help but study the older man closely as he seated himself in the armchair. Trystin looked perhaps ten years older than Van, certainly not forty or fifty years older, and his carriage was that of a young man.

"I'm here." Trystin smiled. "Knowing you, you wouldn't have asked for the meeting unless you were very concerned."

"I am. It started on Korvel. Sherren Myller . . . she'd requested a visit."

"I recall. I handed that off to you."

"She was worried about a unique problem, and one she didn't want to spell out in a message that anyone else could read. There was a tremendous influx of credits . . ." Van went on to detail what he had found and done in Korvel, Islyn, and Beldora systems. ". . . I wrote up what we observed, but not what we did." He extended the datacard. "It's all there."

Taking the datacard, Trystin nodded slowly, as if he had expected what Van had told him.

"You're not that surprised," Van said.

"I am, and I'm not. I'd like to hear what you think, first."

Van looked at Trystin. "I can see what's happening. It's

painfully obvious. The Revs have forsaken outright military conquest in favor of a sort of borderline military action. To begin with, they weaken a system—one way or another—then flood the local economy with credit and set up new businesses or take over old ones. They often take huge losses to gain market share. They begin an effort to undermine the local political structure. I'd guess, but I don't know, that they use their church as an example of a pillar of stability, and they probably do all sorts of good and humanitarian works . . . and appeal to people's need for simplicity in an unsettled time—even when they're creating the unsettling . . ."

"That's a fairly accurate analysis," Trystin conceded. "They've been operating that way for years."

"And you're trying to use IIS to slow or stop them?"

"IIS wasn't created as a quasi-military force to oppose the Revenants."

"Not military, but isn't opposing them a large part of what we're doing? We're trying to strengthen the local multis competing against the Rev-backed takeovers."

"IIS was designed to use economics, information, and systems expertise to strengthen local economic institutions and to guide them into patterns for long-term success." Trystin shifted his weight in the chair. "Long-term is a vital part of what we do. Human beings are still genetically programmed or patterned to look at life in economic terms. Everything we do has economic overtones, and yet most people still want to deny that. I'm oversimplifying enormously, but there are essentially two economic outlooks, again dating from our ancient roots. One is the 'big kill' view, and the other is the 'gatherer' view. The big kill literally comes from that kind of hunting outlook. You kill the biggest game animals possible, and then you use everything from that kill for as long as you can. Some ancient humans went after enormous animals—mastodons, bison—creatures that could destroy a single individual. Others were more gatherers, and later, farmers, gleaning bit by bit, planning. Of course, in some cultures, farmers again went after the big kill in terms of a massive harvest of a single profitable crop—monoculture in the extreme. What does this have to do with us—and IIS? The big kill philosophy doesn't work over time. It doesn't work socially or economically. Steady managed returns work far better, and economic organizations that can develop that kind of approach actually produce higher profits and better products over time. They also instill more personal discipline. But they almost never produce huge windfalls, and there's always someone out there who tries to convince people that the big kill is better." Trystin laughed. "It is better—for the head hunter, if you will, and for a few of those just under the head-hunter. But not for most people and most societies."

Van could understand that, but he wondered. "Where do the Revs fit into your analysis?"

"Oh . . . that's simple, if you think about organized belief systems in economic terms. The Revs are the religious equivalent of the 'big kill' approach. You believe in this one over-simplified system, do what the headhunter—the deity—and his mortal high hunters say, and you will be rewarded with the big kill—paradise in the afterlife, and for those especially privileged in the here and now. The other aspect of this approach is that it also thrives on chaos. The more disrupted things get, the more humans want security and simple answers, and the big kill offers that. No, you don't have to discipline yourself. You don't have to sort out the moral ambiguities of life, the cases where things don't fit in neat little cubes. You don't have to work hard at all the little things along the way. All you have to do is believe and follow directions, and security and paradise are yours." He snorted.

Van hadn't quite thought of it that way.

"The Revenants have always had a habit of portraying themselves as a family-oriented, God-fearing, and moral people," Trystin went on, "even while using every technique that they can get away with to expand their territory and economic power. They bow to superior force, claiming morality and ethics, and then subvert or annex as many independent systems as possible. Those efforts have gone on for years. The larger political entities—the Coalition, the Argenti Commonocracy, the Hyndji Commonality—have looked the other way most of the time, because they didn't want a repeat of economic and social costs of the Eco-Tech-Revenant War. This has encouraged the Revenants to keep expanding, especially in more recent years. IIS has done what it can to discourage that sort of thing, but we don't have the resources, even leveraging them through economic efforts, to do more than slow things down, and really only where the systems themselves need and want assistance. Some systems don't have enough integrity to resist. And there's always the danger that other systems will see the apparent short-term success of the Revenants and decide to follow that path as well. That's at least as big a danger as the Revenant expansion."

Unfortunately, what Trystin said made sense to Van, perhaps too much sense. "So the Revs are creating economic and social chaos, and you're using IIS to create order to stop them? And to offer an alternative to other systems?"

"The alternative, yes. But, as for stopping them . . ." Trystin shook his head, sadly. "It isn't working that way. We've been trying to create islands of order to give examples to people, to show them in practice that true virtue, if you will, has practical and economic rewards."

"And we're not above giving true virtue a little hand with a few torps now and then?"

"In the ancient days some marshal once remarked that virtue was on the side with the biggest battalions. Virtue doesn't have a chance among humans if it's without defenses. Most of us have great difficulty resisting the allure of the big kill. Throughout history, humans have succumbed to that— wasting billions on lotteries where but one person out of hundreds of millions could win, arming themselves abruptly for massive conflicts, then disarming as quickly and losing the peace." Trystin stood and stretched. "IIS does what it can. That's why we're a foundation and not a multi."

"You make it sound . . ."

"Almost hopeless?" An ironic smile crossed the face of the older man. "No. It's far from hopeless. Look at how many systems have adopted the steady gatherer approach. It just seems hopeless at times, I think, because you can't quantify our successes in the way you can a big kill success. They can trumpet a big kill, while the most we can do is to set up organizations and institutions that spread the ethical approach through economic and political success."

"And destroying Revenant warships isn't a big kill?" questioned Van.

"No. We don't tell anyone, and that means no bragging rights. When we can, and it isn't that often, we remove forces that would instill the big kill in more system cultures."

"I hope we're not secretly building a planet-sized dreadnought somewhere to destroy some larger aspect of that big kill," Van said dryly.

"No dreadnoughts." Trystin laughed. "They'd be a terrible waste of resources." After a pause, he added, "In the end, though, it's a matter of personal ethics. If you don't chart a course based on ethics, then you're for sale to the highest bidder—or the most insistent one. That goes for me, and it goes for you." He smiled. "I make it easy. I demand you act ethically and pay you for it. Except it doesn't really work that way. You can't demand ethical behavior from people who have to exercise initiative. You can only reward it, or punish them for its absence. That's true of cultures as well. They can be punished, except most other cultures avoid it, which is often regrettable."

"Speaking of cultures . . . can we do anything more about Beldora?" Van asked, trying to change the subject. Although he tried to act as he thought ethics required, talking about the subject disturbed him.

"You handled that well," Trystin said.

"The Revenants will be back. They may be back already. Unless that coded message brings in Hyndji ships. I made a copy for you to look at. I couldn't break the encryption."

"IIS Cambria can, but it's doubtless a plea for aid from the Hyndjis. The Coalition won't do anything. Beldora's out of the way. It might be considered a jumping-off point toward the inward edge of Hyndji territory."

"Do you think the Hyndjis will respond?"

Trystin shrugged. "I don't know. They're almost as reluc-tant as the Eco-Techs. They'd rather avoid conflict. They might look into it if Beldora would accept a protectorate or something."

"Would the Beldorans accept that kind of arrangement?"

"Given the alternatives?" Trystin looked hard at Van.

Van gave a wry smile. After a moment, he added, "We blew the secondary shield generator in Beldora, and over-strained the primary. I had them replaced at Neuquen orbit control. General Marti was there. He's now a deputy com-mander of the region. He sent us cruiser generators—unasked for."

"He knows IIS. It's easier on them to make sure we've got good equipment."

"He knows you as well. He said you were the best pilot in the Arm. And the oldest." Van grinned. "It sounds like he knows you well—or about you."

"About, I'd judge. I can't recall meeting the man, but it's no secret that Argenti intelligence has been tracking IIS for years." Trystin laughed. "Most of them would like to do more of what we've done to the Revenants, but the Montaje doesn't want a shooting war. Not one out in the open, anyway."

Van decided against pressing that issue too hard. Not yet, anyway. "So what am I supposed to do? Keep trying to expand IIS operations where we can? Close down operations and get out as much in assets as I can in places like Islyn?"

"That's what we've done for years. Do you have a better idea? We can't build a fleet, you know?"

"Not any bigger than we have now," Van countered. "I still have the feeling that the Revenants are undoing more than we're doing—more than all the rest of the Arm is doing."

"At the moment, it looks that way," Trystin admitted. "But things will change."

Van wasn't sure about that, but Trystin had been at it far longer than Van had. "Did you ever get any more information on what caused the Scandyan mess—and are they still lean-ing toward the Revs?"

"There really hasn't been anything new since you took over the *Joyau*. The credits and the clones went back to the Revenants. They denied it, and there was no real way to prove it was more than the excess of a single diplomat." The older man's tone was highly ironic.

"The excess of a single diplomat? And everyone accepts that?"

"Publicly. If they don't, they either have to start a war or admit that they'll let the Revenants take over anything that doesn't belong to major powers. That would make independent systems and lesser powers very uneasy."

"Like the Keltyr and the Republic? They already know that."

"Of course. That was one reason why they retired you."

One reason? "What were the others?"

"You have been effective, when most RSF officers were not, and you are not a holo-perfect RSF officer, and your skin is darker than they'd like. You probably were on the edge of discovering something else, or they thought you were, and, because you weren't one of those being groomed for higher office, they had to find an honorable way to get rid of you."

"Honorable? Murder is honorable?"

"Nonsense. You would have suffered a heart attack, brought on by your injuries, and you would have had a most honorable funeral and memorial service."

Van laughed, not humorously. "What was I about to discover?"

"I have no idea. You do realize, however, that you are the sole survivor of the *Fergus* and that encounter off Scandya?"

Van had realized that, but what significance did that have? Were his nightmares trying to tell him something? What?

"You won't find out unless you find a way to look into RSF headquarters, and going into the Republic could still be dangerous. Very dangerous."

"I could use the Argenti registration and the identity as Viano Alberto," Van suggested.

"You could. Think about it for a while. If you want to, you

might visit some of the outlying IIS offices in the Republic first, places like Weathe, Korkenny, Wexland."

There was something about Weathe. Van tried to recall why Weathe would mean something particular to him, but couldn't recall what that might be. "The RSF doesn't know I'm working for IIS."

"Probably not. If you use the alternate identity for the *Joyau*, and don't hit New Oisin until later, the local RSF commanders may report the visits as routine, if they bother at all."

"You could . . ."

"I couldn't. First, I don't know the culture as well as you do. Second, I'm involved in this energy transfer technology project, and I can't leave it for long right now. The timing is getting critical."

"What is this project?"

Trystin tilted his head, pursed his lips. Finally, he spoke. "I've told you about this before. I've been working on this for years. It's something I shouldn't know, because it's Farhkan, but I persuaded them to help me—blackmail in a way, because I pointed out that if I misapplied it, they might not like it. So now I have a prototype, and I'm hoping to use it— the prototype—as a lever to see if they'll help."

"What is this prototype?" Van asked.

"You might call it a new way of generating and transferring energy."

That didn't exactly answer the question.

"And you managed to get them to transfer the technology to you? The Farhkans haven't been that forthcoming very often."

"That might be because, used improperly, it could be quite dangerous. They might want to make sure I develop it correctly. I don't want to say more. I could look very foolish if it doesn't work out." Trystin smiled. "Then I could look just as bad if it does. Once it's ready to implement, I'll brief you on it."

"What—"

"How is the *Joyau* doing?" Trystin ignored Van's attempt to ask another question.

Van let it go. He tried to find out more in three different ways, and Trystin hadn't told him any more than he'd wanted to. The older man would tell Van when he was ready, and not before. "I'll need to go back to Perdya. I think I have three torps left."

"Your message hinted at that," Trystin replied. "I brought twenty as cargo. We'll have to handle them ourselves, but between the four of us . . ."

Van nodded.

"You will need to go planetside on Kush. Before I'd gotten your message, Nynca took your Winokur templates there, and they're being stored at the IIS office. Now . . . we need to transfer those torps and get you on your way to Kush."

Until Trystin's last words, it hadn't fully dawned on Van that he and Trystin and the techs were the ones who had to shift the torps from the *Elsin* to the *Joyau*. He didn't care much for what the torps represented, but then, he cared even less for what would have happened without them.

Chapter 56

The templates were waiting on Kush, and Van gave Eri the day off when they were shuttled up, then loaded from Kush orbit station. Then he took the next day himself, trying not to feel too guilty about it when he took the shuttle down to meet Emily Clifton for dinner. He reminded himself that he'd paid for the shuttle trips out of his own personal account—and that he'd taken no time off in months, but he couldn't help but worry about what might be happening in the Republic.

He reminded himself that Emily could fill him in on Republic affairs. That reminder helped with his guilt, although he knew that he shouldn't have to find a job-related reason in order to enjoy a dinner, especially with a woman he hadn't seen in years. Then, he couldn't exactly justify spending tens of millions of credits to fly the *Joyau* to Kush just for personal reasons—and he couldn't afford the credits it would take from his personal account.

Emily was waiting outside the truncated pyramid that was the Republic embassy, in the late afternoon heat that blanketed everything, a heat that left all the structures a brilliant white and blurred the horizon with haze. She was wearing a deep green outfit that somehow set off her gray eyes and blonde hair, although Van did notice the tiredness in her eyes.

She looked at him twice before she spoke. "Commander . . . I mean, Commodore."

"Van," he said gently. "Just Van." After a pause, he asked, "How far is the Markesh?"

"About half a klick, but it will be hot, even this late in the day."

"I can manage half a klick." Van noted that Emily's singlesuit, although dark in color, was a lightweight solar-cooling fabric that turned heat energy into cooling. "Shall we go?"

"That might be best. You aren't dressed for this heat."

Emily was right. Van was perspiring heavily by the time they reached the restaurant.

The Markesh was cool inside, but light, which Van appreciated. He disliked places that equated dimness with coolness. A woman led them to a corner table, discreetly screened on each side by low-spreading ferns in large marble pots.

"Would you like something to drink?" The woman looked at Van.

Van looked at Emily.

"Iced almaryn."

"A pale ale. Cold."

"Almaryn?" Van asked after the woman left them.

"A local tea. I suppose it's technically not tea, because it's not from the tea plant, but it has caffeine and tastes better."

"I'll have to remember that."

"The first time you came, you said you really hadn't undertaken all your duties. What else do you do besides pilot?" A faint grin surfaced and vanished as she added, "You must have some idea after two years."

"I'd like to have gotten back here sooner . . ." Van shrugged helplessly.

"We're all at the mercy of what we do." Emily laughed, a sound both ironic and rueful. "If I can't manage at least another few years in the diplomatic service, I won't qualify for immediate retirement. If my RSF time didn't count, I couldn't do it at all." She looked at Van. "I'm sorry. You were saying what you do."

"Besides being chief pilot of the *Joyau*, I'm also a senior director. That means a combination of charm and sales, which I need to improve on, and troubleshooting, where I need even more improvement."

"What do you do when you troubleshoot?"

"Provide advice, and hope it's correct. One office wanted me to come by. They wouldn't say why until I got there. They were seeing enormous credit influxes, totally unanticipated. The director was doing the right thing, but she worried about where it was all leading . . ."

"Which was? Or is?"

"Small multilaterals and wealthy individuals fleeing systems tipping toward the Revenants and all settling into the system where the office is." Their drinks arrived, and Van took a swallow of the ale.

"Too many credits chasing comparatively too few goods and services?"

"Exactly. We worked out a strategy, and then I left, and we both hope it works."

"I don't think it was that simple. I've gotten the feeling that little around you has ever been simple. Not from the time you were a child, although you've never said anything about that."

"I had a happy childhood."

"I didn't say you weren't happy. I said it wasn't simple. I'd also wager that it got less happy as you got older."

Van shrugged, helplessly. "You seem to know so much. Tell me more."

Emily laughed. "I will." Before she spoke again, she took a long swallow of the almaryn. "You don't like it when people are deceptive, but you can use the absolute truth just as deceptively as some people use lies."

Van offered an exaggerated wince.

"You asked me to tell you more."

"Go ahead," he replied with mock-resignation.

"Things nag at you, years later." She paused. "Cordelia said you mentioned that you still had nightmares about the *Regneri*."

"I do," Van admitted. "Not often, but they're still there." And they probably always would be, he reflected, along with those unexplained nightmares about the *Fergus*.

"You're the sort of man that can't let a puzzle or a wrong drop easily."

But hadn't he? He'd never really followed up on the attacks on him. Or the puzzles of the *Collyns* and the *Fergus*.

"That might not be true when they impact you, because you'd feel self-indulgent if you spent too much time on yourself."

Van groaned. "I think I've had enough honesty for the moment." Even if Emily were right, he should have followed up on the missing ships, even if no one else cared. He should have.

"Just for the moment?"

"Let me recover." Van noted a server hovering and glanced around.

"The green button there," Emily said.

Van touched it and was rewarded with a menu projected before him. "What's good?"

"Pretty much everything, but I've never cared for the squish."

Van raised his eyebrows.

"An experiment when they adjusted the ecology during colonization. Squish is short for a squid fish. People here find it very tasty. To me . . ." Emily grimaced.

"Slimy?"

"That's charitable."

Van wouldn't have ordered fish in any case, but he appreciated the information.

The server eased to the table.

"The golden gourd soup, and the rosemary-apple lamb," ordered Emily.

"The salad emeraud, and the lamb, also." He glanced at Emily. "Would you like anything else to drink?"

"The almaryn is fine."

Van nodded, and the server slipped away.

"I wasn't sure I'd hear from you again," she said slowly. "You didn't stay long the last time."

"I didn't have a choice then," Van pointed out. "I told you that."

"I wondered if that were just an excuse to leave."

Van wondered if she were teasing him, just a bit. "Not at all. I'd rather not leave you." He almost flushed at the inadvertent admission.

For a moment, Emily glanced down.

Van took the instant just to look at her. He liked what he saw, but he always had.

Emily raised her eyes. "And this time you're just at loose ends?" Her words were definitely teasing—with an undertone.

"This trip, I made time. I still have to catch the midnight shuttle."

"I feel flattered."

Van wished he were more glib, but he'd never been that quick with women. "You . . . let's say, you deserve to be flattered."

The woman he had thought of as so composed . . . flushed. Then she shook her head. "I can't believe . . ."

"You can't believe what?" he asked with a smile.

"You."

"What . . . I didn't mean to offend you. I hope I didn't . . ."

"No . . . no!" Abruptly, she laughed. "You didn't. Not at all. I hope you don't mind. But I have always pictured you as so calm, so collected. All your compliments at the embassy were just . . . so professional. Even your last visit . . ."

Van wished he hadn't been quite so professional. "Maybe I shouldn't have been so professional."

She reached out and touched his hand, fleetingly. "You were charming . . . at least to me. Cordelia was scared to death of you."

"I never—"

"She said that you'd pilot a ship through a sun to do the right thing, and she couldn't understand that."

Van knew he wasn't that ethical. "I hope I'm never that foolish."

"You know what I meant . . . Van."

He smiled again. "I try, but I don't think I'm *that* ethical."

"No. You're not ethical. Not at all. Let's see. You risked your life to stop the *Vetachi*. You took on three armed men without a weapon to protect a driver you scarcely knew. You threw yourself in front of eight assassins to save the premier. And I don't even know all the other things you've done."

"Those all could be called stupidity or foolhardy."

"They could," Emily replied amiably.

"Thank you for agreeing."

They both stopped as the server appeared with Emily's soup and Van's salad.

Emily immediately took several spoonfuls of the soup. "Pardon me. I didn't have much to eat today."

"You should have told me . . . I could have come earlier."

She shook her head. "I wouldn't have been able to get away earlier." After more soup, she looked at Van. "We were talking about foolhardiness and ethics, but being ethical is always being foolhardy today. It may be that way in any technological society."

"You think so?" Van gestured to the greenery. "Good salad."

"I know. I've had it before." She paused, then continued, "I can't give you reasons or even a good argument. I just have that feeling. Maybe it's because technology speeds up information and the ability to make decisions, and when people act quickly, they don't have to think too long about whether something's right."

"There are still moral people," Van pointed out.

"That's true. How about this? There's a small group of people in any society who are instinctively ethical, and another group that's instinctively unethical, but most people are in the middle. With technology, it's easier to focus on self-interest and what you can do, rather than what you should do, and that pushes all the people in the middle away from being as ethical as they might have been."

"You have a point there. A good point. I hadn't thought about that."

"Do you miss the RSF?" Emily asked.

"Why?"

"You seem happier in a way, and yet . . . wistful." She shook her head. "It's not that. Like something's missing."

Van knew what was missing, or part of what was missing, and that was the woman across the table from him. "It's a rewarding position, in most ways." He tilted his head, trying to figure out exactly how to say what he wanted, without being either obscure or forward. "Effectively, it's so highly integrated—the ship is—that it takes a crew of two."

"You and a tech?"

"Eri's very good, but she's almost old enough to be my mother." Van laughed. "I'm exaggerating. She's older, but more like an aunt, I'd guess."

"Aunt is definitely better than mother." Emily watched as the server took her empty tureen and replaced it with a platter piled with spiced lamb and surrounded by apples that looked neither stewed, nor dried, nor fried, but somehow embodying features of each of those preparations. Then the server took Van's empty salad plate and presented his lamb.

Van hadn't realized how much he'd tired of the limited, if good, food prepared by the formulators in the *Joyau* until he tasted the lamb. "Very good. Excellent."

"It is," mumbled Emily.

They ate in silence for several minutes.

"What's happening with the great and glorious Republic of Tara? There's not been much news about it where I've been."

"You haven't heard?" Emily frowned, an expression that Van disliked on her face. Some people could frown and express mild displeasure. Emily's frown always suggested extreme displeasure, even when she was not that displeased. He didn't like the idea that she might be displeased with him.

"Heard what?" Van took the smallest sip of ale.

"Marshal Eamon is the acting prime minister. There was an attack on Founder's Day . . . at the big celebration. It might even have been like what happened on Scandya. The entire cabinet was killed, including the minister of defense—"

Van repressed a shiver. Like the Scandyan incident? "Did they ever discover who was behind it?"

"They found three of the attackers, but they were killed. They were Republic citizens . . . two with strong Keltyr ties . . . and one from Sulyn."

"That bothers me. I can't imagine a Keltyr tie," Van admitted. "I can't imagine someone from Sulyn, at all, even given the way things have been going, because that's just not . . ."

"Not what?"

"Not the Sulynese way. We learned a long time ago that direct confrontation doesn't work unless you're the one with the power, and Sulyn certainly doesn't have that now." He pursed his lips. "Blaming it on Sulyn bothers me. A great deal."

"It seemed strange. I can't see what either the Keltyr or, now, the Sulynese, had to gain. Neither could the ambassador here, nor Commander McIlhenny."

"I can't either." Van wondered if the Revenants were involved and trying to pit the two smaller powers against each other. "So the RSF is running the Republic?"

"The marshal claims it's temporary." She glanced around and lowered her voice. "I've been looking into establishing residence here. I can't yet, not and claim retirement, and it's too hot, but . . ."

Van understood. "The marshal hasn't scheduled new elections?"

"Before next year, they say."

"Are any of the systems unhappy . . . protesting?"

"From what we hear, most are accepting it, reluctantly. There were some protests on Sulyn." She stopped. "I'm sorry."

"That's all right. I'd rather know."

"They were peaceful, but the RSF still sent in a peacekeeping unit, but no one was hurt. That's what we got. Some systems, the more militant ones, like Gaerloch and Coole, passed resolutions asking Marshal Eamon to run for prime minister."

"That's . . ." Van wasn't quite sure what to say.

Emily looked down, and, for a long moment, there was silence.

"You once started to say something about RSF officers," Van offered, with a smile. "A long time back. I've always wondered what it might have been."

"You remembered that?" Her voice was not quite disbelieving. "From more than three years ago?"

"What were you going to say?" Van pressed.

"Does it matter?"

"It does to me. After all, I am a retired RSF officer, even if I'm only just commander of a private foundation ship. Now. . . . about what you almost said?"

"You don't give up, do you?"

"Not about some things." Van grinned.

"Let's just say that, unlike some techs, I enjoyed working on ships and seeing new planets. My early experience with RSF officers . . . well, that wasn't as favorable as it could have been. My later experiences, especially some of my very later experiences, have been more favorable."

"You saw officers from a less than flattering position."

"The least flattering position is from below. You see the underside of things. You know that." She smiled.

Van just took in her smile, enjoying it.

For a while, he could forget that he had to leave for Korkenny the next day. It had been his choice, but he wasn't looking forward to it. Then, perhaps he could link into a Republic database and find out more about the *Fergus* and the *Collyns*. Maybe.

Chapter 57

Traditionally, one of the fundamental questions behind every considered attempt to define ethical behavior has been whether there is an absolute standard of morality or whether ethics can be defined only in terms of an individual and the culture in which that individual lives.

Both universal absolutism and cultural relativism are in themselves unethical. Not only is the application of universal absolutism impractical, but it can be unethical, because the universe is so complex that there are bound to be conflicts between such standards in actual application, unless, of course, the standards are so vague that they convey only general sentiments.

"Be kind to one another" is good general guidance, but it does not qualify as an ethical standard because the range of interpretation of the meaning of "kind" is so broad as to allow individuals incredible discretion. That does not even take into account the problems when society must deal with unethical or violent individuals.

There is indeed an ethical absolute for any situation in which an individual may find himself (or herself), but each of those absolutes exists only for that individual and that time and situation. This individual "absolutism" is *not* the same thing as cultural relativism, because cultures can be, and often have been, totally unethical and immoral, even by their own professed standards. That a practice or standard is culturally accepted does not make it ethical. There have been cultures that thought themselves moral that practiced slavery, undertook genocide, committed infanticide, and enforced unequal rights based on gender or sexual orientation.

The principal practical problems with individual moral absolutism are that, first, one cannot implement a workable societal moral code on that basis, and, second, that any individual can claim unethical behaviors to be moral in a particular situation, which, given human nature, would soon result in endless self-justification for the most unethical and immoral acts. That said, the practical problems do not invalidate absolute individual morality, only its societal application. . . .

In practice, what is necessary for a society is a secular legal structure that affirms basic ethical principles (e.g., one should not kill, or injure others; one should not steal or deceive, etc.), and that also provides a structured forum, such as courts, in which an accused has an unbiased opportunity to show that, under the circumstances, his behavior was as moral as the situation allowed. Such a societal structure works, however, as demonstrated by history, only when the majority of individuals in the society are willing to sacrifice potential self-interest for the value of justice, and such societies have seldom existed for long, because most individuals eventually place immediate personal gain above long-term societal preservation.

The faster and more widely this "gospel of greed" is adopted, the more quickly a society loses any ethical foundation—and the more rapidly it sows the seeds of its own destruction. . . .

> *Values, Ethics, and Society*
> Exton Land
> New Oisin, Tara
> 1117 S.E.

Chapter 58

Van straightened in the command couch, again checking the EDIs and the monitors, as the *Joyau* came out of jump from Winokur, after a quick delivery of the promised formulator templates. Korkenny system looked normal—no foreign warships, no extra RSF ships, just a set of corvettes, one in stand-down, and two planetary patrollers in high orbit off Korkenny itself.

Finally, after an eight-hour in-transit, during which he half dozed, he initiated contact. *Korkenny orbit control, Coalition ship Joyau, requesting approach and lock assignment.*

Coalition ship, say again.

Orbit control, this is Coalition ship Joyau, requesting approach and lock assignment. Parameters follow. Van pulsed off the mass and dimensional parameters, then waited as the *Joyau* eased toward the orbit control station.

Coalition ship Joyau, you are cleared to charlie three. Request anticipated duration of lock usage. Request Galstan guarantee this time.

Orbit control, anticipate four days, five possible, guarantee follows.

Guarantee received. Interrogative sleds for unloading.

No sleds required until departure, control. Will request later. Van wouldn't need cargo sleds at all, but he wanted to create the impression that the *Joyau* would be waiting for cargo.

In the end, he'd compromised, bringing the *Joyau* in under its Coalition registry, but using his Argenti identity, Viano Alberto. The identity was real, and any cross-check would show Viano Alberto as a resident alien in Silvium, employed by IIS as a director. If someone on Korkenny happened to be looking hard for Van Cassius Albert, they'd eventually wonder. But there was no reason to be-lieve that anyone at all except the RSF cared where Van was. He had to believe that Marshal Eamon and Sub-marshal Vickry hadn't turned the Republic into a complete police system yet, if indeed that was their intent, although Van wasn't inclined to be charitable on that point.

He eased the *Joyau* into position at charlie three, then gave the signal for the dampers to engage. *Control, Joyau locked in charlie three, depowering and linking this time.*

Cleared for station power, Joyau.

Van ran through the locking and standby checklist. Then he unfastened his harness and stood.

"Ser?" asked Eri from the second couch.

Van nodded to the tech.

"You're going to want me to watch the ship." That was a statement.

"Absolutely. I may come flying back here as well. With the political upheaval in the Republic, anything could happen. Including nothing."

"That would be best." Eri's tone indicated the improbability of that possibility.

Van laughed. "All we can do is see." He slipped back to his stateroom and used the equipment there to link into the stationnet. The next down-shuttle to Watford was in three hours, but that would have landed him at four in the morning local time. The next one was eight hours later, and he booked a slot on it. Then he began a search of local political and economic news.

There was little of either. Rather, there was a great volume of stories that revealed little.

Quake Rocks Neatbrooke . . .
PM Eamon Cites Rising Productivity . . .
Korkenny Best Republic World for Health . . .
Eamon Urges Public Service Careers for Grads . . .
Nelson Kidnapper Found . . .
Business Indicators Surge After ES Restrictions Loosened . . .

That headline caught Van's eye, but the details were sketchy, just saying, in effect, that the acting prime minister had lifted the most onerous of the economic security restrictions two weeks earlier, and that already business indicators were showing great improvement and a return to near-normal patterns. Van had to wonder, especially since none of the stories he could call up gave much more in the way of details.

After two hours of searching, nearly fruitlessly, Van stopped, fixed a meal for the two of them, and after eating and cleaning up the galley, called it a day and went to bed. He got the first uninterrupted sleep in days, sleeping so long that he had to hurry to get dressed and make the down-shuttle.

He did not reach Watford until past midday, local time, and was fortunate at that. At times, ship time ended up being not at all in synch with planetary time—or destination time. He had a reservation at the Watford Mark, in the name of Viano Alberto, because he doubted that he'd finish what he needed in one short afternoon, and he carried a small overnight case. A groundcar for hire delivered him to a modest structure in the financial area on the west side of Watford. From the buildings alone, similar but not identical, and with few frills, he would have judged that it was a commercial or financial area. IIS was on the second floor, up a curving ramp carpeted in a gold that had seen better days.

He stepped inside the office.

"Ser?" asked the older woman at the plain console.

Van handed across the IIS datacard. "Senior Director Albert to see Director Henry." He didn't like using his real identity, but it would have revealed even more not to.

The expression of skepticism vanished as she looked at the screen readout. "Yes, ser. Just a moment." She stood and walked to a closed door, which opened to admit her.

Van studied the outer office, empty except for him. A plant, a semifern, stood in the corner by the window, drooping for lack of water, and the waiting area looked untouched, but dusty.

"Director Albert?"

Van turned.

"Director Henry will see you."

Van almost bridled at that. Director Henry had better see him. He smiled. "Thank you." Then he walked through the open doorway, using his implant to pulse it shut behind him.

Morgan Henry was as tall as Van, but heavier, especially in girth, and had faded red hair and freckles that also had lightened. "I must say that I hadn't expected a visit from one of the senior directors." Henry smiled broadly. Too broadly, Van felt. "Either the senior director or the managing director. It's been several years since Director Desoll was here."

"That's true. It's one of the reasons why I was brought on board. Director Desoll felt that he couldn't cover an expanding operation as thoroughly as he would like." Van returned the smile, then took the chair across from Henry without an invitation.

As he sat there, Van used his implant to access the IIS records. The direct key had been blocked, but all IIS officenets had been designed with three additional access points, available only through implants to either Trystin or Van. While Trystin had never mentioned it, it was clear enough to Van that the older man was much more than a former pilot, and that he had probably had extensive systems design training of some sort.

"How are matters going here?" Van asked casually, even as he reached into the files on the main clients, starting with AmalGS.

"It's been difficult, ever since the Founder's Day . . . incident."

"I'd heard about that, but in what ways has it affected IIS and its clients?" Van was trying very hard to look pleasantly attentive, watch Henry, and search the files—all simultaneously.

"Rather hard to explain . . . ," Henry replied.

"I understand how complex things can get, but I'd appreciate your thoughts," Van pressed. As he did, he reached the last entries in the AmalGS file. The multi had accepted a tender offer from DIS, a Taran holding company headquartered in New Oisin. Even at a glance, Van could tell that the financial details made no sense from an economic or a profit point of view. More important, the takeover had been accomplished without advance notice at a routine annual meeting, and that was illegal under Korkenny planetary law, as well as under Republic law. Or it had been.

"They have gotten very complex, Director . . . Albert . . ."

"I can appreciate that. How are your billables? And your

retainers? They appeared somewhat down on the last semiannual report."

"They will be down more."

"Can you brief me on what is happening with AmalGS? I'd be interested in why you didn't vote against the takeover by DIS? That would certainly dilute the earnings . . . and it appears as though the retainer arrangement has been repudiated."

A faint sheen of perspiration had begun to coat Morgan Henry's forehead.

"It's not that simple. Or it is. We didn't have a choice."

"Perhaps we should meet with Managing Director Smythers, then, to discuss the matter."

Henry shook his head. "He retired last month. Gerald Addams is the new managing director."

Van nodded. "That would be satisfactory. Why don't you arrange an appointment for us tomorrow morning?"

"I can arrange it for you, ser. I fear I could not make that. My daughter . . . she's having some delicate medical procedures tomorrow."

"Oh . . . I'm sorry to hear that. What sort of procedures, if I might ask?" pressed Van, if solicitously.

"There's a brain lesion of some sort, very near the part of the cerebellum . . . very delicate."

Van had his doubts, but didn't want to walk in and call the local partner a liar in the first hour of meeting him. "I can see your concerns. If you'd like to arrange that for me . . . I'll just wait here."

"Ah . . . yes. I'll see what Maura can do."

After Henry left his office, Van concentrated on the other client files. He only had begun to study the file on Korkenny, Ltd., when Henry returned.

"Managing Director Addams will be most pleased to see you at ten o'clock, if that is convenient."

"Excellent." Van smiled. "Now . . . I'd appreciate your views on how the Founder's Day incident affected Korkenny and IIS." Van had decided not to force the client issues. Not yet. He'd read, if quickly, the files on AmalGS, and they made little sense. He had the feeling that neither would the others, not without an extensive examination, and he didn't want to use strong-arm tactics on Henry until he knew more.

Henry settled into his chair, forcing a smile. "You know what happened?"

"Only that some extremists assassinated most of the Republic ministers."

"All of them. They even destroyed the entire front of the Parliament in New Oisin. The new PM has already started reconstruction work. It may take years to restore it."

"I understand. How did this affect Korkenny and IIS?"

"Prime Minister Eamon declared martial law. Then he froze all asset transfers outside the Republic until the Intelligence bureau could identify the sources of funding for the assassins. That, of course, stopped our transfers of retainers and commissions to IIS Cambria. The freeze was lifted two weeks ago on all planets except for Sulyn, and, of course, those to the Keltyr. We anticipate being able to make those transfers in the next week or so. We have to wait for others. Because IIS is majority foreign-owned, they could only make payments for direct services provided by the local office . . ."

Van nodded. He had the feeling that the last sentence was the most truthful, and that Henry was hiding more than he was revealing. "There wasn't much news about the freeze of assets."

"No, ser. It was part of the economic security regulations. The Ministry of Economic Security sent them to all multilaterals and financial institutions. The financial institutions had the responsibility for enforcement and for educating their customers . . ."

Van had never heard of a Ministry of Economic Security. It certainly hadn't existed a year before. "Go on . . . What else?"

"We all had to certify compliance. Failure to comply was a class one felony . . ."

The more Van heard, the more uneasy he became. The next day was definitely going to be a trial.

Chapter 59

Van didn't sleep that well, even in the luxury of the Watford Mark, but at least he didn't have nightmares. That might have been because he dozed, hardly sleeping deeply enough to dream. He got up early and used the hotel's system to try to search out more on the economic regulations that Henry had cited. There were thousands of pages of them, covering every aspect of finance and commerce. The first hundred pages were actually a preamble and rationale, beginning in true pseudolegal fashion:

> Whereas the Republic of Tara and its affiliated and associated systems and possessions have been attacked in the most heinous of fashions, and whereas this attack was made possible through funding channeled through financial channels and procedures. . . .

Van shook his head. Hadn't anyone asked how restricting outbound funds had any impact on the inbound transfer of credits for such terrorist activities? Or how restricting financial flows would strengthen the economy? Or what the costs and impacts would be on Taran businesses and citizens?

He did try a search for some sort of summary, but that came up blank. Every way he worded the search referred him back to the regulations themselves. There were so many pages that he hadn't had time to assimilate even a fraction of the regulations by the time he had to eat and get ready for his meeting. Should he have asked for a later meeting? He didn't like that option, either, because the longer he stayed on Korkenny, the more likely the RSF would discover his presence. They might not, and they might not care, but Van didn't really want to risk it.

At the same time, he had to wonder why Trystin had suggested the visits. The older director never suggested anything without a purpose. Trystin clearly wanted him to discover something on his own, and Van doubted it was just that IIS was losing cash flow from the Republic. He just didn't know what it might be.

At nine-fifty, he stepped from the groundcar-hire and into the lobby of the AmalGS building on the north side of the financial district of Watford.

"Ser?" asked the receptionist at the console—flanked by an armed guard.

Van turned. "Yes?"

The receptionist stammered. "Ah . . . do you have an appointment?"

"I'm Senior Director Van Albert of IIS. I believe I have a ten o'clock appointment with Director Addams."

"One moment, ser."

Van waited.

"Ah, yes, ser. The fifth floor."

Van took the liftshaft and stepped off on the fifth floor, only to meet another receptionist. "Van Albert."

"Yes, ser. He's expecting you in the conference room. That's the open door there."

Conference room? That was definitely not good, but Van stepped into the small conference room. Two men were waiting.

"Managing Director Addams." Van inclined his head, not knowing who was Addams.

"Ah . . . yes, Director Albert. I had hoped that perhaps Director Desoll might have come." The heavyset man in a black singlesuit with narrow maroon pinstripes smiled professionally.

"He sent me. We do have a number of planetary operations."

"Yes . . . so we understand." Addams turned to the other man in the conference room, an angular figure in dark green. "Director Albert . . . I'd like you to meet the Honorable Earl Roberts, the newly appointed sub-minister of economic security for Tara."

The Honorable Earl Roberts smiled, warmly. His voice was soft, just short of sibilant, as he spoke. "A slight correction. I am the Republic sub-minister of economic security for Korkenny."

"There is a sub-minister of economic security for each Republic planet?"

"Each system."

"Why don't we sit down," suggested Addams. "Would you like tea or café?"

"No, thank you. Not at the moment." Van surveyed the two again before turning to Roberts. "There is a new Ministry of Economic Security? When was that established?"

"Shortly after Marshal Eamon became acting prime minister, after the assassination of Prime Minister O'Kane. The emergency cabinet enacted it in order to prevent financial dislocation."

"I must admit," Van said, turning back to Addams, "that I'm somewhat confused. Under Republic law, a takeover requires advance notice of at least three months to all stockholders at their main place of business. Neither DIS nor AmalGS provided such notice as required by law. IIS is a principal stockholder, and its main offices received no notice, and now a government ministry is involved in ratifying such a takeover. This seems irregular."

"Irregular times often require unconventional actions," Roberts interjected. "You certainly do not have to convince me that the Economic Security Act was unconventional, but the assassination of the government was even more unconventional. Ideally, one would like to follow the old and well-established patterns. That is not always possible in a time of crisis, and this certainly is a time of crisis."

"It would seem, only from what I have seen," Van said carefully, "that however inadvertently it may have happened, this act amounts to a repudiation of long-standing rights and principles."

"Director, you don't have to convince me," Roberts replied sympathetically. "I understand. I certainly do. Whether I understand is not the question, however. At times, actions are taken in the best of causes which later prove to have been unwise, and at other times, actions which seemed most unwise and unpopular when taken prove to be far wiser. And when something so tragic happens, someone *must* be to blame, and something must be done." Roberts shrugged. "That is most unfortunate, but it is human nature. You understand that, I'm certain."

"I'm still a bit bewildered, Sub-minister," Van replied. "IIS engineered the revitalization and strengthening of AmalGS from a continental multi on the verge of bankruptcy to an economic power. I find it hard to see how an outside takeover strengthens either AmalGS or the Republic."

"Ah, yes," Roberts said softly, almost hissing. "Here, too, we have a problem. As you know, as you must know, representing as you do, a Coalition multilateral—pardon me, a Coalition foundation, all systems in the Arm are facing a threat from Revenant expansion, and that expansion is both economic and military. As a system with a unique culture and contribution to the Arm, we cannot afford to allow ourselves to be weakened."

"I do understand that," Van replied politely, "but I fear that I may have missed something that is obvious to you, but not so apparent from studying the accounts. AmalGS is in a strong financial and economic position here on Korkenny. In fact, it is stronger than any other formulation enterprise."

"Exactly! Exactly, my dear Director. Unfortunately, due to the past unethical and government-supported subsidization of various multilaterals in New Oisin by the Revenants, DIS was in danger of collapse. So, in order to strengthen the economic structure of the Republic, the Ministry of Economic Security used its powers to effect a number of consolidations, and the terms of the consolidations, of course, will ensure that the revenue flows out of the Republic will be reduced to a more . . . reasonable level."

"Despite contractual agreements?"

"Contractual laws are set by the system governments. That is a principle that dates back to Old Earth. And while such legal . . . differences . . . have occasionally caused disagreements, at this time, it would seem unlikely that the Coalition would wish to extend itself around Revenant territory over such a trifling matter." Roberts smiled again.

Van returned the smile. "It is an interesting proposition, but you are obviously quite politically astute. I do have a question. Did anyone consider the ethics of a legal maneuver that is designed to confiscate the assets of anyone whose business is deemed so vital that it receives this kind of attention?"

"Ethics, now, Director? The first ethic is survival, and the Republic, make no mark about it, is in a conflict that will determine its survival."

"There is survival and survival."

"You sound like that old moralist—what was his name . . . Exton something or other. I had him for a professor. That was before your time, I fear. He harbored this illusion that there was an absolute morality to any situation. Of course, he couldn't ever define it, and what good was that? In the end those with the power define the ethics."

Van wasn't about to argue with Roberts. "And the Republic has defined them." He nodded and stood. "I appreciate the clarifications and explanations, and I wish you both well." He looked to Addams.

Neither man replied or spoke until they thought Van was out of hearing distance.

". . . not happy . . ."

". . . can't do anything . . . have to live with it, like everyone else . . ."

Van and IIS might indeed, but he wanted to find out more about what Morgan Henry had been up to before he left Korkenny, and he still had six hours before the shuttle to orbit control.

Although it was still before noon when Van returned to the local IIS office, it was closed, and Morgan Henry and his aide had left. Van walked in, used his passcodes for access, and reset all the security features so that only he—or Trystin— had access to the accounts and the data.

The moment he looked at Henry's office, and saw that all personal items had vanished, he knew that he had locked the doors far too late. Still, he needed to find out just what had happened. After a deep breath, he accessed the files, half-wondering why Henry hadn't just blanked them. Then he shook his head. That would have alerted IIS headquarters even sooner, and it wouldn't have done any good, because the files were automatically duplicated and stored through Cambrian Holdings. Any attempt to change that might have been successful in destroying part of the files, but it would have triggered an immediate alert.

Van got to work.

The AmalGS takeover had occurred three months earlier, but there was no record of any message or notification to the IIS main office on Perdya. Nor was there any record of any communication to either Van or Trystin.

Van began to search, going through all the IIS clients on Korkenny.

The three largest had been acquired by larger New Oisin–based multilaterals, and all in the last few months.

Then Van began to study the office accounts themselves. There was also a pattern there. Large sums had been charged to the office operating accounts, and all to a company that had not appeared on the books before nine months previous—H. Morgan Company—clearly a sham front set up by Henry. That certainly confirmed Van's initial impression of the man. The invoices were for proprietary information research.

Van kept digging. There were no deliverables from H. Morgan, and no records of anything except the invoices themselves. He tried the contact links, but those simply led to a simmie receptionist who delivered a perfunctory request to leave a message.

While there was no way that Henry could have diverted the revenues from the clients, because those were paid directly to the transfer account of Cambrian Holdings, with only a percentage coming back to the local office, in the short run, no one would have objected to invoices for research. That was the IIS business. But Henry must have known that someone would check, and that meant he hadn't expected to be around that long.

Van leaned back in Henry's chair.

What could he do? IIS had effectively lost the majority of revenue from the larger clients, except what it might receive in dividends—if any of the merged multilaterals even paid such. The way the revenue streams were being diluted, within a year, seventy percent of all revenues from IIS investments in Korkenny would vanish—legally under the new Republic law. Without IIS support and information, AmalGS would be far less profitable, but that didn't seem to matter to Sub-minister Roberts.

Van had felt like murdering Roberts, but killing one snake in the pit wouldn't solve the problem. In fact, it would probably make matters worse, because the politicians would quickly seize on such a murder as vindication of their charge that the Republic's economy was under siege.

For the moment, Van's best bet was to transfer all assets of the office to the accounts in Cambrian Holdings and arrange for the office to be closed. He doubted that even Sub-minister Roberts would take on Cambrian Holdings—not as the largest Coalition financial institution and one of the largest, if not the largest, in the Arm.

And then he needed to leave Watford and Korkenny.

Chapter 60

Van sat in the cockpit, trying to use his implant to find out what was wrong with the jump generators, but the diagnostic stated, *Jump generator is normal. No deficiencies detected.* He tried again and got the same message. *No deficiencies detected.*

"The jump system is fine," stated Baile from the command couch. His silver hair glinted, as though it were almost blond, and his face was unlined and composed as he reached for the red jump button.

Van flipped off his harness and lurched to grab the commander's hand, but he was too late.

"No!"

Pain red flared across him.

Abruptly, he sat up in his too-wide bunk, sweating.

Once more, the nightmare had seemed all too real. He sat there in the bunk, blotting the sweat off his forehead, trying to cool down and dry off.

The *Joyau* was on the outer leg of the outbound transit to the jump zone—the part above the ecliptic and well away from the inner planets of the Korkenny system—and Van was trying to get some sleep, with the system set to wake him if the monitors detected anything remotely within range.

Absently, he linked to the ship, but the *Joyau* was still three hours from the earliest possible jump point, and there were no ships in the outer part of the system, except for a handful of belt miners, and they were a quarter of the way around the system and inward.

Van blotted his forehead again.

Why was he having nightmares about the *Fergus*—and Commander Baile?

Abruptly, he stiffened, finally recalling what had eluded him before. Baile had said he was from Weathe. Was that important? His subconscious seemed to feel it was, but the more rational side of his mind couldn't say why.

He stretched out on the bunk once more in the darkness. There was something else about the dream . . . but he couldn't place that either.

After a time, he drifted back into an uneasy doze.

Chapter 61

Just before heading out into Weathe orbit station one, Van stood by the ship lock and looked at Eri. "I don't know how long I'll be gone. If you don't hear from me in two days, seal the ship and send the emergency message."

"I won't have to do that." Eri's look was somber. "Do not stay planetside too long."

"I hope I don't have to. I'm not going as me, and I'm not announcing my presence in advance." Just before leaving the Korkenny system and jumping to Weathe, Van had retuned the drives of the *Joyau* to Argenti standard, then called up the matching registration. The *Joyau* had become the *Palabra*, registered out of Silvium.

"Good," Eri replied.

Van made his made along the gray corridors of Weathe orbit station toward the shuttle. No one paid him much attention, and even with his implant he could detect no unusual communications around him. As in the case of Korkenny, his news searches had revealed little at all, except that membership in the Christos Revivos was increasing and that the Economic Security Act was also in place in Weathe, but from the general sources, Van couldn't possibly tell to what degree it had affected IIS.

As he had told Eri, Van had not sent word ahead. At two o'clock in the afternoon, local time, he just appeared outside the small office off Marquis Boulevard and walked in, past the bored attendant in the main lobby.

The woman inside the IIS office looked up as Van stood there. "How did you get in? We're closed."

Van reached out with his implant, and froze the entire system, except for the comm net. "I'm Director Van Albert, from IIS headquarters." Trystin didn't call it that, but Van had already discovered that it helped. "I'm looking for Jameson Pettridge."

"Ah . . . Mr. Pettridge . . . he isn't here. He won't be back today."

"Can you reach him?"

"Ah . . ."

"I left the communications link open. Tell him I'd very much like to see him. Now. I'll wait in his office."

Pettridge had added a protocol to his door locks, but they were simple enough that Van only stood there for a moment before the door opened. He could overhear the woman.

"Mr. Pettridge . . . there's a Director Albert here . . . has to be him. He took control of the entire system . . . doesn't look too pleased, I have to say."

Van wasn't pleased, although he hadn't yet discovered whether Jameson Pettridge was someone with whom to be pleased or displeased. He settled into Pettridge's chair and unfroze the system, beginning to search through the records.

By the end of the first client record—that of Weathe Mercantile—Van was nodding, especially after he noted Pettridge's successful thwarting of a proposed acquisition by—once again, DIS. Van had to wonder who was behind DIS, relatives of the military cabal under Marshal Eamon? Or was the Ministry of Economic Security just trying to consolidate as many multis as possible to simplify oversight and control?

Van had just started on the records for ForCom when he sensed someone entering the office. He stood and walked to the door.

"This is Mr. Pettridge," offered the assistant whose name Van did not know.

Pettridge was a thin, earnest-looking man, neither young nor old, wearing a conservative blue singlesuit.

"Van Albert."

"I'd hoped someone would come," Pettridge offered, "but I got no response . . ."

"How did you send it?"

"Standard interstellar, encrypted. I've sent one almost every week with updates."

"If you'd show me." Van gestured toward the office, closing the door behind them.

Pettridge called up the comm files, and Van ran through them, projecting a holo of each as he read them. Then he looked over at the younger man. "Very thorough. The only problem is that we never got any of them. That's one of the reasons I'm here."

"You think . . . the government . . . ?" Pettridge shook his head. "I knew they were pushing for nationalization of outside assets. They aren't calling it that, but that's what it amounts to."

"That was when you tried to send the first message."

"I sent it." Pettridge frowned, then fumbled through the office net to the accounts. "There." He projected the communications billings. "We were billed for each of them."

Van nodded. That was something that Pettridge was unlikely to have been able to fake, and Van had the feeling that the man was truly honest. "So you've opposed these efforts?"

"I've managed to throw up every legal block that I can," Pettridge said. "So far, we've kept all but Ensign from being acquired. With the Ensign deal, the terms were so advantageous there was no real way to block the acquisition, but we were able to insist on cash rather than equity. That was closed last week. The IIS share was significant, close to twenty million, and that was deposited directly in the local Cambrian Holdings. I checked on that to make sure."

Pettridge looked almost defiant.

Van laughed. "Actually, Mr. Pettridge, from what I have already seen, you've been very resourceful, and very industrious." Not to mention honorable, Van reflected. "I don't have as much time as I would like. So why don't you take me through each of the clients quickly, and give me a quick report?"

"Yes, ser." Pettridge cleared his throat, then called up the Weathe Mercantile account. "DIS was here on Weathe before the ink was dry on the economic security regulations. They've had—DIS, I mean—terrible cash flow problems, and they've been looking for smaller multis with cash potential all over the Republic . . ."

Van listened for almost two hours. His own cross-checking through the records convinced him that Pettridge had been both honest and effective.

". . . so, even with all the troubles, we've managed to generate revenues around seventy percent of the previous year, and that doesn't count the cash from the Ensign acquisition. That, I feel, is a solid effort in difficult times . . ."

More like miraculous, Van thought. "Mr. Pettridge. You've behaved honorably and well. Unlike some. For that, you'll be recognized and rewarded. Director Desoll and I will do our best to see to that."

"I've done what I thought best, ser."

"You've done well," Van said. "Very well."

"Thank you."

"We need to handle one other matter." Van accessed the office systems, which had far greater scope than anything available to the *Joyau* through the orbit station, and put in an inquiry for Commander James Baile, RSF. The response was near-instantaneous. There were only two references.

Van read the first, then the second, frowning.

"What is it?" asked Pettridge.

Van had the office systems print both even as he reread the second article once more.

James P. Baile, Commander, RSF. 14 Quatre 1131 N.E.
James P. Baile died suddenly of natural causes while on home leave between RSF assignments . . . survived by Merilee Watkins, former wife, and three children . . .

Both articles had the same date, and that date was one month before the *Fergus* had been transferred to Scandya.

Van studied the accompanying holo of the late commander. So far as he could recall, the man was the same, except Baile looked older in the holo image than he had in relieving Van.

Abruptly, Van understood the meaning of his nightmare.

He rose quickly, then stopped. He couldn't catch the upshuttle to orbit control any sooner.

"What's the matter?" asked Pettridge.

"It's something involving another project," Van replied. "I never thought it would come up here, but it's something I'll have to deal with much sooner than I'd ever thought." He tried to offer a smile that didn't appear forced. "You've done a praiseworthy job here under very difficult conditions, and I will make sure the managing director knows this. Thank you very much."

Van paused. He had transfer access, even on Weathe. "Just

a moment." He went to the office systems once more, accessing Cambrian Holdings, and making the transaction. "You'll find that there's an immediate fifty-thousand-credit bonus in your account. Until we see where everything is going, I can't promise more, although I will recommend more. But you deserve immediate recognition for honesty and hard work."

For a moment, Pettridge just stood there.

"Go ahead, you can check it, if you don't believe me."

Hesitantly, Pettridge accessed his account. "I don't know what to say."

"You don't have to. We appreciate your work." Van stood. "Keep doing the best you can. That's all we can ask."

Pettridge smiled, broadly.

"What about your assistant?" Van asked.

"Annabel? She works very hard."

"Say . . . five thousand?" Van asked.

"She would be pleased."

"Tell her that we took your recommendation for her bonus." Van made the second transfer, then picked up his case and opened the office door.

Back in the front office, he turned to Pettridge. "Thank you very much. I appreciate your willingness to come in on such short notice. As I said before, you've done an excellent job under difficult conditions." He looked at the assistant. "Good day, Annabel. Keep up the good work."

The woman smiled, but Van could sense the puzzlement behind the professional expression.

Once outside the building and out in the late afternoon sunlight, Van accessed the publicnet and called for a groundcar. He waited less than three minutes before a green groundcar appeared. He slipped into the car.

"Where to?" asked the woman driving.

"Is there a good restaurant near the shuttle terminal?"

"Alkady's isn't bad."

"We'll try it."

"Alkady's it is."

As the driver eased away from the building, Van noted a

dark gray vehicle pull out, but it dropped back, then turned. Was he becoming paranoid, looking at every shadow?

Alkady's had a green-and-white-striped awning, covering outside tables that were not being used in the coolish fall evening. That was one aspect of interstellar travel that had always fascinated Van—that he could go from summer to winter or spring in days.

The host escorted him to an inside booth, paneled in dark-varnished rough wood. There, Van studied the menu, quickly, and was ready when the server appeared.

"What's the best meal you have that isn't fish?" Van asked.

"The golden pheasant," replied the server.

"I'll have it, with a pale ale."

"O'Reilly's all right?"

"Fine." Van had never heard of O'Reilly's, but he wasn't a connoisseur, either.

The O'Reilly's was an undistinguished pale ale, but not objectionable, and he was thirsty, and hungry. The pheasant was better, although he pushed aside much of the fruit compote, and the red potatoes were excellent.

Later, when Van stepped from Alkady's into the twilight, he glanced around. Parked down the side street was a dark gray groundcar. He wasn't certain, but he thought it was the same one.

Quickly, he stepped back into the restaurant, where he motioned to the host.

"Is there a tube train that goes from the shuttle terminal?"

"Of course, ser."

"Where's the nearest station that's not at the terminal?"

"That'd be eight blocks north, off Pearse. Pearse and Celebration, rightly."

"Thank you."

Van called for another groundcar, waiting inside until a beige vehicle appeared. Then he stepped outside and into the vehicle.

"Where to, ser?"

Van could tell immediately that the groundcar was operated by some security service, with the overlaid comm systems. Immediately, he began to cough, leaning forward for a moment, while trying with his implant to disable the comm-transmitting nodes. Then he straightened. "Sorry. Up Pearse, north, probably six or seven blocks. I'll recognize the place."

"You're in charge, ser."

Heading up Pearse. Says he'll say when to stop . . .

Van smiled to himself, noting that the driver had no idea his transmission had not gone out. He began to explore the comm system, through his implant, and after less than a block, disabled the link between the receiver and the repeater.

The driver concealed a worried expression as the car passed one cross street, then another. Van saw the sign for Celebration and said. "Here."

"Ah . . . ten creds."

Van pulsed the credits to the machine, then counterfeited the acceptance, which unlocked the doors, and stepped out. He walked briskly to the archway and down the ramp, amid a handful of others. No one seemed to be following. Whether his maneuver would work, he had no idea, but he had time to spare. No one looking suspicious—or registering a security-type link—neared him on the platform or on the short ride back to the station serving the terminal. There he walked up to the departure consoles. He had no doubts that they were alerted.

So, standing behind two other travelers, a tallish man and a squarish woman in brilliant green, he began to probe the nets.

"Ser?"

Van stepped forward, speaking in Hispyn, "The shuttle to orbit one, and then, a passage to Lanford on the first shuttle in the morning."

The clerk officer looked blankly at him.

Van repeated his request, again in Hispyn, still probing the console.

She shrugged helplessly.

Van spoke in Old Anglo, slowly, and haltingly. "I would like . . . one passage . . . to orbit one. The next shuttle. Then I would like . . . one passage . . . for the shuttle . . . down . . . to Lanford . . . in the morning . . ."

"Your datacard, ser."

Van extended it, the one with the identity of Viano Alberto, knowing he couldn't block the outgoing, but that he could block any hold coming back in. But, so far as he could tell, there wasn't any alarm.

"You are confirmed, ser. Thank you. You go through the portals there." She pointed.

"Thank you." Van nodded politely.

He watched the portals. Again, no one stopped him.

Whoever had been following and watching him had either been thrown off the trail, or was just watching, or did not want to act in the open. That was clear . . . for the moment.

He also knew two other things. He wasn't about to return to Republic space and control under anything close to his own name. But he was going to return—he knew he had to— regardless of the folly of it, to get answers to questions he had let go for too long, because nowhere else could he discover what had truly happened to the *Fergus*.

And he couldn't spend the rest of his life fighting nightmares or consider himself even halfway ethical unless and until he found that out.

Chapter 62

For all his impatience, Van did not take the *Joyau* straight to Tara, but instead made a jump to another system—one only numbered as Y-3134U—a binary system with uninhabited planets and complex orbitals. There he parked the *Joyau* just outside the no-jump zone.

He'd checked the comparators and made some calculations. Had he made an immediate jump, he would have arrived in New Oisin on a threeday, and that would have meant spending too much time on Tara before he could act. He needed to time his arrival for about noon on a fiveday, New Oisin planetary time. That way he could take down an afternoon or evening shuttle, spend sixday making his preparations, then act over the enddays.

He also needed some time to think.

Sitting in his stateroom, he read over the hard copy of Baile's obituary. The commander had been reported dead a month before he relieved Van, but the "Baile" who had relieved Van had had official orders. Further, the RSF had effectively acknowledged his command, and the fact that the *Fergus* had remained off Scandya orbit station for nearly a month being repaired indicated to Van that "Baile" had not been acting contrary to RSF directives. And Van had even talked to the man. Whatever else it signified, it was clear to Van that "Baile" had been acting under the orders and direction of the RSF, or of someone highly placed in the RSF—or both.

Then, there was the Founder's Day massacre of the Republic government. The general methodology had been similar to that used by the Revenants on Scandya. Van didn't believe that the Revenants had done it, but who besides the RSF in Tara had known that much about the methodology?

Add to that the fact that Van was the only survivor of the *Fergus*'s encounter off Scandya and that the *Fergus* itself was lost or destroyed, or both. He had to wonder. Had someone in the RSF just wanted the *Fergus* lost in order to get support for more modern ships? If so, what did that say about the RSF? And what about the attempts to murder Van himself?

Had Trystin played any role in it all?

Van considered.

He doubted it. There were too many aspects of the mess that Trystin didn't know, and couldn't have known, things that Van alone knew and had never mentioned. Trystin had his own agenda, and part of that was using Van's troubles with the RSF to get Van into IIS and into the clandestine war—and it was a war—against the Revenants. But IIS had offices in many Republic systems, and Trystin hadn't talked or acted against the Republic in the way he had against the Revenants.

Van still worried about Trystin's obsession—or near obsession with ethics, but after dealing with both Morgan Henry and Jameson Pettridge, Van had to admit that he definitely preferred ethics over unbridled self-interest, or what Trystin might have called the personal big kill.

The more Van thought, though, the more he realized that he still didn't know quite enough, no matter what he suspected, and that meant, in the end, he would have to go through with the plan that he only had half-formulated.

He walked back to Eri's stateroom, knocking on the door. "Eri . . ."

"Yes, ser?"

"Tell me again what we have in the way of personal gadgets, weapons, tools, and dirty tricks . . ."

Van hoped some of them would fit into his plans.

Chapter 63

Van straightened in the command couch. He had to concentrate on the approach and docking. What came afterward would be more difficult and nerve-wracking than any space combat he'd been in—at least for him.

Tara orbit control two, Hyndji commercial ship **Daiphur**, *on approach. Request locking assignment.*

Daiphur, *stand by, continue low-power approach.*

Control two, **Daiphur** *continuing approach this time.* Was there traffic he couldn't see, shielded by the bulk of the station, or a ship delocking? Van knew he was being oversensitive, but it was hard to avoid such feelings.

Several minutes passed.

Daiphur, *sorry for the delay. Cleared to charlie five this time. Maintain low-power approach. Standing by for authorization transfer at your convenience.*

Control, *Daiphur.* Authorization follows. Van pulsed the credit authorization, this one drawn on the Dhyli Trust.

Authorization received. Thank you. You are cleared to lock, charlie five. Report depowering and switch to station power.

Control, *Daiphur,* *will do.*

Van guided the ship around the station and into position off lock charlie five, then slowly eased the *Daiphur/Joyau* into the dampers. The faintest clunk echoed through the hull. Van winced. He'd touched in a little hard.

After scanning the indicators, he activated the ship's damper receptors, then dropped the ship gravity to nil.

Control, *Daiphur,* *ship gravity is nil. Switching to station power this time.*

Daiphur, *thank you. Have a pleasant stay.*

Van brought up the ship gravity to one gee on station power. He unfastened his harness and looked at Eri. "I have a few things to do before I head out."

"Then you had better do them." The impish expression followed the words.

"I love you, too."

Eri laughed.

Van walked back to his stateroom. He'd need a shower and fresh clothes. But first, he connected to the Taran net through the orbit control station. He made a down-shuttle reservation, then one for a return on eightday. Then he secured accommodations for S. V. Moorty at the Old Dubhlyner, the luxury accommodations closest to RSF headquarters.

He had decided against making any news or information requests from the ship, except for the most recent general news, the sort of request any ship or business might make. He wanted no trails back to the ship itself, nor did he want to alert RSF security in advance.

Before cleaning up, he scanned the planetary and local New Oisin news. There was little of interest, except for several articles on the increased income tax levies required for the buildup in the RSF—with close to twenty new ships being built over the next five years. Marshal Eamon cited "the threat to the Republic posed by those who would use any tool and any subterfuge to overthrow our way of life and our traditions."

Van wasn't honestly sure which threat was greater—the marshal or the Revenants. He suspected that the marshal was a more imminent threat, and perhaps greater in a way, because if the marshal succeeded in creating a more tightly controlled society, many people might well welcome a Revenant takeover—or just stand by.

He cleaned up and dressed, wearing a tan singlesuit with a deep brown jacket over it, then picked up the carry bag. In the bottom was Van's uniform, under some other clothing and toiletries. Scanners wouldn't show it as any different from other clothing, and he'd put the insignia in a small bag inside the underwear. He'd just have to chance explaining it if he were stopped for a hand inspection.

Also in his long wallet were several datacards, specially created through the ship's capabilities and Eri's skills. He had no weapons, although the carryall contained a nanite bodyshield, its components split into apparently innocent items. With what he planned, weapons would merely be a distraction and a certain way to get in trouble with orbit station security.

He glanced around the stateroom. He wasn't looking forward to the next few days, but if he didn't at least try, he'd regret it and be bothered with it—and the damned nightmares—for the rest of his life.

A rueful smile crossed his face. If he botched it, though, he wouldn't have any life left in which to regret anything. The choices weren't exactly wonderful. He stepped out of the stateroom that had been as much home as anything over the past several years.

Eri was standing by the ship lock. "Don't force your way."

Van smiled. "Not too much, anyway."

She nodded somberly. "I will see you on eightday."

"Eightday," Van affirmed. "Or sooner."

The moment he cleared the *Joyau*'s lock, he could sense the scanners. There was no feedback, and he kept walking along the corridor until he reached the immigration consoles, short of the shuttle area. There, without a word, he tendered the datacard and waited.

"Ser Moorty?" asked the official at the shuttle console.

"Yes?" Van replied.

"Where will you be staying in New Oisin?"

"Three days. I have a reservation at the Old Dubhlyner. That is satisfactory, is it not?" replied Van, using a stiffer form of Anglo, one appropriate to an educated outsider.

"Oh, yes, ser. It's a fine place."

Van bet the poor immigration officer couldn't have afforded a single night there, but then, one of the purposes of spending the credits was to create the impression of a wealthy businessman. Then, in a way, Van reflected, he was, although he'd never thought of it that way before.

He had to wait almost an hour before boarding the shuttle, and once on board, he listened for most of the descent, his eyes closed, and his hearing implant-boosted.

". . . can't believe all the questions they asked . . ."

". . . looking for someone, you think?"

". . . more like they're profiling . . . anyone tall and fair, especially blond . . ."

". . . anyone coming from a Revenant system, you think?"

". . . not at war . . . can't cut off travel, you know . . ."

Van wondered about that.

". . . Sulynese . . . might revolt . . . spoiled people . . ."

". . . bad as the Kelts . . ."

". . . worse . . . ask me . . . never trust black Tarans . . ."

". . . some are all right . . ."

". . . name one . . ."

Van winced at the silence that followed.

Once the shuttle had grounded and glided to the disembarking point, Van moved decisively, but not hastily. When he left the disembarking corridor, he found himself opposite another line of consoles, each manned by another junior functionary. Overhead, there were remote arms emplace-ments, not visible except through Van's implant. Both the remote stunners and the consoles had been added since Van's last trip to New Oisin.

In a strictly logical fashion, neither made sense. But the additions made political and emotional sense, because Mar-shal Eamon could claim that the Republic was under attack and all steps were being taken to protect its citizens.

Van took the console with the shortest line, where he ten-dered, once more, the datacard.

"Ser? What is your purpose in visiting New Oisin?"

"It is business." Van waited. "I am with Vishava Securi-ties."

"Are you carrying more than ten thousand credits or any convertible bonds in excess of that amount?"

"No. We operate through the standard clearinghouses."

"Are you carrying any personal weapons? That includes knives, swords, anything with a blade longer than six cen-timeters . . ."

"No."

The functionary scanned the low holo projection before him, then nodded. He handed Van back the card for S. V. Moorty. "Thank you, ser."

"Thank you." Van nodded politely and picked up the overnight bag, moving out through the portals to find a groundcar. Outside, the sun was beginning to set, and he waited behind a couple and an RSF major. The next groundcar rolled past him, without stopping, as did the one following.

Van frowned. Were they worried about a single dark-skinned male?

The next car, a deep blue with a diamond symbol and the single word MEERSCHAUM within the diamond, stopped.

"The Old Dubhlyner, if you please."

"Old Dubhlyner . . . that it is, ser."

Van studied the groundcar and, with his implant, the simple comm gear. The groundcar was just that, a groundcar for hire.

"Have you been here before, ser?" asked the groundcar driver.

"I have not."

"After ten at night, best you take a groundcar, and from a public place, too."

"There is unrest?" Van asked.

"Been unrest ever since the assassinations. Maybe you didn't hear about them . . . Kelt agents cut down most of the government on Founder's Day. Cruel thing it was, and worst of all was that the one who helped them was from one of our own troubled planets."

"I had heard there had been trouble."

"Well . . . the young hotheads, now they think that anyone who's tall and fair, with dark hair, is a Kelt, and some of them go after anyone who looks different . . . know what I mean."

Van feared he did. He shook his head, both for himself and for the persona of S. V. Moorty. He hadn't planned any physical exploring. He'd actually designed a careful publicnet search for telltale information, the sort that would be in character for S. V. Moorty—mostly—as well as a search of the reports on the Founder's Day incident. That might offer a few keys.

Van hoped it did, but he couldn't rely on hope.

Chapter 64

On sixday, Van was up early, eating in his room, then preparing for the day ahead. His "research" of the night before had been less than conclusive. Not all new members of the government were military, but Marshal Eamon and the RSF controlled the key ministries—External Security, Internal Security, and Finance. They also seemed to have public support. Van could not find even hidden references to unrest—except on Sulyn—and that meant that there wasn't much or that Internal Security had an iron hand on things, or some of each. The lack of symptoms was disturbing enough.

After dressing, Van looked in the mirror—a replica Neo-Yeatsian mirror, typical of the decor of the Old Dubhlyner, and checked the RSF commodore's uniform a last time. He'd never thought that he'd wear it again—and certainly not under the present circumstances. He also never thought he'd have to be wearing a nanite bodyshield as well. Fortunately, the long formal uniform blouse neatly covered the waist powerpack.

There were only a handful of senior black Taran officers, but all of them—and Van—bore a certain similarity—golden bronze skins, rather than black or cocoa, straight hair, and fine features. Even before the more recent troubles, black Tarans with truly dark skins, like Dad Almaviva, had had trouble entering the RSF officer corps.

He waited until the corridor outside his room was empty, then made his way to the lift and down to the main lobby. No one even seemed to look his way as he walked outside and took a groundcar for the less than a klick ride to the RSF headquarters complex on Tarahill, the low-rise on the north side of New Oisin.

Like most military headquarters, the RSF building had compartmentalized security. Any officer could enter the "public" areas on the main floor. But above that and in the rear wings, access was much tighter, with projected screens and even weapons emplacements. The first day's expedition was strictly reconnaissance, and to see if the combination of Eri's tech work and Van's implant could handle the security in the way, Van *thought* they could.

At seven-forty, along with a number of other officers, mainly majors and commanders, Van walked up to the main entryway and offered his RSF datacard, which was but slightly altered, in that it would register as Van on the entry console display, but the memory would show a name picked in rotation through a series of other names of other RSF officers, gleaned from Van's memory and records, and report them as having passed the security checkpoint, leaving no record of one Van Cassius Albert.

The central database would doubtless report the oddity, but unless the RSF wanted to shut down the entire HQ building, and compare person to datacard, one at a time, in an override mode, dealing with close to ten thousand individuals, they'd have great difficulty ferreting out one officer. The guard barely blinked as he scanned the card and nodded. "Good day, ser."

"Carry on." Van moved briskly, at the pace of an officer on his way to work.

He had already decided that Sub-marshal Vickry's office was one target. Vickry had to know what had gone on, and Van doubted strongly that all the information was contained just in Vickry's mind. He did not head for the sub-marshal's office immediately, not with the morning influx of officers and support personnel, but toward the small senior officers' mess, really a glorified set of formulator bays and tables where it would not be out of place for a visiting commodore to stop and sit and wait.

Van used the blank datacard, one with credits on it, and no ID, to get himself a mug of very strong café and a scone. A man with a scone was always less suspect than one with merely a mug of café. Then he took one of the small empty tables near the archway that led to the ramps up to the second level.

There, he slowly sipped the café, with a very occasional bite of the scone, and listened, letting his implant and the analyzer that Eri had programmed that looked like a datacard, scan the security challenges at the top of the ramp.

". . . glad it's sixday . . ."

". . . been a long week . . ."

". . . hear about the Revs trying to take over another blind zone system . . ."

". . . which one this time?"

". . . don't recall . . ."

Van wanted to lean forward. Instead, he took another sip of café and waited, listening.

". . . some place spinward . . . Shannar, that was it . . . halfway between Hyndji and Argenti systems . . ."

Shannar? The name was vaguely familiar.

". . . might as well let them have it . . . if it's a blind zone . . ."

". . . cuts two ways . . . could marshal a fleet there . . . never know . . ."

". . . closer to the Kelts . . ."

". . . can't trust them, either . . . not after the assassinations . . ."

The voices of the two majors faded away as they passed the security checkpoint at the top of the ramp.

Van checked the time again. Eight-twenty. Still not late enough. He took a sip of the now-cool café.

Two junior commanders walked up the ramp.

". . . we still on for tomorrow?"

"Why wouldn't we be? Unless you're getting tired of getting whipped?"

"Last sevenday, you got whipped. Remember? I was thinking about . . ."

"That won't change anything. Vice marshal says everything on Sulyn's quiet now. Same on Kerry."

Quiet on Sulyn? That could have a number of meanings. Van decided to finish the scone and the too-cold café. Before leaving the senior officers' mess, he linked with the analyzer, through the implant, then transferred the information and the recommended protocol. Finally, he stood, brushed off the uniform, leaving the mug and plate on the table as he walked toward the ramp.

The security net reached out, and Van offered the handshake through the implant. Eri's handiwork was good, and there wasn't even a blip or hesitation as the security system announced, *Cleared, Commodore Albert.*

Van walked briskly down the corridor. The entire south wing was devoted to the public affairs section—door after door, all dealing with the presentation of the RSF to the public through the media. He'd passed the offices once before, when he'd been in headquarters to be debriefed and retired, but hadn't really noticed. He wanted to shake his head.

At the end of the south wing, Van turned right and followed the corridor—this time past the offices of the marshal for M&P—maintenance and procurement. All told, there were only four doorways that he passed. An entire corridor for public relations—and just a third of one for the acquisition and maintenance of an entire fleet and all the outlying stations, installations, and associated equipment. Dad Cicero could have expressed it logically. Van couldn't, only that it felt insanely wrong.

Ahead of him, halfway along the west corridor, Van could sense the second security check area—the one surrounding the intelligence and strategy offices.

There was no one ahead of him, and no way to check whether his implant and what he'd gathered so far would work. He paused, glancing around, as if he had missed where he was supposed to go, all the time letting the analyzer scan the screens.

Surprisingly enough, at least to Van, the analyzer reported that the protocols were almost identical to the lower security screen.

Van straightened, like a man who had regained his bearings, and walked straight toward the hidden screens and the equally concealed stunners above them in the high ceiling. Again, he offered the security handshake, linked to his modified ID datacard. He also kept the analyzer focused on the system.

This time, there was the faintest hesitation before the system offered him clearance.

As he walked past the unseen screen, Van just hoped that each successive clearance did not get harder. He also worried about his return, since the systems did not discriminate directionally.

He continued past a closed and unmarked door, one with a separate clearance system that probably belonged to the RSF office of intelligence and strategy. The next door was the one that Van had entered before, the outer office of those associated with Sub-marshal Vickry.

Van paused short of the door, reading the outside inscriptions and letting the analyzer pick up what it could. His implant detected nothing, as if whatever security system existed was independent of the building system and had been placed on standby for the workday.

He continued along the corridor, past the office of Marshal Connolly, the chief of RSF intelligence and strategy. He did not pause this time, but continued to the end of the corridor, where he turned into the fresher facility. Not only did it give him a reason for stopping, but after the café and his nervousness, he needed to use those facilities.

He took his time, then returned the way he had come.

He stopped at the main office of public affairs, where he stepped inside.

"Ser?" asked the young-looking major crossing the outer office.

"I was looking for the hard copy releases—yesterday's and today's . . . the marshal . . ."

Van looked apologetic, with the kind of expression that suggested he knew that there was no reason to want paper copies, but that he'd been asked.

The major laughed. "Yes, ser. It happens. Just a moment."

Within several minutes, the officer returned with a folder, moderately thick. "Every office in headquarters has been down here this morning."

"One of those days," Van replied. "Thank you."

"No problem, ser."

Van took the folder and made his way out, heading down the ramp to the main level, still wondering exactly what happened to be in the folders. That could wait until later. He had a few more "errands" to run, including walking close enough to several other RSF buildings to check out their security systems.

Then, he would have a long afternoon taking apart what he'd discovered. With all that effort, inspiration, and luck, he hoped he could develop what he needed for sevenday.

Chapter 65

On sevenday morning, at eight-forty, before leaving his room in the Old Dubhlyner, Van took a last look in the mirror. The greens would have to do, although he doubted any of the handful of Marine guards would quibble because his uniform was more formal than usual on a sevenday. He had very little in the way of weapons, merely the transparent knife hidden in his left boot and the length of cord within his belt. He also checked the bodyshield as well, one last time, before slipping out into the empty corridor of the hotel, although he left it on standby. Even in fall, it was far too hot to keep on except when absolutely necessary. He carried a thin datacase, in which there was nothing except a thin black tunic.

Between what he'd learned from the analyzer, Eri's observations and instructions, and his own insights from his RSF service, Van was hopeful that he could not only reenter the RSF headquarters, but find the information that he knew must exist . . . somewhere. In most RSF installations, there were always officers who worked the enddays, and a commodore was senior enough not to be questioned and junior enough that his presence wouldn't be noted as unusual.

The night before, he'd read through the hardcopy press releases he'd gathered for cover, particularly because he'd wondered why so many offices had been interested, but the only one that seemed of interest was the budget for the RSF for the coming fiscal year. The proposed increases in the number of capital ships had confirmed Van's feelings about the new government's less-than-peaceful inclinations, although some increase was certainly warranted in light of Revenant activities. The second number that had puzzled Van was the increase in fuel mass expenditures and torps, although the rationale had stated that, given the lack of surplus capacity within the Republic, those items had to be acquired over several years before and during the construction of additional vessels so that adequate supplies would be available. The third number was one that just plain disturbed him, and that was the increased funding for "domestic peace-keeping." The rationale there was given as the growing need to maintain control over systems or areas within the Republic where outside subversion threatened domestic stability and economic growth.

Van pushed those thoughts aside as he stepped out of the Old Dubhlyner to get in the groundcar for hire that would take him to the headquarters building. Once more, several ground-cars passed him by, even though they were empty, and he was in full uniform, before one finally stopped to pick him up.

Once he reached Tarahill, he walked through the morning sunlight of the late fall day toward the Marine guards outside the building. Both guards looked him over carefully, although they had barely given the officers before him a nod, as he proffered the ID. After a look between the two, they passed him through. Van had to wonder. He'd never gotten that kind of scrutiny before, especially since the outside guards had to know that the RSF internal screening systems would catch anything they missed. The real reasons for the outside guards were to maintain appearances and to use their weapons against clearly identified outside attackers.

Still . . . he listened as he passed.

". . . quiet today . . . even for endday . . ."

". . . say the marshals are all off-planet . . . something happening . . ."

". . . commodore there's pretty senior . . . first black Taran officer in a long while . . ."

". . . wouldn't include him . . . not black Taran . . . probably got some paper job . . ."

Van frowned. What could be happening that would take the marshals off-planet? A Revenant threat? Some military operation? Whatever it was, it might make it easier for him, even if he bridled at the suggestion that black Taran officers weren't included.

The ramps and corridors were not quite deserted, except for the public affairs office, where all doors were open, and the whole staff seemed to be working. Beyond those offices, Van passed only a major and a commander. Both nodded to him, stiffly, and Van returned the gesture. He reached the intelligence offices without incident, and, as he had hoped, the door to Sub-marshal Vickry's office was closed. From what Van could tell, no one was inside—at least not in the outer office. The door held a standard receptacle for an ID databloc.

Van inserted the databloc, then pressed his hand against the counterplate, using his implant to override the ID protocol. He hoped what he was doing would override it. After a long moment, the door clicked, and Van pulled it open. He could not sense any alarms, and there was no one inside the outer office.

He closed the door behind him and immediately used his implant to override the lights, leaving the outer office dim. He stood in the gloom, just beside the green leather couch set against the wall, using his implant to search through the controls. Then, bit by bit, he began to make changes to the system, essentially freezing an image in each of the scanners, ensuring that they revealed an office empty of people.

He eased toward the archway to Vickry's inner office.

Even from two meters away, he could sense the detectors and the independent power systems. Vickry didn't want anyone inside his office—that was clear, and also a good indication that what Van wanted might well be there. People—even senior officers—didn't have that much security unless there was something they wanted very secure.

Van eased one of the chairs to a point just outside the independent scanning perimeter. After setting down the datacase, he seated himself, taking out the analyzer once more. He pointed it at the portal to the inner office and let it work.

After almost ten minutes, it pulsed, *Analysis complete.*

Van took a deep breath and began to study what the analyzer had reported, and that was very little. There was a detection field, and three stunners were inset in the portal.

Still, the actual clearance procedure had to be simple. No sub-marshal wanted to have to remember much of anything nonessential. That meant, Van suspected, either some variation on biometrics for the secretary or a direct pulse-code, and possibly a more involved manual overcode for emergencies.

Van studied the portal area. There were no counterplates for handprints, and no scanners for retinals. Voiceprinting was unlikely because an allergy or a cold could change a voice too easily. There didn't seem to be temperature sensors.

He looked over the portal area again, then used his implant to begin tracing power and comm lines of the regular office systems. They registered the portal as a "black" area, except for the single fiberline coming out.

Van smiled, focusing the analyzer on the fiberline.

When he checked the results, he smiled—for a moment. From what he could tell, all he had to do was replicate the twined signal, and there would be no alert signal to the main security system for the building.

All? It took almost an hour before he had duplicated the signal on one of the "spare" datacards. He gave the commands to the office system to block off the signal from the portal and to substitute the one from the datacard. Then he held his breath—figuratively, monitoring everything. There was only the faintest flicker in the status signals, but no alarms went off.

He turned his attention to the portal.

The stunners flared a dozen times in the next fifteen minutes, before Van and the analyzer finally broke the codes. The portal had sent out alarm after alarm—but they'd gone nowhere, thanks to Van's makeshift block.

He stepped through the portal, checking the inner office beyond. Despite the coolness in the office, Van was sweating heavily under the uniform. So far as he could tell, there were no more alarms, but he still had to figure out how to get into the intelligence system.

He and Eri had already figured out the likely structure of

entry protocols and set up the analyzer to run through Van's implant. Before Van tackled that problem, he wanted to check Vickry's spaces and drawers for clues and for anything that might make the job easier.

He didn't find much of anything. The drawers in the left side of the antique desk held only personal items, and few of those—a marble stylus holder engraved to Commander Jon D. Vickry, several packages of mints, a small framed holo image of a young woman, several styli of various shapes, a laser pointer, two blank infocards, and a third infocard with the label SCHEDULE on it.

Van shrugged and looked around the office.

Then he took another deep breath, using his implant to unfreeze the point terminal in the inner office but leaving the connection beyond closed. Slowly, he let the analyzer probe the point terminal.

Protocols retrieved.

Van offered a tight smile. The RSF had been careful to keep the reports on the Scandyan "incident" out of the main databases, which meant that, if such reports existed, they had to be in the secure files. But those files had to be open to Vickry.

After entering the secure system, using Vickry's access, Van immediately ordered a search, entering his own name. Three files flashed up, holo-displayed before him. He didn't try to read them, but transferred copies through the implant to one of the datacards with him. Then he searched for the *Collyns* and the *Fergus*. There were dozens of files, but Van only transferred those dated from three months before he'd been commanded to take the *Fergus* to Scandya.

Then he left the system. Either the files had what he wanted, or they didn't, and if what he wanted was in a deeper or more secure system, he was out of luck, because he'd run to the limits of his implant and analyzer capabilities—and he was getting worried about time.

He slipped back through the portal, restoring it to normal function after he did.

Then he froze against the wall as the door of the outer

office began to open. Quickly, he triggered the nanite bodyshield to full protection.

"Lights are out . . ." hissed a voice.

"Heat sensors said . . ." returned another voice.

Heat sensors? Van hadn't found them.

"Probably just some officer working in the back."

Van decided to bluff it out—or try to—even as he moved closer to the Marine who entered the office.

"You're right," he called out loudly. "I was just leaving. I'd turned out the lights and was headed out."

The first Marine turned and looked at Van, taking in the uniform.

"I had a project for the sub-marshal."

The second Marine stopped in the doorway, shaking his head. "Wish someone would tell us sometime."

"I logged in with security," Van replied.

"That's not your problem, ser." The second Marine looked at the first. "You log it in. I'm headed back to give Gorel a word."

He vanished, but the door remained ajar—only for a moment before a second figure appeared, closing the door behind him.

Sub-marshal Vickry stood there, smiling. "What sort of project, Commodore?"

"Research," Van replied, smiling easily, and gesturing toward the sealed portal into Vickry's private office.

"Now!" snapped the sub-marshal.

Van was already moving. Despite the nanite bodyshield, the impact of the slug fired by the Marine spun him around, and his entire body felt as though he'd been struck from shoulder to knee. Rather than fight the impact, Van let it carry him around in a full circle that he forced right up to the young Marine.

The Marine's eyes widened, and he hesitated for just a moment.

That moment was just enough for Van, and base of his palm connected with the other's jaw. There was a dull snap, and the man dropped.

Vickry had reached for a stunner, but Van was faster, and snapped it out of the older man's hands, following up with a stiff jab to the vee of Vickry's ribs. Vickry staggered back, gasping, and Van scooped up the stunner, triggering it at the sub-marshal's legs.

Vickry went down.

Van could sense the alert pulse from Vickry's implant, but since Van had disabled the receivers in the office, along with most systems, the signal went nowhere.

Vickry grimaced as he levered himself against the wall, his lower body numb and inert.

"I hadn't expected you this late." Van smiled, wondering what he could get out of Vickry. "You have rather elaborate security here."

"How long have you been a Coalition agent?" Vickry asked mildly, although behind his expression of mild curiosity Van could sense both worry and agitation.

"I'm not, and I never have been," Van replied. "How long did you and Marshal Connolly and Marshal Eamon have to work to set up your assassination plot and coup?"

"Coup?" Vickry forced a laugh. "I don't see any troopers on the streets, and there will be elections before long."

"It's amazing how closely events here resembled what happened on Scandya," Van added conversationally.

"How did you do it?" snapped Vickry.

"Do what?" replied Van.

"You've blocked off the office. It might buy you some time, but before long, someone will check on it. The building systems will report it as an exception, and they'll send in a Marine team, and there won't be enough of you left to fill a datacard."

"You already tried that," Van pointed out.

"Sergeant Telford will be back shortly, with more men."

"Maybe," Van conceded. "Why did the RSF have to take over the Republic?" He raised the stunner again.

Vickry looked up. "You're so smart, black man. You figure it out. If you have the brains and time."

Van thumbed the stunner up to lethal and pressed the trigger.

Vickry didn't even look surprised.

Van shook his head, looking down not at Vickry, but at the young soldier's body. Van had been the intruder, and he hadn't wanted to kill the man, not until the Marine had tried to kill him.

He had to hurry. Quickly, he pulled out the green couch, away from the wall, then straightened. His entire body had begun to throb. Ignoring the pain, he slowly dragged Vickry's body behind the couch, then that of the dead Marine before straightening the furniture. While the couch wouldn't conceal the bodies from a thorough search, it would hide them from a cursory look into the office.

Then Van picked up the datacase, walked out, locking the door, and turning off the body-shield, because it would register on the security systems. He made his way along the deserted corridors—except that two doors in the public affairs office were still open, and a major and a captain were calling up holo images and working on something. Neither looked up as Van passed.

He wanted to look around, to see if anyone happened to be following him, but knew that looking worried would alert anyone monitoring the system. So he continued to walk down the ramps, past security—which cleared him—then outside. He kept feeling as though someone would put a laser through his back, although not even his name was in the building security system.

The sky had clouded up in the hours that Van had been in the RSF headquarters building, and a mistlike rain had begun to fall.

He nodded to the guards. "I hope it doesn't rain any harder."

"You and us, ser."

Van smiled and kept walking.

At the end of the open plaza, he hailed a groundcar. Thankfully, this time the first one stopped.

"Orbit station shuttle terminal."

"OST, it is, ser."

Van couldn't sense any communications to or from the driver, and he added a solid tip to the fare when the woman dropped him off. By then, the rain had intensified, and Van was glad of the weather screens as he walked into the terminal.

There he made his way into the public fresher, and in one of the stalls, after using the implant to blank the sensor, changed tunics. The severe black changed not only his overall appearance, strikingly, but even his mien. Van hoped it would be enough. He slipped the datacase into a corner with his tunic and uniform cap inside. While he would have preferred to keep the uniform tunic, he didn't want to risk having it scanned when he departed Tara—if he could depart.

After leaving the fresher, rather than seek a seat on the shuttle in person, Van eased his way to a pubcomm unit, and reserved his place—as S. V. Moorty. He had slightly less than three hours to kill.

Empty-handed, he walked toward the small restaurant on the left side of the terminal, where he managed a seat that looked out onto the open concourse. While the time passed, slowly, he occasionally scanned the open space outside the restaurant, watching to see if any security or military forces appeared.

As he ate slowly, he could discern neither, and finally he slipped from the small circular table and made his way to the departure consoles.

"Ser Moorty, how was your stay on Tara?" asked the console officer.

"Most productive, it was," Van returned.

"You have no luggage? No cases?"

"I brought business materials. They remained." Van shrugged. "It makes the return shuttle flight much lighter."

The woman waved Van through. He kept thinking that someone would try to stop him from boarding the up-shuttle, but no one did. The hardest part was walking without betraying the soreness and growing stiffness he felt. And the growing concerns he was getting for his family.

Chapter 66

Eri was standing just inside the lock to the *Joyau* when Van closed it behind him.

"I'm sore, very sore," he replied. "We need to delock as quickly as we can." He moved toward the cockpit.

"Is someone chasing you?" Eri followed him into the cockpit.

"They could be shortly, and I'd rather not wait and see," Van replied as he settled into the command couch, awkwardly fastening his harness before he began to run through the checklist. He triggered the comm before he finished. *Tara orbit control two, Hyndji commercial ship* **Daiphur,** *requesting delocking and departure corridor.*

Daiphur, *stand by.*

Control two, **Daiphur** *standing by this time.* Van turned to Eri. "We're going to nil gee."

She had already slipped into the other couch and quickly finished strapping in.

Van brought the fusactors on line, ready to wrench the *Daiphur/Joyau* out of the lock dampers if necessary.

More than a minute passed, an interval that felt far too long. Van could feel the sweat running down his back, and the air in the cockpit smelled metallic.

Daiphur, *sorry. Cleared to delock from charlie five this time. Dampers released. Maintain low-power departure until clear of the amber. Suggest corridor two.*

Control, **Daiphur**, *will do. Delocking this time.* Van eased the *Joyau* away from orbit control two, watching the station and the ships in orbit or nearing or departing planetary orbit. He brought up ship gravity to one gee.

He still needed to route funds and messages to his family. From what he'd seen, Sulyn wasn't going to be safe for them much longer, if it even was now. He looked across at Eri. "Would you set up a comm link to the IIS office in New Oisin, secure?"

"Yes, ser."

Van checked the systemwide EDI screen. There were only four RSF ships in the entire system. One of the heavy cruisers was off Burke, the largest satellite of Synge, the gas-giant seventh planet. The other was at the other side of the system. Each of the other corvettes was a quarter of the system from the cruisers, so that each ship covered one quadrant—but there were only four ships—the fewest Van had ever seen.

Departure corridor two ran almost directly toward the cruiser off Burke.

For the moment, Van continued piloting the *Joyau* toward corridor two.

"I have a secure link, ser. But it's secure only to the office. Beyond that . . . when they retransmit . . ."

"I understand." Van pulsed in the codes to send the message to his fathers, then added his own personal billing information.

I'm sorry this will be quick, he messaged, *but I've little time. You may recall my last messages. I would urge you, as well as Arturo and Sappho, to follow through on Sappho's earlier inclination. Material which could expedite that will also be following, through VCA . . .* VCA was the account Van had set up years earlier in order to transfer funds home for investment. Now, the funds transfers would be for a different form of investment, Van hoped. *I'm not likely to be easily reached for a time, but consider my recommendation as one that failure to follow could result in a final curtain call for the opera company and its director and his associates.*

Van was being oblique, to say the least. He doubted that one message among thousands would be pulled out, but there was always the chance that someone in the IIS office might break in and relay the contents—if they thought they were unduly suspicious. In any case, it was the best he could do on short notice, and it wasn't as though he hadn't recommended that his family leave Sulyn before.

He followed the message with the instructions for the

funds transfers from his personal accounts. Those would work, because they went through Cambrian Holdings, and the RSF wasn't about to interfere with a major Coalition financial institution. Not yet, anyway.

Those items completed, Van concentrated on the EDI screen once more, where the RSF cruiser remained on station—not that the scale of the screen would have showed movement, although the relative overlay would have.

Van almost nodded to himself. While the cruiser was not moving toward the departure corridor he'd been assigned, he didn't like the idea of departing the system in a way that would bring him closer to a ship with that much power. For the time being, he left the *Joyau* on course until the ship was clear of the amber protective area off Tara. Then he began to incline the departure course of the *Joyau* "down" from the system ecliptic, but gradually. He didn't want to alert the RSF—not yet.

Then Van unstrapped and walked back to his stateroom, closing the door behind him but still remaining linked to the ship system.

He stripped off the thin black tunic and undershirt, studying his frame in the mirror.

At first glance, his entire torso looked bruised, but a closer scrutiny revealed that only about a third was purplish. That third was enough to make every movement tentative, and probably would come to hurt more before it hurt less. The nanite bodyshield had kept him from getting killed, but it had exacted a price. He changed into a shipsuit, trying not to wince at every movement.

Next, he fed the datacard with the files he had copied from Vickry's office into the reader in his stateroom, creating an isolated directory on the system for it. He hurried back to the cockpit. He could read through those files from the command couch, but he didn't want to leave the cockpit for that long, not in the Tara system.

From the galley, Eri looked out as he left his stateroom. "You will need something to eat."

"Thank you." Van settled back into the command couch

and, using his implant and access through the shipnet, began to search through the files he'd lifted.

The first two were routine.

The third was not.

. . . the commanding officer of the RSFS *Collyns* was informed that a hostile cruiser disguised as the RSFS *Fergus* would be entering the Scandyan system and that the purpose of that entry would be to break the capital space vessel limitation agreement with the Scandyans, thus forcing the RSF into a position where it would be forced either to withdraw from the Scandyan system or to engage in armed conflict with the Scandyan system. Since such conflict was clearly not in the interests of the RSF, the *Collyns* was tasked with destroying the imposter vessel . . . including using drive detuning for an element of surprise . . .

Later information, after the destruction of the *Collyns* by the real *Fergus*, a deplorable occurrence, revealed that intelligence dispatches to RSF headquarters had been falsified by sources believed to have been either Keltyric or Argenti. The marshal determined that revealing this information would have been highly detrimental to Republic security, and the official position remains that the *Collyns* is presumed lost on secret maneuvers . . . With the drowning death of the RSF military attaché to Scandya, further disclosures are unlikely, although it was considered prudent to remove certain qualifications of the attaché from records open to public scrutiny . . .

Van took a long slow breath. He'd been attacked by the RSF and destroyed officers and techs he'd known. And, despite the denials in the file, it was clear enough to Van that Vickry and Marshal Connolly had actually set up the *Fergus*—the real *Fergus*—to be destroyed by the *Collyns*. Worse, there was a clear implication that Cruachan had been murdered because he'd known too much. But why? There had to be more.

He continued to read.

... Taran public had consistently failed to realize the danger posed by greater Revenant or Argenti influence in the Scandyan system ... and the lack of newer and more advanced vessels ... Council recommends that the RSF high command proceed in developing a plan that will make the electorate more fully aware of the critical situation developing ... to prepare public opinion for alliances of necessity, and to develop a contingency plan for more direct action, should it prove necessary ... contingency should also include operations to reduce areas of dissent within the Republic. Public opinion will support such an option [see Report XX-1A] ...

The line that bothered Van the most was the last one. From what little he'd seen and heard, public opinion was definitely in favor of harsh measures against Sulyn, but he didn't know what had changed matters so much. Or had that bias always been there, and he'd just ignored it?

... Commander Van Cassius Albert, commanding the RSFS *Fergus*, former commander of the corvette *Eochaid* in the *Regneri* incident. Also former CO of the *Gortforge*. Considered a good, but not outstanding ship-handler ... Sub-commander Forgael, exec and senior pilot, also competent, but was one of the principal grievants in the Naomi case ...

The Naomi case? Van concentrated, and his vastly improved memory—or memory access ability—brought up the name. Jillyan Naomi had been a major on the *deValera*, who had accused the senior commodore of pressuring junior female officers into having sex with him, promising either better annual reports or unsatisfactory ones. The evidence had been overwhelming, and the commodore had been courtmartialed. Major Naomi had been transferred to the *McCourt*. Two years later, her body had been found at the base of a stone staircase on Sulyn, where she had been on leave visiting a friend. A local magistrate had found that her death had been caused by a broken neck from a fall. The bruises on the inside of her arms had not been explained.

Van nodded to himself and went back to the entry before him.

> . . . None of the pilots on the *Fergus* are rated in the top-level
> of combat effectiveness . . .

Van drew in his breath. The implications were clear enough, but they were only implications, and not solid proof. He laughed softly. What he had wouldn't be admissible in any court, and certainly not before a Board of Inquiry—and he'd never survive to reach a board, not if he went through the RSF. It was clear enough to him that the Marshal's Council had wanted an "incident" in the Scandyan system, and they'd set it up in a way to remove another troublesome officer—him. When that had failed, they had implemented an alternative plan.

He continued to search through the files until he found another hint.

> . . . contingency plans required activation of Commander
> Baile. After the loss of the *Fergus* in transit back to Tara . . .
> only remaining survivor of the *Fergus*'s encounter with the
> unidentified cruiser is Commodore Van Albert . . . recommend
> retirement . . . commodore's health will be known to be less
> than perfect after his medical treatment in the aftermath of the
> Revenant attack on the Keltyr embassy in Valborg . . . would
> not be surprising if he did not long survive once he returns to
> Bannon . . .

The mention of contingency plans and the "activation" of Commander Baile were suspicious. Even so, the pieces fit together, though some were missing. But once again, even if Van could have forced release of the records, they were less than conclusive in a legal sense. Still, although he could not prove what had occurred, he had his answers—or enough of them.

In a practical sense, he could do very little. He couldn't prove anything, and he dared not return to the Republic, not with two deaths on his hands, even though the RSF might never make the connection, and even if one of the deaths was in self-defense and the other certainly justified . . .

But . . . was he just rationalizing? Did his need to know, to discover what had happened, really justify his actions?

He'd done what he'd thought was right for Tara time after time, and in the end, what had he gotten? Any number of attempts to kill him or set him up to be killed, and the sacrifice of at least two RSF ships for political purposes.

He needed to send off a message torp to Trystin and meet with him—again—on Perdya. Between the Revenants and the Tarans, their section of the Arm was looking less and less stable—and Van didn't even know what might be happening with the Argenti and the Coalition.

He checked the EDI screen again.

Neither of the cruisers had moved, but Van changed his own course to move "down" at right angles to the system ecliptic. That would play hell with his jump calculations, and add hours, if not days, to his transit time to Perdya, but there was no way any Republic vessel could reach him before he could reach an area clear enough for the *Joyau* to jump clear. After all he had done, he didn't feel like risking anything more, just in case, unlikely as it was, that in the time since he'd left the RSF headquarters, the bodies had been found and linked to the "*Diaphur.*"

Chapter 67

More than half a week passed before Van managed to lock the *Joyau* into Perdya's orbit station. The off-coordinate jump translation had resulted in the loss of three days in translation time, and an additional two days in nonjump travel because the *Joyau* had dropped into norm space well away from Perdya. Still, Van had preferred the lost time to the possibility of an encounter with RSF warships.

He just hoped that his family had gotten his message—and that they had acted upon it. He couldn't make them, but everything pointed to the Republic becoming more and more inhospitable to black Tarans in the days and months to come.

Once the *Joyau* was safely locked in, Van left Eri on board to handle the maintenance and took the down-shuttle to Cambria, even though the IIS headquarters had already informed him that no one knew where Trystin was—only that he had left word that he was in an uninhabited system engaged in testing equipment.

Joseph Sasaki was waiting when Van stepped off the lift on the top floor of the IIS building.

"Have you heard anything new from Director Desoll?" Van asked. "I'd sent a torp . . ."

"We relayed it via coded standing wave," Sasaki replied. "I hoped you might know where he was. Less than an hour ago, we just got word. The Revenants have just smashed the Keltyr fleet, and are taking over the Keltyr systems . . . or half of them. The other half, the ones closest to the Taran systems, are being taken by RSF fleets . . ."

For a moment. . . . Van just gaped. He felt as if he'd been gut-punched. "The RSF . . . Tara . . . they're cooperating, allying themselves with the Revenants?"

"That's what the Service says, and we're getting coded standing wave messages from the planetary offices in the Keltyr systems. The media haven't reported it yet. I expect that any moment."

Van shook his head. The pieces had been there. He just hadn't expected them to go together that way.

Sasaki stiffened.

Van sensed the incoming and waited.

Sasaki looked at Van. "Let's go to your office. There's a standing wave message for you."

The two walked silently down the corridor. Once in his office, Van used the system to call up and display the message. Decrypted, it was simple enough.

Immediate action: *Joyau* is to take on a complete load of message torps, cargo awaiting at the Aerolis Belt shipyard, and any additional message torps able to be fitted in the *Joyau*'s cargo bay. Make rendezvous with *Salya* and the *Elsin* ASAP.

The coordinates were there, but offhand Van didn't know where they might be, except they looked to be somewhere close to the Revenant systems.

"That says where he'll be," Van said. "And where we'll all be." He pulsed an order for a hard copy of the coordinates, even as he used his implant to burn them into memory.

Sasaki looked back at Van. "I've ordered a private shuttle to get you back to orbit control two. I don't think you'd better wait for the regular shuttle. The private shuttle will be touching down on the grass in front of the building in five minutes."

"That bad?"

"The Coalition knows Director Desoll. They know he's not here, but it won't take them long to think about you and Nynca."

Van didn't even nod. He just retrieved the hard copy of the message and coordinates, folded it and slipped it into his shipsuit, then turned and hurried to the lift. Even so, the shuttle was waiting for him, hovering over the grass.

"Director Albert?" called a crewman in a maroon shipsuit.

"That's me."

"We need to hurry."

Van jumped onto the ramp that didn't quite touch the ground. Even before he was inside, the shuttle was climbing, and by the time he strapped into one of the luxurious leather couches, it was screaming skyward. Van was the only passenger.

The Revenants taking over the Keltyr systems? Given what Van had seen in the last few years, that didn't surprise him as much as the Republic's alliance with the Revs. His own people, though? Should he have seen it? Ashley had as much as told him that matters were getting bad, and that had been two and a half years ago. His fathers' messages had also suggested the same. Then there had been the growing numbers of unfavorable references to the Keltyr that he'd observed.

So why was it so hard to believe?

Because he'd wanted to believe the RSF and the Republic were better than the Revenants? Because, despite the way he'd been treated, he'd hoped for better? Again, he had to ask himself whether the entire Republic culture was what he had thought—or what he had wanted to believe.

He forced himself to try to relax as he waited.

As the shuttle neared orbit control, the crewman reappeared. "The private lock is closer to your ship, but you'll need to hurry. They're debating whether to close Perdya to both outgoing and incoming traffic. A decision could come anytime."

"Thank you." Van nodded and began to unstrap. He followed the crewtech to the lock, where he stood waiting.

There was a muted *thump* as the shuttle eased into the locking bay, followed by the hissing of pressurization.

As Van started to step out of the lock, the crewman grinned. "We're all behind you."

Van accepted the words with a nod and another, "Thank you." Behind him—or IIS? For what? To take on the Revenants?

He hurried down the station corridors to lock charlie three.

Once more, Eri was waiting.

"We're leaving immediately?" she asked.

"For Aerolis." Van pulsed the lock closed and headed for the cockpit. Rushing back to the ship was getting to be too much of a habit. "To pick up torps and cargo, and then rendezvous with the *Elsin* and the *Salya*." Van paused. "Did you hear about the attack on the Keltyr?"

"Yes. Joseph linked here just a while ago."

"We need to get clear before the Coalition decides to

freeze traffic." Van slipped into the command couch.

Eri laughed. "We should hurry, but they will wait until we're clear."

"Because they know IIS."

"Because they know Trystin," she replied.

Chapter 68

From the beginning of written human history, there has always been a debate over the ethics of ends and the ethics of means. Can a good and ethical solution result from the use of unethical or immoral means? Does the end justify the means? Virtually all ethicists would agree that, of course, it does not, because, first, actions should be ethical in and of themselves, and, second, because corrupt means almost invariably result in corrupting the ends.

One difficulty with this position has been discussed in some detail, and that is the problem of war. War is evil, yet wars have been fought to combat and correct greater evils. If one accepts the premise of the ethicists, then greater evil will always triumph because the ethical soul will not stoop to an unethical action, even if it precludes a greater evil. The necessary evil of war against a greater evil has become accepted as the necessary compromise, in practical terms, and nation after nation, political system after political system, has gone to extreme lengths to "prove" that each was only acting to prevent a greater evil when it has gone to war.

This conflict between practice and theory obscures a more fundamental question that both ethicists and politicians have avoided whenever possible: Are there societies and cultures that are so evil that they do not deserve to survive? Certainly, at times in human history, scholars and politicians have judged that certain societies fit that criterion, but almost always comfortably in academic retrospect or in grandiose political statements that lead nowhere except to public office.

Unfortunately, that is all too often where the public discussion ends.

What of the other problem—the case where unethical ends lead to ethical results or where truly ethical means lead to an unethical result? We see few discussions about either possibility, particularly about the idea that ethical and moral people or principles can in fact create unethical ends. Yet how much suffering has been created by truly good men pursuing ends they thought ethical and moral? Is it not possible that such pursuit could lead to true evil?

> *Values, Ethics, and Society*
> Exton Land
> New Oisin, Tara
> 1117 S.E.

Chapter 69

The trip outbound from Perdya to the outer Belt had been quiet, although Van had noted several Coalition warships also traveling outbound. Mason Jynko had had both a dozen armed torps, a half dozen message torps, and ten large smooth-finished crate-boxes—each roughly two meters long and a meter in height and width—waiting for the *Joyau* at the Aerolis complex.

Two short hours had been all that it took them to load the *Joyau*, although the mass of the unmarked boxes was significant.

"What's in them?" Van had asked.

"I don't know," Jynko had replied. "These are the last ones. He brought them in sealed. The mass calculations are on each, but I don't know what they are."

So Van was carrying ten crate-boxes, each one massing

close to two hundred kilos, plus ten spare torps, in the cargo bay.

As they cleared the Belt complex, outbound, Van scanned the EDI screens. There were more warships gathered, a fleet in each outer quadrant, than Van had ever seen before in one system, and all were Coalition ships.

"The Coalition isn't exactly happy," he observed, looking across at Eri, strapped in the second seat.

"That is an understatement. The last conflict with the Revenants almost destroyed the Coalition. Now . . . with the Taran Republic as an ally . . ."

"I can't believe the Republic stooped that low . . ."

"Stooping low is easy," Eri commented dryly. "Rising above baseness is rarer."

"You're right about that. But . . ." He checked the outbound course again, easing the *Joyau* another ten degrees to port, just to make certain they would reach a jump point well away from any of the gathering Coalition warships. He still had trouble understanding either how he had been so blind or how things had changed so much and so quickly in the Republic.

Before they had even reached Aerolis, Van had checked the rendezvous coordinates and verified them. The *Joyau*'s destination was a system without even planoformable planets, but a system high in the Arm, well "above" most of the human systems.

"We all want to believe better of where we were raised, I guess," Van continued. "At least, I do."

"Like . . . Director Desoll, you are an idealist," Eri said evenly.

"Is that bad?" asked Van, half-wondering why Eri was suddenly so talkative, even as he checked systems and screens again. They still had another two hours before they would reach a position far enough from the gravitational fluxes with a low enough dust density to permit a jump.

"Most revolutionaries and many tyrants began as idealists."

"So why did they change?"

"Because they expected too much from the common people. Director Desoll, he protests that he does not. But he does."

That was another disturbing thought, at least to Van. "In what way does he expect too much of people?"

"He expects that they will act in their own interests. They do not, because they do not know what is best. They only know what they want."

Van nodded, thinking of his fathers and the conversation they once had had about most people being creatures of appetite rather than of thought.

"Someday he will do something that is terrible and wonderful," Eri said. "Again."

Again? Van straightened in the command couch. "What did he do before?"

"I do not know. Nynca said that, but she would not explain."

"What exactly . . . is she his daughter?" Van blurted.

Eri smiled. "No. I do not know, but . . . she may be the daughter of his granddaughter. I do not know this, but from what they have said, I think it may be so."

Van frowned. Marti had said that Trystin was old, but Nynca was older than Van, and, if she were his great grandchild, that meant that Trystin had to be well over a hundred fifty. He looked fifty at the most. Marti had suggested that Trystin might be one of the handful of immortals, and Van had to believe that well might be the case . . . unsettling as the implications were.

Chapter 70

Van was on full alert when the *Joyau* came out of jumpspace, scanning the system, but there were only two EDI traces in the entire system. One was a comparator beacon, and the other matched the profile of the *Elsin*.

He was still wondering what Trystin had done that was so wonderful and terrible, and whether it could really have been either. Even with the power of IIS behind him, Trystin hadn't done that much, not in the larger scheme of things. Between them, over the past few years, they'd destroyed perhaps ten Revenant vessels. While those losses might have been significant to the Beldorans or the Keshmarans, that number was a mere annoyance to powers like the Revenants, the Coalition, or the Argenti, and slightly more than a minor problem to the Republic.

Still scanning the screens and checking monitors, Van turned the *Joyau* toward the *Elsin*.

"Two hours, I'd guess," Van said to Eri in response to her unspoken question. "The *Salya*'s not on the screens yet."

"Nynca will be here," Eri predicted.

"She won't be happy, but she'll be here."

"She is less certain than he is."

Van almost laughed. Trystin did have an air of certainty, of complete assurance that what he did was the right thing to do. "I'm in her camp."

Eri only nodded.

Van's thoughts dropped back to his fathers, to Sappho and Aelysa and their children, and to Arturo. He couldn't help worrying about them, hoping that they were all right. But, at the moment, he couldn't do any more than he'd already done. He'd warned them, and he'd sent funds, but there was no way he could land on Sulyn without either taking the *Joyau* or without a fleet behind him—and neither was possible. He couldn't just spend millions he didn't have or spend IIS funds to jump halfway across the Arm because he was worried.

As the *Joyau* neared the *Elsin*, Van kept checking the screens, but the system remained as empty as before, with just the beacon and the two IIS ships showing.

Finally, he pulsed, **Elsin,** *this is* **Joyau**, approaching for rendezvous.

*Just lock to the **Elsin** and come aboard,* Trystin replied.

Commencing approach for locking.

We're standing by.

Once the approach and locking was complete, Van set the shipnet on remote and made his way to the lock. From there, he stepped from the lock of the *Joyau* into the *Elsin*.

Trystin stood there. For the first time, he looked older, his face almost gaunt, with deep and dark circles under his eyes. Van did not see Alya, who had been working as Trystin's tech.

"You've been working hard," Van observed.

"Some things take more effort." The older pilot gestured toward the captain's stateroom.

Van followed, but this time took the console chair, leaving the more comfortable armchair for Trystin.

"Let's start with you," Trystin began. "You had asked to rendezvous."

"You know about the Revenant and Republic attack on the Keltyr systems?"

"That's why we're here. We'll get to that. Why had you asked me to meet you?"

"Some of it's not so important now. It makes more sense, though. The RSF staged a coup, using the same sort of techniques that the Revenants did on Scandya—except they were successful in New Oisin . . ." Van went on to summarize his experiences, and his information raiding expedition. ". . . and when you look at it in light of the assault on the Keltyr systems, it all makes sense. They've been trying to push out and minimize the Coalition presence in the Republic, as well as using confiscatory legislation and economic policies to appropriate assets. I'd bet that those assets have gone into ships, supplies, and training."

"How do you feel about it?" asked Trystin.

"Upset . . . worried. I'm afraid my family's still on Sulyn, and that's one of the places where internal security has been putting down unrest."

"Betrayed?"

"That, too," Van admitted. "That's been going on longer than I'd guessed. I know it all happened, but I still find it hard to believe."

"That's because not enough people said, "No." To stop

evil, someone has to say no. At times, if the society's strong, more than one person says it. At the present, none of the major societies in the Arm are strong. As I told you, it took years to find someone suitable for IIS."

"That's not why you rescued me from the RSF. Or why you prodded me to go back there." Van said quietly. "You've wanted a good combat pilot from the beginning, haven't you?"

"Yes, because I knew that IIS would run into more and more dangerous situations. It's been getting worse for years. There's more and more reliance on force, rather than order or cooperation." Trystin cleared his throat. "I didn't prod you to take a look at the systems in the Republic. Suggested. That's because I knew you needed to come to some resolution about that."

Van doubted he really had come to any internal resolution about how he felt about the Republic. "I still don't know why you picked me."

"Like a long-ago mythical figure who took a lantern, I went looking for an honest man. There aren't many, not even in as many stars as the Arm has. Not honest able men who will act."

"I'm not one."

"Honest men always say that."

"I'm not honest," Van said. "And I've blood on my hands. More than I'd ever thought when I was a bright-eyed lieutenant so many years back. There's more every year. I killed that Marine in RSF headquarters . . . Vickry and all those in the Revenant ships—and in the *Collyns*."

"You can't wash away the blood," Trystin replied. "I know that. I wouldn't take too much guilt for it, either. Let me ask you a few questions. First . . . that Marine in RSF headquarters. He shot to kill you, not to capture you. What was so important in that building that he had orders to kill? Second, why do you feel guilt at all about the *Collyns*? The ship attacked you, and if you hadn't destroyed it, you'd have died—"

"But in a way it was futile. Everyone but me died anyway. And it's still blood."

"It is," Trystin agreed, looking squarely at Van. "Every minute of every day, we spill the blood of something, either directly or indirectly. And we know it. We try to repress it, to sanitize it. But to live, an animal must kill, and shed blood, directly or indirectly. Even in a high-tech society, we do it. We just do it indirectly. We take the resources and use them. What we take someone else cannot use. Oh . . . it's more sanitary that way, but it's still killing."

"I'm not sure I . . . Aren't you justifying the Revenants? They're direct, and they're honest in that way. They'll lie, steal, and murder to expand their systems . . . Anything that will maximize their survival and expansion."

"No. Ethics is the progress away from murder, from destruction and rapine, toward the indirect methods of survival that disturb other life and other cultures the least. The goal is to use technology to re-create life in harmony—

"Every so-called utopia has ended up a dystopia. It can't be done."

"You may be right," Trystin said quietly. "But isn't it worth the blood? Isn't it worth the struggle?"

Van paused. *Isn't it worth the struggle?* Wasn't that really what life was all about? "So . . . tell me again how what IIS, how what we're doing makes it better?"

Desoll shook his head. "*You* tell me. Tell me how what you did in Islyn or Beldora or New Oisin makes a better Galaxy."

"I don't know that it did," Van protested. "In Islyn, all I ended up doing was salvaging as much of our assets as I could. In Beldora, I destroyed three Revenant ships and a bunch of mining tugs . . ."

"You kept the Revs from bombarding the planet and killing most of the population. Three ships for an entire population. Wasn't that an improvement?"

"Only for the moment. I couldn't stay around. The Hyndjis *might* send some ships to stop a second attempt."

"In the end . . . everyone dies. All we can do is what we can do now."

For Van, that didn't seem like near enough.

"You don't think that's enough?"

"I didn't say that."

"You might as well have," Trystin pointed out. "It was inscribed on your face." He paused. "I'm going to ask you to do what you just indicated you wanted done."

"What?" Van was confused.

"I'll get to that in a moment." Trystin fingered his chin. "Would you say that ethical civilization is in danger now? In grave danger?"

"Danger? Yes. Grave danger . . . I don't know."

"Danger of destroying all that has been built up here in the Arm?" pressed Trystin.

"I don't think we're in that much danger now."

"Let's see," mused the older man. "The Coalition has refused to act against the Revenants for so long that the Revs have been able to build up huge and hidden fleets. They've taken over system after system, either through economic or military means. In effect, through pressure and fear, they've subverted your home system, and are now in the process of smashing and taking over the Keltyr systems. Now . . . you could make an argument that this conquest isn't necessarily bad—that it is a necessary means to a good end." Trystin smiled ironically. "Do you think that the Republic is a better, fairer, and more ethical place to live now than it was a generation ago?"

"No."

"Do you think most people would rather live under the Revenant theocracy?"

"No. But that doesn't make it a grave danger to all humanity in the Arm."

"It doesn't?" asked Trystin. "When the end result will be self-destruction of the higher ideals and the subjugation of reason and tolerance to the code of an outdated deity?"

Van just waited to hear what more Trystin had to say.

"Self-destruction comes in many forms. One of the most deadly is when ethical collapse is combined with technological advancement. You can study all of human history, and that pattern is the most deadly. Almost invariably, it results in massive devastation."

"So . . . you seem to have an idea. Just what are we going to do—with our three ships that aren't quite light cruisers—against the Revenants and all their massive fleets?"

"The Coalition is massing its fleets, isn't it?"

"How did you know?"

"It's on standing wave." Trystin smiled coldly. "The Coalition cannot afford to wait any longer. They've already waited too long. The Revenants have been building fleets and hiding them in uninhabited systems—like this one. If there is an all-out war, and unless we can influence its outcome, the destruction and devastation will be massive and will drag in all the inhabited systems in the Arm."

"What can we do about it?" Van asked again, wishing Trystin would get to the point.

"We're going to fry their entire communications network. All their standing wave transmission capabilities, and all in-system communications in the Jerush system."

Van just stared at the older man.

Trystin smiled.

"Even if that were technically feasible," Van said, "how would the Revs ever let us close enough to do that?"

"It is feasible, and possible. It's an offshoot of the energy transmission project I've been working on. Focused properly, it can stir up enough of a jumpspace flux to disrupt all communications in a system, and the feedback and returned energy will burn out any transmitter that they attempt to use for days, perhaps weeks."

"And we're the only ones who can undertake this heroic and near-impossible mission?" Van couldn't blunt the sarcasm in his voice.

"No. We're the only ones who will. If you and Nynca will help."

"Where is she?"

"She just finished her jump. The *Salya* should be here in, say, three hours. Then I'll outline how we'll do it." Trystin stood. "Go get something to eat and get some sleep. Once we get started, you won't have a chance for much of either."

Van stood. Again, Trystin radiated confidence, but there

was something behind that confidence. Sadness? Was that it? Van wasn't sure, but why would Trystin be sad about disrupting Revenant communications to allow the Coalition forces a greater chance of victory?

"We'll talk more when Nynca gets here," Trystin added.

Van nodded in response, then turned to head back to the *Joyau*.

Chapter 71

The three commanders sat around the mess table in the *Elsin*. Nynca's face was almost as drawn as Trystin's although she didn't have the dark circles under her eyes that Trystin did.

Van listened, trying not to think about what might be happening to his family with the unrest in the Republic, and whether anyone would trace his actions back to them.

". . . the paired generators shoot out thousands of what might be called jumpholes—they're miniature extrusions of nothingness—and inverted matter . . ."

"Antimatter?" asked Van.

"Inverted matter's not quite the same," Trystin explained. "It wouldn't be stable even in an antimatter universe. The paired flows create massive surface disruptions to any sun's fluxes and magnetic fields."

"Massive solar storms, then?" Nynca's voice was matter-of-fact.

Trystin nodded. "They'll be strong enough to burn out the interior of all standard comm equipment inside the orbits of the gas giants. With the photon blasts, Orum and all the satellite bases and orbit stations will be blind for days. The underspace flux ripple effects will stop standing wave transmissions for several days, at least. Another effect will be that the jump distance will increase for several weeks, and that will delay ships entering and leaving the system."

"How will this stop the Revenants from completing the conquest of the Keltyr systems?" Van asked.

An ironic smile crossed Trystin's face. "A good portion of their reserve fleet is in the Jerush system."

"How do—"

"I looked. It made sense. Theocracies are tightly controlled. Also, with the rest of their fleets in Keltyr territory, they'd certainly want to protect the capital system—home of the Prophet and the Temple." He shook his head. "Too bad they didn't keep listening to the latest incarnation of their Prophet."

"People forget," Nynca said quietly. "In time, even the strongest examples of a prophet are forgotten and pass into legend."

"Legend." Trystin snorted. "Legends have to be reinforced. Or replaced."

Van sensed that he was missing something, but he didn't know enough even to ask a general question.

"You've explained what this equipment will do," Nynca said quickly. "How are you going to get it in place, and what do you want from us?"

"That's simple enough. We use an escape pod, with its onetime jump generator. It translates the equipment, which has shields, into the sun—"

"Into the system sun?" asked Nynca. "How long will the shields last under those conditions?"

"Five seconds, if my calculations are correct," Trystin replied. "Twice as long as the ship's shields would . . ."

Left unsaid were two facts. First was that a jump in-system would destroy the jump generators, and second that, even had the generators survived, nothing could jump out of a solar mass. So any trip was strictly onetime, one-way, and that meant that the escape pod had to be programmed and directed precisely.

"That's if you don't translate into the core, and that's why the translation has to be made from as close to the sun as possible—just on the fringe of the density drop-off."

"Can you get that kind of accuracy?" asked Nynca.

Van marveled at their cool discussion. He was still having trouble with the entire idea of sending an untested chunk of equipment into the sun of the Revenant home system to disrupt communications enough to leave the home system blind—and vulnerable to an attack, presumably by the Coalition.

"I've tested it. Burned out two generators. It works. Once you've got the hardware, it's not all that difficult," Trystin said, looking at Van. "Your cargo is the spare set. I wanted it here, in case something went wrong. It has a complete set of instructions inside."

Van hadn't even looked inside the boxes.

"What do you want from Van and me?" Nynca asked.

"Cover," Trystin replied. "I'll need some time to get the pod ready, and I can't do it if I have to fight off Rev patrols. They'll be there, probably not so far out . . . but that doesn't mean they won't come after us . . ."

"How long will it take?"

"Between thirty and forty-five standard minutes. We'll be on the system fringe."

Nynca nodded. "Thought as much."

"Assuming . . . just assuming that we pull this off," Van asked, "what do we do afterward? I can't imagine we'll be terribly welcome anywhere in the Arm, except perhaps Santonio or Silvium, or . . ." He shrugged.

"If it works as planned," Trystin replied, "the Coalition and the Argentis will be too busy to worry about us, and we should regroup at Aerolis. But . . . if there's any trouble, we should make for Dharel."

"The Farhkans?" asked Nynca. "Why?"

"They like to look into how we mess things up," Trystin said dryly. "Also, if there's trouble, someone might try to find us. That's one place where no one will think of—or want to follow."

"You're worried about how well this will work, aren't you?"

"Not about how well it will work," Trystin replied. "It will. What will happen afterward is another question. Also, we don't know what sort of shape the ships will be in, either."

"Because we might have to fight our way into position?" asked Van.

"That's really a matter of luck." Trystin shrugged. "They can't have enough ships there to cover the entire system. No government can. What protects a system is the fact that an attacker has to come out of jump hours, if not days, away from the habitable zone, and that allows defenders to move into position. We don't have to get anywhere near the habitable zone. We'll have to work from the jump zone, and even if we come in close to a Revenant patrol, we'll likely have a good twenty or thirty minutes."

"Do you have the coordinates?" Nynca's voice was resigned.

"You have a better idea?" asked Trystin.

"No. That's the problem. No one listened to the better ideas—nor to you—when they would have worked."

"And you took care of the messages?" Trystin looked to Van. "I asked her to have some messages sent on a delay basis to both the Argentis and the Coalition. They suggest that the Revenants may be having severe communications problems—and that a number of their ships in the Jerush system might not be usable in combat—"

"Because their sensors might also get fried?" asked Van.

"That's right." Trystin cleared his throat. "That means one other thing. If we don't jump before the wave front reaches us—the flux wave front, not the electromag wave front—then we'll be stuck in the Jerush system."

"We could shutter."

"Some of their ships will certainly do so as well." Trystin looked from Nynca to Van. "I'll give a countdown to jump. You'll have less than thirty seconds. Do you understand?"

Both Nynca and Van nodded.

"We'd better get moving," Nynca said.

"Do you need any help with the equipment?" asked Van.

"It's ready to deploy." Trystin stood.

Van also stood.

"You go first," Nynca said to Van. "It's easier that way."

Van inclined his head, then turned.

He did not look back as he headed to the lock, but he couldn't help but sense the hug Nynca gave Trystin, or the words that followed.

". . . be careful . . . wish it hadn't turned this way . . ."

". . . do what I can . . . my responsibility . . ."

Van frowned. *What* was Trystin's responsibility? What IIS had done? He couldn't have meant the Revenants were his responsibility. No man could take responsibility for a culture, especially one not his own. Could he?

Chapter 72

Although the *Salya* jumped first, followed by the *Joyau*, when Van came out of jumpspace, the *Elsin* was already moving in-system, and the *Salya* was nowhere to be seen. Van checked the comparator beacon. He was definitely on the outskirts of the Jerush system.

The shipnet monitors had already begun to bring up the EDI traces, and Van could see almost fifty vessels, half of them light cruisers or larger vessels. His initial scan showed none of the heavier vessels near the two IIS ships, but two corvettes were within a thousand emkay. They had not reacted—yet.

Van extended the photon nets full, but did not draw on his accumulators, as he brought the *Joyau* after the *Elsin*.

"Eri . . . full combat restraint."

"Yes, ser." Eri's voice was strained.

The brightening of the corvettes' EDI traces indicated that they were adding power. After a moment, Van checked their courses—toward the *Elsin*, predictably enough. The *Salya* was still in transit, and while Trystin was doubtless a better combat pilot than Van, Trystin couldn't very well set up his device for delivery while under attack.

The Revenant corvettes continued to accelerate toward the *Elsin*.

Van increased his own acceleration, closing the gap as the *Elsin* decelerated. That meant that Trystin felt he couldn't move farther in-system.

The Revenant corvettes began to launch torps, in sets of two, salvo after salvo, all arcing toward the *Elsin*. Van counted sixteen.

As the torps closed on the *Elsin*, Van could see the other IIS ship's shields flare to maximum as Trystin transferred all power to them. But the *Elsin* launched no torps as a counter. Was Trystin so loaded with equipment that he carried no torps? Did the setup take both him and Alya?

Van kept checking the closures. He also noted four torps impacting the *Elsin*'s shields at once, and the slight shiver of amber flashing through Trystin's shields. He continued to concentrate on the Revs, and was almost within torp range when the two corvettes changed course, trying to bracket the *Joyau*.

Van sensed the slight raggedness in the shields and drives of the Revenant farther from the *Elsin* and turned the *Joyau* onto a head-to-head. He smiled, knowing that the corvette pilot would realize shortly that the *Joyau* could crush the smaller ship with screens alone. He also hoped that the pilot continued to think that the *Joyau* was either unarmed or unequipped for conventional combat.

The Revenant was brighter than that, launching a double salvo of torps, then making a tight turn back in-system. Too tight, Van realized. He immediately launched his own torps.

The Rev's screens flared amber, and Van sent a third torp.

The Rev tried to flip his shields to bring the heavier forward shields into play, but the strain on drives and shields was too much, and a flare of energy replaced the overstressed corvette.

Even before the energy dropped from the monitors, Van angled the *Joyau* toward the remaining corvette. The pilot, reacting to what he had seen, began salvoing his torps at the maximum rate—but that meant only eight torps before he seemed to exhaust his supply. Van cut all power to the drives and screens, redirected it to the shields, and shuttered everything.

Two minutes later, the *Joyau* was through the wash of energy and closing on the Revenant, who had turned insystem. Van redirected power to the drives, and with half shields, began to overhaul the Revenant.

Three torps were enough to take out the smaller vessel.

Van turned his attention back out-system toward the *Elsin*, seemingly stationary in the system. The shipnet monitors indicated that one of the Revenant cruisers had turned and was accelerating out-system toward the IIS ships, with a CPA of twenty, plus or minus five.

Status green? Van pulsed toward the *Elsin*, not wanting to give an identity.

Green, affirmed Trystin. *But the concussions shook up my packages. May take longer than I'd thought.*

Do you want me to bring over my packages?

Negative this time. Take longer to set them up than to set things right here.

Van studied the screens. The oncoming cruiser was pushing everything to reach them.

With a tight smile, Van swung the *Joyau* into a tight turn, one that would sweep through the area where the second corvette had disintegrated.

Interrogative assistance, came from the *Salya*, now moving in-system.

Stand by, Van replied. *Cover number one.* He'd never worked with Nynca before, and two uncoordinated ships were at greater risk than a single vessel.

Will do.

As the photon nets pulled in the molecular debris from the second corvette, Van monitored the strain on the ship systems. He was carrying a mass load close to design limits, but that wouldn't matter if the strategy worked. If it didn't, then the *Joyau* couldn't hold off a heavy cruiser for all that long.

Interrogative time necessary? Van pulsed to the *Elsin*.

Twenty, with luck.

Stet.

Van frowned. A corvette had appeared out-system of the *Salya*. Had one of the Revs used a short jump? That was almost suicidal—except that it had worked.

Nynca changed course to put the *Salya* between the corvette and the *Elsin*.

Van went back to concentrating on the oncoming heavy cruiser, a vessel that massed twice what the *Joyau* did. Since both the Revenant cruiser and the *Joyau* were on a closure course, the CPA had dropped to less than fifteen.

For an instant, he focused on the *Salya* and the Revenant corvette. Nynca had launched torps, and two of the Rev's torps had flared harmlessly against the *Salya*'s shields.

Another cruiser had turned out-system, but according to Van's calculations, would not reach the *Joyau* for close to thirty minutes.

Van watched as the *Joyau* and the closer Revenant cruiser neared each other. The Revenant began to launch torps even before the two ships were within effective torp range. The first four flared away harmlessly a good emkay short of the *Joyau*'s shields.

Van dropped all power to the drives and gravs, and transferred it to the forward shields.

The next set of torps—four in all—impacted the shields, but not simultaneously, and the shields shivered, but remained in the green.

Because the *Joyau* still wasn't close enough for what Van needed to do, he shifted power to the drives for a moment, then returned it to the shields before the cruiser's next salvo arced toward the smaller IIS ship. Again, the *Joyau*'s reinforced shields held, staying in the green, if barely, as Van kept his course head-on-head with the cruiser.

The cruiser shifted course, not by much, less than five

degrees, as if to avoid a collision. Van shifted his course to return to a steady bearing, decreasing range. There was less than five minutes to CPA, although it was unlikely to be a collision, given the relative velocities and speeds. Van just wanted to be close enough to use the *Joyau*'s nets and torps to full advantage.

The cruiser's next salvo brought the faintest trace of amber into the *Joyau*'s shields.

Van checked the closure—still not near enough.

Within another minute, the two vessels would be within less than twenty klicks, flashing toward and past each other.

Van slewed the *Joyau* across the projected course line of the cruiser, then flexed the photon nets, released all the matter gathered there, and followed with two quick salvoes of torps, then another.

The Revenant cruiser's shields flared bright green as the cruiser impacted the wave of matter Van had flung, then dropped to amber, but held.

Van loosed another double salvo of torps.

The cruiser's shields held, momentarily, and in the amber, but they held. Van could see the Revenant's EDI drive indicators flickering, and he let loose another set of torps. He hoped they'd take out the cruiser, because, until he and Eri could manually reload the spare torps in the cargo bay into the firing bays, the *Joyau* was down to two torps.

The cruiser's drives flickered off, but the screens remained amber.

Van fired his last two torps, then swung the *Joyau* out-system.

Behind him, the cruiser's screens collapsed, and the cruiser flared into energy.

Van checked the wider monitors.

The *Salya* had taken station near the *Elsin*, and there was no sign of the Revenant corvette, but another cruiser had turned out-system to follow the one that was only fifteen minutes from intercepting the three IIS ships.

After another five minutes, Van was close enough to pulse the *Elsin*.

Interrogative status?

I've had to improvise here, but everything's go. Countdown beginning at sixty. Departure in thirty. Beginning countdown at sixty. Departure at thirty.

Van let out a slow breath. *Affirm departure in thirty.*

In thirty, affirm, came from the *Salya*.

. . . thirty-six, thirty-five, thirty-four, thirty-three, thirty-two . . .

The transmission from the *Elsin* broke off. Van stiffened. The *Elsin* had vanished—gone jump. He scanned the EDIs, then the system screen.

Van froze, if but for an instant. The EDI screen showed—impossibly—an enormous flare surging out from Jerush—the sun itself—what looked to be a major flare.

"No . . ." murmured Eri from the second seat.

Van froze, if but for a milli-instant. The release of energy shown in the EDI screen was not just a massive solar wind, a comm disruption, but something with enough energy, heat, and power to broil the sunward side of Orum, or burn it to a crisp, strip the atmosphere away. The image of eight white towers melting down instantaneously flashed across his mind, followed by the screams of millions of men, women, and children, walking, talking, one moment, and then . . .

Convulsively, Van initiated the jumpshift—hoping that he had not been too late, and hoping that Nynca had not waited so long as Van had.

The *Joyau* twisted, and Van felt his guts being ripped in different directions, pulled out from inside him, even as they simultaneously were being crushed into the internal equivalent of a black hole.

Black flashes alternated with white flares, and the entire ship shuddered in the endless and yet instantaneous moment of jump.

The *Joyau* staggered—that was the only word that fit—out of jump. Van checked the systems, half-surprised that they had made it anywhere. The ship was somewhere on the fringes of the Perdyan system, but well out beyond normal jump emergence.

Then he just sat in the command couch, shuddering, as image after image ran through his mind, of oceans instantly boiling away, of waves of flames incinerating everything before them, before the air vanished, of the strongest buildings being flattened, just before the very ground turned to molten rock, of mountains melting down like candles in a wildfire, of seas boiling away in an instant . . .

While trying to cope with those images, he automatically ran diagnostics. Both jump generators were inoperative. The secondary screen generator was down. He tried to spread the photon nets, and got fifty-seven percent of maximum extension.

The *Joyau* was headed in-system, and Van sat stunned in the command seat, images jumbled together, images of shuttles being dashed from the skies, of orbit stations being vaporized, of all the Revenant ships in-system knowing the wave front was accelerating toward them, and those in the inner system unable to move fast enough to reach a place where their shields would protect them, and those in the outer system, half-blinded, unable to jump, their habitability systems failing . . . slowly, inevitably.

. . . and the millions upon millions of people . . . gone . . . dead . . . instantly.

Van couldn't stop shuddering, even though his entire body felt bruised and sore, and each shudder racked him.

Across from him, Eri was unconscious, but breathing, and the medical scan indicated no severe physical trauma.

Sometime later, an hour perhaps, Van pulled himself out of his stupor and checked the monitors, finally realizing that something had been nagging at him. He checked the systemwide EDIs. There were only about twenty Coalition warships—and all were drawn up in a defensive formation around Perdya. The other ships that had been mustering before he had jumped out-system were gone.

Where? They certainly hadn't gone to Jerush. The Keltyr systems?

Van continued to monitor the system as the *Joyau* built up

speed, headed in-system. Van reminded himself that deceleration would also take longer.

After another twenty minutes, Eri groaned.

Van unstrapped himself and went to the galley, where he started the kettle and the café maker. He tried not to think about what had happened in the Jerush system, but images still flashed across his mind. After the kettle boiled and the café was ready, he carried two mugs back to the cockpit.

Eri took the tea, but just cupped it between her hands.

"Why?" she asked.

"Why what?" Van took a sip of café. "The damage to the *Joyau*?" He didn't want to address the bigger why. "I waited too long. We did make it back. But we're outside Perdya, well outside, with no jump capability, and a little more than half drive capability. I'd guess close to twenty-plus hours to reach Aerolis. That's where we're headed because the *Joyau*'s in no shape to go anywhere else."

The tech nodded. She was pale. Finally, she sipped the tea.

Van checked the system again, but nothing had changed. It would be hours before they reached the normal jump exit zone. For a time, he just sat there. So did Eri.

"I was on the shipnet," Eri said. "When . . . he . . ." She shook her head.

Van swallowed. He hadn't even thought that Trystin had actually used the *Elsin* to deliver his device to the Revenant sun. "You think that he . . ."

Eri nodded. "He could not be certain otherwise."

"But Alya, I can't believe . . ."

"Was she on board? Did you see her?"

"No," Van admitted, "I didn't. I didn't hear anyone either." That would also have explained the extra setup time that Trystin had needed. "But why?"

"He needed to be certain," Eri said bleakly. "He always needed to be sure." She looked down at the mug she held.

Van couldn't say he understood. Trystin had never struck him as the martyr type. And Trystin had never lied to him. After a moment, Van laughed softly and bitterly. Trystin hadn't lied. He just hadn't told the entire truth—and that had happened before.

The Revenants—if not destroyed—were broken. Their home planets, their great Temple, and their defense fleet were all destroyed. The Coalition forces—and perhaps the Hyndjis and the Argentis—wouldn't hesitate to finish off the Revenant invasion fleets. Without those fleets, most of the planets taken over in recent years might well revert to their previous belief and social systems. Then, again, Van reflected, they might not.

He frowned. Except for him and Eri, and Nynca and her tech, who would know what had happened? Massive solar flares did happen. They were rare enough that no one could be sure exactly of the cause. Was that what Trystin wanted? A proof that the Revenants were not God's chosen people? A seemingly natural occurrence that cast massive doubts on the divine support of the Revenants?

Van took refuge in the shipnet, checking the system EDIs and the ship systems.

He still couldn't say he understood, especially after everything that Trystin had said about ethics—and the totally ethical way in which he had treated people. Van just hoped he would be able to understand when he knew more. If he could learn more. If he could put aside the images.

Chapter 73

Nynca and the *Salya* had reached Aerolis before Van and the *Joyau*, and Nynca was waiting at the tower lock once he had the *Joyau* docked.

Van wasn't certain he wanted to see her. The more he'd thought about what Trystin had done, the less he understood. The images still flashed through his mind. How could anyone believe that destroying a world, a system, with half a billion people, was ethical? Had Trystin been, at the end, a madman, as José Marti had suggested? How could he have been otherwise?

Where did that leave Van? He couldn't return home, not with what he'd been a party to, and not with the situation in the Republic. And he also didn't have a ship that was going anywhere, not anytime soon. Could he make amends through IIS? What would happen to IIS?

He pushed those thoughts aside as Nynca stepped into the *Joyau*'s lock. Her eyes were still reddened, and she had deep black circles under her eyes. Without a word, she walked into Van's stateroom and waited for him to close the door. Then she spoke. "Privacy. No recording."

Van nodded and triggered the little-used privacy cone.

"How much have you figured out?" she asked, without sitting down.

"He had it all planned." He cleared his throat. "Alya wasn't on board, was she?"

"No. He sent a burst coded message to me just before . . ." Nynca's lips tightened, and she looked down at the stateroom floor, at the synthetic parquet flooring.

"He wanted a natural occurrence to destroy the Revenants," Van offered. "One that would cast doubts on either their sense of divine mission, or one that would imply that their God disapproved of their actions. Maybe both." Van paused. "That's all I can really say that I truly understand. I don't . . . I can't . . . understand . . . there must have been five hundred million people . . . How could anyone . . . ?"

"That is the danger of age," she replied.

"The danger of age?" Van replied stupidly.

"How old do you think he was?" Nynca asked.

"At least a hundred fifty. There are some who thought he was an immortal."

"He was close to three hundred years old. He created IIS two hundred years ago, when it became clear that his first attempt to shift the course of Revenant history had failed."

"His first attempt?"

"He was the last prophet—the one who immolated himself in the Temple and ended the Coalition-Revenant War. He didn't, really, but that was the impression he left." Nynca swallowed. "He kept trying, using economic pressure, force . . . you've seen it all. Half the independent systems in the Arm wouldn't exist today without him and IIS."

"But . . . all those people . . . ?"

"He grew up in the first Great War. You must have read about it—where the Revenants sent millions of missionary troops across the Arm in troids. They sent millions. Their casualties were never totaled, but it was estimated that the Revenant systems lost over two hundred million young men and women in fifty years. The Coalition lost thirty million, or more. His sister—the *Salya* is named after her—was killed when a troid attack wiped out all civilians in a system being terraformed. It wasn't the only system treated that way by the Revenants."

"But . . . five hundred million?"

"How many systems have been taken over by the Revenants in the last two years—that you know of?"

"Five, six . . ."

"And what happened to those who don't want to become Revenants?"

"They're marginalized."

"Marginalized. That's a polite word, Van." Nynca's voice hardened. "What it means is that they lose their businesses, their jobs, and their homes. Sooner or later, they lose their lives. Most of them aren't executed. They just lose so much they wish they were. That still leaves millions who die in one way or another."

Van was silent.

"Trystin . . . he saw that beginning to happen again. The Coalition didn't want another war . . . they didn't want to deal with another thirty or forty million people lost. The Argentis didn't either. Both built up their forces, but no one wanted to go to war to save the Keltyr, or the Samarrans, or the Nraymarans, or Beldorans, or the Aluysons, or in a few years, the Scandyans. And that wasn't the only danger. What about your Republic? Wasn't it already leaning toward an alliance with the Revenants? That's what your reports indicated. The RSF felt they couldn't survive unless they made an alliance. How many people died or will die in those systems? Are their deaths any less important because they died in small groups or alone one at a time?"

Van was silent.

"What was he supposed to do, after everyone forgot what happened the last time? What was he supposed to do, when what he had attempted before had failed, and when everyone else stood around waiting? When IIS reported to everyone— we sent that information to every major government—and no one did anything except wring their hands?"

"And he felt it was his responsibility?"

"He hated the idea of his being responsible for their current culture. About ten years ago, he began to feel that by ending the war the way he had done he'd just made matters worse. That was when he built the *Elsin*, then commissioned the *Joyau*. He looked for someone like you for almost that long."

"Like me?"

"You're more like him than you know, Van."

"If you're worried—"

"I'm not worried about you saying anything. You wouldn't. He asked me to make sure you understood if he didn't get back. But he was only being gentle. He knew he wouldn't be back. You're the new managing director of IIS."

"Me? Why me? I'm still wrestling with . . . the magnitude of what he did. You're his great-great-granddaughter."

"You've left out several 'greats' there, even if I was named for his mother." Her voice was dry again. "You're not the only one wrestling. I argued against it. But I didn't have the answer to his last question." She paused. "He just asked, 'Who else will act for all the innocents that the Revenants will kill or destroy? Tell me, Nynca, who else will act?' That's what he asked." She looked hard at Van. "I didn't have an answer. Do you? Is it right . . . Gramps would have asked if it were ethical . . . to allow hundreds of millions of people to lose their freedoms and their lives because to stop it would require an equal or greater cost? Are principles only weighed by bodies alone? Is it not ethical to act ethically if it causes pain and suffering? You tell me before you judge him."

Van stepped back.

"I can't judge," she added in a low voice. "I know I couldn't do what he did. But I didn't stop him because I couldn't refute him. But I couldn't do it." She looked at Van. "I can plan for IIS, and I can support you, and I will. But . . . I'm not meant . . . I can't do what you and Gramps did."

"I don't know that I could do—"

Nynca laughed, harshly. "You already have. It's just on a smaller scale. I've read the reports on the Scandyan embassy affair and the *Regneri* incident."

"Isn't the threat . . ." Van let the words trail off.

"It's not over. It's never over. Who will make sure that the Argentis, or even the Coalition, don't pick up the mantle of divine support?"

"Mantle of divine support?"

"That's what he called it—the illusion that a culture is the chosen one, that its members can do no wrong."

Van could appreciate that terminology. He'd seen enough of that, both with the Revenants, and even in the Republic, especially lately.

"You need to get to Perdya to assure everyone that IIS will continue. We'll be leaving in two hours. The Coalition will be watching us closely, but they're allowing both in- and out-system transport."

"Thank you." Van studied Nynca, and the chill she projected. "I'm sorry. I didn't know that he'd planned to deliver his device . . . personally. I'd just never thought . . ."

"You couldn't have known. I've worked with him for years, and I didn't know. I knew he was more and more worried about the Revenants, and what they stood for, and about what they were doing to all cultures."

"All cultures? In reaction to them, you mean? That people can become exactly the same as their enemies in outlook and action?"

"You see? You understand."

"But . . . me?" Van said again.

"You're best for the job, and someone has to do it. Besides, it's what Gramps wanted."

"I wasn't looking . . ."

"I know." Nynca paused. "I'm not angry at you. I'm not angry at him. But I'm angry that things have to be the way they are."

That Van understood.

He just sat in the console chair, looking at nothing, long after Nynca had left.

In time, there was a tap on the door. Van sensed Eri beyond. "Come on in, Eri."

The diminutive tech stood there. "I wanted to tell you, ser . . ."

"I'll need a new tech?" Van asked gently.

She nodded. "I have done this long enough."

Van also understood that.

After Eri left, he began to pack a duffel, almost in a daze, knowing that was a luxury that he could not long indulge.

How could Trystin . . . all those millions? He frowned, shaking his head. On the other hand, how could he not . . . ?

Were there any answers? Real answers?

JUDGE

Chapter 74

Van eased the *Joyau* back out-system, checking the systems. Once more, he realized that he had no torps left, not a one, and there were at least two more cruisers headed out after him and the *Salya*.

Van studied the monitors, then pulsed, *Interrogative status?*

Had to improvise here . . . everything's go. Countdown beginning at sixty . . . fifty-nine, fifty-eight . . .

The numbers marched down slowly, and Van struggled to recall . . . something . . . there was something wrong about those numbers, something he should know. He glanced around the cockpit, familiar and yet unfamiliar . . . trying to remember . . .

. . . thirty-six, thirty-five, thirty-four, thirty-three, thirty-two . . .

The transmission from the *Elsin* broke off, and the *Elsin* had vanished.

And Van knew, his eyes frozen as the shipnet called up in his mind the energies flaring off the sun Jerush . . . and the wave fronts that would scour the planet of Orum clean of all life, and freeze the jumpships in place, unable to leave the system . . .

Could he jump the *Joyau*? After what would happen, could he?

He wanted to think, to come up with another answer. But it was already too late, and the black-white timelessness of jump washed over him.

Van sat up, soaked in sweat, breathing heavily.

Slowly, he swung his feet over the side of the luxurious bed in the top-floor apartment, and sat there for a time, trying to slow his heart and his breathing.

The same nightmare, seemingly every night.

But Van hadn't *known* . . . just as he hadn't known about the *Fergus* . . . or the *Collyns*.

"Should you have known? Shouldn't you have guessed?" he murmured to himself. But a nova device?

After several moments, he stood, then walked from the bedroom out into the sitting room, moving to the wide south window. Most of the city of Cambria looked dark, even in the damp winter, because the lights were designed to shine out and down, and not upward in a way to be visible from the sixth floor of the IIS building.

Ethics? How could Trystin have talked so much about ethics? Yet Dad Cicero had warned Van about men who trumpeted their ethics. Yet until the end, Trystin had acted for what Van might have called the greater good. It was better to destroy Revenant raiders than to allow them to terrorize systems that could not defend themselves. It was better to help businesses and small multis in ways so that they could compete and hold off, if not surmount, the subsidized and state-supported competition from Revenant institutions.

But . . . did that inevitably lead to . . . something like the Jerush flare?

Trystin had said that the technology was Farhkan. Did that mean . . . could they have somehow programmed the older man to destroy the Revenant home system? Trystin hadn't seemed programmed, not in the way that the clones in Scandya had been.

Van paced away from the window, still damp with sweat, then turned back.

Could he honestly continue to manage IIS? Could he not? What would happen to all the independent systems . . . or to the fringe planets even in the Argenti or Hyndji loop . . . if someone, something like IIS, didn't offer another alternative?

Or was that mere self-justification?

Van took a deep breath.

He hadn't done any of the things that plagued him in nightmares. Was he having the nightmares because he hadn't acted *after* he had learned? But what could he have done besides what he had? Walking away—from the RSF, from IIS—that didn't make things better. It was a meaningless symbolic act, as if to say that Van wasn't responsible. Was the guilt in what he felt because he hadn't seen and should have—and should have acted?

Just as he hadn't seen, or hadn't wanted to see, what had been happening in the Republic until it had been too late?

Van slowly looked from side to side and back again, his eyes facing the window, but not really seeing the city or the darkness beyond.

Chapter 75

In the late morning of fiveday, Van sat at the conference table in the ISS Cambrian office, in the position where Trystin had once seated himself. Van still didn't feel like the managing director of IIS, even after more than a week in Cambria, but everyone looked to him as that, probably because Nynca had made it absolutely clear that Van was indeed the managing director. Van had checked the records, and Trystin had only made the changes in the leadership contingency plan for IIS a month before his death—and he'd never told Van.

Van wondered if they all would have looked to him had they known of the nightmares and doubts that plagued him. Then he could see from the lines and the darkness behind Nynca's eyes that at least some of those demons tormented her as well. And Eri had simply left IIS, claiming her stipend.

"I've read your report," Van began, looking at Laren, the dark-haired woman in charge of research in Cambria. "It's good." It was good, even if Van didn't like the facts it contained. The Jerush system was uninhabitable, and would be for years, if not centuries, even with remedial planoforming. Uninhabitable . . . such a clean word to use after the death of over five hundred million people.

The Coalition forces, with assistance from the spinward Argenti fleets under General Marti, had defeated the Revenant fleets and destroyed most of the ships. A joint Argenti-Coalition task force was administering the Coalition "protectorate" over the former Revenant systems.

All that, Van could understand and accept, if reluctantly. What he had trouble accepting was the joint Coalition-Argenti decision to allow the Republic of Tara, scarcely a Republic any longer, to complete its annexation of the defenseless Keltyr systems.

"Thank you," Laren replied.

"What I don't quite understand is *why* the Coalition forces allowed the Republic to annex all the Keltyr worlds."

Laren glanced from Van to Nynca, then to Joe Sasaki, before responding. "Everything collapsed so suddenly. We were left with all the Revenant systems, and no one wanted them to rebuild in the same mold. That meant resources being spent on governing the central Revenant systems—for years to come. The Republic fleets were drawn up in good order and suggested the compromise. No one wanted to fight another series of battles, and the Argentis didn't want the Coalition annexing the Keltyr systems, and we didn't want the Argentis expanding there. Then there was the power vacuum problem . . ."

"That's the problem that, before the Revenant defeat, neither the Republic nor the Keltyr were strong enough by themselves?"

Laren nodded.

"So some genius on the Coalition general staff decided that allowing the Republic to consolidate all the Keltyr systems would keep them occupied and build up a counterforce to the Argentis." Van snorted. "And the Argentis agreed to it for the same reason—to keep the Coalition from becoming too strong."

"Essentially, yes."

"Idiots. Didn't they see that the Republic is just a smaller version of the Revenants, except with even less ethics, and without a religious foundation?"

"I thought you didn't care for the Revenants' religious base," said Joe Sasaki, his voice expressing puzzlement.

"I don't," Van replied. "Neither did Trystin. But, believe it or not, some systems can be even worse." And the Republic was headed that way.

"No one else wanted to get involved," added Laren. "Not in a major way. The Hyndjis reasserted their claims to some independent systems like Beldora and Goilhen. The Argentis did the same spinward. We did with the areas near Keshmara."

Van nodded slowly. "We can't change what the space forces did. Not immediately, and not directly, in any case. So we'll have to change our focus. We'll start with reestablishing or strengthening our offices in the newly independent systems that have been taken over by the Hyndjis or the Argentis—or by the Coalition. Once our ships are operable. That shouldn't upset anyone in the Coalition, should it?" He looked to Nynca.

"No."

"No," replied Laren.

"I don't think so," said Sasaki.

"When will the *Joyau* be ready?" Van looked to Joe Sasaki.

"Not long after you will be. The External Commerce Subcommittee of the Assembly has asked that you testify on the activities of IIS two weeks from tomorrow."

"About what?"

Sasaki shrugged. "The invitation is general. I think they want some assurance that you will remain as closely linked to the Coalition as Trystin was."

"I don't exactly have a choice. I'm persona non grata in the Republic. I might even be on an assassination list."

"I wouldn't mention that."

"I don't intend to." Van looked around the room. "What else?"

"Do you want to commission a replacement vessel for the *Elsin*?" asked Joe.

"Yes. But we probably can't handle that kind of credit drain immediately." Especially not with major repairs needed for both the *Joyau* and the *Salya*, neither of which was capable of an interstellar jumpshift until Aerolis finished a great deal more work—and IIS paid a significant amount of credits. "We also don't have anyone to command it. I can't learn what I don't know about Trystin's job and find that person at the same time."

"We could offer a commission, with construction beginning in a year," suggested Joe.

"How long will it take to build the ship?"

"Three years . . . could be four."

"How about a commission, with a modest deposit, for Aerolis to begin construction sometime between a year and eighteen months from now?"

"We could do that."

"Then we should." Van was acting on instinct, but with the unsettled state of the Arm, he had the feeling that he and Nynca would be hard-pressed before long.

"We'll also need to change the credit arrangements for a number of offices, the ones in systems affected by the protectorate and settlement terms . . ."

A good hour passed before the meeting ended and Van returned to his office with Nynca.

Once there, she looked at Van. "You didn't mention an assassination list before."

"Trystin suggested I go back and look into the background of the Republic. I did." Van went on to explain most of what he had found, including the Revenant-like coup and the transfer of command to the "dead" Commander Baile.

"No wonder you weren't pleased with the Coalition decision. What do you think we should do?"

"For the moment, I'll have to treat the Republic in the same way Trystin treated the Revenants. I'm certain they know I'm connected to IIS, and that would put anyone we sent there in danger. We'll just have to manage the offices left in the Republic through communications and intermediaries—if we can. The way the Republic is trying to confiscate outside assets, it's not a place where I'd recommend doing much business. Or trying. Not until matters settle, if they do, and until we've cleaned up the other messes." Van looked at Nynca. "You're the director of planning. What do you think?"

"You're right. We'll need to scope out a more detailed strategy before you testify."

Van had almost forgotten about that. He wondered how many more duties he had that Trystin had handled. Nynca and Joe would make sure he knew. Of that, he was certain.

And . . . he still couldn't help but worry about his family. But for the moment, and for at least weeks to come, there was little more that he could do. He had no ships, and commercial travel to Tara and Sulyn had been suspended—at least from the Coalition. Even if he had tried a roundabout routing, it would have taken weeks or months, with no guarantee of even getting there, let alone evading Republic security if he did reach Sulyn.

But he still worried.

Chapter 76

Van was in the office early. He sat at the table desk, looking out into the distance beyond Cambria. After a second week in the office, he was more than ready to return to the *Joyau*, except that he couldn't, even without the hearing ahead, because Aerolis hadn't finished the repairs.

In addition, he'd had to work out a redefined strategy for IIS, not that it had been that difficult, not with Nynca's considerable assistance. The hard part had been working out the implementation plans. Then Laren had brought them the new notification requirements imposed by the Coalition, and Joe had brought in the latest financials—worse than any of them had expected, and Van hadn't been that sanguine to begin with. The only saving grace was the reserve fund that Trystin had built up, and Van insisted that IIS only use a third of it in the next year.

Besides that, he had yet to testify before the External Commerce Subcommittee, and he couldn't afford to alienate the Coalition, for all too many reasons.

He smiled, sadly, thinking of Trystin, then looked down at the hand-written message that Trystin had left, his eyes going over the words he had read so many times in the last days.

This is for you, in the event matters do not work as well as I hoped. I hope you do not see this, but a good commander plans for the worst. A long time ago, I thought I could fix something. I did, but it didn't stay fixed, because as my father said so many years ago, a tree truly bent is never straight again. He was a far better gardener than I.

About most things, the Farhkans are probably right. About other things—like human nature, which they believe can be changed, because they have changed their natures—I have my doubts. Some aspects of human nature and some cultures can never truly be changed. There are trees that need to be uprooted so that better trees can grow, and I have taken that upon myself, because, much as I have tried to prune and shape and direct the Revenant culture from without, there is a core that is wrong. I have watched, and asked, and questioned, and waited, but the tree has again grown twisted and crooked, and in many ways, worse and more hypocritical and evil than before. Were anyone else to see this, they would doubtless decry my arrogance. I may well be arrogant, but I am willing to act when others will only wring their hands.

I ask that, once read, you destroy this. Not because I am concerned about posterity, but because ascribing what hap-

pened to human action will only reinforce the determination
of survivors to regrow the same twisted tree. So long as there
is doubt about what happened and why, there will be questions, and questions are the very basis of truth. Questions
denied are truth denied.

Van read the words a last time, and then set the single sheet
of heavy parchment in the decorative bowl he had borrowed
from a table in the hall. He focused the miniature gas torch on
the corner of the note and flicked it. Flame licked the creamy
parchment, creeping toward the words set in black ink.
Before long, only ashes remained, as Trystin had requested.

Had the device not worked as Trystin had planned? Or had
he just gotten tired in the end? Or had he taken too much to
heart the feeling that he had been responsible for the
Revenant resurgence? Nynca seemed to be the only one who
knew, and she wasn't saying.

Then how was Van any different, worrying as he did about
where the Taran Republic was headed?

Incoming out-system for you, Director Albert.

Accept. Van could feel himself tense. What now? What
other problem was coming home to roost on his shoulders?
Van looked at the office screen, then called up the message.

His sister Sappho's image appeared on the holo projection.
He could see the tiredness in her eyes, and the darkness
behind them.

"Van, the local IIS office here in Kurti gave me this address
and said that they would forward my message to you. Yes, Aelsya and I and the children made it to the Kushite systems, and
we've settled in here on Meroe. It's hotter than we expected,
but we've certainly been welcomed. That's the good news . . .

Van winced, but continued to listen.

". . . we were already set to leave when your funds came
through, and Dad Cicero made sure they were all retransferred

to our names with the Nabatan Trust . . . Aelsya and I begged them to leave Sulyn with us, but they both said that . . . that everything that meant anything to them—except us—was in Bannon. Dad Almaviva shoved us onto the first out-system flight we could get. I couldn't believe the cost . . ."

Van could. He knew those costs all too well.

". . . I've tried to find out what happened after we left. At first, even the Republic embassy here wouldn't tell us anything, but there was a woman there who recognized your name, somehow, and she's been very helpful . . . this morning . . ." The image of Sappho swallowed. "This morning . . . she gave me a hard copy report . . ."

Van waited for the image of his sister to go on.

". . . I can't believe it . . . They . . . they executed Dad Cicero and Dad Almaviva . . . and it was Arturo . . . he was the one . . . He claimed that they had supported you, and that you had killed a sub-minister in New Oisin . . . and had committed treason against the Republic. The RSF just came and took them away, and they shot them for treason . . . and I know they . . . they wouldn't have done that. You wouldn't have done that . . ."

"They've already killed hundreds, and it could be thousands, and no one even raised a weapon . . . it's hard . . . how could anyone . . . ?

"I sent a message to Arturo, asking him what happened . . . how it could be so . . . I haven't heard anything back. Maybe I never will . . . Oh . . . the woman at the embassy, she didn't believe it about you either. She said that you'd never do anything that wasn't right. She didn't say how she knew you, but she did . . ."

Van stood there, cold inside, watching the blank holo projection for a long time, before his eyes dropped to the bowl and the ashes there.

Chapter 77

Threeday of the following week found Van walking into the hearing room of the External Commerce Subcommittee of the Commerce Committee of the Constituent Assembly of the Eco-Tech Coalition. A youthful-looking staffer gestured toward the console and chair before the antique style desk-dais, behind which sat six delegates. Three positions were vacant, Van noted, as he seated himself. He also noted that the session was closed, with no audience. That did bother him.

"For the record," opened the chairman, Delegate Inaru, "please state your name and position."

"Van Cassius Albert, managing director of Integrated Information Systems."

"You are a resident noncitizen, are you not?"

"That is correct, ser Chairman, but my official residence is here in Cambria."

"For how long?"

"It's been almost three years—three years in Octem."

"Thank you. I understand that you have been the managing director of Integrated Information Systems for less than a month."

"That is correct, ser Chairman. Since Director Desoll was lost with his ship. That was unexpected."

"You were the number two officer at IIS prior to becoming managing director?"

"That is also correct."

The chairman looked directly at Van. "IIS has been noted for undertaking a number of enterprises and activities that would be considered, shall we say for lack of a better word, most unconventional by other governments. Since these activities have always ended in beneficial results for the Coalition, and indeed for most of the Arm, and since they generally lie outside the purview of this committee, we will not intrude into this area, although the committee would like to note that the Assembly does retain that right."

"I understand and appreciate the committee's power and discretion," Van replied, wondering what would come next.

"The committee will also note that it is highly probable that there were IIS vessels near the Jerush system in recent weeks, but that, unless other information should come to light, it appears unnecessary to pursue the matter."

"We defer to your insight and understanding, ser Chairman." Van understood that part of the message very clearly, and the reason why the hearing was closed.

"The committee would also like to suggest that the value provided by IIS lies in its unconventional approach, and this committee would certainly not wish to suggest any change in the IIS operations."

That was a slight surprise, but Van nodded as he answered. "I cannot foresee any changes in the operational outlook and plans of IIS."

"Do you plan any *specific* and significant changes in the operations of IIS?"

"Director Desoll had developed a system and a plan for IIS that worked exceedingly well, ser. I see no reason to change the overall operational outlook or structure of the foundation. With the . . . change in the political and economic structure of the Arm, IIS will have to shift or close some planetary offices and open others, and we will need to change certain operational plans to reflect the changed economics. But I do not foresee any significant departures from the overall basic operations of the foundation."

"That is good to know. In the past, IIS has been most forthcoming in sharing information with the Assembly. Do you foresee any changes there?"

"The function and mission of IIS is to provide information, as you know, ser Chairman. We would be most remiss if we did not share as much information as we could, and we intend to continue the policies that have worked so well in the past." Van was very glad that Laren had briefed him on the types of questions he was likely to face.

"What position does IIS intend to take with regard to the Revenant protectorate?"

"IIS will review each planetary system as it has always done, in terms of economic opportunity and the chance to foster equality in competition—"

"A question, ser Chairman." The interruption came from the minority side.

"A question for the representative from Jiaku," the chairman announced. "One question, Delegate Mitsui."

."Thank you, ser Chairman." Mitsui looked gravely at Van. "Under your predecessor, IIS was known to accept large contingency repayments from foreign multilaterals. Some members of this committee have questioned whether this was proper for a foundation that pays no taxes on such revenues. Do you intend to continue this questionable practice?"

"As you know from the detailed reports IIS files with the committee and the government revenue office," Van began, "IIS is not a business entity that pays returns to shareholders. Nor do we pay profits taxes, since we have none. We do pay employee support and welfare taxes, as well as real estate and other services taxes. In fact, IIS pays more of these taxes than a number of Coalition multis. I believe the committee received a report on this from Director Desoll. If there is any public question on the level of taxes, I would be more than happy to make that report public.

"I might also add that, while some of the payments for our expertise might appear high, our expenses in providing that expertise are also extremely high. Our contribution to the Coalition is measured in far more than credits. In all planetary systems where IIS has developed a strong presence, Coalition financial and commercial interests have also prospered, and the index of personal economic and social freedoms has increased in the vast majority of those systems. Increasing economic and social freedoms in the Arm are aims clearly spelled out in our charter, and I believe it is fair to say that we have generally been successful in those efforts. Not in all cases, but in the majority. Neither our charter nor the laws of the Coalition restrict our revenues, only their use. We have fully complied with both the charter and the laws, and we have reported diligently on our revenues, expenses, and accomplishments. I believe, as did my esteemed predecessor, that our usefulness and effectiveness should be measured by the results we have achieved and not by merely assessing the flow of credits." Van inclined his head politely.

"Ser Chairman . . . ?"

Chairman Inaru glanced toward Mitsui. "I believe the director has been most responsive to your inquiry and to his responsibilities to the Coalition. Our past investigations have shown the overall cost-effectiveness of IIS to be quite high. That is especially true in terms of the information provided continually to the committee." Inaru turned back to Van. "You do intend to continue the reporting practices of your predecessor?"

"I could not imagine doing otherwise, ser Chairman."

Van had the feeling that the hearing was going to be very long, and that he would end up answering many of the same questions, again and again, if in slightly different words amounting to the same response. He smiled politely and waited.

Chapter 78

The *Salya* slid into the docking tower at Aerolis, kissing into position without so much as a click or a muted *thump*.

"Excellent docking." Van unstrapped from the second seat and looked at Nynca. "Thank you."

"My pleasure." She smiled wryly. "I may not say that after this tour you've scheduled for me. You did Gramps proud."

"I gave you the ones you knew," Van protested. "You were

the one—the planning director—who told me that we needed to reestablish the offices that the Revenants had forced shut as soon as possible and reopen—"

"Laren and the legal staff said it was necessary to claim what assets we could and to ensure we didn't get charged with effective abandonment or neglect."

"Always the legalities." Van shook his head. "Never what's right."

"The advocates don't like ethics, Van," she said quietly. "They're too dangerous. Legal codes are more predictable."

"Only when they're backed by ethics and power."

"They don't like to remember that," she pointed out.

"Most don't." Van smiled wanly as he reclaimed the duffel and the small carry bag filled with datacards necessary to update the information on the *Joyau*'s shipnet. "Alya and I will clear out and leave you to your tasks."

"You have the harder ones."

In some ways, he did, Van reflected, but Nynca had more stops to make.

Mason Jynko was waiting for Van and Alya in the docking tower beyond the lock.

"Director . . . we had more to do on her than on the *Salya* . . . but she's ready now."

"Good." Van slung the carry bag over his shoulder and followed the ship contractor hand over hand down the tube.

They took another tube to the third docking tower and climbed back up to the locks joining the *Joyau* and the tower. There, Jynko stopped and looked at Van. "We've managed to incorporate the standing wave equipment by cutting a meter off the port rear cabin and half a meter out of the hold. It's not like a satellite-based system, ser. Your receiver is just as sensitive, but—"

"I know," Van replied. "I read the specs you sent. What you're telling me is that the transmitter's only good for *very* short bursts, and that I've got to be in jump areas for it to work at all, and it will take all the power of the fusactors for five minutes—poured into that special accumulator."

"That's about it, ser. It was tough working out the reverse flow from that."

That had been one of Van's ideas. If he had to have another accumulator, he wanted to be able to throw the power back into the ship's drives or shields, if necessary. In effect, the additional power would hold the shields another three minutes against a dreadnought. What good three minutes might do . . . Van didn't know, but he'd seen how power cross-connections had worked for Trystin and later for the *Joyau*.

"As you ordered, ser," Jynko said, "we've stored the boxes that were in the cargo hold in the conditioned warehouse space."

"I've told Joe to expect the billing," Van replied. "Compared to the cost of refurbishing the *Joyau*, it won't be much, but I need them kept safe."

"We understand, ser. We've been supporting IIS for over a century."

Van nodded. "Everything checks out?"

"Yes, ser."

"I'm sure you're right." Van pulsed the ship lock open and stepped inside. He could smell the odors of fresh coatings, and electrical work.

Even before he reached his stateroom, where he stowed his gear, he had linked to the ship and was running his own diagnostics. Even as Jynko had promised, everything checked. Alya had made for the tech spaces.

Still, it was almost two hours before Van was ready to delock.

From the second seat, Alya, olive-skinned, green-eyed, and willowy, despite also being nearly as old as Van and having raised two children, looked at him.

"Thank you," he said.

"For agreeing to be your tech? I like the job. I like IIS. I like working with you." She smiled. "You told me where we were going . . . but not in what order."

"I've had a few things on my mind." Van grinned sheepishly. "The Farhkan system—Dharel—first. Then Keshmara, Meroe in the Kushite Association, and a long list of small places, but the order after Meroe depends on what happens as we go. We have a lot of offices to investigate and rebuild." After he talked to the Farhkans—if they would talk to him.

Van squared himself in the command seat. "We might as well get on with it."

A-prime, this is Joyau, ready to delock this time. Van checked the locks and seals, then the ship's power, before dropping the internal grav to nil.

Joyau, you're cleared to delock and depart.

Stet. Delocking. Will maintain low-power departure.

Thanks, Commander. Like to keep those towers for a few more years.

Van laughed. *Like to see them when we get back.*

He used the barest touch of the steering jets to ease the *Joyau* away from the tower and the asteroid to which it was attached. The monitors still indicated a heightened level of Coalition warships in the Perdyan system, and a lesser amount of commercial travel.

Once the ship was headed out-system and well clear of the Belt and any other traffic, Van turned in the command seat. "Can I ask you . . . what Trystin said . . . when he put you off?" Van's words were tentative.

"He didn't say much," Alya replied. "He said that what he was doing was dangerous, because the technology hadn't been tried. He said that he'd already felt too guilty for all the others who'd suffered for him . . ."

"I found out about his sister," Van offered.

"His mother was killed in the anti-Rev riots of the Coalition-Revenant War. She looked Revenant, and she died protecting a niece. That bothered him."

When he heard Alya's words, although he knew how long ago that had been, the time frame was still a shock to Van. "He told you that?"

Alya shook her head. "Eri did. He never spoke about it to me."

"What about his wife?"

"No one knows. Or no one will say."

Van pondered as he checked the screens and systems

again. "Did he give any hint that he was going to . . . deliver the device . . . personally."

"No. He even talked about taking some time off later."

Had Trystin just run out of time, and made a decision on the spot? Trystin had also made contingency plans of all sorts, so that his arrangement for Van to succeed him didn't necessarily mean that he had planned a suicide attack.

Van wondered if he'd ever know.

Chapter 79

Van glanced around the cockpit, knowing something was wrong, terribly wrong.

Countdown beginning at sixty . . . fifty-nine, fifty-eight . . . The numbers marched down slowly, and Van struggled to think . . . Something . . . there was something wrong about those numbers, something he should know. He tried to recall . . . to remember what he should do . . .

. . . thirty-six, thirty-five, thirty-four, thirty-three, thirty-two . . .

The transmission from the *Elsin* broke off, and the *Elsin* had vanished.

Van sat up abruptly in the wide stateroom bunk, his ship-suit soaked through. He'd just tried to get a short nap on the inbound leg to Dharel, but the same nightmare had caught him. It wasn't every time he slept—when he could sleep, and at times, he couldn't—but it was still all too often.

He peeled off the damp shipsuit and took out another, as well as clean underwear, and headed to take a shower, not that he would feel that much cleaner. Less than ten minutes later, he was back in the cockpit.

Alya looked at him. "You're not sleeping that well."

"No," Van admitted. "I'm worrying a lot."

"So did . . . so did Commander Desoll. He only slept in snatches."

"Did he ever say why?"

"Not directly. He talked about how people kept repeating the same patterns. He said that the Revenants were locked in an unethical pattern, but they perceived it as ethical, and that nothing short of a catastrophe or divine action would change them. Then he laughed, and said that made it difficult, because in his long life, he'd never seen any direct divine actions."

Van nodded. He could see Trystin saying that. "I haven't either." Then, Van recalled, Trystin had once been a prophet, and prophets acted for deities. But for what deity?

A silence settled over the cockpit, and Van went back to scanning screens, systems, and monitors—and found nothing out of the ordinary.

Another hour passed, and the *Joyau* neared the Farhkan outer orbit station.

Farhka Station Two, this is Coalition ship **Joyau,** *code name Double Negative, pilot Albert, patron Rhule Ghere, inbound for consultation and information.*

The minutes passed, and then more minutes passed. Would the Farhkans even acknowledge his transmission? Van studied the monitors. There were no ships in the system except two Farhkan vessels in-system of the station, both with EDI signatures that resembled dreadnoughts. Neither had changed its course, and neither was headed anywhere close to the *Joyau.*

Another five minutes passed.

Ship **Joyau,** *pilot Albert, you are cleared for approach and locking. Do you have the beacon?*

Farhka Station Two, that is affirmative. We have the beacon. Proceeding as cleared.

Van tried to ensure that his approach and docking were smooth, although he couldn't help worrying. Trystin had said that the Farhkans could be standoffish, and that their technology was vastly superior to the best of human developments. The solar flare device had proved that.

Human pilot Albert, you may proceed to the first conference room. You will be met.

Station Two, thank you. Proceeding this time. Van nodded to himself.

"They'll talk to you? That's something," Alya offered, as Van unstrapped.

"What they might say is another matter."

"You'll know what to do."

"Let's hope I do." Van slipped from the command couch.

He took a few minutes in his stateroom to clean up again before he walked back to the lock and opened it. When he stepped into the gray-green and featureless corridor of the Farhkan station, the musky odor that he had forgotten washed over him. Not unpleasant—just different. He pulsed the lock closed and began to walk. The corridor was empty, as it had been before.

A single doorway lay open ahead. The Farhkan who waited in the room—a space devoid of furnishing and furniture—did not feel the same as the one who had operated on Van.

Van bowed. *Thank you. I do not believe we have met.*

We have not. You may consider me as Erelon Jhare. Your patron remains Rhule Ghere.

Van Cassius Albert. Van wasn't quite certain where to begin.

Why are you here? Pilot Desoll applied technology beyond your human capability. The results killed many hundreds of millions.

Van thought for a time before he answered. *To seek some understanding.*

Jhare barked the Farhkan laugh. *You seek . . . absolution . . . for what you did not foresee and did not do. None can grant that.*

Are you one of those who studies humans and ethics?

Anyone who truly studies anything must study ethics. After a moment, Jhare added, *I study technology, the technology that Pilot Desoll . . . .* There was a long pause before the Farhkan continued. *. . . used in an unethical manner in the* *hope of achieving an ethical resolution to an insoluble difficulty.*

The Revenant culture was an insoluble difficulty?

Is it not obvious? That culture is predicated on the existence of a deity. Rules of conduct are ascribed to that deity. Those rules preclude free choice. No deity can preclude free choice. The society developed under the ascription of those rules is fatally flawed.

Societies must have rules. They do not survive otherwise, Van protested.

The Farhkan laughed. *You are correct. Societies must develop rules. Rules that are imposed in the name of a deity are always flawed. They are flawed because they are inflexible. The universe changes. Even the laws of the universe are not inflexible.*

Van had to think about what sort of flaws the Farhkan meant. *Without firm guidelines, human beings can bend anything in any fashion.*

Is that not true of any creature that develops intelligence and the ability to reason?

That wasn't exactly an answer, was it? *You're saying that there are no moral absolutes?*

A solar flare explodes from a sun. A culture, a species dies. This happens in the universe. Is this unethical? How can it be? That is how the universe is. A human finds a way to create a solar flare; he uses it to destroy a world. Why is that any different from what the universe does time and time again?

It is different, Van protested.

The result is the same. Do you claim the universe is unethical?

Intelligent beings have the right . . . the duty . . . to create order and ethics.

For whom? The universe? Do you have this duty to create or impose your order upon me? Or upon all Farhkans? Do I have the duty to impose such order upon you? Upon all humans?

Van could sense a combination of irony, coldness, and yet even humor in the projections of the Farhkan.

Are you saying that there is no such concept or requirement as ethical actions? he asked.

Did I ever suggest that? You are confused if you think so. Think upon what Pilot Desoll did. Until you do, there is little more that you will learn.

Van doubted that he had learned anything—except that the Farhkans seemed strangely indifferent to Trystin's use of the nova device.

We are not indifferent. There was a sense of both regret and amusement. *Never have we been indifferent to those who struggle with ethics. Why would you think we are indifferent?*

You helped . . . you allowed . . .

Is there any difference between imposing a rule or forbidding an action? When are either effective or useful?

Van knew he had an answer, but was still struggling with what it might be.

We have allowed you to question. That we never allowed Pilot Desoll. The universe changes. You must ask yourself why he acted as he did, not us. There was a long pause. *You may go.*

The room shifted, and Van blinked.

When he finished blinking, the room was empty, the door leading to the corridor open once more. He looked around, but the room remained. He left the chamber and began to walk down the musky, clean-smelling corridor back to the *Joyau* . . . slowly.

Why had he come? What had he hoped for?

Answers. He had wanted answers.

The Farhkan had thrown the questions back at him, as if to say that Van knew or could find those answers. Or *the* answer to why a man Van had thought ethical had murdered five hundred million people.

He frowned, realizing that they had given him something. Jhare had as much as said that there was an answer.

But was there? Or were the Farhkans playing a far deeper game, one that menaced the entire human race? Yet why would they do that? They clearly had the resources and the technology to wipe out any human system they wanted.

Van kept walking. Questions or not, answers or not, he had too many systems to visit, beginning with Keshmara. And then Meroe.

But there were answers . . . weren't there?

Chapter 80

A tall man in shifting white robes and a turban—probably the same aide Van had seen the last time he had been in Keshmar—ushered him into the fifth-floor waiting area.

"The minister will be with you shortly." The tall man bowed and turned, leaving Van alone.

Van made his way to the wide armaglass window offering a west-facing panorama of the planetary capital. The morning sun gave the River Khorl a deep blue appearance that highlighted the plaza beyond and the domed and templelike buildings that seemed to be everywhere in Keshmar.

"Director Albert?" offered a heavyset man in white robes, who stood by the doorway to the inner chamber. "The minister will see you."

Van entered the minister's receiving office, with its circle of stools set around a low table.

Minister Sahid, a good head shorter than Van, stood before the chairs and table. "Director Albert . . . a pleasure to see you again."

"It is equally one to see you, too, Minister Sahid." Van bowed.

"Please be seated." The minister gestured to the stools.

Van waited until the older man seated himself. Almost as soon as he had, a young man carried a tray with two small cups upon it into the room, presenting the tray first to Van. Van could smell the strong black café even before he picked up the cup.

"I was most sorry to hear of the death of Director Desoll. You are kind—and diligent—to come to see us."

"You have always been supportive of IIS, and we share the same objectives in seeking to maintain the independence of smaller systems."

"Your efforts have been most valued in the past." The minister offered a crooked smile. "There are some who would say that times have changed and that we have no need of them now."

"There are those, I am sure," Van replied. "There are always those who advocate throwing away that which has served well following any apparent success."

The minister laughed. "You sound just like him. Not in your words, but in the sentiment of those words. I share that sentiment. Yet . . ."

Van nodded gravely. "There is a time where one must bend. You believe that perhaps a token reduction in the annual retainer . . ."

"My opponents, and I do have such, Director, they would wish more than that."

"I am most certain that they would. Yet there are many who need our services . . . and once we are committed . . ."

"I have said as much, and they asked if I would request more than a token reduction." The minister offered a helpless shrug. "You can see that such places me in a difficult position."

"Most difficult. That I can understand." Van smiled, although he hated the kind of bargaining that he was being required to do. "There are many systems regaining their independence, and they will also need services such as IIS provides. We must supply those who are willing to pay for our services, much as we would prefer to continue to work with those whom me know and trust."

"Ha! You would make a strong man weep, and I am not a strong man. The Council of the Sidarte, they would need some changes, some hope that we would not need to spend so much . . ."

"IIS can be flexible over time," Van replied, with a shrug.

"A lower retainer, but a higher charge for emergency services. It would need to be a much higher charge."

The Minister sighed, dramatically. "The council . . . fifteen percent less, they might accept for the retainer . . ."

Van considered, recalling the options he had calculated earlier. "Fifteen percent . . . that would require a fifty-five percent increase in emergency service charges, based on the past probabilities of services. That will be difficult, because there is a higher probability that you will need those services more than once in a year."

"A higher probability?" Sahid was clearly puzzled. "When the Revenant forces can no longer raid our systems?"

"When renegades are more free to operate? When you have the Republic of Tara taking over the Keltyr systems? When both the Argenti and Coalition forces are occupied in pacifying and controlling the new protectorate? With your experience, I am most certain you have thought of these possibilities, but have the members of the council?"

"They may not fully understand what you have explained. Under these circumstances, it might be possible that they would consider a decrease of as little as ten percent in the retainer, if there were no significant increases in the emergency charges . . ."

"I would have to calculate, but perhaps we could work an offset . . ." Van smiled politely, once more. He had hoped for a relatively quick renegotiation; but like everything, it seemed, that process was going to be neither quick nor easy.

Chapter 81

As soon as the *Joyau* was docked at Meroe orbit control, Van put through a link to the Taran embassy. He was fortunate, because Emily was there. Her image filled the holo screen in the stateroom. Van took in the short and severely cut blond hair, the straight features, and the gray eyes. The severity vanished from her face with her words. "Van . . . where are you?"

"At the moment, I'm locked to orbit station one. We've just arrived."

"Are you coming planetside?"

"I'd planned on that. Is there a possibility we could have lunch or dinner, or something? What time is it there?"

"It's midafternoon."

Van frowned.

"Is that bad?"

"No . . . but I need to meet with my sister . . ."

"That's Sappho?"

"Yes, and thank you for helping her."

"I was glad to." Emily paused. "I was sorry to hear about your fathers. I really was."

"Thank you." After a moment, he asked, "Do you know any more? She only told me that they had . . . been executed."

Emily's face clouded.

"You think it's something you'd rather discuss in person?"

"That might be better. I'll meet you. That would also be best."

Van understood. "A late dinner? Twenty hundred local? You name the place."

"D'Oro Real—it's not that far from the embassy, on the Plaza Dulein. I'll make reservations."

"Thank you. D'Oro Real on the Plaza Dulein at twenty hundred . . ."

Van held her smile in his mind for a moment after the link faded.

Although he had Sappho's codes and physical address in Kurti, he wasn't about to call her until he talked with Emily. There was too much he didn't know. So his next link was to the local IIS office.

He got the simmie receptionist. "If you would please . . ."

"This is Managing Director Albert. I'd like to speak with Miryam Adullah as soon as possible . . ."

The simmie vanished, to be replaced with Miryam's oblong dark face. "Van. Where are you?"

"Orbit station. We just docked a few minutes ago."

"We heard about Trystin . . ."

"That's one reason why I'm here."

"How long will you be here?"

"How long do you need me here?"

Miryam smiled, but there was a sadness in the expression. "He picked well. We do need to talk."

"Tomorrow morning?"

"You have something?"

"There's another problem. I'm meeting with someone from the Republic embassy tonight. And I'm trying to track down my sister."

"Your sister? The one—"

"Yes. She and her partner left Sulyn, but I haven't talked to her since our fathers died . . ."

"I understand." Miryam nodded. "We do need to talk. Nine o'clock tomorrow morning?"

"I'll be there." Van smiled. "And sometime while I'm here, you can take me to G'zai's."

"I will take you up on that. Especially since you remembered."

"How could I have forgotten?"

That brought a momentary smile to Miryam's uncharacteristically somber face. "Until tomorrow."

After he broke the link, Van took a quick shower and changed into a pale—almost white—bronze singlesuit. He packed several days' worth of clothes into a single bag, then went to look for Alya.

She met him in the passageway outside his stateroom.

"You can have the next two days free to go planetside," he said. "Just make sure that the ship is totally sealed. Charge the shuttle and any hotel to the operating account, but meals are on your own."

"We're not going to be called off somewhere?"

Van shook his head. "The local IIS office needs me for things for at least two days. You might even get more time than that." He paused. "Let's do it this way. Meet at the local IIS office in Kurti at ten hundred two days from now, and we'll see where we stand."

Alya smiled. "You're certain?"

"Certain," he affirmed.

"Thank you, ser."

"I should have thought of it earlier. I've had a lot on my mind. If you hurry, you can make the next shuttle."

"I think I'll wait for the one to Omdu. It's in two hours. I've always wanted to go there."

"Then . . . just call the IIS office at ten hundred two days from now. No sense in your traveling cross-continent."

"That would be all right?"

"Just go. Enjoy. I don't know that you'll get much of a break after we leave Meroe."

"Yes, ser." Alya smiled more broadly as Van turned to leave the *Joyau*.

The down-shuttle to Kurti was almost on time—leaving a mere ten minutes late, but the suite at the Takwar Grande was warm enough that Van had to turn down the temperature before he washed up and left to find the Plaza Dulein.

Even so, he managed to walk into the D'Oro Real at nineteen-fifty.

Emily was waiting at the corner table where the young host escorted Van. She was wearing a loose deep green blouse that set off her skin and hair.

Van couldn't help but smile as he bowed. "Emily."

There was the faintest flush as she replied. "I'd . . . hoped you'd make it back to Meroe before too long, but . . . it was a while . . . quite a while, the last time."

"Two years, more or less," he replied, sliding into the seat across from her. "I hadn't thought it would be quite so long." Then he grinned, and said, "I've done better than seven years, though."

Emily flushed. "You . . . you are . . . impossible. I never should have told you."

"I like your middle name, and it fits."

Before Emily could respond, beyond a deeper flush, a

server dressed in loose white trousers and tunic with a silver-green vest appeared.

"You're having?" Van asked. "Almaryn?"

"Not tonight." She looked to the server. "Chellis."

"A pale ale. Cold."

The server vanished with a nod.

"I could have met you at the embassy," Van began, not quite certain where he stood.

"It would be better if you didn't come to the embassy."

"Less uncomfortable?" asked Van.

Emily laughed. "These days, I could care less who I make uncomfortable. I've been accepted for permanent residence here, and my tour ends in a year. I think I've lined up a position as a junior media person with a local multi, and I'm eligible for a deferred diplomatic retirement in another ten years. I could get immediate retirement if I stayed another five, but I wouldn't last.

"No . . . it's for your sake. Mostly, anyway. You're wanted, supposedly for questioning, but the RSF has let it be known that anyone who gets you into custody in Republic territory will be very highly regarded."

"And an embassy is Republic territory."

"I don't think most staffers would do it. You're still a hero to most of the diplomats, and the lower staffers, but Commander Omeara—he's the new military attaché—he follows the RSF line to the last letter and last period."

"Will you get in trouble for not luring me into the embassy?" asked Van.

Emily shook her head. "The ambassador and the first secretary weren't pleased with the coup—pardon me, the change in government. They haven't said much, but I can tell."

"What do you think about it all?"

"I think my actions say how I feel. I don't know that Meroe is the ideal place to be, but where else could I afford to go? If I went back to Korkenny . . ."

"You don't want to go back there," Van said gently.

"Oh?"

"I was there several months ago. They've fallen in totally

behind the new government. They've already starting confis-
cating half the assets and profits of all non-Republic multis
under the new Economic Security Act, or whatever it's
called."

"That allows that? And the Parliament passed that kind of
law?"

"Under the . . . new government. Has anyone said what
they want to question me about?"

"No, but there are rumors—" Emily stopped as the woman
server returned and slipped a goblet of a silver-white wine
before her, then a frosted glass with Van's pale ale before him.

"We haven't—" Van began.

"Why don't you look at the menu while I order," Emily
suggested.

Van called up the projected menu and scanned it.

"I'll have the house salad, and the herbed flank steak."
Emily looked to Van.

"I'll have the same." Van wasn't totally sure, but the dinner
wasn't about food. He waited until the server departed before
continuing. "You were saying . . . about the rumors . . ."

"They were saying that you had sneaked into the RSF
headquarters and done something horrible . . ."

"I did," Van admitted. "I broke into their records." He
paused. "Do you want to know what I found out?"

"I've always been an incurable snoop." The brilliant and
warm smile appeared. "But I'm not a gossip."

Van knew that. He shrugged. "The RSF set up the *Fergus*
to be attacked by the *Collyns*. I upset their plans by destroying the *Collyns*. They were going to claim that the *Fergus* was
a Keltyr cruiser that was breaking the Scandyan space restrictions. Oh, and there's a strong indication that Commander
Cruachan was murdered by RSF operatives because he knew
too much about what was going on." He glanced at Emily.
"You don't look surprised."

"From that group . . . no. So they sent someone out to kill
you?"

"I don't know about that—not on Scandya, that is. They
did send an assassin after me in Bannon after I retired. He

was stunned, and I left quickly. But . . . that wasn't the worst. They used a clone—stage three, I'd guess—to impersonate an RSF commander. My replacement on the *Fergus*. You might recall that the *Fergus* vanished on its return to Tara?"

"I recall that—only because I knew you'd been on the *Fergus*."

"I'd been doing some research, and on Weathe I ran across an obituary. It was of a James P. Baile. It even had his picture."

"Why was that surprising?"

"He was listed as dying of natural causes one month before he relieved me of command."

Emily offered a wry smile. "In your somewhat skeptical mind, I take it, you find it hard to believe that there are that many James. P. Bailes with the same age, rank, and looks in the RSF who undertook command duties in health after they died."

"I did find that hard to believe, especially from the same home planet."

"Couldn't they just have faked his death?"

"They could have. Either way, it's wrong. But I have my doubts about a faked death. A clone would be much easier to program to send the ship into a fatal jump."

"How do you make a fatal jump?"

"Translate into the center of a sun. Change the jump coordinates. There are fail-safes, but the commander has to be able to override them."

Emily looked down, started to speak, then waited as their salads arrived. "You realize this is not exactly totally private? I doubt that we're monitored directly, but . . ."

Van shrugged. "It doesn't matter, not here. It won't make the RSF think less of me, since that's not possible. I had a little difficulty in leaving New Oisin . . ."

"The same sort of trouble as on Scandya . . . as the prime minister?"

"This time I was better prepared, but there were casualties . . . That's why they want me. They tried to kill me, and the RSF doesn't allow self-defense, not when their cover-up might be disclosed."

Emily nodded slowly. "I'm not surprised." She reached across the table and touched his hand. "It must have been hard for you."

"I like working for IIS . . ." He shook his head. "I never told you."

"Never told me what?"

"The managing director—his ship was caught in the Revenant mess. He didn't make it through. I ended up as the head of IIS. That's one reason I'm here." Van stressed the word "one" ever so slightly. He swallowed, and added, "You're another."

Emily laughed softly. "Even if I'm only one of several reasons, that's one of the most flattering things said about me in many years—that a man actually piloted a ship from systems away to have dinner with me."

Van could feel himself flush, although he doubted that Emily would see his reaction in the muted light of the restaurant. "I wanted to spend more time with you the first time I came through, but I couldn't. I didn't control the schedule. In a way, I still don't."

"That happens."

"I still remember the tour we took of Cliff Spire."

"It seems so long ago."

"Not for me," Van blurted.

"You are more of a romantic than anyone knows," Emily said. "Why didn't you ever find someone?"

Van looked into the half-empty pale ale, and then into her gray eyes. "It just took longer."

This time, she was the one who looked down. Then, she looked up and smiled. "I suppose I asked for that."

"No . . . you didn't. I've never been known for subtlety in personal matters."

"It might be better if you didn't try to prove it again. Not immediately." But there was a twinkle in her eyes.

"Not immediately," Van agreed. "Oh, before I forget. Would you mind if I asked for a small professional favor? I think it's a small favor."

Emily lifted her eyebrows.

"News . . . news from Sulyn and Bannon. I'd also like anything you can come up with about or by a mediacaster named Ashley Marson. And about my brother Arturo, if you can."

"I can see. That shouldn't be that difficult. It will take a while. It seems to be hard to get news or information about Sulyn."

Van was afraid of that. "If you would just send it to the local IIS office. Miryam Adullah is the director, and she'll get the information to me."

"She's a formidable lady, everyone says."

"I know. I'm meeting with her tomorrow morning."

They both paused as their entrées appeared.

Van took another sip of the pale ale, then nodded to the server for another. He stopped. He couldn't recall the last time he'd needed a second.

"Tell me again that you came all these light-years to see me."

"I came more than all those light-years to see you." Van offered the statement deadpan.

Emily laughed, warmly.

"And I love your laugh."

"It's too direct. My mother always told me that a lady never laughed like she meant it."

"That's terrible . . ."

"She was very old-fashioned."

Van took a bite of the flank steak, barely tasting it as he watched and listened to Emily—his Senta. He hoped.

Chapter 82

Miryam Adullah looked across the conference table at Van. "He told me that you'd be his successor, but I didn't expect it so soon."

"He didn't bother to tell me," Van said. "I thought Nynca would be his successor."

"What did she say to you? You asked her, didn't you?"

"We talked about it. She said she could plan, but that she wasn't suited for the position."

"She's not ruthless enough."

"Ruthless?"

Miryam smiled, a wide but sympathetic smile. "I'm not a big believer in coincidence, Van. Whatever happened to the Jerush system has Trystin's aura all over it."

"A solar flare? How could that be?"

"The timing was rather suspicious, and if anyone could coax a sun into flaring, he could. There's a great deal about Trystin that's more than mysterious. I'm pushing sixty, and I've known Trystin since I was nineteen. He looked the same then as he did the last time I saw him. He's the only human with an open entrée to the Farhkans. He also opposed every aspect of the Revenant expansion, and he was getting more and more frustrated with the unwillingness of the other major Arm powers to rein in the Revenants."

"That doesn't mean he could make a sun flare."

"I've read the reports. It wasn't anything like a nova—but a major flare. There's a big difference. Not to the people. They're all dead. But to the system. It's still there."

"Five hundred million dead and the system uninhabitable for years, at least without planoforming."

"You know I'm right," Miryam said. "There's no point in talking about it more."

Van shrugged.

"You'll see. And don't be too surprised when you decide that he was right." Her dark eyes fixed on Van. "That's done. You're here, and you can't stay that long. I've got a schedule laid out." A holo field appeared in the center of the conference table. "Let's go over it. If you think something's not necessary, let me know."

Van doubted he would have any objections. She knew Meroe and the Kushite systems far better than he did, and he'd seen the accounts.

All in all, Van spent two hours with Miryam and did not leave until she had extracted a commitment for almost all of his time for the following four days, beginning the next morning.

Then, feeling more than slightly tense, he made his way to Sappho's house on the west side of Kurti. He'd debated calling ahead, but decided to risk not alerting her.

Of course, she wasn't home.

So Van found a small restaurant and ate, then called the house.

When she answered, he broke the link and made his way back.

He didn't get to the door before she opened it, standing there tall and glorious, golden red hair flaming.

"That was you, wasn't it?" Her smile was wan.

"I'd come by earlier, and you weren't here."

"You could have called to find out when I would be."

"After your message, I wasn't sure how welcome I'd be. I thought it might be harder for you to say no if I showed up in person."

His sister shook her head slowly. "I never said I was angry with you. You're always welcome." She stepped away from the doorway. "Come on in. The girls are at school, and Aelsya's at work. I don't start until next semester. Things are still a mess here. I get tired more quickly."

"It's the heavier gravity."

"The heaviness of more than that."

Van waited to say more until she had shut the door. "I'm sorry I couldn't get here sooner. We had a problem."

"You've always had problems, brother."

Van accepted the slightly bitter words. "First, the head of IIS died in a ship accident. Second, my ship was badly damaged, and third, I was requested to testify before the Coalition Assembly. I left as soon as the ship was ready. We docked at orbit station late yesterday."

Sappho sank into the new armchair in the sitting room, but one that seemed similar to one Van recalled from her house in Bannon.

Van took a straight-backed chair. "Have you heard from Arturo?"

"I haven't heard a word."

"I stopped by the embassy. Well . . . actually, I met with the third secretary outside the embassy. She's going to see what she can find out."

"Do you want to tell me why you didn't go to the embassy?"

"Do you want to know the whole story?" he countered.

"It might be easier."

"It's a long story," he began. "It actually started on the *Fergus* . . ." Van told her almost everything about his encounters with the RSF, including Commander Baile, and the effects of the Economic Security Act, and his efforts at RSF headquarters. He avoided the Revenant issue. ". . . and that's probably why they want me for questioning—because they don't know what I know or who might know. Otherwise, they'd just have people looking to shoot me. They may anyway."

Sappho studied him for a long time. "You always looked like Dad Cicero. The same things bother you, too, but he was a thinker. You're a doer."

"That's not always good," Van pointed out.

"It's better that way, but it's never easy on the people around you. Or those who love you." She paused. "Do you still have a job? You said that your boss . . ."

"I have a job. He named me his successor. I'm the head—the managing director of IIS. That was another reason it was hard to get away."

"You . . . you're the head of one of the biggest foundations in the Arm, and you've only been with them something like three years?"

"It's absurd, when you look at it that way," Van agreed.

"I wondered where you got all those credits you sent." She shook her head. "You didn't borrow those?"

"No. I had a healthy stipend as the senior director, and I never had a chance to spend much of it. So I sent everything I could."

"You've always been generous that way. I remember when you came up with—"

"I had the credits, and you needed them."

"You never told Cicero and Almaviva, did you?"

"No. There was no reason to."

Sappho shook her head. "You haven't changed. You still tell people what you think they need to know."

Van glanced around the sitting room, taking in the thick white walls and the high ceilings. "It's a good house."

Sappho smiled tightly. "It's better than anything we could have bought in Bannon. I worried about using the credits. They weren't ours. Aelsya kept telling me . . . that . . . not spending them . . . would be wasting them . . . that my fathers didn't want us or their grandchildren to live in poverty because of what happened to them, and that you wouldn't have wanted that, either."

"No . . . I'd hoped . . ." What had he hoped, exactly? "I'd hoped they would have come."

"They couldn't leave. You know that. No matter how bad things got."

"I didn't realize . . ."

"They weren't always that bad . . . and you believed . . . you wanted things to be better. That's one thing where you and Arturo were alike."

Van didn't want to think about that. "I still hoped they'd come with you." Hope always warred with experience. Van knew that, but he'd never wanted to deny hope, no matter what experience said. After another long silence, he finally spoke again. "Sometimes, I just wonder. I never wanted to hurt anyone. But there never was a place for me in Bannon. At least, I never thought there was, and I never found it. Now, Dad Cicero, Dad Almaviva . . . they're gone . . . and we're here. I can't help thinking . . ." His words trailed off.

"Whatever caused it all, big brother, it wasn't you. I can't condemn you for wanting to live free. For not wanting always to look over your shoulder. That's what I want. I didn't know it until I got here. It's sad, though. Other people shouldn't have to suffer, or die, because we want freedom. But that's one of the prices. You warned us. Dad Cicero and Dad Almaviva—they understood and chose. Arturo never understood. He always thought that education and position would protect him. That they should protect him. Life isn't like that."

"What about Arturo?" Van already had a good idea, based on what Emily had already told him, but he wanted to hear what Sappho said.

"You've already guessed. It's in your eyes."

"It's a guess. I want to hear what you know."

"Arturo was angry with you when you left. He complained that all the publicity and all that you had done was making life harder for him, and for all of us. He said . . . he said that you had always done what you wanted, and you didn't care how it affected everyone else. You just had to do what you wanted to do."

"In some ways," Van admitted, "he's right. Go on."

Sappho looked down. "He kept saying that you never thought about what it would do to the rest of us. When the credits came in, Dad Cicero said that they should be split, because that was what you wanted. Arturo got furious. He said that you couldn't buy him, and that he hoped he never saw you again."

"Unless he leaves the Republic, he'll get his wish," Van replied.

"That's sad, too, because he never will. You know that."

"I know."

There was another long silence.

"Oh . . . I almost forgot. Just a moment." Sappho turned and left the room.

What could she have forgotten, Van wondered.

Sappho returned almost immediately with a packing box. She extended it to Van. "Dad Cicero insisted I bring it. It has all your decorations in it, and that beautiful box from the premier."

Van swallowed. His dads had wanted him to have them. He just wished that they had come with Sappho and her family. Finally, he said, "Thank you."

Another silence fell over them.

"Thank you for coming."

"I had to . . . and I could."

Sappho glanced toward the door. "The girls won't be long. I know you must be busy . . . but . . . we really . . ."

"The rest of the day is yours," Van said.

"You mean that?"

"I wouldn't have said it, if I didn't."

Starting early in the morning, Van still had to meet with Daidae Mubarca at the Nabatan Trust, and with the Candace Bank, to clear up the linked IIS accounting, not to mention all the meetings set up by Miryam, as well as any other clients she felt needed the personal touch of the managing director of IIS.

But for the evening, he could stay . . . and would.

Chapter 83

Clearing up all the loose ends on Meroe had not taken a few days, but well over a week. Part of that had been beneficial, since the word that IIS was now headed by someone with a darker skin and heritage had resulted in meetings that had, in the end, gained IIS several new clients—if smaller ones. Still, with the state of IIS revenues, Van wasn't about to overlook such possibilities. Miryam wouldn't have let him, in any case.

Then, as a reward, Van had promised himself one last treat . . . or more than treat, and that was why he sat at a table in the Nubeya, just before noon, waiting for Emily.

"What would you like to drink while you're waiting, ser?"

"Almaryn, thank you."

Van glanced toward the entrance, but Emily had not yet appeared. He hoped that she hadn't had to cancel because of some crisis at the embassy. He wished he'd been able to spend more time with her, but he couldn't just drop everything, like an adolescent, and blurt out that he wanted to marry her. They'd been together . . . what . . . perhaps five times in four years . . . and he still had a responsibility to IIS . . . and Trystin.

While he waited, he perused the menu. After several minutes more, he looked back toward the front of the restaurant again, but while several people stood there, all but one in shimmering white robes, Emily was not among them.

Possibly three minutes passed before Emily stepped into the lobby area, looking around, but they felt like ten. Van raised his arm, and she nodded, smiling, hurrying toward his table.

Van watched as she appeared, wearing a deep turquoise green suit that brought out her eyes and hair. He couldn't help smiling as he stood.

"You look happy," she said, smiling as well.

"I'm always happy to see you."

Emily seated herself without quite looking at Van.

The server appeared moments after Emily did, delivering the tall frosty glass of almaryn to Van, then looking to Emily.

"Almaryn, also." She looked to Van. "Much as I'd prefer chellis, I do have to go back to work this afternoon. You're leaving, also, aren't you?"

"Immediately after lunch."

"Another good meal before venturing forth?"

"Not exactly . . . another good meal with delightful company."

"I don't know how delightful I'll be. I've put in the inquiries about your newsie friend, and about your brother, and I've been searching the incomings, but . . . so far there's nothing direct." Her face turned severe.

"When you get that expression," Van said, "it's generally not good news."

Emily nodded, with a rueful smile. "That's why I'd never be more than third secretary. My face reveals too much."

"What's happening on Sulyn?" Van questioned.

"It doesn't look good . . . Van. I'm sorry."

He waited.

"The local planetary parliament . . ." She shook her head. "I'd better start at the beginning. The system government demanded that Sulyn abide by all the emergency laws. The Sulynese parliament refused. Politely. They pointed out that the charter of incorporation reserved certain rights to the planetary authorities forever. Prime Minister Eamon insisted that such rights could and should be abrogated in a time of crisis, and that no planet was above the laws of the Republic."

Van set down the almaryn, then waited as the server reappeared with Emily's glass.

"We'd better order," he said.

"Unfortunately. Do you know . . ."

"I already looked."

"You order, then, and I'll make a quick decision."

Van looked to the server. "The lamb special, with the risotto and apples, and the alstora soup."

"The same, except I'll take the house salad instead of soup."

The server nodded and slipped away.

"The prime minister insisted," Van prompted.

"The Sulynese stood fast, and we received word this morning that RSF fleet elements are proceeding to Sulyn, along with another domestic peacekeeping unit." Emily held her almaryn, but had not taken even a sip, her gray eyes on Van. "I'm sorry."

He shook his head. "What good are rights, if they can be abrogated at the will of whoever's in power? It's all an excuse. I understand what's happening, but not why." He paused. "Maybe I should say that I understand it intellectually, but not emotionally. Sulyn has always been the freer-spirited part of the Republic, where the arts flourished, and where discussion was always more open, and every time it got too open, the government tried to crack down. Most times, it backed off . . . but there's always been a conflict and resentment . . ."

"Part of that is because the majority of the Sulynese community is black? Is that what you think?"

"It's easier to target a group that's visually different," Van pointed out. "Even if the Sulynese cultural leaders weren't black, Sulyn would be targeted because it has a tendency to speak out more, and it's pretty clear the government doesn't want any disagreement. But it's gone further than that. Gangs in New Oisin are now attacking anyone who looks different. It's not just the government. The government's playing on existing feelings . . . and that's the frightening part."

"For the first time, at least in my life, it's somehow sad to be Taran," Emily said. "How did it happen?"

"You told me, remember? How technology undermines ethics and morality . . ." Van stopped as his soup and Emily's salad arrived.

Van took a spoonful of the soup. "It's good."

"I'll have to try it, the next time we come." Emily smiled.

"I'm glad you're granting me a next time."

"How could I not?" Emily flushed. "I mean, you're the only man who's crossed the stars for me."

"With a middle name like yours, how could a ship's captain refuse?" Van asked lightly. "Even if I do have to sail off."

"I won't throw myself off a cliff," Emily replied.

"I'd never give you the chance," Van blurted. "I mean, even if I am leaving after we eat . . . it's not as though . . . I will be back . . ."

"You'd better not wait seven years," she said dryly.

"Not seven years," he agreed. Somehow, he would get back, far sooner than that, next time, and with better planning.

They both smiled.

Chapter 84

Van had hated to leave the Nubeya—and Emily. Despite the overtones of what was happening throughout the Arm, it had been a respite of warmth and laughter, and one all too short.

Back on the *Joyau*, while he waited for Alya to return, he had used the time to catch up on news and work on the itinerary and the associated needs and strategies. He'd decided that the next stop would be Samarra, partly since Nynca had suggested that Van visit Samarra to assess the viability of reopening the IIS office there and partly since it was a convenient stop before the *Joyau* headed more spinward along the Arm.

He also couldn't help thinking about the Republic, and the idea that the government was not composed of leaders, but followers, followers of prejudice, and, as Trystin had put it, simplistic "big kill" beliefs. Had that been the problem with the Revenants as well? That Trystin's earlier actions had influenced leaders, but the leaders couldn't overcome the biases and beliefs of the people? Was the Republic already following that course?

He tried to concentrate on getting ready for the IIS business ahead and managed to get some of his preparations done before he sensed the lock opening.

Alya was smiling as she reentered the cockpit of the *Joyau*. "Good afternoon, Commander."

"I can tell you had a good time," Van commented dryly.

Alya flushed before she replied, "And you didn't?"

"I had a good time—part of the time. The rest was necessary and useful." Van paused. "I'm glad you had a good time. We're headed to Samarra, and you'll probably have to sit the ship there."

"Samarra? Didn't the Revs take that over three–four years back?"

"They did, but we've gotten word that once the Coalition smashed the Rev fleets, the Samarrans revolted and took back control of their system. It's still unsettled."

Alya looked quizzically at Van.

"If we reopen the office there now, we can help with the rebuilding—and we might get opportunities we won't get later."

"And headaches."

Van laughed. "They go with opportunities."

Alya strapped into the second seat.

Meroe orbit control, this is Coalition ship Joyau. Request delocking and departure this time.

Stand by for delocking.

Standing by. Van reduced internal ship gravity to zero, brought the fusactors on line, and delinked from station power.

Joyau, clear to delock and depart this time. Traffic departing in the orange.

Control, delocking this time. Have traffic in screens. Departing low-power. Van eased the *Joyau* away from the station and onto an out-system course.

He even got some sleep in the outer reaches of the Kush system before they reached the jump zone. And thankfully, no nightmares.

Jump was normal—black-white, eternal and timeless simultaneously.

Once back in normspace, Van studied the monitors.

Unidentified warships closing. Less than one hundred emkay.

"Strap in tight, Alya. We've got company, and they don't look friendly." His attention shifted to the EDI screens. The two ships making for the *Joyau* had Revenant drive signatures. One was a frigate, and the other a corvette.

Van decided to play dumb and continue in-system, but he double-checked the torp bays and the shields . . . then watched and waited as the two Revenant vessels neared.

Unidentified ship, drop all shields and stand by for boarding.

Request identity and authority, Van pulsed back, ready to reinforce his own shields as necessary.

Our authority is that of the Prophet. This system remains Revenant territory.

On behalf of the Coalition, Van pulsed back, *I would be pleased to accept your surrender. If you choose to surrender, drop your shields immediately.*

The only response was a salvo of torps.

Van dropped the internal gravs, diverted power to the shields and turned head-to-head toward the corvette. For a moment, the smaller ship continued toward the *Joyau*. Then it fired two torps.

The four torps did not arrive simultaneously, and the

Joyau's shields barely flickered. Van diverted some power to the drives and accelerated toward the corvette, which turned toward the frigate.

Van slewed the *Joyau* toward the corvette, accelerating more, then cut the drives and flexed the shields outward until they touched those of the smaller ship. The corvette rebounded from the *Joyau*'s shields, carried back by the greater mass of Van's ship and by the strength of the shields, toward the frigate, which had not fired any more torps.

Van fired two torps, one at each vessel, timing them so that they would reach the other ships—he hoped—at the same time as their shields touched.

The Revenant shields intersected—and flickered, just as the first torp neared the corvette.

The corvette disintegrated in a shower of energy.

The frigate's screens went amber.

Van fired another torp.

A flare of energy marked the frigate's demise.

"That wasn't bad," remarked Alya.

"They'd already taken some damage, I think. The frigate's shields just collapsed, and it was low on torps." Van was glad that he hadn't had to use many torps, and he almost felt sorry for the Revs. Almost, but he had trouble with any fanaticism that required single-minded dominance over others, and one that effectively required suicide rather than allowing others freedom.

He eased the *Joyau* back on a direct in-system course toward Damcus, the fourth and only inhabited planet in the system.

"I'll fix something to eat," Alya volunteered.

"Thank you." Van leaned back in the command seat. What would they find at Damcus? Confusion, chaos? The one thing they wouldn't find were other interstellar ships. Of any kind.

The EDI indicators showed no ships anywhere in the system.

Six hours later, after another nap and another formulated

meal, Van was back in the command couch, scanning the approach area to Damcus.

*Damcus orbit control, this is Coalition ship **Joyau**, request approach clearance and docking.*

*Ship **Joyau**, say again.*

*Control, **Joyau**, request approach clearance and docking. Inbound for resumption of commercial operations.*

***Joyau**, wait one.*

*Control, **Joyau** standing by. Continuing approach this time.*

Van checked everything nearby, but could find no other traffic, not even in-system patrollers.

***Joyau**, interrogative combat out-system.*

Van wondered. Samarra system was supposed to be under the new Protectorate. Had he been mistaken? *Negative combat. Coalition cruiser provided escort, destroyed raiders.*

***Joyau**, appreciate information. Raiders destroyed Argenti corvette on station for Protectorate. Oh . . . cleared to charlie one this time.*

Understand cleared to charlie one. Reducing power for approach this time. Full identification follows, with Galstan authorization.

***Joyau**, interrogative status of Revenant systems.*

Jerush system destroyed by unpredicted major solar flare . . . Coalition and Argenti fleets have occupied most Revenant systems.

Good!

The force of the emotion behind that single word rocked through Van, and it took a moment for him to return full concentration to the approach.

Orbit control. Have acquired beacon.

***Joyau**, lock charlie one is operative and ready. Welcome to Damcus!*

Thank you, beginning locking.

Van did not open the *Joyau*'s lock to orbit control, although he did put the fusactors on standby and link to station power.

His first effort was to link into the planetary comm channels and begin to scan them. Before he set foot outside the ship, he wanted to know exactly what had occurred on Damcus. He began to jump from channel to channel and net to net.

. . . the interim assembly has urged restraint . . . calling the massacre of women and children in the Revenant compound beside the Damcusan High Temple 'barbaric' and 'unworthy' of the people of Samarra . . . The screen showed the smoldering rubble of a structure that had been situated on a hill overlooking a city.

. . . the last of the moral reeducation camps was bulldozed yesterday in Telfor as hundreds looked on and cheered . . .

. . . shortages of cereal grains in the plateau region . . . shipments of food seized from the Revenant Revealed Center in Dosodi have been diverted . . .

. . . fighting continues in the eastern highlands . . . more than ten thousand armed Revenants have seized Remorya after their defeat on the plains of Dhar . . .

Van continued to switch and study. After going through more than a hundred different channels in an hour, he was convinced that Samarra was not under Revenant control. On the other hand, he wasn't certain whose control it was under, although the planetary capital of Alion was reported calm and under the control of the interim or provisional assembly.

He began to make links planetside.

All in all, it was two days later—filled with link conversations, agreements, negotiations, and what amounted to institutional bribery—before he finally left the *Joyau*. Within his shipsuit was a small military stunner, and at his waist was the nanite bodyshield and powerpack. The gray corridor outside the ship bore several long dark marks, as if lasers or other weapons had been used, and not thirty yards from the lock was a large and irregular synthetic patch, clearly recently applied.

He'd only gotten a dozen steps from the *Joyau* when three

figures in shipsuits appeared. One, in a maroon suit, carried a military stunner slung over her shoulder. The other man and woman wore green, with orbit control logos on their chests.

"Ser? Commander Albert?"

"I'm Commander Albert," Van replied.

"Ser . . . we just wanted to thank you, and to ask if you could carry messages outbound. We'll pay double the interstellar rate." That was the woman in green.

"The standard rate will be fine. IIS is a commercial operation. We don't normally carry message traffic, but we're equipped to do it. We'll have to download at a spinward hub for retransmission, though. Would that be satisfactory?"

"Yes, ser."

Van used his implant to access the stationnet and then the *Joyau*. *Alya, Commander Albert here. We're going to upload message traffic for later download at the next out-system hub.*

We can only take a standard single load, ser.

I'll tell them. Van turned to the three. "My chief tech tells me that we're limited to one standard single load."

"We won't have that much. We've just gotten the station back in operation. Less than a week, ser."

"You had to use shuttles to attack?"

The guard in maroon nodded.

"You'll be going down to Alion on a station shuttle," added the man. "We don't have the commercial operations back yet. When you're ready to return, just link to station operations, and we'll send one down to pick you up." He paused. "You'll need to use paper credits. The transfer links don't operate planetside. Better stop by the credit stall here."

The three walked Van to the credit stall, where he obtained a thousand Samarran credits, hoping they would be enough, then to the shuttle bay. The woman guard accompanied him onto the shuttle.

An hour later, Van stepped outside the shuttle terminal in Alion—and was overwhelmed with the swirl of freezing air and smoke—smoke that held odors of burning wood, powder, hot metal, charred flesh, chemicals, plastics, and other synthetics exposed to excessive heat. For all that, there were three groundcars waiting, each with a driver gesturing.

Van stepped forward and took the first driver. He was glad he had the nanite bodyshield, and that terminal security had allowed him to bring down the stunner.

"Drohya building on the Occident."

"Ah . . . I know that one . . ."

Van certainly hoped so. "How has the last week been?" he asked, once the groundcar pulled away.

"It has been terrible, but we have seen worst. Never . . . never will we bow to outsiders again. Better that the sky melt down and turn us all to ashes."

Van tried not to wince at the response.

"Soon . . . all of Damcus will once more belong to Samarrans, and not an infidel invader will remain."

The groundcar whistled past a block in which all the buildings were blackened hulks, then along a stretch of boulevard where every third or fourth building had huge gaps—antique shell holes, Van thought. Fine white flakes of snow drifted out of a gray sky.

"What happened there?"

"The infidel Revenants, they said we would not destroy the royal row and the children's home. They stayed behind the walls, and they had children as hostages. They died. We saved some children. We had to. The last time we tried to save all the children, we lost everything."

The groundcar came to an abrupt halt opposite a squat fortresslike building set between two other structures with broken windows and traces of fire on the upper levels.

"Drohya, it is here."

Van offered a fifty-credit note.

"It is too much. I will wait." The driver smiled. "I am Reduaro."

"I'm likely to be here a long time, Reduaro."

"Who else will I drive?"

Van smiled and handed him another fifty.

"I will wait until the moon falls from the sky."

Van walked toward the entry. It had taken several fund transfers to obtain a lease on the first floor of the building and nearly thirty links to track down Jahil Monsa—the former manager. A gaunt figure in an expensive singlesuit that was far too large stepped out of the entryway.

"Jahil?"

"The same. Director Albert?" Jahil Monsa walked slowly forward. His left arm was in a sprayed cast, and he limped.

Van nodded.

"I cannot believe that you got us an office so quick. And equipment."

"It will take a week or more before they'll have more than a single comm line."

"Longer than that," snorted the slightly built man.

The two walked inside.

The front part of the long room inside the door had been turned into a waiting area, with a couch and several chairs. Behind the waiting area were ancient bookcases, used as dividers, with the boxes of office equipment behind.

Jahil gestured to a solidly built young man in a maroon jumpsuit who had set down a heavy box of something. The jumpsuit showed places where insignia and patches had been removed. "This is Harad. He's a former Samarran commando. He knows comm systems, too. He's been helping me get this place organized."

"I assume you're putting him on the payroll," Van said.

"I wanted to ask first." Jahil frowned slightly. "There are few credit facilities . . ."

"I made a substantial deposit with the Bank of Samarra. We already have a message contract with the provisional government. I reopened the IIS planetary account. You have draw privileges. No one else but you."

Harad smiled, interrupting almost apologetically. "You are . . . were a soldier?"

"Deep-space pilot for the Taran Republic."

Harad looked to Jahil. "I told you. Others would wait."

Jahil shrugged.

Van was afraid that Jahil would collapse, so frail and worn

did he appear. "Let's sit down and sort things out." Van took one of the straight-backed chairs. "You look like you've been through quite a trial."

"I survived. Most who were sent to the faith reeducation camps did not."

"Faith reeducation?"

"We needed to learn the ways of the Prophet." Jahil snorted, and looked as though he wanted to spit.

"Which ways?" asked Van.

"That we should give more credits to the Temple, and that our women should serve strangers before they serve us, and that those who do not believe as they do . . ." Jahil broke off.

Van looked at the slender man and nodded. "And those women who love women, and those men who love men are cursed and reviled?"

Jahil looked up sharply.

"I came from a family with two fathers," Van said quietly. "I am not like them in that, but I love them and understand. My sister married her woman partner, who is a doctor."

Jahil smiled ruefully. "You see much." A brighter smile crossed his face. "With Director Desoll, I was never certain. What happened to him?"

"He was killed when his ship malfunctioned. He was testing some experimental equipment. It was very unexpected. I had not expected to succeed him." Van shook his head, then offered a smile. "How do you feel? Are you up to rebuilding the IIS operations here?"

"I feel much better over the last week, and even better today." Jahil grinned boyishly, and Van could see that he had once been extraordinarily handsome. "I should not hate. So I will not, but I am glad that the Coalition and the Argenti fleets came to Samarra, even if they could not stay. I am most glad it happened when it did. Another six months, and I would have been dead. It is hard to conceal what one is, and after they shot Ibrim, I was in shock . . ."

Van had not known about the Revenant "faith reeducation camps." Trystin might have, but Van could not recall any mention of them, nor had he found any references to them in the IIS files. "We have a great deal to do. I've laid out a general plan. It's only general because you know Damcus better than I do. It will take work." Van smiled. "I think it will generate millions of credits over the next ten years, and help Samarra become stronger than before. It will also make you very well-off . . ."

Jahil smiled. "Tell me more . . ."

Chapter 85

Van stood in the shade of the rear portico, looking out at the garden, past Dad Almaviva's greenhouse. The morning sun was bright, but to the northwest he could see dark clouds rising over the badlands, and the distant rumble of thunder rolled toward him.

Almaviva straightened from the row of beans, and gestured to Cicero, who was pruning the pear tree at the edge of the garden.

Abruptly, from nowhere, four troopers in green fatigues dashed past Van, as if he were not there, then stopped at the edge of the garden. Without a word, they leveled their slug throwers at the two men and opened fire.

"No!" Van yelled, but no words came from his mouth, and none of the troopers turned. Van tried to move, but he was rooted in place.

Then, as suddenly as they appeared, the armed troopers turned and marched out of the garden. Lightning flashed, and thunder rolled, and Van stood on the plaza before the Parliament House in New Oisin, with red rain falling all around him.

As he watched, a tree began to grow from the center of the building, an oaklike tree that began to slant to the right as it grew. Then a branch thrust itself down, as if to try to keep the tree from overbalancing itself, and the oak grew more massive and more gnarled and twisted. With each moment, the oak leaned more and more.

Van watched, transfixed, as the giant tree began to topple. The enormous roots pulled out of the Parliament building, and building stones were flung across the plaza, slowly bouncing. A spark from somewhere ignited the fallen and splintered tree, and within moments, the plaza was an inferno.

Van threw up his hands . . .

He sat up in the wide bunk of the commander's stateroom aboard the *Joyau*. Sweat streamed down his face. Slowly, he swung his feet to the side and stood, walking deliberately to the fresher, where he washed his face, then blotted himself·dry.

He walked slowly around the stateroom, barefoot, until he cooled down, then slipped back into the bunk, on the side where the sheets were cool and dry, and not damp.

In time, he woke, and washed, and dressed, and made his way to the cockpit.

There he settled into the command couch and studied the monitors. He could feel himself frowning, knowing something was off, not quite right.

Van glanced around the cockpit, again, and then again.

Countdown beginning at sixty . . . fifty-nine, fifty-eight . . . The numbers announced themselves slowly, death-marching downward. Van tried to focus his thoughts, thoughts that felt so sluggish. Something . . . there was something wrong about those numbers, something he should have recognized. He tried to remember what . . . and what he should be doing . . .

. . . thirty-six, thirty-five, thirty-four, thirty-three, thirty-two . . .

The transmission from the *Elsin* broke off, and the *Elsin* had vanished. Energy flared across the boards, searing Van with its heat. Somewhere, in the distance, eight gleaming white stone towers began to melt before exploding into vapor . . . and the screams of millions echoed through Van's mind.

Once more, Van bolted up in the bunk.

This time, he did not even think of trying to get more sleep as he rose to take a shower and don a clean shipsuit.

After leaving Damcus behind, after almost two weeks there, Van could have expected nightmares with shattered buildings, with gaunt figures like Jahil, or empty-eyed children, and the shapes of burned-out buildings, or the smell of ashes and death, but nightmares about his fathers—and trees?

The nova dream was familiar, at least, if unwelcome, but the dream about his fathers and the giant tree bothered him more—far more—even if he could not say why.

Chapter 86

Van shifted his weight in the command couch as the *Joyau* approached Angslan, a formerly independent system that had been "annexed" by the Revenants nineteen years earlier, although they had not closed down the IIS office in Ingelar until four years later, according to IIS records. That was still fifteen years ago, Van thought to himself, wondering what he would find.

Angslan control, Coalition ship Joyau, for approach and locking.

Joyau, request registration.

Control, registration information dispatched. How tight was the Coalition control of Angslan?

Wait one, Joyau. Continue approach.

Continuing approach this time. Van checked the monitors and EDI indicators. There was one other commercial ship in-system—and the drive signature was Hyndji. But there were three Coalition frigates and four corvettes—most of them near Angslan on what looked to be a former out-system base.

*Coalition ship **Joyau**, your registration is approved. Clear to charlie one this time. Be aware that no incoming cargoes are being allowed planetside, except equipment for Argenti and Coalition forces. No travel planetside is permitted, except for Coalition and Argenti forces and support groups.*

*Control, **Joyau**, no cargo to declare. Bearing message traffic for rerouting. Interrogative outbound cargo.*

Message center is operative for other stellar destinations. Planetbound traffic will be delayed and screened. Outbound cargo is embargoed at this time.

Stet.

Van eased the *Joyau* through the docking and locking process almost silently. He'd hoped to get planetside, but it didn't look that likely. So the stop at orbit control was going to be useful only for messaging, reenergizing, and for whatever information he could gather.

Once the ship was locked in place and on station power, he took a deep breath.

"Not good, ser?" asked Alya.

"They've got the entire planet quarantined. They're not calling it that, but that's what it amounts to. Go ahead and get the mass tanks topped off. I'm going to see what I can find out."

He unstrapped and walked back to his stateroom, where he called up the files on Angslan. There wasn't anything obvious, except that the annexation by the Revs had been peaceful.

After a moment of reflection, he pulsed through a message to orbit control administration—and got a simmie, dressed in a white uniform.

"This is orbit control administration. How can we help you?"

"This is Van Albert, commander of the *Joyau* and managing director of IIS. We're a Coalition foundation, and we've traveled here to try to reopen our office planetside." Van waited.

The simmie smiled politely. "Let me see who might best help you."

Van waited for several minutes before the holo projection switched to the figure of a Coalition commodore in a wrinkled singlesuit. Her face was drawn, her eyes tired, and set in circles of black.

"Commander Albert. Or should I say Commodore Albert?"

"Commander or director. The commodore doesn't count for much anymore."

The faintest smile crossed her face. "Commodore Yoriki. I'm in charge of the restoration work here. I understand you had hoped to go planetside to reopen an office?"

"That had been my hope. I've just finished a similar project in another system."

"It would have been my hope as well, Director Albert. But the Coalition has been forced to adopt an embargo of Angslan. That precludes commerce and travel."

"Might I ask why, and how long this might be expected to continue?"

Yoriki shrugged tiredly. "The Revs smashed the local culture, then sent in waves of their most fervent believers. They're still a minority, but they control all the local institutions. We aren't about to risk Coalition forces. So we'll just keep the place isolated until they adopt the political changes the Coalition requires. We've also grounded all air transport until that happens." Her smile was simultaneously wry and cold.

"What political changes?"

"The restoration of the open representative democracy, the abolition of required polygamy . . . the physical destruction of all reeducation centers . . . and the return of all commercial establishments to their original owners or heirs. In addition, any religion must permit open access to all buildings and establishments."

"I take it that these changes are being resisted."

"You might say that."

"I'm certainly not opposing your requirements and actions, and neither is IIS. In fact, I would think that IIS could be of great assistance—"

"I understand that. I'm very sorry, Director Albert. The Service knows how much you and IIS have done to support us, and you've been most supportive of the Coalition, but you must understand that if we broke the embargo for you . . ." Yoriki shrugged.

"I understand. I appreciate your explanation." Van paused. "Is this the policy for most of the systems recently annexed by the Revenants?"

"We're taking it on a case-by-case basis. If there's a change, a real change, we're just monitoring. But on the older planets, this is pretty much standard. They just don't get it."

And they probably won't for a long time, Van reflected. "Thank you. I do appreciate the explanation."

"My pleasure, ser. And thank you for all you've done."

The holo projection blanked.

Van leaned back in the chair. After a time, he searched to see if the station had access to planetside comm channels. Since it did, he began to scan them, seeking out the media news outlets and stories.

. . . joint enforcement effort of the Argenti-Coalition forces again refused to lift the ban on air transport anywhere on Angslan. High Bishop Truman yesterday denounced the ban as genocidal and inhumane, citing the death of fifteen-year-old Elton Christensen as an example. Christensen died before ground transportation could reach him and take him to the trauma center in Ingelar . . .

. . . In his capacity as minister of public health, Bishop Hansen offered statistics showing that over five hundred people have died needlessly as a result of the embargo . . .

. . . the first president of the Angslan Quorum rallied his congregation in Susseks . . . part of his speech . . . excerpted and broadcast continentwide . . . "What did we ever do? We have worshipped God in our own way. We have taken care of the sick . . . and all we have ever required is that those who partake of the goods God has provided follow his commandments and give him thanks and share that bounty with others. Is that so much to ask, for we owe all to God . . ."

Van thought about the reeducation centers on Samarra, and presumably those on Angslan. Somehow he had trouble with a culture that believed in destroying the lives of people who didn't agree with a given theological view. But was the Republic any different? The true "beliefs" of the Republic were more political; but the means were the same, if directed so far more at individuals than at whole planetary populations.

He called up another news story. He'd record and study what he could, but, from what he had already seen, it would be a long, long time before there would be an IIS office on Angslan.

Chapter 87

Once out of jump, and on the outskirts of the Islyn system, Van headed the *Joyau* in-system before checking the coordinates with the system comparator. He'd gotten almost as close as possible.

"Short trip in," he said to Alya.

"That would be nice."

"For a change, you mean?" Van teased.

"I didn't say that."

"You thought it," he countered.

On the inbound trip, Van reviewed the records of the principal clients, as well as the recent revenue transfers. Camryn Rezi had done exactly as he promised. Now the question was how to handle someone who had had the majority share of ownership of the planetary office. It would have been easier to let matters alone, but he either had to ratify the arrangement, obtain a modification, or pull IIS out. He couldn't just let the problem sit. Letting things fester just made them worse. He was seeing that firsthand with the Revenant problem.

As the *Joyau* continued in-system, he kept checking the net, the EDIs, and the far-screen monitors—which showed a

Hyndji ship, and one Argenti battle cruiser, in addition to the handful of Islyn Defense Forces ships—three corvettes and two frigates. As he took in the Argenti battle cruiser, he smiled. The good general Marti had wasted no time in sending a reminder to the Islyn Quorum that Revenant power had waned in the Arm.

When he could study no more, he left Alya in the cockpit, set the alarms, and tried to take a nap, hoping he would sleep soundly. He was getting quite the repertoire of nightmares, what with those about the *Regneri* or the *Fergus*—more infrequently—and the newest two.

He was tired enough that he woke abruptly with the alarm. *Unidentified object . . . .*

He shook himself and walked to the cockpit, more to clear his head.

"It's just debris, I think, ser," Alya offered.

Van settled into the command couch, checking the monitors, and altering course slightly to give a wider berth to the asteroid ahead, before studying the EDI and the system plot. The only out-system ships remained the Argenti battle cruiser and the Hyndji ship.

Then he leaned back and called up the recommendations prepared by Laren's staff once more. He hoped Camryn Rezi was still as cooperative as before—and would be interested.

Hours later, as the *Joyau* neared the approach to Sandurst, he squared himself in the command couch and began the contact with orbit control. *Sandurst orbit control, Coalition ship **Joyau**, requesting approach clearance.*

*Ship **Joyau**, interrogative purpose.*

*Orbit control, Coalition ship **Joyau**, purpose of visit is business.* Van pulsed the standard Coalition ID.

*Ship **Joyau**, cleared to charlie three. Continue approach this time.*

Van couldn't help but smile. It was amazing how much more cooperative the controllers had become since his previous trip. *Understand cleared to charlie three. Authorization follows.*

*Thank you, ship **Joyau**. Interrogative beacon.*

We have the beacon.

Only a minute or so passed before another transmission filled the net. *Coalition ship Joyau, this is the Bolvara. Interrogative Commodore Albert.*

Van cocked his head, then replied. *Affirmative, this is Commodore Albert, commanding.*

General Marti requested we convey his regards if we saw you.

Thank the general for us.

He said to tell you that madmen can also be saints.

A wave of sadness washed over Van, unexpectedly, and he did not reply for a moment. *If you would thank him for that as well.*

We will, Commodore. If you need any assistance, the Bolvara stands ready.

Van understood that message, sent in the clear, was a message to Islyn as well. *Your support is most welcome, although we trust we will not need it.*

The *Joyau* had begun the final approach to lock charlie three when control transmitted, *Welcome to orbit control, ship Joyau.*

Thank you, control. Commencing docking this time.

Once the *Joyau* was locked, using station power, Van brought up ship gravity.

"Smooth approach, ser," Alya said.

"Thank you. I won't know what we'll be doing until I talk to Director Rezi." Van unstrapped.

"That's fine, ser."

From his stateroom, Van accessed the planetary commnet, first scanning through the news and media highlights. He started with Islyn political news.

Commerce Ministry Looks for Resumption of Info-Trade . . .
Cairen Volcano Quiet . . . Guard Units Released . . .
Quorum Repeals EEA . . .

Van hoped the story was what he thought. It was. The Islyn Quorum had unanimously repealed the Economic Equalization Act on the rationale that the economic and political situation in the Arm had changed with the recent joint-access treaty signed between Islyn and the Hyndji and Argenti governments.

"Court Affirms Decency Act . . .

Van nodded to himself. Some things would not change.

The rest of the news did look more encouraging, and definitely better than the situations in Samarra and Angslan. Van pulsed the local IIS office.

As before, he got the simmie receptionist. "This is IIS, Kahla. May we help you?"

"This is IIS Managing Director Albert. I've just locked in at orbit station—"

The simmie's image was replaced by that of the dark-haired Rezi, who wore a cream singlesuit with dark brown cuffs and trim.

"Director Albert, it's good to see you again."

"We're on orbit station, Director Rezi."

"Will you have time to make a tour of the office and visit some of our clients?" Rezi offered a broad smile. "Matters have changed much."

"I had hoped that might be the case," replied Van cautiously.

"For the past week, I have been working out the transfer paperwork, now that the need for my duties as custodian for IIS is passing . . ."

That was a clear and welcome message.

"You endured a great deal, Director Rezi," Van replied, "and I'd like to discuss some changes in those terms in order to ensure that you receive adequate and permanent recompense for your efforts and the risks that you undertook."

Rezi bowed slightly. "IIS has always been known for rewarding loyalty."

Van couldn't help grinning.

"This time, you must come with me to Sian's for the most wonderful meal."

"I think I'd like that. Is it a favorite of members of the Quorum?"

"One or two of the ministers eat there, and if we find them there, they will be most pleased to see you. They are looking forward to a wider range of trade and commerce."

Van understood that reference as well, but he would still wear his personal nanite shield. "This evening, perhaps?"

"That would be most possible." Rezi bowed again. "I look forward to seeing you . . ."

After they discussed the details and locations, and Van broke the link, he stood, shaking out the stiffness as he pondered his next steps.

He would have to give Rezi a share in the outbound revenues, and he needed to calculate what was both fair, and what was workable. Still, if he and Rezi could come to an agreement, that would mean another functioning office, with ongoing projects and revenues, and one less headache for him, for Nynca, and for Laren and the rest of the staff.

Chapter 88

After turning left off the main corridor of Neuquen orbit station two, Van walked briskly along the corridor to The View. This time, the cherry-paneled walls felt both tired and affected, an attempt at evoking a time and place that had never been.

Van had been fortunate—he thought—that Marti had actually been in the Neuquen system, and that he only had been required to wait ten hours for an evening meeting with the general.

"You are with General Marti?" asked the waiting maitre d'hotel.

Van nodded, then followed the man to one of the private booths. Marti stood and stepped out of the booth as Van approached. Even from meters away, Van could see and sense the tiredness in the other's face and carriage. Even Marti's uniform shipsuit lacked its usual crispness.

"Commodore Albert . . ."

"General . . . you're kind to take the time."

Marti reseated himself. "For you, it is worth every moment." A wry smile appeared. "It is also good to get away."

Van slid into the booth and sat opposite the general. A tall pale ale was waiting. "You look as though you've been busy."

"Fighting too many battles that are not battles." Marti shook his head, then looked at the waiting server. "I will have the greens, the consummé, and the ascadoro con arroz."

Van had to pick up the menu and scramble through it. "The greens, wild mushroom soup, and the duck cassis."

Marti picked up the wineglass, half-empty. "And another glass of the cabernet."

The server bowed and turned.

Van took a sip of the still-cold pale ale. "What sort of battles?"

"The kind that one cannot fight." Marti took a long swallow of the red wine before setting the wineglass on the white linen. "If one insists that the fanatics accord nonbelievers equal rights and access to education and services, the fanatics riot because we do not respect their way of life. If we do nothing, nothing changes, and all will revert to what was the moment our forces withdraw, whether that is in two months or two centuries. If we embargo the planets that do not meet the terms of the protectorate, then the fanatics murder their dissidents and unbelievers, and matters are worse than before. All this is true in systems long held by the Revenants. In those systems held only for a few years, the same thing is true, except on the other side. The local people so hate the Revenants that without threats, they would murder them all—or enslave them." Marti drained the last of his wine, but did not lift the second glass delivered by the server.

The greens followed the wine.

"That was an interesting message you sent," Van offered with a smile.

"Message?" Marti's voice was absolutely deadpan.

"The *Bolvara* conveyed a message from you, something about madmen also being saints. I assumed that a battle cruiser commander would not convey such without absolute certainty of its contents and source."

Marti laughed. "At times, Commodore, you are so serious." He continued to smile. "I did think it was an appropriate message." He lifted the wineglass, but, this time, only took a small sip.

"Intriguing, but cryptic," Van pointed out. "Saints have often been madmen, but a label does not change facts."

"That depends on the value of the label, my friend. It also depends on how much force lies behind it. I fear we all underestimated the force behind the label known as IIS."

"Oh?"

Marti snorted, then took another sip of wine. "You know what I mean."

"I know several things that you could mean," Van parried. "Guessing which it might be could be dangerous to my health."

"I will be blunt, then. I would earnestly hope that IIS does not plan to use whatever device the late—he is late, is he not?—Commander Desoll used on Jerush as a means to Galactic empire."

"You seem rather certain that the flaring of Jerush was not accidental," Van replied. "I don't know of any way to create a solar flare, and so far as I know, no one else does, either."

After taking another sip of his wine, Marti laughed again. "That offers some reassurance . . . if not complete reassurance . . ."

"Why do you feel that Commander Desoll had anything to do with the unfortunate events befalling the Revenants." Van took a sip of the pale ale.

"There was a remarkable confluence of events . . . First, Commander Desoll made a change in the procedures for IIS administration and succession just before he disappeared . . ."

Van managed to sip his ale without choking. How did

Marti know that? Van hadn't even known that until he'd looked at the records afterward. And how had Marti found out so quickly that Trystin had disappeared?

"Second, he left his chief technician behind. Third, that technician is now the chief technician on your vessel. Fourth, there are reports that all three IIS vessels, three light cruisers in effect, all vanished from known space at the same time. Now one adds to that the fact that Commander Desoll did not care for the Revenants, that he had armed his vessels, and that over the years large numbers of Revenant warships vanished when his IIS vessels were nearby. I might also add that you, my friend, are known as a superb combat pilot, and a number of Revenant vessels have also vanished when your ship was in their general area. Nothing conclusive, but I have a most suspicious mind . . . Generals, I have discovered, must be most suspicious . . ." Marti raised his eyebrows.

"You're doing that very well, General," Van said. "You have decided that one man, alone and without human assistance, invented a technology no one has seen or knows about to create an effect that only time and nature have been able to do so far. You have also decided that the man who supposedly did this either vanished or destroyed himself after doing the impossible, and you imply that I know things that I don't."

Marti laughed. "Commander Desoll chose well, I can see. You have not said an untrue statement ever. Neither did he." He took a small sip of wine before setting it down next to the plate containing the salad that he had eaten without Van's even noticing it.

"I don't lie well," Van admitted. "So I try not to." He took the last few bites of his salad.

"Most of us do not." Marti's smile turned wry. "So I would like to know what you and IIS intend to do with the Republic of Tara."

"The Republic?" Van wasn't sure what Marti meant.

"You have not heard?"

"Heard what?"

Marti nodded. "At times I forget that what I see is not what everyone can see. No matter. It will be on all the media nets before long."

Van waited.

"The Republic claimed that the Keltyr space forces refused to surrender."

Van's stomach tightened. He could feel his face stiffen.

"I see you are beginning to understand." After a pause while the server removed the salad plates and presented the entrées, Marti went on. "The word is that none of the Keltyr ships survived." Another moment passed. "Not a single one. That is an even more remarkable . . . coincidence than those surrounding Commander Desoll."

Van forced himself to take a moderate and slow swallow of his ale before he replied. "That is, as you say, remarkable. I cannot see how it applies to me, though. I am unwelcome in any Republic system, and the RSF certainly has little interest in listening to my views."

"That is a pity." Marti took a bite of his meat, a dish Van did not recognize except for the rice on the side. "They refused to heed your views before, as I recall."

"A number of times," Van said dryly. "I can't say that it seemed to harm them." He tried the duck, piquant and tasty, but not oily.

"Not for now. The Revenants did not heed Commander Desoll, and the cost was high."

"I can't see how not heeding me would increase the Republic's costs."

"Is there a state faith in the Republic?" asked Marti.

"No. Not unless it's the blind worship of wealth and power."

"You see?" Marti laughed, gently.

Van didn't have to feign confusion.

"You do not wish to see, but you will," Marti added. "Because you are what you are, you will not be able to avoid it."

"I'll take your word for that."

"That is most kind of you." The general's voice conveyed gentle irony. "So few do these days. It will be generations before the Revenant problems are resolved, if they ever can be, and doubtless my successor will insist that I could have done everything better." He snorted. "Of course, today, no one has any suggestions. But, after I fail, there will be many who insist they did."

"I don't see you as failing," Van said.

"It does not look that way. For that, I am grateful, but . . . one must take care not to delude oneself. We have millions of people who believe and cannot think if anyone raises a single word that conflicts with that faith. We have millions to whom the word of an ancient deity must be followed to the last syllable, even if it means killing or enslaving those who are exactly like them, except for their faith. And those who have been enslaved know—from their bitter experience—that one cannot reason with millions of fanatics. One can only kill them." Marti shrugged. "What am I to do? What is any general to do? I cannot command the resources to isolate and educate every child of each side for generations—and that is what is necessary."

Van nodded slowly. He wasn't certain he agreed fully, but Marti had a definite problem.

"It is barbaric. It is cruel. But who is to say that if the flare that destroyed Orum had occurred five hundred years earlier that the Arm would not be a more peaceful and worthwhile place?"

"You don't mean that."

"My friend, that I do. How many millions have died? How many millions have had their lands, their businesses, and their children taken from them? We are human. We do not ever wish to admit that some people and some beliefs will always lead to evil and cruelty. We believe, or we convince ourselves, that in some way, if we could only reach such fanatics, that we could change matters. But one cannot reach an entire culture of fanatics. When such a culture has grown as vast as the Revenants did, the result is always death and disaster, if not by a solar flare and then by our fleets, then eventually by disintegration and collapse and greater violence, dragging down an even wider net of peoples. Let us just say that the Revenants had learned to create such flares. Then what could others expect? If we, the Argenti, obtained such power, would you trust us?"

"Probably not," Van replied.

"Good, because I would not. Nor would I trust the Coalition. And, pardon me, my friend, but I would certainly not trust the Republic in these days and times."

With that, Van certainly agreed, as he slowly finished the remainder of his duck. He hadn't fully trusted the Republic as it had been. He took another sip of the ale.

"But . . . my friend," Marti said with a smile. "I have been far too serious, and in this uncertain Galaxy, who knows when we will next share a meal. Did I tell you that next month my wife and I will get a week together? And that I do not intend to talk of ships and sealing wax, or faith or fleets . . . ?"

"You deserve that time together." Van thought that Marti deserved more than that and hoped that the general would get it. He tried not to think about Marti's words about how some cultures were doomed to create evil, tried to avoid equating them to the RSF and the Republic.

Chapter 89

Van closed the stateroom door, although he remained fully linked to the shipnet. The *Joyau* had come out of jump from Neuquen well outside all system bodies, and well clear of all system traffic. The marginal standing wave equipment had taken in three short messages from IIS headquarters. Two had been quick updates on Nynca's efforts.

In turn, Van had sent his own updates. He'd scanned Laren's other message, but he wanted to read it again, even though he was so tired that his eyes were beginning to blur.

He called it up and began to read. Certain phrases and paragraphs leapt out at him.

... reports confirm that the Keltyr warships that survived the initial Revenant-Republic assault were later destroyed to the last man and vessel. RSF sources claim the Keltyr ships refused to surrender ... some doubt of that ... likely that surrender was not allowed ... RSF has not disclosed its own losses to date.

... martial law remains in force on all Keltyr planets. All outspace installations now held and controlled by the RSF ...

... Keltyr political leaders and families allowed to depart Keltyr systems ... reports indicate that departure was not voluntary in all cases, but no political deaths have been reported.

Van understood that. Without political deaths, there were no martyrs, and seldom did the deaths of military forces generate much political unrest. He didn't like the rest of the implications, not at all. But he couldn't dictate to the Republic.

From what he'd seen recently, no one was successfully dictating much to anyone.

He stood and walked to the bed. He could use some sleep. After a moment, he lay back back on the wide bunk. He closed his eyes, still thinking, although he remained linked to the shipnet. The *Joyau* still had a good four hours on the inbound leg before he would need to be in the cockpit.

Marti's words kept coming back to Van ... "If we do nothing, nothing changes ... None of the Keltyr ships survived ... one cannot reason with millions of fanatics ... one can only kill them ... some beliefs and some people will always lead to evil and cruelty ... always lead to evil ... always lead to evil ..."

Always? Were people that stupid and shortsighted?

Van tried not to yawn. It had been such a long day, and he

probably should not have left Neuquen so soon . . . but there was still so much to do. So . . . much to . . . do . . .

Darkness swirled around him, and Van stood in the rain before the Parliament House in New Oisin, thunder buffeting him. He watched once more as a tree grew from the center of the building. The oak slanted as it grew, both more angled, and more gnarled.

As quickly as it had grown, the giant tree—towering over the plaza and the city—began to topple. The trunk and roots pulled out of the soil beneath the city with such force that the stones of the Parliament building flew in all directions. Before the topmost branches of the tree struck the scattered building stones, the twisted limbs and shattered trunk had burst into flames, and ashes showered down around Van.

Van rolled over breathing heavily. He should have expected the nightmare. He was tired.

He checked the time. Less than fifty minutes had passed. He got and stretched, walking around the stateroom and cooling off.

He needed the sleep. He knew that, but he was reluctant to lie down again.

In time, he did, and his sleep was dreamless—until he found himself back in the cockpit, in the command couch, wondering how he had gotten there.

Had he been so tired that he had been sleepwalking?

He squinted, trying to focus his thoughts on the shipnet and the monitors. He felt himself frown. Something was off, not quite right.

. . . thirty-six, thirty-five, thirty-four, thirty-three, thirty-two . . .

The numbers, in Trystin's voice and from the *Elsin*, stopped. The *Elsin* had vanished. Energy flared through the cockpit, searing Van.

He sat up slowly in the bunk and checked the time. He'd gotten another two hours' sleep before the second nightmare.

A shower might help. It might.

Chapter 90

Van had debated going back to Korvel in order to see Sherren Myller, but there was no real reason to do that. She doubtless had the situation in hand, and there were other systems where IIS needed to reestablish its presence. That was why Van had brought the *Joyau* to Denaria and why Alya was still on board monitoring any possible communications.

Denaria had been one of the systems that Van had meant to check out before the Revenant attack on the Keltyr systems, but he'd never gotten there. Since it had never been under Revenant control, although close to the ill-defined border of the de facto protectorate, it had remained an open system.

Van had not had any trouble in getting cleared into orbit control or arranging shuttle transport, and he was walking out of the shuttle terminal at nine-fifteen on a threeday morning—local. Under a clear blue-green fall sky and carrying just a datacase, he moved toward the line of groundcars for hire, to get a ride to the IIS office in Aureum Plaza, when he was brought up short by the piercing ululation of a siren. Van looked to his left to see an open lorry—filled with men and women—moving down the boulevard. Military vehicles with riot cannons preceded and followed the lorry.

As he watched, he listened to those lined up in front of him for groundcars.

". . . last of the Revvie bastards, I heard . . ."

". . . just people, Imri . . ."

". . . can't trust 'em . . . would have taken everything . . ."

". . . they have children, like we do . . ."

The couple entered a groundcar, and Van took the next one.

"Where to, ser?"

"Aureum Plaza, Moon Tower."

"Moon Tower . . . You must be out-system." The ground-car eased away from the terminal.

"Why do you say that?" asked Van.

"That area's high-trade."

"How has business been?"

"Much better the past week. Off until the government rounded up the last of the Revvies."

Van just nodded and sat back, wondering how many Denarians held the same attitudes.

In less than ten minutes, the groundcar pulled into an underground and enclosed reception portico.

"Fifteen, ser."

Van pulsed the credits and stepped out. He walked through the entry, pulsed an ID to the system. After a moment, a lift door opened, and he stepped inside and rode up to the seventh level.

A dark-haired man with ivory skin stood waiting.

Van recognized him from the holo images when he had set up the appointment. "Director Vincenzio. It's good to finally see you."

"And you, Director Albert . . ." Vincenzio turned to his left, leading Van down a wide corridor floored in highly polished green marble. Vincenzio had a corner office twice the size of Van's office in Cambria with a view of the city to the south.

"Quite impressive," Van acknowledged, adding, "I'd hoped to be here earlier, but when I got off the shuttle and was going to get a groundcar, there was a slight delay. A lorry full of prisoners—"

"Those were probably the last of the alien Revenants—the ones who never applied for Denarian citizenship. The government is sending them to an internment camp in the Mysera Islands until they can be repatriated somewhere."

"Had they caused a particular problem here?"

Vincenzio smiled indulgently. "What didn't they do? Without IIS and the Ghendi Foundation, Denaria would have been an occupied world under the protectorate."

"It's a good thing that didn't happen." Van smiled politely. The reports he'd received and reread before coming planet-side indicated that there had been recent Revenant invest-ments, but nothing to compare to the sort of problems systems like Islyn had faced.

"Good for us and good for IIS. I have to tell you that next year looks especially good. We put in a bid on Wyal, and the government accepted it."

"I can't say I'm familiar with that multi," Van temporized.

"You wouldn't be. I should have explained. The Revvies pumped credits into a group of local sympathizers starting about ten years back—not that we knew any of this back then—and they began to acquire smaller formulators in the high-end building supply business, folding them into Wyal. By last year, Wyal controlled thirty percent of the building supply trade . . ."

"They were Denarian citizens or Revenant citizens?"

"They claimed Denarian citizenship, but the government invalidated it when it discovered the plot to monopolize the industry and run out true Denarian businesses."

Van forced himself to nod.

"Anyway, IIS Denaria now owns Wyal."

"I see. Have you done anything about changing the man-agement?"

"Well . . . we'll need new top managers. Most of them were interned."

"I'd suggest, then, that you don't make any significant changes among the employees . . ."

Vincenzio looked puzzled. "But they're Revvie sympathiz-ers. They have to be."

Van looked squarely at the younger man. "They had thirty percent of the business. The government took care of the ones they thought dangerous. If you get rid of any more, you'll lose both too much talent and the institutional memory those employees hold. They're scared. You keep them and treat them well, and they'll line your pockets. You don't, and what you bought won't be worth a third of what it was in less than a year." Van smiled politely. "I know that with everything that's gone on, that might take some considerable political skill on your part, but it's clear that's an area where you excel . . ." As he talked, Van just hoped he could steer Vincenzio away from more useless vengeance.

Chapter 91

Three days later, Van, Alya and the *Joyau* had left Denaria and headed out-system. Just before jump, Van had retuned the drives to Argenti standard and changed the ID and authorization packages.

"Ser?" Alya had asked.

"We're headed for trouble—Setioni—one of the fringe Keltyr systems. I need to see what's happening there."

"You know best, ser." Alya's tone conveyed great doubts about the wisdom of Van's decision.

Entering a Keltyr system wasn't necessarily wise, especially if the RSF had ships deployed, but, the way Van felt, it was necessary. Are you sure it's necessary, a part of his mind asked. Van pushed the question away and jumped the *Joyau*.

After the black-turning-white and white-turning-black endless moment of eternity, the *Joyau* dropped back into normspace and headed in-system. Van scanned the monitors, the EDIs, and the farscreens. After almost fifteen minutes, he had picked up a small Republic flotilla—two battle cruisers, four frigates, and six corvettes. The two nearest corvettes had changed to a course line and inclination that would intercept the *Joyau* in less than a standard hour.

Van checked the other vessels, but none followed the corvettes.

"I don't think we're going to make Setioni orbit control, ser," observed Alya.

"Probably not, but I'd like to see what they have to say."

"Are you certain that they won't use their torps to begin the conversation?"

"I don't think they'll fire on an Argenti vessel without giving a warning, and our shields are strong enough to handle two corvettes."

"I need some tea, ser. You?"

"Café, if you will."

Van continued to wait and watch, sipping first one mug of café, then a second.

In time, he walked to the galley for a moment, washing and racking the cup, before returning to the cockpit, where he strapped in.

So did Alya. "How long?"

"Any moment."

Unidentified vessel, Setioni is a closed system at present. Interrogative registration and purpose.

Van cut the internal ship gravs to free more power and stood by to throw full power to the shields. Then he responded. *This is Argenti ship Palabra, inbound for commercial purposes. Interrogative ship.*

RSFS Pylmer, stabilization patrol. Palabra, request registration this time.

Van didn't intend to argue. Not yet. *Pylmer, registration information dispatched.*

Wait one, Palabra.

Van continued toward the corvettes, ready to use his heavier shields and his torps, as necessary, although he hoped neither would be.

Palabra, your registration is cleared. You may depart system this time.

Pylmer, interrogative departure. Palabra bound for Setioni.

Palabra, Setioni system is closed to non-RSF vessels at this time. Request your immediate departure, or we will be forced to fire.

Stet. Commencing turn and departure.

The corvettes followed only another few minutes before turning in-system.

"Where to, now, ser?" asked Alya.

"Back to Perdya." Van doubted he'd like what the IIS staff had discovered there, either.

Chapter 92

Once the *Joyau* was locked to Perdya orbit station two, Van had given Alya two weeks well-deserved leave, sealed the ship, and headed to Cambria. The first night there, he'd tried to get a good night's sleep, but even planetside in the penthouse quarters above the IIS offices, he had had more of the nightmares.

In the end, he was one of the first in the offices the next morning, and that was after he'd run five klicks and done a half hour of exercise, then cooled down. His first task was to review the IIS financial figures—the ones he almost feared to see, given the events of the past year.

Fortunately for him, Laren wrote well, and while the numbers were not wonderful, neither did they reflect a complete disaster. Laren did offer the caution that the negative results caused by the collapse of the Revenant government would drag on for at least several years. The reason why IIS was only marginally affected was simple enough. IIS only had had a handful of offices in the Revenant systems. The negative effect of the Taran Republic's Economic Security Act promised to be far worse on future IIS revenues and operations, unless its effect could be mitigated.

There was also an update on the military situation on the Revenant planets. The Coalition was continuing to embargo and isolate systems that did not make reforms, leaving the locals to work out the details. There was one notable exception—the Leiphi system. There, some on-planet military types had modified a magshuttle, loaded it with something, and accelerated it into a Coalition frigate in orbit. The frigate commander had clearly been lax, but he had paid for that with his life—and that of the crew. The system commander sent a message back—with torps launched down at the planet. Large holes dotted numerous hilltops where once Revenant temples had stood.

The Argenti forces had opted for a case-by-case approach, leaving more options to the local system commanders. They'd also suffered more casualties, without much better results.

The problem was, Van reflected, that the Revenants had taken over so many planets, and with the high birth rate of their faith, they had always had fanatics and bodies to spare.

Laren peered in the open door. "Do you have any questions, ser?"

"A few." Van collapsed the holo screen onto which he had projected the information he'd been studying. "How much more will the revenues drop off?" He motioned her into the office.

Laren eased in and took a chair across from him. "We only get about two percent from Revenant worlds. I'd judge that we might get increases from some of the former border systems, especially those near the Argenti protectorate."

"What aren't you telling me? The Republic and Keltyr numbers?"

"The offices on Republic worlds only amount to ten percent of revenues, but we could lose all of those. Also, if the Republic starts to expand . . ."

"That won't happen immediately," Van said. "The RSF has most of its ships tied up in the Keltyr worlds. For now."

"The Keltyr worlds . . . Let's see." Laren frowned, concentrating. "We only have five offices there, but in the independent systems surrounding them, we have eight."

"You're telling me that the Republic's policies—over time—could cost us between, say, five and fifteen percent of total revenues?"

"We can't project that . . . there are too many variables,"

Laren pointed out. "But, yes, we will lose revenue. We'll also lose access, and information." She smiled politely. "Is there anything else?"

"Not for right now." Van had thought he understood. For the moment, he didn't need hard numbers, just an understanding of the overall picture. But before he made any hard decisions on operations, he would need those numbers.

Chapter 93

On fiveday, Van was in his office early again, as he seemed to be every day since he had arrived in Cambria. He'd called up a holo projection of the Arm, one that presented the areas of political control in color, and was studying it.

Incoming out-system for Director Albert. Sender, IIS office, Meroe.

Accept. Van wondered what Miryam Adullah had for him.

The face that appeared on the holo projection was not Miryam's, but that of Emily Clifton, her blonde hair pulled back severely.

Van waited.

"I couldn't let all this come without a personal message," Emily's image declared. "I used my personal leave as terminal leave so that I wouldn't have to go back to the embassy. The ambassador understands. Miryam Adullah said it would be acceptable for me to give the Meroe office of IIS as a return, since I don't have a commcode of my own yet."

A somber look followed.

"I've enjoyed being with you, more than you could know . . . this is hard . . . Please don't shoot the messenger, Van. I care, and I can't tell you how sorry I am."

Without another word from Emily, the holo began to display what were clearly media images, stock scenes of locales, interspersed with talking heads.

> With great regret Prime Minister Eamon announced that the unrest in Bannon has been resolved. In a written statement, he deplored the self-indulgence and treasonous behavior of those in Bannon and throughout Sulyn who had no understanding of the dangers that had faced and continued to confront the Republic . . .

> . . . the use of heavy weapons by Republic Marines in house-to-house fighting turned more than ninety percent of the city of Bannon and the outlying residential areas into little more than rubble . . . The Ministry of Internal Security expressed regret that the rebels had not seen fit to accept the rule of law that governs all civilized societies . . . but had tried to take that law into their own hands . . . preliminary estimates indicate that more than ninety percent of all structures and dwellings have been destroyed . . .

Van swallowed. Sulyn had the highest percentage of black Tarans in the Republic, and Bannon had held most of the more distinguished figures—such as his fathers.

Emily's face reappeared, and her voice trembled slightly as she spoke. "I managed to get some of the casualty figures . . . it appears as though over three thousand RSF Marines have been killed, and more than three million civilians. That could be low . . . there are twenty million people in the areas attacked, and independent media reports are claiming death rates of eighty to ninety percent . . ."

Emily's image vanished and was replaced by a talking head, and then by a scene of smoking rubble, klick upon klick of it. Van recognized the badlands at the northern edge of the screen as those beyond where his fathers' house had stood—as had Arturo's. Had stood, because it was clear nothing had been left standing.

A report from the Argenti news service Verdad claims that the Taran Republic executed scores of media personnel during the crackdown on unrest on the planet of Sulyn. The executions centered on those reporting the high levels of casualties, now estimated to exceed five million . . . Among those executed was noted mediacaster Ashley Marson . . .

Ashley, too? Was that because Ashley had been unbiased? Or because he had been tied to the Albert family?

. . . Verdad states that unidentified sources have confirmed that the Ministry of Internal Security had held secret military trials for a number of media types, including Marson. Marson was allegedly convicted of treason on the grounds that he had incited civil unrest and rebellion in Bannon. The Ministry of Internal Security had declined to open the military trials to the media, citing Republic security, and has kept the verdicts sealed, despite widespread reports of executions of scores of mediacasters, advocates, and academics who had opposed the government's actions to restore what it termed civil order . . .

. . . Verité reported yesterday in Marsay that virtually all Taran professionals of color or 'external ethnicity' had either fled the Republic of Tara, been placed in work camps, or executed under the pretext of treasonous activities. This report was immediately denounced as untrue and as inflammatory propaganda perpetuated by the enemies of the Republic by the Taran ambassador to the Frankan Comity . . .

Taran Prime Minister Eamon announced that elections will take place tomorrow . . . .

Van calculated that with the time delays those elections had doubtless already taken place.

. . . and that the new parliament will be sworn in and be ready to take up the government's agenda for social and economic reform, as well as the prime minister's proposal for strengthening the Republic Space Force. High on the government agenda is a proposal to strengthen the Economic Security Act..."

...Minister of State Shirlen dismissed as sheer fabrication reports that two ambassadors had defected and that more than thirty diplomatic personnel had sought asylum in other systems...

When he had finished the message, Van collapsed the holo projection. He sat there, thinking.

Then he began a series of searches. Had there been any comment from the Argenti government? The Coalition? The Hyndjis?

The best he could find was a statement from the Coalition Assembly's minority leader.

"We are deeply concerned that, in an effort to deal with internal instability, the interim government of the Republic may have resorted to the use of more force than necessary. We would hope that such will not continue...

That was it.

More than five million casualties... almost all of them black Tarans. Mediacasters who tried to reveal what was happening. The Keltyr fleet massacred to the last officer and tech. Was it just the Republic government?

Almost no one was saying anything. Why? Because the Coalition and the Argenti were unwilling to get involved in another war so quickly? Because it didn't affect them and wouldn't for years?

And how had it happened so quickly? Except had it? Hadn't the signs been there all along? Ashley had certainly called them to Van's attention. And now... Ashley was dead, and probably Arturo as well.

Van shook his head.

Was it just the RSF takeover? How could it be? The government hadn't put lasers to the heads of groundcar drivers and told them to avoid blacks. It hadn't demanded that street gangs terrorize foreigners on the streets of New Oisin. And there weren't protests from anywhere outside Sulyn or the minority community—except for a handful of mediacasters and outsiders.

What could IIS do?

Another series of assassinations? That wouldn't work—not when it was clear that the officers underneath the marshals believed the same way. Not when most civic-minded citizens agreed with the prime minister. Besides, Trystin had tried that—and regretted it for centuries.

Van looked out the window for a long time.

Then, he pulsed Joe Sasaki. *Do you have a moment?*

I'll be right there, ser.

Sasaki walked into the office and stopped. He looked at Van.

Van looked back. "I'm going out to Aerolis this afternoon. I want to talk to Mason Jynko about the possibilities for another ship."

"Laren said that the financials are better than we had thought, but starting construction now . . ."

Van forced a grin. "I didn't say I was going to authorize starting another ship, Joe. I understand the numbers. But I need to see if I can get some more flexibility from Aerolis. I also want to see if some modifications can be made to the *Joyau*, things I've thought about over the past year and kept putting off."

"You don't have to go out there . . ."

"It's better in person." Van laughed. "That's what I do best. You and Laren are the analysts. I can't do that much here."

"You provide the fire and the leadership."

"I provide it best, I suspect, in small quantities of personal presence here, and by example traveling in obscure systems."

"You aren't doing yourself justice . . ."

"I'm doing you all justice. Trystin didn't spend much time here, and that was for years on end, and matters continued just fine." Van smiled again. "You can always reach me at Aerolis, and I can be back in a matter of hours."

"Ah . . . yes, ser."

"If there's anything that absolutely needs my presence or approval, you've got until fifteen hundred."

"Yes, ser."

Van felt simultaneously worried and relieved as Joe left the office.

Chapter 94

On sevenday, Van stood in a maintenance shipsuit in the conditioned and full-gee warehouse room within the asteroid headquarters of Aerolis. Somewhere above him was the locking tower that held the *Joyau*. Before him were ten sealed containers, set in racks in a row.

"You sure you don't want any technical help with that equipment there?" Mason Jynko asked.

"If I do," Van said with a smile, "I think I can find you."

Jynko laughed. "Sound just like Trystin, you do." He cleared his throat. "About the design of the new ship. That's going to cost a good twenty percent more than the *Joyau* did. Could be more, if we're not going to start for another nine months. Have to check out the specs for certain."

"Let me know. You know where I'll be."

With a nod, Jynko turned and left.

Van walked over to the line of containers. There were no external labels on the gray sides, except a single numeral on each. The numbers ran from one to ten, predictably. Van studied the first container, then noted the almost flat pouch below the numeral "1."

He eased back the opening strip to find a sheet of permabond—addressed to him. Although he nodded to himself, he could still feel the shock of finding the message.

After a moment he smoothed out the sheet and began to read.

> Van—
> If you are reading this, one way or another, I'm not around.
>
> The boxes contain a complete duplicate of the various components of the sun-flare device that I attempted to employ against Jerush. Obviously, if I'm not here, something went wrong, and you'll need to be exceedingly careful.
>
> Please make certain that, if you are thinking about using this device, there are no other alternatives.

Just think about whether there are any alternatives. The perfunctory nature of the caution told Van a great deal, including the fact that Trystin himself had come to feel that at times there were no viable alternatives. At the thought of "viable alternatives," Van smiled ironically.

> Under the pouch in which you found this is a concealed cardreader. It is designed to accept your IIS card and no other, and will read the card against your biometrics. If any other card is used, and if the biometrics do not match, the contents of the first case will melt down. Without them, the other cases are effectively junk.

"More suspicious than he ever let on," Van murmured to himself.

Still, Van found it interesting that Trystin was only willing to turn the duplicate device over to Van, and to no one else. Why?

Because he felt only Van understood? Or because Van was the only one who might actually consider using it? Either way, it was a chilling thought.

Van looked at the container, knowing the hell it contained. Yet . . . what was he supposed to do? Spend the rest of his life on useless palliatives while the Republic replicated the mistakes of the Revenants, sowed the seeds of greater oppression while everyone else stood by, because they had bigger issues or domestic concerns?

The strongest words expressed against the Republic had been "deeply concerned" with a vain hope that the atrocities would not continue.

Van took out his IIS datacard.

Chapter 95

By sixday of the following week, Van had a far greater appreciation of Trystin's abilities. Without the detailed instructions that had come with the flux generator, it would have taken Van weeks, if not months, to assemble the equipment and set it up within the *Joyau*'s escape pod.

Even with what amounted to a step-by-step manual, and with equipment that had been designed and created in a modular structure, Van had worked sixteen-hour days for over a week. On more than one occasion, he'd had to call in Jynko for technical help. He had managed to explain the equipment as an out-system emergency power generation system, although he wasn't sure that Jynko believed him. Jynko had looked dubious, but at least had not called Van on the description, which was, in a fashion, correct.

By late afternoon, Van had finally returned the escape pod to its normal position at one end of the *Joyau*'s main cargo lock, where he was resetting the emergency quick-release restraints.

Message from incoming vessel—that was the relay from the shipnet.

Accept. Van had a good idea who that might be.

Van . . . you've got no image.

That's because I'm not near a scanner, Nynca.

Where are you?

In the cargo bay, checking things out. Dock at the other tower and come on over.

I'll be there in thirty minutes.

Van finished resetting the last of the quick releases, and then, given his sweaty condition, returned to his stateroom, where he quickly showered. He'd pulled on a clean shipsuit and ship-boots, and had even gotten into the galley. The café and kettle were beginning to steam when Nynca appeared at the tower lock. Van slipped from the galley to the lock and opened it.

She looked at his still-damp hair and laughed. "You and Gramps."

"What about us?"

"He didn't like to meet people unless he was clean and groomed and dressed."

"There's nothing wrong with that, is there?" Van pulsed the lock shut behind Nynca.

"No. It's a pleasant formality, but one that's not always followed these days."

"When formality vanishes, so do ethics," Van quipped. "That's a quote from Exton."

"He might have something."

"Do you want tea or café?" he asked. "The kettle's on, and the café's made."

"Café."

Van led the way to the galley, where he poured two mugs, then walked to the stateroom. He took the console chair and let Nynca have the more comfortable reading chair. Van's eyes strayed to the shelf on the far bulkhead, where the restrainers held the decorative box from the prime minister of Scandya. He wanted to shake his head. That had been so long ago, and he'd been so innocent.

Nynca looked at him. "What is it?"

"Nothing. Just thinking about how much has happened in the last few years."

"It has." She paused. "Joe said I'd better meet you here. He didn't say why. He did say that you came out here without Alya."

"He doesn't know why," Van said. "He just knows that I'm here, and that I didn't give him a good enough reason. I didn't bring Alya because I'd given her two weeks off, and for what I'm doing, I didn't need her, and she didn't need just to sit around. I'll need her more later."

"That's good to know," Nynca said dryly. "That you'll need her later. Why *are* you here?"

"Checking out equipment, and going over the *Joyau* with Morgan." All that was true.

"You're sounding more and more like Gramps." Nynca laughed. "Everything you say is the truth, and I don't know any more when you finish than when you started."

"That's possible. I think we had a few things in common. Tell me more about him," Van suggested.

"About what."

"Start with more about why he felt the way he did."

"I don't know. Not really. I'm not sure that anyone could know, except maybe Ulteena. From what I've heard, she didn't say anything either." Nynca sipped the café. "This is good."

"Thank you. Who was Ulteena?" That was a name Van hadn't heard.

"She was his wife. She was also a senior commander in the Service. They were married late, and only had one child." Nynca smiled. "I come from a long line of single children, and, like all the others, I have one."

"A daughter?"

"A son actually. He's at Cambria University."

"And he'll be a Service pilot, too?"

"He says not."

"Was Trystin around when you were growing up?"

"He was there, but usually not when my father was. He made my father nervous."

"Your mother's the Desoll, then?"

"Yes. He—my father—didn't like the idea of the name going down, but there were a lot of things he didn't like." Nynca straightened in her chair. "Something's nagging at you." She didn't ask what. She just looked at Van.

"On the last time out, I tried to get into the Setioni system. It's one of the outlying Keltyr systems. The Republic has a small flotilla there. Two battle cruisers, frigates, and corvettes."

"You're thinking of building a battle cruiser?" Nynca arched her eyebrows.

"I thought about an IIS version—until I checked the costs. I settled on a more powerful version of the *Joyau*—when we can afford it." Van laughed. "If I wanted to get everywhere I'd like to go, I'd need a dreadnought." He paused. "Did Trystin think about it?"

"That was why he built the *Elsin*. IIS needed ships powerful enough to take on the Rev corvettes and frigates, but anything larger was cost-prohibitive. Also, it would have been far too obvious." She studied Van. "What about the Keltyr system?"

"It's not just that. I can't confirm it, but it's almost a certainty that the Republic wiped out my fathers and my brother and his family. Then, you saw the analysis Laren did. The RSF effectively massacred the Keltyr fleet . . ."

"What are you trying to say?"

"I guess . . . I'm not sure I see any real difference between the Revenants and the Republic." Van shook his head. "Oh, there are lots of differences. The Republic doesn't have Temples and a state faith, and it doesn't indoctrinate all its citizens into one belief system. But they both seem devoted to amassing temporal power and marginalizing anyone who is opposed or gets in the way. Neither wants people who are different with any degree of freedom or power. With each year, it gets worse. Just like the Revs, the RSF is using clones as disposable tools. Just like the Revs, they're wiping out groups that don't agree. The total is over five million already—"

"Five *million*?"

"That's just on Sulyn. It doesn't count the Keltyr fleet and whatever's happening on the former Keltyr planets." Van cleared his throat. "Just like the Revs, they're using economic and social tools to expand and consolidate power. And just like the Revs, they've decided to change the rules of society whenever necessary to accomplish that, by taking away the rights of those who would oppose them. Did you know that they've started holding secret military trials, and that they've executed mediacasters and advocates who criticize the government?"

"I didn't know that, but there have been scores of governments in history, if not more, that have done the same thing."

"I know. But this is where I grew up. These are the people I defended. For me, that makes it different." Van took a sip of the already-cool café. "Trystin had the knowledge that at least the evil ones were the enemy."

"Not completely," Nynca replied. "I was told that once he was followed and almost arrested in Cambria because he looked like a Rev. That was one reason he was never more than a commander in the Service."

"That just makes matters more complex." Van shook his head. "How can you stop evil when no one wants to pay the price?"

"People have never wanted to pay that price. They only rally to stop it when it doesn't cost too much, or when their own survival is threatened. Why do you think Gramps used his device on the Jerush system? No one else wanted to act, and they wouldn't have, not until the Arm had been turned into four major powers, with all the independent systems gone."

"Do you think what he did will work?" asked Van.

"What do you think?" countered Nynca.

"Mostly . . . it did. It will take years for everything to settle out, but the Revs can't use unified economic power to push into smaller systems. That means, unless someone turns into the Revenant model, the smaller systems will become stronger, and there will be more of them. The Argentis are fairly live-and-let-live, and so is the Coalition . . ." Van paused. "Was that why he did it?"

For the first time, Nynca looked puzzled.

"He was afraid that the Coalition would have to go to war, and then all the freedoms, all the tolerance, all the economic openness would vanish . . ." Van waited.

Nynca's laugh was sad—and wry. "I didn't think of it that

way, but that was the way he thought. That's why I said you're more like him than any of us are." After a moment, she said, "Van . . . let things settle out. The Arm needs IIS, and IIS needs you. If you try something like Gramps did . . ."

"I promise you I won't translate the *Joyau* into a sun, or do anything like that," Van said. "I'd like to think that I'd accomplished something positive, and I'd like to have time to do it. And there are . . . things I really want to do."

"Is that a promise?"

"It is."

"So what *are* you going to do?"

"That's why I'm out here. I've been talking to Mason and trying to figure out what else we can do with the ships. I also needed some time to think. But whatever I do, I want to be around for a good long time, and I want my life to reflect something positive." All that was absolutely true. Van just had to figure out how he could do what he had to do and still do what he wanted to.

"I'd like to believe you," Nynca said.

"But Trystin said the same thing." Van paused. "Or did he?"

She frowned, then was silent for a time. "No. He really didn't. Not this last time."

"You see?"

"With you, I'll believe it when I see it."

Van shrugged. "I'll have to spend years proving it, then."

"See that you do."

Van laughed helplessly.

Chapter 96

After Nynca's talk with Van, she had not stayed at Aerolis, and Van had finished his preparations on sevenday, including restocking on torps. Early on eightday, he eased into the command couch and went through the checklist.

He looked at the blank board before him. *Do you want to go through with this?* The next question was harder. *If you don't, will you spend years like Trystin, crisscrossing the Arm and trying to clean up cancerous outbreaks of tyranny and repression everywhere? Will you end up old and feeble, and unable to do anything, regretting losing the chance that you had?*

He cleared his throat and linked. *A-prime, Joyau ready to depower and delock.*

Van dropped the ship grav to nil and waited.

Joyau, cleared to depower and delock.

Depowered. Delocking this time. With the gentlest touch of the steering jets, Van eased the *Joyau* clear of the locking tower. *Outbound on minimum power.*

Till the next time, returned Jynko.

Till then.

Once clear of the asteroid complex, Van turned the *Joyau* on an out-system course.

From what he had learned earlier, and updated while he'd been both in Cambria and at Aerolis, the "new" Republic government was being sworn in the next morning in New Oisin, and would be addressing the legislative and legal "reforms" proposed by Prime Minister Eamon. As Van had surmised, the RSF slate of candidates had won overwhelmingly, and the news permitted out of Tara trumpeted the results as a victory for "the people" and "a new era" for the Republic. Van had snorted at that.

Hours later, once he was clear of Perdya system, Van put the *Joyau* into jump immediately. The first jump from Perdya system brought him to an uninhabited system in the nebulous area bordered by Coalition, Argenti, and former Revenant systems.

There Van rechecked his equipment—and his calculations—then walked around the ship and stretched before settling back into the command couch.

The second jump brought the *Joyau* out into normspace close to the Taran system ecliptic, and well beyond the cometary belt—which was not at all where Van wanted to be.

He scanned the EDIs and the farscreens, but he was so far out that only a handful of RSF ships—those out beyond the gas giant Yeats—were showing.

Van calculated, then decided on a short jump—as short as he could make it—which would place the *Joyau* at an equal distance from Solis—Tara's sun—but at right angles and directly "below" it.

He initiated jump.

What was black turned white, and white turned black, and every color was its opposite, and yet itself. Time stretched endlessly, and yet the jump was over instantly.

Van winced as the *Joyau* dropped back into normspace. For whatever reason, shorter jumps seemed to leave him more disoriented than longer ones. He'd heard the same thing from other pilots over the years, but the technical types had always dismissed what the pilots felt. Van supposed that had been true back in the dark ages, when the only piloting had been atmospheric.

He immediately began deceleration, since the lower the velocity of the *Joyau*—and the escape pod—the more accurate he could make the pod's in-system jump. Then he studied the screens and EDIs, but nothing had changed, except that the jump had left the *Joyau* both in better position and farther away from the RSF ships patrolling the system.

Van scanned the in-system fleet—three dreadnoughts, six battle cruisers, eight frigates, and twelve corvettes—enough for an invasion force of a smaller system, and a clear sign that the Republic was at least slightly worried about either the Argentis or the Coalition. Next, he checked the system comparator, and nodded. It was twoday, as it should have been, and that meant that the Parliament would be in session, working on Prime Minister Eamon's agenda.

It took more than an hour of deceleration for him to bring the *Joyau*'s relative velocity down within the limits he had earlier calculated, but finally he was satisfied. Less difficult was the last-minute wrestling with himself.

The questions and counterquestions echoed and reechoed through his thoughts.

If you don't do anything, who will? But do you really think that destroying New Oisin will change matters? How can you possibly justify such an action? After all that the Republic has done in the past year, and the way it's treated the Keltyr systems, how can you not stop them from becoming another Revenant empire? Besides you, who will do anything? Didn't the Argentis and the Coalition surrender the Keltyr worlds to barbarism rather than take a stand and risk any of their ships and personnel? But does one set of barbaric actions justify another such act? Aren't you taking too much on yourself?

Van shook his head.

Except that . . . no one else was doing anything, and if millions had already died on Sulyn, how could there not be millions more dead in the years ahead? There wasn't any good answer. That much was clear. What was also clear to Van was that no one else was going to do anything, not anytime soon. The protectorate and the abandonment of the Keltyr systems to the Republic confirmed that.

Finally, he pushed away the questions and checked the farscreens and EDIs one last time. None of the RSF ships had made any course changes.

Van finally left the command couch and walked aft to the lockers next to the cargo hold. There, he donned the space armor and made his way into the cargo space. After sealing the helmet, he closed the lock doors. Then he loosened the quick-releases on the escape pod. If he had used the quick release bolts in their emergency mode, the pod could have come out tumbling, and that would have made the final adjustments and settings close to impossible.

When the pod was loose, he attached his own tether to one of the cargo restraint loops near the outer lock door. Then he attached the second and third tethers to the pod and then to a restraint loop on each side of the cargo lock. Only when he was satisfied that the tethers were secured did he send the command to the shipnet to reduce internal grav to nil.

Then he depressurized the hold, and opened the lock doors. As he had hoped, the rush of air broke loose the pod from the deck, at least enough that Van could lever it out of the lock doors. He used as little force as possible, not wanting to put too much strain on the tethers or the restraint loops.

The pod reached the end of the tethers, stretching them slightly, but the one-way nature of the tethers stopped the rebound, and the pod came to rest ten meters outside the cargo lock door.

Before proceeding, Van linked with the shipnet once more, calling up the EDIs and farscreens. A single corvette had begun to accelerate outward toward the *Joyau*, but Van's quick calculations showed that the corvette would not even near torp range for nearly three hours. He ran another calculation, and found himself frowning inside the shipsuit. If the corvette wanted to risk a high-dust-density jump, it was likely that the RSF ship could make a short jump in an hour. The jump accuracy for that short a jump was problematical, which was why Van hadn't tried another jump to get closer in-system, but he couldn't assume that the corvette would jump wide.

That meant, in the worst case, he had less than forty-five minutes to set up the pod for an in-system translation jump—with enough accuracy to avoid the solar core, a process analogous to threading a needle with a hundred-meter pole. With a deep breath that momentarily fogged the helmet view, Van began making his way, hand over hand, out along the tether that led to the escape pod.

Once there, most carefully, he unclipped himself from his own tether, clipping the tether to the ring on the pod. The lock into the pod would barely accommodate the armor, and one locking would almost exhaust the pod's extra-atmospheric capability. But then, no one would be needing that after Van adjusted the controls and settings.

Once inside the pod, stripped of all couches and habitability save basic atmospherics in order to accommodate the welter of equipment that Van had to move around, Van opened the helmet, and removed the gauntlets. Then he eased into position, half-floating before the control panel—and the even larger panel above it that controlled the flux generator.

The link to the *Joyau* was faint, but clear. Van ran a check, then took the positional information from the *Joyau*. Using the pod screens and comparing them to the relayed information, Van pulsed the steering jets until he had the pod oriented on Solis. Next came the course line settings, and then modifications to the jump generator. Then he had to set up the remote operation. Sweat pooled inside the armor, especially on his back, giving him the sense that he was wearing an icy jacket.

After another twenty minutes, he was ready to leave. Slowly, and carefully, he eased away from the controls, making his way back toward the minuscule lock. He sealed the helmet and donned the gauntlets once more, then slipped into the pod lock, careful to seal the inner door.

Atmosphere puffed out around him as he emerged from the pod. He had to be careful to clip the return tether to his armor first, and then unclip the other two tethers from the pod without exerting force on it, so that it floated free of the *Joyau*, but in the orientation most favorable for the programmed course.

Then Van pulled himself back to the *Joyau*, where he reeled in the other two tethers and closed the cargo lock. He repressurized the hold and waited until the heat indicators reached amber before he took off the helmet. The air still froze his nostrils as he took a breath.

Even before he was out of the armor, he linked into the shipnet.

There were three corvettes coming at him from out-system, with less than ten minutes before they were within torp range. Van had no idea where they had come from, unless they had translated from the far side of the system, but that was an academic question. He just left the armor on the floor of the passageway and dashed to the cockpit and strapped in.

Then he ran the checklist for the pod and began the sequence—a sequence that would take three minutes.

Eight minutes before intruders are within torp range, the shipnet informed Van.

That left Van with less than five minutes. He couldn't move the *Joyau* far from the pod, not without risking disturbing it and disrupting all his work—and the chances for success.

Are you sure you want to do this? Van pushed away that

thought, recalling the devastation the Republic had created
on Sulyn and the massacre of the Keltyr ships that had not
been allowed to surrender—ships that had never even tried to
attack the Republic.

One minute before the pod was go.

Van began to bring up full power on the *Joyau*'s fusactors.
At the same time, he set up the precalculated jump coordinates. They'd be off some, but he wasn't going to have time
to refine them, not the way matters were going.

The pod vanished, and Van instantly poured full acceleration through the drives, a force that pressed him into the command couch, because he'd sacrificed the power for ship
gravity to the drives and shields.

The monitors showed the three corvettes converging on the
Joyau, and Van could see that he was moving all too slowly.
The three corvettes had fired their torps simultaneously.

Van checked the EDIs, focused on Solis itself, looking to
see whether the device had worked. But the screens went
blank under the flare of energy that sheeted over the *Joyau* as
the RSF torps began impacting Van's shields. The secondary
generator flared amber for a long moment, before slowly
dropping back into the green.

Another wave of torps was on the way, but in the momentary clearing, Van could see the massive EDI surge from
Solis, and he gave the command. *Jump!*

At that moment, energy from the second salvo of Republic
torps flared against the shields, and Van could feel the secondary generator fail even as normspace vanished. The very
jumpspace around the *Joyau* buckled, and the ship seemed to
bend in half, then collapse inward, squeezing Van into a point.

Black turned a searing red, a blood-and-pain-filled red that
was somehow also white, even as white turned to an icy-deep-
space-freezing black, and the pain from both ran through
every nerve in Van's body, an endless nerve-electric torture.

The *Joyau* dropped into normspace with a sickening lurch.

Van could barely breathe, and he could feel the entire shipnet burning through his nerves. Every sensor pulsed along his
arms. Miniature knives twisted themselves deep into his

skull. Every energy source shown on the EDIs pulsed pain. Through the pain, he could sense that the ship was mostly structurally sound. At least, he thought it was.

Where was he?

Slowly, he tried to remember. Minutes later—or was it hours?—he recalled the jump system coordinates—the uninhabited system on the return to Perdya. Except . . . he had the feeling that he shouldn't be heading to Perdya.

What could he do?

Trystin had mentioned . . . something.

Slowly, concentrating on a thought at a time, he programmed the *Joyau* for a jump to Dharel. Each mental pulse sent an echo of pain back through his neck and skull.

Finally, he thought he could order the jump.

Jump.

The second jump was worse than the first.

Colors and temperatures jumbled into flashing, searing extremes that lasted forever, yet did not, before pummeling Van into a deep blackness.

At some time, he slowly woke, his breathing ragged, held in place only by the acceleration harness of the command couch. He lifted his head.

Electric pain surged through every nerve, and another wave of blackness engulfed him.

The second time he woke, countless spiderwebs of pain seared through his arms and legs, and the emptiness of the Dharel system pulsed through his optic nerves like a dance of infinitesimal and unending needles.

He made one course correction, then another.

In time, and it could have been hours or days, the *Joyau* neared the gas giant around which orbited the unseen and unseeable Farhkan installation.

Van had to concentrate on each word he pulsed into the darkness beyond the *Joyau*, hoping that the station was there, somewhere. *Farhka station Two . . . Coalition ship* **Joyau,** *code name* **Double Negative** . . . *pilot Albert* . . . What else was he supposed to say? What else . . . oh, the patron . . . . . . *patron Rhule Ghere, request assistance . . . medical assistance . . .*

Van had to close his eyes, but that barely helped against the pain that seemed everywhere within him. Time passed.

More time passed.

Ship Joyau, pilot Albert, you are cleared for approach and locking. Do you have the beacon?

Farhka Station . . . affirmative . . . have the beacon. Proceeding . . .

Van made each correction deliberately, carefully, but he still slewed the *Joyau* into the dampers, and for a moment, feared the ship would rebound. The Farhkan dampers held, unlike human ones, Van thought.

You . . . may unlock and enter the station . . .

Van fumbled with the harness. He had to visualize each movement to get his fingers to move. Then he floated up in the null gee and slammed into the bulkhead aft of the command couch.

He did manage to check the atmospherics before cracking the lock.

He took one step beyond the lock, into full grav, and his legs collapsed.

Van just sat there in the gray corridor that smelled musky and clean until the blackness tapped him on the shoulder, and he fell over.

Chapter 97

The blackness lifted, but the grayness that replaced it was filled with white-and-red pain. Then a greenish coolness swept across Van, followed by a deeper darkness. Words and thoughts marched through him from somewhere, but he could understand none of them, not before the restful green carried him away once more.

Van woke abruptly, his head clear. He lay on something that was neither a recliner nor a medcenter bed, but partook of both. A thin sheet of something lay across him, folded back to his waist. The first thing he noticed was that he didn't hurt. Looking at the gray bulkheads didn't send knives into his skull, nor did thinking and wondering where he was. After all that had happened, he felt relatively good. He should have been sore, aching, not to mention discouraged, overwhelmed, and depressed. He didn't, and that worried him. What had happened? Was he truly in the Farhkan station?

You may dress. Do not be alarmed. Someone will be with you shortly. The all-too-clear words scrolled through his mind. They had the Farhkan overtone, the one he could not describe, but felt so clearly.

Van sat up, looking around, finally locating his shipsuit, hanging from . . . something beside the bulkhead. Beneath it were underclothes, and his boots. He eased back the thin grayish covering. His body, what of it he could see without a mirror, looked normal, without scars, without change. He eased off the med-table-recliner. His legs held him as he walked to the clothing. He dressed quickly and pulled on the boots.

A Farhkan appeared. Van did not see how he entered the room, but he did recognize Erelon Jhare. The clean/musky scent intensified.

I must be better, or I'd be seeing Dr. Fhale.

Dr. Fhale has already seen you and done what was required.

What was that?

You were injured. Your gross physical injuries were not excessively severe, but the damage to your nerve and mental systems would have rendered you unable to function normally and caused you to die at an early age, even for a human. That was judged to be unacceptable. So Dr. Fhale reconstructed those aspects of your being in a more durable fashion.

He rebuilt me? Van glanced down at his chest and abdomen. *I didn't look any different.*

You would not.

While the Farhkan's words had not been spoken, as had also been the case the last time he was on the station, Van now sensed them far more clearly than ever before.

That is true. Your implant has been removed and integrated into your neural functions. It is more effective that way.

Thank you. I don't think I would have made it back to Perdya.

You would not have. You created some damage in docking here, and your ship was failing. We repaired that as well.

Have I been here that long? Or could the Farhkans do miracles with ships as well?

You have been here some time. Several months of your time.

Thank you.

It is a form of payment.

Payment? I didn't do . . .

No . . . you must repay the debts incurred by the other and by your own actions. You would not have lived long enough to do so had Dr. Fhale not reconstructed and strengthened certain of your aspects . . .

Debts? Is that why you're here?

You will need many centuries to rectify what you have done. You misapplied the technology the human Desoll obtained. So did he.

What would you have had us do? Let more millions be enslaved and murdered over generations?

Always . . . you think in terms of absolutes.

Those words ignited an anger close to fury in Van. He forced his response to be as cool as he could make it. *No. I do not think in terms of absolutes. Neither did Trystin. But all too many humans in positions of power do. They exploit the nature of other humans to seek and obtain simple and absolute answers. The universe does not allow such simple answers. The result is unethical, immoral, and impossibly cruel behavior. Trystin worked for years trying not to use absolute means, but absolute means were often necessary to prevent worse evils. He died believing that his greatest failure lay in not applying such absolute means to the Revenant culture far earlier, before that culture could create such evil and disruption. I could see the same pattern emerging with the Republic, except a pattern of more cruelty and evil even sooner.*

You would elevate yourself to a deity?

Trystin wouldn't have claimed that, and neither would I. We're a species of toolmakers, and we grabbed and used the biggest hammer we could swing because nothing else had worked.

In your arrogance, you assume that a solution to your nature is possible.

That stopped Van for a moment, not only the words, but the cold certainty behind them.

In your arrogance, he finally replied, *you assume that no solution is possible because you cannot envision it. Is it not better to try than to admit failure?*

The Farhkan snorted the ironic laugh. *You will have many, many years to try. More years and more lives than you would ever wish.*

A cold chill ran through Van as he understood the import of the Farhkan's words. How they would work it, he had no idea, but he understood fully that he would not be afforded the inadvertent option exercised by Trystin.

You may go. The Farhkan turned away, then stopped, and turned back to Van. *Should you prove us wrong . . . your sentence will be in your hands.*

Van blinked, and Jhare had vanished.

Should you prove us wrong . . . should you prove us wrong . . .

Van swallowed as he looked at the doorway that had opened in the wall, a doorway leading back to the *Joyau . . .* and exactly what he did not know, except that he had a debt to pay, and that it would take longer than he could possibly imagine.

For a moment, he swallowed, recalling Dad Almaviva, a powerful black man standing in the light, singing words Van had not understood then, and still did not, save that the character Almaviva had sung, Daland, had been a captain and a pilot, doomed to travel forever on his ship, until . . . until what?

That . . . Van feared he would discover, as had the ancient *Holländer*.

Chapter 98

Van had barely stepped out of the lift on his office floor of the IIS building in Cambria when Joe Sasaki and Laren appeared.

"Welcome back, ser," Joe said. "It's good to see you. We were worried."

"You look good," added Laren.

"Thank you. Thank you. We'll meet a little later. I'd like to catch up on a few things . . . and I need to talk to Nynca." He glanced around. "She said she'd be here."

"I'm here," said Nynca as she walked past the central lift-shaft toward Van. She did not look directly at him.

Van did not look at her either, as the two walked down the corridor to Van's office. He ignored the looks and the outright stares from the staff, although he would have to deal with them later. Once inside his office, Van closed the door behind them and, without Nynca's asking, activated the privacy cone.

He said nothing, but sat down in one of the chairs before the old-style table desk.

Nynca sat in the other. "Three months," she said. "Three months, and not a word, except a message from the Farhkans saying that you had been injured and were recovering. I thought you promised."

"I promised not to try anything suicidal," Van said. "I got attacked by three corvettes as I was leaving the Taran system. The energy scrambled me and the jump."

"You know that there's nothing left there. Whatever you

did . . . it wasn't just a superflare. It was close to a full nova. In fact, two of the nearer Republic systems will suffer damage in the next few years from the radiation. The underspace is still disrupted enough that no one can jump close to the system."

Van nodded. What could he say?

"Aren't you going to say anything? Doesn't the death of two hundred million more people mean something? Two hundred million more."

"It does. Enough that words don't mean very much."

"I find that hard to believe, when you saw what happened when Trystin . . . used . . . it . . . and then you just did the same thing."

"That's why I did," Van said slowly. "Because of something that he said, because I felt he was right."

"Right? How can killing seven hundred million people *ever* be right?"

The words burned forth from Van. "How about when it prevents killing millions more? Especially millions of innocents? Or when it stops injustice after injustice? Or when it stops a system of repression that will only grow across the Arm like a cancer? Or when it's the only recourse, because those with the power to stop the injustices with fewer deaths won't pay the price, because those being repressed and killed belong to other systems and other beliefs? And because they value the lives and freedoms of their own people above those of other people?"

Nynca sat stock-still.

"And remember this. Trystin was from the Coalition and attacked and killed the Coalition's enemy. I addressed the evils of the society in which I was raised. I stopped those evils before the Republic could replicate the example of the Revenants—before hundreds of systems were either tyrannized or before the entire Arm was plunged into war."

"You don't know that."

"No. I don't. What I do know is that Trystin saw more than I did, and he thought that he had done wrong to wait so long to act, and that no other powers would act. And they didn't.

What I know is that everyone looked the other way when the Republic massacred the survivors in the Keltyr fleets, and when the Republic closed off the Keltyr systems, and when the Republic massacred millions of its own people on Sulyn because they protested peacefully against tyranny. What I do know is that evil that is not confronted grows. What I know is that Trystin was right, that some trees are so misshapen and evil that they will never grow straight, and that it is better to topple them before they grow so large as to threaten all around them."

"I don't think we'll ever see eye to eye on this." Nynca said.

"We probably won't. Do you want my resignation as managing director?"

Her laugh was bitter. "You can't resign. If you do, IIS is disbanded and the assets turned over to the Coalition government."

"What?"

"Trystin was very clear on that. It's in the charter, and the way it's written, if the succession determined by the managing director is changed other than by that managing director, or by the successor he named, the charter is voided."

"I could appoint you to be my successor."

"No, thank you. I never wanted to run it, and I especially don't want to, now. The whole center of the Arm is a mess. The Argentis pulled out of their half of the protectorate, and it won't be long before the Coalition does the same with its half. The Argentis claimed that the protectorate was unnecessary now, but it's more likely that they want to use their ships against all the raiders and renegades that have appeared. You made this mess—even if no one could prove it but you and me and the Farhkans—and it's up to you to clean it up and prove you were right."

Van found an ironic smile crossing his lips. "That's what they told me."

"The Farhkans?"

"They said I had a lot to do."

"Then you'd better do it." A wry smile appeared, but

Nynca's eyes remained bleak. "There's going to be a greater demand for IIS services, especially for our secure shipping services. If the *Joyau* is still operational."

"The Farhkans repaired the ship as well as the pilot." Van looked at her. "How about if you become managing director of programs?"

Nynca frowned.

"I'll be managing director of operations. I do better with a ship." Van frowned. "I'll have to work out of a ship now."

"Have to?"

"Payment for my rehabilitation. The Farhkans were most unhappy."

Nynca studied Van for a long time. Finally, she spoke. "Like . . . gramps?"

Worse, Van suspected, but he only nodded slowly, wondering if he could avoid ending up like the historical HOLLÄNDER. Wondering if he could still reach out . . . and not turn his back on all those he had affected—who still lived—and to Emily, who might yet be his Senta.

He had time. That, he did.

LOOK FOR

FLASH

BY

L. E. Modesitt, Jr.

NOW AVAILABLE IN PAPERBACK
FROM TOM DOHERTY ASSOCIATES

A DATE WITH THE OTHER SIDE

"Do yourself a favor and make a date with the other side."
—Rachel Gibson, *New York Times* bestselling author

"One of the romance-writing industry's brightest stars . . . Ms. McCarthy spins a fascinating tale that deftly blends a paranormal story with a blistering romance . . . Funny, charming, and very entertaining." —*Romance Reviews Today*

"If you're looking for a steamy read that will keep you laughing while you turn the pages as quickly as you can, *A Date with the Other Side* is for you." —*Romance Junkies*

"Just the right amount of humor interspersed with romance."
—*Love Romances*

"Quite a few chuckles, some face-fanning moments, and one heck of a love story." —*A Romance Review*

FULL THROTTLE

erin mccarthy

BERKLEY SENSATION, NEW YORK

THE BERKLEY PUBLISHING GROUP
Published by the Penguin Group
Penguin Group (USA) LLC
375 Hudson Street, New York, New York 10014

USA • Canada • UK • Ireland • Australia • New Zealand • India • South Africa • China

penguin.com

A Penguin Random House Company

FULL THROTTLE

A Berkley Sensation Book / published by arrangement with the author

Berkley Sensation Books are published by The Berkley Publishing Group.
BERKLEY SENSATION® is a registered trademark of Penguin Group (USA) LLC.
The "B" design is a trademark of Penguin Group (USA) LLC.

For information, address: The Berkley Publishing Group,
a division of Penguin Group (USA) LLC,
375 Hudson Street, New York, New York 10014.

ISBN: 978-0-425-26174-3

PUBLISHING HISTORY
Berkley Sensation mass-market edition / December 2013

PRINTED IN THE UNITED STATES OF AMERICA

10   9   8   7   6   5   4   3   2   1

Cover photo of "Young attractive couple leaning on their car" © Kristian Sekulic/Getty Images.
Cover design by Rita Frangie.
Interior text design by Kristin del Rosario.

FULL THROTTLE

CHAPTER

ONE

"I double-dog dare you."

Shawn Hamby stared at Eve Monroe-Ford and remembered exactly why they had gotten in so much trouble together back in the day as the only two girls on the tween racing circuit. Eve had grown up with brothers and was a master at taunting manipulation. Shawn had grown up with an indifferent sibling and was eager for camaraderie, with an inability to keep a straight face. The combination had resulted in broken bones and many a grounding from their honked-off parents.

"I'm not falling for that," Shawn told her now with a laugh. "I'm not going to talk to a random guy in a fetish club because you dared me to." She wasn't twelve anymore, and she didn't need to prove anything to anyone.

Which didn't explain why she was here in the first place.

Damn. Maybe she hadn't changed all that much.

"Oh, come on," Charity McLain said, lifting her cocktail to her mouth as she leaned against the bar. "We're here because of you, so you might as well have the full experience."

They *were* here because of her, in a roundabout sort of

way, and as Shawn looked around at the dimly lit club, she fought the urge to giggle, which was her usual reaction to situations that made her uncomfortable. How a book club meeting had resulted in her and three friends being at a place called The Wet Spot—and no, they weren't talking about spilled beverages—she couldn't imagine.

"All I said was that people don't really do what the chick in that book was doing. I didn't say let's go to a fetish club and see if it's true or not." It had just been a little hard for Shawn to believe that their fiction selection for the month had any basis in reality whatsoever, regardless of how enjoyable a read it had been. Average suburban women didn't just up and go to a sex club after years of lame sex and let a total stranger blindfold them. She was sure of it. Not in Charlotte, North Carolina. Not in a day and age when true-crime shows about serial killers and date rape drugs were on TV every day, all day.

Not only did it seem dangerous but it also seemed kind of silly. She wasn't so sure what would be hot about having a man boss her around. Hell, she had that every day at the track, and it just frustrated her. There was nothing sexy about it in the least. Not to her anyway. Hence, the curiosity.

Harley, Charity's twin, tucked her blond hair behind her ear, glancing around nervously. "Let's just leave then."

"No!" Charity rebuked her. "Shawn needs to admit that this is real, that people go to clubs like this."

"I admit it," Shawn said easily. She wasn't exactly sure what people were doing here, or what drew them to the club, whether it was curiosity like the four of them, or a genuine interest in BDSM or other fetishes, but she'd seen enough.

There were only so many adult men and women being pulled on dog leashes she could look at before she lost it and started laughing. It wasn't like she found other people's choices amusing. It was that it just looked . . . fake. Like a movie being filmed. Like a giant skit being played out for her benefit. None of it seemed real, from the girl on the red velvet sofa allowing two different men to swat at her backside with a paddle to the extremely thin man who was shirtless and wearing nipple clamps, SLAVE tattooed across his chest, a lollipop in his mouth.

"This isn't really what I pictured," Eve said, scrutinizing the room. "I guess I thought it was going to be more tawdry. Nobody is having sex or anything."

"Do you want to see people having sex?" Shawn asked, because she didn't. She didn't even really get the appeal of mirrors in a bedroom. Sex was not a spectator sport. Not that she remembered what sex was like, given how long it had been since she'd had it. Eve, on the other hand, was married to a sexy jackman, so she had no business being curious in Shawn's opinion.

"No, I do not. I don't even want to be here. My husband's going to start to think our book club is a front for checking off items on my Bad Girl Bucket List. Last month we got drunk on margaritas and took a pole-dancing class, which was a huge leap from reading Margaret Thatcher's biography. The month before, you goaded me into waxing my cooter, though Nolan wanted to write you a thank-you note for that one."

Eve had a point. Shawn wasn't sure how this kept happening. She thought it had something to do with the prevalence of wine at their book club gatherings and the fact that she and Eve felt every one of the five years they had on the twins. Or maybe they were just repeating their childhood of stumbling into Bad Ideas together, though she had to primarily blame Charity for this particular outing. She was the one who had asked Siri on her iPhone where to find a fetish club in Charlotte, and suddenly here they were.

"We can go at any time," Shawn said. "And I get to pick next month's book selection. Plus it's my birthday month, so you'd better have cake for me." She was turning thirty-three, which, while not noteworthy, was fairly appalling. "Red velvet."

"Fine. I'm going to the restroom first," Eve said, setting down her beer and heading off.

Shawn wasn't sure going alone was totally wise, but Eve could take care of herself. She was known around stock car racing as having a razor-sharp tongue and no hesitation whatsoever in using it to slice offenders to ribbons. It was a talent Shawn did not possess. She was the goofy girl, the one who cracked a joke at the wrong time, the one who nobody took seriously.

"I'm kind of disappointed," Charity admitted. She and Harley were identical twins, but only in appearance. While Charity was outspoken and wore significant makeup and teased and highlighted her hair, Harley was quiet and completely natural-looking. When they stood next to each other, it was like seeing a before-and-after pageant shot of the little girls on *Toddlers and Tiaras*. "I was hoping for something more glamorous."

"I think if you join one of those members-only clubs, you get glam. Otherwise you just get skimmers," Harley said. "People dabbling in the scene. Not that I know anything about it, really. I'm just speculating."

"None of these guys are even cute," Charity complained.

Shawn would have to agree, except right at that moment, a guy came around the corner from the other room, and he wasn't just cute. He was beyond cute. He was smoking hot. He was wet-panty-producing sexy.

"Hubba hubba," she said, before she could stop herself. "Now there's a fine male specimen."

He was ripped, but not bulky, filling his button-up shirt and jeans to perfection. Just a perfectly hard, muscular lean man with a confident step and an intense stare that swept the room and landed on her.

"Oh, damn, he is hot," Charity said.

"And he's looking at us," Harley breathed, sounding panicked.

He was.

And then he strode right over to them, his eyes locked

4

on Shawn. On her. Yikes. She swallowed and tried not to fidget. She didn't really want to do this. She wasn't prepared to talk to a guy here. It was all just a dumb idea to even set foot in this place, and she certainly didn't want to encourage any attention from a guy who would clearly be interested in areas outside her expertise and comfort level.

She would have to politely dissuade him.

Before he even spoke, his hand slid out and took hers, his thumb stroking across her palm, causing a shiver of arousal to take her totally by surprise.

"You should dance with me," he said, already pulling her toward him.

"Okay."

So much for turning him down flat. Why the hell had she just agreed to dance? Because he was hot. And there was something commanding about him that appealed to her. Which was annoying.

"I'm Rhett," he told her.

Of course he was. Shawn squeezed her mouth shut so he wouldn't see her desperately trying not to laugh. She imagined using a fake name was what you did in a place like this, but seriously? Rhett?

"Well, then I guess that makes me Scarlett," she told him.

RHETT Ford saw the dark blonde the minute he came around the corner. She was smiling at her friends, and she looked relaxed, casual, dressed simply in jeans and a purple sweater that had fallen off one shoulder. Her friends were dressed similarly, and given that he'd never seen her at The Wet Spot before, he suspected she was someone just like him—curious and turned on by kink, but not sure where to start.

Aside from the fact that he was immediately attracted to her, she also didn't appear to be the type that he'd always gone for, and which had always resulted in total disaster. He had a firm habit of choosing the shy, unassuming girls, like the blond twin currently standing next to the woman who had caught his eye, and invariably he scared the shit out of every single one of them. They all ran, terrified. Like his latest mess of a relationship with Lexi.

So this was a conscious choice, to be approaching a woman who looked confident and amused by her surroundings. He didn't even mind that she thought he was giving her a fake name. Though God knew, if he had a choice of names, he never would have picked Rhett. It had been the bane of his existence almost since birth. If he went for an assumed identity, he probably would pick Bill or Dave. No one could poke fun at a Dave.

Leading the woman by the hand to the back bar where there was a dance floor, Rhett glanced back at her. She was checking out his ass. Now that was promising. He had never actually hooked up with anyone he had met here, since for the most part, he had just been observing and working out his own personal sexual interests, but he was definitely intrigued by this so-called Scarlett. When they got to the small dark room, where only half a dozen people were moving to the baby-making music, he pulled her into his arms and studied her face.

She met his gaze steadily, her hands snaking up to wrap around his neck. He was tall, but so was she, and while he had to bend down to make eye contact, it wasn't significant. Her eyes were an amber color, and they were shining with amusement and, if he wasn't mistaken, attraction. As they swayed, his hands lightly on her trim waist, he gave her a slow smile.

"So what brings you here?" he asked her.

Her response wasn't flirtatious, nor was it cryptic. It was just matter-of-fact. "Information."

"Are you a reporter? A blogger?"

"No. We're four women who like to be right. This is my friends' attempt to prove me wrong."

Interesting. Bored housewives? He couldn't check her ring finger to see if she was married, but then again, if she was looking for a good time, she would take her ring off anyway. If she was, he would be disappointed. Married women weren't his thing. He was loyal and committed to a single woman at a time, and he had no desire to serve as an itch scratcher for a restless spouse.

"How so?"

"I didn't think people came to places like this. Apparently they do." She gave him a wry smile. "So why are you here?"

He had no problem being honest. Another lesson hard learned. He needed to be up-front about his desires. "I'm looking for the right woman for me. One who likes to be led in bed."

She gave a little laugh. "Oh, really?"

"Really."

"Uh-huh."

Rhett wasn't sure if he should be offended or not. He did know he was turned on. There was something very compelling about the way she never broke eye contact. What could be hotter than a woman submitting to his desires but doing so out of titillation, boldly? Nothing, as far as he was concerned. But he was getting ahead of himself. Which was evidenced by her dropping her arms to halt his creeping progress lower and lower on her back. He was at the curve of her ass when she reprimanded him, gripping his hand to stop it.

"Hey now, sport, watch the sticky fingers."

Rhett grinned. "Don't you mean wandering hands? I'm not trying to steal your wallet."

"Whatever," she said dismissively. "You know what I mean."

"I do." He kept his hands far above the erogenous zone, wanting to respect her limits. "So give me your number." The song was almost over, and who knew what would be played next. She might use a booty-grinding song as an opportunity to leave the floor and return to her girlfriends. He didn't want to waste time.

7

Her eyebrows shot up. "That's a little presumptuous, don't you think?"

"You never get what you want if you don't ask."

"How old are you?" she asked suddenly, putting more space between them as they swayed to the bass pumping R&B.

So that was it. She was older than him. "Old enough to know what I want."

"You're younger than me." It wasn't a question. She seemed certain of it.

"Frankly, Scarlett, I don't give a damn." Might as well make his stupid name work for him.

She gave a short laugh, smiling at him. "Nice. Corny, but effective. What's your real name, by the way? I only give my number to Clark Kent, not Superman."

He liked the sound of that. She was going to cough up her phone number, and he was suddenly glad she'd shifted away slightly because he was getting hard. There was something about her that he found seriously arousing, and she didn't seem intimidated by what he'd told her, which further turned him on. "It really is Rhett."

A flicker of annoyance crossed her face.

But before he could pull out his driver's license and prove it, her friend approached them. "Shawn!" she said, urgently.

So her name was Shawn. It suited her. Unusual, unique. The tomboy who grew up to be a sexy woman. Or so he would guess, given the muscle tone of her waist and arms, and the perky lift of her backside. This girl liked sports, or at least the gym.

"Sorry to interrupt, but we need to leave. Emergency. Let's go, now."

Shawn stopped moving to the music entirely and dropped her hands to her sides. "What's wrong?"

"Nothing. We just have to go. Come on." The blonde wouldn't look at him at all, and when there was a hesitation on Shawn's part, she actually took her friend's hand and pulled her away.

"Wait," Rhett said. "I still want your number."

But to his disappointment, Shawn just gave him an apologetic smile and a wave. "Nice to meet you," she said, as she was dragged away.

Rhett was left standing on the dance floor having a whole hell of a lot of sympathy for Prince Charming when he'd been ditched. But unlike Cinderella, Shawn didn't leave any clues behind.

"*WHAT* is going on?" Shawn asked Charity, fighting the urge to glance back at the hot hunk of man flesh she'd left on the dance floor. Despite ticking her off a little with his refusal to give a real name, she had to admit, her interest was peaked. Along with her nipples.

"We have to go because of that guy you were talking to."

"What? Why? And where are Eve and Harley? And stop yanking on me. You're going to pull my arm out of the socket." Shawn followed Charity out the front door, the cold February air hitting her with a smack as she pulled on her coat that Charity shoved at her.

Eve was pacing to the left of the door, looking anxious. She darted her eyes behind Shawn. "He didn't follow you, did he?"

"No. Why would he follow me? And what is the big deal about that guy?" Had Eve seen him on *America's Most Wanted*? Was he a *Gone with the Wind*–inspired serial killer? First he dressed you in drapes, then he threw you down the stairs?

As they started walking toward the car, Eve said, "*That* was my brother-in-law. When I came back from the restroom, I saw you with him. There was no way I could let him see me there. And there was no way I wanted him to know I saw *him* there."

"Your brother-in-law? You mean, like, Nolan's brother?" She could see how that would be more than a little awkward for Eve. It wasn't just the corner pub they'd been in.

"Yes." Eve beeped open her SUV and they all climbed in. She turned toward Shawn in the backseat and gave a snort of laughter. "Nolan's little brother, Rhett."

"That guy's name is really Rhett?" she asked in amazement. Now she felt like a jerk for doubting it. "I thought he was making that up!"

"No, it's really his name. He's twenty-five years old and he's in a sex club. Oh, my God, how am I going to look him in the face?"

"Twenty-five?" Shawn squawked, horrified. "Good Lord, he's a fetus!" Who she had been contemplating pursuing so she could get a serious look at him naked. Her cheeks burned. "He looked older than twenty-five. He looked too hot to be that young. And I thought Nolan's little brother was well, little. It never, ever occurred to me that the fake Rhett could be the real Rhett. You always talk about him like he's seventeen."

"To me, he might as well be. He's Nolan's little brother! What the hell was he doing there?" Eve asked, pulling out of the parking lot.

Oh, Shawn had a funny feeling she knew exactly what he was looking for. She might not be particularly knowledgeable about the lifestyle, but she could pick up on a clue or two. "I think he was a Dom looking for a submissive," she said, not at all sure how she felt about any of this.

"*What*?" Eve said, moaning. "Oh, shit, I'm going to die. I do not want to picture that. God!"

"I should have let you give him your number," Charity said ruefully from the front passenger seat. "But I panicked."

Still stunned, Shawn murmured, "I told him my name was Scarlett. I thought he was giving me a code name."

As Eve cruised to a stop at a red light, they all looked at one another and burst out laughing.

"So what are we reading next month?" Harley asked.

Shawn figured it could only be a letdown after this selection. She settled back into her seat, shivering, and tried not to think about a certain guy who was too young for her, with the most intense green eyes she'd ever seen in her life.

It worked for about three whole seconds.

CHAPTER
TWO

RHETT swiped a handful of nuts from the crystal bowl on the coffee table as he stepped over three of his nieces coloring on the floor, the smell of his mother's enormous Sunday dinner cooking in her kitchen. Frowning, he searched the crowded room for his sister-in-law, Eve, wanting to discuss the plans they had going for the upcoming racing season.

But he had the distinct feeling that she was avoiding him today for some reason. Every time he got close to her, she disappeared, and other than a quick wave and a half smile, she hadn't made eye contact with him once. It was weird.

A wail sounded from the carpet, and he realized that he had stepped on Georgia's yellow crayon and snapped it in two. His niece was only three, and frequently at the mercy of her older siblings. Being the youngest of nine kids himself, Rhett sympathized with her.

Immediately, her older sister Jessa started mocking her. "Stop being a baby. Baby, baby, cry baby."

"I'm not a baby!" Georgia's face was red, her eyes and nose leaking fluid. Rhett bent down and scooped her up under his arm, slinging her back and forth.

"Sorry, G. My fault. I'm sure there is another Macaroni and Cheese crayon in this house somewhere."

Tears trickled off into giggles.

He gave Jessa a look of reprimand. "Be nice. You don't like your stuff getting broken either."

Hearing his niece's laughter usually made him smile, but he felt off today. Having a hell of a time falling asleep last night after going to The Wet Spot, he had woken up with a start and a giant boner that morning. He had dreamed of the woman from the club, Scarlett, aka Shawn. It was likely she'd never show up there again, and while her first name was unusual, without a last name or any information about her at all, he had no way to locate her. It was a huge downer because there was something about her that had gotten under his skin. Or at the very least, in his pants. He wanted her, and knowing he would never get her made him grumpy.

His brother had already picked up on it. "So what's your problem today?" Nolan asked him as he let another niece, Asher, climb on his back.

"Your face," he told him lightly, because that's what you said to your brother. "Where the hell is Eve, by the way? I wanted to ask her if she's talked to Evan about when we're getting the car."

"She's around here somewhere. Probably in the kitchen. She loves Mom's cheese balls."

"I think she's avoiding me," Rhett said as he pulled Georgia up to rest on his hip. It made him concerned there was a problem with their plan. Last fall, Eve had quit her job as a PR rep for her brothers, both highly successful stock car drivers, Elec and Evan Monroe, to pursue her own career as a driver. She had chosen to try to tackle the truck series and was already a few weeks into her inaugural season. Rhett had left Evan's pit crew to join Eve's, knowing it would afford him more free time to pursue his own passion—dirt track racing.

If all this went south, he was going to be less than thrilled. Not to mention out of a job.

He didn't really know his new sister-in-law all that well, since they had only fleetingly crossed paths over the past couple of years. It was just since she'd married Nolan a few months earlier that he had started to spend more time with her, but they weren't particularly close. Maybe he was reading her wrong.

"You sound like a middle school girl," Nolan said. "No one is avoiding you."

If he hadn't been holding Georgia, he would have called his brother a dick, but he was, so he had to settle for punching Nolan on the arm.

"Dinner! Find a chair," their mother called from the kitchen.

They were easily twenty for dinner that night, which was still only half the family, but in a small ranch house, it made for tight quarters. Rhett tried to maneuver himself near Eve, but she hightailed it to the very end of the long folding table, which came out on Sundays to accommodate their large numbers. With six kids and Nolan between them, there was no way Rhett was going to get a seat anywhere near her.

He was not imagining that her behavior was off.

It did not improve his mood.

Nor did his mother's decision to ask him about his love life.

"So I was hoping we'd see Lexi here tonight," his mother said to him across the table, ruining his appetite entirely.

"We broke up," he reminded her. "It's been six weeks, Mom. Let it go."

To change the subject, he turned to his sister Danny. "Give me the mashed potatoes."

His sister made a face at him, and he realized that sounded way ruder than he had intended.

"So bossy, for crying out loud," his mother said. "I hope you weren't bossy like that with Lexi."

If only his mother knew just how bossy he had been. The thought amused him.

Down the table, Eve started choking on her wine.

His nephew Simon whomped her on the back.

"Good Lord, are you okay?" his father asked her.

"Fine, fine," she said, holding her hand up.

But then she made eye contact with Rhett and started, glancing away quickly.

What the hell?

"I just think," his mother said, circling right back around to his failed relationship, "that maybe you're not *nice* enough to your girlfriends. Nolan was the opposite, always falling in love in a minute, showering the girls with gifts, but you don't smile enough. It makes the girls feel so insecure."

"So I should smile more and I'll nab an unsuspecting female? Okay, thanks, Mom." He wanted to roll his eyes, but there was really no point. She meant well.

"You showered the girls with gifts?" Eve asked Nolan, her eyebrows raised, the corner of her mouth turned up in a teasing smile. "I don't seem to recall that happening with me."

"Oh, I meant when he was young," their mother hastened to amend. "You know, cheap things, like teddy bears and chocolates."

"I bought you leopard-print underwear and that crap wasn't cheap," Nolan told Eve.

"Nolan!" That was their mother, horrified.

Rhett grinned. He did enjoy a good Sunday dinner.

"Why are you so eager to marry Rhett off anyway?" Nolan asked their mother. "With me, you were always telling me not to rush into anything."

"Because you were always impulsive, and you wear your heart on your sleeve. Rhett doesn't attach very easily. It worries me."

"Rhett is in the room," he said, annoyed all over again. It wasn't that he didn't attach easily, nor was he opposed to marriage. The truth was, he was often guarded with women because he did attach. He was intense. Once he was in, he was all in, and he'd yet to find a woman capable of handling that facet of his personality and needs. They all eventually became frightened by his passion.

He was starting to conclude that he was just a whole lot of too much for the average twenty-three-year-old woman.

"It's just because you're the last one," his sister Jeannie said. "Nine kids and eight are married. Mom wants to close the folder on her parenting."

Yet another one of the joys of being the youngest.

Though most of the time, he didn't mind it. His childhood had been happy, and his sisters had all doted on him, carrying him way past the age when he needed to be carried, and slipping him treats. He'd been their mascot of sorts and had satisfied their desire to role-play as mommies. But there was no question his parents had been a bit worn out by the time he'd been coming up, and he had never quite gotten over his resentment about his name. It had given him countless bloody lips and bruised knuckles on the playground when he'd been forced to defend himself against bullying.

Maybe he could let the whole thing go if just once his mother admitted that perhaps it had been a poor choice, but she didn't. She still thought his name was the shit.

"She can do that whether or not I'm married. I have my own apartment. I have a job. A social life. It's all good." He glanced at Eve again, but she was cramming a dinner roll in her mouth.

"Speaking of social lives, or lack thereof. Eve, do you still have your book club?" Danny asked. "Can I join it? I would love to do something like that and get out of the house a little."

Nolan laughed. "Eve's book club is a front for getting together with her friends and drinking wine. She had it last night and they wound up in a bar."

"I'm in," Danny stated emphatically. "I need one night to be an adult. Who else is in the group?"

"It's not a front," Eve protested. "We read all the books

and we do discuss them. It's just, why not discuss them with wine, right?"

Nolan scoffed. "That still doesn't account for the bar. And don't tell me that was Harley's or Shawn's idea, because I seriously doubt either one of them would suggest it."

Shawn? Rhett set his fork down and looked down the table at his sister-in-law. How many women named Shawn could there be in this town? Who had been in a bar the night before? With female friends?

"Are you suggesting it was me?" Eve asked hotly. "Nolan Ford, you are going to pay for making me sound like an alcoholic in front of your mother. It was actually Charity's idea, because Shawn said that a place like that doesn't exist."

Rhett went still. The Shawn in the club had said virtually the same thing.

"Bars don't exist?" Jeannie asked.

Shawn. Four girlfriends. Skepticism about a fetish bar.

Holy shit, Eve had been in the club the night before with the woman he had danced with.

Eve suddenly seemed to realize what she had revealed. "Oh, sh–, I mean, shoot. I mean, like a specialty bar. Never mind." When she glanced at him, her cheeks were burning red, confirming that Rhett was one-hundred-percent right.

Whattya know. Rhett grinned at Eve.

While his initial reaction was one of mortification that his sister-in-law had seen him out at a fetish club, it paled in comparison to the rush of excitement and satisfaction he felt knowing that he now had a way to find out who Shawn was and where he might be able to see her again.

Rhett took the platter of sliced pork tenderloin his brother-in-law passed him and served himself a hearty helping. His appetite had suddenly returned, full force.

EVE couldn't look at Rhett without picturing him paddling a simpering female. It was pissing her off. She liked her brother-in-law, damn it. They worked together and were just starting to get to know each other. They were essentially starting a new business venture together, and she did not want to know about his sex life. It was like walking in on your parents having sex. Or seeing your husband's father naked in the shower. She didn't care what Rhett did in his private life, she just didn't want images of it popping up in her head every time someone used the word "bossy." Or "dominate." Or "whip."

There had to be some sort of mental trick she could use to disassociate Rhett from sex. Like every time she started to conjure up inappropriate imagery, she could think of dead rabbits or something. That might work.

As long as he never knew that she knew, they would be cool.

Speak of the devil, when she opened the door to the kitchen from the garage, having gone out there to snag a beer from the overflow fridge, he was standing there, smiling at her. He gestured for her to go back into the garage and then he pulled the door firmly shut behind him.

"So Eve, how did you like The Wet Spot?" he asked.

Crap on a cracker, how did he know? Never one to back down from what she'd done or a challenge, Eve just shrugged nonchalantly. "It was alright. A little underwhelming, to be honest. I take it you saw me there?"

"Nope. But I put two and two together, given that the woman I danced with was named Shawn, and she was with three friends out strictly to satisfy their curiosity, not pick anyone up." He leaned against the door and crossed his arms over his chest. "But you saw me."

"Yes, I did. And we don't have to discuss it in any way. Ever." It was cold in the garage, given that it was the beginning of February, so she gestured for him to move. "Now let me in the damn house, I'm freezing."

"Who is your friend Shawn? That I danced with."

Uh-oh. Eve recognized that look on Rhett's face. She

saw it on Nolan every night when he climbed into bed with her. Lust, plain and simple.

"I don't think so," she told Rhett. "You are not pumping me for information, because I have no idea if Shawn would be okay with that or not." Though the truth of the matter was he was going to figure out who Shawn was soon enough, given that he was set to start racing at her track come spring.

Nonetheless, how and when Shawn wanted to encounter Rhett was up to her, not Eve. She would warn her, then Shawn could proceed however she chose.

"Oh, come on." Rhett's nostrils flared. "I could just go and ask Nolan, you know. He'd tell me before he'd even know why he should or shouldn't."

"That's low, Rhett," Eve told him with disapproval.

"I'm legitimately interested in her," he said. "Please?"

Pleading sounded about as sincere on him as it did on her—which meant not at all. Eve snorted. "You met her for like sixty seconds."

"So? How long were you dating Nolan before you married him?"

Ouch. The kid was good. She'd give him that. "Don't be an asshole. Look, I'll talk to Shawn and see if she's interested in hearing from you, okay?"

His tense posture relaxed slightly. "That's fair. Did she mention me at all?"

Eve grinned. Rhett had a crush. It was actually kind of adorable, except that the object of his alpha affection was one of her oldest friends. "Yes. Then she wrote your initials in a heart on her notebook."

"Fuck you."

Nolan opened the garage door in time to hear this last annoyed remark from his brother. "Excuse me? Did you just tell my wife 'fuck you'? I think you need to apologize or you'll be eating my fist for dessert."

Rhett was taller than Nolan, but her husband had bigger biceps. They glared at each other, chests puffed out. Good

Lord. Eve rolled her eyes. Though she couldn't really pull off the pious act since most of her childhood she and Evan had fought like a couple of rabid dogs. The fact that she was a female hadn't factored in at all. There had been fists involved often, much to her mother's dismay.

"It's fine, babe. I deserved it. I was giving your brother a hard time. I know you find that difficult to believe, given how generally sweet and passive I am."

Nolan raised his eyebrows and took a step back from his brother. "About what?"

"It turns out Rhett was in the same bar as us last night and he's taken a shine to Shawn. He wanted to know how to contact her."

"Really?" Nolan eyed his brother. "She's too old for you."

For some reason, that annoyed Eve. Shawn was actually a year younger than *her*. And while she one hundred percent agreed that she wouldn't want to date a guy Rhett's age if she wasn't married, she didn't want a man dismissing her or her friend as too old. It got her back up.

"That's not the issue here," she told her husband. "Men date younger women all the time, and no one says a damn word about it."

"Sure they do," Nolan protested. "Everyone says she's a gold digger."

"So they call younger women dating older men gold diggers and older women dating younger men cougars. Yet no one says anything about the men at all. That pisses me off."

"I never called Shawn a cougar," Nolan told her easily. "Frankly, my point was she's too mature for Rhett. I don't think he can keep up."

"Hey." Rhett frowned. "How exactly am I so immature? God, you and mom both. I have a job, an apartment."

"That was my apartment," Nolan pointed out. "I let you take over the lease when I got married and moved in with Eve. And I'm not saying you're immature, just not as mature as a woman who runs a dirt track almost entirely on her own."

Ah, shit. There was no way Rhett wasn't going to be able to figure out who Shawn was now.

Eve gave her husband an annoyed look and pushed him into the house. "I'm freezing. Plus, I want pie for dessert."

The garage door swung down slowly on automatic hinges and Rhett leaped inside before it shut. "Wait a minute," he said, the wheels clearly turning. "That was Shawn Hamby, wasn't it?"

Eve didn't answer, and she put her hand on her husband's mouth before he could further blow it. But it was too late.

Rhett broke into a grin. "It is. There can't be two women you know named Shawn who run a dirt track. Damn. Who knew the owner of Hamby Speedway was so freaking hot?"

"She's too old for you," Nolan said again.

Eve didn't say anything at all. She just pulled her phone out of her pocket. She needed to warn Shawn she was about to be stalked by a horny member of her pit crew.

"*YOU* cannot be serious," Shawn said, staring at her grandfather's lawyer, Clinton Oiler, across the desk of her office at the track. "There is no way that is even legal."

"Oh, I can assure you it is. Your grandfather owned this track, and he had the right to do whatever he wanted with it."

Shawn fell back against her chair, sending it rolling a foot to the left and colliding with a box of leftover programs from the previous season on the floor. Her office was a contender for putting her on an episode of *Hoarders*, but she wasn't detail-oriented. She was a big picture person, and she loved this dirt track, had loved helping her grandfather run it until his death three months earlier.

Losing Pops had been rough for her. She had known it was coming. He'd battled cancer for two years before losing the fight, but he had always managed to seem like he would beat it. Until the very end, he had still been at work, and she had deluded herself into thinking he would never be gone. Then in the blink of an eye, he'd taken a turn for the worse and he was gone. But what had comforted her after he died was that she had been entrusted with his legacy, this track. It was her home, her heart, her passion.

But apparently her grandfather had thought her passion was slightly misguided.

"Are you sure it wasn't a joke? Pops had a sense of humor."

"No, it's no joke. You don't inherit the track unless you're married. Plain and simple."

Married. Good God. Her grandfather was blackmailing her into marriage. Unbelievable. Shawn stared at Clinton, suddenly speechless. This was the most insane thing she'd ever heard.

The lawyer pulled off his wire-frame glasses and rubbed the sagging skin under his eyes. He and her grandfather had been friends for sixty years, and he probably knew him better than anyone. "We had several conversations about it, Shawn, and I have to tell you that I told Jameson I didn't approve of this, but he was adamant. He thought that you spent too much time at this place and that you needed more balance in your life. He wanted you to be settled and have a family, like your brother does."

Shawn blinked. "So forcing me to marry some dude off the street is going to give me balance? That makes no sense whatsoever."

"I imagine he had Sam in mind, not some stranger off the street." Clinton steepled his fingers and pressed them to his lips. "Everyone always thought you and Sam would get hitched."

"Well, we didn't," Shawn said, pointing out the obvious. "And there was a very good reason for that. Sam cheated on me. Three times. Now I may be the forgiving sort, but even I know that three times is not the charm when it comes to infidelity." She realized her hand was shaking and she was starting to think she might get sick. She sat on her hand to stop its tremors and regain some control. "I would rather stab myself in the eyes than marry Sam."

"Oh, dear," Clinton said. "I don't think Jameson knew about the cheating."

"I never told anyone. It's a bit personal." And humiliating. And so two years ago. She was completely over it, and frankly, was completely happy on her own, aside from the lack of sex. Rhett Ford popped into her head and she resolutely shoved his image aside. That was the last thing she needed to think about right now.

She had been embarrassed to realize that she was pleased and more than a little turned on when Eve had texted her that Rhett was asking about her and wanted permission to contact her. Shawn had said she would think about it, but truth be told, she had wanted him to do it anyway. She didn't want to be the one who called the shots, because agreeing to it made her responsible. But if he pursued her and she happened to flirt back, well, then it wasn't her seeking out dating a twenty-five-year-old. It was accidental cougar-ing. In her mind, anyway.

But she hadn't heard from him, so all the mental gymnastics had been for nothing.

"Your grandfather figured Sam would be the perfect partner to help you out with the running of this place," Clinton told her.

Sam couldn't manage having an affair in secret so he certainly couldn't keep on top of running a business venture. "That's misogynistic and insulting. Why is it that no one can accept that women can run a business just as effectively as a man? God, racing is something I love, yet how many female drivers and team owners are there? A handful. It's incredible." Shawn freed her hand and shoved her hair back off her forehead.

"No one is saying that. But even a small dirt track like this is a lot to handle, and while enthusiastic, you're not the most organized woman on the planet." Clinton looked around pointedly at the chaotic state of her office. "The season opens in two months, and if it isn't successful financially, all of this will be a moot point anyway. Hamby Speedway will go bankrupt, and you'll have to shut it down or sell."

Shawn swallowed hard. She knew they weren't rolling in profits. She had worried about it constantly for the last two seasons, and she was aware of every dime that went in and out the door at the track, but hearing it said out loud by Clinton forced her to admit the truth to herself, which was damn difficult. "I know it's bad, Clinton, but I also know what I'm doing when it comes to this business, messy office or not."

"The bottom line is the business is failing."

Shawn winced. Hearing it put so boldly, all her fears, was hard to swallow. "So you're telling me if I don't get married, I'll lose the track, and if I do get married, I could still lose the track?"

Clinton nodded.

"Why aren't you just a ray of sunshine today?" she said ruefully.

"Sorry, sweetie. But if you pull in some bigger names, you'll do alright. You'll make it through this year."

"Only if I have a husband." The thought made her more than uneasy. There was no man of her current acquaintance that she was willing to enter into a legitimate marriage with, and no man who would be insane enough to do it in a business-type arrangement. It wasn't like she had much to offer financially, and she was not about to have sex with a man she wasn't in an actual relationship with or was not attracted to. Besides, what man would agree to marriage just for some nookie? There were plenty of women giving the milk away for free because getting milked was a good time. So if a man was buying the cow it was because he really liked the cow, right? Not to increase his milk intake.

Great. She was thinking in farm metaphors. Which were just as sexist as what her grandfather was attempting to do to her.

Panicking again, she looked at Clinton. "I could just hire an actor, you know." Not that she had that kind of money, but maybe struggling actors worked for cheap. Or she could pay him after she secured her inheritance.

"Why don't I tell you the stipulations and requirements?" Clinton pulled out his electronic tablet and adjusted his glasses, amusing Shawn. The man was seventy, and he was using technology that made Shawn want to break out in hives. Tablets had everything organized and that scared her. She begrudgingly used spreadsheets, but most of her daily tasks where catalogued in her head, not anywhere else.

"Okay. Hit me. It can't get any worse." Basically, she was facing losing everything she loved unless she complied with her grandfather's clearly nutty last wish. There had to be a loophole, a way around this whole mess. Because marriage wasn't something you just jumped into.

At least she didn't.

"You have to be married by the start of the season, April fifteenth."

"That's two months from now!"

"However, if you marry immediately, prior to February fifteenth, you will receive additional funds from the estate to hire a marketing director for the season."

"That's two weeks from now." Shawn picked at the front of her sweater, suddenly uncomfortably hot. The idea of a marketing director was extremely appealing, she did have to say. But two weeks? It wasn't possible. "By the way, why is this just coming to my attention now?"

"Your grandfather didn't want to upset you in the immediate weeks after his passing."

"How thoughtful," she said weakly. It still didn't change

that she felt like she was eight years old again and was being punished for tormenting her little brother with wet willies.

"The marriage must be legal in the state of North Carolina, and it must last a minimum of one year. You must reside in the same house as your husband for at least the first six months."

Gross. Even if she hired someone as her fake husband, she wasn't sure she could deal with someone living in her space.

Feeling like her loopholes were rapidly disappearing, Shawn didn't say anything. A sense of defeat settled over her. She was going to lose the track and then what?

This couldn't be what her grandfather truly wanted for her. Unemployment and misery.

"Your husband must pass a criminal background check conducted by myself prior to the marriage, and he must be employed. He cannot be an actor or a stripper."

That almost made her giggle. Almost. She really couldn't picture her grandfather and Clinton discussing her blackmail marriage in such detail. The old buzzards were thorough, she'd give them that.

After that, she started to tune Clinton out as he passed a copy of the will across the desk to her, outlining the monies and insurance policies she would receive upon her marriage. She was numb. Stunned.

Even when the lawyer left with an apology and a look of concern, she just sat behind her desk, not sure what to do. What to think. Hell, there was really nothing she could do, was there?

There was no man she could or would marry.

A knock on her door had her jerking out of her stupor. "Yes?"

The door opened and a head popped in. Holy shit, it was Rhett Ford. Looking sexy as sin.

"Well, hey there, Scarlett." He gave her a slow, naughty smile. "Do you have a minute?"

No, she really didn't have a minute. Her whole life was basically crashing down around her, and she wanted to either scream or curl into a ball and cry. "Sure. Come on in."

God, why did she do that with him? The last thing in the world she needed at the moment was to deal with a virtual infant hitting on her.

And yet, she'd invited him in, just like that.

He came in. Shutting the door firmly behind him.

Her heart started to pound unnaturally fast.

Lord, she was in trouble.

CHAPTER
THREE

RHETT leaned against the closed door of Shawn's office and drank in the sight of her. She had the same impact she'd had on him Saturday night. There was something just inherently sexy about her. It was the way she tilted her head slightly when she spoke. It was in the careless tumbled look of her soft, shiny hair, currently pulled atop her head in one of those weird twist buns that women did when they didn't want to deal with it. Tendrils curled over her graceful neck, and her face was free of makeup, her lush lips naturally a deep pink. She didn't seem aware of her looks. She didn't carry herself with that in-your-face sexuality that some cleavage-baring, fake-eyelash-wearing women did. Nor was she sweet and shy and demure, unable to meet a man's eye.

Maybe it was that she seemed to know exactly who she was and was completely comfortable in her own skin, which he found very hot. Even now, coming face-to-face with a man she had briefly met in a fetish club, she didn't look particularly uneasy. She stood up and stuck her hand out, clearly in her element in her own office.

"Maybe we should formally meet, even though you clearly know who I am."

He moved forward and took the offered hand, keeping it longer than was strictly appropriate. "Rhett Ford."

"Shawn Hamby. Sorry I didn't believe your name was Rhett. I thought you were being coy."

"I'm not cheesy by intention. Just cheesy by birth." He finally let her hand go when she gave it a pointed look. "My mom was living out some fantasy, and I pay the price every day."

"I bet it makes you lucky with the ladies."

Oh, that was just too good of an opening. "Not yet today. But there's still time."

She rolled her eyes. "So is it true? You're driving a Monroe car in the Modifieds this season?"

"Yes. I believe I am on your schedule here at Hamby Speedway." Rhett gestured for her to sit down, himself taking the seat in front of her desk. "Ironic, isn't it? That we would meet where we did."

"I suppose it is." She tightened the bun on top of her head, making it lopsided. "I am looking forward to the season. I'm planning a big media blitz, and if you're interested, I'd love for you to play a big part in that. I think your story will get a fair amount of attention."

"My story?" He wasn't aware that he had a story, nor did he really want to talk about one. He was there to ask her out, not talk racing.

"Yes. Your decision to leave one Monroe crew to join another, and to start racing yourself. That's all a bit nuts in the world of racing, you know."

He knew that. He'd heard it from just about everyone he knew in the business. "Yeah, well, I don't see any point in staying somewhere I'm not completely happy. Guys compete for those pit crew positions and it wasn't fair for me to be taking it."

"You didn't like it? Yet you're not leaving being on a crew."

Rhett noted the way she moved constantly, fidgeting in her seat, her hands always fluttering, running over papers on her desk, up to her necklace, on to her hair. The more still he was in his chair, the more she seemed to move. "I guess I like things a little more down and dirty, a little more real. Without the big money and the engineers."

It was true. He liked the grit of dirt track racing. The money sucked, which was why he was still running a crew for Eve Monroe. But it wasn't about the money, it was about besting himself out there. The pure competitiveness. It was like fencing versus ultimate fighting. Both required major skill, but he preferred it raw.

No shocker there.

"I wouldn't mind a little money either," she said, laughing nervously. "But I get what you mean. I like the passion of dirt track myself. You have to love it to be in it." Then she tilted her head. "I mean, of course, those in the cup series love it, too, I don't mean that. And I don't mean that they, or me, are moneygrubbing or anything. It's just that money is necessary when you're dealing with such expensive tracks and cars and marketing. But it's not like they don't deserve it. Or that dirt track drivers and owners don't deserve it, too. It's just a different thing, but both have their place and no one is better than the other."

Rhett let her babble on, waiting until she petered out. She was cute when she was trying not to offend. "You don't need to be politically correct with me, Shawn. There's enough of that bullshit in this world. I knew what you meant."

"Oh." She cleared her throat. Her cheeks bloomed with color. "So, uh, how can I help you?"

He gave her a slow smile, enjoying more and more the reaction she was giving him. He made her nervous, not because he thought she was an anxious person, but because she was attracted to him the way he was to her. It gave him clear encouragement to tell her exactly why he was there.

"I came to ask you out. Dinner or a drink, or both, your call. Eve said you didn't say yes, but you didn't say no, so

I figured the door was open enough for me to wedge a boot into it and plead my case."

"I don't think I should," she said immediately. "I mean, you're Eve's brother-in-law, and I own the track, which is potentially a conflict of interest, and you're younger than me. It's just not a good idea. At all. It's a very bad idea, actually."

"Then we won't call it a date. We'll just call it two people having a drink. Come on, let's go." Rhett stood up.

"What, like right now?" she asked in astonishment. "But . . ."

"But what? It's almost seven o'clock. You can't still be working. If you are, you shouldn't be." He liked that she looked confused and disarmed. It would work to his advantage. She wouldn't be able to formulate an excuse fast enough.

"I've had a really terrible day," she said, hand going up to pat the back of her bun nervously.

"Even more reason to get out of here." Rhett came around the desk, amused when she backed her rolling chair up so quickly it hit the wall. He reached out and took her hand into his. "Beer or wine?"

"Beer," she said without hesitation.

It didn't surprise him. And it pleased him. Both that she had understood what he was asking, and that she was the kind of woman who preferred a bottle to a glass.

"I probably shouldn't, but you know what? I don't give a shit," Shawn said, standing up. "Today was like ass on an ass cracker, and I deserve a drink."

He wasn't really sure what an ass cracker was, but it didn't sound like anything he wanted to be served.

"That's the spirit." Whereas Shawn would have dropped his hand immediately, Rhett held it firmly in his so she couldn't break contact. "I'm sorry you had a lousy day. Care to talk about it?"

"Not yet. Maybe after a few beers." Shawn shook her

head at him and smiled. "You may find yourself sorry you asked me that question. In fact, you may be sorry you walked in this door."

She gave another tug on her hand as she grabbed her coat and they moved out of her office into the cold dark hall. But when Rhett refused to relinquish his grip, she seemed to accept it. He had to admit, it turned him on. He liked that she had opinions, that she protested, but then gave in to him. It made the moment of capitulation all that more intriguing to him, all that much more arousing. He didn't know her well enough to guess how any of this would translate to the bedroom, but he was definitely interested in finding out. His gut told him he had met the woman who could keep up with him and give him exactly what he wanted.

"I sincerely doubt I'll be sorry," he told her, studying her lips, wishing his mouth was on hers right now, teeth sinking into her tender flesh.

As they pushed through the doors and into the parking lot, Shawn stopping to lock the building behind them, she yanked her hand away from his and shook her head as she inserted the key into the lock on the glass door. "Let's get one thing clear, Rhett. I may have been in the club the other night, but I am not submissive. It's just not my nature." She straightened and turned to face him, eyes slightly narrowed. "I am used to being a girl in a man's world, and if anything, I'm aggressive, not the other way around. So don't think that I'm the type of chick to lick your boots, because I won't do it."

"Who said anything about bootlicking? There is humiliation and then there is submission. They're two different things." Rhett actually suspected a woman like Shawn might enjoy not having to be a woman in a man's world for a change. But he didn't know that any more than she did, apparently. What he did know was that he was curious enough to explore the possibility, and clearly she was, too, or she wouldn't have bothered to mention it. She would have just turned him down flat and had herself a beer at home, solo. "But I thought we were just grabbing a beer and venting about a bad day."

Her cheeks flushed with embarrassment and anger. "Oh, really? So that's all you want? To just sit on a bar stool next to me for an hour and have a Bud? Okay, we can do that."

"That's not all I want," he told her, hands in his front pockets as he watched her tugging the two sides of her coat closed over her chest. "But I don't want to scare you." The dark thoughts that were crowding his mind—of tying her up in his bed and cracking the palm of his hand on her bottom until it reddened—were not something you mentioned on a first date. Or a first not-even-date yet.

"I don't scare easily." She brushed the tendril of hair the wind had whipped across her face out of the way. "Especially not when it comes to men young enough to be my . . . younger brother."

Rhett couldn't help it. He laughed. She looked so indignant and fiery. "I'm sure you don't scare easily. But if I told you the thoughts I'm having, they might not scare you, but they would definitely sound rude considering the short length of our acquaintance. So let's just leave it at that for now, okay?"

"Fine. But you're a terrible flirt," she told him, brushing past him.

"I can't disagree with that." He was. His mother had even picked up on it. He didn't have the easy charm of his brother Nolan. His thoughts were too intense, his expressions too serious, his manner too straightforward. It unnerved women, and while he wished it didn't, he had given up on trying to change himself. Forcing himself to smile and joke when he didn't feel it, just made him look weird, like an escapee from a state psychiatric ward. Like he could potentially kill his dates and eat their organs, and really, that wasn't the vibe a guy looking to get laid wants to give off. So he'd decided while him in his natural state wasn't exactly going to charm the ladies, it was better than creeping them the hell out, which was what faking it did.

It was what it was.

She could either take it or leave it.

It seemed Shawn was going to take it. She gave him a brief smile. "Well, I appreciate your honesty."

"It's my best asset," he assured her. It was. Along with something else he wasn't going to mention.

Shawn's smile spread into a grin. "Well, an honest man would certainly be a first, but it's too freezing cold out here to discuss that any further. And because I'm feeling generous, I'll let you drive. We can go to Milt's place across the road. Beer is cheaper than water there."

She was putting a power struggle into play. He wasn't sure if she was aware exactly of what she was doing, if she knew she was baiting him. But either way, it was making him hard.

Shawn let Rhett take her hand again and lead her to his truck. What the hell was she doing? She was engaging in some kind of verbal sparring with a man she absolutely could not date. Not only was he way too young, he was a driver, her friend's brother-in-law, and he was the type of guy she didn't even understand. She had always gone for the big talkers, the loud, friendly, work-a-crowd guys who never met a stranger and could work any angle, whether it was in a boardroom or on the golf course.

Rhett was . . . intense. He didn't say a lot, and he smiled infrequently, yet somehow she felt like when she was with him, she was his only focus. That his stare could set her on fire, which was frankly annoying. Unnerving. She felt off-kilter with him and that was the last thing in the world she needed to be feeling given that she was about to lose everything.

But maybe that was why it was so easy to let Rhett steal her attention—if she was distracted by him, she didn't have to contemplate life after Hamby Speedway. Because that reality was something she didn't even want to consider, yet she had no choice.

Unless she got married.

It was insane.

So really, the last way she should be spending her evening was with a man who made her nervous, yet here she was.

"Sounds like a plan," he told her, pulling his keys out of his pocket. "This is my truck here."

Of course he drove a truck. He was essentially comprised of testosterone, so nothing else would be acceptable. But he was also a gentleman. He opened the door for her and helped her into the truck, which while not necessary was certainly helpful, because while she was no shorty, there was some serious air between the ground and the seat.

"At the risk of sounding like your father," Rhett said as he got in and started up his truck, "you know you really shouldn't be hanging out in the track offices by yourself in the dark at night. I just walked right in, and if I could do it, anyone could."

Shawn wasn't offended by his concern. He had a valid point, and most of the time she was more careful. "I'm not usually there alone. I have a couple of employees who leave at the same time as I do. If I am there alone, I try to keep the door locked, but today my lawyer had just been in to see me so the door was open."

"Hence the bad day?"

"Oh, yeah." She fiddled with her seat belt and debated how much she could or should tell Rhett Ford. She was dying to blurt it out to someone—to have them sympathize with how appalling the whole situation was, and maybe let her bounce some ideas off them on how to increase her profits this season. Yet at the same time, she really didn't think it was a good idea to have more than a couple of people know the reality of the situation. One, because she didn't want anyone to think less of her grandfather. Two, because she didn't want anyone to think they could swoop in and try to buy the track from her at a rock-bottom price. Three, because if she decided to fake a marriage, the less who knew the truth, the better.

Not that she was planning to fake a marriage, because how would she do that? But it seemed best to proceed with caution. She may not know what the hell she was doing when it came to men, but she knew her way around the business world, thank you very much, despite what, apparently, her grandfather thought.

That, she had to admit, was at the crux of her dismay and shell shock. She'd thought her grandfather trusted her with the business—to find out he didn't was salt in the wound of her grief.

"How was your day?" she asked Rhett inanely, suddenly realizing she didn't want to talk about Clinton's visit, because then she would have to say out loud that she was going to lose the track because her grandfather hadn't trusted her.

"It was a day like any other," he said, shifting gears and gunning it across the four-lane road to the opposite parking lot. He handled his truck like a driver, and she was attracted to that, to the way his hand rested lightly on the gearshift, fully in control, forcing the truck to bend to his will. "Running some trials on Eve's car. It's running loose, but she has a great mechanic in Sheppard. He'll tighten it up, no problem."

It was an addiction, this sport, this career, this lifestyle. She knew that, and she wouldn't have it any other way.

She couldn't walk away without trying. She just couldn't. There was no way. It was in her blood.

A crazy idea popped into her head. A very insane, she couldn't be serious, idea. Yet she couldn't help but follow the thought through.

She quickly calculated some figures based on the insurance information Clinton had given her. Rhett Ford was hard up for money, he had told her that. He also understood the love of racing. He was attracted to her, he was single, he was clearly a man who did what he wanted, with no regard for anyone's opinion about it. He was a risk taker.

But was he desperate enough for cash to marry her?

And could she go through with it?

It was ludicrous, the very concept.

But once the idea had taken hold, Shawn couldn't shake it. She could save her livelihood, the last connection to her grandfather, a sport that she loved. If Hamby Speedway closed, there wouldn't be a regional dirt track in the area, and that would be a crying shame.

To do that, she needed to get married.

Why not Rhett?

As he parked and came around and opened her car door, then the door to Milt's, when he pulled out her bar stool, and took her coat from her and hung it on the back of her chair, she debated with herself, her heart pounding at twice its normal rate as she contemplated blurting out such a bizarre business proposition to him.

"What kind of beer would you like?" he asked her.

"I'll take a Guinness."

"That'll grow hair on your chest. I'm impressed," he said with a close-lipped smile, his eyes assessing her.

She laughed, a sound of pure relief that she hadn't screamed out a marriage proposal. Yet. "That hasn't been the result for me, thank God. I like dark ales. When I'm feeling really sassy, I like a good Irish Car Bomb. Jameson dropped into Guinness is a taste like no other."

"Now I'm really impressed." Rhett put his keys on the scratched-up bar top and said, "I'll do one if you do."

Uh-oh. "Are you daring me?" How could he have figured out already that was her weakness?

"I'm definitely daring you. In fact, I double-dog dare you."

Damn it. He was either psychic or Eve had been telling tales.

Shawn slapped her purse on the bar and said, "I'm in." No matter that she hadn't eaten dinner and, on an empty stomach, was very likely to get snookered from whiskey at the end of such a stressful day. She could not turn down a dare.

Rhett grinned and flagged down the bartender. "How competitive are you? Think you can drink it faster than me?"

"Oh, I know I can." Hell, she had paid half her living expenses in college from bets on how fast she could shoot a beer. "It's all about opening up the throat to take it all down," she told him confidently.

His eyebrows shot up. "Now that's a mighty fine talent to have."

Oops. That did sound a little sexual. Shawn felt her cheeks heat. "Don't be rude."

"What? I didn't say anything."

"You were thinking it."

"Thinking what?"

Damn it. He was good at this. He wasn't going to say it, that they were both thinking about her giving him a blow job. Neither was she going to say it. "Just take your drink."

He gave her a slow grin as the bartender set the glasses with the Guinness down on the bar in front of them, three-quarters full. A shot of Jameson was next to each glass, waiting for them to drop the shot glass down inside the Guinness. "On the count of three."

Shawn picked up her shot of whiskey and let it hover over the Guinness, which she held in her right hand. From experience she knew to throw back with her dominant hand. Her coordination was better. She eyed Rhett as he counted, making sure he wasn't going to cheat.

"One," he said, and for some reason she shivered.

There was something about the way he stared at her. It was like he could give her an orgasm with the sheer force of his will, just from the intensity of his gaze. She shifted uncomfortably.

"Two."

Shawn licked her lips, her hand shaking slightly. She wanted to look away, but she couldn't. She was trapped by his eyes, which were such a deep green they were almost emerald. He was . . . arresting. That was the word for him.

It threw her off her game and she felt her wrist slacken a little, her girl insides warming in arousal.

"Three."

Shit. He had gained an advantage by being sexy. Shawn dropped, lifted, drank, the sting of the whiskey masked by the smooth maltiness of the ale. She opened the back of the throat, let it all flow down, and slapped her empty glass back on the table while she finished swallowing.

Rhett was a few seconds behind her.

"Ha! I was first!" Not that she was one to gloat or anything. Much.

"Wow," was the bartender's opinion. "I've never seen a woman drink a car bomb that fast." The bartender was big and brawny, covered in tattoos, his beard enveloping the bottom half of his face in bushy salt-and-pepper hair. Shawn took it as a serious compliment.

"Thanks." She beamed a little.

"That was impressive," Rhett agreed.

"Well, you were no slouch yourself," she said, wanting to soothe his ego a little. "But I might have forgotten to mention that I supplemented my income in college from bets over how fast I could down a car bomb."

Rhett's eyebrows rose. The bartender laughed.

"You've got to appreciate a woman who can shoot whiskey."

"Well, my grandfather's name was Jameson. It seems disrespectful not to be able to handle his namesake, you know what I mean?" Shawn suddenly felt melancholy. God, she missed Pops.

The bartender fist-bumped Rhett. "You're a lucky man, brother."

"Not yet, but I'm hoping," Rhett told him.

"Ah. Well, good luck." The bartender winked at Shawn. "Make him work for it, hon."

Except the truth was, she needed Rhett Ford more than he needed her, so she wasn't going to be forcing him to dance on a string. If anything, it was about to be the other way around. Or more like her crawling on the floor for him with a gag ball in her mouth.

Oh, God. There were going to have to be some ground rules on this fake marriage thing. Which she really needed to discuss with him. Her palms started to sweat, the liquor heating up her extremities. In her mind, one way or another, it was already a foregone conclusion. That's how she was. She made a decision, and everyone else needed to fall in with it. Somehow she didn't think Rhett Ford was the falling-in type.

Not having any idea how to reply to the bartender, she cleared her throat, wishing she were like Eve, who was never at a shortage for words.

"Where did you go to college?" Rhett asked her as the bartender moved on to other customers.

Not that Milt's was jumping. There were only a couple of guys in their fifties at the end of the bar. Good. Fewer witnesses when she asked Rhett to marry her and he started laughing.

"I went to the University of South Carolina." Then, because it would be expected, and because she already had a slight buzz from the whiskey she added, "Go Cocks."

She expected Rhett to laugh or make a crack in return. It's what people did whenever she referenced USC's mascot, the gamecocks. It was funny. Juvenile humor, yes, but funny. It was the only legitimate way to say "Go Cocks" in a conversation in public ever.

But Rhett didn't laugh. In fact, his eyes darkened. "Say that again," he told her. It wasn't a request, it was a demand.

Shawn felt her face and chest burn, from the alcohol, from desire. "What?" she asked him, bewildered. "What do you mean?"

"Say 'cock.' I want to hear you say it."

It could have been a creepy request. But somehow it wasn't. It was just a complete and total turn-on. It was the oddest thing to her, that all Rhett had to do was look at her, his gaze trained on her and only her, and he commanded her full attention. Commanded her.

"Cock," she whispered, licking her lips nervously.

"Louder."

"Cock," she said more confidently, aware of how he subtly shifted toward her, his body firm and masculine, his knee brushing hers.

He made a sound, in the back of his throat, that told her what she'd just said was as effective as if she'd gripped his cock itself with her hand. Her nipples beaded, and she realized that he might be younger than her by more than a couple of years, but he was fully mature and in control of himself and his desires. Possibly more so than she was.

It was so sexy, so hot, that she did exactly what she had been hoping she wouldn't. She blurted. Instead of approaching him with a business proposition, the words just spilled out of her mouth like ice water on a flame.

"Will you marry me?"

CHAPTER
FOUR

RHETT blinked at Shawn. All the blood had gone south to his cock just watching the dirty word roll off Shawn's plump lip, so maybe he was at less-than-full mental capacity, because he could have sworn she had just asked him to marry her. Which could not be what she had said. Hell, he'd had to talk her into a beer.

"What?" he asked, wanting to shake his head and rattle it into a reset like they did in old-school cartoons. "What did you say?"

Shawn blushed. She looked down at the bar, fiddling with her empty Guinness glass. "See, here's the thing. I need a husband. I'm offering money. Are you interested? A business deal, pure and simple."

He was not following her at all. "Why the hell would you need a husband?" This wasn't the fifties. If she was knocked up, no one was going to think anything of it. It couldn't be for any sort of tax advantage. God knew, she was better off being single if she wanted a break from the IRS, so he didn't understand.

Her eyes finally met his, and she looked emboldened, determined. The shift was dramatic, and it had his body responding again. There was something so damn sexy about her, vulnerable yet strong at the same time.

"Let's just say that if I don't get married, I'm going to lose something that means a lot to me. It's ridiculous, but there it is. I'll give you a hundred grand if you stay married to me for a year."

Rhett actually felt his jaw drop open. A hundred thousand dollars? Was she serious? That was more money than he could ever hope to see at once. While he had made a decent living on Evan's pit crew, he'd taken a pay cut to switch to Eve's crew, and he'd be lucky if he made five grand off his dirt track racing this year. There just wasn't a lot of cash at this level, and he wasn't expecting to win right out of the gate. He was aiming more for breaking even on his car and expenses. A hundred grand. Damn. That was a lot of cheddar.

But he shook his head. "I need more details. That's a lot of money, and this doesn't seem above board to me, Shawn. I don't want to get involved in something illegal. Or be some sort of pawn to make a boyfriend jealous."

Now it was her turn to look surprised. "I would never involve you in something like that! Either of those things! I wouldn't ever do anything illegal. Hell, I don't even jay-walk. And I am not the kind of woman to play games in relationships."

She looked so indignant that Rhett instantly trusted what she was proposing was something that, while not exactly typical, wasn't sketchy either. "So then tell me what it really is."

Shawn sighed. "I guess I can't expect you not to have questions. I shouldn't have just blurted it out like that. But the thing is, I'm desperate. I'm not sure if you heard, but my grandfather died in November."

She paused, jaw working, he suspected both from grief and from struggling to find the words for what she needed to say.

"I'm really sorry, Shawn. That must be very difficult."

His own grandparents were all still miraculously alive, and he knew he was fortunate in that regard.

"Thanks." She ran her finger around the rim of the glass, slowly, methodically, her nails painted a rich, ruby red that surprised him.

He would have expected something more natural, clear polish or a pale pink. The image of those red nails on her pale flesh popped into his head. He wanted to see them splayed over her breasts, trailing down her belly to bury inside her hot, moist inner thighs. Rhett cleared his throat and shifted on his stool. He needed another drink. Preferably with ice he could pour down his jeans to cool him down.

"Pops owned the track and ran it for forty years. I've been working there since my midtwenties. It's my . . . life." She looked pleadingly at him, as if she were begging him to understand.

He did understand the love of racing, but he still didn't understand what she was getting at. "You love racing. I get that, Shawn. It's my life, too."

She nodded. "I assumed the track was left to me. Or at least a portion of it, so that I would continue to run it as operating manager. My father hasn't been around since I was a kid, and my mother hates everything about racing. My brother is an optometrist, go figure, and he was never big on being a Hamby anyway. So it was always me and my grandfather, playing in the dirt, as he called it. But it turns out he didn't leave me the track free and clear. His lawyer read his will to me today, and it seems the only way I can inherit is if I'm married." The grimace on her face showed him exactly what she thought of that.

"Are you serious?" Rhett could see why she was having a bad day. "Why would he do that?"

She gave a bitter laugh. "I guess he thought I was devoting too much time to the track and racing. He wanted me to settle down and breed, like a good girl."

Oh, yeah. That was bitterness. He couldn't exactly blame her. "Jesus. And I thought my mother was bad, always dropping hints about how I should get married sooner than later."

"She does? But you're only twenty-five."

"I know. But she thinks that I should be married and have a baby by now, like she did. You have to start early to rack up nine kids, you know. She's always on my case about it, giving me advice in front of my whole family."

"What kind of advice?"

"She thinks I should smile more," Rhett told Shawn. "She says I scare women." It was true and he knew it. But somehow he didn't think he scared Shawn much.

In fact, Shawn laughed. "Now that's funny."

"Clearly, I don't scare you."

"Only a little," she admitted. "But that's more because I can't figure out why I'm attracted to you."

"I mean, who would be?" he asked ruefully.

Shawn smacked his arm. "That's not what I mean! It's just bad timing, you know? But then I thought, well, maybe it's not bad timing. If I have to be married to save the track, maybe you'd be a good candidate. But now it just sounds crazy and rude and creepy. I don't know what I was thinking. If anyone should be frightened here, it should be you." She fussed with her bun, which was sliding south. "You must think I'm a total freak, popping the question to a guy I just met."

"I'm flattered." He actually was. Yes, it was crazy. It was crazy that her grandfather would expect her to jump into a marriage. It was a plan bound to fail. But he respected that Shawn was willing to do whatever it took to save her property, to save what was meaningful to her. He would probably consider doing the same thing, though he wasn't exactly one to like being told what to do. But he admired her guts and her businesslike approach to the problem. Instead of crying, she'd sought a solution. "And I'm not saying no straight out. I just need to hear what would be expected of me."

"You're not saying no?" she asked, eyebrows shooting

up as she froze with her arms above her head, tightening her hair thing.

"No, I'm not saying no." He wasn't. Insane or not, she had just dangled a hundred grand in front of him. Not to mention, he'd been looking for a good excuse to get to know her better, both with clothes on and off, and what could be a better excuse for that than marriage?

Was marriage a huge commitment that he shouldn't take lightly? Yes. But this wasn't a real marriage. He didn't think. "What does this marriage mean exactly? Is it paper only? We would never see each other?" He wasn't down with that. He couldn't walk around and be secretly married, shagging other women and taking money for something he hadn't really *done*. It all just seemed too dishonest to him. He liked his cards out on the table. If he was going to be fucking anyone, it was going to be Shawn.

His wife.

Oh, damn. He should walk away. This was dicey.

Yet, he wasn't. He flagged down the bartender and said, "Can we get two more shots of Jameson? Skip the Guinness this time." This was a straight-up liquor conversation.

Shawn took a huge breath. "The deal is this. We have to be married for a year, but we have to live together at least for the first six months. So you would have to move in with me. I have a guest room that you can use, and I suppose the positive is, you'll be saving on rent for six months."

That was an attractive thought, he had to admit. He'd only been in Nolan's old apartment for five months, and while he loved the freedom, the rent was kicking his ass. "Guest room, huh?" So he wouldn't lose his own space, exactly. But he wouldn't get the ultimate benefit of marriage—having a warm woman in his bed every night.

"Yes. If we get married before February fifteenth, the will states I get the funds to hire a full-time marketing director for the upcoming season, which would really be helpful, so that would be my preference. To get married before then, I mean."

Rhett watched her face carefully. She seemed to have shifted into efficiency mode.

"I can have my lawyer draw up a contract outlining what I just described and that you'll receive payment upon completion of the year. I will pay for the divorce. I will pay for the initial marriage license fees and all of that. So there is no risk, no hidden cost to you. We both enter and leave the marriage with what we came with, save the hundred grand fee."

No hidden cost?

Just a year of his life.

Could he commit a whole year to a woman who didn't really want to be involved with him, even for money? Or did she?

Those were the real questions on his mind.

"I'm not the tidiest person, I'll admit, so if you're a neat freak, that is something to consider," she added.

That wasn't a factor he cared about it. He had more important concerns.

"I wouldn't want it to be a secret," he told her. "I can't live like that."

"It has to be a secret," she said. "No one can know about the money. My grandfather's lawyer said I can't marry an actor, a stripper, or a criminal, and he'll be doing a background check. We can't let anyone know we're faking it, that it's not a real marriage, or it's null and void."

"A background check? I don't have anything to hide." Rhett took the whiskey from the bartender with a murmured thanks, and threw the shot back. It burned going down, and he welcomed the distraction. "I meant, I can't keep the marriage a secret. I wouldn't be able to date and tell women I'm free and available when I'm not, regardless of the circumstances."

"Oh." Shawn lifted her own shot glass and bit her bottom

lip. "I guess I just assumed we wouldn't . . . see other people. But now that you say that, I realize that's a lot to ask. I suppose if you're discreet . . . I mean, it's not a real marriage and you have . . . needs."

Hell, no. Rhett shook his head. "That's not how I roll, Shawn. Real or not, I'm not interested in any woman who would sleep with a man she thinks is married."

"Celibacy is a lot to ask. Even for a hundred grand."

Rhett gave a low laugh, sliding his hand over to rest on her thigh. She jerked slightly. "Who said anything about being celibate?"

"Me?" she asked, suddenly sounding unsure of the whole thing.

He shook his head slowly. "No. If we do this, sex will be a part of the equation."

"But . . ." She took a sip of her whiskey. "I would feel like I was paying you to sleep with me."

Now that was the dumbest thing he'd ever heard in his entire life. Hell, he would pay her for sex, not the other way around. "You wouldn't. It would be entirely voluntary on my part."

"What if I don't want to?"

Was she serious? Or did she just want him to work for it? Spell it out. "I won't do anything you don't want me to. But we both know you want me to."

Her eyes widened. "That's really ballsy."

"It's true." Rhett moved his hand higher, stroking through the denim of her jeans, feeling the heat at the juncture of her thighs, his thumb rubbing over the seam. "I give it two weeks, tops, before we're fucking."

"What makes you so confident?" she asked, her expression annoyed.

Yet she didn't push his hand away. Nor did she deny it.

"Because you want me as much as I want you. I can practically smell how wet you are for me."

Without hesitation, she tossed her shot of whiskey into his face.

It missed his eyes, fortunately, because that shit would have stung. It didn't particularly surprise him, nor did it piss him off. He just slid his hand over his face, pulling the random drips of liquid off his nose and cheek. He licked his lips.

"You're an asshole," she told him.

But she still didn't push his hand away. In fact, she had spread her legs a little, her hips moving forward so his light touch was more intimate, the pressure greater.

Oh, yeah. She was exactly the kind of woman he needed. She was going to fight it, yet she could more than handle his proclivities. She was going to enjoy them. And he was going to enjoy teaching her how much she could take pleasure from submission.

"I accept your offer," he told her. "And I'm changing my estimate to one week."

SHIT fire, Shawn was in trouble. She was breathing a little too raggedly from both agitation and arousal. It was entirely possible that she was in way over her head with Rhett. Because her impulsively tossing a drink in his face didn't seem to anger him one bit. If anything, he seemed even more confident, more pleased with her. His movements were slow and methodical, and he was still resting a hand between her legs and she was letting him.

But he knew precisely how to push her buttons—all of them, good and bad.

"Is that a challenge? A bet?" God, she needed to work on her inability to back down from a dare. It was going to land her in a marital bed with Rhett Ford, her ankles over her head.

Though maybe that wouldn't be such a bad thing, now that she considered her vagina. Nope. Not such a bad thing.

The corner of his mouth tilted up in a slow smile. "Yes. I'll marry you, and we're going to have sex within the first seven days, because you want to."

"I can resist you," she bluffed. "One week is nothing." Then because she couldn't look him in the eye when she was so blatantly lying, she turned and flagged down the bartender. "Could we have more napkins? My whiskey seems to have spilled on my friend's face."

The bartender nodded. "I saw that. We're not going to repeat that, are we? Or I might have to ask you to leave."

She was going to get kicked out of Milt's, a dive if ever there was one? The thought almost made her laugh. "No, there will not be a repeat. I was just making a point."

"We'll take another round," Rhett told him. "We just decided to get married."

The bartender looked more than a little skeptical as he handed a napkin to Rhett, who swiped it over his damp face. "Huh. Well, good luck with that. Methinks you're going to need it."

Rhett laughed. "Probably. But she's worth it."

He was almost convincing. Shawn was suddenly amused at the absurdity of the whole situation. If she had to do something so insane, she might as well enjoy what she could get out of it.

"I won't have sex with him until we're married," Shawn said. "And then not for seven more days. Isn't he devoted?" She shared a grin with Rhett, thinking that the truth was way more ridiculous than the story she was spinning.

And she was definitely going to have sex with him and reap the benefits of this odd arrangement. After seven days. There was no way she was losing this bet. But after that? All bets were off and all beds were on.

"Very devoted. To her physical and mental well-being." Rhett leaned closer to her, violating her personal space in a way that was territorial. "Sometimes I know what she needs even before she does."

He was talking about sex again, clearly, and her nipples knew it. Damn it, how did he manage to do that so easily? She moistened her lips and tried not to pant in anticipation.

They needed to get married soon because the seven-day grace period was going to be hell on her. So the sooner they got to it, the sooner she could be feeling his touch everywhere.

Which was the most ass-backwards logic she'd ever used in her entire life, but there it was.

"If you don't mind my saying, I think y'all are fucked up," the bartender said. "Relationships don't work when you're playing games." Then he promptly walked away, clearly wanting out of their conversation.

"Oh, I don't know," Rhett told her, nudging her knee with his. "I've always enjoyed Follow the Leader. That usually works for me. If I'm the leader."

"You're a very dirty boy, Rhett Ford. But didn't your mother teach you that you can't always get what you want? I think I'm the leader in this case." They were playing games, definitely. But what difference did it make? It wasn't going to be a real marriage, and they might as well enjoy the sexual tension strung out between them.

She was going to save the track and get some action.

After seven days.

If they were really doing this. Were they really doing this?

Her cheeks felt hot at the very idea.

"I don't think you're in any position to make threats or demands," he told her. "You are, in essence, the damsel in distress, and I'm rescuing you. You can't be nagging me about my dragon-slaying techniques."

That doused her libido quite effectively. "You're no hero. You're a hired mercenary, remember? I'm not in your debt, emotional or otherwise, when I'm paying you a hundred grand."

His hand fell off her leg, and he sat back so quickly the air around her actually cooled. Despite her annoyance, she found herself regretting his retreat. Which meant it really was a good thing he had distanced himself. She couldn't afford to want anything other than to save the track from being sold, and she needed to remember that.

"Let's get one thing straight, or I'm not doing this," he said, words slow and determined. "When we're in public, I play the role of your legitimate husband, and yes, then I'm your mercenary. Your hired hand. But when we're alone in your place, what happens between us has nothing to do with money and nothing to do with any of the legalities or any contract I signed. It's strictly about what you and I both want. If you can't keep the money out of the bedroom, then there's no deal."

Shawn sat stunned by his vehemence. She hadn't meant that she would be tossing the payoff in his face every time he hit on her. In fact, that was the opposite of what she wanted. It would be profoundly awkward to be thinking about how much money she was paying him while he was between her thighs.

"I don't want that either," she assured him. "I agree entirely that *if* anything happens between us, we keep it totally separate from our business arrangement." If she stopped to think about it, she would have to admit that doing that would be damn near impossible, but she just refused to think about it. There was too much at stake to worry too much about the finer points.

He gave a slow smile that made her wish his hand were still between her thighs. "Then we have a deal. Get over here and seal it with a kiss."

Shawn gave a nervous laugh. Because she was going to do this. And because she wanted to do this. It was a smart business decision. It was a monstrously stupid personal one. But that basically summed up her life over the last decade—she could run a business, but she had no clue how to handle men.

Maybe that's why Rhett was so damn appealing. She didn't have to handle him. He wanted to handle her, and he gave step-by-step instructions on how to do it.

So she shifted her butt on her stool, inching forward,

maneuvering between his open legs, her right hand gripping the bar top. Her lips parted in anticipation and she watched him as she leaned, watched the way he watched her, his stare never wavering, his eye contact so complete, so intense, it was instinctive to look away. But she didn't. She forced herself to continue, even when she wanted to drop her gaze to her lap in confusion, view him under the demure protection of her eyelashes and a tilted head.

When she was close enough for him to reach for her without stretching, he did, putting the palm of his hand firmly on the back of her head and drawing her to him, with a commanding, but not harsh, pressure.

Then they were kissing. It wasn't a kiss. It was kissing. It wasn't tentative, or curious. The minute their mouths met, it was like they'd been there before many times, and both wanted more. Shawn had thought kissing was pleasant before, that it was a nice gesture of affection, or a precursor to the passion of sex. But never had she known that it could be this—a hot, wet explosion, an all-consuming tangle of tongues and desires, her breath ragged and desperate, his hand digging into the remains of her bun, yanking her hair harder with each passing second.

Just when she was reaching for him, wanting to slip her arms around his neck, wanting to snuggle in closer to brush her body against his, he seemed to sense her need and let her go so quickly she almost fell off her stool. Rhett stared at her, panting, his eyes hooded, expression unreadable. She stared back, unsure what to say, wanting to regain the upper hand, but feeling too confused, too aroused, to form a coherent sentence. She knew if she tried to speak, she wouldn't be able to achieve the casual nonchalance she wanted to project. He would hear her nervousness.

Because he had made her nervous. Afraid that she might lose the bet. Afraid that she might lose even more than that before the six months of living with him was out.

What she really wanted to do was say something funny that would break the intimate spell between them, but she couldn't think of a damn thing to say, which further confused her.

She settled on, "What date are you free to get married?" It was businesslike, efficient, and her voice only wobbled a little on the last word. The *M* word. Her stomach flipped like a pancake. She had not been a girl who had fantasized much about her wedding, but she had assumed that she would at least *want* to get married, not be terrified.

But hearing herself ask him the question like she was an employer asking when a new employee could start work, she felt significantly better. She could handle this.

"We'll get married this Friday, which gives your lawyer time to draw up the papers. Then we'll have a party to celebrate on Valentine's Day," he told her. "It will make it seem like a romantic elopement, totally legit. And you can wear sexy red lingerie on our wedding night. I prefer garters and corsets."

He never ceased to amaze her with his arrogance. Or the fact that he was right about the dates. Both made total sense. But if she agreed, she was feeding his ego. "Oh, really? I agree with the elopement nonsense. But you can forget the corset. I'm not trussing myself up like a Victoria's Secret model for you, because I won't be having sex with you."

Rhett reached out and ran his thumb along her bottom lip. Shawn wanted to jerk away, but she didn't want to look petulant. Besides, it was causing her to shiver in places she hadn't even known she could shiver.

"We already placed that bet—you don't need to reiterate it." He shrugged. "I'll buy you the lingerie and we'll see who wins."

Shawn calculated four days until the wedding and seven after it to be the victor. Holy hell. It was going to be the longest eleven days of her life.

She was screwed. Quite literally.

CHAPTER
FIVE

"ARE you sure you want to do this?" Shawn's lawyer asked him point blank in his stuffy office loaded down with mahogany furniture. Rhett didn't like rooms like this—it was dark and oppressive and formal. It made him long for the acreage of his parents' property, or the freedom of being behind the wheel on the track.

Clinton seemed like a nice enough sort of guy, and he was clearly concerned about Shawn's well-being. It was obvious he wasn't buying their sudden desire for marriage, when four days earlier Shawn had told him she wasn't dating anyone.

"I'm sure," Rhett told him confidently, just wanting to sign the paperwork and get the hell out of there.

He'd thought of virtually nothing else for the last seventy-two hours, and he hadn't changed his mind. He needed the money, otherwise he was going to have to give up driving a car after this season. He knew that. He also knew that he and Shawn collectively could generate attention and media and create a buzz for the track this year, guaranteeing greater success for her and him both. At the end of the year they would both walk away with their dreams secured. It was win-win. Plus, he would have potentially months to explore a sexual relationship with Shawn. After that kiss the other night, there was no way he was going to deny himself that pleasure.

Clinton sighed. "Alright. I guess I can't gainsay Shawn at this point. She's technically doing exactly what her grandfather wanted her to do. I swear if he wasn't dead, I'd kill him myself for doing this to her."

It was nice to see that Shawn inspired such protectiveness. Rhett understood the feeling, and he'd spent very little time with her so far. They had only spoken briefly since her unexpected proposal the other night, and it had only been about managerial details, like when they would tell their families and when he would move in to her apartment. And where she actually lived so he knew where to move to.

"I think Shawn is going to be just fine. You don't need to worry about a woman as savvy and strong as she is," he told Clinton. He meant it. Any woman who was willing to go through with a fake marriage to keep her business was tenacious as hell.

"Just don't run around on her and embarrass her," Clinton said, giving Rhett the stink eye.

"I have no intention of running around on her." He didn't. If he was working up an appetite at home, he fully intended to eat there as well.

"Guess there's nothing to do then but sign on the dotted line." Clinton pointed to the bottom line of the contract Rhett had already skimmed and handed him a pen.

Rhett signed his name with a flourish. Rhett B. Ford. Done.

He shook Clinton's hand and left the office, feeling pretty damn pleased with himself.

Then he called his brother Nolan. "Hey, bro."

"Hey, what's up?"

"You busy on Monday?" It was their day off from racing, usually their only one.

"Not particularly, though I was planning to sleep in. Why?"

"I need you to help me move." Rhett crossed the parking lot and beeped his truck open, unable to prevent a grin. He enjoyed shocking his brother. There was just something really damn fun about it.

"What? Where the hell are you moving to? You just took that place over from me. God, are you moving back in with Mom and Dad? That's lame."

"No. I'm moving in with Shawn." He was going to save the whole marriage thing until after the deed was done, but he did need to get the muscle lined up for moving day, or he was going to be trying to carry a couch by himself.

There was dead silence on the other end. Followed by, "What the fuck are you talking about? You just met Shawn like five minutes ago!"

"We met on Saturday, technically," he said cheerfully.

"You're kidding me right?"

"No. There's just something about her. She blew me away." She had. That wasn't a lie.

"But you're not impulsive. You don't attach easily."

"That's just Mom's opinion. I actually attach extremely easily." Which might concern him if he stopped to think about it. He chose not to. "Just save your opinions and psychological analysis and show up on Monday, okay?"

"Does Mom know?"

"Not yet. Don't worry, I'll tell her before Monday."

"Jesus Christ, Rhett. She's going to flip her fucking wig."

"She can handle it. She handled nine kids. I'll talk to you later. I have plans with Shawn in twenty minutes." To get married.

Shawn was pacing in the courthouse hallway when he arrived, a gift bag in his hand, a ring box tucked in his coat pocket.

"I thought you weren't coming," she blurted, then seemed

to be annoyed with herself for admitting that. "Anyway, how did it go with Clinton? He e-mailed me last night that everything was in order with your background check."

"Yep. We're good to go." He pulled the ring box out of his pocket. "For you."

Her eyes widened. "You bought a ring? Holy crap, you didn't have to do that! I figured we'd just get cheap bands from Walmart."

"So I can look like a tightwad? Screw that." If everyone thought it was legit, he didn't want to look like an ass. Besides, when he had walked into that jewelry store, he had wanted to buy something delicate and beautiful for Shawn, something that went with the elegant grace of her long fingers and her fair skin.

There was something about Shawn's features that intrigued him endlessly. She was strong and athletic clearly, yet parts of her, like her fingers, her lips, her tiny nose, were so profoundly feminine that he couldn't look away when he was with her. It may be a fake marriage, but she should be wearing a beautiful ring to match her delicateness.

Yeah. This was him not attaching. Fuck.

But when she opened the box and let out a gasp, it was worth it.

"Oh, my God, this is stunning. It's so pretty, Rhett."

It was vintage-inspired, white gold, and narrow, the band crusted in diamonds, meant for the elegant hand of an elegant woman. The fact that Shawn was that and a former driver and current track owner and racing enthusiast, made her just about the perfect package.

Too bad none of it was real and he was essentially a warm body she'd hired.

"Let's do this thing," he told her, because he found himself doubting the intelligence of this move. He was starting to feel a brooding mood coming on, and that wasn't going to look good in the wedding picture.

"I like your wedding jeans," Shawn told him with a smile as her eyes swept over him, the ring box closed again in her hand.

"Thanks. I even washed them before I put them on." He owned exactly one suit, and he felt like a gigantic ass wearing it, so he'd opted out. He had put on a button-up shirt, though truth be told, it was wrinkled. Hey. It was Friday and two in the afternoon. Who was there to give a shit?

"How thoughtful."

"You look pretty," he told her truthfully, though the minute he said it, he hated how lukewarm it sounded. So he added, "But I wouldn't have objected to some cleavage."

She was wearing a narrow skirt, tights, and boots, with a red sweater. It was kind of officelike, but it was February and a fake wedding, so he hadn't expected her to pull out all the stops either. But it wasn't exactly screaming "We're in love, I'm so excited."

Rolling her eyes, Shawn told him, "You should be looking at the doughnut, not the hole."

Say what? Rhett got an erection instantly just thinking about her hole. "Do not say things like that in public. Seriously. I mean it."

Her expression took on a mulish quality. "You can't tell me what to say. It's a free country."

"It's also illegal to have sex in a hallway, so unless you want me to shove you into the restroom and fuck you against the stall wall, I suggest you not talk about your hole or your creamy edges." A man could only take so much. Surely she could understand that.

Her eyes widened. "Why do you have to be so gross about it?"

That made the tension in his shoulders ease just a little. Shawn was clearly deluding herself if she actually believed she thought it was crude. The truth was, she liked it when he was honest and straightforward about his lust. It was there in her body language, the way she leaned in toward him, the way her breath caught. The tightness of her nipples beneath her sweater.

"Your disgust isn't even remotely convincing," he told her. Suddenly he wanted nothing more than to be done with the ceremony and back at her place. He was convinced he could get her to let him inside her with just a little coaxing.

Her knuckles were white on the ring box. "Are we sure we want to do this?"

No. He really wasn't.

Marrying Shawn might be akin to opening Pandora's box. It might let out feelings, sexual and otherwise, that he wouldn't be able to contain again.

"Are you getting cold feet?" he asked, because it bothered him more than he cared to admit that she might bail. "Runaway bride does make for an interesting end to our short-lived relationship. Met me to left me, all in one week."

Her response was as predicted. Shawn bristled. "Of course I'm not bailing! The track means everything to me. Everything."

"Then let's go." He took her hand firmly in his. "Repeat after me: I do. That's all we need."

Shawn looked up at him, her eyes wide with fear. "I do. Don't I?"

It almost made him laugh. He led her down the hallway and through the glass doors to the reception area to let the clerk know they were there. "Do you have the marriage license?" he asked her.

"Yes."

Five minutes later they were married. It was easier than renewing his driver's license. Easier even than getting a flu shot, and for the most part, less painful.

Rhett looked down at Shawn, gauging her mood as he leaned down to kiss her. She looked like she'd hit the wall at Talladega at one hundred and forty miles an hour. Stunned. But when he brushed his lips over hers, she wrapped her arms around his neck and clung to him like a wet kitten.

It was a convincing embrace.

"You okay?" he murmured to her.

That snapped her out of her terrified fog. She said defiantly, "Of course. Why wouldn't I be? This was my idea."

"Excellent." Rhett turned to the clerk. "Can you take our picture with my phone?" He wasn't sure why it seemed important. It just seemed like someone would ask at some point if they had proof of the ceremony. Or maybe he just wanted a picture of them. He handed her his phone from his pocket and showed her the button to push.

"Sure. Say 'wedding night!'"

Shawn dutifully repeated it as they smiled at the camera. But Rhett just held her hand, his finger brushing over the ring he'd slipped on her, and tried to smile. It wasn't his strong suit. Repeating a cheesy phrase was definitely beyond him.

It was possibly the worst wedding picture ever. He was grimacing and Shawn looked like she was being held prisoner by a madman and forced to pretend otherwise.

Shawn gave a nervous laugh as she peered down at the screen on his phone. "Wow. I don't think that will be our Christmas card next year."

"Probably not."

Shawn suddenly seemed to realize how far away Christmas was and that they would in fact be married nine months from now if she wanted to keep her business. Her entire face leached of color. For a horrifying second, he thought she might hit the floor. But she rallied. She thanked the clerk and tugged him by the hand, hard, into the hallway.

"So, you're moving in on Monday?" she asked as they headed for the parking lot. "I'll make sure I clear some space for you." She dropped his hand like he was a disease carrier. "I'll text you tomorrow."

Even though he had known she was going to try to ditch him, he hadn't expected her to look quite so eager to get rid of him. But while he understood her desire for space, it wasn't going to prevent him from angling for her time, and body. They were both feeling unnerved by what they had just done—hell, they'd gotten married—but what better way was there to ease that tension than by spending the rest of the afternoon in bed together?

"I want to see you tonight. Say 'wedding night,'" he said as they came to a stop next to her car, giving her a genuine smile.

"I was planning on meeting Eve and my other girlfriends for a drink, to tell them our wonderful news."

Sarcasm wasn't a good look for her. It suited Eve more so than Shawn.

"Oh, yeah? Where at?"

"That Mexican place on 150." Then she got suspicious. "Why?"

"Just being polite, and trying not to be jealous of your friends," he told her, striving for casual. She didn't need to know that he was just as tenacious as she was. She didn't know that he had no intention of letting her walk away that easily. He dropped the gift bag in her lap. "For you."

Then he leaned forward and kissed her lightly. "My ring looks good on your finger," he told her, then opened her car door for her. "I'll talk to you soon."

Shawn frowned. Her mouth worked, like she was going to say something, but then stopped herself. "Okay. Have a good night."

"I intend to."

SHAWN let Rhett slam her door shut as she turned the ignition to her car. Then he waved and walked away. Her husband. He walked away. Which was what she had wanted him to do, but now that he did, she suddenly felt discontent.

They had gone through with it. They'd gotten married, and she had a whole year to save the track from financial decay. A whole year to be married to Rhett Ford and have his green eyes boring into her on a daily basis.

She had to be totally and completely insane.

The ring on her finger felt foreign and monumental, a total Frodo moment, like it might change her forever. It wasn't an epic *Lord of the Rings* journey, but it felt damn close enough to her. It was marriage and she had just defiled the institution by marrying for all the wrong reasons. The right reasons to her, but the wrong reasons in general.

She peeled back the tissue paper stuffed in the gift bag and promptly jammed it back in once she saw what was under it. Red lace. It was underwear of some kind, though she was choosing not to look too closely at the moment.

Her head hurt and she wanted a drink as big as her kitchen sink.

Instead, she took an Advil PM and took a nap before she had to face the book club girls at seven. Probably not how most women would spend the afternoon after tying the knot, but it worked for her.

By the time she arrived and ordered her first margarita, she felt more calm and in control. Capable of faking it.

"So what is this big news you texted us about?" Charity asked immediately as she peeled off her coat and plunked down in the seat next to Eve, across from Shawn. "I'm dying of curiosity."

"Thank God, you two are finally here," Eve said. "She wouldn't tell me until you got here."

Shawn sipped her margarita and wished she could tell them the truth about the situation. But Eve had a mouth the size of Texas and Rhett was her brother-in-law. She wasn't going to approve of their motives for marriage, nor was she going to be able to keep it a secret. Her tirade would be heard in three counties. Charity was a gossiper, and she couldn't be trusted either. Harley could keep a secret, but she would worry and end up with an ulcer tearing through her stomach lining. Shawn couldn't do that to her.

This was her secret. Hers and Rhett's.

So she had to be convincing.

"Obviously, you know that Rhett Ford is the guy we saw at the bar last weekend and that he asked Eve about me?"

"Unfortunately, yes," Eve said dryly. "Did you give him the go-ahead to call you or whatever?"

"Not exactly. He showed up at the track on Monday."

"What?" Eve pushed her caramel hair back off her forehead and reached for a chip to dip in guacamole. "What a little shit! I told him it was your call. But he is kind of aggressive that way."

"Oh, he's definitely aggressive," Shawn said, her cheeks heating up as she thought about what she could be doing tonight if she had just agreed to see him. But there was a principle at stake here. He wasn't the boss of her. How mature did that sound? She mentally eye-rolled herself. "We've been, uh, spending a lot of time together."

Not true, but it was the only way to explain what she was about to say next. Which she had purposely chosen to announce in public so that Eve couldn't swear at the top of her lungs.

Eve's eyebrows shot up. "I don't think I want to hear this."

"I do," Charity stated emphatically, leaning forward on the table.

Harley, seated next to Shawn turned and gave her a concerned look. "What is it you're trying to tell us, Shawn? Did he hurt you in some way?"

"What? No, of course not." Not yet anyway.

No. Never. She was not going to get hurt. If she got hurt, it was her own damn fault, not Rhett's. She was the one who had coerced him into this ridiculous farce. Actually, if she got hurt it was her grandfather's fault for setting up this bullshit game of emotions in the first place.

"We got married today. Isn't that awesome?" Ba-dum-bum. She felt like a bad comic.

Three faces stared at her in complete silence and shock. The busy restaurant bustled around them, and they looked like they had been frozen in place by a witch's spell. A tortilla chip was actually dangling from Charity's lip, her mouth gaping open.

Any second now, Shawn would be hearing crickets.

"Isn't anyone going to say anything?" she asked, when it became apparent they were not.

Eve exploded. "*What*? You cannot be serious! You just met him! Are you insane?"

Oh, yeah, she was, but Eve had no room to talk. Shawn had an ace up her sleeve, and Eve had dealt it to her. "How long were you dating Nolan before you got hitched in Vegas?"

That really had been insane, because Eve and Nolan had gotten married spontaneously without a legal contract, unlike her current situation. So who was the crazy lady here, huh? It made Shawn feel a whole lot better.

"That is not the same thing," Eve said indignantly. "I knew Nolan for two years before we started dating."

Shawn snorted. "You probably said hello to him in passing once a week. You did not know him at all. You just happened to know who he was."

"What . . . how . . . ?" Harley sputtered and reached for her wineglass. "What prompted you to go get married today, a Friday, in the afternoon? I mean, are you in love with him? You must be, right?"

Love? Hardly. Shawn didn't even believe in love at first sight. Her triumph at besting Eve's argument was short-lived.

Charity answered before she could. "Of course not! There's no way. It's lust, pure and simple. He must be hung like an ox."

Well, now that was slightly insulting. The assumption that she would get married based purely on the size of a man's penis made her seem profoundly shallow. She might get married for business reasons, but not for penile size. Sheesh. Give a girl some credit.

"We are in love. Desperate, maddening, cannot-be-explained love. I mean, seriously, ladies, he is seven years younger than me and not my type at all, but sometimes, you just get swept up off your feet." And hand her a fucking Oscar, thank you very much.

"Yeah, and onto your back," Charity insisted.

"Jesus, Mary, and Joseph," was Eve's opinion. "My mother-in-law is going to shart herself. Both her precious sons eloping in the same year. I hope like hell you and Rhett know what you're doing."

Not a clue. But fake it till you make it. "I'm not going to worry about it. None of it. People's opinions don't matter when you're happy." She almost choked on her own cheesiness, but she forced it out.

"And when it all goes south, you just get divorced. No biggie," Charity said cheerfully.

Her thought exactly, which suddenly made her sad. Was she cynical about relationships? She hadn't thought so, but maybe she was. Her own father was a douchebag, and her flaky mother had run through a string of lousy boyfriends over the years, so maybe Shawn had gotten used to looking at relationships with expiration dates on them. Was it so impossible to think that marriage could last? Eve and Nolan had started off with an impulsive and improbable beginning, and they seemed quite happy.

"Don't be a Debbie Downer," Harley told her twin.

Eve looked torn. "I want to be supportive. I do. I mean, damn it, you're right. Was it really that different with me and Nolan? But . . . you and Rhett? For real? He's such a demanding brat." She leaned forward on her elbows, studying Shawn carefully. "Are you happy?"

"Yes," she said truthfully, because she was. She was scared. Nervous. But she was happy. Hamby Speedway was still hers and she was going to make a success out of it. That was all she had ever wanted. She was also going to have an orgasm, or multiple ones, in a week or so. Rhett looked like he could put some air in her tires, and she was looking forward to that. So, yeah. She was actually good, now that she thought about it, even as fears and moral implications stewed in the back of her brain. "And I don't think he's a brat at all." Demanding, perhaps. But he was always very honest and straightforward, and she respected that.

"Rhett looks pretty damn happy, too," Charity said, pointing to the doorway. "Here he comes with Nolan."

What? Shawn twisted toward where Charity was gesturing. Yep. That was Rhett, looking sexy as hell in his wedding jeans, which cupped his buns quite nicely, she might add. Nolan, whose nostrils were flaring in agitation, walked in behind him. What the hell were they doing there?

"I would say 'smug' is a better word for it," Eve said. "Rhett does smug well."

That he did. Shawn felt the now-familiar rapid heartbeat and hardening of the nipples she experienced whenever Rhett was around her. It was something about that expression he wore . . . not just the confidence he exhibited, but the way he made her feel, that he was looking at her, and only her, that made smug sexy.

But what he was doing strolling into La Ranchita was a mystery. She should have known he had a reason for asking specifically where she was going.

It made her uneasy.

Yet he was giving her a smile. He raised his hand in greeting and peeled off his coat as he approached their table. He leaned over and kissed her possessively on the mouth. Without missing a beat, he turned and asked the table at large, "Did Shawn tell y'all the news?"

Nolan was shaking his head as he gestured for the hostess to bring them two more chairs. "I would say so, given the looks on their faces."

"Did you seriously marry my oldest friend in the middle of a Friday afternoon six days after meeting her?" Eve asked. "Because I just want to be clear about what I'm hearing."

"I did." With a smile for her, Rhett took the chair the hostess brought over. "Thank you, ma'am, appreciate it."

He nudged it in alongside Shawn, so that when he sat down, his leg was nice and snug against hers. "And there wasn't even any alcohol involved."

Just a legal contract and serious greenbacks. But never mind that. Shawn took another swallow of her margarita, then instantly regretted it, remembering the saying about tequila and clothes falling off. She didn't need to lose her drawers and the bet tonight. It was a situation she had very little control over, this whole business with the track. So the bottom line was, she wanted to delude herself into thinking she had some kind of control over Rhett. By proving she could hold out on sex.

Yeah. This was all just brilliant.

"For the first time in her life, my wife is speechless," Nolan said wryly as he sat down next to Eve on her free side. "But I guess congratulations are in order, Shawn. I have to say I'm more than a little surprised, but who am I to stand in the way of true love?"

There might be more than a little sarcasm in his voice, but Shawn chose to ignore it. If Charity or Harley had strolled in and announced they were married to a man they had just met, she was sure her reaction would be similar to the ones they were being given.

"Thanks, bro," Rhett said. "Now I think you should buy me a drink."

"I can do that. Anyone else?" Nolan asked. "This round is on me."

"That's it?" Eve asked. "That's all you're going to say? Your brother marries a total stranger, and you offer to buy him a drink?"

"I'm a total stranger?" Shawn asked, indignant at Eve's choice of words.

"You know what I mean."

"No, I don't. It's not like you don't know I'm a decent person. What do you need to protect Rhett from, exactly?"

"Yeah, it's not like she's a gold digger," Nolan joked. "Rhett doesn't have a pot to piss in."

Next to her, she felt Rhett shift uncomfortably. "Way to sell me, Nolan, thanks."

"What? You're already married. You were smart enough to lock her in before she figures out all your faults."

Eve laughed. Her husband grinned at her.

Shawn wasn't particularly amused. Rhett didn't look like he was enjoying the stand-up comedy routine either. He was frowning, and when the waitress asked him if he would like a drink, he ordered a double shot of tequila. Holy firewater, amigo. Shawn looked at him in amazement.

"Maybe you shouldn't order that," Eve told him. "You don't want whiskey dick on your wedding night. Or technically, tequila dick. But that just doesn't have the same ring to it."

She and Nolan both laughed again, enjoying their little shared humor at Shawn's husband's expense. She had to say, she did not care for that one bit. "That's not a problem for my husband," she said, and damned if she didn't sound like one pissed-off wife, legit.

Everyone else must have agreed because Eve's laughter cut off and Charity was staring at her wide-eyed.

"It was a joke," Eve told her. "Truth be told, I don't give any thought to your *husband's* dick."

"Well, that's a relief," Nolan said.

"Are we having fun yet?" Charity asked, holding up the basket. "Chip, anyone?"

"I'll take some," Shawn said, reaching in and grabbing a massive fistful. She suddenly felt the urge to stuff her face before she said something that was rude and uncalled for to her friends.

Rhett's hand squeezed the top of her thigh. He leaned in close to her and murmured, "Thanks for defending my prowess, babe. I appreciate it."

She made the mistake of turning to look at him. He was

closer than she realized, his mouth inches from hers. "Well, I can't have people talking smack about my husband."

Then she jammed a chip into her mouth to combat the salivating desire to kiss him in La Ranchita.

His hand came up and cupped her cheek. "God, you're gorgeous," he told her earnestly.

A warm wet pool of desire formed deep inside her. Did he have to be so sexy?

Harley coughed next to her. When Shawn looked up, she saw four faces staring at them, with varying expressions, ranging from horror (Eve) to envy (Charity).

"Is that your wedding ring?" Harley asked as Shawn reached for her margarita. The diamond band was glaringly obvious in the multicolored lights of the fiesta décor.

"Yes, it is. Isn't it beautiful?" That wasn't an exaggeration. It was a stunning ring, delicate and vintage-inspired. Oddly enough, she didn't think she would have chosen it for herself, yet it fit her perfectly. She liked that it wasn't showy or attention-demanding. It was something her grandmother would have worn, which made her feel a little melancholy. Her grandmother had died when Shawn was twenty, and she and Pops had enjoyed a fifty-year marriage.

The thought of their love and commitment had her reaching for her margarita again.

"It's gorgeous," Harley agreed. "Rhett, did you pick that out?"

"Yes. It just looked like it would suit Shawn."

"Are you going to have a reception or anything?" Charity asked.

"We're having a party, not a full-blown reception. On Valentine's Day," Rhett told her.

As he spoke, his hand covered hers, his finger stroking over the wedding band with a clear display of possessiveness that made her uncomfortable. What was he doing here, by the way?

"If you need any help, let us know," Nolan said mildly,

like it was perfectly natural for any of this to be happening. "We have the race on Sunday, obviously, but V-Day is Wednesday this year, so I can help you out on Monday and Tuesday."

"Thanks, I appreciate that." Rhett looked genuinely touched by his brother's support.

Shawn pictured this evening times ten at a wedding reception on Valentine's Day, of all days, paper hearts and doilies barfed all over her house, congratulations, curious stares, and the knowledge that she was a massive fraud, and she just wanted to get drunk.

But when she reached for her margarita, Rhett actually moved it out of her reach. "What are you doing?" She stretched further, and he put his hand over hers to stop her progress.

"I just did a double shot of tequila. I think you should drive us home, not me."

Was he fucking kidding her? "I didn't tell you to take a shot!" And what was this about going home anyway? Whose home? She had fully intended to spend tonight alone with her rabbit. The vibrating kind, not the furry kind.

"But I did. So would you mind driving us home?"

His tone was even, but his eyes said something she didn't understand. Shawn felt confused, miserable, and in desperate need of an orgasm. If she said yes, she did mind, she would just sound petulant. Besides, she probably shouldn't argue with her fake husband on her wedding-night outing with friends. It would look a little sketchy.

"Of course I don't mind." Big. Fat. Lie. "Though I guess we should discuss these things right off the bat, shouldn't we?"

"Communication is key to a successful marriage," Charity said confidently.

"How the hell would you know?" Eve asked. "You're not married."

"So?"

They started to argue, and Shawn sat back, glad the spotlight was off her. An hour later, she was more than ready to leave and massage her cheeks out of their lockjaw from fake smiling.

But of course, that presented a different set of issues. Rhett held her coat out for her, and when she slipped her arms into it, he said, "Just let me get my bag out of Nolan's truck, then we can go."

He really was coming with her, and she couldn't ask him what the hell he thought he was doing in front of everyone else. That it was manipulative and rude.

After hugging her friends and smiling and waving in the parking lot, she climbed into her car and wished for death. It would be preferable to this bullshit. Why had she thought she could do this?

This was the stupidest, most ill-conceived plan ever on the face of the planet, and she was going to be struck by lightning and die for lying to her closest friends. Either that or end up in prison after murdering Rhett. A girl was entitled to her cocktail, thank you very much, and if he valued his junk, in the future he would not do that. It was patronizing and it pissed her off.

She was going to have to establish some ground rules.

He got in the passenger seat and smiled at her. "That went well."

Why did his smile disarm her anger? Maybe because he didn't really smile all that often. When he did, she felt . . . special. Gag. The tension was causing her to lose it. "Not really."

"I'm not really sure it could have gone any differently. All things considered, everyone reacted pretty calmly."

Whatever. "Why did you show up there? And why are you in my car? You could at least give me a little warning, you know." So she could have been somewhere else.

Rhett just gave her a very calm, very matter-of-fact shrug. "Because you would have tried to talk me out of it. Or you would have gotten way too nervous waiting for me to show up. And the truth is, no one was going to believe this marriage is real if we didn't go home together tonight. What bride and groom don't want to be together on their wedding night?"

He had a point.

Shawn threw her car into reverse. "You're pretty damn good at this, you know that? Have you been fake married before?"

"No. This is my one and only time. So I plan to make it count."

A shiver tripped up her spine, and it wasn't from the winter temperatures. It was from anticipation.

CHAPTER
SIX

RHETT knew that Shawn was stressed out. He also knew that she was expecting him to hit on her and that if he did, she would resist. So he was going to sneak around and try to enter from the back door. Not literally. That would keep for a while. He'd give her a week at least on that one. No, he meant he was not going to approach the subject of sex head-on. He was going to come at it from an unexpected direction by trying to get to know her.

It wasn't game playing. He was curious about her. But he knew she wasn't expecting it, and it would help her let her guard down.

"So you said you have one brother," he said as they pulled out of the parking lot. He probably could have driven—the tequila hadn't really affected him at all—but better safe than sorry, and he had wanted to establish that they were a couple now in everyone's eyes. They needed to communicate and act the part. "What's his name?"

Shawn glanced at him, clearly startled. "Will. He's an optometrist and he's married. His wife is Kate. And they were married before the Prince of England and Kate Middleton, so it's just a coincidence."

"I never would have thought about the prince, trust me. I'm not one to follow royal gossip." Any gossip for that matter. He couldn't tell you who was dating who in Hollywood, and he didn't give a rat's ass. "Is he older or younger?"

"Younger. By two years. My mom and grandparents raised us. My father lit out when I was four."

Her fingers gripped the steering wheel tightly in the ten and two positions, but it was clear she was comfortable with her car. She drove a stick, which was the only way to drive as far as he was concerned. "I'm sorry. That sucks. I have no respect for a man who can knock a woman up, but not stick around."

"Me either," she said wryly. "But I don't remember him, so no big deal. My grandfather was a good role model. The only mistake he ever made was putting this dumb marriage deal in his will."

"I guess we'll just have to make the best of it." He fully intended to. At the end of six months, he wanted to look back and say that he'd fully explored Shawn and their relationship, no matter what the end result was. If they had to act married, why not attempt to be married, in a manner of speaking?

"I guess so." She glanced over at him at the red light. "Rhett, I should say thank you. I mean, I know I'm paying you, but this isn't easy. It's a big deal to tell people we're married. To move in with me. I appreciate you keeping it together and handling the details. I'm a big-picture type of girl, and this is all a little overwhelming for me."

"No problem." It pleased him that she recognized he had been trying to pave the way for her. He wasn't someone who got much credit for being thoughtful, because he didn't smile and laugh and flirt all the time. Serious seemed to equal selfish to a lot of people, when the opposite was true. If he cared about someone, he was loyal, and he busted his ass to make her happy. He couldn't crack jokes like Nolan, but he'd change your oil, wash the dishes, and make you come five times, all in the same night, and he thought that was nothing to sneeze at.

Shawn was already someone he knew he could care about. She was by far the least irrational woman he had encountered, and when she got angry, it blew over faster than a summer storm. The fury seemed to come and go in under five minutes. She didn't whine, she didn't cry, as far as he could tell, and she was honest, which was maybe his number-one requirement for a healthy relationship.

"Where are we going?" he asked suddenly when he realized they were heading out of Mooresville, not that far from his parents' house.

"To my house," she said, sounding bewildered. "Isn't that what you wanted to do?"

"For some reason, I thought you had an apartment in town. I'm not sure why." He had pictured her in a modern new-build apartment, with a perky little balcony in a complex called Symme's Landing or some other similarly vague name. But he could see he had been way off base when she turned off down a dirt road.

"No. I live in my grandparents' old house. I like not having the neighbors too close. Is that a problem?"

"Hell, no." He was actually relieved. "I prefer this. I like having some space myself." Aside from the fresh air, and the room to tinker on cars, it meant no one would hear Shawn when he made her scream in pleasure. It was perfect.

"The house isn't exactly up-to-date, and it's only two bedrooms, but it's cozy. I like it."

"My parents raised nine kids in a three-bedroom ranch. If the plumbing works, that's the only amenity I need."

"It does. The toilet may be powder blue a la 1950, but it works just fine."

"Perfect. It sounds manly."

"So what was growing up with eight siblings like?"

"Noisy." Rhett craned his neck to see the house as they pulled up to it. It was a brick ranch with an aluminum awning, surrounded by trees. The garage was set back and had a dilapidated basketball hoop. It was a hell of a lot like the house he'd grown up in. "But I have no complaints. Being the baby, my sisters, well, babied me. I didn't have to walk unless I really wanted to until I was about five, because there was always someone to carry me."

She laughed. "I have a hard time picturing that."

"Every picture of me under the age of three is on a sister's hip, with a sippy cup or a pacifier or a lollipop in my mouth. It was a tough life." Though until he was at least four, he'd thought his name was actually Rhettie-poo. His reality was bad, but at least not that bad.

"Apparently." Shawn parked her car alongside the house and turned to him. "Maybe that's why you grew up getting what you want. You're used to it."

"Maybe." But he didn't tend to think about the psychology of how he was raised. He liked to be in charge in the bedroom and that's just the way he was. It didn't require diagnosis. "Since you weren't expecting me until Monday, I'm sure my room isn't ready. I can sleep on the couch."

That seemed to throw her. "Okay," she said, but she looked troubled.

Exactly as he intended. He wanted her to invite him into her bed.

Rhett opened the car door and pulled out his bag. They walked the few feet to the side of the house, Shawn pulling back the squeaky storm door and propping it with her shoulder. He took the weight of it, holding it for her.

"Thanks," she murmured as she shoved the wood door open and flicked on the hall light.

It was a typical ranch, with the side entrance opening onto a tiny landing with two steps up to the kitchen, and a narrow steep staircase straight in front leading to the basement.

Before she could step inside, Rhett dropped his bag on the gravel and dirt drive, and kicked the metal bar on the bottom of the screen door with his foot so it would hold the door on its own.

"What are you doing?" she asked, looking down at the propped door.

"Carrying you over the threshold," he told her, no smile, just all serious intention. It may be a fake marriage, but that didn't mean a girl didn't deserve to have a little romance. He wanted her to feel comfortable around him, comfortable with her decision to have him in her home, her life, for six months bare minimum. He wanted her to like him enough to open her body to him and let him inside so they could both gain as much pleasure as possible from their arrangement.

"Oh, God, please don't," she said, her cheeks turning pink. "It seems so fake. Forced."

"I don't believe I asked you for permission," he told her, reaching over and gripping her under her backside and lifting her into his arms.

She was light, but she shrieked and instantly squirmed and flailed. "Put me down!"

"I intend to. In your bed," he promised. And that's where he was going to leave her. Alone, aroused, wishing for his hard cock.

SHAWN really didn't want to be in Rhett's arms being carried over the threshold like a blushing and happy bride. But neither did she want him to drop her down the basement stairs, so she realized it would behoove her to quit jerking around. Given his spot on Evan Monroe's pit crew as a gasman, he had killer biceps and excellent strength, but he probably didn't work out by wrangling giraffelike women with thrashing limbs, so if she valued her skull, it seemed best to at least get into the kitchen before putting up a fight. Because she had to put up a fight to get out of his embrace or she was going to find herself in bed with him on top of her, and then how the hell was she supposed to say no to nekkid fun?

He wouldn't ask. He would just start stripping her, and

it was so damn hard to say no to him. It was like she was looking at a shaman or something, the way he stared at her so intently, like he was digging into her sexual soul. Saying no would feel bad, but she would have to, and really she just wanted to avoid the whole situation. But she could allow herself one tiny moment to relax and feel very feminine and very womanly captured in his rock-solid embrace. He was doing it—watching her, while his grip on her was firm. He smelled good, like skin and heat and nothing more.

When they got up the two steps to the kitchen, she didn't bother to fight. It felt kind of good, actually, and why deny herself? "Do I get a sippy cup next?" she asked. Then realized immediately there was all sort of naughty directions he could take that question, regarding other things she could put in her mouth.

But he didn't, surprisingly enough. He just said, "No." But then he did add, "It's bedtime, young lady."

Oh, God, that shouldn't have turned her on, but it did. She heard herself giggle nervously, and was appalled. She was a giggler, she had to admit, but Rhett wasn't the guy you giggled with. He wasn't going to laugh back.

Nope. He definitely didn't. He just kept walking, in the dark, through the kitchen and past the living room and down the hall, like he knew the house. "Don't you want to turn a light on?" she asked. "I don't want you to trip."

"I'm fine."

"My room is the . . ." Room he was already going into. "How do you know your way around my house?" she tittered. Now she was tittering. Good God. Next she'd be simpering.

"Common sense."

Of course. It wasn't like all ranches didn't have about the same basic floor plan. Shawn said, "Just set me down next to the bed, thanks."

But he didn't. He deposited her on her bed, brushing her hair back off her cheek as he bent over her, his hip close to hers, warm breath rushing over her face. Shawn waited, teeth clenched and shoulders tense.

"Can I use the bathroom first? I just need five minutes," he said.

Now that wasn't what she was expecting him to say, but it made sense. He probably wanted to brush his teeth. Not that he had bad breath, because he didn't. But he probably wanted to before bed, and he wanted to dig a condom out of his bag, sure he was going to get some. Which he wasn't. She put a stop to her pointless panicky thoughts and managed a casual, "Sure."

"I can find it myself." He stood up, the air around her suddenly empty.

He went into the hallway, partially closing her door on the way out, which was courteous. Shawn lay on her bed, forcibly letting her body relax, one muscle group at a time.

He was coming back, wasn't he?

An hour later, it was evident he was not. She'd heard the toilet flush and the sink run, then there had been silence. Nothing but silence.

She had kicked off her shoes and gotten under the covers, but she was still wide awake, waiting for him to creep into her room and hit on her, so she could tell him no. Which she now realized wasn't going to happen. So eventually she found herself doing the creeping, climbing out of bed and down the hall to the living room to confirm what she knew—that he wasn't coming into her room. There he was, fast asleep on the couch, in his jeans and no shirt, on his side, hands tucked under his cheek in a way that was pretty damn cute. The bare chest wasn't cute, it was smoking hot. She cursed the fact that he'd left the light on by the back door, because otherwise she wouldn't have seen what she was missing.

And Lordy be, wasn't he cold? It was February after all.

Shawn took the USC afghan off the easy chair and slowly, carefully draped it over Rhett.

"Thanks," he murmured, eyes closed.

She jumped. Shit, he was awake. Sort of. His breathing was even and steady, like he was already sliding back into sleep. Shawn stood there for a minute, waiting for something to happen. Nothing did, so she went back to bed. Alone. And cursed herself to the ends of the earth for falling for another double-dog dare.

It was cold and lonely and very unsatisfying in her queen-size bed solo.

IT didn't help when Rhett came in at seven in the morning, fully dressed, and gently shook her awake. "Shawn."

"What?" she asked crossly, running on about zero sleep, her dreams plagued with erotic images of Rhett stroking her to orgasm, over and over.

"I have to go to work. I just called a cab. Are you going to be home later when I get back, or can you leave the door unlocked for me?"

Oh, my God. Details. More effing details. They were killing her. "I'll be home." Masturbating, apparently, since she was even hornier now than when she'd gone to bed. "And I can drive you to your car if you want. You're going to need it, obviously." Even though she would rather walk through a fire anthill naked, she would get up and drive him. Right after she pried her eyes open. They felt slightly glued together, but she managed to focus more clearly on him.

He looked wide-awake and sexy. Bastard.

"Don't worry about it, babe. I'll have Nolan take me to my car. You sleep in."

She tried to find something asshole-ish in any of that, but there wasn't anything. Geez. He was making this so difficult. "Are you sure?"

He smiled. "Yes, I'm sure. See you later. And I'd love steak for dinner if you were wondering what to fix."

That had her eyes popping back open. "Excuse me?"

Rhett actually laughed. "I'm kidding. God, the look on your face was great."

"You're not allowed to joke," she told him, completely serious. "It's out of character."

That just made him grin even wider. "Go back to sleep, Shawn."

He leaned down and kissed her, which made her squawk in alarm. She had saliva in the corner of her mouth, damn it.

Not that it mattered. It was a very brotherly sort of kiss. Or grandson to grandmother on her birthday. Coupled with his complete lack of interest in nailing her the night before, she suddenly felt very grumpy as he left her alone in her bed. What the hell was going on? Yes, she was fully intending to reject him, or more accurately fend him off for the next six days in order to prove her point, but the thing was, he was supposed to be making it necessary to fend him off. There was no need to fend, because he wasn't trying anything. What was up with that?

Was she just no longer attractive to him? Did he see this as a purely business deal after all? The idea of being forced into celibacy for the next year was more than a little horrifying. Never mind that it had been a year since she'd had sex anyway, at least then she'd had the *option* of sex. But if Rhett didn't want to diddle her, then she was going to be diddle-less.

That was not going to fly. Shawn shoved the covers back and decided she was going to brew some coffee, and then she was going to make Rhett Ford want her more than any woman he'd ever met in his entire life.

RHETT pulled up to Shawn's house at six, exhausted and admittedly a little bit irritated. It had been a long day at work, juggling his usual responsibilities with having to repeat explanations over and over that yes, he had gotten married. No, he wasn't an idiot. Yes, his new wife was older than him, and why did that matter? It had been harder than he had expected because he wasn't really the kind of guy to share his feelings with anyone, least of all his coworkers.

What he would really like to do to turn his mood around was walk inside that house and bend his wife over the kitchen table and bury his frustration inside her wet and willing thighs. Only she was acting skittish and like she regretted this fake marriage, even though it had been her idea. It both insulted and hurt him, which just further increased his bitter mood.

There would be no easy conversation, no cuddling, no ball-draining endless nights in her bed. At least not yet. It was going to require patience and finesse he wasn't entirely sure he had to coax Shawn into understanding this would all go a whole lot faster if they spent some of it in bed.

It had him wound tight, and he shoved the side door open harder than he intended.

What he saw in the kitchen was very possibly the only thing on earth that could have improved his mood.

Shawn was bent over the oven in a short dress and heels, pulling a couple of T-bone steaks out of the broiler. As he kicked off his muddy boots on the doormat, she turned. The front view was even better than the back. Her dress plunged in a V, and her breasts had been pushed up and together, like a couple of perky grapefruits in the grocery, on display perfectly. Just for him.

She smiled. "Oh, good, you're just in time for dinner."

Hello. "Well, then good thing I'm hungry."

Fanning herself with the oven mitt, she said, "Whew, the broiler made me so hot. I think I need a cool drink." She tugged her dress down lower, exposing enough cleavage to have his cock standing up to take notice as he went up the steps to the kitchen.

"Can I get you anything? A beer?" She picked up a cherry that had been used to garnish a pie—a fucking pie—and sucked the syrupy sauce off it, the plump fruit between her lips, a sassy glint in her eye.

Seriously? What alien had abducted Shawn and replaced her with this little flirt?

He wanted to ask her if she had hit her head, but the truth was, he didn't really want the answer to that question. Whatever her game was—and it was clearly a game—he didn't want to prevent her from playing. In fact, she sparked his competitive nature. If there was a game going on, he was bound and determined to win it. That was why he liked to be behind the wheel racing instead of on a crew. He liked to control the situation.

So he went over to her, still wearing his coat, and immediately gripped the back of her head with his hand, pulling her to him for a kiss, a hot, wet, tongue-plunging kiss that transferred the cherry from her lips to his mouth, where he bit it, then shared the sweet tangy juice with her.

Then he broke away and told her, "I stole your cherry." He swiped the remnants of the juice that were clinging to her swollen lip and sucked it off his finger. "Mmm."

"You didn't even ask," she said, her voice husky with desire. Her nipples jutted out prominently in her stretchy black dress, and her hair was loose around her shoulders. If he wasn't mistaken, she was wearing more makeup than usual, her eyes carefully outlined in a charcoal gray.

Someone was trying to mess with him.

"You didn't stop me," he told her. "By the way, I like this dress. What's the occasion?" He fiddled with the neckline, following the trail as it descended to her rib cage, his flesh brushing against the creamy exposed hills of her breasts.

"Just trying to get off on the right foot," she said, leaning back on the counter. "We have to live together for a while. It would be better to do it in harmony."

"It would be better to do it naked," he told her, slipping a finger inside the dress to stroke lazily across her swollen nipple. "Pull your dress down, Shawn. Show me your breasts."

"What? No!" Her cheeks pinkened from more than the blush she'd put on them.

Like he believed her indignation. "Why not? You clearly want me to notice them, otherwise you wouldn't have put this dress on, and this bra that so nicely thrusts them out in my direction. So pull down the neck and let me really see them."

"No. Does being so bossy work for you?" she asked, even as her hand fluttered up to her chest, her fingers playing with the fabric of the neckline, which was really more of a navel line, the plunge was so pronounced. "Because you're very good at it."

"Not really," he told her truthfully, shifting his leg in between her ankles. "I haven't met a woman strong enough to handle me yet."

"Strong enough? Don't you mean passive enough?"

He shook his head. "No. That's been my mistake. I only scare those women. What I need is a woman strong enough to trust me, confident enough to enjoy obedience. I don't want you to pull your dress down at my command and feel ashamed to do it. I want you to do it and be turned on by it, aroused by my demands. It's a big difference." His lust was dark and swirling inside him, a hot desire on his tongue, and he wanted her with an urgency that had him clenching his fists by his sides, his cock thick and throbbing in his jeans.

Her breathing had grown deeper, her eyes wide. "Oh. I guess I get that. But I'm not having sex with you tonight."

"No," he agreed. "You're not having sex with me until I say so."

She wouldn't like that. At all. But it was true.

Then she did exactly what he had known she would. She peeled down her dress, taking her bra with it, so that her breasts sprang out, her nipples just barely in view. "Is this what you wanted to see?"

What she didn't realize was that in her attempt to thwart him, to exert control, she had in fact submitted to him. It was immensely sexy.

She was also wearing the red lace bra he had given her, if he was not mistaken, which was deeply satisfying.

"Yes, that's what I wanted to see." Rhett just drank in the sight of her, color high in her cheeks, head held tall and proud, ripe breasts gloriously bare, a mere foot in front of him. If he leaned over, he could suck the taut bud up into his mouth and sink his teeth down on it, turning them both on with the sharp tang of her pain before he soothed her with his tongue. But he didn't.

Instead, he kissed her mouth, a soft, gentle, worshipping kiss, but not of the fervor of their earlier tongue tangle. Her hands were trapped behind them, her breasts pushed against his chest between them. "Thank you," he told her as casually as he could manage. "Now let's eat this dinner you were so sweet to make before it gets cold. Where are your plates?"

He moved out of her personal space and opened a cupboard to look for plates, knowing she would be baffled by his withdrawal. Just like he wanted.

CHAPTER
SEVEN

SHAWN wasn't sure exactly what had just happened, but it definitely wasn't what she had intended. Yes, she had purposely dressed in an outfit that would get his attention, and she had made dinner to throw him off-kilter. The only one in this damn kitchen who was off-kilter was her. Somehow, he had effectively turned the entire situation to his advantage.

Now she was just sopping wet and aching to be taken by him.

She had proved to herself that he was interested in her, and wow, wasn't that a satisfying victory? Not. He seemed to want her, alright. Wanted to torture her.

It wasn't every day she flashed a guy. It seemed like it should be a little more noteworthy than "Where are the dinner plates?" But maybe that was just her.

"In the cupboard next to the fridge." Shawn bent over again to retrieve the twice-baked potatoes out of the oven, hoping that Rhett was looking so he would see that she had logged a lot of time at Zumba and yoga classes to get these legs.

He hadn't even noticed that she was wearing the bra he

had gifted her with the day before. She was also wearing the matching thong, not that he was going to see it.

"I hope you like twice-baked potatoes and asparagus," she said, using tongs to pull the broiled vegetables off the pan and onto the two plates Rhett brought over to her.

"I do." He stood next to her, facing her, while she was facing the counter, which brought him in close and intimately. "Thank you again. I appreciate this." And he tucked her hair back behind her ear, a personal gesture that made her want to step away, retreat.

But she held her ground, and she transferred potatoes to plates. "You're welcome. So does everyone know we're married? Did you tell your parents?"

He nodded. "They were more than a little surprised. And we're the subject of gossip at the track. Most people seem to be of the opinion that you're pregnant."

"What?" Shawn carried the two plates over to her kitchen table and set them down. "I guess I'm not surprised, though nothing could be further from the truth." According to seventh grade health class she couldn't get knocked up from a toilet seat, and it wasn't going to happen any other way, so she was safe.

"Good to know. I'd hate to think I was your cover for having an illegitimate child. I don't really want to end up on the *Maury Povich* show. Rhett Ford, you are *not* the father."

Shawn laughed. "Yeah, me either. Do you want some wine?"

"What I want is something that's not on the menu," he told her, even as he glanced down at his steak. "Though this looks very tasty."

She shouldn't ask. She knew what he meant. It wasn't exactly subtle. But for whatever perverse reason that meant she probably needed therapy, she wanted to hear him say it out loud. "What is it that you want?" she asked, ignoring her own plate of food as she walked across the kitchen, her heels clicking on the linoleum floor as she went for a bottle of merlot.

Any other man she'd ever dated would have said, "You" or "Isn't it obvious?" or something generically similar. She knew that wouldn't be Rhett's answer. He would give specifics, and they would make her wish she hadn't asked at the same time they would turn her on. A lot.

She was right, and she did like being right.

He said, "I want you, Shawn. I want you out of that dress, strewn across this table with your legs spread for me so I can lick your pussy until you scream. Until you beg me for my cock. You'd like that, wouldn't you?"

Shawn froze in front of the wine rack she had mounted on the wall next to the fridge. It was a rhetorical question, she supposed, and she knew what her answer was, but if she said it, well, would that mean she'd lost?

Then again, what would she lose? A bet that had no stakes, really? Or her dignity? No. He wasn't trying to strip her of that.

More likely she would lose control, that's what she was afraid of.

It was going to be a very long six months if she was terrified the entire time.

So she turned around and very slowly, she nodded. "I probably would like that."

He smiled. Then said, "Sit down, babe. I can get the wine for you."

"I'm fine. I have it." Turning away, Shawn used her automatic bottle opener to uncork the wine and poured herself a healthy glass of red. This was nuts. How was she going to do this for half a year? "So I suppose I need to make a key for you. And you are free to come and go as you please, you know. No need to feel like you have to check in with me. I don't want to . . . interrupt your life."

Rhett pushed his chair back and stood up, and when he came toward her, Shawn shivered in anticipation. She had a feeling he was going to pull her dress down and suck her nipple, which was really a perfect way to kick off any dinner, wasn't it? But he actually walked right past her and stared at her, expression curious, as he yanked open the fridge and rooted around, before emerging with a beer.

"Is that what you would like? For us to be roommates, accidentally sharing the same space?" He shook the beer. "Should we have separate shelves for our food and take turns supplying the toilet paper?"

When he said it like that, it wasn't particularly attractive-sounding. "I'm trying to be accommodating."

"Let's not make rules. Let's not stress out. Let's just feel our way through it." He popped open the beer with his bare hand, no bottle opener needed, apparently. "Now come sit down and enjoy the dinner you were so wonderful to make."

What the hell was she supposed to say to *that*? He really left her very few options. She was just going to have to relax and behave like they were friends. It was maddening. Confusing. Because now she really had no idea whatsoever what it was she wanted. Did she want to sleep with him? Did she want him to go away? Did she want to sleep with him, then have him go away?

Good question.

She had no choice but to sit down and eat her meat. The answers would come later or never. Much like her.

The interesting thing was that Rhett was an easy conversationalist. She wouldn't have expected that. She wasn't sure why. It wasn't like the guy could smolder 24/7. At some point he had to make conversation. Presumably.

Which again made her feel at some sort of disadvantage. So he could toss out sexual comments and invade her personal space and then switch gears and talk casually about the weather and tell anecdotes about his family. It left her no way in which to gain the upper hand.

Though he almost never laughed. Maybe instead of trying to play a sexual cat-and-mouse game by wearing a sexy dress—a game she would most definitely lose—she could disarm him by making him laugh.

Shawn mentally eye-rolled herself. What was she going to do, dress like a clown? Do stand-up? *So a priest, a driver, and a parrot all went into a bar.* He'd think she was a freak.

She was starting to worry she was.

She was also full. Pushing her plate back, she said, "When I was a kid I always wanted a huge family. I felt sort of ripped off that it was just my mom, Will, and me. At the very least I wanted a sister." Truthfully, what Shawn had wanted was some attention, any attention. Her mom had checked out emotionally the day her dad had left physically.

"You can borrow one of mine if you like. Seven sisters is a bit excessive." Rhett had eaten everything on his plate, including the potato skin.

"They're going to hate me, aren't they? For 'eloping' with you?" Not that it mattered, since it wasn't a real marriage, but hey, Shawn liked to be liked.

"I doubt my sisters will care. They just want me happy. Frankly, they'll appreciate not having their kids dragged into a wedding as flower girls and ring bearers and whatever."

"How many nieces and nephews do you have?"

"Fourteen. No, fifteen." Rhett frowned. "Wait. Then Owen was born. Sixteen?" He started murmuring names and counting on his fingers. Finally he said, "Hell if I know. You'd have to ask my mom."

Shawn couldn't even imagine having a family that big. "I'm surprised someone doesn't go missing on a regular basis. That's a lot of kids to keep track of."

"Once when I was five, my parents left me home by accident. They took two cars to go to my grandma's house, and both thought the other one had me in their car. I was in my room getting my Power Ranger to take with me, and when I came out, the house was empty." He gave a wry look. "It was my *Home Alone* moment. Thank God they just went down the road, not to France."

"Were you upset? Did you cry?"

"No. I watched TV and ate chips, grateful for the silence. When the phone rang, I answered 'Ford Residence,' feeling pretty badass about the whole thing. It was my mom, and she burst into tears and told me to lock the front door, that they were on their way home."

"Aw, your poor mom. I can only imagine how worried she was."

It wasn't hard to picture Rhett as a solemn, curious child, watching everyone, not reacting with any fear. In total control of his emotions.

Shawn had never been in control of her emotions. It was why she was so willing to dive into stupid situations.

"I bet you were a sassy little girl," Rhett said, draining his second beer.

"I was the kind of kid who got into a lot of scrapes. Climbing trees, crawling in drainpipes, trapping snakes. Yeah, that was me. Eve and I were a force to be reckoned with on the junior racing circuit." The memory made her smile. "Picture two dusty little tomboys talking smack, and that was us."

"I have no problem picturing that. But Eve is more the smack talker than you. I bet you got your way with your charm."

She snorted. "What charm? Though after I heard Eve had kissed Junior Spaulding behind the grandstand at the county fair the summer we were thirteen, I decided my life wouldn't be complete until I got Ty McCordle to do the same with me. So I carefully laid the foundation with clumsy flirting all week at the track." She shook her head, remembering all the hair flipping and lip gloss that had gone into that summer. She had walked around looking like she'd dipped her lips in the fry oil.

"So what happened? He kiss you?"

"Of course," she told him. Hey, she may be thirty-two, but she wasn't above a little bragging still. "Though it didn't go off without a hitch. He was chewing gum and it ended up in my hair. I had to use peanut butter to get it out, and for days I smelled like a peanut butter cup."

Rhett laughed. "Smooth, McCordle. I wish I knew him better so I could give him shit about that."

"Well, the peanut butter seemed to make me instantly desirable. Boys were crawling out of the woodwork the rest of the summer because I smelled like a candy bar."

"Or maybe because you were the thirteen-year-old version of hot."

"Or because they heard I was up for tonsil tango." Shawn grinned at the thought of that summer. She had been skinny, flat as a board, and sporting braces. Probably not every teenage boy's fantasy. Then again, she hadn't looked much different from the other girls. "I was taller than most of the boys my age that year. They needed serious motivation to overcome the embarrassment of coming up to my chin."

"I bet. That's a scary thing for a guy." He gave her a look, the one that usually meant she was about to be sorry she had taken that bet. "Did you wear cowboy boots? I always had a thing for girls who wore cowboy boots."

"I might have." She'd had three pairs that she had rotated on a regular basis. She'd been particularly fond of a red pair, but he didn't need to know all her secrets. "I bet you were a father's nightmare in high school when you came sniffing around his daughter."

He didn't deny it. "I was harmless. For the most part. Like now."

Harmless as a rattlesnake. If you didn't get too close you wouldn't get bit. Otherwise, you were dead. "Uh-huh," she said noncommittally.

Rhett stood up. "Can I get you more wine?" He collected her plate and took it with his to the sink, where he rinsed them and loaded them into the dishwasher. For a second, Shawn thought she might have an orgasm just watching that. A man who cleaned up without being told? Without bitching about it?

"No, I'm fine, thanks." Shawn stood up quickly, wanting

to do . . . something. The truth was, she wanted to be near him. How utterly lame was that? His presence was so powerful that when he moved away, the air seemed colder.

And she was clearly drunk.

But that didn't change the fact that the dishes still needed to be washed. She'd left the detritus of the broiler pans on the oven and several mixing bowls in the sink. Edging him aside with her hip, she rapidly pumped soap onto a sponge. And actually, she wasn't drunk at all, she was just acting like she was. She only wished she could legit use it as an excuse.

She started scrubbing like a madwoman, wanting the heinous chore over and done with. This was the downside of cooking a decent meal. It also didn't help that Rhett was still next to her and he had suddenly decided it made sense to run his tongue along her bare shoulder. His tongue. On her shoulder.

"What are you doing?" she asked shrilly.

He didn't bother to answer.

Of course he didn't answer. He didn't seem to think being polite was necessary when it came to sexual advances. Yet he cleaned up plates, opened her car door, and treated her with respect. How in the hell was a woman supposed to respond to that?

Well, Shawn's response was to let out a little involuntary moan. She didn't mean to. But that licking was so suggestive, so intimate, as his tongue traced the path of her clavicle bone up to her neck where he nuzzled into her flesh. How could she stay immune to that? Only a robot could remain unaffected, and hell, even a robot might short-circuit it was that hot.

Then he stepped back. "Here, I'll rinse, and then we can watch a movie."

On. Off. On. Off. He was killing her.

"Sure. Great idea." Mr. Suckity-Suck. He was doing this on purpose, she was convinced. He would rev her engine, then stay in park. He wanted her to cave, to beg him to have sex with her. That was not going to happen, no matter what her lady parts had to say about it.

So she held strong as they sat on her sofa together, perilously close, his hand stroking across her thigh. He chose a thriller to watch, but it also had several steamy sex scenes in it, with lots of moaning and dewy skin, and arching backs as the hero of the movie pumped hard into his love interest. The woman was clearly enjoying it, given her pronounced moans and bouncing breasts, but Shawn wasn't feeling it.

Or rather, she was feeling it too much.

It was almost impossible to sit still next to Rhett, where she could hear him breathing, could feel his thigh touching hers, and watch a couple having way more fun than she was. Shawn bounced her foot rapidly. Bit her nails. Cleared her throat. And finally jumped up.

"I need a glass of water. Can I get you anything?"

His smile was slow and suggestive, and while he didn't say anything, his expression told her exactly what he was thinking.

"No," she told him sourly.

He laughed.

He didn't protest, but when she sat back down, his hand started at her knee and ended up under her dress dangerously close to the end zone.

Shawn pushed it back down as something exploded on the TV screen. Or maybe that was her resolve going up in flames.

He switched tactics. He shifted sideways and pulled her against his chest, so that she was resting between his legs, her butt nestled on his crotch. Yeah, that wasn't helping. Because he either had a hair spray can down his jeans or he was happy to see her.

By the time the movie ended, she was a hot, aching mess, and he looked as calm as usual.

"I'm going to bed," she announced, flipping the TV off. "I made up the guest room for you. See you in the *morning.*" Just in case there was any doubt that she was not letting him into her room, her bed, or her vagina. Tonight anyway.

He didn't respond. He just watched her as she retreated to her room and closed the door with a sigh. Then she went straight to her nightstand drawer where she kept her vibrator. This was an emergency situation.

RHETT knew that Shawn was well aware of how much he wanted her. She was choosing to ignore that and her own desire. He was willing to let her. For now. Because it was obvious that she was an impulsive person, and all it would take was the right moment, a certain look, the perfectly placed touch, and she would forget about her irrational need to win a no-stakes bet, and she would open herself up to him. He could be patient for a little longer.

The payoff of having her come to him desperate and ready would be worth it.

He might be in a bit of blue-ball hell in the meantime, but he could handle that.

What he could not handle, though, was the realization that Shawn was in her room touching herself. He knew she was because when he walked past her room to the bathroom he heard the very faint sound of something battery-operated and her anxious breathing. Damn it, those walls were thin, and now he had an image he just couldn't shake. Pausing, he listened for another second, which confirmed his suspicions, his mouth growing hot, cock thickening with need.

She hadn't even waited five minutes.

There was something immensely satisfying in that. Not however, as satisfying as pounding her would feel.

Rhett knocked on her door. She gave a tiny squawk from her room, then called out in a shaky voice, "Yes?"

Peeling his shirt off, he dropped it on the hallway carpet before shucking his jeans as well. "I want to take a shower and I can't find a towel."

"They're in the hall closet," she said.

"What? I can't hear you," he lied, and he opened the door. It was a dirty trick, but then again, he'd never claimed to be a Boy Scout, and they were married after all.

"What the hell are you doing?" she asked. "You can't come in here!"

"I couldn't hear you." He moved closer to her bed, hiding his amusement over the fact that she was clutching her covers to her chin. But there was still the faint sound of her vibrator humming away under the blanket.

"Hall. Closet." Her teeth were clenched, and her hair was looking a little wild.

Had she been rolling around under there, rocking herself onto her vibe? Rhett pulled his fingers into fists at the notion.

"What's buzzing?" he asked her.

The hall light was strong enough to illuminate the horrified expression on her face. "What do you mean?"

"I hear buzzing. What is that?"

"I don't hear anything," she said, voice high, grip tightening on the comforter. Her gaze dropped down to his lower half. "Oh! You're not dressed."

"I was going to the shower. Are you dressed?"

"I'm wearing a T-shirt."

Somehow that was even sexier than if she were totally naked. It meant she was secretly pleasuring herself in the dark from under the hem of her shirt.

It also meant he could flip that comforter back.

"Seriously, what is that? It sounds like . . ." And Rhett peeled the side of her comforter back, not exposing her, but exposing her little friend. Who was not so little. It was a healthy-size purple sparkly vibrator, with rabbit clitoral stimulation. Fuck yeah. "A vibrator."

Shawn screamed, "Rhett! Get the hell out of my bedroom!" She tried to flip the comforter back over the sex toy, only he had a firm grip on it, and they engaged in a brief tug of war over the fabric before she gave up and changed tactics, grabbing the vibrator and stuffing it under her pillow. "Go. Away."

He would, if he could walk. But he was afraid he might injure himself if he tried to move. "Shawn. I'm going to ask you a very serious question. Why are you getting yourself off with a vibrator when I could do that for you? We are married, you know. Married people have sex."

She finally let her death grip go on her comforter. She wasn't lying about the T-shirt. It was a ginormous hot pink number, with a pocket over her breast. It said, "I love Mr. Darcy." Who the fuck was Mr. Darcy and did he need to be jealous of him?

"It's the principle," she told him. "I don't want you to think I'm easy."

Rhett raised his eyebrows. "With all due respect, sweetheart, I'm not sure how your date with the purple pussy eater is making you look disinterested in sex."

"Uh!" Color rose in her cheeks, and she picked up her pillow and smacked him with it. "I thought you were decent enough to respect my privacy and not enter a room with a closed door! And didn't your mother tell you not to mention to a lady that she is using a vibrator? It's rude!"

That made him laugh. "That is not a conversation I've had with my mother, no. Generally speaking, we steer clear of politics and battery-operated sex toys in our chats."

She hit him again, harder this time, the pillow making a nice thumping sound in the quiet room.

Rhett ripped the pillow out of her hand. "Knock it off."

"Fuck you."

"I wish you would."

Shawn grabbed another pillow and hit him with it, right across his face this time.

"You're really pushing it," he told her, wanting to give her fair warning that he wasn't above a pillow fight with a girl if she started it. She packed a serious punch to her swings.

"So are you." Her eyes were snapping with anger and lust. She swung again, nailing him in the chin. The pillow exploded, a cascade of feathers raining over his chest and down onto the bed. Shawn's expression changed to one of amusement, her mouth twitching as she started to laugh.

So she was going to laugh at him? Rhett grabbed the pillow she had hidden her sex toy under and hit her in the chest with it.

"Hey!" she said, but she was giggling now.

It was a look he liked on her. He enjoyed the way she couldn't hold on to anger, the way she was so easily amused. The pillow fight wasn't having quite the same effect on him. He was just getting more and more aroused.

She hit him again, grinning, more feathers escaping the hole in the seam of the pillow, coming up on her knees to get more leverage and put more bite into her swing. Rhett whacked her on her ass with his pillow. He could see her thighs but not her panties, the T-shirt still covering them, but it was enough skin, enough to know that there was very little between him and her sex, that her breasts were bare under the shirt, to stir his desire even more.

"You can't hit me there," she said, breathless, whacking his arm and sounding more aroused than indignant.

"You hit me in the face." And so he hit her right between her thighs.

"Rhett! You can't do that."

He wasn't sure how the rules went if she was allowed to do whatever she wanted and hit him anywhere, but he had restrictions.

When she raised her arms again for another assault, he pulled the pillow out of her hands and tossed it on the floor. "Now what?" he asked with a smile.

She went for a backup pillow behind her, but he tore that out of her hands, too. So laughing, breathless, she tried to strip him of the one he was holding.

"I don't think so, little girl." He kept a tight grip on it.

"Little girl?" she asked with a snort. "I'm eight years older than you."

For which he was definitely grateful. She was hanging in way better with him than the younger women he'd dated.

"You're right. You're a woman. But you still can't take this pillow away from me, no matter how hard you try." He knew she would. He'd already pegged that aspect of her personality, and he found her tenacity admirable. And he had to admit, he enjoyed baiting her.

"Oh, yeah?" She lunged for him, and she was faster than he expected.

He almost lost the pillow to her nimble fingers, but he clamped down harder on it and raised it high above his head so that she had to stretch for it.

"Oh!" She glared at him in frustration, but there was a definite twinkle in her eye.

Then she did something he never in a million years would have predicted. Nor was he at all prepared for it.

She reached out with her left hand and stroked right across the front of his boxers, down the length of his cock. He was so shocked that he loosened his grip on the pillow. Which she snagged and then scooted backward on the bed, laughing, removing her hand from his erection.

Rhett was stunned. And turned on. And filled with a new respect for her quick thinking.

"Oh, so that's how you want to play it, huh?" he asked, nudging his knee between her legs and pushing on the pillow so that she fell backward onto the bed on her back. He dropped his forearm onto the pillow, pinning her.

She squirmed, trying to push him off her, but he wasn't budging. They were going to finish this to both their mutual satisfaction. Rhett leaned down and kissed her, but she turned her head to avoid it, so he ended up kissing her cheek. Frowning, he pulled back to gauge her mood. She was still giggling, a nervous reaction that she seemed unable to control.

"What? What's so funny?"

"It just popped into my head that you're about to go Dom on me, and it makes me laugh."

"Why?" He didn't bother to correct her that he wasn't a Dom. Not technically.

"Because it's funny. Sex is funny." She looked up at him innocently, like she genuinely believed her words. "It's so dorky when you think about it."

"Not the way I do it," he assured her most sincerely. He had never once thought of sex as dorky. Or funny. "Who the hell have you been having sex with that just the thought of me fucking you makes you giggle?"

Shawn's eyes were a dark amber, but now they seemed lighter, almost glassy as she looked up at him, her chest heaving beneath the pillow. "I don't know. I guess mostly I have buddy-buddy relationships with men. I don't think I'm their sexual fantasy any more than they're mine."

He had to admit, that surprised him. No wonder she always looked at him a little nervously, yet determined. She must instinctively know that it would be different with him. Which it was going to be. He was going to show her exactly how she'd been let down by the men she had dated. Then again, maybe it wasn't entirely their fault. Attraction was a mysterious thing.

"You're my sexual fantasy. When I'm here, with you, in bed and naked, you can trust that you're the only woman I'm thinking about, that you're the only woman I'm interested in." Something deep and intimate and territorial rose up in him.

She stared up at him, her smile smoothing out into something thoughtful, curious. "I want to believe you. But I also still want to giggle."

It was a start. "Go ahead and giggle if you want, and get it out of your system. But trust me."

That was, after all, the key to a healthy and satisfying relationship, particularly given his tendencies. She needed to trust him to pleasure her, to let him steer the ship. Rhett eased up on the pillow and watched Shawn, waiting for her answer. If she resisted, he would leave her bed tonight. He wanted her all in. He wanted her acquiescence, her eventual surrender.

He knew he would get it.

The question was just if it would be tonight or not.

CHAPTER
EIGHT

SHAWN looked at Rhett, unnerved by his calm, by the way he was doing it again—staring steadily at her, making her the entire focus of his attention. She'd never really experienced that kind of intensity. She had been telling the truth in that most of the men she'd dated had likely been picturing supermodels when they'd been in bed with her. Obviously Sam had, given his wandering eye. She had never been in love with a man, had never emotionally connected on that level with someone. She'd had laughs and good times and respectable sex. But never all-consuming, earth-shattering pleasure.

Never had she looked up and felt like a man wanted to consume her, to eek every last drop of desire out of her body and swallow.

Until now.

Did she trust him?

She did, though there wasn't necessarily any logic to it.

He was borderline rude, definitely bossy, and determined to get his own way.

But he was also honest, straightforward, fair. And most important, he never pushed her.

So yes, she did trust him. And even if it meant she was going to lose a little face by caving five days early, a mere forty-eight hours into their marriage, she knew beyond a doubt that his goal was to make it worth it for her.

"Okay," she whispered, well aware that she was giving in to a course of action that would change the way they interacted over the next six months. But she wanted this. She wanted him. Inside her.

Then he smiled and it was so beautiful, she sucked in her breath, her heart beating almost as loudly as the vibrator that was still buzzing a few feet away from her right ear.

The least she could do was try not to laugh.

So when he bent over to kiss her again, his arm pressing into the pillows, she tried, she honestly tried not to think about the fact that her arms were contained beneath white linens, like a mummy. Or that if she wiggled her hands, they would pop out the bottom of the pillow like T-Rex arms. She twitched, a snort coming out as she tried to contain her nervous laughter.

Rhett paused. "Really?"

"I can't help it!" She took a couple of deep breaths. "Okay, I'm good. Sorry. I'm fine now."

But she really wasn't, because when he stroked his thumb across her bottom lip, she squirmed from need. Not sexual need, but the hysterical urge to reach out and snap at him with her teeth. Suppressed laughter made her nostrils flare and she knew she was about to totally lose it.

She was in no shape for sex clearly.

Rhett sat back, giving her a dark look. When he retreated off the bed, she was disappointed and annoyed with herself. Why couldn't she be normal and artfully pose and come on to him? Why did she have to act like a ginormous goofball and ruin her chances of actually having an orgasm?

Sighing, she rolled over and turned off her vibrator. No sense in wasting the batteries, and she didn't think she could go back to it with the right attitude once he was gone. But Rhett didn't leave her room like she thought he was going to. Instead, he yanked open her dresser drawer and started rooting around. Hello. Her panties and bras were in there.

"What are you doing?"

He turned back to her, a pair of her tights in his hand.

Wait a minute.

He wasn't going to . . .

Oh, but he was. Rhett crawled on the bed and lifted her head so he could put the tights behind her and around her jaw. For a second, she felt a flash of anxiety, but before he gagged her, he kissed her softly. "Trust me."

Unable to speak, her mouth thick with saliva, she nodded. She'd never been gagged before, but it had certainly robbed her of the obnoxious need to snort with laughter.

Rhett wasted no time in tying off the tights so that she couldn't open her mouth. It was a strange sensation, not nearly as vulnerable as she would have thought. It was actually sort of . . . freeing. She didn't have to say anything. She could focus on the pressure of the spandex pushing against her lips and breathing through her nose. It calmed her down, and when Rhett slid his hand up her thigh and under her T-shirt, his lips caressing her neck with soft, seductive kisses, she had no desire to laugh. Instead, she sighed, relaxing back against her mattress.

Rhett brushed over her thighs, her belly, the underside of her breast, his other hand pulling stray hairs gently free that had been caught under the tights. His callused thumb moved across her cheek, tracing her mouth under the tights, his eyes on her facial features, like he was studying each inch of her.

There was something almost worshipful about the way he touched her, like she was fragile. Or beautiful.

She suddenly remembered that legally he was her husband.

It was a very, very strange thought.

The pillow had fallen off her chest and he hovered over her, his bare chest tantalizingly close. He was muscular, like any man on a pit crew should be, free of tattoos and covered in a light dusting of caramel chest hair. Shawn wanted to touch him, both to explore that hard plane, and to keep a slight barrier between them. To hold on to control.

But he clearly sensed that because when her hands came up, he shook his head, cupping them to push them back down. "No. Lie still."

The question was, did she do as he told her, or did she do what she wanted? Given that she would still be chortling like a donkey if he hadn't taken charge of the situation, she realized that while it went totally against her every instinct as a competitor and an independent businesswoman, there might be some value in doing as he said. At least this once, to see if it brought her a different experience, if it allowed her to experience pleasure from a new perspective.

So she left her hands at her sides where he had placed them and waited further instruction. The very idea of that actually brought a rush of warm desire to her inner thighs, the heat pooling deep in her womb. His hard masculinity trapped her beneath him, and though she couldn't feel it, she knew his erection was mere inches from her. Part of her expected him to shove her shirt up and push into her hard, claiming her before she changed her mind.

But that wasn't what he did. Instead he ran his hand up her thighs, slowly and steadily, slipped under her shirt to brush over her breast, then descended again. He caressed her inner thigh, but never moved over the front of her panties, and after three passes up and down the length of her body, Shawn no longer felt the urge to laugh. His feathery touch was pulling goose bumps from her skin, and she quieted down, her body relaxing as he coaxed a simple awareness of her body from her. She wanted him to touch her more intimately, to push her panties back and bury his finger deep inside her wet body. That was what she expected, an aggressive dominant approach of going straight for the gold. He would use his finger, then his cock to get her off, and it would be over and done in a hot burst of ten minutes of passion.

That wasn't what he was doing, clearly.

He was taking his time.

And it was driving her nuts.

She couldn't even complain because her mouth was covered.

"Your skin is very soft," he told her, eyes trained on her.

It didn't require an answer, though under usual circumstances, Shawn would have said something in response. She would have most likely made a crack about having a boyish figure or how winter brought on alligator-skin syndrome, both of which would have however unintentionally and however minutely altered the mood, never allowing either of them to fully surrender to pleasure.

It was an interesting realization. As she was forced to lie still, which was not her most coveted or easy position, there was no running commentary of words from her mouth to distract her. There was nothing but her skin and an awareness of her rising desire that she had never experienced before. She could feel the prickle of each goose bump rising on her flesh, hear the soft rush of her breathing out of her nostrils, smell his masculine scent as he lay over her, his knee wedged between her thighs. Rhett played a little with her nipple, just teasing his thumb and forefinger over its hardness, his lips brushing across the delicate flesh under her ear.

When he pinched her nipple, unexpectedly, Shawn was stunned at the sharp kick of desire that she felt acutely in her stillness, her body quiet, able to process in its entirety the sensation of pleasure through the sting. She had never kept her hands at her sides, had never understood that if she did, she would feel the distinct ache in her womb, feel the slow trickle of hot desire easing out of her to soak the front of her panties. Her breathing grew more anxious, and she reveled in the new experience at the same time she started to panic. Involuntarily, her hand came up to push against his chest, to pull off her tights.

Rhett pushed it back down. "Shh. Not yet. Just give me a few more minutes. But if you really want me to stop, I will. I won't hold your hands down."

Did she want him to stop? Given that his thumb was now stroking against the skin at the apex of her thighs, so tantalizingly close to her clitoris, she decided she could keep it together for at least a few minutes. If he didn't tie off her hands, she could also escape. She did trust him.

As long as he didn't demand she crawl across the floor, she was okay with what they were doing. In fact, she was more than okay with it, and that's where the fear sprang from. She wasn't sure she'd ever been quite this aroused from so little actual contact.

"Are you okay with this? I need your permission. Nod your head."

So she nodded her head.

"Good girl."

Rhett kissed her on the lips, the nylon tights between them. It was an odd sensation, one that made her yearn to feel his taste, his tongue inside her. She moaned a little, the sound muffled, her nostrils flaring. Then his thumb slipped under the satin of her panties and slid up and down in her slickness and she arched her head back, closing her hands into tight fists so she didn't move them, reach for him. It felt so odd, to be a non-participant, but more involved and attuned than she had ever been. She wasn't sure how that was possible, but as Rhett massaged up and down her swollen lips with his thumbs, his tongue teasing into her ear, she marveled at that reality. She was agonizingly turned on, and she could already feel an orgasm building, and from what? A few finger strokes? She usually required the launch-to-orbit setting on her vibrator or a man who knew how to use his tongue for extended periods of time.

She didn't come from a single finger, nowhere near her clitoris.

Without realizing she was doing it, she started to squirm, wiggling her hips.

"No moving," he told her, pinching her swollen labia, his stroking ceasing. "Or you won't get my tongue."

Oh, God. Shawn's chest heaved, her breathing anxious and frantic sounding to her own ears as she desperately tried to quiet her body, the thought of his tongue motivating her to follow his directives. If his finger could do this, what could his tongue, his lips, his *teeth* do down there? The thought prompted a rush of liquid desire, soaking over his thumb, trapped by the barrier of her panties. She knew if she looked down, she would see the satin stained with her arousal, and he knew it, too. He was looking at it. He had bent over to study her, pausing to wait for her compliance.

It almost killed her, but she relaxed, letting her legs drop apart, keeping her head back on the bed.

Her reward was him removing his hand entirely. Aghast, she tried to cry out in protest, but the words were lost behind the tights.

But he shook his head in disapproval. "Trust me. Or I'll leave you here like this, wet and aching."

Shawn wasn't sure she could do this. She didn't know how.

But neither did she want to be left alone feeling like she was on the cusp of something, like she was about to be treated to intense satisfaction, only to have it denied to her because she couldn't relinquish control.

It was an ironic paradox and she fought with her emotions, while Rhett startled her by pulling up her T-shirt and gently lifting each of her inert arms through the holes, then lifting it up and over her head, leaving her gloriously free and bare to his gaze.

"See?" he told her. "That's what I was going to do. I wasn't trying to torture you."

Oops. Hey, how was she supposed to know? Shawn felt the cool air of her bedroom on her naked skin, her nipples pert, her breasts rising and falling rapidly with the urgency of her breathing. There was nothing between her and Rhett's gaze, his touch, but the wet scrap of her thong that he had bought and she had worn to torment him. Funny how the tables had been turned.

He peeled the tights back long enough to surprise her with a hot kiss and a plunge of his tongue, before he was gone again, his mouth descending on her breast. She gasped, her eyes fluttering shut, her heels digging in to the bed, her hips squirming again before she realized she wasn't allowed to do that. Knowing he would stop if she did, she immediately stilled her actions, sliding her hands under her ass so she wouldn't be tempted to reach out and claw at his briefs to free his penis.

This time her reward was him reaching down and with both hands, snapping the strap on the side of the thong so that the satin front panel fell away, exposing her entirely to him. That was definitely worth sitting on her hands. The move was so hot she felt her mouth fill with saliva, excitement rushing through her like a shot of whiskey on a cold night.

It was just the beginning. When he bent down, he traced the inside of each of her thighs with his tongue, a teasing caress so close to the core of her desire.

"This is how this works," he murmured against her skin. "You only come once I give you permission. If you're getting too close, you can move your hand to tap my head to let me know you don't have control over yourself and need a pause. But I *will* give permission, and you will come when I think you're ready, so don't worry about that . . . I don't get off on leaving you unsatisfied. I want the opposite."

Shawn wanted to protest that his rules weren't particularly fair, but she didn't want him to withdraw his touch, nor did she want to waste time worrying about particulars when he was essentially promising to bring her to orgasm.

"Nod your head."

So she did, and the minute she did, she knew it was a

delicious decision. His tongue shifted to her pussy, his fingers gently tugging her lips apart so he could lick her deeply and thoroughly.

Shawn almost came, but she remembered the rules and managed to tap him on the shoulder, frantic and disappointed all at once. She didn't want to fail. She didn't want to have to move. She wanted to play by his rules and win the game.

Rhett stopped, his eyebrows raised as he stared at her over her pubis. "So soon? Really? Damn, Shawn."

Her cheeks flushed with the heat of her embarrassment. She didn't like to disappoint. So she slowed her breathing, pulling her knees in closer so that the arousal wasn't quite so intense, and relaxed her head back. When she had control, she returned her hand to behind her backside so he would know she could again accept his plunging tongue without careening into an unallowable orgasm.

It was then, as he first began to use two thumbs to massage her lips up and down that she wondered what the punishment would be if she did accidentally orgasm. And then she wondered at her sheer excitement at the thought of him taking his palm to her bottom and spanking her in retribution. Oh, God. Shawn fought to stay in control, fought to keep her body relaxed. Even if the punishment was sweet, she couldn't unless it was purely an accident. She had to obey.

She had to obey.

It was the dirtiest, sexiest, hottest thought she'd ever had.

One that almost made her come.

But she wrangled herself back from the edge by biting her bottom lip behind the tights so hard that she felt the wet trickle of blood. The sting distracted her enough to prevent her from rushing over the edge too soon.

It was a wise choice, because in the next second, Rhett gripped her thighs and split her legs apart, his tongue flickering over her clitoris for the first time.

"Mmm," he said. "So pretty. So swollen. You're doing so well, Shawn. I'm very, very pleased."

That shouldn't sound nearly as exciting as it did.

But when he licked her clitoris again, before dipping his tongue inside her, she didn't care about whether it made sense or not. She was too busy yanking her hand out to smack wildly at him so he would stop.

It was too late. His tongue was lazily lapping at her, and by the time he started to lift his head, she was screaming behind the nylon, and gripping his head with both hands so he wouldn't stop. She came hard and fast, cramming his tongue into her with a ferocity that startled her. It was a tight, unsatisfying orgasm, a wild desperate constriction of her tight inner muscles, a single ice cube on a blistering summer day. It momentarily cooled her, but then simply left her wanting much, much more.

Plus, she had broken his rules and she knew it.

Instantly, as her body shuddered to its final completion, her pussy still aching and wet, she let go of his head and fell back, afraid. Not afraid of him hurting her, but that the punishment might be that he would deny her his erection plunging into her. Because she knew that she really, really needed that. That she would actually possibly beg if it was required.

This night could not end until he had filled her to capacity.

RHETT wasn't surprised that Shawn had come. Exactly what he had wanted had happened—she had let go entirely. She had let go through allowing him to control the situation, and it was the hottest thing he'd ever seen. He had a steel grip on his own desire, but his cock was throbbing and the taste of her was on his tongue. He wanted her, but her wanting him was even better.

But if he wanted to continue the way they'd begun,

which he definitely did, he couldn't just sink inside her and stroke them both to satisfaction. He had to follow through.

Knowing she needed some fresh air, he pulled the tights down around her neck. She gulped in air and before he could say anything, she was speaking an achingly sweet apology, her eyes wide in the dimly light room.

"I'm sorry, I'm sorry, I didn't mean to . . . it's just I haven't had sex in a while, and it just came over me and by the time I realized it, it was too late and I already was, and then I didn't want to ruin it, so I grabbed—"

Rhett covered her mouth again. "Shh. I know." He brushed her damp hair back off her forehead. She was flushed, eyes darkened still with her desire. "But you do need to be punished. Do you agree with me? Do you need to be punished?"

She knew what he was asking. If she said yes, he would continue the way he had started. If she said no, he wouldn't. Even if she said no, he would still make love to her, but in a more traditional sense. He wasn't a masochist, nor did he want to leave her unsatisfied. But he would prefer it if she said yes. He would prefer it deep down into the very depths of his soul, and as the seconds ticked by, the agony of the wait gripped him in the balls and his throbbing cock, still trapped behind the cotton of his briefs. He hadn't realized how much he had wanted this, wanted Shawn, until it all rested on what happened next.

Wanting to hear her speak her desire, Rhett fully undid the gag hanging around her neck, tugging it until it fell to the mattress beside her ear.

"Do you? Answer me."

If she said yes, then he was certain Shawn was absolutely the perfect woman for him.

"Yes," she whispered, her chest heaving, the sweet scent of her desire rising between them. She swallowed hard. "Yes, I need to be punished."

Rhett felt a massive swell of satisfaction and desire, intermingling with each other. Fuck, yeah. She was on board, and he was going to make her damn glad she was.

Then she added, with a boldness he wouldn't have expected of her at this point, "I promise I won't come again."

That was possibly the best news he'd ever gotten. He kissed her, a deep, worshipful kiss, his palm cupping her cheek, the feel of her mouth opening for him, tugging at him in a deep, intrinsic way.

"That's perfect," he told her. "Exactly what I wanted to hear." He skimmed a hand down low, over the strip of dusky blond hair covering her soft folds. She sighed.

"You're so beautiful, Shawn."

She was. He liked her like this, flushed and dewy, color rising above her breasts, her lips parted on a sigh. He also liked her laughing, that saucy spark in her eye, that devilish glint. And he was going to like her on her knees.

So he pulled his hand away. "On your knees, facing the wall. Hold on to the headboard."

Her eyes widened as the reality of his words sank in and she felt the loss of his touch. He thought she had the courage to go through with it, but he wasn't sure. He was asking her to take a total leap of faith, to trust him. A man she admittedly didn't know that well.

But he was her husband.

Though he wasn't going to use that title now. He knew how far to push, and bringing that up would cause her to bristle. She was still an independent and feisty woman who ran a business. She would have a point where she would balk, and likely that would be it.

While she pressed her lips together and slowly rolled over onto her stomach, her gaze darting back at him over her shoulder, Rhett came up on his knees, debating whether stripping his briefs off would reassure her or scare her. He didn't want her to think in any way that he would actually hurt her. So he left them in place for now and leaned over her shoulder and murmured, "I really won't hurt you,

Shawn. I'll never hurt you. And you can always say stop at any time."

Just to show her he was serious, that he would always be respectful, he skimmed her hair off her shoulders onto her back and trailed his fingers down the bumps of her spine, skimming her hips, and the perfect curve of her ass. Then he gave her a light smack. She jumped a little, but before he could get a second swat in, she was dragging herself up into the position he had demanded—on her knees, hands gripping the headboard.

Thick saliva filled his mouth and for a second, his vision actually went black as the enormity of her submission hit him. Then he smacked her perfect, tight ass, harder this time.

A tiny gasp flew out of her mouth, and her knuckles whitened as she gripped the bed more thoroughly. With his left hand on the small of her back, Rhett moved one knee in front of her, the other behind, so he could get the perfect motion. With each smack, he took it a little harder, the slap of his palm on her skin a loud crack of satisfaction in the quiet night. With each spank she let out a little cry and jerked forward from the momentum of his swing. But she always tilted her ass back up for him ever so slightly, whether she was even aware she was doing it or not. She took it, and came back for more, until her backside was a stinging red, and he couldn't go much harder without leaving her with more than a lingering soreness.

Caressing the apple-smooth ass cheeks, he leaned forward and whispered gruffly, "Is that enough punishment, or do you deserve more?"

Shawn rested her head on her arm against the wall and gazed back at him with eyes limpid with desire, her breathing hitched, words a strangled whisper. "That's for you to decide, not me."

And with that, he knew that she was absolute perfection, and everything he could have ever asked for in a woman.

CHAPTER
NINE

SHAWN stared back at Rhett, her excitement and confusion and shock at her own response all swirling together and leaving her waiting in breathless anticipation for his next move. She didn't understand why she was allowing his dominance, why she was so titillated at the idea of him allowing her pleasure, as opposed to her taking it freely, but she was. Rhett ran his thumb over her bottom lip, over the laceration her teeth had left when she'd torn into the flesh to prevent her orgasm.

"You're right. It is up to me whether you need more punishment. But I think that shows I can stop here for now." Teasing his hand over her bottom he slipped between her cheeks and stroked into her soft heat. "But stay in this position."

It wasn't an order, exactly, it was more of the way it was. He was in charge, and holy shit, she liked it. She did. She had of course in the past wanted the men she'd been with to take pleasure in sex with her, but she had never wanted to please them, exactly. The difference was subtle, but profound. She wanted to please Rhett, give him the greatest satisfaction possible.

The feelings were scary and intense, but the overlying pleasure was so great, her aching body so desperate for the feel of him, that she thought she might agree to do just about anything. The palm of his hand on her ass had stung, the pain a little more acute with each strike, but she had enjoyed it, no question. It had made her more aware of her skin, her body, the bounce of her breasts and the tightness of her clitoris. Everything he did made her feel as if she were discovering nerve endings and depths of her body that she had never known existed before.

Clinging to the top of the bed, she moaned as he skillfully used his fingers to stimulate her even more, two fingers going deep inside before dragging down between her legs, soaking her with her own desire, before one of the two fingers slipped inside her backside. The unexpected invasion caused her to jerk slightly, but she bit her lip again to cut off the protest. She wasn't allowed to protest or she would be punished again. Only if he was hurting her.

Which he wasn't.

It felt . . . decadent. The tightness of the passage gave his strokes greater impact and she relaxed into the touch, a small moan escaping her mouth. Just when she got used to the feeling, he was gone, back up to tweak her clitoris with his other hand, before pushing into her pussy again, then slipping down and back into her ass. Shawn closed her eyes, her head lolling onto her arm. "Oh, God," she murmured. "You're . . . ah."

The incomplete thought wasn't worth finishing. She just panted through the intense pleasure, her inner muscles starting to quiver from all his attentions. She wanted to come, but didn't, knowing it would be better if she waited until his cock was in her. Which would surely be soon. He had to be as turned on as she was. But she could still feel the brush of his briefs on her thigh, indicating he was still dressed and had control that she couldn't even comprehend. She started to claw at the headboard, arching her back and thrusting her hips back to take his finger deeper.

This time he didn't correct her. He let her go at it. "You're fucking my fingers, aren't you?"

She nodded, beyond embarrassment.

"Would you like my cock instead?" His voice was gruff, and he was already tearing the remains of her panties down her thigh where they'd gotten trapped by her bent knees.

She nodded again. Did she ever. It was probably the stupidest question she'd ever heard.

He removed his touch and she could hear him removing his underwear, his legs brushing against her bare backside. Anticipation had her limp, resting on her hands.

"Let me hear you say it," he ordered.

"Yes. I want your cock." The words made her flush, but she didn't hesitate to say them. She had to if she wanted him inside her. She knew that.

The reward was feeling the press of his heat, the smooth tip of his penis at the entrance to her vagina, a teasingly light touch.

"Are you on birth control or do I need a condom?"

Oh, right, protection. "I'm on the pill," she murmured, swallowing hard.

"Good. I want to feel all of you." Suddenly her head was jerked back as he yanked on her hair. "Sit up. I don't like your face hidden."

Tears rose in her eyes from the pain of having the roots of her hair pulled, and she didn't see how sitting up meant he could see her any better since she was facing the wall and not him. But she didn't protest.

Because there was something undeniably sexy about what was happening between them. It was like she'd been having sex in the dark her entire adult life and now the lights had been turned on. It was sex in high def.

His hand twisted into her hair, keeping a tight grip on it, her shoulders arching back toward him as he pushed into her with one single thrust. Shawn groaned, the unexpected invasion an arousing agony that almost brought her to climax.

"Oh, shit," she whispered because it was overwhelming.

His left hand covered hers on the headboard, his right in firm command of her head, but not hurting her, his hips aligned with hers as he rested deep inside her. She could feel his throbbing heat, could smell the saltiness of his sweat, hear the sharp strain of his labored breathing. He was maintaining his control, and to prove she could as well, she kept herself still, the only movement the involuntary flexing of her vaginal muscles onto his cock.

His mouth was close to her ear and when he spoke, she shivered. It didn't seem like a time for conversation, but then again, nothing with Rhett was what she was used to.

"Just so we understand, when we're not in bed, you're the one in charge, Shawn. You tell me what you want, where you want me to be, how you want me to act. I'll wash dishes, take out the trash, be the perfect husband in public, give you your space in private, whatever you decide. You call the shots. But here, in bed, I'm in charge. You have no say. You get to ask no questions and you have to obey, but I promise you, you'll never go to sleep unsatisfied. Do you understand?"

A shiver rushed up her spine and she swallowed hard, his words sinking as deeply as his cock into her and she nodded. "Yes," she whispered, because she couldn't say no. If she said no, he would pull out of her and leave her with the most profound sense of emptiness she'd ever experienced.

When he began to stroke inside her, she knew it was the right answer to give. She couldn't imagine not having this, him, pumping into her with a perfect rhythm, his hands dropping to her hips so he could pull her back against him with each thrust, the slap of their bodies ringing in the room. Each push came so fast that she barely had time to breathe, none to moan, her eyes rolling back in her head as she struggled to keep her body from shattering.

Rhett leaned forward and skimmed her hair back from her ear and cheek with callused fingers, his rhythm never breaking. "You can come now," he told her, and his voice was softer than she expected, almost worshipful, like she had pleased him.

"Thank you," she said most sincerely, because she couldn't contain it any longer. She let go, and immediately burst into the most intense orgasm she'd ever experienced. "Oh, God!"

It was all-consuming, and Shawn cried out again and again as the waves of satisfaction rolled over her, her awareness of her own body, her own pleasure, the most acute it had ever been. This wasn't just an orgasm, this was something else, something she didn't understand, and she felt like Rhett was ripping something raw and elemental and powerful from her. As the climax quieted, she blinked, and felt the tear roll down her cheek as she sucked in deep, ragged breaths.

Oh, God was right.

RHETT had never enjoyed a woman's orgasm as much as he had Shawn's. The fact that she had waited until he gave permission, then literally came thirty seconds after he granted it was the hottest thing he'd ever experienced. She was exactly what he wanted—strong and able to control herself, her willingness to submit more arousing because she wasn't normally passive.

He had introduced her to the game, and so far, she seemed to find it to her liking.

Her tight pussy gripped his cock, massaging him through the throes of her orgasm, wet heat surrounding him. It was harder to maintain his own control with her, because she felt so amazing, but he had already discovered that the harder he had to work to maintain control, the more electric his whole body felt.

When she shuddered to the end of her climax, he tilted her chin slightly so he could see her, and he was shocked to see that her eyes were wet with tears, a single streak sliding over the flushed skin of her cheek. Her lip was swollen, the dried blood in stark contrast to her normally silken perfection.

The last thing he wanted to do was actually hurt her. Worried, he asked quickly, "Are you okay?"

She shook her head slightly. "What just happened?" she asked, her voice trembling.

Then he understood. He hadn't hurt her. She had just felt what he had, that something had shifted between them. That their connection was strong, elemental, intimate.

He didn't give her an answer. He just started to move again, watching her face to see how quickly the needs of her body would crowd out her confused thoughts. It didn't take long. Within a minute or two, she was sighing in renewed pleasure, her shoulders relaxing. Rhett took a slow, languorous pace, closing his eyes and allowing himself to experience the full feeling of her body open for him, for him only.

When he felt her responding, wetness soaking him, her inner passage tightening, he didn't want her to fight it. "Yeah, that's it, baby, come for me again. I love to feel you come."

Her orgasm was quieter this time, soft sighs and loose hips, and Rhett allowed himself to indulge in the satisfaction of having gotten her off three times, her second time so intense it had brought tears to her eyes. Because of him. He had pleasured her that thoroughly. He thrust harder. She moaned a little in ecstasy. She was his to command in this bed, yet the thing he wanted more than anything was for her to be satisfied, and that she was, and so relatively easily, had him pounding harder into her willing flesh.

This was only the start of the pleasure he could give her.

Still maintaining a tight grip on his own desire, because he never allowed himself full loss of control, Rhett exploded in her with a hot pulsing orgasm, gripping her hips tightly.

Hell, yeah.

He stopped moving, letting his heart rate slow down. When he gradually withdrew, he ground his teeth together in both satisfaction and the need for more. But it was enough for now. Shawn wasn't ready for more.

Still on his knees, he leaned over her and ran his hands down her arms to where she was still gripping the bed. Rhett pulled her up, massaging her hands, pressing his chest to her back so they were perfectly aligned, flesh to flesh, his lips on the nape of her neck. Bringing their entwined hands together in front of her stomach, he breathed in the scent of her, holding her close, enjoying the feeling of sexual satisfaction, the knowledge that he had been granted an unexpected and extraordinary gift.

The next six months were going to be amazing.

"You tired?" he asked her.

"Yes."

He kissed her cheek. "Then let's get some sleep."

He released her so she could settle down onto the bed. Her hands were shaking as she pulled the bedding they had destroyed into some semblance of order.

Handing her the T-shirt he had torn off her earlier, Rhett knew she was feeling vulnerable, so he stood up and went to get her a new pair of panties. He found a pair that looked like simple everyday-use cotton and handed them to her. She met his gaze, her cheeks pink, but then she looked away, already in her sleep shirt. He wanted to sleep naked, but he didn't think she was in the right place for that, and he wanted to respect her feelings.

"Can I get you a drink or anything? I'm running to the bathroom."

"Water would be great." Shawn lifted her knees and her bottom to slide on the new panties, and Rhett caught a visual reminder of his orgasm, a wet trail down her inner thigh.

She clearly wasn't intending to go clean it off, and he felt a hot punch of possessiveness. He liked to see his come rolling down her leg. It made her his. His wife.

Unnerved himself, Rhett moved out of the room abruptly.

In the bathroom, he cleaned himself off and stared at himself in the mirror, the harsh fluorescent lighting forcing him to squint. He was going too far. He already knew it. He was attaching.

He frowned at his reflection, hands on the smooth marble countertop, the cold a sweet relief to the heat of the bedroom. This should be a warning. He should dial back on the sex with Shawn, take a more vanilla route with her.

Instead, all he wanted to do was go back in the bedroom and start on her all over again until she was quivering with want and coming at his command.

But when he returned with a glass of water for her, she was already asleep.

He tried to tell himself it was for the best, but he didn't believe it.

CHAPTER
TEN

SHAWN woke up with a start, hot under the covers and desperate for a drink. She'd been dreaming about being chased by a tiger, who had backed her into a corner and bared his teeth at her. Heart racing, she rolled onto her side and realized why it was so unusually warm. Her body was being heated by Rhett's, who was sleeping a mere two inches away. She could feel the warmth radiating off him like a toaster oven. The sun was starting to come up, a sliver of light spreading across the carpet of the bedroom floor.

Swallowing the thick lump that was in her throat, she pushed her hair off her face and studied him. She didn't know if he was naked below the waist, but he was on top, his arms both out from under the comforter, his head turned toward her. She felt a tender urge to reach out and stroke his cheek, his jaw, but she squashed it, her feelings too muddled. Last night she had done things, said things, allowed things that she didn't understand and she felt vulnerable, stripped bare.

When he shifted a little, she quickly looked away, afraid he would wake up. There was a glass of water on her nightstand, clearly brought to her by Rhett. She didn't remember falling asleep, just that when he'd left the room, she'd been relieved. Relieved to be back in protective cotton, the covers over her, her cheeks itchy from crying, her inner thighs hot and sticky. She hadn't been able to get up, afraid her legs wouldn't work, afraid she might actually start crying in earnest.

A week ago, she had woken up alone, happy, healthy, content for the most part, heir apparent to the speedway, a single, confident businesswoman.

Now she was . . . what? A wife? A submissive? Terrified? Exhilarated? More sexually satisfied than she had ever been?

She didn't know. All she knew was that last night she had surrendered to him and enjoyed it.

"Morning," he murmured from behind her, his hand coming up to rest on her shoulder, caressing down her arm.

Shawn fought the urge to jerk away. Or worse, to give in and turn to him and beg him to take her again the way he had the night before.

"Morning," she managed back, staring at the wall before reaching for the glass. The movement forced his hand to fall away from her. "Thanks for the water."

"You're welcome."

The second she settled back on the bed, he was touching her again. Acutely aware of every inch of her body, Shawn's heart started to race, and not in a good way.

Rhett kissed the side of her head. "Damn it, I have to go to work."

Thank God. "That sucks," she lied as she glanced back at him. "Do you want some coffee and eggs or anything?"

"I can fix myself some coffee. You stay in bed, beautiful."

The bed creaked as he sat up and she struggled to find fault with him. He was considerate. And naked. Very, very naked. With an incredibly tight set of buns. He turned. And a very erect, above average penis. No wonder she was sore this morning. Not that any lingering awareness prevented her from wanting him to pound her again.

She forced her gaze upward again, aware he was speaking and she had no idea what he was saying. "What?"

The corner of his mouth turned up in a smirk. "Distracted you, didn't it? Don't worry, there's plenty of time for you to check it out when I get home."

Home. Ugh.

He seemed to realize what he'd said because he added, "Unless you have other plans tonight."

She shook her head. At the moment, she wasn't sure if that were a good thing or not.

"Good." He came back to the bed—still naked, hello—and leaned over her to kiss her fully on the mouth. "Want me to bring home Chinese food? I'll be back around seven."

"Sure. Thanks. Have a good day at work." Could she be any more inane? Could this be any more bizarre?

"Thanks." He ran his finger across her bottom lip, where she had torn into the flesh the night before, and then gave her a soft kiss. "Last night was very sexy. I'm glad you enjoyed yourself."

She nodded. Apparently she had not only given complete sexual control over to him, she'd become mute.

"Alright, I'm outta here. See you tonight, Scarlett."

And that made everything just all that much worse.

Shawn lay in bed for fifteen long minutes, afraid to move, afraid he might come back into the bedroom, until she finally heard him go out the side door, the screen slamming behind him.

She heaved a sigh of relief and jumped out of bed and virtually ran for the shower, locking the door behind her, something she never did in her own house. Turning on the water, she didn't even wait for it to heat before she jumped in, intent on washing the scent and feel of him off her skin. Using a loofah, she scrubbed every nook and cranny on her body, cheeks burning as she remembered the night before, wondering how she could have let him do those things to her.

Wondering how she could survive if she didn't let him do it again.

When she got out she was toweling up and feeling more calm. Coffee would help even more.

Then she heard a knock on her front door. That better be a Jehovah's Witness leaving a pamphlet or she was going to scream. The knocking continued as she pulled on her yoga pants and a sweatshirt. Rushing through the living room, she saw it was Charity and Harley standing on her front step.

Let the fun continue.

"Where the hell have you been?" Charity asked. "It's colder than tea bagging in ice water out here."

Shawn blinked, both at that image and at the uncertainty as to why her friend was pushing past her into the living room on a Sunday morning. Charity wasn't exactly known as a morning person.

"We were at the side door, but for some reason the doorknob is locked, so we couldn't get in. You never lock your door."

"Rhett must have locked it," she said, running her hands through her damp hair. "He left for work and he doesn't have a key yet."

Talk about it like it was normal. Make it normal.

Charity grinned. "Dude, you're insane, do you know that? I never thought you had it in you."

Harley looked more worried than anything else as she closed the front door behind them, the blustery February wind cutting through Shawn. She wanted coffee and a pair of socks. "So what brings you two by today? Do you want some coffee?"

"We're here to help you plan your wedding party, remember? We made plans yesterday."

"Oh, shit, that's right." She had totally forgotten about Harley's offer to help with her fake Valentine's Day love-fest celebration. Gag. "My brain is fried."

"You're probably running on no sleep. I'm surprised you can actually walk after two nights of Mr. Wet Spot." Charity flopped on her sofa.

Shawn tried not to blush, but it was an epic failure. "So how do we plan a wedding party? Not that I really want a wedding party, but I'm sure Rhett's mother already hates me, so I don't want to make it worse. He said she'll be hurt if we don't have a party."

"You have to have a party of some sort," Charity told her. "Come on. How many times do you get married? Twice, maybe three times tops. The very first one at least should warrant a little boogying down."

"I think this is it for me," Shawn said truthfully. There was no way she wanted to do this again once she and Rhett got their divorce a year from now. Then again, when would this bizarre set of circumstances ever present themselves again? "I'm putting some coffee on."

"The whole house smells like coffee already," Harley said, following her into the kitchen. "Do you have an automatic coffeemaker?"

"No." But she had a *husband*. Who in addition to giving her three orgasms, left hot coffee in two thermoses on the kitchen counter, a note next to them.

"Hot coffee for you. XO R"

XO? Hugs and kisses? Shawn studied the scrawl of his handwriting and tried to interpret the meaning behind it. He hadn't known there would be anyone there to witness the note, so why would he write that?

Her head hurt. Her chest hurt. Her cooter hurt.

If this was marriage, it blew donkey balls.

"Ah, that's so sweet," was Harley's opinion.

Donkey balls were sweet?

Oh, she meant the note. "Yes. Yes, it is." Because that's what she was supposed to say. And it was sweet. How could she argue that it wasn't?

"Do you ever wonder if Rhett has an ulterior motive?" Charity asked, joining them in the small kitchen.

"Charity!" Her twin squawked, clearly appalled. "It's a love-at-first-sight thing! It happens!"

Probably not, but the truth was a lot less shiny.

"What kind of ulterior motive could he possibly have?" Shawn asked Charity, actually feeling a little insulted. How nice to hear that her friend thought no guy would fall head over ass for her.

"Maybe he thinks the track is worth more than it is. Maybe he's after money and sponsorships." Charity shrugged. "I'm not trying to be a dick, but you have to admit, this is just cray-cray. Totally out of left field for you."

"He signed a prenup before we got married on Friday. He can't touch the track. He doesn't get anything." Except the hundred grand she'd promised him. "Don't be so cynical. Maybe I was just ready."

"Ready for what? To marry the first guy who asked you?"

"Charity . . ." Harley said in a soft voice, the warning clear.

Shawn felt herself bristling, but she beat it back. The truth was, if either of the twins had done what she just had, she would be concerned herself. However, she suspected she would be a bit more tactful than suggesting a man had married her for money. Or that she was so desperate she'd grab the first male to show interest and get hitched.

"Seriously, Charity, I'm going to pretend that what you just said wasn't nearly as rude as it sounded. I think it is possible that I'm smart enough not to just marry any man who asks me. If I wasn't, I would have eloped at fourteen with Bryan Johnson when he told me he'd marry me if I blew him."

"Was that what Rhett offered?" Harley said, in a rare comedic moment for her.

Shawn laughed. "Something like that."

"Wait, you blew Bryan Johnson?"

"No! That is not what I meant!" Shawn went into the cupboard for a mug. She clearly needed her coffee. Now. "I wasn't blowing anyone at fourteen." In fact, she wasn't blowing anyone now. That had not entered into their bed sport the night before, which Shawn found curious. In her experience, men were forever trying to wave their pecker in her face, and yet Rhett hadn't at all. He had spent the majority of the night focusing on her.

Hmm. That was interesting.

"So how many people are coming to the party?" Harley asked, leaning on the counter as Shawn unscrewed one of the thermoses.

Good question. "Well, Rhett has seven sisters and a brother, plus all their spouses." Though, truthfully, she had no idea if they all lived in the Charlotte area or not. "Plus sixteen nieces and nephews. His parents. My mom and my brother and his wife. You two. Debbie, Linda, and John, who have all been working at the track for years. Rhett's fellow crew members. How many is that?"

"I think we're at forty-seven," Harley said.

"Holy crap." Shawn poured coffee into a mug that read "If only Mondays were as easy as I am." The mug had been funnier a week ago, she had to admit. "That's a lot of people for a small party."

"You always wanted a big family," Charity said. "It looks like you have one now."

Except it wasn't real. Shawn bit her lip and took a sip. She realized that someone was knocking on the side door. "Okay, now who is that? Eve is at the track today, so it can't be her."

"I'll get it," Harley offered. The minute she opened the door, a gust of wind and an older woman rushed in.

Arms instantly enveloped Harley. "Honey, it's so good to meet you. I'm your momma-in-law."

Oh, God.

Harley automatically hugged her back as Rhett's mother continued, "Now I can't say I'm thrilled that you got married so suddenlike and at the courthouse, but you know what? I say who cares when what really matters is that my youngest has found the right woman for him." She pulled back. "Let me look at you, Shawn. Oh, you're just too cute. Exactly Rhett's type."

Shawn coughed, not sure whether to be amused or offended. Harley sputtered a little, her head shaking.

"Oh, I'm not Shawn."

"I am," Shawn volunteered, raising her hand a little and really wishing she were wearing a bra. "It's so nice to meet you, Mrs. Ford."

"Oh." Rhett's mother swung her view from Harley to her. "You're Shawn?" she asked, incredulous. "Oh, goodness, well, of course. It's just you're not Rhett's usual type." Then she laughed. "Of course, he didn't marry any of those girls, did he?"

Shawn laughed weakly. Except that he hadn't intended to marry her either until she'd offered him money. So girls like Harley were normally his type, huh? Petite, blond, natural-looking. Clearly sweet, clearly passive. Unlike her. She was tall, her figure more athletic than traditionally feminine, her hair a low-maintenance, tousled shoulder-length mess. She couldn't be bothered to flat-iron it or curl it. Or really even cut it all that often. Nor was she particularly passive. At least, not generally speaking.

The memory of Rhett spanking her popped into her head and she shoved it aside. So she'd been passive in bed. What of it?

She was not going to feel inadequate because she was independent and something of an adult tomboy. Hadn't she come to terms with that self-esteem crap twenty years ago?

So she moved away from the counter and toward Rhett's mother. "Come in, come in. Let me take your coat."

"Oh, thanks, hon."

Shawn found herself enveloped in a hug before being handed a basket. "I brought you some muffins. I know, it's not much, but I didn't have a lot of notice." She wagged her finger at Shawn and gave her a rueful look.

"Thank you, Mrs. Ford." Shawn took the basket and set it on the counter.

"Oh, Lord, call me Sandy. Technically, we're both Mrs. Ford now."

Oh, God, she was, wasn't she? Wait. She didn't have to change her name. That would be stupid, because then she'd just have to change it back in a year. She was still Shawn Hamby and always would be. Feeling a profound sense of relief, she gestured to her friends. "This is Harley and Charity. They're here to help with planning the wedding party."

"Nice to meet you girls. Perfect timing then!" She peeled off her coat and handed it to Shawn. "Unless you don't want your mother-in-law's opinion."

"No, of course, I would love it. I have no idea what I'm doing." That was the truth, without a doubt. "Would you like some coffee?"

"I'd love some."

Shawn poured coffee for everyone, then took out the muffins and plated them, and they all retreated into the living room. Sinking into an easy chair, she marveled at the sheer oddity of the circumstance. She was sitting here planning her wedding reception with a woman she'd never met. Her husband's mother. If only Pops could see her now, he'd realize what a foolish idea his will had been. They were making a sheer mockery out of the institution of marriage.

"Rhett's father and I have been married for thirty-six years," she started.

Oh, and that made her feel better. Not.

"Congratulations, that's wonderful."

"The house is a little empty these days, but it's good to know all my kids are married themselves and happy and healthy. I wasn't sure about Rhett, you know. He's always been so serious."

"He's no stand-up comedian," Shawn agreed. "But the good thing is he always knows what he wants."

Charity coughed into her hand.

Shawn shot her a sideways glare. She knew exactly what Charity was envisioning, and damn it, she was right.

"That is true. So where were you thinking of having the party? And when?"

"Valentine's Day. Rhett thought it was . . . romantic." She almost choked on her tongue, but she forced the words out. Fortunately, her blush could be taken as that of a new bride, and not the lying poseur that she was. "I have no idea where to have it. I think it's going to be about fifty people, and given it's winter, we can't exactly have an outdoor barbecue in the yard."

"What about a hall or a restaurant?" Charity asked.

"That sounds expensive to rent." She was already shelling out a hundred grand to be Rhett's wife, she wasn't going to drop twenty K on a wedding reception on top of it. The point was to be financially solvent in the end, not bankrupt after going through all of this. "I was thinking wherever it is, people can bring potluck instead of wedding gifts. I want it to be casual, fun." Cheap. Over.

"What about the track?" Rhett's mother asked. "Hamby Speedway has plenty of room indoors, right? It wouldn't be glamorous, but it's free and it seems fitting."

She had a point. Plus the publicity would be phenomenal. "Hm. That's a great idea. I think it could work."

"It's so . . . dirty," Charity said, in horror. "It's a dirt track."

"We're not talking about throwing a party on the track itself," Shawn protested. "We have a party room for corporate and media events." It could work.

"I think it's a great idea," Harley reassured her.

Charity looked skeptical, but then again she always did.

But once her twin pulled out a notebook and started making a to-do list, Charity seemed to realize this was happening with or without her opinion, so she might as well add it. Which was good, because ultimately Shawn found she had no opinion herself. It was more overwhelming than anything else.

Frankly, she'd never been the little girl who fantasized about her wedding, and she was no great party planner either. She was more of a show-up-with-a-bottle-of-wine-and-hope-someone-did-all-the-work kind of person. Given that this wasn't even real, and she was already feeling guilty for essentially duping her friends and family, she really didn't care whether they used peonies versus roses.

"So I'll call the catering company for linens, Charity is handling the flowers, and Mrs. Ford is going to organize the food. Shawn, what is your mom going to want to do?"

"Drink." Shawn shrugged. "No, seriously, I don't think she will want to be involved in any way, but I'll ask her."

"She's not going to want to be involved?" Mrs. Ford looked horrified. "Why ever not? You're her only daughter."

"Mom is kind of a free spirit. Mostly my grandparents raised me. She's happy for me." Which wasn't even true. When Shawn had called her to give her the news, her mother had told her she was an idiot to get married and tie herself emotionally and legally to a man who would most likely screw her over in the end. It hadn't been a helpful chat. "She doesn't like details," she added.

"Neither do you," Harley pointed out. "It's like pulling teeth to get you to offer an opinion on cake flavors or a décor theme color."

"Which is why I can't fault her for it." Hey, she could admit that she was missing a craft gene. She had no interest in hand-cutting decorative paper signs for the milk-and-cookies bar Harley had thought would be supercute. She agreed. The concept was supercute. But that didn't mean she wanted to cut shit.

Nor did she think Rhett was really the milk-and-cookies type. He seemed more like whiskey and caramel sauce. But then again, what the hell did she know?

"Don't worry about it. You're the bride. We'll handle everything," Rhett's mother assured her. "I have six daughters living here in Charlotte. We'll knock this out in a few hours, and with Charity and Harley's help, you won't need to worry about a thing."

Shawn would think that was marvelous if it wasn't for the fact that she felt guilty as hell. "Thank you. Y'all don't know how much I appreciate this, seriously. I couldn't do this without your help."

"Should we do a slide show? You know, like pictures of you both growing up, then pictures of you together?"

Shawn gave Charity a look that hopefully conveyed how totally freaking stupid that was. "That's going to be a short slide show. To my knowledge, there is only one photo of Rhett and me together, and it's not one I would ever show anyone."

"Oh." Charity made a purring sound, tossing her blond hair over her shoulder. "Naughty, naughty."

Really? Harley was about to find out what life as a single birth was like because Shawn was going to kill Charity. "I don't mean *that*! Gawd. My mother-in-law is here." It may not be real, but it still held all the trauma of the title for her. "I just meant it's the shot from the courthouse when we got married and the lighting sucks. I look translucent and Rhett is scowling at the photographer."

"That's just the way he is," Mrs. Ford said, waving her hand. "But you make a good point. We need to have a photo shoot done with the two of you."

Shawn sat up straighter. "Oh no! That's not what I meant. We don't need to do that. It's fine. I'm not very photogenic."

"Oh, good grief. Of course, we're doing it. I'll call a friend of a friend and we'll have it set up for this week."

Well, if Shawn got her lack of organization from her mother, it was safe to say that Rhett got his heavy-handedness from his mother.

"Now what can I get the two of you for a wedding gift?"

"Oh, nothing, really . . . I mean, you're giving me all this help with the party. That's honestly enough. We don't need . . . anything," she finished lamely. Why the hell did Rhett have to work today? She couldn't believe that she was being forced to deal with this on her own.

Of course, this whole farce was her idea, so technically, she should be the one dealing with it. Damn it.

And this morning, she had wanted him to leave because she'd been feeling vulnerable after last night.

"Dishes? Towels? Maybe some new bedding?"

Well, new bedding wouldn't hurt. Her comforter was the same one she had used as a teenager, and according to the calendar, that was a long-ass time ago. "Bedding would be lovely, but don't feel you have to." Get anything for the greedy whore.

Oh, this was dicey moral ground.

"What size is your bed? A queen?"

"I'm not sure. It might be a double."

"Well, let's go take a look." Sandy was up on her feet before Shawn could protest. "Which room is yours?"

"First door on the right." Shawn scrambled to follow her.

She was already in the doorway, assessing. "That's only a double, honey. Good grief, talk about close quarters. Young love is certainly cozy."

"It doesn't seem to be a problem." It hadn't. Yes, she had woken up with a body temperature of a thousand degrees from Radiator Rhett, but she would just use a thinner blanket. If he even intended to sleep in her bed again. Which he might not want to. Or she might not want him to.

"Regardless, you do look like you could use a little refresh in here. I'm happy to see that you're practical and don't waste your money on things you don't need, but sweetheart, let me buy you some new sheets."

Shawn glanced into her room over Sandy's shoulder. It was a tired-looking bedroom she had to admit, with worn beige carpet and equally worn beige walls. She'd hung a picture of a sunset on the wall about a decade ago, and it was now crooked. The bed was even tilted at an odd angle from the wall, like they had shifted it last night during sex, and the sheets were destroyed. There was also a purple vibrator on the nightstand where she had tossed it after Rhett had gone to use the bathroom.

Oh. My. God.

With any luck, Sandy hadn't noticed.

Then she turned, with pursed lips, and Shawn knew she most definitely had noticed.

Shawn wanted to die. She wanted to peel back the dingy carpet and bury herself under it.

Not that Sandy would say anything. But just knowing that she knew was horrifying enough.

Except she did say something.

Which meant that Shawn's plunge into awkward hell was one hundred percent complete.

"Shawn, is Rhett not . . . satisfying you?" she asked in a low voice.

Yep. Hell. Certainly her face was on fire. "Of course he does," she managed, wondering if she could pretend this was about a reference to say, something like his ability to meet her emotional needs. Not about why she needed to use a vibrator two days after her marriage.

"Because I know that Rhett can be selfish. He's been spoiled, I admit, and that's my fault. He was my youngest, my baby, and I knew we weren't having any more, so I definitely cut him more slack than I should have." Sandy put her hand on her chest. "His last girlfriend told me that he's rude and demanding, and it breaks my heart to hear that."

It was breaking Shawn's that they were having this discussion. And who was the bitch who had run to Rhett's mother and whined? Geez. Deal with your shit, honey, don't go running to your boyfriend's mother.

Feeling defensive on Rhett's behalf, she told Sandy quite honestly, "Rhett is actually very thoughtful. He opens the door for me, he washes dishes, he makes coffee. I don't find anything rude about him at all." She was not discussing their sex life. In any way, shape, or form. And she was going to resolutely pretend there was no vibrator anywhere near them while they were discussing anything other than her sex life.

His mother looked pleased. "I'm glad to hear that. He has a good heart. He's very loyal. But he doesn't smile enough, and sometimes people misinterpret that as having ill intentions."

A strange feeling settled over Shawn, one that she didn't understand. She felt something in her chest that was unrecognizable, a tight grip. "He's a wonderful man, Sandy," she said, and she meant it. "You should be proud of him."

Sandy squeezed her hand. "You should see him with the kids and his siblings. That's when he relaxes."

"So you really don't mind that we eloped?" It was a stupid, masochistic question to ask, but she found herself seeking approval from Rhett's mother. Maybe it was because her own mother had been so casual and flaky when she'd been growing up. Maybe it was because she missed her grandparents, who for all practical purposes had been the heart of her family. Maybe it was also because Eve had indicated that Mrs. Ford had been very unhappy with her own unexpected marriage to Nolan.

"I honestly don't mind. Now with Nolan, it worried me a little because Nolan fell in love more times than I can count. But in the end, once I saw him with Eve, I knew this was different, something special. She's the right woman for him. With Rhett, I trust that if he chose to marry you, you're the woman he wants to spend his life with. He holds his emotions back, so when he opens up, it's honest."

Yeah, she shouldn't have asked. Because now she felt like complete and total crap. Honest? Hardly. Neither one of them were being honest, and she felt lousy about deceiving Sandy, who clearly had her son's best interests at heart.

Shawn also felt something that was suspiciously similar to jealousy. She envied the woman who would capture Rhett's heart someday, who would have all that intense loyalty, that straightforward, never-wavering devotion.

She didn't know what to say, afraid that if she did speak, she would either confess the truth or admit that she was suddenly wishing she were Rhett's type. Fortunately, she didn't have to respond, because Charity called to them from the living room.

"You have got to see this dress, Shawn! I think you should wear this to the party."

Relieved and horrified all at the same time, she gave Mrs. Ford a sheepish smile. "I hadn't even thought about a dress."

The truth was, there were a lot of things she hadn't thought about before she had gone and asked Rhett to marry her.

EVE watched her brother-in-law moving around the garage and frowned. She had known Rhett for years, but only in the last three months had she really spent any time with him. Initially, she had thought that he was arrogant, a charmer, who didn't show you who he really was. She still thought he kept himself private and remote, but she knew now he wasn't arrogant, and, frankly, he wasn't particularly charming. He didn't play games with women or his co-workers, and he really only spoke if he had something to say that was relevant.

Whereas Eve's own husband could work a crowd, laughed easily, and was almost never angry, Shawn's new husband simmered quietly beneath the surface with something Eve had never quite understood.

Even more so, now she wondered what really went on in his head.

Nolan, who had a rare weekend off from working on her brother's pit crew, had come to the track with her to see her new engine. She had placed fifteenth the day before, and they were all pretty excited at the possibilities. Her truck was running well, and she was getting the attention she had wanted on the circuit. Her two-year plan was to break into the cup circuit and garner a major sponsorship, and so far, so good.

Even better, her husband appreciated her new engine.

But now she was worried about Rhett and Shawn, because well, she was a worrier. "I don't know about this," she told Nolan for about the twentieth time in the past three days.

"Eve." Nolan put his hands on her shoulders and rubbed her through her sweatshirt. "Rhett is a grown man. Shawn is a grown woman. They know what they're doing."

All she could do was shake her head. "Something is fishy here, Nolan. It's not like Rhett to just dive into a wedding on a minute's notice with a woman he just met."

"He is pretty intense, you know that."

As Rhett came toward them, Eve stepped slightly away from Nolan, rocking in her sneakers as she pondered what was really going on. Shawn was impulsive, sure, but Shawn didn't fall head over ass for men. Her starts tended to be more about racing and drinking, not about relationships. While she was perfectly willing to get a tattoo with Eve, she had never even let a guy live with her. But now she had eloped with a virtual stranger? It didn't add up.

"Hey, can I knock off early today?" Rhett asked as he came up to them. "I just got a text from Jeannie that Mom went over to Shawn's, and I would like to head over there and save her from being endlessly grilled."

"Sure, no problem." Eve felt a pang of sympathy for Shawn. "Your mom must be pissed off. I don't envy Shawn right now. Sandy was suspicious of me for a good three months. She thought I had ulterior motives." Fortunately, now she and her mother-in-law had come to a mutual respect and admiration for each other, but at first it had not been easy.

"She thought you were nuts for marrying beneath you," Nolan said with a grin.

Eve snorted. "Hardly. But I'm sure the prenup didn't

help her opinion of me." She still regretted bringing that stupid document to Nolan to sign.

He groaned. "Oh, God, let's not bring that up again. It almost destroyed our marriage before it barely started."

"I still don't get why you cared," Rhett said. "I signed one and it's not a big deal to me. Shawn has the right to protect her assets."

Eve felt her jaw drop. "You signed a prenup? When the hell did you have time to do that?"

"On Friday, before we got married."

He looked like he thought it was completely normal. Inconsequential. "See you tomorrow at the apartment, right?" he asked Nolan.

Her husband nodded, then Rhett was gone with a wave.

"What the frickety-frack?" Eve asked, the second he was out of earshot. "Who the hell elopes after knowing each other for five minutes, which would indicate massive amounts of passion and insanity, yet still has enough time and a business head on their shoulders to whip together a prenup? No one. That's who."

"No one but Shawn and Rhett." Nolan shrugged, but he looked puzzled, too, staring off at his brother's retreating back.

"This is not right. Something is off. I feel like Rhett and Shawn are lying to us about something." None of this added up.

"What the hell would they be lying about?" Nolan rolled his eyes at her. "She can't be pregnant. There hasn't been time."

"Or has there?" Eve narrowed her eyes at her husband. Was Shawn pregnant with someone else's baby? No, that didn't add up. She would have told Eve, and she hadn't been dating anyone for quite some time. But there was definitely something off. "What is really going on here? Because I feel like they're pissing on my leg and telling me it's raining."

"Mind your own business, Eve."

"When have I ever done that?" she asked him, incredulous.

Nolan smiled. "You got me there, babe. Now can we go home? I need you to hold me before the shit hits the fan tomorrow."

Eve laughed. "Oh, yeah? So I need to comfort you with sex?"

"Now that you mention it . . ." He gave her a cute, pleading look.

"You're ridiculous." But he was her kind of ridiculous.

CHAPTER
ELEVEN

RHETT had driven to Shawn's faster than was strictly legal.

He wasn't afraid of a lot in life—not snakes or spiders or confrontation—but his mother still scared the shit out of him on occasion.

This would be one of them.

God only knew what she was saying to Shawn. Or worse, what she was asking her.

He had promised Shawn Chinese food but he was way earlier than expected, and he'd take her out to dinner as an apology for being subjected to a sneak attack from Sandy Ford.

Damn it. His mother's car was still in the driveway. Not good.

He was covered in motor oil from being jostled by Travis, an eighteen-year-old kid who was nervous and still learning his way around a pit crew. But he was not going to disappear into the shower until he had a good measure of Shawn's misery and he could politely send his mother home.

When he entered through the side door, kicking off his

dirty boots on the rag rug, he heard something unexpected. Shawn and his mother were laughing. He had expected cold tension, his mother voicing all her objections to their impulsive marriage, while Shawn pursed her lips in stoic silence. But no, they were yucking it up in the living room. What the hell could be so damn funny?

Coming around the corner, they both looked up at him in surprise.

"Oh! You're back early," Shawn said. She didn't look like it mattered one way or the other to her.

"Rhett," his mother said, her expression . . . guilty? Her reading glasses were perched on her nose. "I stopped by with some muffins for Shawn, and we've been making wedding-party plans. Her girlfriends just left."

And that was funny?

Feeling suspicious, he skirted the coffee table and kissed his mother on the cheek. "Thanks for stopping by, Momma." When he wasn't there. And when she had never met Shawn before.

His mother wrinkled her nose. "Good Lord, you smell bad enough to gag a maggot. Go change your clothes, and then we can show you what we've been up to."

He wasn't sure he wanted to know.

But he did have the urge to kiss Shawn. To show her and his mother both that he was relevant here.

So he came around to her side of the couch and gave her a smile that she could interpret however she liked. "I got off work early because I missed you."

Her eyes widened in surprise but before she could respond, he kissed her. Not a brief kiss of greeting, but a firm, drawn-out kiss that put a pink tinge to her cheeks. "I'm sorry I stink," he told her as he straightened up and out of her space.

"I don't mind," she said. "You smell like gas and rubber. I associate those scents with speed. Winning."

It was the kind of answer that made him wish his mother were nowhere near them. If she weren't, Rhett would have eased Shawn back onto that couch and peeled down those yoga pants to show her what winning really felt like.

But his mother most definitely was three feet away and Rhett nodded, turning abruptly so neither woman saw his growing erection. Screw dinner. He wanted Shawn more than lo mein noodles.

In the bedroom, he stripped off his smelly clothes and pulled on a clean T-shirt and jeans. The dirty ones bunched in his hand, he came back down the hall and asked, "Where is the washing machine, Shawn? I'll throw these in."

"Oh, here, I'll show you. Excuse us for a second," she told his mother. "It's in the basement."

She led him through the kitchen and down the steep stairs to the cold and poorly lit basement laundry room. "Sorry, it's gross down here."

He could care less. He flipped the lid on the washing machine and dropped the clothes in. "Listen, I'm sorry about my mom. I had no idea she'd just show up here. I hope she didn't give you too much of a hard time."

Shawn shook her head. "She's being really nice, which is almost worse. She's happy for us, and I feel like a jerk."

"She's happy?" That was something of a head-scratcher. His mother had nearly had a heart attack when Nolan had eloped with Eve. She had ranted and raved for days.

"Yeah. She says she wants you happy and that since you're not impulsive, she trusts that you know what you're doing."

That was interesting. His mother trusted him to choose his life partner wisely. Maybe she knew him better than he had realized.

Though she clearly didn't know what was really going on here.

"I feel like shit, Rhett, honestly." Shawn poured some laundry detergent in the machine on top of his clothes, looking flustered. "I didn't know how bad I would feel about lying. I didn't think about it at all, frankly."

Rhett moved in behind her and brushed her hair off her

shoulder so he could kiss her neck. He didn't like to see her so stressed. He didn't particularly like lying to his mother either. But his interest in Shawn wasn't feigned, and he intended to focus on that. "This isn't a purely business transaction, you know. We are having a relationship." His erection grew as he pressed her against the machine, her pert backside a soft cushion for his thighs.

She shivered. "Rhett . . ."

"Yes?"

"It's not the same thing," she protested, even as her ass angled to give him a better position, his cock resting between her cheeks.

"No, it's not." He nibbled on her ear, loving the delicate skin there. "I don't want you unhappy, Shawn. If you want, we can pull the plug on all of this. Right here, right now. We can say it was a mistake, and walk away."

While he waited for his words to sink in, he ran his hands down her sides, letting one reach around to stroke down between her legs, the cotton pants giving him access to every curve of her body. He bit her ear gently, then soothed it with his tongue.

"We can?" she asked, growing breathless, her hips starting to rock back and forth, teasing her clitoris against his hand, and brushing her ass into his erection.

"Of course we can. We can do whatever you want." He actually would be disappointed if she said she wanted to annul their marriage and forget this whole thing had ever happened. He tried to tell himself it was because then he wouldn't have access to her in bed every night, but there was more to it. He and Shawn hadn't finished exploring each other, physically and emotionally. There was something there between them, besides sex, and he wasn't entirely sure what it was, but he was curious to find out.

"I'll lose the track," she murmured.

"Yes, you will. And you'll lose my cock," he added, before slipping his tongue into her ear.

She gave a small gasp. "I will?"

"Yes. If we end this marriage, then it wouldn't make sense for us to see each other again. I'm not designed that way. I'm either all in or all out."

"It's a lot to lose."

He could only hope that longing was at least in some small way for him along with her family business.

"It is. But it's your choice."

"I started this. I need to finish this. It's not fair to you otherwise."

Rhett turned her around so he could see her. He laced his fingers through hers. "Shawn. This is about what *you* want. Don't do this out of fairness or concern for me. Do what you want, what's right for you." He meant that. He wasn't worried about anyone's opinion, and he saw no sense in doing something you already knew you would regret. Life was too short.

She stared at him for a second then gave a short nod. "You're right. I'm already in. I want to stay in."

The relief he felt surprised him. So he buried his hand in the back of her hair and tugged her to him. "The passion between us is real. That's all we have to show people."

"It is, isn't it?"

"Very real." He kissed her, a deep, plunging mating of their mouths, a demand and a promise all at once. He wanted to bury his cock in her the same way, a wet tangle of desperation. As soon as he felt her give in, her arms snaking around his neck, he broke off the embrace. Establish control. Choices outside of the bedroom were hers, but sex was his arena.

She gave a moan of disappointment.

"We need to go back upstairs," he told her with a swat on her backside. "Come on."

Her eyes darkened at his touch, and he knew she was remembering exactly what he was thinking about—his palm slapping against her bare flesh, her bottom raised for his pleasure, for her punishment.

They were so not finished with what they had started.

Last night had only been the beginning of what he could make her feel.

As he took her hand and pulled her up the steps, he felt the hot, thick taste of anticipation in his mouth and something else he couldn't define.

SHAWN let Rhett hold her hand as they walked up the basement steps, more confused than ever. What had she just agreed to?

To continue this sham of a marriage, deceiving everyone important in their lives. For what? The track? Was it really that important to her?

Weren't the people in her life more important than a business?

But the truth was, they were all intertwined in her life. Business was pleasure and the track was the people she had grown up with, driven with, worked with now. Racing was her life, and it was to the majority of the people she considered the important friendships and influence on her life.

She also didn't want to lose Rhett. Not yet. Not when she was experiencing something she never had before, not when she was realizing that there was a world of pleasure she had never even tapped into. Not when she was curious as to what was happening between them, wondering how far it could go, wanting to see what made Rhett tick as a man.

Plus, she also had to admit, that just for a little while, she wanted to borrow Rhett's family. She wanted to belong, to fit into a large, boisterous family who cared so deeply about one another. She missed her grandparents, and her brother and mother were no cure for the void. In fact, her mother was quite the opposite. Being married to Rhett, Shawn got to voyeuristically fill up her familial well, and while that was no doubt wrong of her, she couldn't help but enjoy it now that she was in it.

Even if it meant wedding-party planning.

Rhett's mother was on the couch, scrolling through her cell phone. She gave them a look that indicated she knew precisely what they had been doing. "Did you get lost?"

"Shawn was just showing me how to use the washer."

Sandy snorted. "You know how to do laundry. You've been doing it since you were six. But I understand, you're newlyweds. I'll get out of your hair."

"Oh, you don't have to leave, Sandy," Shawn protested, embarrassed by how long they'd been gone and remembering that she had seen her vibrator earlier. One afternoon and her mother-in-law knew more about her sex life than she cared to contemplate.

But Sandy waved her words off. "It's time for me to go home and cook for Senior. He gets cranky if dinner is late."

"What were you two laughing about anyway?" Rhett wanted to know. "I'm a little scared to find out."

"We were looking at designer tuxes from these bridal magazines the twins brought," his mother said. "They're ridiculous. I don't know a man in Charlotte who would wear a skinny tux in red."

Shawn grinned at Rhett's expression. He looked like someone had suggested removing his testicles.

"Neither do I," he said emphatically.

"And I showed Shawn a baby picture of you we might use for a slide show."

"Oh, Lord," was his opinion. It was accompanied by a wince.

"We scheduled a photo shoot for you on Thursday out at our house," Sandy continued.

Now Rhett looked like he had indigestion. "A photo shoot? For what?"

"For your wedding announcement."

"Jesus," he muttered. Then louder, he added, "I'm not photogenic, you know. Do we really need to do this?"

Shawn grinned, feeling a whole lot better now that he was aware of what she'd been subjected to all afternoon. "You'd take better pictures if you smiled."

He glared at her.

Sandy nodded in agreement. "That's what I always tell him!"

"I can't smile when someone is shoving a camera in my face. It's so fake."

"Well, buck up," was his mother's final opinion. "You're doing it. What are you going to tell your kids someday if there isn't a single picture of the two of you together?"

That knocked the grin off Shawn's face. Kids? Good God. The unexpected image of a couple of toddlers bouncing on their bed popped into her head. For a split second, she could have sworn she actually felt a fluttering in her womb, like it was yawning awake after a lifetime of slumber, shaken to awareness by the idea of procreation with Rhett. Holy crap. Not good.

"I don't have an answer for that, honestly," Rhett told his mother.

"You are going to have kids, right? And sooner rather than later. I understand that Shawn is already in her thirties."

Huh. The fluttering stopped. In fact, her uterus might have cringed in horror at that reminder.

"Mom!" Rhett gave his mother a stern look. "I'm not discussing our procreation plans with you two days after our wedding. In fact, I'm not discussing our procreation plans with you ever."

Because there would be no procreation plans.

She should feel relieved.

Instead, she just felt unsettled. She was only thirty-three, or would be in two weeks anyways. That was young still. She had a decade before the factory would shut down. Or at least seven years. Four, if she really wanted to have the best shot at a quick conception. Two, if she didn't want to be considered high risk.

Holy shit.

When had this happened? When had she even cared about having children? Now she was suddenly realizing that by the time this marriage with Rhett was over, she would have to start over dating, as a divorcée, and then who knew when she could even contemplate starting a family?

"That doesn't change the facts. Shawn, you want children, right?" Sandy asked her.

Unable to speak, she simply nodded, her stomach in knots.

"Then it's silly to wait five years. Rhett wants kids, too."

She cleared her throat and managed to choke out, "Rhett is only twenty-five. Maybe he's not ready."

"Then he shouldn't have married a woman almost ten years older than him. Your fertility is dropping like a stone as we speak."

Now she was officially speechless. Sandy made her sound like her eggs were petrifying, ovaries deflating like a fallen soufflé. She had never felt quite so old or quite so past her expiration date.

"Mom." Rhett used a tone that brooked no arguments. "That is way out of line. You've hurt Shawn's feelings."

Sandy did look contrite, but Shawn still felt stung, with no clue what to say.

"I'm sorry, dear, that didn't really sound right, did it? It's just that children are such a blessing."

"We're not having nine, I can guarantee that," Rhett told her.

Hell, no. Because even if this were a real marriage, which it wasn't, Shawn was clearly too old to have nine kids unless they were three sets of triplets. God, she had a headache again. The aspirin from the morning had clearly worn off.

"And you already have enough grandkids to bankrupt you at Christmas, so just chill out. Let's just focus on being married for a while, and getting to know each other and each other's families." Rhett gave a rueful look. "If Shawn is still interested in getting to know the Fords after that introduction."

"Shawn knows I just have your best interests at heart, don't you, dear?"

She nodded, even if she had no idea what Sandy's intentions really were. "Of course," she managed to say.

Rhett still looked put out. "Momma, if and when we get pregnant, you'll be the first to know. Otherwise, I'm telling you with all the love in my heart to butt out."

"Your brother would never talk to me like that," she sniffed. But to Shawn, her expression looked like she wasn't genuinely put out. If anything, her love for her youngest son shone through. She admired him for standing up for his wife, it was obvious.

"No," Rhett agreed. "But he wouldn't let you make Eve feel bad either. He would just say it in a more charming way." Rhett turned to Shawn. "And now you've witnessed the Ford family dynamic. I'm sorry to say you did not get the charming brother."

Something stirred in Shawn that she did not want to examine too closely. "No, I got the loyal one." Leaning over, she kissed his cheek before she could stop herself.

She had the satisfaction of seeing that she had actually caught Rhett off guard. That wasn't easy to do, yet he looked downright sheepish. His mother was beaming.

"And on that note, I'll leave you two to your dinner and newlywed shenanigans." Sandy gave each of them a hug.

Shawn hugged her back and tried to forcibly shove the phrase *if and when we get pregnant* out of her head. This wasn't what she had signed on for, but what was more disturbing than anything was her confusion and reaction to marriage, babies, family. She must be missing Pops more than she realized. Or the sex had gone to her head.

As Rhett walked his mother to her car, Shawn busied herself shoving the bridal magazines into a pile and cramming them into the desk in the corner of the living room. Then she carried dirty coffee mugs to the kitchen and filled the sink with soapy water.

"You're always doing dishes," Rhett said when he came back in. "Why don't you use the dishwasher?"

"It's broken. I don't have the money to replace it." It was a hated chore, but then again, weren't all chores hated by most people?

"What's wrong with it? Did it actually die, or it's just not getting dishes clean?"

"It's not getting the dishes clean. There's dried old food on them after an hour of water spritzing them. It makes no sense." Though she wasn't sure why they were talking about this.

"The jets are probably clogged."

Before she realized what was going on, Rhett was on the floor, dishwasher door open, parts being inspected. "Where are your tools? I need a screwdriver."

Was he for real? Shawn swished her hand to make the suds inflate. "You don't have to fix my dishwasher."

"It's no big deal. It'll take me ten minutes." He smiled up at her. "Besides, if you're washing dishes ten times a day, it's going to cut into our sexy time."

Oh, geez. She should have known. "I'm not planning to be horizontal the majority of my day. I don't think doing the dishes is going to ruin our sex life."

"Just a little insurance." He stood up and kissed the back of her head. "Where is the screwdriver? And a drill would be helpful."

"In the basement. Next to the washer and dryer." She should have left it at that. But she wasn't wired that way— she was a button pusher. So she added, "And who says I have any intention of having sex with you again? Just because you fix my dishwasher doesn't mean I will lie down for you any time. I may need some convincing, you know."

He stopped on his way across the kitchen and studied her. "You like to play this game, don't you? You want me to get aggressive and throw you down on the floor and prove you like my attention."

Maybe. "No, of course not. I have no idea what you're talking about." Hell, the truth was, she did want him to throw her down and make her forget that they were married. Which was messed up, she had to admit.

"Liar." He laughed softly. "But the answer is no. Because I don't dance on a puppet string. If you want me to fuck you, just ask and I'll decide if I want to give it to you or not."

Shawn felt her jaw drop. "You'll decide? Oh, you'll decide? Screw that!" Any sort of tender feelings she'd been having toward him disappeared pronto. She was sorry she'd let him gag her. Shawn Hamby was not to be gagged. She had things to say, damn it. Opinions that mattered. "I am not the kind of woman who is going to beg you for sex."

"Who said anything about begging? I meant I think you're strong enough to ask for what you want without dancing around in passive-aggressive style. Don't hint, then expect me to do all the work. It doesn't suit you." With that, he went down the basement steps.

Shawn was tempted to throw a coffee mug at the back of his head. "Asshole," she muttered in frustration, and it felt good. She didn't understand him. At all.

Wouldn't he want her to be sly about sex? Wasn't that the point of a man who wanted to dominate? She was supposed to be coy and shy, and he was supposed to grab her and do her? He was right, she was willing to play that game. But this one? She didn't even know what game they were playing, let alone what the rules were.

Which pissed her off. She didn't like to lose. She was a born competitor.

So when he came back upstairs with tools in hand, knelt down, and leaned into the dishwasher, she couldn't let it go. "I thought you wanted to do the work. I thought that was the whole freaking point. So what am I supposed to do, Rhett? What am I *allowed* to do? Not that I ever agreed to be your submissive, but what does a submissive do exactly if it's not flirt, beg, hint, or demand?"

His head popped out of her dishwasher. "You're supposed to trust me. You're supposed to trust me enough to be honest and direct with me."

It wasn't an answer that was going to satisfy her. Ever. "How is this for direct? You can sleep in the guest room tonight."

Rhett didn't say anything, which further annoyed her. He just fiddled and unscrewed and pulled something that looked like a dead mouse—holy shit, was that a mouse?—out of her dishwasher. Shawn waited until he had dropped the pile of yuck he was holding, expecting him to answer her. But he didn't.

"Aren't you going to answer me?"

"I wasn't aware that was a question," he replied.

She threw her soapy sponge at him. "Don't be a smart-ass."

The sponge bounced off his knee, leaving a trail of suds down his shin. He didn't even look up. "You told me I'm sleeping in the guest room. I told you that this is your house, and I'll do whatever you say. So I'm sleeping in the guest room tonight."

That was a deflating response to her anger.

No. She definitely did not understand Rhett Ford.

"What happened to ordering Chinese food?" It was an emotional hook to hold on to her anger, she knew that. Was fully aware of how juvenile it was. Yet couldn't stop herself from seeking some sin to lay at his feet.

"I came home early. But I can order it now if you'd like. I can go and pick it up."

Said the man very respectfully as he fixed her dishwasher. She was stymied. "We can just get it delivered."

Finishing the dishes, Shawn dried her hands off and reached for her cell phone. While Rhett worked, she found herself dialing for delivery, asking him what he wanted.

By the time the food arrived, he had finished with the dishwasher and was washing his hands. "We can test it with the Chinese food dishes," he told her. "But it should run just fine now."

"Thanks." Because she was grateful and sheepish and uncomfortable. What was happening between them? It was something. It was nothing. It was nothing she'd ever encountered and nothing she understood.

She wanted to trust him, but to what end? She didn't know. And she wasn't quite there yet.

While eating, they talked about the track schedule and about Rhett's car and who to hire as a marketing director. His advice was sound, his tone respectful. After watching the cup series race on TV, Shawn went to bed.

Alone. Rhett just said good night and gave her a yawn, still on the couch.

It should have felt like a victory.

Instead it just felt unsatisfying. Like diet ice cream.

In her PJ bottoms and a USC T-shirt, she poked her head out of her room and called down the hallway, "Do you need help moving tomorrow? I can come to your apartment and help you pack, or clean the apartment, or whatever."

"No, that's okay," he called back. "I'm sure Nolan and I can handle it."

That wasn't satisfying either. "No, really, I can help." She wasn't a total bitch. She was helpful, a hard worker, a good friend. She just didn't like being told what to do. But she could offer. "You want the apartment clean or you won't get your deposit back."

"Yeah, Nolan would probably appreciate that since it's his." Rhett was just in her line of view, even though he was twenty feet away. She couldn't read his expression. "Thanks, Shawn."

"You're welcome. And thanks again for fixing the dishwasher."

"My pleasure."

She hovered in the doorway, feeling like an idiot. Then

she said, "Good night," yet again and retreated, closing her door behind her.

When she climbed into bed, she swore she could smell him on her sheets.

The vibrator stared at her in the dark from the nightstand, mocking her, while her vagina berated her for being so stubborn.

Maybe her pillow would like to insult her while they were at it. Shawn punched it so it wouldn't get any ideas, and threw her head down, feeling bitter, determined not to think about Rhett.

So far marriage was a dress that didn't fit her.

She'd much rather be naked.

With Rhett. Naked, him thrusting into her again, her cries trapped by the tight fabric over her mouth . . .

Uh-oh. If this was her not thinking about it, this was going to be a long night.

Because she knew from experience that he would not come into her room.

And she was right. He didn't.

CHAPTER
TWELVE

RHETT threw the last of his clothes in one of the boxes Nolan had brought with him and surveyed his empty bedroom. He wasn't sorry to be leaving this small and dark apartment, though he was sorry he'd been relegated to Shawn's guest bedroom. But it was for the best, for now. He wasn't going to live with that passive-aggressive shit, where she poked at him and circled around what was bothering her and jabbed with sly, underhanded comments. So he would stay in the guest room and hope she would learn to trust him, learn that she could say whatever she was thinking, feeling, and he would respect that.

He wanted to make her happy. It was that simple.

But he wasn't going to be put in a position where he never knew if a sponge, or worse, was going to come at him.

Was he demanding and intense? Yes, he was. He couldn't change that, and he was honest about it, had been from the first minute he met her. But he was also fair, helpful, polite. So he liked to think. So why was Shawn fighting him so hard at every turn? It was like she was determined to wrest power from him.

"You okay?" Nolan asked him, appearing in the doorway. "You look like you could chew glass and like it."

Rhett shrugged. "I don't know, man. Why didn't you warn me that marriage was complicated?"

Nolan's eyebrows shot up. "Because I didn't know you were going to elope about three minutes after meeting Shawn. If I had, I might have suggested you wait a month or twelve and get to know her before getting hitched. But you did, so you're in it now. What's going on?"

"I feel like Shawn is trying really hard to hold on to her independence and prove that she can't be controlled. But I don't want to control her. I just want to be partners, and when you're partners, sometimes one is the leader and sometimes the other is, depending on the situation. It's natural." That was what he had seen with his parents' and his siblings' marriages, and he wanted that for himself. He wanted to lead their intimate sexual relationship and let her lead the rest. Why was that so difficult? Hell, he'd think a woman would jump at that.

"You're right, it is. But maybe because this is a brand-new relationship, you're going to need time to sort that out. Moving in together is a big step, let alone getting married, so cut Shawn some slack."

Nolan was right. Especially considering they weren't really even married. What the hell did Rhett really expect from her? "You're right. And I am figuring her out, that's for sure. She'll be here in a few minutes because she feels guilty about getting short with me last night. She's the kind of woman who throws something out there in anger and impulse, then immediately does something thoughtful that's totally unrelated because she feels bad."

"I think she and Eve are friends for a reason. They're similar personality types. But I don't get the sense Shawn worries as much as Eve does."

"Oh, I think she worries plenty." Rhett dropped the box on the floor and lifted the mattress from his bed off of the box spring so he could start to disassemble the bed frame.

"Funny, neither of us married a woman like our mother. Momma never worries. She has total confidence the world will bend to her will."

"Ha, that's true. But I'm not surprised you didn't. You're basically Mom, you know. I'm more like Dad. But I have a need to mediate, calm things down. I think Eve and I are a good fit that way."

Rhett realized that marriage had already changed his relationship with his brother. They were talking man-to-man, friend to friend, instead of big brother to little brother, or adult to child. As of yet, they'd barely even made fun of each other in the last hour. It was nice to be able to share with Nolan, yet there was a limit to how long they could talk about their feelings without a drop in testosterone.

"I am not my mother. That's disturbing." He shoved the mattress against the wall. "Now are you going to stand there and scratch your nuts, or are you going to help me?"

Nolan grinned. "Definitely nut-scratching."

His sister Jeannie and her husband, Mark, were in the living room, picking through the remains of Nolan's old furniture that Rhett had inherited and no longer needed. They were trying to furnish their finished basement on a budget. Rhett figured when he and Shawn divorced and he moved out of her house, he would just start fresh with new stuff. It would be a small reward to himself for surviving the six months intact.

The doorbell rang. "Come in!" Rhett yelled as loud as he could, already wresting the box spring up.

They could hear Jeannie greeting someone and Nolan took the box of clothes and went out into the living room, leaving Rhett alone with the box spring, which, while not heavy, was awkward for one person to maneuver. "Thanks, dick!" he called at his brother's retreating back.

Nolan's response was his middle finger thrown over his shoulder.

Yep. They were back to being brothers.

A second later, Shawn's head popped into the bedroom. "Hi," she said, sounding breathless, her dark blond hair tousled from the wind.

Rhett smiled at her because, the truth was, he was glad to see her. He liked the companionship between them, despite the speed bump of the night before. He wanted their relationship to work. He didn't know what he meant by that exactly, but he did. He wanted to be with her, in some legitimate capacity, for whatever time they had together.

"Hey, beautiful, how was your day?" He slammed the box spring against the mattress propped against the wall, and bent down to get his wrench out of his toolbox.

"It was good." She sounded surprised by that fact. "Eve had some great suggestions for PR, and I posted the job listing for a marketing rep. I cleared more stuff with the lawyer, and I signed vendor contracts for the season. How about you?"

"I slept in. It was awesome. Then I worked out. And now here I am, breaking down a bed I don't need."

"What are we going to do with that and the furniture in the living room?"

"Oh, my sister is taking the couches and my other sister is taking the bed. And yet another sister is taking the kitchen table. All I have is my clothes and some sports equipment. Once I put out the word that I had free stuff up for grabs, the Fords descended faster than a hot knife through butter. It's one of the pluses of a big family."

"Oh, okay." Shawn was worrying her bottom lip with her teeth, her arms across her breasts. "Aren't you going to, uh, wish you had that stuff later?"

He liked the jeans she was wearing. They were snug, and her hip was jutting out to the right as she leaned on the door frame. Her breasts were pert beneath her fuzzy gray sweater, and she was wearing shiny lip gloss on her full lips. Abandoning his Allen wrench, Rhett decided he needed to kiss her. She just looked too juicy and irresistible. As he stood and moved toward her, he shook his head.

"It's old and it was Nolan's. I'm not particularly worried about it."

For a second she looked like she wanted to bolt, obviously aware of his intent. But when he put his hand on the back of her head and gently massaged her scalp, urging her to him, she gave in with a sigh. The kiss had his eyes drifting closed, his body leaning in to Shawn. God, she tasted good. Felt good.

He didn't want to argue with Shawn. He wanted her to smile at him, with that special smile she had where her mouth was wide and her eyes crinkled in amusement. He wanted to settle down into their relationship and just enjoy each other. So maybe he was like his mother in that regard, because he wanted what he wanted and he assumed he was going to get it.

"Thanks for coming to help," he said, brushing his lips over her jaw. "Did you meet Jeannie and Mark?"

"Yes," she said, her neck tilting back. "They're very nice."

"Jeannie wants to talk to you about the wedding party, or reception, or whatever we're calling it."

"Oh, Lord," was Shawn's opinion. "I'm sorry this has spun so out of control."

"I don't mind." He didn't. Because if he were honest with himself, and he always was, he wanted it to be real. He knew that he could be happy with Shawn, and he wanted this to be real. Wanted to work toward ensuring that it was. "But I understand how you're feeling. It's a lot to take in. Just let my sisters and mom handle the whole thing."

"Oh, I intend to. I may be a control freak in some regards, but planning a party is not one of them. I don't know squat about girly stuff like decorating and cakes, as you can tell from the state of my house."

"I like your house. It's comfortable, cozy." Rhett lazily stroked her backside, nuzzled in her hair. He could touch her for hours and never get tired of the feel of her skin, her body.

"Are you moving or making out?" Eve asked from the hallway. "Get the lead out, Rhett, I want to go home before midnight."

Rhett smiled and took a step back from Shawn. "And with that, Eve shatters the mood." He glanced over Shawn's shoulder at his sister-in-law. "Carry this mattress set out to the truck, Eve, and we're all set. Show us your muscle."

"You think I can't?" Eve rolled her eyes. "I've got this."

Rhett stepped aside, pulling Shawn with him, as Eve and Nolan came in and hauled the mattress back out, Eve swearing but not looking like she was overly strained.

"You did that on purpose," Shawn said to him, clearly amused as she lifted one of the boxes off the floor. "You played Eve."

"We're all competitive. It's not hard." Rhett picked up the other box and grinned at Shawn. "We both know all I need to do is dare you to do something, and you fall for it every time."

She laughed. "I can't deny it. All I can do is hope you don't abuse your power."

"I'll never dare you to do anything that matters, I promise." He grew serious, wanting her to understand. "I'll never dare you in bed, I hope you know that. That wouldn't be fair."

Her smile disappeared. "This is that trust thing again, isn't it?"

"Yeah." He nodded. "I want to sleep in your bed tonight. Not to have sex, but just to be near you, to hold you. Do you trust me not to initiate sex?"

She stood, bulky box in her arms, and moistened her lips, her brown eyes darker than usual. "What if I want you to initiate sex?"

He felt a sharp kick of lust. "Do you?"

"Yes. I do."

That was what he wanted to hear. He wanted her to be straightforward, honest with him. No game playing. "It would be my pleasure, then."

Even with the dual boxes between them, he leaned over and kissed her. "I'm going to make you come harder than you've ever come," he promised her, voice low, his desire intense.

"You'd better," she told him. "I'm trusting you."

That right there turned him on. It meant everything to him that she trusted him. "You've put your trust in the right man, Shawn."

Shawn hoped so. She did trust Rhett, though she still had a niggling concern in the back of her mind that she was going to regret this marriage, their relationship, the sex. That when all was said and done, she was going to get hurt. But she couldn't stop it. There was no way she could live in the same house with him, pretending to be his wife in public, and not want as much as she could have. His green eyes were so intense, so serious, so committed, that she knew she couldn't spend night after night with him down the hall in the guest room while she yearned for another immersion into the pleasure he had shown her.

It wasn't logical. Nor was it smart. But it was what she wanted.

"I know," she told him, and it was true. She had asked him to enter into a marriage of convenience with her days after they had met. She could have found herself in a disastrous situation with a guy who would manipulate and use her need for secrecy to his advantage. She could have wound up with a slob or a mooch who expected her to be his housekeeper. She could have found herself having to ditch the whole insane idea, losing the track, and facing public humiliation.

So yes, she trusted Rhett.

It seemed stupidly obvious now to her.

Her fear of regrets didn't stem from concern that he would in some way make things difficult for her, it was that he wouldn't. Her fear was that she would fall for him, and that in the end, it would hurt to let him go. That if she allowed him to be a part of her life, it would be lonely when he left.

But it was too late to worry about any of that. She was in and, much like him, once in, she was all in.

Nolan and Eve reappeared for the box spring. "Seriously?" Eve complained. "You two are doing nothing but making moony eyes at each other. I'm starting to get pissed."

"My wife is very romantic," Nolan told them.

"Sorry," Shawn muttered. "We were just making some plans."

"That don't include the two of you," Rhett said. "So we would like to thank you very much for helping out, but I know you're both busy, so you can head home now."

Well, that was a little obvious. Shawn followed Rhett down the hallway, wondering if he was going to give that same speech to his sister and her husband. Though truth be told, there wasn't really anything left in the apartment, aside from a lonely vacuum, which Jeannie was using on the worn carpet, and a random floor lamp.

"I should be offended, but I'm just grateful," Eve said. "I want to get a run in before I collapse for the night." But then she added, "Shawn, can I talk to you for a second before I leave?"

"Sure." Shawn looked at her expectantly, no idea what Eve would want to say, but suspecting it wasn't anything particularly positive.

"Alone," Eve said bluntly.

Wonderful. "Sure," she said, less enthusiastic. She turned and went down the hallway, figuring they could use the now-empty bedroom.

Once inside, she rounded on Eve, arms crossed, unable to prevent her defensiveness.

"Whoa, tiger, pull back your claws. I come in peace." Eve held up her hands. "I just want to ask you if, you know, everything is okay. If you're happy." Then without waiting for a response, she winced. "God, that sounded so asinine. Sorry. I just want you to know that if you regret your impulsive decision to marry Rhett, we can get you out of it. This isn't like the tattoos we had done when we were trying to best each other with our obnoxiousness. We don't need laser removal, a physician, and a few grand to get you out of this. A hundred bucks on the Internet and we can have you divorced."

Shawn almost laughed. Almost. Because she was still annoyed about the tattoo ten years after the fact, she didn't. "It's your fault we have such bad ink, you know. I'm never going to admit otherwise."

"It's your fault, too!" Eve protested. "You started it by egging me on about coming in last at the fair when I entered a shooting contest and slipped on a discarded onion ring and shot the light out."

"Yeah, then you told me that the only way I was going to get a guy between my thighs was if I tattooed one there. And that Stoney White, who you know I had a massive crush on, had called me lanky and had mimicked a pelican walking. That was bullshit."

"I did you a favor. Stoney White was a loser. His name was Stoney, for Chrissake. Plus I didn't make you take that car bomb. Or the second. You were bound and determined to prove to Stoney that you could do a shot of whiskey in thirty seconds."

Huh. Perhaps she hadn't matured as much as she thought in the last decade. It seemed her seduction techniques had not improved. "Well, I could. It wasn't just bragging. I still can, you know."

"And I still have a tattoo on my inner thigh that says 'Open 24 hours.' "

Shawn grinned. "That was a beautiful night, wasn't it? We were such idiots, but damn, we always had fun." She wondered why Rhett hadn't said anything about her tattoo. He had certainly been down between her thighs, so he had to have seen it. Most men burst out laughing the first time they got a glimpse of it.

Eve laughed. "Maybe a little too much fun."

"Nah. Truth is, we let too much fun slip away from us. We grew up and both became workaholics."

"I've been working on a better balance myself. Nolan helps. How about you? Seriously, not to sound like your mother—or rather like anyone's mother but yours—how is it going? You still haven't answered that question."

"It's intense," she admitted, much preferring to be as honest as she could without having to lie to her best friend. "It's hot, it's sexy, it's new, it's an adjustment. But it's good. For real. No worrying about me." She would worry about herself a shit ton, so no need for someone else to get in on the action and stress themselves out.

Eve studied her for a minute. "Okay. Cool. I won't get in your business anymore. You know you can talk to me about anything, and it won't matter that Rhett is Nolan's brother. I'm a steel trap."

"Unless we're going head-to-head. Then you'll spill every secret I have if it will throw me off my game."

"That is not true," Eve protested. Then she grinned. "Much. But you know I'll only tell embarrassing secrets, not painful ones."

"Thanks for the distinction. But I can't exactly bitch you out, because I'm the same way. It's ultimately why we get along."

"Alright, let's go get laid." Eve fist-bumped her. "To the power of the V. And whiskey. And shitty tattoos."

"To finishing first. And friendship. To the Brothers Ford."

"Amen, sister."

That was as warm and fuzzy as she and Eve were ever going to get. They were essentially guys with vaginas. But they had both come to terms with who they were years ago.

"I think this was our middle school fantasy, you know, to marry brothers," Eve said with a laugh as she headed back down the hall.

Unfortunately, it was still a fantasy.

Shawn fought the urge to sigh.

"So I have to ask . . . is he kinky?" Eve said, looking both super curious and super horrified. "Does he have . . . contraptions?"

"I am not talking to you about that other than to say there are no contraptions." Good Lord. She didn't even want to consider what Eve was envisioning.

"So he's kinky." Her eyes sparkled and she gave a choking laugh. "Shawn, if only Stoney White had known you have a penchant for kink, he could have been all yours. In all his idiotic meathead glory."

"Shut up, Eve," was her opinion on that.

Eve just laughed harder.

"I can keep my clothes and stuff in the guest room," Rhett said as he surveyed the space, or lack thereof, in Shawn's bedroom. She wasn't a housekeeper to his mother's standards, that was for sure, and she had odd things propped in the corners of her bedroom, like a large stuffed gorilla and a hunting rifle, which didn't contain bullets. He'd checked when she was in the bathroom.

"No, it's okay. I can clear some space in the closet for you," she said. Which she promptly did by shoving her clothes to the right until hangers were jammed out at awkward angles and her sweaters looked like they were choking one another. Then she ripped a black-and-white dress off the hanger and balled it up and tossed it on the floor of the closet. "I hate that dress. It makes my ass look big."

"Somehow I doubt that," he said wryly as he pulled clothes out of his box and hung them up in the three point five inches of space she'd given him. He was no neat freak himself, so he couldn't say the chaos of her closet and bedroom bothered him. He just wasn't sure he was ever going to find a clean shirt again.

"So I have a question for you." It was something he hadn't wanted to ask in the intimacy of bed, because he had a feeling it was going to embarrass her or make her laugh.

"Yeah? What?"

"Why do you have the face of a little boy with curly hair tattooed on your inner thigh?" He had to admit, it had given him a start the other night, but he had managed to ignore it. Now it was generating a lot of curiosity. He couldn't figure out what crazy story was behind it, and he knew there had to be one.

Shawn made a face. "It's not a little boy! It's Justin Timberlake, back in the day when his hair looked like a chia pet."

"Really? Okay, so why would you tattoo a portrait of him diving into your vagina? Any particular reason?"

"It was a bet, and no, I'm not going to tell you the full story. Let's just say that Eve didn't fare any better than I did."

Rhett raised his eyebrows. He didn't even want to consider what was between his sister-in-law's thighs.

"I've thought about getting it removed but it's expensive, time-consuming, and painful."

"You could cover it with another tattoo. The right artist could make JT disappear."

"Yeah." She gave a noncommittal shrug. "It is kind of fun to see the reaction of the gyno when I get my Pap test, but I have gotten some negative reactions from former boyfriends. That's probably why I keep it."

Rhett laughed. "Why does that not surprise me?"

"Now that I think about it, you're the first guy ever who didn't stop and ask me about it." She looked over at him, curious. "But you obviously saw it."

It was his turn to shrug, pleased that she had made the distinction. It had been a conscious choice to ignore that silly tattoo in the heat of the moment. "It wasn't worthy of my attention right then. The only thing worthy of my attention was you."

"Oh." She cleared her throat.

Rhett put his baseball bat and glove in the corner. He didn't play much these days, but back in high school he'd loved cracking that bat against a ball. He didn't want to part with the option that he could play a ball game for fun.

"What's with the gorilla?" he asked, because as he studied it, he realized he and Shawn had gotten busy the other night with the big lug watching them. He wasn't sure how he had missed it in the first place, but now that he'd noticed, he didn't like it. The gorilla had a creepy smile, and Rhett had seen enough horror movies to dislike it.

"I won it for selling a crapload of Girl Scout cookies. I had to win it, you know, once I saw him in the prize brochure. He was calling my name." Shawn bent over the dresser, yanking open a drawer and pulling out socks, which she dumped on the bed. "His name is Coconut."

"He has a name?"

"Of course."

"Can we, uh, turn him to the wall while we sleep? I don't like the way he's looking at me." Rhett decided he didn't want his baseball bat next to Coconut. He moved it next to the bed, where he could easily access it.

"Are you serious?" Shawn blew her hair out of her eyes as she finished emptying the drawer and closing it again. She then opened the one below it, stuffing the socks back into it, ignoring the fact that there wasn't really any room for them. "Does the gorilla actually bother you?"

"Yes." He wasn't going to lie about it. "He's fucking creepy. I don't need him staring at me while I sleep."

"He's not real," Shawn said with a grin, trying to shove the overstuffed drawer closed. It only made it halfway. "He's a stuffed animal."

"I know. That's why he's creepy. Why does anyone need to make something so realistic-looking as a stuffed toy? I don't like it." It was like some of the dolls his sisters had played with as kids. They were freakish in their attempt to look like real babies. It had disturbed him then, and it disturbed him now.

Shawn laughed. "Okay, then. I never would have guessed you had a secret fear of stuffed animals."

"It's not fear." Why was she failing to see the distinction here? "It's like seeing someone have their fingernails pulled out. It's disturbing."

"How would you know what it looks like to see someone's fingernails pulled out? Do you have a secret past as a terrorist interrogator?"

She was lucky he found her so cute. "Yes. So don't piss me off."

"Did you just make a joke?" Her eyes lit up in delight, and she laughed. "I love it. And don't threaten me, Ford. I'll sic my monkey on you."

He walked toward her and was amused to see her back up against the dresser, darting her gaze around for an escape route. "Gorillas aren't monkeys, and who is threatening who?"

All he had to do was reach his arm out for her, and she shrieked and tried to rush past him. Laughing, he didn't find it a particular challenge to halt her progress. Despite her athletic strength, he was happy to say she was no match for him. "Where are you going?"

"I have to, uh, put the grounds in the coffeemaker for tomorrow morning." She wiggled in his hold. "Let me go, you oaf."

"Oaf? Okay, Gran, I'll let you go." Rhett was amused by Shawn, by their banter, by how comfortable he felt around her. He was also aroused by the way she was willing to tease him, the way she didn't cower and back down, the way other women had with him.

"Gran?" she asked indignantly. "Is that a cougar slur?"

"No." He grinned at her, pulling her tight against his

chest so she would quit squirming. "I actually forgot you're a cougar. Though I'm not sure you qualify since I initially approached you."

"Well, I did ask you to marry me in exchange for money, so I think that makes me a model cougar." Her expression was wry, but she did stop struggling.

"For totally different reasons. Not because you couldn't score me all on your own. Because you could have. I would have been eager and willing." He leaned forward and bit her bottom lip, just to hear her expression of shock and the follow-up sigh of pleasure.

"Really?"

"Really. And I'm eager and willing right now to make you scream with pleasure." Rhett rested his hand on her waist and pulled her hard against his erection. "Now you have four minutes to deal with the coffeemaker and get back here."

Her eyes darkened and her voice was husky. "Oh, yeah? What happens if I don't?"

"I'll come into the kitchen and I'll punish you for making me wait." His heart started to pump quicker at the thought of what he could do to Shawn, at how amazing it would feel to bury his cock inside her wet and willing pussy. His blood thickened, and saliva filled his mouth.

"You'll spank me again?" she asked, and she sounded titillated by the idea.

Rhett shook his head, because it was important to keep her guessing, to maintain the control. "Probably not. You'll never know what your punishment is until I hand it out. It could be anything."

Her response was a low sound in the back of her throat. But then she disarmed him by kissing him sweetly and saying, "My time starts when you let me go."

Holy shit, she was so hot it made his body ache in ways he hadn't known were possible. Rhett released her and stepped back. "Go."

She moved quickly to the door, not pausing to look back.

Rhett checked the time on his phone. He wasn't sure if he would actually hold her to the four minutes or not. But he didn't think he would have to make that decision because Shawn was too competitive to miss the mark.

Waiting for her, he stripped off his sweatshirt and the tee beneath it and tossed them over Coconut's face. He took his watch off and set it on the nightstand. He knew a lot of guys had quit wearing watches, but he liked the feel of it on his wrist. But not when he was going to be sliding his hands over every inch of Shawn's body. He was cracking his neck, taking his chin in both hands and twisting it left, then right, when Shawn returned.

"Are you limbering up?" she asked, with a small smile. She was slightly out of breath from her efficiency.

Rhett glanced at his phone. "Three minutes. Impressive." He didn't answer her question, because he didn't need to. "Good job."

"Thanks." Her gaze raked over his chest, his abs. "Do I get a reward?"

He should have known she would take it to that conclusion. It was her personality. Shaking his head, he told her, "No. Your reward is not being punished."

Her lips parted, her eyes flashing with something close to irritation, and he waited for her to protest. It would be logical for her to protest, given Shawn's need for control.

But she didn't, and that was by far the sexiest response she could ever give him. "So what should I do?" Her hands were fiddling with the bottom of her sweater, like she wanted to strip it off and dive onto him. It was there in her expression. She wanted to take charge, shove him back on the bed, and climb on and ride him to a fast orgasm.

Efficient.

Get off and get on with it.

That's the sex life Shawn had experienced before him. But Rhett wanted more than that. He wanted submersion, loss of control, total capitulation to the pleasure between them . . . the kind of pleasure where she forgot her name, what day of the week it was, or where she was.

So the erotic dance had to start where it had the night they'd met, with his hand taking hers and guiding her onto the dance floor. "You dance with me."

"There's no music."

He scrolled through his phone and hit play, taking a guess that babymaking R&B music could cause her to giggle. He went classic rock, and as The Doors filled the room, her eyebrows went up in surprise, and pleasure. He held out his hand and she took it, her head tilting in a way that almost read as shy as he pulled her into his arms. He suspected not a single man had ever truly taken the time to seduce Shawn, and he intended to make up for that.

As they swayed to the music, he nuzzled her ear and told her, "I'm very, very glad I saw you that night at The Wet Spot."

Fingertips lightly on his shoulders, she whispered, "I am, too."

Hooking his index finger on the collar of her sweater, he dragged it down so that her chest was partially exposed. He had the long, lean lines of her clavicle and the rise of her breasts to explore with his tongue while they moved to the music. Her grip on him tightened as he lazily explored her jawline, her neck, her breasts. She started to move her hands down his shoulders to his biceps, her fingers trembling, tentative, like she expected to be stopped any second. Or maybe because she'd never allowed herself the indulgence of touching a lover in curiosity. He didn't know. But he did like it, did want her to express herself, take tactile pleasure for herself.

She seemed particularly fascinated by his abdominal muscles, brushing back and forth over them in a way that was causing him to count backward in his head to hold on to his control. She was inches above his waistband. And he was well aware of the fact that she hadn't touched his cock yet. But he wasn't going to allow it now.

He set her away from him. "Take off your sweater."

Without hesitation, Shawn complied, though she looked disappointed to have her exploration interrupted. "Put your hands in your pockets," he told her, wanting to heighten her arousal, to tease her.

Color rose in her cheeks and she looked on the verge of protesting, but instead, she dropped her sweater on the floor and slowly pushed her hands into the front pockets of her jeans, her tongue moistening her bottom lip. She seemed to recognize that sometimes initial denial created greater satisfaction in the end. That it felt good to play his game.

He wanted to heighten her anticipation until she was beside herself with want, until nothing would ever satisfy her until he pounded his cock inside her.

So he kissed her, a teasing slow kiss that he took his time with, his hand in her hair, his tongue stroking a response out of her. He liked the way their hips rested near each other, but not entirely touching. Likewise with her chest on his. Her bent elbows prevented them from coming completely in contact with each other.

"You're such a good kisser," he murmured, because she was. So many women wanted to press, then pull back, press, then pull back. They didn't want to dig in to the kiss, to commit to it, to find that the tangle of tongues and breath and desire has its own appeal. Shawn opened herself to his kiss, and he appreciated that.

"Thank you," she said, her lips shiny, eyes slumberous. "I don't think anyone has ever told me that."

"That's because they were idiots. You make a man want to kiss you all night and then start again in the morning." He did. He wanted to disappear inside her kiss, lose himself in her warmth, her taste, her willingness.

"Whatever you want," she told him, the sincerity almost bringing him to his knees.

Shawn got what he craved. She understood it. That he didn't want a woman to kowtow to him, to do what he wanted out of fear, that he wanted her to do it out of trust, out of the understanding that her surrender would bring them both more pleasure than they'd thought possible.

"There's something really very perfect about you, Shawn." He rubbed both her nipples to tight peaks with his thumbs, enjoying the dilation of her eyes and the lazy backward tilt of her head, her hips reaching for his. "I want you to know that there is nowhere I'd rather be than right here, right now."

"I feel the same way. I didn't expect to, but I do."

"Good." Rhett kissed her neck, the curve of her breast. He sucked at her nipples through the satin of her bra, first one, then the other. He trailed his tongue down her belly, dipping into the depression of her belly button, enjoying the little jerk she gave. Moving lower, he scraped his teeth on the fabric of her jeans, knowing she would want to grab his head, guide him to the perfect location. That she would want to thrust herself onto him.

The whimper she gave was evidence he was right. "Would you like to touch me?" he asked her, murmuring against her clitoris, his breath hot on her jeans.

"Yes," she whispered.

"No," he told her, pulling the zipper down and flicking his tongue inside.

This moan was more pronounced and she shifted on her feet.

She was wearing cotton panties, already damp with her arousal, and it was easy to soak the fabric with his tongue and wiggle his way to the swollen button. He popped the snap on her jeans so the waistband would slide farther apart, giving him more depth to his invasion, but still containing her hands in the pockets. Spurred on by the sounds she was making, which were growing increasingly desperate, Rhett peeled her panties down from the top and sucked on her clit.

Shawn let out a cry of ecstasy, which turned to despair as he snapped the panties back in place and stood back up. He took her hands out of her pockets. She watched him with hooded eyes, her breathing labored, cheeks and chest flushed pink. Keeping his gaze locked on hers, he undid the catch, then jerked her bra down her arms before moving behind her and tugging her wrists back toward him. He tied her hands together with the bra and let them rest on the curve of her ass.

When he shifted in front of her again, he asked in a tight voice, "Okay?" He didn't want her to do anything she wasn't comfortable with.

She nodded, swallowing hard. Her breasts were pert and tempting, her hair tumbling into her eyes, her lips slightly parted. Her jeans were sliding a little on her hips, giving him a tantalizing view of her stomach and hip bones. There was something demure, coy, about the tilt of her head, her gaze meeting his from under her lashes. Goose bumps raced across her arms.

He suddenly wanted to devour her. He wanted to eat and bite and lick every inch of her. He wanted to lose control and consume her with his lust, to take and tear them both apart with frantic passion. Knowing he couldn't unleash the full force of his sexual need, he settled for biting her earlobe, his teeth sinking in deep enough that he heard her gasp in pain. He didn't want to hurt her. It brought him back under control, just as he had known it would. He soothed his actions with soft kisses and murmured words of nothing, his fingers teasing into her panties, enjoying the warm, wet welcome he received when he drove two fingers deep inside her.

"Shh," he said when she gave a whimper, her hands jerking instinctively against the restraints.

He swallowed any further protests with a kiss as he coaxed and teased pleasure from her, seeking her G-spot. When he found it, sliding across the sensitive spongy spot, she jerked again, her mouth breaking away from his, her forehead resting on his shoulder as she fought against an orgasm. He could feel her muscles straining, feel the tightness of her nipples against his chest, hear her ragged breathing. She had remembered to wait, and that gave him immense satisfaction.

"Do you need to come?" he murmured in her ear, enjoying the brush of her lips on his shoulder.

"No," she whispered.

"Do you want to come?"

"Yes. And no."

Holding the back of her head, he slowed down his stroking, not wanting her to tumble into an orgasm. "Which is it?"

"Of course I want to. But I also know it will feel good to be driven crazy."

That was his girl. "Then we'll go with door number two. Because Shawn, you're right. It will feel good when I drive you crazy. You're going to scream my name before we're finished."

And when she did, he had a feeling that for the first time ever, he wouldn't despise the name he'd been given.

CHAPTER
THIRTEEN

SHAWN nodded, no longer able to speak. She was concentrating too hard on not losing control and coming on Rhett's finger. It was too soon. She wanted to draw out the anticipation, but he was so good at setting her on fire, stroking her into hot ecstasy that here she was, struggling to hold on.

It wasn't just his touch, though he had found her G-spot in about thirty seconds. It was having her hands behind her back. It made her breasts jut out in a way she wouldn't naturally do. It made her exposed, unable to fold forward, to embrace, to touch. It made it all about her. That was the most shocking and sensual realization of all. She never would have thought that making herself vulnerable would make her powerful, yet it did.

Sensation was heightened, intensified.

Rhett had slowed his movements to a steady hypnotic glide, moving away from her sensitive spot, but intuitively understanding that if he just jerked away from her entirely, it would catapult her into an extremely unsatisfying orgasm. Breathing deeply in and out, she calmed herself down, regained control of her body, and managed to pick her forehead off his shoulder so she could see his face, gauge his expression.

His green eyes had darkened, and he was watching her with an expression she didn't understand. It looked . . . tender. Unnerved, she tried to pull away but his hand was still in her pants, his finger still inside her, other hand cupping the back of her head. Holding her firm, he shook his head, just a slight shake of disapproval and she felt a flush of . . . what? Disappointment in herself for disappointing him?

Oh, hell, no.

Now she was really freaked out. She started to rear away from him, full-blown panic rushing over her. Given that her feet were entangled with his and her hands were tied and he was holding her, she ended up stumbling backward and would have fallen if he hadn't prevented her from going down. Which made it worse. She realized that without her hands to brace her fall, she would have landed hard on her ass, or worse, on her face.

"Shawn." He gripped her steadily, bent his head to make eye contact, but she couldn't look at him. "Shawn, look at me."

She stared at the wall, breathing hard, overwhelmed and confused. If she looked at him, he would see that she was suddenly terrified. Of how he could make her feel. Of how she could easily come to depend on him.

That wasn't her. She didn't depend on anyone. Because they would let you down. Leave. Like her father, and in ways so much more hurtful, her grandfather checking out and putting conditions on her inheritance.

Oh, God. Tears rose in her eyes, and one leaked, inching down her cheek, and she couldn't even wipe it away. She was mortified.

"Baby, talk to me. What's going on?" Rhett gently lifted her chin, forcing her to look at him. When he saw the tear, he wiped it with the pad of his thumb and then sucked the droplet off his finger.

That disarmed her. "Why did you just lick my tear?" she asked, yanked out of her maelstrom of emotion. Sometimes Rhett was just freaking weird.

"I don't know." He shrugged. "I just wanted to taste it."

She gave a desperate sort of laugh. "You're really bizarre."

"I know. I've never tried to hide who I am."

No, he hadn't.

"Why are you crying?" he asked, wrapping his arms around her waist, but loosely, like he knew she would bolt if his grip was too tight.

Which she would.

"I don't understand what you want from me."

He studied her for a long, uncomfortable moment. Awkward to her anyway. His stare was intense, as it always was. It stripped her bare, made her long to look away again, to hide from him.

"I don't want to *take* anything from you. You don't need to *give* me anything. I just want to be with you. Does that make sense?"

"I don't know," she said honestly. "It's just . . . you looked at me and I didn't get it. It was like you . . ."

Shawn stopped herself. She couldn't say it out loud. She would feel like an idiot. A presumptuous idiot.

"Like I what?" he urged.

When she still didn't answer, he frowned, the smooth skin between his eyes forming a deep trench that told her his expression was frequently one of concentration. Which she knew.

"I don't know what I look like," he told her. "But I know what I'm thinking. And what I've been thinking as I kiss you and touch you, is that you're an amazing woman and I want to give you pleasure, make you happy. And you know what that means?"

She shook her head. Sometimes it was really hard to believe that Rhett was so much younger than her. He had an easy confidence in who he was, what he said, that she envied. Yet at the same time, he made her feel very feminine, very cherished, something she'd never experienced before.

"It means I care about you. It means that if you believe in fate, it guided us both to that bar that night because we're supposed to be here, together, doing this. This is right, Shawn, me and you. And you can't tell me otherwise, because I won't believe you."

Oh, God. She had never been particularly romantic, or gushy, or emotionally exposed. But she could have sworn that everything in her just heaved, like her soul sighed in pure bliss. She even heard the exhalation of air from her mouth, a soft rush that proved she did in fact believe him. She trusted him.

That's what was so scary.

He kissed the corner of her mouth, first right, then left. "Say something, baby."

She shook her head. "No. Because if I do I might ruin this moment." It didn't have to be forever. It just had to be now.

So she kissed him. She reached out and poured her overflowing feelings into a kiss, which he accepted and deepened. As their tongues teased over each other, their moans eager and increasingly desperate, Rhett undid the bra locking her wrists together behind her back.

"I want you to touch me," he murmured, his voice rough and gravelly.

She wasn't going to argue with that. Greedily, she ran her hands over the hard plane of his abdomen, over his chest, his biceps. He was so hard, so solid. Like the man himself. There was nothing soft about Rhett, physically or otherwise. Indulging herself, she felt up his ass through his jeans. Equally solid.

When she shifted her touch to the front of his jeans, finding his erection with ease, she was feeling down the length of it, awed by its steely quality, when he broke off their kiss and covered her hand with his.

"Not yet, baby. Let me make you come first. You'd like that, wouldn't you?"

With any other man she would have given a flippant response. A casually tossed "Duh" or the equivalent. But she wasn't even tempted to be snarky with Rhett. It would be, well, disrespectful. So she said simply, "Yes."

He kissed her neck and it caused goose bumps to rise all over her arms. She was lost to him, and she knew it. When he guided her back to the bed, she let him lay her out and she waited, in a sort of warm and squishy state of anticipation as he stripped her jeans off, followed by her panties. There was no rush on his part, no rough jerking of clothes, just a steady progress, the drive on his face clear. He was a man who focused on one thing at a time, she had learned. He didn't start something and not finish it. He didn't talk to her while scrolling through his cell phone checking e-mail and social networking sites. He didn't watch TV and jump up at every commercial to do a chore the way she did.

One thing at a time, that was Rhett. He focused on a task until it was completed, and right now, his goal was to pleasure her.

He was achieving it. Shawn moaned in abandonment when he pulled her thighs apart with a firm grip and went at her with his tongue. She wasn't sure what he was doing, but it was something about the steady rhythmic, yet erratic, movements that kept her guessing, unsure of where his flickering heat would land, that had her gripping the sheet, terrified that he would stop. She had always enjoyed oral sex, had never been particularly shy about receiving it, but with Rhett, it was more than simple enjoyment. It was clawing, agonizing and desperate. It was base, primal. Wet.

But then he pulled back and wiped his mouth, breathing almost as hard as she was as he paused to stare at her sex, a finger absently trailing over her inner moisture.

It was on her lips to ask what the hell he was doing, her thighs quivering from the tension she was putting on them, when she remembered the rules. She wasn't supposed to ask questions. If she did, he wouldn't finish this. He wouldn't let her orgasm.

That, too, turned her on. The thought that he understood her body, her needs, better than she did. If it were up to her, she would come in the first five minutes, let him pump her for another three, then hit the showers, the edge taken off. But that really denied herself the intensity of pleasure that came from extended foreplay, that came from Rhett teasing and denying her.

It almost brought greater intimacy between them. She had engaged in sex by rote with Sam, a familiar choreography of clothes off, kisses, a few hot touches on each other's erogenous zones, then in and out. Sleepwalking sex.

This was so much more, it wasn't even on the same plane of existence.

She wanted to beg Rhett.

She wanted to grab his head and bury him in her.

She wanted to cry out that she was empty and she wanted him. She needed him.

But instead, she reached over and grabbed the pillow and buried her face in it so she wouldn't be tempted to cry out.

He didn't allow it. He tore the pillow from her and threw it against the wall. "Say what you need to say. It's okay. I want to hear it."

"Please," she whimpered, and her voice sounded ragged and strange to her ears. "Don't stop, please. Oh, please, don't stop."

"Put your ankles over my shoulders," he told her.

She did, without question, assuming he was going to plow into her with his cock. She welcomed the thought, wanted something to ease the deep ache. But that wasn't his plan. Instead, he slid his hands under her ass and lifted her clear off the bed, right up to his mouth.

"Oh, God!" she cried out when he made hot contact with his tongue on her clitoris.

The assault continued until she was twisting her head back and forth, fingers numb from her frantic grip on the sheet, skin crawling with goose bumps. "Rhett," she whispered, all the blood rushing to her head, her leg and butt muscles tensed from the position, her agonized ecstasy rendering her incoherent. She had something to say, only she didn't know what it was.

He lifted his mouth and looked down at her, his head framed by her thighs. "Say my name again," he told her urgently. "Scream it."

"Rhett," she said, struggling to keep her eyes open. "Oh!" she said involuntarily, when he plunged his tongue into her again.

His movements stopped and she whimpered.

"Louder."

"Rhett!" she called out, the name half plea, half question. It sounded electric to her, ringing in the quiet room, an embarrassing burst of her succumbing to him, to the needs of her body.

But it clearly wasn't that loud, because he lifted his mouth again and used one finger to pinch her ass cheek. "Say it like you mean it. Don't be ashamed, Shawn. Scream for me."

So she did. She let go of everything inside her and screamed over and over while he worked her. She came with his name on her lips, echoing in the room around them, her throat going hoarse, her pleasure transcending her body, dragging everything out of her.

And when he levered her legs down onto the bed, still tasting her, as the last strains of tight fulfillment were wrung from her, Shawn blinked, her eyes, her mouth, her heart all open to him, frozen in the profound moment of pure abandonment.

Rhett undid his jeans, watching her with a predatory expression as he voiced his approval. "That was perfect. You're perfect."

She was stunned, tremors still rippling through her.

* * *

STANDING up so he could shove his jeans and briefs off, Rhett stared down at Shawn, her breasts heaving, her cheeks pink, skin dewy from exertion. Her fingers were fluttering upward, reaching for him, but on the bed, like she wasn't even aware of what she was doing. She looked like she was in shock.

He felt a little that way himself. Something had happened to him when he had listened to Shawn scream his name, with the tangy taste of her on his tongue, legs wrapped around him. Something had shifted, and he didn't know what it was. He only knew that he had never wanted a woman as much as he wanted her, that he had never known the kind of satisfaction he had felt when she had opened her throat and cried out her need, her pleasure.

His tongue was thick, his cock hard to the point of painful, his control hanging on by the merest of threads.

If she touched him, if he felt the feathery, soft touch of her fingers on his back, if her milky thighs wrapped around him, he wasn't going to be able to contain himself. He was going to lose it in her, and he needed a second.

So as he divested himself of the remains of his clothes, he told her, "Hands above your head. Legs spread. No touching."

Her eyelashes fluttered in confusion, but after a second, she did as she was told. The eroticism of her obedience humbled him, stoked his arousal to a fever pitch, and he moved between her thighs. Her body was displayed to pure perfection, arms above her head, neck long and graceful, breasts rising up, her legs spread wide for him, her blond curls dark and damp. When he sank into her, she cried out, then looked up to him for approval. For instruction.

He paused, the agony of the thick, pulsing desire, the primal pleasure from her surrender, almost unbearable. He shook his head, indicating no speaking, because he couldn't speak himself. He wanted to experience his invasion of her body in silence, her screams of his name still echoing in his ears. She understood without any words from him, and her teeth sank into her bottom lip to hold back the moans as he began to move inside her.

Never had he felt this kind of connection, this deep of an intimacy with a woman, and he bent over to kiss her, wanting her to taste the lingering scent of her own body on his tongue. "Say it again," he murmured softly against her mouth, his gaze locked with hers.

She knew what he meant. "Rhett," she whispered, and the sweetness of his name on her lips broke his control.

He thrust deep and just said, "Shawn," hoping she would understand that this was something different, something important happening between them. "Touch me."

As he pushed in and out of her warmth, he expected her to lock her ankles behind his ass, to dig her nails into his back.

But she didn't. Her legs stayed spread wide for him.

While her fingers reached up and stroked his cheeks.

It disarmed him entirely, that soft caress, her smooth hands cupping his face, while she mouthed his name in silence, the sentiment hitting him harder than when it had been torn from her on a shout.

Turning his head, he kissed her fingers, dragging one into his mouth, biting the tip before pulling it down onto the bed and intertwining her fingers with his. When the rush came, when he exploded inside her, their eyes never left each other, and Rhett knew that they had just crossed a line that couldn't be taken back.

He didn't want to take it back.

He wanted to stay there forever, bodies meshed together, emotions real and honest.

CHAPTER
FOURTEEN

"SO what is this, Take Your Hot Husband We Didn't Know You Had to Work Day?" Linda asked Shawn Monday morning after she had introduced Rhett.

"Ha ha. I'm so glad my staff has such a sense of humor."

Linda shrugged, looking remarkably not contrite. "Friday you left at noon single, or so I thought. You been hiding him in your bedroom?" She eyed Rhett over her reading glasses. "I know I would."

Shawn was surprised that more than annoyance, what she was actually feeling was a prickling of pride that her accounts receivable employee thought her husband was hot stuff. Because the truth was, he was hot stuff. He was gorgeous, built, he focused on her in bed, and he made coffee.

He was a keeper.

And she had gone from being entirely freaked out to wondering if, in fact, this relationship could be something more than a matter of saving her track and getting some booty at the same time.

Maybe it was the afterglow, but she was feeling just fine, thank you very much. Nothing Linda said was going to irritate her. "Maybe I have," she said airily.

Rhett gave her a sly smile, and she knew he was remembering exactly what she was—last night and this morning's repeat performance. Her body still ached in places she didn't know she could ache.

Linda snorted, and dropped her reading glasses down onto her ample chest. She was a feisty woman in her late fifties, and she favored cheetah prints and cherry-red hair dye. She had been working at Hamby as long as Shawn could remember. In fact, when Shawn was little, she had been in awe of Linda, who had seemed like an exotic bird, with her eighties shoulder pads and jumbo hair, lips shiny and red, eyes painted with glittery shadow. Now she was settled into her desk chair behind her computer, eyeballing Shawn with no small amount of curiosity. "So I never pegged you for being able to keep a secret, girl, but apparently you've been mum about your dating life. How did you meet?"

"Through Eve Monroe, my sister-in-law," Rhett told her.

That was a bit of a stretch, but it could be true. Frankly, it would have only been a matter of time before they had crossed paths. The only reason they hadn't was because Eve had been married to Nolan just a few months and she had been busy changing careers, and Shawn had been dealing with her grandfather's illness. They hadn't seen each other much lately, other than at book club, and never with Nolan's family around.

"Hmm. Well, congratulations then," Linda said, and that seemed to be the end of it. "So are you actually working today, or did you bring your man candy just for show and now you're bugging?"

"I'm working, thank you very much. And his name is Rhett. Show a little respect," she told Linda, but since she was grinning, the admonishment wasn't going to have much impact. But she couldn't help it. She was feeling, well, like a new bride. It was embarrassing, but she couldn't stop it.

Linda rolled her eyes. "Sure thing, hon. I'm on it."

"We're having a party on Valentine's Day, and you're invited."

"Open bar?" Linda asked.

"Cash bar." There was no way in hell Shawn was paying for her friends and family to get liquored up and line dance to *Cotton-Eyed Joe*.

"What?" Linda was appalled.

"Maybe we can work something out," Rhett said. "We'll see how long the guest list is."

They left Linda sputtering at her desk about the nerve of some people, and they went into Shawn's office. Rhett closed the door firmly behind him and said, "Give me a kiss."

"Another one?" she teased, though she was more than willing to comply. Wrapping her arms around his neck, she kissed him deeply. "Mmm. Wakes me up better than coffee."

"I thought it was my cock pounding you that woke you up this morning."

"That, too." Her nipples hardened at the memory of how he had awakened her with kisses and a teasing hand over her breasts, her sex, dragging her out of sleep and into languid pleasure before entering her with a decisive thrust. "I don't usually like Monday mornings, but then again, they've never started like that."

He patted her backside with a familiarity that came from having seen and touched every inch of her, and Shawn felt perfectly comfortable in his arms. It was odd to think that she was more intimate, more connected, with a man she had known ten days than with a man she'd spent three years dating.

"We have a new tradition, then."

Neither one of them mentioned that this was supposed to be temporary. They were clearly both determined to just enjoy it, and Shawn was willing to reside in Delusionville for a while longer. "Thanks for coming in with me on your day off."

"I'm glad to. I want to see what you do, see the behind-the-scenes here at the track."

She kissed him again, because she couldn't seem to get enough of his lips. "Hm. Then I guess we'd better open this door back up and behave ourselves, or the only work that will get done today will be of a more personal nature."

He sighed. "Alright, let's get cracking." He nudged her forward and opened the door back up. "But later we'll pick back up where we left off."

"I don't doubt it for a minute," she told him most sincerely. Then aware that several of her employees were craning their necks to gawk into her office, she went around her desk and sat down, indicating he take a seat himself. "So this is my cave, where I spend the majority of my time. Glamorous, isn't it?"

"About as much so as the inside of a stock car." Rhett settled into his chair and glanced around at her many stacks of papers, the old promo posters that had been tacked to the wall and were now faded. "So how is business?"

That was the crux of all her problems. "Business is slow. We're two-bit in a crowded field. I hate to admit that, but it's true. We run a variety of races, from vintage to moto to modifieds, but they're local and regional. They don't draw the big crowds, so we don't get the big vendors or the big sponsors. No big dollars coming in from corporate, and ticket sales alone can't turn a profit, nor can entry fees for drivers." Shawn settled back in her chair, letting it swivel a little. "It's hard for me to talk about this—it feels disloyal to Pops—but the truth is, racing has changed. This isn't the seventies, when it was good ole boys throwing down on the track for shits and grins. This is about money. Survival."

Rhett nodded. "I understand that, and I appreciate that you're willing to discuss it with me. Family businesses are more than dollar signs or bricks and mortar. It's a way of life. It's about heart, not money."

"Exactly." She felt relief that he got it. Got her. "But heart won't pay the electric bill, and I'm concerned that we're losing ground every year. We won't make it if I don't make some changes."

"You need to go national." Rhett steepled his fingers in front of his chin and leaned toward her desk. "You need sanctioning from the big dogs."

Shawn nodded. "With their stamp of approval, and the possibility of earning national points here, as well as a track title, we'll pull bigger drivers, bigger sponsorships, bigger vendors. But I don't even know where to begin with that. I'm not a wheeler and dealer. I'm not a public relations expert. I've basically been the events coordinator. Our staff is small. I don't know where to start."

"I don't either. But I can guarantee Eve does. Didn't you say she offered some recommendations for new hires?"

"Yes. I have to contact them and do some interviews. I feel like I'm in over my head, I'm not going to lie. We need a new website. New promo photos. Social media networking. We need to be modern if we want to succeed, while still holding on to the idea that Hamby is a family track, run by a family, for families to enjoy together."

Rhett smiled. "I totally agree. And what better way to kick off the new season and a media blitz than with our wedding here at the track? Pit crew member marries track owner in a wedding attended by some of the hottest names in professional racing. The new Hamby Speedway dynasty. We'll spin the shit out of it."

Shawn started to get excited and nervous all at the same time. "But the hottest names in racing won't be at our wedding, that I'm aware of. We said family and closest friends only."

"I say we broaden the circle a bit. You grew up with Evan and Elec Monroe, and Evan was my boss. Eve will be there. I'll invite Evan's crew chief, since he and I worked together for two years, and he's a fan favorite. Doesn't your friend Harley work for Cooper Brickman? She can bring him as a date."

The thought of Harley inviting her boss, one of the most

notorious playboys on the driving circuit, as her date, made her laugh. "I think Harley would curl up like a pill bug if we suggested that. She does not like the spotlight."

"But you get the idea."

"We're going to turn our wedding into a media blitz?" It made total sense, but somehow it offended her. It was a wedding, not a business opportunity. Except it wasn't a real wedding, so she was clearly being ridiculous.

"Yes." Rhett had a calculating look on his face that she recognized. It meant he was focused on the idea and was going to devote his energy to making it successful. "We'll do this, Shawn. We make the track a success and your Pops will be proud, toasting you with a glass of whiskey up there in the racetrack in the sky."

Her heart melted like ice cream in August. "Thanks, Rhett. I appreciate you helping me. You don't have to, you know."

"I don't have to. I want to." He smiled at her. "We're in this together. You and me. I care about you."

"I care about you, too," she said.

Which was probably the greatest risk of all, but she was willing to take it.

RHETT sat across the table from Shawn at a steak house, watching her cut her beef into bite-size pieces and eat them, her eyes sparkling, expression animated. He loved a woman who wasn't afraid to eat some meat and potatoes. He loved the way she smiled at him, like he was the only person in the room. Except for when she would occasionally glance up at the TV to check the score on the Gamecocks basketball game playing over the bar.

He felt as if their landing in this situation, married, falling for each other, made about as much sense as a trapdoor in a canoe, but he wasn't going to question it. He was just going to enjoy this time with her.

With his wife.

She gave a cheer as the Cocks got a three-point shot. "Did you go to college?" she asked.

"No. Some of my sisters did. But they paid for it themselves, and I didn't have that much ambition, or more accurately, I didn't care that much about school. I was already in vocational school by tenth grade, working on engines. I knew that's what I wanted to do." He had never regretted that choice. "I'm not cut out to sit behind a desk or work with people. I'm not really a people person."

She laughed. "You act like you're an ogre, which you most definitely are not. But it's good that you understood yourself."

"I did. I still do." Rhett took a long swallow of his beer. "Did you ever want to do anything, like be a nurse or a flight attendant or something?" The image of her serving drinks to restless passengers was hard to conjure.

"Nah. I grew up at the track. It was a part of me. There was nothing else I wanted to do, even once I stopped racing."

"Why did you stop racing?"

"I stopped winning." Shawn grinned. "I may have had a bit of a problem with being too impulsive. You have to be more disciplined than I am."

Rhett grinned right back at her. "Well, isn't that what we've been working on? Your discipline?"

She blushed, like he knew she would, her eyes fluttering down briefly before meeting his again. She was the perfect mix of feminine and demure, yet strong and independent. She would hesitate, she would blush, but she always rose to the challenge. He found her to be the sexiest woman he'd ever met.

"Not the same thing, Ford." She stuck her fork out at him. "And you shouldn't speak to your elders that way."

That cracked him up. "That's not precisely how I think of you. In fact, it's not even close."

The waving fork came over to his plate and swiped some

of his mashed potatoes. "Hey. Eat your own food." Though he didn't mind at all.

"Us old ladies need our food smashed up."

"Why, do you have dentures?"

That had her hastening to say, "No, of course not."

He laughed. "I know that, you dork."

She made a face. "Okay, just verifying. I liked teasing you until it came to that. Then I realized I don't actually want you to think of me as old, so why the hell am I bringing it up? Maybe I should bite some corn on the cob to prove it."

"That's going to prove you're still young?" Her thought processes boggled his mind.

"No! It will prove I don't have dentures."

"Shawn, I've kissed you. I've slept beside you. I look at you a good portion of every day. I know you don't have dentures. And even if you did, I would still think you're hot as hell. Now, why are we talking about this?"

She didn't answer that question. Instead, she said, "Hey, how come you've never had me give you a blow job?"

Rhett almost choked on his T-bone. She was killing him tonight. "Is this really the place to talk about it?"

She shrugged. "The acoustics suck in here. It's louder than fight night at the honky-tonk. No one can hear us."

"First of all, does it really bother you that you're older than me? Do you feel like I'm not mature enough for you?" He was curious about that, given how frequently she'd brought up their age difference.

But she shook her head. "No, I think you're actually very mature. In some ways, you have it together more than me because you never second-guess yourself. I guess it just seems like society cares about women being older. Maybe I'm bracing myself for the reactions I'm going to get. Maybe I need reassurance that you don't care."

"Why would I care? I don't. Trust me. In fact, I like that you're a woman in her thirties. You know yourself.

Who gives a shit what other people think? They're just jealous that you snagged a younger guy." He winked at her.

She laughed. "Well, there is probably truth to that. I thought Linda was going to leap over her desk and lick you."

Oh, God, there was a terrifying image. That had been a lot of cheetah print and bold accessories. He wasn't sure he could handle that kind of bling coming at him. "Please save me if that ever happens. I'm not sure I would know what to do in that circumstance."

She went back into his mashed potatoes. He turned his plate so she would have easier access.

"You can handle yourself just fine. So what about my question?"

Tenacious, she was. It was going to serve her well as they took the track in a new direction. But she didn't want to talk about the track. She wanted to know why she hadn't been asked to suck his cock. The thought had him shifting on his seat, an erection springing to life. "Because when you're having sex the way we've been having it, when I'm asking you to give complete control over to me, for me personally, I feel like having you suck me borders on the line of degradation. I want a woman to suck me because she wants to, not because I ordered her."

"Even if I say I want to?"

He shook his head. "Doesn't matter. Because the whole point is, you've agreed to agree, so you have to say you want to. Plus you can't initiate it. So it doesn't work for me. I don't get off on that."

She seemed to mull that over. "Oh, I think I understand. It's complicated, huh?"

"I've given a lot of thought to what I want, very precisely." Maybe too much thought, but it was his sex life. Why waste time being unsatisfied or choosing the wrong partners?

"Have you, um, done this with lots of other women?" Then immediately she looked angry at herself for asking.

Rhett wanted to reassure her. He wasn't offended by the question. It was natural to want to know, and he wasn't going to tease her in such a vulnerable moment, the way he imagined a lot of guys would. Shawn had had enough of that in her dating, she needed a man who would respect her needs and questions. "No. Not lots of women. And never like this. Never the way it is with you. Never this amazing."

Shawn nodded, thoughtful. "Okay."

He waited, but that was all she said. "Okay? That's it?" Not to be an emotional pussy, but he was kind of hoping she'd throw him a compliment back. Hell, he needed to hear that he was pleasing her, too, even if he knew it when they were in bed. Which only proved that he was falling hard for her if he needed to hear it in words.

"What? Oh, I've never done this with anyone before."

He knew that. "That's not what I meant." He turned and glanced at the TV, wondering if the game was distracting her, but it was a commercial break. He wanted to hear her say that it was different with him, that she thought it was amazing as well.

Looking back, he realized she was watching him.

"I can't say it yet. I want to, but I can't." She smiled sweetly. "But I will say this—I owe the Bitches Book Club a huge thank-you."

He smiled back. It was enough for now. "You call yourselves the Bitches Book Club?"

"Yes. To distinguish ourselves from soccer moms."

That had him laughing. "I would say that would do it. That and the post-meeting stop off at a fetish club."

"Well, you know, if you're going to discuss a book, you might as well really dig into it. We coordinate food around the book themes, too."

Why did that not surprise him? "What did you eat that night? Oysters and hot sauce?"

"Cupcakes with whips and cuffs on them. The fondant work was pretty stellar."

And this was his wife. The sweet and sexy, all mixed together. Rhett raised his beer to her. "Well played, Shawn. Well played."

CHAPTER
FIFTEEN

SHAWN figured it was a toss-up who was more miserable—her, Rhett, or the photographer, who literally winced every time she glanced down at her screen to check the shots.

What could she say? Getting engagement shots taken for what was essentially a wedding for marketing purposes was not high on her list of fun things to do. She felt completely ridiculous, and it was clear that Rhett felt the same way because he was stiff beside her, his hand clammy as he clasped hers per the photographer's instructions.

Sandy was watching them with a look of pure horror. "Oh, hell, no. This is not going to work."

"What?" Rhett asked in annoyance.

"You look like you have gas!" was his mother's opinion.

That made Shawn crack the first smile in the past thirty minutes.

"Momma," Rhett growled, "I'm trying. But I'm getting blue balls out here. Can't we do this in the house?"

"So people can see our shabby living room suite that your father has been promising to replace for me and never does? Absolutely not. It's beautiful out here with the barn in the backdrop."

"It's February. We're standing in mud with bare trees behind us. This is not nature at its finest."

"Do we have a shot we can use?" Sandy asked the photographer, whose name was Erika. The poor woman probably wanted to give back the deposit and go home.

"Not really," Erika said, scrolling through the digital shots. "I'm not getting any genuine emotion out of them."

"The only genuine emotion I'm feeling right now is irritation," Rhett said.

"It shows."

Shawn snorted. She was glad he was as uncomfortable as she was. First she'd had to debate what to wear, then had settled on casual, then Erika had insisted they take their coats off, so she was freezing. A thin sweater was no match for forty degrees.

Jeannie was over with her kids for dinner—the door opened and the kids came tumbling out to play in the yard. "How's it going?" Jeannie asked.

"It isn't," her mother told her. She turned to Erika. "You know what? Let's give Shawn and Rhett a few minutes to regroup. Why don't you snag some shots of the kids playing?"

"Thank God," was Rhett's opinion as he relaxed beside her. "My face hurts from forced smiling."

Shawn turned and reached out to massage his cheeks. "Our lives are so hard, aren't they?"

"They really are." He grabbed her hand again, this time with a smirk on his face. "Come around the corner and make out with me."

Laughing, Shawn let him drag her a few feet away. "You're naughty."

"That's the rumor on the street."

"Were you a bad little boy?" she asked him, smiling, curious as to what Rhett had been like as a child.

"I don't think so. Though I was good at silent maneuvering when I did want something, or was where I wasn't supposed to be. When you're quiet, you can get away with murder."

"Shoot, that's what I did wrong." Shawn figured he had a point. "I was always about as subtle as tie-dye. Fortunately for me, my mother didn't believe in discipline."

"What do you mean? How can you not believe in discipline? Is that even possible?"

"When your mom is a self-proclaimed hippie, it's very possible. She didn't want to stifle our moral growth with preconceived notions of right and wrong." It sounded as cracked to her now at thirty-two as it had at ten. "I say she's lucky we didn't grow up to be hard-core criminals."

"I guess you proved her theory, though. She probably takes credit, doesn't she?" Rhett looked amused.

"She does. And it's annoying. I'm sorry, every kid needs boundaries. There's a big difference between enforcing a bedtime so they're not nuts in school as compared to corporal punishment. My mom lumps them all together. But my grandparents saved us. They taught us not to burp in public and that bathing has its merits."

"I'm very grateful for that. The bathing part, that is. You can burp all you want." Rhett took both of her hands in his and rubbed them gently. "Damn, it's cold out here. I bet all the other kids envied your freedom. When I think of all the hours I could have wasted watching *Power Rangers* if my parents hadn't limited my TV time. I could be a superhero today."

Shawn laughed. "What a tragedy. But while I didn't have a curfew, TV was a no-no, and processed foods were not allowed in the house. Everyone else had a snack cake in their lunch, and I had raisins. It's just not the same, trust me."

The horrified look on his face confirmed this.

"So which Power Ranger did you want to be?" she asked him.

There was no hesitation whatsoever. "Red."

Then he did something she wouldn't have ever in a million years pictured him doing. He threw out his arms and went into a karate stance. "Go, go, Power Rangers!"

Shawn loved it. "Okay, that is the most awesome thing you've ever done."

His eyebrows went up and down. "Ever?"

She laughed. "Okay, maybe not *ever* because you do rock my socks in bed. But that's pretty awesome."

Rhett stood back up and pulled her close against his chest. "Thanks. You cold?"

"Freezing."

"Let me warm you up." He pulled her even tighter into his arms and kissed her.

"Better than hot chocolate," he said.

It was.

SANDY Ford watched her grandkids playing and jammed her hands into her coat pockets.

"Were they that bad?" Jeannie asked.

"Oh, they were worse," Sandy assured her. "I know Rhett hates having his picture made, but good Lord. He looked like he did when he had the stomach flu."

Jeannie laughed. "Maybe you should just let it go. You can't force him into anything, you know that."

Did she ever. He was by far the most stubborn of her kids. "I hate to accept defeat, but I may have to."

"So what do you think of Shawn?" Jeannie asked.

"I like her." Not that she knew her particularly well, but it was clear Rhett was happy with her, and that made Sandy happy. Glancing over at her son, she nudged Jeannie and murmured, "Look at him."

He was doing some kind of role-playing thing, flinging his arms around and going into a crouch, while Shawn's laughter rang in the yard.

"What the . . ." Jeannie sounded as stunned as Sandy

felt. Given that Jeannie had been well into her teens when Rhett was born, she was more than aware that her brother was not the most animated Ford·offspring.

Quick, before the moment was lost, Sandy reached out and snagged Erika, who had been taking shots of the kids. In a low voice, she murmured, so Rhett and Shawn wouldn't hear her, "Five o'clock. Take the shot."

It sounded like she was in a Jason Bourne movie, but hell, whatever it took. She wanted one decent picture of her son clearly in love.

Fortunately, Erika was a good enough photographer to understand this could be her one and only crack at going home with something for her portfolio, because she immediately swung around and started shooting. Rhett pulled Shawn into his arms and kissed her with a tenderness that brought a tear to a mother's eye. Sandy was even willing to ignore the fact that Shawn was in her thirties if this was how her baby boy felt about her.

Erika gave a sound of triumph as she clicked through the pictures on her screen. "Look at this."

It was a great shot. They were gazing into each other's eyes. "I love it."

"That's beautiful," Jeannie agreed.

"Rhett, come over here and see this," Sandy called to her son. She was ready to go back in the house and drink some coffee to warm up. Mission accomplished.

RHETT had forgotten his mother was anywhere near them. He pulled back from Shawn and made a face, realizing they were still stuck doing the photo shoot. They wouldn't be allowed to go back inside until his mother deemed a picture romantic enough. He was starting to think he'd go down on a knee in the damn mud if it got this business over with. He wanted to take his wife home and snuggle on the couch for a couple of hours until he could strip her naked and have his way with her. It was the way the last three days had gone, and he was digging it, he had to say. This marriage business was damn convenient.

The whole getting-to-know-you thing was sped up by them living in the same house. The majority of the time, when Rhett wasn't at work or the gym, he was with Shawn, and already their days had taken on a predictable pattern of dinner, a little TV or a beer at the bar up the road, maybe some darts or pool, then a few delicious hours in bed together before they fell asleep. Honestly, he wasn't sure he could ask for anything more perfect.

And the more time he spent with Shawn, the more he realized that his initial attraction to her was growing into something more, deeper, truer.

Hell, he was falling in love with her.

When his mother called him over, and he and Shawn saw the image Erika had captured with her camera, it was there for him to clearly see. Oh, yeah. He was falling in love with her.

Given the way she gazed up at him with limpid eyes in the photo, Rhett was inclined to think he wasn't the only one suffering from the affliction. Shawn looked . . . soft. Gushy. Wide-eyed. It made his heart swell all over again.

"What do you think?" his mother asked. "Isn't this a great shot?"

"That was devious, Momma," he told her, his throat tight. He didn't trust himself to agree with her assessment, or he might get overly emotional.

"It's candid, honest," his mother protested. "This is way better than anything we could have gotten with you posing."

"I can't argue with that," Shawn said.

Rhett glanced down at her. Her face was pale, nose red from the cold, and she looked thoughtful, teeth digging into her bottom lip.

"Well, let's go in the house, then, before we lose our fingers."

His mother was all smiles, promising coffee and cookies. Jeannie grinned at him. "You've made her day."

"That was my goal," he told her sarcastically. "What is she going to do with these pictures anyways?"

"Hang them on the wall with the pictures of the rest of us from our engagement shoots. And I have to tell you, I'm jealous. Photography is so artistic now. When I married Mark, we had those horrible canned shots with his hand on my shoulder, and we're wearing matching sweaters. I mean, seriously?"

Rhett laughed. He had spent some time as a child studying his mother's hall of marital fame photos marching along the beige wall to the bedrooms, and he had to admit he'd been entertained by some of the fashions. "Sammy's picture was worse than yours. Bill's holding the cat, for Chrissake. Shawn, you have to see these pictures, seriously. It's like an alley of awful."

"Hush," his mother yelled back to him.

But that only made him laugh more, glad the mood had lifted. Shawn was smiling as they went into the house and kicked off their shoes. He led her over to the hall that started with his oldest sister Sammy and descended on down to Nolan, the last Ford to get married.

"I don't think I realized how big your family really is until just now," Shawn marveled as they strolled down the hall, checking out his sister Rachel's underwater scuba engagement shot, to Dawn and her husband sitting on a horse fence holding hands.

Nolan was smiling in his picture, Eve tucked up against his chest. She wasn't smiling, which was typical Eve, but the way she clasped his hands tightly against her rib cage spoke volumes if you knew her. There was an empty spot next to them on the wall, and suddenly it wasn't so funny anymore. Rhett knew that his picture with Shawn would be printed out, framed, and hung to fill the final spot in the Ford family puzzle. Only it wasn't real. And in six months, he would be the first Ford to get divorced and break his mother's heart.

Not to mention his.

Suddenly, the full impact of what he had done, agreed to, hit him hard, and he squeezed Shawn's hand.

Most people didn't fall in love in two weeks.

But he wasn't most people.

He couldn't expect her to feel the same way anytime soon. But he could give her reasons to eventually feel that way. He could be the best damn husband anyone could ever ask for, in bed and out.

Shawn looked up at him, puzzled. "What are you thinking?"

"You don't want to know," he told her. They were thoughts that would probably scare the living shit out of her. Thoughts of forever and love and family.

"I can't believe we have this wedding party in eight days."

"Yeah. Me either."

If the party didn't scare her senseless, Rhett had five months to convince her to consider that their relationship might be real. He was confident he could do it.

He wasn't letting Shawn go, now that he had found the woman for him. End of story.

SHAWN knew Rhett was right—she probably didn't want to know what he was thinking. It was probably something along the lines of being horrified that he had agreed to this fake marriage and how guilty he felt over duping his family. Shawn didn't really want to hear that said out loud, because then she would feel even more guilty than she already did.

Every day she spent with Rhett, she grew more and more confused. If this was a business arrangement only, then it was a shitty thing to be doing to the people in their lives, loss of Hamby Speedway or not. But if it wasn't just a business arrangement—which most of the time it sure didn't feel like that—then what the heck was it?

Rhett, despite his reputation as being serious and intense, was the easiest man to be around she had ever encountered. All her previous relationships had felt like she was jockeying for position, a teasing game of one-upmanship, communication centered around taking jabs at each other under the guise of joking. Like two guys in a locker room, not a man and woman who claimed to care about each other. It wasn't like that at all with Rhett. He was kind and considerate, he asked her opinions, and he listened to her woes and worries. He offered useful advice, and he got excited over her successes.

Then in bed, well, there were no words to describe how absolutely sexy he made her feel, and how totally absorbed by pleasure she was when he was of a mind to have sex with her.

So what did it all mean? She had no clue. All she knew was that the last week had been one of the best of her life. She was pumped about the opportunities she and Rhett were planning for the track, she was pleased to have a partner to even discuss them with, and while she'd never been lonely in her house before, Rhett fit into her home perfectly.

But here at his parents' house, the images of his siblings and their spouses blending on one long wall of happiness and expectation, Shawn felt torn between wanting this to be real and horror with herself for violating something so clearly sacred. The Fords weren't her family. They respected marriage. Shawn found that she herself did, more than she had ever realized before all of this.

"What did we get ourselves into?" she asked with a laugh that was intended to sound casual, jovial, but sounded shaky instead. She meant regarding the party, but the truth was, it could be said for the entirety of what they had been, and were, doing.

But Rhett just shrugged, still looking at the pictures, not her. "The party will be fun."

She wanted to scream that that wasn't what she meant. She wanted to very pathetically ask him how he really felt about her. She wanted to say that she was grateful to him.

Instead, she copped out and joked, "At least we can get drunk. We're practically obligated to drink champagne, so we might as well take advantage."

Rhett finally looked at her. The corner of his mouth lifted slightly. "Good point. It will loosen you up." He leaned closer to her, his breath caressing her cheek and causing her to shiver. "Then I can take you up the ass like I've been wanting to."

Hello. Shawn had never engaged in that particular activity, and she wasn't sure she wanted to. "We'll see." If he wanted to kick up the kink, honestly, she'd prefer they dust off her vibrator. The back door had never been a fantasy for her.

But he just gave a slow, seductive laugh that had her hoo-hah heating up. "Since when do you call the shots? We do what I want, and you'll like it."

The fact was, she probably would. He hadn't been wrong yet.

CHAPTER
SIXTEEN

"OH, no. No. Absolutely not. As in hell no," Shawn said, in case there was any doubt in anyone's mind. She was not going to ride the mechanical bull. "This isn't a real bachelorette party because I'm already married, so I do not need to act like an idiot."

She was perfectly content to sit at the sticky table in the country western–themed bar and drink her beer while she moved her feet to some Tim McGraw tunes. Simple. Worked for her.

Charity had other ideas. She was dressed in nothing but a denim vest with fringe dangling at her ta-tas, a tiny denim skirt, and hot pink cowboy boots. "Don't be a spoilsport!" she said, wetting her lips with yet more lip gloss and fluffing her blond hair. "Cut loose a little."

"I think you're being loose enough for all of us," Eve told her with a grin.

"Bitch." Though Charity didn't look particularly hurt. "I want to dance! You old ladies can sit here like a bunch of lame-os, but I'm going to dust off my two-step. Harley, you coming?"

Her twin shook her head rapidly. "No." She looked like

she would prefer to paint her naked body with honey and go strolling through a bear's den than dance on the floor with a multitude of skimpily dressed women and one drunk fifty-year-old man who was aiming too high with his flirtations.

Shawn was with Harley on this one.

Eve shook her head when Charity asked her. "I can't dance. I look like I'm being electrocuted." She sipped her beer and glanced around. "Man, I do not miss being single. This is a meat market, and not the freshest cuts, I have to say."

"Thanks," Harley said with a frown, pumping her straw furiously up and down in her fruity drink. "That's very helpful to those of us who are single."

Oops. "You don't want anyone here anyways," Shawn protested. "There isn't a guy here worthy of you."

"That argument gets stale when you haven't been on a date in a year."

"I can sympathize with that," Shawn said. "Before Rhett I was on a dry spell that had the trees begging the dogs to lift a leg. When you least expect it, you'll meet someone."

"I doubt it," Harley said. Then she smiled, "But this is your night anyway. Though I have to admit, I'm having trouble keeping track of Rhett and Nolan's sisters. There's just so many of them, and their names all seem to end in 'y.'"

"Tell me about it," Shawn agreed. Five of Rhett's sisters had come and were at the bar ordering drinks. "They all look similar, too, and the only one with a stand-out name, Rachel, is the one who lives in California. The rebel."

Eve snorted. "Yeah, she's so rebellious that she works as a CPA."

"You know, to people like Sandy and Nolan Senior, and my grandparents, and your parents, leaving the Carolinas is akin to seceding from the South. Unless you move to Georgia."

"Then they just think you're being stubborn." Eve grinned.

Danny, Sammy, Andy, Melissa, and Dawn, the Ford sisters, came back to the table, various drinks in hand.

"It's too bad Jeannie couldn't make it," Andy said. "But Asher was projectile vomiting." Given the way she was swaying her hips to the music and grinning, the sympathy seemed more like relief that it wasn't her stuck at home with a sweaty kid.

"So tell us gossip about Rhett as a kid," Eve said. "So we can shame him tomorrow."

Danny laughed. "He was spoiled, I can tell you that. Dad wanted another son, which is why half of us girls have male nicknames. I don't think Mom cared one way or the other, but there is no question he was her baby. And ours. We used to put him in our old dresses."

The image of Rhett dolled up made Shawn snort. "That must have been a sight to behold. He's so . . . masculine." Immediately, she felt the heat in her cheeks. That didn't sound right. It sounded very smitten and girly. Yikes.

Melissa rolled her eyes, lifting her drink, which looked an awful lot like straight bourbon. "He wasn't born six two with rock-solid biceps, you know. He was a scrawny enough little kid. With a freakish ability to never blink. For a while we were sure he was Damian from *The Omen* reincarnated. Mom was a little pissed about that when we started calling him JB, for Jackal Baby."

Eve laughed. "That sounds like something I would have done. I love it."

"Would have done?" Shawn asked. "Hell, you still would."

"True."

Danny set down her drink and stripped off her hoodie. "Okay, I never get out of the house. Ever. I am going to dance. I may be too old for this shit, and I may be happily married, but sometimes a woman still needs to shake what the good Lord gave her."

"Charity is already out there. She's the one surrounded

by a cloud of White Diamonds. She thinks wearing an Elizabeth Taylor scent will attract older men with money."

All the sisters went out to the dance floor. They didn't try to drag Eve, obviously knowing their sister-in-law well enough to realize she couldn't be dragged anywhere, not even out of a burning fire if she had decided she wanted to stay and get a tan. Harley was no match for them, though. One tug, and they had her. Shawn bailed by saying she wanted to talk to Eve. Which she did, so it wasn't a total lie.

"Do you really want to talk to me?" Eve asked, shifting her chair closer to Shawn's to be heard over the music. "Or were you just trying to get out of dancing?"

"I wanted to ask you something." It was a weird thing to ask, but hell, Shawn was curious. She'd never been married before. "How often do you and Nolan have sex?"

Eve spit out the beer she'd been sipping and choked. "Goddammit, Shawn! Will you fucking warn me if you're going to ask something like that? I almost drowned from my Heineken."

"Sorry. But I am serious. Like, what is normal when you're married?"

"Well." Eve wiped her mouth with a cocktail napkin and then rubbed it down the front of her tight shirt. "I would say on average, it's three times a week. It would probably be more like four or five if our schedules didn't keep us apart. Why? Is Rhett falling asleep watching TV instead of banging you? He's only twenty-five, for crying out loud."

Shawn coughed. "No. Um, it's kind of the opposite. We've had sex every day for the last ten days. I was just wondering if, you know, that's normal. And if, maybe at some point, it's going to slow down."

Eve's jaw dropped. "Ten days in a row? Are you serious?"

Shawn nodded.

"Are they quickies, or are they like actual sexual events?"

Oh, they were not quickies. "Actual events. Usually at least an hour, most closer to two." And every day had been a little more freeing, a little more arousing, a little more all-encompassing. She'd never been so in tune with her body, never had so many orgasms in such a short span of time. It was amazing and wonderful and, frankly, scary as hell.

"Holy crap. I think I need to have a word with my husband." Eve laughed. "Though, honestly, at some point I think that would just be overkill for me. Nolan and I have a rocking sex life and that would just cut into my sleep schedule. So, how do you feel about it? Is it boring or something? Is that why you're asking?"

That most definitely was not the problem. "No, it's not boring at all. I love it. It makes all the sex I've had before look like child's play. I was just wondering if at some point we're going to have a sexual crash, and then it will be nothing. Or if I might be doing harm, you know, like wrecking my vagina or something. I would think it needs a break at some point."

"It's not a Walmart worker. It doesn't need an hour for lunch." Eve made a face at her.

"I know." Shawn laughed. "It just seems like it can't be good for it."

"Well, ask it. Like 'Hey, vag, how are you feeling today?' If it feels beat up, tell Rhett to give it a rest for twenty-four. Otherwise, I think you're good. I mean, isn't that what it was designed for?"

"True." Sucking down her Guinness, she shook her head. "Who would have thought I would be worried about getting laid too frequently? Sam and I had sex once every two weeks."

"That's because he was banging random chicks the other thirteen days."

"Thanks for the reminder. See? This is why I question Rhett's behavior. It's out of my realm of experience."

Eve laughed. "I think you just need to enjoy the fact that your husband is so into you. Though now when I look at him I'm going to be watching to see if he's popping Viagra or something. Two hours? What the hell?"

"He's twenty-five," Shawn reminded her. "He is erect or semi-erect on average eighteen hours a day."

"I'm going to puke," was Eve's opinion.

Harley came rushing back to the table and dropped into a chair, her eyes wide.

"What's wrong?" Shawn asked her.

"Cooper's here."

Uh-oh. "Your boss?"

"Yes. He's dancing."

Cooper Brickman was a man-whore driver who Harley had just started working for as a nanny/prison guard for his obnoxious twelve-year-old niece. It was safe to say Harley had a King Kong–size crush on him, though he seemed like the last person on earth she would be interested in. But there was no accounting for attraction. Shawn was just worried she was doomed to unrequited lust.

"So dance with him," was Eve's suggestion.

"He's my boss!" Harley looked aghast and downed half her rum runner in one gulp. "I can't dance with him! Besides, he's dancing with Charity. I need another drink."

"You might want to sip the next one," Shawn suggested. "And tell Charity you have a thing for him so she isn't horning in. You shouldn't have to sit here and watch them dancing together." She could see them out there on the crowded dance floor. Charity was engulfed in Cooper's octopus grip, his hands lower on her back than was strictly appropriate.

"You're identical twins and he's hitting on Charity. Don't you think that means he's actually interested in you?" Eve asked.

"No! There is nothing identical about Charity and me." And she crossed her arms over her chest in a clear signal that she wanted to pout about it, not talk about it.

Danny and Sammy came back over, tossing back their hair and laughing. "Come on, we're riding the mechanical bull! Who's in?"

"I'll do it," Eve said, tossing a smirk her way. "And I dare Shawn to do it."

Damn it. One of these days she was going to pass on a dare. She was going to be mature enough to realize it didn't matter in the slightest if she didn't rise to the bait. That her worth as a human being was not based on how many challenges she could accept and accomplish.

That day was not today.

This was her bachelorette party and she was not going to be shown up. So she shrugged in total nonchalance. "I'll do it. It looks easy."

Eve laughed. "Talking smack, huh? Twenty bucks says you can't stay on for forty-five seconds."

Shawn tried to remember her previous experiences watching other women ride the bull at various bars around town. Usually they took it easy on them, preferring the setting that bounced the bull up and down, creating a crowd-pleasing breast jiggle. Once she'd had the misfortune to see a woman get tossed off in a miniskirt, flashing the whole bar her girl bits. Shawn was wearing jeans, and she had enough strength in her thighs from playing volleyball and doing yoga that she was confident she could hang for forty-five seconds.

"No problem." She turned to her sisters-in-law. "Who wants to lay down their money? Me or Eve, who can stay on the bull longer?"

"Oh, Lord," Harley mumbled.

Purses were flung open and money was waved around.

Shawn eyed the bull from across the room and sized up her competition. Eve had the advantage of wearing jeans with some spandex in them. Otherwise, it was a level field.

She cracked her knuckles and strode over to sign the waiver.

RHETT watched his brother-in-law going for some kind of basketball shooting record and decided he was bored out of his mind. He didn't want a bachelor party with strippers or to wind up puking in the backseat of Jared's car, but hell, he wanted something a little more exciting than an adult-oriented arcade. His sister's husbands all had kids and didn't get a night to themselves very often, so they were all pumped to be drinking beer and playing Skee-Ball, but Rhett was feeling understimulated. Nolan didn't look to be having that great of a time either, though he had managed to score a boatload of tickets off the water pistol game.

"What do you think the girls are doing?" he asked Nolan, when his brother came strolling over to him, tickets dangling out of his back pocket like paper sausages.

"I think they're getting drunk at the bar and egging each other on to see who can dance the most like a stripper."

"I wish we were there to see that." He did. Most sincerely. He missed Shawn. He didn't want to deny her the fun of a girl's night, but he thought they would both have more fun if they were together. "We should crash their party."

"Are you crazy? Do you want to lose your nuts the day before you get married? Or celebrate being married, since you are already married?" Nolan shook his head. "You'll just piss Shawn off, you know."

"I don't think so." He didn't. "She'll think it's funny. The guys did it in *Mamma Mia* and every woman in existence loves that movie."

"*Mamma Mia*?"

"The musical. The dudes crash the bachelorette party."

Nolan gave him a long sidelong glance. "I've never seen it. And it scares me that you have."

"That's because you're like a hundred years older than me. When I was a kid, I had a pack of sisters who wanted to see every chick flick in existence. I saw *Bridget Jones's Diary* at ten years old. *Pretty Woman* at five. Five years old." He held one hand up to make his point. "That ain't right. And they conned me into *A League of Their Own* by telling me it was a baseball movie."

Nolan snorted. "Well, why did you go?"

"Because I didn't have a choice. The girls were babysitting me."

"Where was I? I feel kind of bad, little brother. I should have tried to save you from time to time."

"You were always at the track or chasing tail."

Nolan grunted in acknowledgment of the truth behind that. "Where was Mom?"

"I don't know. Nailing Dad?" They looked at each other and cracked up. "That was their Saturday afternoon thing, you know."

"Oh, I know." Nolan watched Mark throw his arms up in triumph. "And I wouldn't call me old around your wife, you know. She and I were born the same year. You'll have your ass handed to you on a platter if you're not careful."

"Good point. But come on, let's go to the bar they're at. You want to see Eve drunk, don't you?"

"I've seen it. It's highly entertaining."

"I can't say as I've seen Shawn drunk."

Nolan glanced at his cell phone. "By now, they're probably challenging each other to a drinking contest or who can deep throat the penis straw. You know how they are."

"And you don't want to see that? Because I do." Rhett was hard just thinking about it. He loved the competitive side of Shawn. And deep throating a penis straw? He was in.

"You make a solid case." Nolan finished his beer. "You okay with it if Shawn gets mad at you?"

"Yeah." Rhett gave him a smug look. "I know how to handle her."

"Oh, big words, little man. We'll see." Nolan clapped him on the back. "Hey, guys!" he called to the rest of the group. "Let's roll!"

There was resistance from the others, who were envisioning very pissed off wives waiting for them, but in the end, since Rhett was the new groom, he made the decision.

Which is how he wound up walking into the Silver

Buckle just in time to see his wife throw one leg over the mechanical bull and hoist her sexy ass up onto it.

His sisters were hooting and hollering, and Eve was standing on the edge of the pen, arms crossed.

"Uh-oh," Nolan said, coming up beside him. "Eve has her psyche-out-the-opponent look on her face. Twenty bucks says the girls have a bet going already."

"You want me to bet you that they're in the middle of a bet? That's stupid." All Rhett wanted to do was grab a seat and watch the action unfold for a while, unnoticed by the women. "Hold back for a minute. Let's not let them know we're here yet."

Considering there were six of them, it wasn't going to be easy to stay incognito, but they could manage five minutes.

"I hope to God my wife isn't planning on riding that bull," Dave said. "I can see it now—she'll throw out her back, and that will be the end of life as I know it for the next two weeks." He shook his head, glum.

Rhett nudged him. "Come on. She's not that stupid. She knows her limits. Unlike my wife."

"Your wife is riding like she was born with a bull between her legs."

"Excuse me?" Rhett glared at him before swiveling his gaze quickly to see Shawn, her slim thighs straddling the bull as it slowly reared up and then back down. Her posture was loose, her body fluid, moving in harmony with the mechanism. She looked relaxed and hot as hell.

"Sorry, that didn't sound right."

"No, it sure in the hell didn't." Rhett unzipped his athletic jacket and put his hands in his front pockets. "You can go get me a beer to make up for it." He was too busy watching his wife to hit the bar himself.

The bar employee had turned up the bull, much to everyone's delight, and Shawn was working harder now to stay on, her thighs clamping in a way that made his tongue thick, her breasts bouncing with a vigor that got his blood pumping.

"Fine," Dave grumbled.

"Dawn. Straight ahead," Nolan told him.

Their middle sister had spotted them, and she was picking her way through the crowd. "What the hell are you guys doing here?" She glared at her husband. "You guys can't crash a bachelorette party!"

Rhett didn't respond, mesmerized by Shawn as she held on but then lost control and sailed off the bull in a graceful dismount, landing on her perfect bottom. She bounced up immediately, and there seemed to be some haggling going on between her, Eve, and Charity.

"It's a free country," Nolan told her. "Hey, what are they doing, besides the obvious? Do they have a bet going on? Eve has her serious face on."

"How can you tell the difference?" Rhett asked.

Nolan punched him in the arm.

"They have a bet to see who can stay on the bull longer. Best combined total time out of three runs."

"Seriously? Leave it to them to not be satisfied with just a sudden-death one-shot ride." Nolan grinned. "God, I love my wife."

Rhett had to say he loved his as well.

He started. He loved her?

God, he did. He wasn't sure when it had happened, maybe gradually, one laugh, one orgasm at a time, but over the last ten days, he had fallen hard for her. He admired her gumption, her strength, her sweetness. He took immense pleasure in giving her pleasure night after night, in making her more and more his.

"Shawn will win, I can guarantee it," Rhett told his brother.

Nolan's eyebrow shot up. "What makes you so certain? Eve is as stubborn as they come. If anyone can make a mechanical bull her bitch, it's her."

"Oh, good grief," Dawn snapped. "You're going to turn their competition into a secondary competition? You're worse than my kids, I swear."

Eve was up on the bull now, and she pulled an impressive ride, one that was arguably the same length, if not longer than Shawn's. When she fell off, she leaned over and mimicked "Call me" to the bull with her thumb and pinky up to her ear.

Nolan let out a laugh. "That's my girl."

"This is Shawn's last run," Dawn said.

While Rhett's cock grew harder and harder with each bounce and jolt of Shawn on the bull, her thighs clamped on like she was riding him the way he had instructed her to the night before, hands behind her back. Damn. He loved his sexy wife.

"You look feral," Nolan told him. "Ease up, brother."

"What? Shawn is hot, I can't help it."

She lost control and flew off the bull. There was haggling and an intense discussion to the side, with Sammy clearly the timekeeper. She raised Shawn's arm, declaring her the winner, as Shawn whooped in triumph. Eve didn't look pissed. She was grinning.

"Should we announce our illustrious presence?" Nolan asked him.

It appeared Dawn already had. She'd rejoined the girls, and there was finger-pointing in their direction. Eight sets of female eyes swung their way.

"We're in for a world of hurt," was Jared's opinion.

"If this were a musical, this would signal the start of a dance number," Rhett said, amused by the thought. "Angry girls sexy dance in unison around the bull pen. Men stride up and grab a partner to a choreographed tango."

Nolan held his hand out. "Give me your man card. You have never sounded more like a girl than right now."

"Screw you," Rhett told him. "It's a joke. It's funny. Now you bitches can stand here quaking in your boots about what your women might do to you. I'm going to *get* my woman."

He started to walk, moving toward his wife.

He heard Jared ask Nolan, "How does he get that caveman shit to work for him? I would get my balls ripped off and stuffed in my mouth if I pulled what he does."

"Beats the hell out of me."

Rhett smiled. He knew exactly how he got away with it.

Shawn knew he respected her above all things. Shawn trusted him.

And it was time to tell her that he had fallen in love with her and wanted their temporary marriage to become a very real one.

CHAPTER
SEVENTEEN

SHAWN was glowing in the triumph of beating Eve by exactly two seconds. Eve was taking it well, joking that she had thrown it so that Shawn could win at her own bachelorette party.

"It was the only kind thing to do," Eve told her. "And by the way, I have a feeling my thighs are going to be killing me tomorrow. Good thing it's Sunday. I have a few days to recover."

Shawn grinned at her. "Yeah, it's harder than it looks, I'm not going to lie."

"Look behind you," Dawn said, pointing. "It looks like our party has been crashed. I swear, what were they thinking?"

Shawn and Eve turned and there were Rhett and Nolan and the other guys, watching them from across the room. "How long have they been here?" she asked, her heart starting to race. Just the sight of her husband got her blood pumping.

"Long enough that they caught both your final rides. Voyeurs." She sounded disgusted.

Shawn wondered if she was a disgrace to wives that she

actually wanted her husband to be there. And that it actually turned her on that he had seen her ride a bull. "I wonder whose idea it was to come here?"

"It had to be Rhett or Nolan. The other guys, one, know better. Two, they don't really want to see us. Y'all are still in the honeymoon phase, but never fear, the need to see each other all the time will wear off."

Somehow Shawn didn't think she would be like that. Given that her adult relationships had never been particularly all-encompassing, romantic, or devotional, she found that with Rhett, it was totally different. She both loved and was terrified by her need, her want, to be with him.

"Maybe I don't want it to wear off," she murmured as Rhett started toward her, his stride confident, Nolan immediately falling in step behind him.

"It's not practical," Dawn stated.

Something about her tone had Shawn wondering if Dawn and her husband were not quite okay. But she wasn't about to ask her here, not now.

"If Shawn doesn't care that the guys are here, then I don't suppose you should," Eve told her. "It's her bachelorette party."

"I don't mind," Shawn said.

In fact, when Rhett came over and smiled at her, immediately pulling her into his arms, she didn't want to do anything other than kiss the stuffing out of him. So she did.

"Mm. That was an awesome greeting," he murmured in her ear, stroking his hands down her back. "Nice bull riding."

"I have strong thighs."

"Something I've always admired about you."

"So what are you doing here?" she asked him.

"I was bored. I missed you. I thought if we're already married, why shouldn't we spend the night partying together, instead of separately?"

"Sound logic," she told him. "Though you may have pissed your sisters off."

But he just shrugged. "It's not their night. It's ours. And I found myself wanting to dance with my wife."

Oh, damn, he was just so . . . much. It wasn't charm, it wasn't being smooth, it was something else. Something . . . more. He looked at her like that, and she melted. She gave in, she opened to him, she forgot who she was, and wanted nothing more than to be with him, to please him. It was exhilarating. Awful.

"Are you asking?" she said, to remind him that outside of their bedroom, she called the shots, so to speak. Not that she did, really. Rhett was by nature a dominating personality, and even when he was being polite and thoughtful and offering to cook dinner or change her oil or take her to the movies, he tended to initiate the order of their days. She didn't mind, not really, because if she said no to anything, he would change gears without question. If she wanted pasta instead of steak, he would go to the grocery store and get pasta, so she didn't care that he had a strong personality.

But she worried that she should.

"Yes. Will you dance with me, Shawn, my beautiful wife?"

"I would love to." The ease with which he used the word *wife* made her feel warm inside. It made her wonder if he was wondering what she was wondering—that maybe they shouldn't automatically dismiss their relationship as temporary, as fake. That maybe it could be, should be, something real.

As they swayed to the music with more feeling than any particular skill, Shawn smiled up at him. "Are we going to survive this party tomorrow?"

"It will be fun."

"I've never seen you in a suit."

"I've never seen you in a wedding dress. I'm not sure my blood pressure will be able to handle it."

His hands were warm on her waist, and he was inching farther south than was really appropriate for a public place, but she let him for now. Once he reached her ass, she would stop him, but for now she was enjoying his touch. "I don't think you're that delicate. You'll be fine."

"There is delicate, then there is vulnerable. You have no idea how vulnerable I am with you," he said, his voice low and near her ear.

Shawn shivered, the pulsing beat of the country ballad reverberating through her feet, her breasts, her inner thighs. Or maybe that was just him. But the room was warm, the lighting low, their bodies close and intimate, and she was barely aware that anyone else existed.

"I don't see how I can make you vulnerable," she whispered, inching her fingers up to stroke the back of his neck. He smelled like cologne and beer. He didn't usually wear cologne and she found it appealing, like he had kicked his own manly scent up a notch. "I think it's the other way around and sometimes it pisses me off."

He frowned. "What do you mean?"

She hadn't really meant to say that, or to get into a discussion about their relationship on the sticky dance floor, but her doubts were getting the best of her. She wanted so much to be with Rhett in a way that was real, yet at the same time it freaked her out. Shouldn't she want to be independent? Shouldn't she be ticked like his sisters that he had crashed her girl's night?

"I don't know," was her cop-out response.

But Rhett shook his head. "Don't pull that. You know you can trust me. Tell me what you're feeling."

Shit. How did she explain her jumbled thoughts and feelings?

"It's just that . . . well, I think about you every day, Rhett. I want to please you, I want to be with you all the time . . . I feel like I'm being *absorbed* by you. It scares the shit out of me."

Just hearing her own words had her heart rate increasing. It sounded crazy. She was crazy for him.

He didn't look particularly alarmed. His nostrils flared and if anything, he looked aroused. "That's funny, because

I feel the same way, yet my understanding was that this is how falling in love works, Shawn."

"Falling in love?" she asked dumbly. Was he saying he loved her?

"Yes. Falling in love. Which is what I'm doing." He softly brushed her hair off her cheek. "Do you think that is what you're doing?"

"I don't know," she whispered. "Maybe. Yes." Way to commit. She mentally kicked herself. Then she took a deep breath and added, "Yes. I am falling in love with you."

She'd never said those words to anyone. Not even to her high school boyfriend, who she had been sure she would spend the rest of her life with. She'd never told a man she loved him. While this was still one step away from that, it was pretty damn close. Her cheeks burned with the overwhelming realization of what was happening. This was it. This was major.

He smiled at her. "So what do we do now?"

Hell if she knew. "I guess we dance. And we live together. And tomorrow we have a wedding reception."

Rhett's thumb rubbed over her bottom lip. "So pragmatic. Where's the romance, darlin'?"

That made her grin back at him, relieved that he knew her so well already that he was lightening the mood. That he was allowing her to steer this conversation. "Read a novel," she told him. "You're barking up the wrong tree if you want a gushy girl."

"Oh, I think I can get you to gush a little . . . you get more romantic in bed than you realize."

"I wasn't aware that begging was romantic," she said wryly.

But Rhett shook his head. "That's not what I was referring to. I was thinking more about the way your eyes darken and your skin flushes and the way your fingers trace my face like you can't quite believe I'm real."

It was true. She did all that. And she blushed anew to realize that he was so aware of her and her reactions. "Sometimes I wonder if you are real," she whispered. "Sometimes I think that I'm going to wake up with the clock rewound and find none of the last two weeks has happened."

"How would that make you feel?"

"Heartbroken," she told him truthfully.

"Me, too." His green eyes were shiny with sincerity.

A tap on her arm made Shawn jump. She glanced over and saw Eve and Nolan watching them in amusement.

"You do know you're slow dancing to nothing, don't you? The music stopped sixty seconds ago."

Oh, Lord, she was right. The dance floor was completely empty except for them.

"But the rhythm of my heart is beating like a drum," Rhett said, deadpan.

Shawn lost it, laughter spilling out. That was such a Rhett comeback, and she loved it.

Nolan shook his head. "Bro, my hat is off to you. You managed to find the one woman in the world who doesn't think you're a freak."

RHETT opened the back door of Harley's car for Shawn and eyed his wife's backside as she climbed in.

"I saw that," Eve told him, sliding past him to follow Shawn into the car.

"I don't care," he told her with an unrepentant grin. "And why aren't you going with Nolan? Not that I don't enjoy your presence thoroughly, but I would think you'd want to go home with your husband."

"He has to drive Jared home. He's shit-faced. I'm dead on my feet, so I'll get back faster this way."

"So Harley's dropping you first, then us?"

"Yes. It's on the way," she said defensively.

It was a toss-up whether it was or not, but Rhett didn't care to argue. He was damn happy. Happy as a dead pig in the sunshine. So he just smiled at her and got in the car. "Switch seats with me, Eve. I want to sit next to Shawn."

"Kiss my butt," was her reply. "You can fondle her later. I'm not climbing over the top of you so you can sit next to her. God, so high school."

"You are tired," he commented. That was a bit sharp even for Eve.

"I'm exhausted. I drank just enough to dance like a fool, but not enough to not feel the crash. So don't piss me off or I'll cream your corn."

"I'm not afraid of you, big talker." Rhett leaned around her to talk to Shawn, intentionally getting his elbow in Eve's face. "Baby, I hope we don't need to be anywhere first thing tomorrow because I'm not ready for sleeping yet. I've got at least two hours in me."

"Gross," was Charity's opinion from the front passenger seat.

He just laughed. Shawn smiled at him, bundled up in her coat. Eve pinched his arm.

"Move it," she said.

Settling back, he found himself feeling very conversational. "So Harley, you're quiet up there. Did you have fun?"

"It was fine," was Harley's clipped reply from the front seat.

Charity snorted.

"Wrong question, hon," Shawn told him in a warning voice.

Was it wrong that he was more interested in the fact that Shawn had called him "hon" than whatever was bothering Harley?

The thought guilted him into saying, "I'm sorry, Harley. Didn't mean to poke a sore spot."

"I didn't know you were crushing on him," Charity exploded at her sister. "If you would actually share something with me once in a while, I wouldn't have kissed him. You know, it's really very hurtful that you won't let me in, Harley. I tell you *everything*."

"Wait, so this is my fault?" Harley asked in shock, taking a turn a little hard and running them over the curb.

"Maybe I should drive," Rhett suggested. "Were you drinking, Harley?"

"No. I cut myself off three hours ago because that's what I do," Harley said. "I am the driver and the wallflower while Charity gets drunk and dances half-naked with the guy she totally knew I was into!"

"I'm out," Rhett said, turning to Eve. "I can't do the girl-fight thing."

"Don't look at me," Eve said, shrugging. "My suggestion to arm wrestle it out isn't really practical at the moment."

But Shawn had it under control. She was already leaning forward, murmuring to the twins, reassuring Harley that Charity had not known about the guy and suggesting to Charity that if she wanted her sister to confide in her, she should consider allowing her a word in edgewise on occasion.

Rhett leaned against the window and watched her sort the whole mess out in a matter of minutes. After they pulled into Eve's apartment complex and Harley parked the car, there were tears and hugs and apologies, and then suddenly all was okay. It was, in his eyes, as miraculous as Moses parting the Nile.

"That's why I leave this stuff to her," Eve told him. "See you tomorrow with my happy face on." She gave him a smile and got out of the car after he opened the door and stood up to let her pass.

"Thanks. Shawn is pretty amazing, isn't she?"

"I'm glad to see you realize it," she told him. Then with a wave to her girlfriends, Eve went into the apartment building she and Nolan had recently moved into after the sale of her condo, and Rhett waited to make sure the door firmly closed behind her.

"Eve's in. We can roll." And with his sister-in-law safely home, he could cuddle with his wife. His wife. That's right.

She came willingly when he urged her to tuck in up against his side.

"I'm freezing still," she said. "It must be thirty degrees out tonight. I know I can always count on you to warm me up."

He moved his eyebrows up and down.

She laughed. "Well, yeah, there's that, but what I really meant was that you radiate heat all the time. Your body temperature must be ten degrees higher than most people."

"I think I would be dead if that were the case."

Shawn rolled her eyes. "Smart-ass."

He really enjoyed that Shawn was perfectly comfortable giving him shit. It was one of the things he loved about her.

Love. Funny how that very small, unexpected word could change everything. Rhett bent over and murmured in her ear, "I love you."

Shawn started and gazed up at him. Her eyes were wide in the dark backseat of Harley's car, but they were open and honest. "I love you, too."

What more could a man ask for? Nothing, as far as Rhett was concerned.

When they went inside and kicked off their shoes and hung up their jackets, Rhett loved the way Shawn waited for him at the top of the kitchen landing, her hand out for his.

There was no question in her eyes.

She knew he was going to make love to her. She knew that whatever he did to her, he would put her pleasure first, that she would be satisfied. The way she let him lead her down the hallway, the way she waited in the doorway for him to undress her, the way she kissed him with a deep fervor and abandonment, satisfied Rhett in return. He had never known that he could be this happy, that the restless agitation that had burned inside him would be eased by Shawn's open affection and perfect willingness to submit to his aggressive desires.

He urged her back down onto the bed, reaching back to

flick on the light so he could see her body. She blinked as the harsh overhead light hit her eyes, but she didn't complain. She knew he wouldn't go down on her if she did, and that made his mouth hot, his cock throb. Stripping off his own clothes, Rhett took his time, touching her everywhere with teasing, light touches, skirting her clitoris until he felt her quivering, goose bumps on her skin, her need growing more and more urgent.

"Put your ankles on my shoulders," he told her. He suddenly needed to be inside her.

She did so without question and Rhett entered her, and even without stimulating her with his fingers or tongue, he found her wet and welcoming. Knowing that she got aroused just from his fingers brushing over her bare skin, that she knew her pleasure was a guarantee, was almost as arousing to him as the tight fist her pussy made around his erection.

Breathing hard as he gripped her shins and pumped them both to desperation, Shawn sought his permission with her eyes.

"Yes?" he asked, willing to grant any request she might have at that moment, his body tight and alive, his heart swollen with the knowledge that she loved him.

"Can I come? I really, really need to come." Her lips were wet, her eyes glassy, her hand lifting off the mattress, then fluttering back down as she remembered she could not do whatever she had been planning to.

Rhett wondered if she'd been intending to bite one of her fingers, to suck it, or if her plan had been to twist and tweak her own nipple with the pads of her fingers.

"Not for another minute," he told her. "I want to come with you. You'll know when."

"Oh," she panted in agony, her head turned to the side, her legs trembling from the position.

"Suck on your finger," he told her. "It will help."

She did without hesitation, though the widening of her eyes and the clasping of her body onto his cock told him that it hadn't made it any easier for her to hold back. It had made it worse, which was his intention, he had to admit. Watching her struggle to hold off her orgasm, her lips frantically wrapped around her finger, sucking it in and out like she was substituting it for his cock, heightened his own frantic desire.

When he squeezed her legs tight and let himself go, pumping his hot ejaculation into her, Shawn was immediately there with him. Her orgasm blended with his, her cries of anguished ecstasy ringing in his ears, as he held her and gave in to his body, gave in to her. She owned him, there was no question about it. Shawn had his heart and his body, and hell, even his soul, and he felt the most profound satisfaction and sense of triumph that he'd ever felt in his twenty-five years of life.

As he fell onto the bed next to her and pulled her into his arms, their bodies warm and sticky, her fingertips fluttering over his chest, he was inclined to believe there was such a thing as destiny. "Scarlett, you're one hell of a woman," he told her.

Her response was to kiss his shoulder. But a moment later, she asked, "What's your middle name?"

He was so content, he didn't even get annoyed with his least-favorite subject. "I'm sure you can guess."

"Your mother seriously named you Rhett Butler Ford?"

"Yep."

She didn't laugh. "I'm named after my father, who took off and left my mother and two little kids living in an RV."

"I guess it doesn't really matter where a name comes from, it's whether you live up to its original intention." Rhett yawned and reached down to drag the blanket up over their bodies.

"True. Which is why I was wondering how you'd feel about me being Shawn Hamby Ford."

Rhett looked at her in astonishment, his heart squeezing. "I would be honored."

This was real. And they both knew it.

"Now are you going to turn the light off?" she asked.

He grinned. "I was hoping you would."

"I didn't turn it on," she pointed out.

He couldn't argue with that. As he sighed and lumbered out of bed and across the cold room to flick the switch, he said, "Next week, I install the Clapper."

She giggled. "I dare you."

"Done." Then he was back in bed, and she was in his arms, and the world was a perfect place.

CHAPTER
EIGHTEEN

SHAWN looked at herself in the mirror, Eve and the twins hovering around her, fussing with the long, flowing skirt of her white dress that Charity and Sandy had chosen off the rack at a retail store. She looked like a real bride.

And she promptly burst into tears.

"What's wrong?" Harley asked, reaching out and taking her cold hand in hers.

"You'll mess up your makeup!" Charity shrieked, horrified.

"I'm sorry." Shawn managed to stop the tears almost as soon as they started, sniffling and widening her eyes to keep herself under control. "I can't help it. I miss my grandparents."

It was the truth. But she also was realizing that not only did she look the part, she *felt* like a true bride. She was in love with her groom. She wanted to spend her life with him, regardless of the reasons they had come together in the first place.

How nuts was that?

Rhett had told her he loved her the night before, and she believed him. For the first time ever in her life, she had looked into the eyes of a man and seen that she was cherished by him. It was wonderful. It was wacky. It was overwhelming. She wasn't sure how a woman was ever supposed to be prepared to fall in love, but she hadn't been. Instead of enjoying their mutual emotions, she was still a ball of anxiety, because who was to say what was going to happen when six months had passed? It was too soon to ask Rhett for a real commitment, regardless of their legal marital status. Pressuring him or even asking could smother the spark of their newfound love. It had merely been the post-sex relaxation that had allowed her to say something about taking his last name, and while he had agreed, it could have been purely because he knew his family would expect it.

Despite everything he had told her, he still hadn't said what was going to happen when he had a hundred grand in hand.

It was a lot to have swirling in her head when she was staring at herself in the mirror, looking every inch the part of a woman pledging her love and her life to her new husband.

"I'm going to puke," she said, her stomach suddenly clenching in a violent spasm, bile clawing up her throat.

"Holy shit!" was Eve's opinion as they all glanced frantically around the lounge area of the restroom of the Hamby Speedway banquet room for some kind of receptacle.

Sandy had come into the room in time to hear Shawn's last words, and as Shawn covered her mouth and desperately breathed through her nose, Sandy cut through the girls and took charge. "Give her some space!"

Taking her firmly in hand, Sandy pushed her down into the deep sofa opposite the vanity area, and she sank down gratefully.

"Head between your knees," Sandy said gently, pushing her shoulders forward and kneeling down to lay the back of her hand on Shawn's clammy forehead. "You're okay, you're going to be fine. Just try not to swallow so much."

Shawn started to calm down at the soothing tones of her mother-in-law.

"What's wrong?" Harley asked. "You're already married, no need to be nervous."

"She's not nervous," Sandy said, running her hand down Shawn's cheek in a way that made her realize in thirty-two years she'd never gotten that kind of touch from her own mother. It made her miss her grandmother even more. "You're pregnant, aren't you, sweetie?"

Shawn sat up straight at those words. "What? No! I mean, I don't think so . . ." Was she? She supposed it was possible. She and Rhett had been having sex like it was going out of style. She was on the pill, but she tended to take it at various times of the day, which was a bit of an instructional violation. But still, what were the odds? Rhett would have to have supersperm.

Given he had eight siblings, and six of them had produced sixteen children, maybe that wasn't so out of the question. Fertility was a Ford virtue.

"Well, we'll know in a week or two. But for now, I think you should skip the champagne tonight and stick to ginger ale to settle your stomach."

"Yeah, okay." Truthfully, the thought of alcohol did make her want to gag. Oh, Lord. What if she was pregnant?

"Whoa," was Eve's opinion on the matter.

Sandy hugged her and Shawn melted into the warmth of that embrace. "Welcome to the family."

"Thank you." She meant that most sincerely. She had deceived Rhett's family, and they were showing her nothing but love. She was truly grateful for that.

Especially given that her own mother chose that moment to come into the room. "What's going on, Shawn? Why are you serving so many beef products?" she said by way of greeting.

Raising her head, Shawn swallowed hard. "Mom, please. Everyone was nice enough to help me with this party, I don't want to hear any criticism."

"I'm just saying." Her mother pouted, her long hair loose from its usual braid, gray streaked throughout since she didn't believe in using chemicals to dye it. Her dress was more of a wrap-and-sari combination in a vivid purple, which Shawn knew was not a color that could be achieved with natural dye. So, as usual, her mother selectively chose her moments to be environmental.

Still feeling a little weak, she took a deep breath and was standing up, holding on to Sandy's arm, when Rhett came into the room, with a pointless knock on the door as he was already entering.

"This is the ladies' room," Charity told him.

"I'm coming to see what's taking so long. Everyone is here, and they're devouring the appetizers."

He looked very handsome in his suit, his tie straight, a jaunty red for the Valentine's Day theme, and Shawn willed him to meet her eye. She needed him to look at her, to reassure her. He did, giving her that sexy smile that she had first noticed in The Wet Spot, her insides turning to liquid.

"Hey, beautiful. You ready to do this thing?"

She nodded, immediately feeling better, then immediately after that freaking out that she needed him to make her feel better.

He held his hand out for her.

She took it.

SHAWN looked a little green, but Rhett knew she was nervous about being the center of attention. He found it interesting that for a woman who ran a business and had spent all those years on the youth racing circuit, she wasn't comfortable with entertaining. Parties and anything that could be classified as an event seemed to generate nerves. Yet in his mind, every weekend at Hamby Speedway during the season was an "event."

Maybe it was just that she didn't really like wearing dresses, which was a damn shame, because she was a knockout in them. Especially this one. It looked every inch what he would imagine a bridal gown to be, from the strapless fitted top, to the flowing skirt that looked a little like soft-serve ice cream to him. He wanted to lick her.

"You hungry?" he asked her, as they moved down the hall, her friends and their mothers following them. "There is enough food in there to feed the fans at the Daytona 500."

It was an inane thing to say, but he wanted her to relax. He squeezed her hand a little and she squeezed back.

"I actually have an upset stomach," she said. "I think I'm having stage fright."

"It's just our friends and family. And the hard part is over. If you didn't faint in that courthouse," he murmured to her, "I think you'll be fine. I mean, let's face it, it takes a strong woman to agree to put up with me for even six months."

She gave a brittle laugh, but the tension lines in her forehead smoothed. "True. You are a whole lot of something, Rhett Butler Ford."

He winced. "Don't trot out the middle name unless you're pissed off at me. Or I may not contain my spankings to the bedroom."

"You wouldn't dare."

She smiled up at him, and he was glad to see she was genuinely amused and looking less sallow. "Don't try me," he teased. Then he pushed open the doorway to the banquet room that his sisters had spent the last two days decorating.

"A big Charlotte welcome to the brand new Mr. and Mrs. Rhett and Shawn Ford!" his brother-in-law Mark boomed as they stepped into the room.

Mark had gotten a microphone from God knows where, and he appeared to have nominated himself for MC/DJ, an iPod and speakers set up behind him.

Even Rhett wasn't quite prepared for the loud pronouncement of them as man and wife and the thundering applause and hoots and hollers that followed. For a second he just blinked.

Shawn murmured, "Good Lord, it looks like Cupid shart in here."

Rhett choked back a laugh and managed to smile and raise their clasped hands together in a victory shake. Then he fought the urge to drag Shawn through the crowd and the explosion of pink and red hearts, and took a nice, steady pace instead. He wasn't exactly sure where they were supposed to go, so he took the opportunity to just stop every few feet and greet guests and receive hugs from ancient great-aunts and his grandmother.

Suddenly he wasn't sure this party had been such a fabulous idea after all, because while he knew for certain he loved Shawn and she loved him, they had gone about this all ass backwards. Instead of taking their vows in a church with family present, meaning each of those words they'd spoken, they had stood before a judge and lied through their teeth. It left the stain of dishonesty on this party, and that pissed him off. He didn't want there to be any whiff of falsity to the night, and while he was used to being hugged and cosseted from female family members, the truth was, he didn't have his brother's easy charm. Playing host wasn't any easier for him than it was for Shawn to tackle the hostess role.

So as soon as they had reached the head table, crowded with giant vases of red flowers, he deposited Shawn in a chair and went for some liquid fortification. Shawn shook her head when he asked if she wanted a drink, already turning away as her mother swooped down on her like a purple dragon. He'd barely exchanged five words with her, and he had to say quite honestly, he despised her mother. From her made-up first name of Mati, stolen no doubt from the legendary spy, to her insistence that marriage was for the weak-minded, she grated on his nerves.

Rhett had kind of always thought marriage was for the monogamous, but go figure. He ordered a shot of whiskey from the bartender.

"Eight dollars," the bartender told him.

He didn't even have his wallet on him. "I'm the groom."

"I'm sorry, sir, that doesn't matter."

"Are you fucking kidding me?" Rhett turned to go find someone to bum a ten off of, when he almost ran into his father.

"Let me buy you a drink, son."

"Thanks, Dad," he said, more relieved than he cared to admit. He wasn't usually one to crave alcohol, but neither did he usually have this much emotion churning inside him like a cement mixer.

"Whatever he wants," his father told the bartender. He handed the bartender a hundred dollar bill. "For the rest of the night so we don't have to keep doing this every time he or his bride need to wet their whistle."

"Thanks, Dad." Rhett was touched.

His father smiled at him and held his hand out. They shook. "Congrats. I hope you and Shawn will be as happy as your mother and I have been."

Yeah, that was a lump the size of a baby's fist in his throat. "Me, too," he said. He meant it with every bone in his body.

"My youngest married." Nolan Senior shook his head. "Damn, I must be old."

"Nah." Rhett clamped him on the shoulder. "You still have a lot of Saturday afternoon delights with Mom ahead of you."

"Don't be smart, boy." But his father did laugh, even if the tips of his ears were a little pink.

Rhett grinned and raised his glass. "Cheers." He drank the shot of whiskey and felt the slow burn down his throat, knocking through that lump in there like Drano. That was better.

Somehow as various brothers-in-law and uncles and cousins came up for a drink, Rhett found himself trapped at the bar for over an hour. During which he might have done another three shots. Feeling pleasantly buzzed, he finally made his way over to the buffet of food and attempted to load himself up a plate. After he dropped the slotted spoon in the green beans three times, his Aunt Trudy took his plate from him and not only spooned up his beans for him, but went down the whole line, loading him up with eats.

"Don't trip on your way to your table," she told him with a wink. "And lay off the whiskey if you want to make your bride happy tonight."

Ha. As if that was ever an issue. His chest inflated with more than a little manly pride. "How do you know I've been drinking?"

"I married your Uncle Georgie, didn't I? That man has pickled his liver."

Rhett couldn't really argue with that. Georgie was a pretty hard-core drinker. He'd been known to fall asleep with his forehead on the bar top in his local watering hole, then rousing long enough to order another one before passing out again.

"I smell it on you."

"Oh." That was his stellar whiskey-stunted brainiac reply. "Good party, huh?" he asked, feeling satisfied with the way it was turning out. Sure, there was an excess of pink and Ford relatives, but everyone was happy and having a good time. Mark was spinning tunes, or more accurately, had hit play on the playlist, and there was some early dancing starting up, still a little timid and demure at this point. Another hour, the jackets and the ladies' shoes would come off, and the hip shaking would begin in earnest. Just like a real wedding. It felt like a real wedding.

Which reminded him. He hadn't seen Shawn in quite a while.

"Excuse me, Aunt Trudy. I need to find my beautiful wife."

"Where the hell have you been?" Shawn snapped at him when he returned to the table, balancing his plate with one hand while swiping a deviled egg off the pile with the other.

"I went for a drink." He pointed to his plate. "And food. Do you want me to get you some?"

"I want you to not abandon me again like that. God, I just met a thousand relatives all on my own. Eve brought me a plate." Shawn was sitting down, and her dinner was really just a pile of shredded biscuits with some uneaten ham next to it.

"Do you want something else?" he asked. "I can go back up for you." He sat next to her and kissed the side of her head. "Sorry. I got waylaid by congratulations."

"Are you drunk?" she asked him, sounding very suspicious.

"No. I am buzzed. There is a big difference." He shoveled pasta into his mouth. He was suddenly very hungry now that his nerves had worn off.

"Oh, Lord," was her opinion.

"Aren't you drinking?" he asked her. "You didn't drink much last night either. Just a couple of beers."

"I have a headache and my stomach is queasy. Plus I don't want to embarrass myself in front of your family, so no, I'm not drinking."

"I doubt you would do that. You're the king of the car bomb, remember? You can hold your liquor. Have a drink if you want one." It might do her some good.

"I'm fine."

"Okay." See how good he was at being a husband? He was already agreeing to everything she said.

There was a violent clanking of forks on glasses throughout, and Rhett grinned at Shawn. "They want us to kiss."

She leaned forward and gave him the most chaste kiss they had ever shared, then waved in acknowledgment to the crowd.

"What kind of a kiss was that?" he complained. "Next time, I think you should slip me some tongue. Show me you mean it."

"Rhett, don't piss me off right now, seriously."

"What?" he asked in bewilderment. "I'm sorry, babe, are you really feeling that awful?"

She nodded, her eyes suddenly welling up with tears.

Seeing her expression, he felt horrible, and he reached over and brushed her cheek with the back of his hand. "Did you take any aspirin?"

"No. I didn't bring my purse."

"Honey, there are thirty females in this room. We could medicate a small hospital once they open their purses. I'll get you something."

"Thanks."

"And as pretty as your hair looks, maybe you should loosen that knot thing it's in. That can't be helping."

She nodded, and he went off in search of pain relievers. Within five minutes he had them and had brought them to Shawn. But then he was called over to the bar by his father, who was telling a story to a group of cousins involving Rhett's first dirt bike and a certain accident involving his jeans.

"Dad, this is not a roast. It's my wedding. You can't be telling about every stupid thing I did as a kid."

"The hell I can't. It's a father's privilege once his son is grown. Someday you'll understand that yourself. Let's do a shot."

It was that suggestion, paired with the idea of fatherhood, that had Rhett willingly reaching out his hand.

Which might explain how by the time he got back to Shawn, he was well and truly on his way to being drunk.

SHAWN could not believe that Rhett was wasted. In all the time she'd known him, which admittedly was not that long, she'd never seen him drunk. She'd seen him drink wine, beer, whiskey, and never even get a buzz. But here, at their wedding party on freaking Valentine's Day, where she had a headache and was paralyzed by fear that she might be carrying his child, he chose to get bombed.

So annoying.

Another night she might have found his whistling, his wolfish drunken smile, his loosened tie, and his uninhibited dancing quite entertaining. But while her nausea had disappeared, she was still not in any position to enjoy the ridiculousness.

It seemed everyone but her was freely imbibing. The dance floor was packed with the young and the old and one brother-in-law was swinging his jacket around over his head. The kids were drunk on sugar and excitement, which was in evidence when Danny's son Simon stuck his entire face in the chocolate fountain, earning hoots of laughter from the adults. When he pulled back and shook like a dog, chocolate flew in all directions, scattering on the floor, the table, and three girls in front of him. Still no one yelled at him, which spoke volumes at the amount of alcohol consumed, in Shawn's opinion.

She had floated from table to table, always seeking a chair. She was tired. Clinton, her grandfather's attorney, sank into the seat beside her, and all it took was a very slurred greeting and a glimpse of his glassy eyes to realize he was just as drunk as the rest of the room.

"Hey, Clinton," she answered, giving him a wan smile.

He leaned forward and clasped her hand in his large, warm one. "You look beautiful, my girl, just beautiful. Jameson would have been so proud to see you as a bride."

That almost did her in. "I miss him, Clinton."

"Me, too." He squeezed her hand. "Shawn, are you happy? Is this marriage really what you want?"

Puzzled, she studied him. "All things considered, it's the best solution, yes." He knew she had paid off Rhett to marry her. He was the only person alive who did.

Clinton shook his head. "This was wrong, all of it. I shouldn't have been any part of it, and I should have told you the truth, Jameson's wishes be damned."

Shawn stiffened. "The truth about what?"

He leaned even closer, almost falling into her lap. "You didn't have to get married. You could have contested the restrictions placed on that will, and I don't doubt for a minute you would have won. You might have had to split ownership with your brother as dual heirs, but you would have won."

The heat of the room suddenly felt stifling. For a very brief moment, she actually thought she might faint, but she was made of sterner stuff than that. "So you're saying I didn't need to get married?"

"No, probably not. I mean, it would have taken a few months and thousands in lawyer's fees to contest the will."

Thousands? Not a hundred thousand, which is what she owed Rhett when all was said and done. She couldn't believe what she was hearing. She absolutely could not believe it. Save a few months of paper pushing and probably ten grand in legal fees, she could have achieved her goal of ownership free and clear? She wouldn't have given a damn about sharing ownership with her brother. He wasn't interested in the track. He wasn't even particularly interested in her. He had sent his apologies for not attending this very wedding party, because he had claimed he'd been unable to get a sitter for the baby. When she had suggested he bring the baby, he had said she was afraid of crowds.

Shawn could have taken the hundred grand she was giving Rhett and could have bought out her brother. There wasn't a doubt in her mind that he would have jumped at the chance to have the cash.

"You really think I would have won?"

"I'm certain it would have all shook out in your favor. You're the obvious heir, and the will stated you were to inherit, just under stipulations that most judges would deem inappropriate."

"Why didn't you tell me this before?" she asked, finally freeing her hand from his hot and sweaty grip. God, when she thought about the anxiety she had felt, the panic, the fear that she was going to lose the last connection to her grandfather, Hamby Speedway, she wanted to scream at the top of her lungs.

"I was trying to respect Jameson's intentions. I kind of figured you would marry Sam after all, but then when you didn't and you were all set to get hitched with the younger Ford brother, I started to think that you might be making a huge mistake. I should have come to you, but I thought, well, hell, I'm an old man and what do I know about your dating life? Maybe you're happy with Rhett and this just sped things up. You're happy, right? I'll never forgive myself if you're not."

Though she was mad as hell, Shawn couldn't help but feel bad for Clinton. None of this ridiculousness had been his idea, and he had just been trying to respect his best friend's dying wish. But he clearly felt guilty and he looked genuinely worried about her. She'd let him off the hook, but she wasn't the least bit happy about his information.

"I'm happy," she told him simply to ease his guilt, though she wasn't sure she was, exactly. She was head over ass for Rhett, but she wasn't precisely sure she was happy. It was exhilarating, but it certainly wasn't peaceful. But maybe that's how love went. She didn't know, because she'd never been in love before.

Part of her questioned if she was even in love. How did one recognize that it was legitimately that elevated emotion? For all she knew, she was making that classic mistake of confusing lust with love. It wasn't like this was a long-standing relationship. In the course of an average lifetime, she would spend more time renewing her driver's license than the time she had been married to Rhett. What did she really know about love?

This felt like love.

Didn't it?

She sought out Rhett across the room, but she didn't see him.

"I'm glad to hear it, girl, glad to hear it."

"Thanks, Clinton." Feeling distracted, Shawn was actually hugely relieved when someone called out that the car service had arrived to safely shuttle home the bride and groom and anyone else who had been drinking.

Rhett appeared. "You ready to go?" he asked, holding on to the back of her chair like the room was swaying a little.

"Yes. Beyond ready." Shawn stood up and braced herself for the round of good-byes that were about to commence when suddenly Rhett tried to pick her up. "Ack!" She swatted at him and scurried out of his reach.

"What? I want to carry you to the car."

"Hell, no. You're drunk, and I don't want to be dropped on my ass."

"I could carry you in my sleep," he retorted.

That statement was so stupid Shawn didn't even bother to reply. She just wanted to go home and go to bed. And not to have sex, to close her eyes and sleep.

But Grabby Hands was already trying to knead her ass cheeks like he was baking bread as they paused to speak to his parents. She smacked at him, irritated. He seemed to have forgotten their small wedding party had grown to seventy-five people, and most of them were watching them leave.

Sandy was handing her a large silver box.

"What's this?" she asked.

"It's filled with the cards everyone brought."

"Oh." Shawn blinked. "Oh, thank you . . . I didn't think . . . I didn't realize." People had given them cards and probably some included money. Could she feel any worse? Not that she wanted to test the theory, because she felt pretty much like a huge asshole right now.

Sandy hugged her. "We'll talk soon." She rolled her eyes at her son when his hands slid across her backside again. "Rhett, wait three more minutes, for crying out loud. You're embarrassing your wife."

He didn't look particularly concerned, and when they walked outside into the cold night air, Shawn's jacket just draped over her shoulders, he opened the car door for her.

Murmuring, he said, "You'd better give your heart to Jesus, because your ass is mine tonight."

What irritated her more than anything else was the fact that despite her annoyance, his words still aroused her.

And she wasn't sure how she felt about that.

CHAPTER
NINETEEN

RHETT wasn't as drunk as everyone seemed to think he was. He could still walk a straight line and get an erection. That was all that really mattered. In fact, he already had an erection as the driver took them home, his hand making inroads into Shawn's inner thighs through the soft fabric of her dress. Or rather, not making inroads. He kept getting caught in folds of slippery whiteness.

"Damn it," he complained. "This dress is multiplying."

"It's drunk-groom-proof," she said, and her tone was not particularly lighthearted.

Rhett was starting to get the impression that Shawn was not best pleased with him. "Honey, I am not drunk. I'm relaxed. Relaxed Rhett. Everyone always tells me I'm too serious, so here I am, letting my hair down."

"I've never said that," she said, though the corner of her mouth did turn up slightly.

"How is your head?" he asked, suddenly remembering she'd complained about it hurting.

"It's a little better, but I just feel exhausted."

"Let me massage your head." Because there was no way he was letting her go to bed without a wedding bang.

Shawn shook her head. "Don't worry about it."

But she did undo the bun and let her hair down. It fanned around her face in some weird hair-sprayed clamshell effect. Rhett was suddenly glad he hadn't come of age in the eighties. That hair was terrifying.

"If you're tired, lay down." He urged her down onto his lap and was surprised when she didn't protest. "Just don't fall asleep."

"Why not?"

"Because I have a thing or two I'd like to say with my tongue before you sleep." He waggled his tongue down at her so she could get the rather obvious hint.

Shawn rolled her eyes. "This may be the first night in our relationship that I'm immune to your heavy-handed charms."

Uh. No. He didn't think so. It was their wedding night, or their second wedding night. Which didn't sound right. But the point was, he was not going to waste a good buzz and a hard-on tonight of all nights. "Heavy-handed? Is that what we're calling it? I'll give you heavy-handed."

"Shh," she whispered, her finger over her lips, and her head tilted to gesture to the driver.

"I think he probably has a good guess what we're going to do. I don't think you need to worry about being seen as tawdry. It's our wedding night." Rhett was starting to lose his buzz. Something was off with Shawn, and he didn't like it.

It was obvious when she didn't even wait for him to pay the driver, instead letting herself into the house and actually shutting the door behind her while he was still in the driveway. The driver shot him a look of sympathy, and Rhett felt his irritation spike.

When he went in the side door, Shawn had tossed her coat on a hook in the entry and was holding on to the kitchen counter, peeling her shoes off with a sigh.

"Is there a reason you just shut the door in my face?" he asked her, striving for an even tone.

"I wasn't sure how long you'd be and it's cold out there."

That was clearly an excuse. She was bordering on petulant, and he didn't understand why.

"Let me help you." He shucked his suit jacket and tossed it over a kitchen chair. Bending over, he undid the buckle on her other shoe and pulled it off. He pressed his lips to her ankle, sliding his tongue up the firm calf. "You have amazing legs."

Normally she went liquid under his touch, but she remained stiff. Rhett rose again, pulling the fabric of her dress with him so that her legs were exposed from the thigh down. "What kind of panties do you have on?" he asked curiously. He was picturing a white scrap of lace.

Which contributed to his total astonishment when he reached under the silky folds of her dress and discovered some sort of one-piece bodysuit that was clinging to her skin like a wet suit. "What the fuck are you wearing?" He immediately retreated. He didn't want to touch that. It was like stroking a seal.

"A body shaper. So there are no lumps under my dress."

"There aren't any lumps anywhere on you. Except for this." He cupped her breasts. "First order of business is getting you out of that contraption."

But when he reached for the zipper on the side of her dress, she wiggled out of his reach. "No, I'm not going to have you take this off. Getting out of a body shaper is almost as difficult as getting into it. There's a lot of tugging and . . . flopping."

He held up his arms, palms out in surrender. "Okay, hands off."

"You can't watch either."

"Are you kidding me right now?" This seduction was not unfolding at all the way he had intended.

"No."

Rhett tore his tie off and dropped it on the counter. "Do you think this counts as disobedience?"

For the first time all night, he saw her breath hitch with

desire. But she shook her head. "No. You said that you would never force me to degrade myself. Shoving this off my body while you watch constitutes degradation."

Rhett laughed. "I can respect that." He ran his finger over her lip. "Thank you for being honest with me. Thank you for being you."

But for some reason, his words didn't have the effect he had assumed they would. She pulled a face.

"What?" he asked.

"Nothing."

Studying her expression, he couldn't read her. She wasn't even meeting his eye. "Then go take your dress off."

There it was again, another face. "I suck at these parties. I was awful tonight. I'm sure your family is wondering what you see in me."

It wasn't like Shawn to dive into a pool of self-pity, and he was taken aback. "I'm sure they'll love you like I do."

Then she totally threw him when she suddenly reached out and started to undo the buttons on his dress shirt, with a sort of manic fervor. He had no idea what this was about, but he wanted no part of it. Something was going on, and they were going to talk about it, not bury those feelings behind sex.

He took her hands firmly and pulled them down by her hips, pinning them in place. "No."

SHAWN wasn't even sure what she was doing. She had just suddenly been overcome with the need to prove herself, to be independent, to be in charge of something because it felt like her whole life had suddenly skittered out of her control. Why did everyone else get to determine her future? Hell, her orgasms.

Feeling mutinous, she pulled a pout, ready to protest.

But Rhett shook his head and gave her a very unexpected crack on her backside. "No pouting, Shawn. You're better than that. Pouting is for three-year-olds wanting a cookie."

Maybe he had a point about the pouting. But she was not in the mood for submissive sex play. "You're not my father."

"No. I'm your husband. And I'm just trying to get you to see that you're really much more amazing than you give yourself credit for being. If something is bothering you, tell me. None of this avoidance crap."

This just wasn't the way she had operated most of her adult life. She was used to wheedling with the men she dated and using a circular back-door approach to get what she wanted. Rhett despised that.

Which she could understand. But there was direct, then there was just being a dick. She didn't feel like playing the game tonight, and he should know to back down.

"What I'm feeling is that my husband is an asshole," she said. The night had been too much. Clinton's confession. Rhett's lack of attentiveness. Her own guilt for frauding everyone and their mother. It was all just too much and she wanted, needed, to lash out, irrational or not. "Stop treating me like a student whose behavior you need to correct."

He studied her in that careful way he had. "If I say no or you say no, then the other one should respect that, right?"

She was not in the mood to have him speak carefully to her. She wanted to scream out her emotions, all these unexplained feelings, all this fear, and she wanted him to crack, to break down, and lose it like her. "Of course. But this is about you telling me I'm doing something wrong and I'm tired of it."

"It's called communication. When I left a wet towel on the floor, you made it pretty damn clear to me that I was in the wrong, and if I did it again there would be consequences. How is this any different?"

He had a point, but she wasn't going to admit it. "Because I was pointing out something that is easy to fix and it's not personal. You were correcting something about *me*."

"Tomato, *tomato*. It's all the same thing. It's a matter of letting each other know how we feel so the other can respect it."

"Well, I don't feel like being told what to do tonight." With that, Shawn picked up her swirly bridal gown and stomped off in the direction of the bedroom, tears in her eyes.

She was breaking down. She couldn't do this. She didn't want to feel inadequate.

"Where are you going?"

"To Paris to see the Eiffel Tower. Where do you think I'm going? To take my dress off."

"Come back to the kitchen when you're changed."

"No!" she hurled over her shoulder. "I am not having sex with you tonight, so stick that in your libido and smoke it." She wasn't sure what that even meant, but it felt good to say it.

Going into her bedroom, she slammed the door shut behind her and locked it. It was a challenge to get the zipper down solo, but Shawn wrestled her way out of the dress while Rhett rattled the doorknob and said, in a very calm voice, "Open the door. Now."

"No."

"You're being childish."

"I am well aware of that, thank you very much! But I don't give a shit." Huffing and puffing, she yanked and shoved and peeled the body shaper until it finally gave way and her entire body let out a huge sigh of relief. All her hills sprang forth like an army of flesh unleashed on the enemy. Instantly her stomach felt less queasy.

Balling the torture chamber of spandex up, she threw it into the corner, where it landed in Coconut's lap.

Naked, she was stepping into a pair of panties when the door flew open, wood splintering as Rhett broke the lock and shoved his way in with his shoulder. She jumped about three feet and almost fell over, given that she was one foot in, one foot out.

"Are you fucking crazy?" she shrieked at him. "You just broke the door!"

"I'm well aware of that," he said, echoing her words. "But I refuse to be shut out until we discuss what is bothering you."

Hurriedly pulling her panties up and into place, she tried to figure out what the hell to do now. She felt vulnerable, her literal nakedness exemplifying her emotions. "I can't do this," she admitted. "I don't want to do this."

"What *this* are you referring to? This discussion or something more than that?"

"I don't know. I think all of it. I feel like everything is spiraling out of my control, that everyone else is dictating what happens in my life. First my father by leaving, then my mother by being a flake, then my grandfather for the stipulations in his will, now you. I need to be the one calling the shots for a change."

"If you wanted to go straight to bed tonight, you could have just said that. I would never force you to have sex if you're not in the mood. It was a long day."

Was he deliberately misunderstanding her? Shawn crossed her arms over her breasts and watched him unbutton his dress shirt and peel if off his shoulders. What the hell was he doing? "What are you doing?"

"Going to Paris to see the Eiffel Tower. Or undressing to go to bed."

Okay, that had asshole written all over it. And he called her passive-aggressive? "Why are you so afraid to let me have some control, Rhett? Why is it so important to you?"

He paused with his fingers on the zipper of his dress pants. "It's just a sexual preference, Shawn. Don't psychoanalyze me."

"You called me a three-year-old." Shawn turned her back on him to get herself a T-shirt out of the dresser.

He came up behind her and kissed the side of her neck. "I am not trying to control you. I told you I would be a model husband outside of bed, and I meant it. Just tell me what you need from me."

Shawn shuddered, the agony of her emotions overwhelming her. "Maybe I need to slow down. Maybe I need you to give me some space."

He stiffened, then his hands fell away from her arms. "Do you want me to sleep on the couch tonight?"

She nodded. "I would appreciate that."

"I'm only agreeing to this because I know you're tired. We're not done with this discussion," he warned her.

That was the problem. Her anger spiked all over again. "We're done with it if I say we're done with it!"

He didn't even respond to her. He just zipped his pants again, then started toward the door.

"My lawyer says I don't need to be married," she hurled after him, because the secret was weighing on her like ten thousand tons of concrete.

He stopped walking, but he didn't turn around. "Is that true?"

"Yes. He said that I could contest the will and would most definitely win."

When he turned around, his expression actually froze her in fear that she had just done something irrevocable. "Is that what you want?" he asked, and his voice was cold, even, devoid of any emotion.

"Maybe." She was so deep in shit now, she didn't know where to walk to get out of it.

Rhett slowly shook his head. "It doesn't work that way. You're either in all the way, or you're out all the way."

She swallowed hard, not sure what to say, not sure what she felt.

"I don't believe in hedging my bets, or taking it slow, or living separate lives that we invite each other into on occasion. If you love someone, 'me' becomes 'we.' That's it. One car, two drivers."

Could she do that? She didn't know. She honestly didn't

know. "I can't . . ." She wasn't even sure what she was going to say, but Rhett sighed.

"Yeah, I guess I know you can't. But the truth is, I can't do this if you can't commit to me. I love with everything, Shawn, not in bite-size portions. And I do love you."

Anxiety crawled up her throat. Shawn opened her mouth, but nothing came out. She just stood there in her underwear and made nothing but a tiny nonsensical sound.

Rhett nodded. "I'll sleep on the couch. Tomorrow I can move out."

That startled her into speech. "Move out? What do you mean?"

"Well, what do you think we're going to do? Float along, not totally committed to each other, playing house, each wondering when the other one is going to bail? I can't do that."

"But . . ."

"We had an agreement, right? Yeah, we did. But that was before I fell in love with you."

"But . . ." Shawn didn't know how to deal with this. She didn't want him to move out. She would miss him. But she knew it was unreasonable to expect him to stay when she had no clue what she was doing or how she really felt.

"I don't want you to submit to me. I want you to submit to love." With that, he went out of the room, pulling the door closed behind him.

Shawn was left standing in the middle of the old carpet, wondering how to fix something when she wasn't even sure what was broken.

RHETT woke up, his head pounding and his heart aching. He was slightly hungover and he had a crick in his neck from sleeping on the couch, but more painful than either of those was knowing that Shawn didn't really want to be married to him. It had been on her face the night before at the party, in her panicked eyes, and the stiffness of her body. He had thought it was just nerves, but it wasn't.

The truth was, she had learned to give in to her desire, to jump off the cliff and trust him, but she couldn't trust his love, their marriage.

He couldn't do it. He couldn't stay there day after day wanting something more from her, trying to drag it out of her, until she withdrew and he resented that his needs weren't being met.

Sitting up with a muffled groan, Rhett pulled on his dress pants and pushed off the blanket. Trying not to make any noise, he went down the hall and crept into the bedroom to find a shirt to wear. Shawn was sleeping soundly, her mouth open on a slight snore, her hands tucked under her cheek. He loved her with everything in him, and for that very reason, he knew he had to let her go. He would emotionally bleed her dry. She didn't feel the same intensity of emotion that he did, and he couldn't make her feel it.

Without opening the closet, he wasn't going to be able to find any shirt other than the dress shirt from the night before, and he didn't want to risk waking her up, given how rough the day before had been for her. So with a sigh, he pulled on the crumpled-up shirt and by the side door shoved his feet into his work boots. He would call Shawn later.

He left the house, but his heart stayed behind, tucked up beside the only woman he knew he could ever love.

NOLAN was in the kitchen, eyeballing the coffeemaker through bloodshot eyes, wondering how it was possible he was even awake when there was a knock on the apartment door.

"Eve?" he called. "Can you tell whoever that is to go the hell away?" It was his wife's specialty, telling people off. Besides, she was closer, curled up on the couch, still where they had landed after the party, ripping each other's clothes off and making pro wrestling look like a low-contact sport. They had never made it to the bedroom.

"My pleasure," she mumbled.

As Nolan poured grounds into the filter, he heard the door open. Then Eve yelled back to him. "Uh, Nolan, it's your brother. You might want to come in here."

"What?" Nolan abandoned what he was doing and went into the living room in his underwear. Rhett was in the doorway wearing his rumpled wedding clothes, the shirt not even buttoned, his feet in boots, his hair standing on end, his face weary. "What the hell are you doing here? Did you get arrested last night or something?"

It was the only explanation his brain could produce for why his brother was dressed like that and at his apartment at eight in the morning the day after his wedding reception.

"Where's Shawn?" Eve asked, wearing nothing but Nolan's own dress shirt from the night before.

They were quite the trio of post-party fashion Don'ts.

"She's sleeping still." Rhett came in and shut the door, then fell into a chair, his hands going into his hair. "We broke up."

Oh, Lord. Nolan was going to need coffee for this. "What are you talking about? You got married two weeks ago. Last night you were celebrating." Though now that he thought about it, Shawn hadn't exactly been a beaming bride. She had mostly sat and looked like she was mildly nauseated.

"She doesn't want to be with me," Rhett said, sounding hungover and miserable.

"I'm going to put pants on, then I want to know what the hell you're talking about," Eve said. "That girl is crazy about you."

"Eve's right," Nolan said as his wife went down the hallway. "Whatever you said last night when you were drunk doesn't matter today. Talk it out, bro."

Rhett shook his head. "It's over. Can I stay here for a few weeks?"

Hell, no. Nolan sat down on the couch, his head pounding a little bit. He started to worry that this was more serious than Rhett and Shawn having a drunken fight. "Look, I'm going to give you the same advice you gave me when Eve and I had a disagreement about a minute after we got married—go home and deal with your wife. You can't stay here."

"You're a dick." Rhett scowled at him.

"You were right, you know. Eve and I talked, and look at where we are. You need to talk to Shawn, sort this out with emotions calmed down."

Eve came back out of the bedroom in yoga pants. "I agree. I've never seen Shawn fall for someone this hard."

"Except it's all bullshit," Rhett said. "We only got married because if she wasn't married by next month, she wouldn't inherit the track."

Nolan blinked. "Excuse me?" God, he really needed that coffee. He hadn't even put the water in and turned it on, yet he clearly needed it because his brain didn't seem to be firing at full capacity.

"I mean it was a set-up. She offered me money to marry her, and I agreed because I know how important the speedway is to her. And I wanted an in to her bed, I admit it."

"*What?*" Eve exploded. "Are you both insane? Marriage is not something you play around with!"

Nolan recovered from his initial shock to second that opinion. "Holy shit, Rhett."

"You two have no business judging us. You got married impulsively."

"Impulse is one thing—for money or sex is another." Nolan couldn't even believe what he hearing. "Oh, my God, Mom is going to die. She thinks the two of you are in love."

"You can't tell anyone for fuck's sake. It still has to be a secret, for Shawn's dignity. And the truth is, we do love each other. We fell in love, which in a way, was my plan all along. But that doesn't mean every plan works out in the end."

"I don't even know what the hell you're talking about."

"I knew something was fishy," Eve said, pacing back and forth, her hands on her hips. "I told you, Nolan. I said Shawn didn't do shit like this, and I said the whole prenup thing was a red flag."

"You did." Nolan should have trusted her suspicions. Then they could have all been spared a wedding reception that was based on a complete lie. "So you're telling me that even after starting a marriage based on something as mercenary as cash and sex, you do want to be with Shawn."

"Yes." Rhett said this like it was obvious.

"If there was no money, would you still want to be with Shawn?"

Now his brother looked downright offended. "Of course."

It was a legit question. This whole thing was crazy. "Then tell her that."

"I did. She just stood there and stared at me. I can't do this, man. I can't be in love with her and have her unsure if she wants to really be with me."

"So you snuck out of the house in your wedding clothes while she was sleeping? Bro, seriously. Go talk to her."

"I told her how I felt. The ball is in her court."

Oh, God. "I need some coffee."

"Can I sleep on your couch for a few hours?"

"Yes. We had sex on it last night, though, just full disclosure."

Rhett made a face. "I'll sleep on the floor."

"Fine."

"I'm going for a run," Eve announced. "I need to clear my head."

If Nolan knew his wife, she was going over to Shawn's.

Which was confirmed when she went and got her keys. Last time he checked she didn't need her car to jog. Hopefully, Eve would have more luck talking sense into Shawn than he had with Rhett.

Total disaster.

He scratched the tattoo of his wife's name on his chest as he stumbled back to the coffeepot. The path of true love never ran smooth. More likely you ran out of gas, blew a tire, and hit the wall before you crossed the finish line.

But you were always glad you entered the race.

CHAPTER
TWENTY

SHAWN wasn't even sure how she had managed to fall asleep, because after Rhett had closed the door, she had spent the first few hours lying in bed staring at the wall. She had debated going out into the living room and talking to him about a hundred times. Every single time she had chickened out.

Of course, when she had gotten up, he was nowhere to be found.

Now she was exhausted, miserable, and confused as hell as she sat on the couch, picking through the box of cards from all their friends and family. Every single one, with its well wishes and words of congratulations, were a new knife in her heart. There was a lot of money. Thousands of dollars, and as she calculated in her head, her guilt and disgust with herself grew. Marriage was a serious covenant, not something you jumped into without zero thought and for practical purposes.

So she might have lost the track, which would have been horrible. It hadn't been worth the damage she had done to her own conscience and how the people she cared about would feel when her split became known. If there had been no marriage, she might have dated Rhett and they might have gotten to the same destination in the end. But there was no way of knowing that, and no way to go back. Second-guessing was painful and futile.

The truth was, they might have managed to create a relationship together despite the odd origin, if she had been able to unlock her lips the night before and tell him she loved him.

But then again, she did have a legitimate point—once in a while she wanted to feel in charge.

Though on the other hand, when had he ever really truly been bossy out of the bedroom?

She clutched the box to her chest and cried silent tears.

Which is how Eve found her.

When she heard the side door open she thought it was Rhett, and she felt her hope soar, only to realize it was her best friend.

"Okay, start explaining," Eve said by way of greeting. "Rhett is at my apartment saying that the two of you got married so you wouldn't lose the track."

The blood drained from her face. "What?"

"Don't worry. I know it's a secret. It's crazy, but I won't tell anyone. But tell me what this is all about." She sank into the chair opposite Shawn.

So she told Eve everything, starting with the will and how she had impulsively chosen Rhett because she was attracted to him and because she figured he could use the money. "Then the thing is, we did fall for each other for real. We really did. I am in love with him."

"Okay, so I'm just going to let all the ridiculousness of how you ended up married go for now and focus on the immediate issue. So if the love is mutual, what the hell is the problem?"

"I'm worried about losing my independence."

Eve blinked. "Why would that happen? I married Nolan and I'm the same person I was before. I didn't suddenly start wearing pearls and an apron."

"Rhett is different than Nolan." Shawn bit her lip. "He's . . . intense."

"I'm not going to talk about your sex life, or at least I'm going to try not to. Are you saying he wants you to be like a submissive all the time? Like an actual lifestyle choice? Because I can understand you might object to being led on a leash or whatever."

"No! Not at all." Shawn set the box down on the couch next to her and leaned forward. "I'm afraid to be too much in love."

"You're afraid to be your mother," Eve said shrewdly.

Shawn winced. "There is probably truth to that. She never recovered from my dad leaving. I'm afraid to give my heart like that."

"But in trying to avoid being hurt like your mother, you have become the post-divorce version of your mother— apathetic. She can't bring herself to care more than superficially about anyone, including her own kids."

That was definitely true. But the realization that she could wind up like that punched Shawn in the gut. "Oh, God, I do not want to be my mother. She's miserable, and she makes everyone else around her miserable, too."

"Let me ask you this very simple question. Would you rather be alone or with Rhett when you go to bed every night? And when you wake up in the morning and you're having your coffee, would you rather be alone? Or would you like him there?"

Shawn didn't even hesitate. "I'd rather be with him."

"Then stop treating every little speed bump like the end of the relationship. Marriage is a learning curve. But you can't learn anything if you both just bail the second that it gets tough. Give it a shot, work on being together, then in six months, get married for real, with vows you actually mean when you speak them."

"You think so?"

"Girl, I'm Eve Monroe Ford. I know so."

Shawn laughed, suddenly hopeful. They could work on

their relationship. So Rhett was all or nothing. But maybe he would understand that when you skipped a step or five, you were all in, you just weren't at the end goal yet. "What should I do?"

"Go to my apartment and surprise him. I'll text Nolan and tell him to make up an excuse to leave Rhett alone. Just tell him how you feel. You've got nothing to lose. I went after Nolan, and look at how that turned out." Eve sat back, smug. "We've basically cornered the market on awesome marriages."

"And modesty, too."

"Yeah, well, you're one to talk. Now get dressed and go talk to Rhett, or I'm going to post on Stoney White's Facebook wall that you have never gotten over him."

She rolled her eyes and stood up. "You aren't even friends with Stoney White."

"How do you know?"

Shawn ignored the question and asked one of her own. "How can something that's so amazing be so scary? I never thought of myself as chickenshit, but this loving someone—it's terrifying."

"Tell me about it. But I combat the fear by drag racing with Nolan. It takes the tension out."

That wasn't going to work in her case, since Shawn hadn't driven in years and Rhett would leave her in the dust. But she had a better idea. "Good call, Eve." She went to get dressed and go lay her cards on the table. She had taken a huge leap of faith in asking Rhett to marry her. Now it was time to make another one.

RHETT was dozing in and out of sleep on the floor, his head on a throw pillow from the armchair, his headache between his eyes and misery pronounced. The door to the apartment opened and he sighed, guessing it was Eve back from her jog, or Nolan back from the doughnut shop. He'd said he had a post-drinking hankering for fried dough.

Hopefully, whoever it was, they wouldn't speak to him. He wanted to be left the hell alone.

But his eyes flew open when he realized whoever it was had stopped next to him and was dropping onto their knees. It was Shawn, and in another second, she was on the floor, aligned next to him.

"Hi," she said, with a soft smile.

"What are you doing here?" he asked, even as a seed of hope began to sprout. He rolled onto his side so he was facing her. He wanted to touch her, but he restrained himself.

"I came to apologize for my behavior last night. You wanted to know what was wrong—the truth is, I'm not entirely sure. But the closest I can figure is that I'm afraid. I'm afraid of these feelings, Rhett. I've never been in love before, and I'm afraid of losing Shawn in our relationship."

Her eyes were glassy with new tears and her voice was quiet, words spoken with conviction. "But I'm willing to risk it. I'm all in if you are."

The words were everything to him. Her sincerity was clear, and he was willing to work on whatever they needed to make this work. He gave in to his urge and ran his finger across her bottom lip. "I'm all in. I love you."

It was that simple.

"I love you, too." Her hand started to wander across the front of his dress pants.

"What are you doing?" he asked with a smile as he kissed her chin, the corner of her mouth, her ear.

"Something I've been wanting to do for a while." She unzipped his pants and reached in with eager strokes and freed his cock.

Rhett gritted his teeth. "What if Eve or Nolan come home?"

"Eve texted Nolan and told him to leave and not come back until further notice. She came over to my house to bitch me out. They won't be back until we give the word."

Rhett grinned. "Smooth, Hamby. I like your style." He stilled her hand. "But you know my stance on oral sex."

"I can appreciate your opinion. But this is what I want, and sometimes, Rhett Butler Ford, you're just going to have to do it my way." Her mouth descended and wrapped around his erection.

"Damn it, that feels good," he said, laying back and closing his eyes for a second and enjoying the hot stroke of her mouth over him. "But I'm not going to stop being dominating in bed, I hope you understand that. I can't turn it off."

Shawn looked up at him over the length of his cock, her lips clearing with a slick popping sound. "I understand, and believe me, I enjoy it, too. I had no idea how very much I would enjoy it. But on occasion, I'm asking you to let me have my way with you."

It was a fair compromise, especially given that a second ago she had been sucking him, and now they were merely talking. "I can live with that. Now get up here and ride me."

"Uh-uh. Give me a minute."

Shawn's mouth covered him again and he groaned, letting her have her way with him. He had to admit, it was a sensation that drove him crazy, and the view was amazing. He let her go at it, both enjoying it, until his control was threatened. But for once, he didn't mind. He wanted to lose control with her, he wanted to be swept away on a wave of emotion with Shawn. His wife.

He gripped her arms and hauled her up the length of him. "Come here." A second later he had her pants down and her astride him. He didn't bother to tell her what she should do. He let her sit up and start a slow, eager rhythm.

"Rhett?" she asked, eyes dilated with desire, hips pumping.

"Yes, Scarlett?"

"As God is my witness, I will never go horny again."

If he weren't so turned on, he would have laughed. "And that is one of the many reasons I love you."

CHAPTER
TWENTY-ONE

"*IT'S* very irregular," the clerk said. "I can't believe the minister agreed to do this."

It was because Rhett had paid him two hundred bucks, but he just shrugged. "He didn't see what the harm was."

He and Shawn were in a wedding chapel, renewing their vows, with true emotion in their hearts this time. They had been legally married for five weeks, and every day their union solidified a little more. It was an education, that was for certain, and they were learning how to communicate, but the amazing moments overshadowed and outnumbered any brief flashes of confusion and misunderstanding. They had been working together on new ideas for Hamby Speedway, and Shawn had started the ball rolling to get national affiliation. It was going to be a great year for racing, and they were definitely working together as a team.

Getting married again had been his idea, and she had readily agreed. They hadn't told anyone, and it was just meant to be the two of them speaking their commitment to each other out loud.

Shawn was beaming, a beautiful bride, part two, in the dress she had worn to their wedding reception.

"I do," she said clearly, her eyes shining, lips parted in a wide smile.

"I do," Rhett said when it was his turn, and he meant that to the depth of his soul. He held both her hands in his and looked deep into her eyes.

When it was time to seal it with a kiss, Shawn threw her arms around him and opened her mouth to him. Rhett picked her up and gave her a spin, grinning. This was it for him—he couldn't imagine being any happier or that any other woman could make him feel so amazing.

As they walked back down the aisle of the slightly shabby chapel, Shawn told him, "I have a gift for you." She handed a box to him that looked like a bracelet would fit in it.

"What's this?" Puzzled, he lifted the silver lid. For a second, he had no idea what he was looking at. Then he realized it was a pregnancy test. A positive pregnancy test. His vision actually went black momentarily, then his hand started to shake. "Is this what I think it is?"

She nodded with a smile. "You have supersperm, there's no other explanation for it. I'm actually very excited, now that the shock has worn off. I never thought much about being a mother, but I can't wait. I hope it's okay with you."

"Are you kidding?" He grinned. "This is amazing!" He pulled her close against him and decided that he was probably the luckiest man on the freaking planet. "God, I love you."

Shawn snuggled against her husband and watched in astonishment as her super serious, alpha male husband got a little watery-eyed as the reality of his impending fatherhood sunk in.

Just one more reason she loved him.

"If it's a boy, I think we should name him Jameson after your grandfather," Rhett said, holding her tight. "He brought us together, after all."

Oh, yeah. She loved this man. Now she was blinking back tears, too. "And if it's a girl, Margaret."

"Margaret?" he asked, clearly puzzled.

"After Margaret Mitchell."

He let out a laugh. "We can discuss that one." He took her hand and they started out of the chapel. "You want to have everyone over for dinner this week and we can tell them?"

"I would love to. Any day but Friday. That's book club night."

"Oh, God," was his opinion. "You hitting up The Wet Spot again?"

"Of course not!" Shawn let him put her coat over her shoulders and accepted the sweet kiss he gave her.

"Damn. I was hoping to go separately and hit on you like I was a total stranger. It would be fun in a place like that to start making out." He made a sound in the back of his throat. "I'm getting hot just thinking about it."

So was she. "It doesn't have to be book club to do that. How about tonight?"

"I love the way you think. Among other things."

The feeling was mutual.

Turn the page for a special look at

True

and

Sweet

Two new adult contemporary romances by
Erin McCarthy, available digitally from InterMix.

TRUE

GETTING drunk was not in my plans for Friday night. Neither was admitting to my roommates, Jessica and Kylie, that I was a virgin.

But they left me alone with Grant.

I knew what Jessica and Tyler, Kylie and Nathan were going to do in the guys' respective bedrooms. Well, it's not like I actually knew from personal experience what they were doing—but I hoped their sex fest wouldn't take that long. I had studying to do for an inorganic chemistry exam on Monday. Plus, I had to read six chapters of Hemingway about boozy, washed-up writers and their cheating wives, which was always a challenge for me, since I preferred the facts of math and science. Puzzling out literature and the social dynamics of characters struck me as a waste of time, especially given their activities.

Alcohol and sex. Ironic, really.

But Jessica was my ride. It was too far to walk back to the dorms, and it was the kind of off-campus neighborhood that had my dad raising his eyebrows and suggesting I go to college in some cow town like Bowling Green, where there were no dirty couches on sagging front porches and no residents smoking crack in full view of the street.

So walking back was not happening, because I didn't smoke crack and I was no risk-taker. At all. Yet sitting there alone with Grant while my roommates were off having a good time almost seemed riskier than strolling through the ghetto. It was sort of like perching over a public toilet seat without actually touching anything. It was difficult. Awkward.

Plus, it was very, very quiet. He didn't speak, and I didn't either, so there was a lot of sitting and a lot of awkwardness and a lot of trying to be entirely motionless so I wouldn't be moving more than him. Since he was barely breathing, this was a hard thing to do.

I actually felt sorry for Grant, which was just crazy because I wasn't exactly the Girl Everyone Wants to Be. But Grant was cute, with long hair that dropped into his eyes, long cheekbones, and thick, girlish eyelashes. He was too thin, his black T-shirts always tight and wrinkled, with various rude expressions like BITE ME and WHAT THE F ARE YOU LOOKING AT? His dirty jeans hung off nonexistent hips that rivaled Mary Kate Olsen's, and not because he was looking to be fashionable. I don't think he ate enough, honestly. Nathan had told me Grant's father was a drunk, and his mother was a freak who stabbed her coworker at Taco Bell with a pen and was in some psych ward downtown. No one was shopping for vegetables at Kroger in Grant's house.

So I had kind of an awkward girl crush on Grant because the situation smelled of possibility. Like, it was not totally out of the realm of possibility that he could actually want to be with me, in some sort of male-female capacity.

"Smoke?" Grant asked, holding his pack of Marlboro Reds out to me, gaze shooting around to avoid the connection with mine, as we sat in the main room of Nathan's apartment.

"No, thanks." It was the eyes that made me understand

that here was someone I didn't have to be afraid of, didn't have to feel threatened or intimidated by. Because even though his eyes never met mine, Grant had haunted eyes. Aching, vulnerable, gray eyes.

I wanted him to kiss me. Even as I took a huge swig out of the beer he had given me five minutes before, I was thinking that if only he would recognize what I saw, everything would be awesome. We were absolutely perfect for each other. Two totally sensitive, pale, quiet people. I'd never shove him around the way Tyler did, under the guise of bro wrestling. I'd never embarrass him or set his clothes on fire for fun like his alleged best friend, Nathan, did.

His hand shook a little as he flicked his Bic on to light the cigarette he'd stuffed in his mouth. There was an oak end table between us, each of us perched in a plaid easy chair, a movie playing on the TV screen in front of us. Some sort of bad Tom Cruise drama. I've never liked Tom Cruise. He always reminded me of someone's creepy cousin who smiles too big before he touches your butt and whispers something gross in your ear with hot whiskey breath.

Grant was studying the TV, though, very seriously, his smoke floating out into nice, sexy ovals. He could make smoke rings.

I thought my only talent was converting oxygen to carbon dioxide, though to give myself credit, I did really well in school—I always have. I was in the honors scholar program, and I was on track for magna cum laude, which made my rooming with Jessica and Kylie even more ironic than me reading Hemingway. They were social superstars, while if there were a subject called Casual Conversation and Flirting 101, I would have been flunking it.

I'd never had a boyfriend. No sweaty, hand-holding, note-passing, middle-school boyfriend. No guy in high school who had me wear his football jersey to pep rallies. No TA in college who suddenly recognized the value of a quality brain and spent coffee-shop nights studying with me. None of the above.

I wasn't exactly sure why, because I didn't consider myself ugly with a capital "U." Maybe slightly plain, definitely quiet, but not repulsive in any way. No body odor, bad breath, or strange growths in obvious places, no bald spots or facial tics. I did have a few guys who wanted to make out and attempt to shove their hands down my pants, but no one wanted to date me.

Which is why I knew I should make a move on Grant somehow. Because here was my chance to score a boyfriend. To have make-out sessions and share popcorn at the movies, to text each other on a minute-by-minute basis using sickly sweet nicknames. Just to see what it was like, a relationship, to try it on for size like a great pair of sexy heels.

Maybe it would even result in having my name tattooed on Grant's bicep. It was a short name, Rory, so it would fit on his skinny arm. Something permanent that said that someone else in this world thought enough of me to ink me into infinity.

In reality, Grant and I had remained completely silent for fifteen, twenty minutes. He'd even stopped asking me if I wanted another beer. He had the uncanny ability to sense when I'd drained one without even looking over at me, and he immediately offered another by just holding out the can. I didn't really want this many, but I couldn't bring myself to say no. His silent offer was the only thing connecting us at all, besides the fact that we were both human and happened to be sitting in the same room.

I was starting to feel a serious buzz from the three back-to-back beers I'd had, and I was wondering how much longer until my supposedly large brain managed to put forth a flirtatious comment for me to sling at Grant with an artful hair flip. A lot of girls I knew talked more as they drank, but so far, my tongue still seemed to be stuck to the roof of my mouth, and my ears were ringing.

"Do you think . . . ?" Grant started to say, his whole body suddenly turning to me.

Startled, I choked a little, beer going up my nose. I didn't know he was going to look at me. Not prepared. No coy smile in place. I blinked at him, hoping that just maybe he'd say something that could lead to something, and I would have a turn at this strange mating game we all seemed to want to play.

"Do you think Tyler and Jessica are serious about each other or are they just hooking up? Or could I, you know . . ."

I sank back into the burgundy plaid. My turn was not today. I was stupid to think it ever would be.

"No," I managed to say. "They're definitely serious." Even though I knew it wasn't true, that Jessica wasn't serious about anything right now. But I was feeling mean and a little sick, and drunk in a not-so-good way. It was rare for me to get angry, but I suddenly felt just that.

Because even Grant, who was like a terrified grasshopper clinging to the windshield of a speeding car, was too good for me.

I lifted my beer to my mouth and sucked hard, eyes focusing on Tom on the TV and his cheesy grin.

"She says she adores him," I added, to emphasize my point, driven to speak by an itchy humiliation that prickled over my skin. It wasn't a lie—she had said that. But Jessica adored her Hello Kitty slippers, and her iPhone, and Greek yogurt. It was her catchall word for anything that was pleasing her at that very moment. Tyler had been pleasing her half an hour ago. Whether he still was now was anyone's guess.

Grant looked down the hallway, toward the bedroom. He didn't say anything, but I could see it. That pathetic, hopeless wanting. The desire for what you want but can't have. The need for someone to like you.

I recognized it because I saw it in my own face every day.

So I drained my fourth beer completely, my teeth starting

to numb, my breath sounding loud and labored to my ears. I knew I should slow down, drink water, stand up, but it was easier to feel sorry for myself, hidden behind a beer can, deep in the recesses of the plaid chair, my new best friend.

When Grant leaned over and suddenly covered my mouth with his, I was so shocked I made a startled yelp and dropped the nearly empty can in my lap, dribbles of cold beer spilling onto my jeans. Grant had eaten up the distance between the two chairs and was leaning on the oak table with one hand, grabbing the back of my head with the other. Confused, I sat there unresponsive for a second, my beer brain chugging along slowly, processing. Grant was kissing me.

I kissed back. Because, well, this is what I wanted, right? Grant to kiss me.

But then I remembered Grant wasn't really interested in me. He was into Jessica. I knew that. And his mouth was hard, his tongue thrusting and swollen. I started to pull back, desperate for air. He tasted like stale cigarettes, and he smelled like he did laps in a swimming pool of Axe body spray.

"Pass that on to Jessica," he said, panting hard, tossing his hair out of his eyes.

I blinked. I may have been the awkward girl, but I didn't want to be second-best. A sexual stand-in for my hot roommate. Humiliation flooded over me, drenching my skin in heat from head to toe as I flushed with embarrassment and anger. When he started to move in again for another kiss, I put my hand on his chest to stop him.

"Tell her yourself," I spat out, standing up, the beer can tumbling to the dirty carpet. I wasn't sure where I was going, but away from him.

Only Grant grabbed me by the arm as I walked past and pulled me down onto his lap. Before I could react, he had his arms completely around me, his warm lips on my neck, the hard nudge of what I figured had to be his erection at the back of my thighs. Fear flooded my mouth. He didn't look this strong. He didn't look strong at all, yet his grip on me was tight, his sloppy, wet kisses trailing lower down my chest, under my T-shirt.

When I tried to stand, his hands held my arms so tightly it felt like my wristbones were being snapped, and I was too out of it from the beer to have great coordination. Trying to back up, I ended up sliding down his lap, between his legs and to the floor.

"Now that's what I'm talking about," he said, loosening his hold on me to take down his zipper. "Good girl."

When he pulled out his erection, a mere foot from my face, I couldn't believe what I was looking at, all smooth skin and dark hair, just out there, all casual. Right in front of my face. I realized he thought I was going to give him a blow job. That I was actually offering to give him oral sex, for no reason, with no conversation or lead-in, just a few shitty kisses when he referenced my roommate. That somehow he was insane enough to think that I would willingly go down on him. Nauseated, I turned my head, so I didn't have to look at his junk.

The beer was going to come back up. I drank it too fast and it was sloshing around in my gut, ready to rush up my throat in a Bud Light tsunami, crashing out over my teeth onto his lap if I didn't get some fresh air, didn't get away from him.

"Let me go," I said, trying to get my feet on the floor so I could stand.

But he had my hair at the back of my head, and I realized the only way out was to go low, not try to stand. But if I fell to the floor completely, then he could fall *on* me, which meant that if I didn't get out of this in the next sixty seconds, I might wind up having sex on the hard, filthy carpet of this crappy rental apartment. I'd rather give oral sex than lose my virginity to this douchebag, who I had thought was nice, who I had thought would never victimize anyone because he'd been the victim.

Neither was a good choice.

But if I faked oral, I could bite him instead. Sink my teeth down into his most sensitive spot and get away. Call a cab. I was just panicked enough that I figured I could actually do it, get away or at least go down fighting.

So I tried to stand instead of falling down, and he yanked my hair so hard tears came to my eyes. I had long, dark-red hair, which made it easy for him to entwine his fingers to control my head and my neck, holding me so I couldn't move.

"Stop! I'm serious." I braced my knee on the bottom of the chair, my hand on his chest to keep my head as far from him as possible. "I'm going to be sick," I added, because it was true, and I figured no guy wanted to be puked on.

But he ignored me and said, "Open your mouth."

So I punched his wrist, trying to break his hold, desperate, panicked, my vision blurred from tears and too many beers, my stomach churning violently. "No! Please, don't!"

"Let her go, Grant. *Now*."

He did, and I fell to the ground, gasping, scrambling backward, my floral rain boots giving me traction to butt-scoot out of his reach. Tyler was standing in the hallway, not wearing a shirt, a beer in his hand. He had clearly been to the kitchen, clearly seen what had been happening, clearly planned to stop it.

Relief had my hands shaking and I zipped up my hoodie, wanting my T-shirt covered, wanting all of me covered, gone.

"Mind your own fucking business," Grant said.

"No. I won't. She said no." Tyler was tall, broad-shouldered, his chest and biceps covered in tattoos. He looked at me, and I shrank back a little. His eyes looked angry in the fluorescent glow of the stove light. "Did you say no, Rory?"

"Yes. I said no," I added, wanting to clarify.

Grant's foot came out, and he kicked my arm, hard. "You did not, you dick tease."

He kicked me. I couldn't believe that he just kicked me. I yelped, and before I could respond, Tyler was between me and Grant, pulling him to his feet.

"I heard her say no. Now get the hell out of here. Go home. What is wrong with you? You don't treat a chick like that."

They scuffled a little, Grant shoving Tyler's arms off him as he made his way to the door. "Man, I was doing her a favor. No one else wants her."

Tyler's response to that was to punch Grant in the face, knocking him into the wall. "Shut the fuck up, or I'll beat your ass into tomorrow."

Grant peeled himself off the wall, shot me a look of hatred, then left, the door slamming hard behind him. The tears were rolling down my face, whether I liked it or not. The realization that I was almost raped settled over me, and his hateful words lay on top of that, a final insult. He was right. No one wanted me. But that didn't mean I could be treated like shit. It didn't mean I wasn't a person, that I should toss over my dignity and accept whatever attention I got, no matter how selfish and crude it was.

"You okay?" Tyler asked, popping open his beer and holding it in front of me.

I shook my head. Because I didn't want the beer. And because I wasn't okay.

"I'm sorry. I didn't know he would do something like that. I feel really bad." He set his beer down on the end table. "Do you want me to give you a ride home? Jessica's asleep."

Great. All I wanted to do was retreat to our dorm and cry in my bed, but Jessica was taking a post-coital nap. It was bold for me, but I decided to accept his offer, even though I knew I was putting him out. "Yeah, if you don't mind."

"Sure, no problem. Just let me get my keys." He made a face. "And a shirt. It's cold out there for October."

He went back into the bedroom and when he came out,

Jessica was actually with him. "Rory, are you okay?" She rushed over to me, blond hair flying behind her, dressed in men's pajama pants and a huge sweatshirt. "Tyler told me what happened."

Her arms wrapped around me and I let her hug me, grateful for the contact and her concern.

"What an asshole. If I see him, I'm going to cut his dick off and shove it down his throat. Let's see how he likes cock crammed in his mouth."

Her vehemence made me feel better. "I should have . . ." I started—but then stopped myself. I should have what? I shouldn't have done anything differently. I was just sitting in my chair and he made a world of assumptions and I said no, and that was the truth of it. I wasn't going to blame myself that he'd taken a fist to the face.

"No, screw that," Jessica said. "You didn't do anything wrong. And I'm sorry I left you alone with that prick."

"I'll be right back," Tyler said, his phone buzzing in his hand. He retreated into the bedroom as Kylie came out, her hair a hot mess, makeup streaked.

"What's going on?"

"Grant tried to rape Rory," Jessica said in such a loud, matter-of-fact voice I couldn't help but wince.

"What? Are you effing kidding me?" Kylie could have been Jessica's twin. They were both tall, blond, tan, toned. They were getting vague degrees in Gen Ed and would probably wind up as wedding planners and golf wives, while I was intending to go to med school to be a coroner. I was more comfortable with dead people than living ones. But for whatever reason, they liked me. And I liked them. Their reaction cemented that feeling. They both looked like if they had had a baseball bat and five minutes alone with Grant, he'd wish he'd never been born.

I didn't want to fight Grant. I just wanted to forget it had ever happened. "I did kiss him," I said, because I felt guilty for that. That was leading him on, a little.

"So? A kiss is not a promise of pussy," Kylie said.

She was right. "I know," I said, miserable, confused, stomach upset. I sat down on the end table, looking at my boots. "But I mean, it's not like I haven't thought about being with Grant. I have. But he was so . . . and I don't want it, my first time, to be like this . . . and I should have done . . . something."

So much for telling myself I wasn't going to do that. There I was, worried, feeling like I'd had some part in what had happened.

"Your first time? Wait a minute, are you saying you're a virgin?" Jessica was staring at me blankly. "For real?"

Oops. I hadn't really meant to share that. It wasn't exactly a deep, dark secret, and it really couldn't have been that much of a shock to her, but it wasn't necessarily something I wanted to go around talking about. "Um. Yes. I just haven't . . ."

Had the opportunity.

"There hasn't been anyone . . ." I reached for the beer Tyler had abandoned and took a sip. I was drunk, but not nearly enough to not suddenly feel completely and totally middle-school mortified.

"Oh." Kylie looked bewildered. "Well, that's cool. Lots of girls make that choice."

"It hasn't been a choice. Not exactly. I mean, if I could, I think I would." I did. I was twenty, and I had all the same physical feelings as other people. Just no one to explore them with. In a way that wasn't a quickie on the stained carpet.

"Well, why can't you?" Jessica asked.

"Because no one is offering. I guess technically Grant offered, but I don't want it like that." I was sorry I'd brought it up at all. It wasn't a discussion I wanted to have with Tyler and Nathan a few feet away.

"So you want, like, romance?"

Was that what we called it? "I guess."

Tyler came back into the room, pushing his cell phone into his front pocket. "You ready?"

"Yeah." I found my cross-body bag on the floor and put it over my head.

"Tyler, Rory wants romance," Jessica told him. "What do you think of that?"

My face burned with embarrassment. I didn't want to be the subject of discussion. I didn't want Tyler to stare at me the way he was, dark eyes scrutinizing mine. He was the typical bad-boy type—which was why Jessica liked him—and I was the kind of girl he would never notice. And he hadn't ever noticed me, not really. I was the quiet friend of Jessica and Kylie whose presence he tolerated. But now his eyes were sweeping over me, assessing, and I couldn't read his expression.

"I think she should have whatever she wants." He reached out and took the beer can from my hand, his fingers brushing mine. "But nothing says romance like a six-pack. I need to pick up more beer."

I shivered from his touch and from the inscrutable look he was giving me.

"I'm staying here," Jessica stated. "It's too cold outside to go home. See you tomorrow, Rory."

Kylie was already curled up on the couch, in a praying position, half-asleep as she gave a weak wave. "Bye, sweetie."

"Okay, bye," I said, shoving my hands in the front pockets of my jeans, wishing I had worn a thicker coat. I was cold and I wanted a hot shower to wash away the beer and the fear and the feel of Grant's wet lips on me. But first I had to sit in the car alone with Tyler. A perfect ending to a crap night. Awkward small talk with my roommate's Friend with Benefits, who had punched his own friend on my behalf.

As I followed Tyler down the metal stairs, the smell of fried foods strong in the hallway, I thought that was the end of any talk about my virginity.

I didn't know it was just the beginning.

SWEET

I couldn't go home for the summer. I just couldn't.

Going home would mean endless worried looks from my mother, and reminders about following curfew and the dangers of alcohol and pre-marital sex. My father would force me to volunteer—which was *such* an oxymoron—to teach Sunday school at his church, and threaten to throw out all my revealing clothes. Like shorts. Because wearing shorts in summer was so scandalous.

I couldn't deal with it, a whole summer ruined with their good intentions and their high moral standards that only a saint could live up to. And I'm no saint.

So I lied and told them I was spending the summer in Appalachia building homes for the poor with a Christian mission group when I was actually staying in Cincinnati and working at a steak house. I know. That was kind of a shitty lie.

But it was the only one that would have worked, so I had gone with it and there was no turning back now. Maintaining my freedom was worth a little guilt that I wasn't actually helping people in need, though I suppose I could argue I was at least fueling the economy by serving beef. So the only thing still unresolved was where I was going to stay for a week in the gap between when I had to leave my dorm and when I could take over a sublet on an apartment June first.

I had a plan. Turning the doorknob, I stepped inside and assessed the situation. My roommate Kylie, snuggled with her boyfriend, Nathan, who lived in the apartment. Tyler and my other roommate, Rory, also cuddling. The sap-factor in the living room was huge, with Kylie on Nathan's lap, their fingers entwined, while Tyler did that weird thing he was constantly doing where he played with Rory's hair and made me want to smack his hand away on her behalf. She always seemed okay with it, though, go figure.

"Hey, Jessica!" Kylie said brightly. "Cute top."

"Thanks." I had put the tight red tank on absently, then had wondered if more cleavage would be better for what I had in mind, then had been disgusted with myself for even thinking such a thought. So then I had decided no cleavage was necessary to my self-respect and pulled a Union Jack shirt on over the tank. Appearance was such a process. "What are you guys up to?"

"I'm watching *Inglorious Basterds*," came a voice from the kitchen. "Everyone else is engaged in foreplay."

Ugh. Trying not to sigh, I turned and saw Riley Mann, Tyler's older brother, popping the top of a beer can. He was not who I wanted to see.

"Jealous?" I asked him lightly, forcing a sardonic smile. Everything about Riley annoyed me, from his sarcasm to his inability to ever be serious, to the fact that he was hot as hell and so clearly knew it. I didn't see him very often since he worked full-time in construction, which was perfectly fine with me. It was easier to breathe without his testosterone choking the room.

He shook his head. "No. Sex is not worth the headache of a relationship. And my hand doesn't expect me to text it twenty times the next day."

There was mental imagery I did not need, though I couldn't argue with his opinion that relationships were a crapload of work. I made a face. "You're always so charming. Is Bill here?"

"He's studying in his room," Nathan told me. "He has a physics final tomorrow. God, I'm so glad I'm done with my exams."

I was done, too, which was why housing was becoming something of an issue because I only had two days until I had to vacate the dorms. "Okay, thanks." I started down the hall to Bill's room.

"You're going in there?" Nathan called after me. "I'm warning you, he's in a mood."

"I'm sure it's fine. I just want to say hi." Bill had been crushing on me for six months, ever since his girlfriend from high school had dumped him for a basketball player at Ohio State. We had hooked up a few times, but I had been totally clear about not wanting to date. I was not in the market for a relationship at all.

Without knocking, I went in to Bill's room. He was at his desk, and with the exception of the books and papers spread out in front of him, his room was neat as usual, bed made, no sign of finals stress. Until you got to his hair. Then the tension was evident in the floppy curls sticking out in various directions, looking like he hadn't made nice with a hairbrush in days. His glasses were sliding down his nose when he looked up, and he was a very cute, modern interpretation of the absent-minded genius.

"Hey," he said, looking vacantly at me.

"Hey. How's studying going?" I propped a hip on the corner of his desk and smiled.

"Not bad, but I still have a lot to go through. Did you need something or did you just want to hang out? Because I can't until tomorrow."

"I wanted to know if I can stay here with you, in your room, for a couple of days." Okay, so it was more like eight days, but who was counting?

"What?" He frowned. "What do you mean?" He tapped his pen on his lips and blinked up at me.

"I need a place to crash until I can get in the apartment I subletted. There's no way I'm sleeping on that couch in the living room. It's like chain mail. But I can sleep in your bed with you, right?" I smiled and used the tip of my finger to push his glasses up. "I promise I won't kick you in my sleep like I did last time."

For a second, he didn't say anything. Then he shook his head. "No."

That was definitely not the answer I was expecting. "What? Why not? Okay, so I know I can't promise to have control over my limbs when I'm sleeping, but you can always kick me back. I don't mind." He couldn't be seriously telling me no. My heart rate started to increase, anxiety creeping up over the back of my neck.

"I don't care if you kick me, it's not that." Bill sighed. "Look, Jess, we both know it's no secret I like you, and you've been totally straight up with me about not returning the sentiment, and I appreciate that. Maybe it's insane of me to say no, because sometimes I do manage to talk you into hooking up when you take pity on me, but I can't share a bed with you every night for a week and not feel like shit about it. I just can't."

My jaw dropped and I felt a hot flood of shame in my mouth, which made me angry. I hadn't done anything to feel bad about, despite what my dad's opinion about it would have been. "You make it sound so sketch. We're friends. We've hooked up when we both felt like it, not because I was desperate and you were my only option, or because I felt sorry for you. I'm not that nice of a person that I'll blow you out of pity. I just like you as a friend and I think you're cute. We have fun. Apparently, I was totally wrong in thinking you felt the same way."

"I do feel the same way," he insisted. "The problem is, I feel more than that, and I'm just not into torturing myself.

I want you to be my 'girlfriend.'" He made air quotes. "Pathetic, I know."

The thought of being anyone's girlfriend made me want to throw up in my mouth a little. There was no way I wanted to give a guy that much control over my emotions and my time. I had finally gotten away from that for the first time in my life.

"I'm sorry. It's not pathetic, it's just . . ."

"It's you, not me." He rolled his eyes. "I know. You can save the let-him-down-gently speech for another dude, I get it."

I had to admit, that was kind of a relief. "This is awkward," I told him.

"Probably more for me than for you," he said with a nervous laugh. "Look, you can stay on the couch."

"Except now it will be weird." It already was.

"No, it won't. I won't be needy or anything. I just need to have some self-preservation."

"Okay, I understand." I did. But it made it different. I couldn't casually touch him anymore. I couldn't flirt without feeling like I was leading him on, and I would have to be careful around him. I fought the urge to sigh. Why did everything have to be so complicated between guys and girls? Curse hormones. "Good luck on your final."

"Thanks." He gave me a smile, then he returned his attention to his book.

I left, feeling deflated and oddly sad knowing Bill and I couldn't quite be friends in the same way we had been. But then again, maybe we'd never really been just friends, because I had always known he liked me. And why did that suddenly make me feel so guilty?

"That was fast," Riley said the second I came into the living room, his feet up on the coffee table, expression bored. "I guess that's why they call it a quickie."

"Shut up," I said with more vehemence than I intended. I was feeling bad and I couldn't precisely figure out why

Bill's rejection had bothered me so much. I didn't need Riley judging me.

"What's wrong?" Rory asked, peeling herself off Tyler's chest where she was splayed like plastic wrap.

"I just don't have anywhere to stay for the next couple of weeks, that's all." I didn't want to say in front of Riley that Bill had turned me down. It would be like handing him the material for a ten-minute stand-up routine at my expense. No, thanks.

"You can stay here," Nathan said.

"Thanks, but I don't think that's going to work."

"Why not?" Kylie asked.

I shot her a look, hoping she'd get the hint.

"Did you and the nerd have a fight?" Riley asked. "Is he not putting out enough for you?"

It really wasn't fair that such a beautiful face was on such an asshole of a guy. Riley was a little shorter than Tyler, just as muscular, but whereas Tyler had a certain hardness to his face, Riley had been gifted with adorable dimples and large eyes. It was almost tragic he was such a jerk-off. I ignored him, but it wasn't easy, because he seemed to take great pleasure in pissing me off. I really wanted to throw something at him. Like my fist. Right into his cocky face.

"You can stay at my house," Tyler offered. "The boys and I are going to Rory's dad's for a week, remember, so you'd have a bed to sleep on."

There was a thought, though it was an intimidating one. "Is it safe?" I asked, before I thought about how rude that actually sounded. Tyler and Riley lived with their two younger brothers in a lower-income neighborhood in a house the bank was in the process of foreclosing on since their mother had died. Riley had lived in a basement before that, but once his mom had overdosed, he had moved back in. I'd never been there, but I was picturing a crime-infested neighborhood with drive-by shootings and prostitutes on every corner. My parents lived in a mini-mansion in a small town, so I didn't exactly have street cred. My experience with poverty was limited to movies and episodes of *COPS* on my laptop. It was like a bear walking through the desert, I had no previous exposure.

"I mean, won't the neighbors think I'm breaking and entering?" I added, as a very lame cover to my initial question.

"Princess, I don't think anyone is going to think you've broken into our shithole and are squatting," Riley said, rolling his eyes. "If anything, they'll just think you've come over to score drugs."

"Rory stays with me all the time," Tyler added. "No one will even notice. People keep to themselves in our neighborhood."

"I never feel unsafe there," Rory said. "But then again, I'm never sleeping there alone. Tyler is always with me."

"I've never lived alone," I said. Even for a week, the thought had a certain appeal. No one's opinion but my own. No rules. No guilt. No feeling bad that I could never live up to anyone's expectations. It sounded awesome, and scary. I wanted to try it, just to see what it would be like. "That sounds great, Ty, thanks for offering."

"Have both of you forgotten something?" Riley asked, picking up his beer.

"What?" I said, wary. I just knew I wasn't going to like whatever he was going to say.

"I'm not going to Rory's dad's to swim for a week like a kid at summer camp. I'll be here, working. Living in my house."

Oh, God. I couldn't help it. I made a face.

The corner of Riley's mouth turned up. "That's exactly how I feel about it, Princess."

"I think it will be good for you guys," Kylie said, an eternal optimist. Or suffering from massive delusions. "You can become better friends this way."

"Maybe we don't want to become friends," Riley told her. "Maybe we like not liking each other."

I almost laughed. There was a certain truth to that. I basically felt like I'd seen all I needed to see to know I didn't need to see more. But if I said that, Kylie's head would explode. She was a very honest and kind person, and she didn't always get my point of view. Or anything involving math.

"How much will you even see each other? You both work and it has three bedrooms," Tyler said. "It seems stupid to sleep on a floor somewhere when there's plenty of room at the house."

"It's up to Riley," I said, because that only seemed fair. It was his house. "Maybe he wants some alone time with all of you gone."

I didn't mean that to sound quite as weird as it did.

He laughed. "Does that come right after Me Time and Circle Time?" He stood up and moved further into my space than was strictly appropriate.

It was a game of chicken and I lost by instantly backing up. Damn it. He smirked in triumph.

"I'll be fine. I can handle it if you can."

I was playing right into him and I knew it, but I couldn't stop myself. "Of course I can handle it. What's there to handle?"

He stared at me, his eyebrows raised, a challenge in his deep brown eyes. The stubble on his chin was visible and I could smell the subtle scent of soap and a splash of cologne. He looked and smelled very, very masculine, and I was suddenly aware of my body in a way that made me seriously annoyed.

"Bring some beer."

"I'm not twenty-one." Not that it had ever stopped me from drinking, but I wasn't going to give Riley anything I didn't have to. I did not want to feel like I owed him. It was Tyler who had made the offer of a place to crash, so if anyone deserved thanks, it was him, not his arrogant brother.

For a second, Riley's eyes roamed over my chest, like he could gauge my age by my boobs. Such a tool.

But then he just said, "You can borrow my ID."

And I couldn't help it. I laughed. "Because we're practically twins."

He nodded. "Though I am *slightly* better-looking."

I snorted. "I have better hair."

"I can drink more whiskey than you."

"I'm smarter."

"I'm stronger. We should mud wrestle so I can prove it."

I bit my lip so I wouldn't throw a scathing response back at him, or worse, laugh. He didn't deserve the attention, or knowing he'd gotten under my skin, which was what he wanted.

But for a split second I wondered if I should sleep on Nathan and Bill's couch after all. Because Riley seemed to be the one person who could get an emotional response out of me, even if it was just anger.

And emotion was dangerous.

It led to being trapped, like my mother, in the pretty prison of my father's house.

I was never going to let that happen.

"I call dibs on the bathroom for the mornings," I told Riley.

Then to let him know that he did not intimidate me, and that I was always in control, I turned and walked away.

She's holding tight. He's hanging loose.
And they both have the same drive.

FROM *USA TODAY* BESTSELLING AUTHOR
ERIN McCARTHY

JACKED UP
A FAST TRACK NOVEL

———

Eve Monroe is a stock-car PR pro who puts her career first—until
an on-track wardrobe malfunction reveals more than the sexy smile
of jackman Nolan Ford. The video's become an Internet sensation,
and it's Eve's job to calm the sponsors and put a spin on the unexpected exposure.

It may be a public relations job, but now that Eve's seen what's
under Nolan's crew suit, it's gotten personal. After a few dates,
she has Nolan pretty revved up. Nolan's sure that the spontaneous
birthday bash he's throwing for Eve in Las Vegas should loosen her
up. Somewhere between cocktails and a smoking-hot motel-room
derby, it does more than that...

PRAISE FOR THE FAST TRACK NOVELS

"The sexiest series I've ever read."

—Carly Phillips, *New York Times* bestselling author

"A wild ride...buckle up, ladies."

—*Romance Reviews Today*

erinmccarthy.net
facebook.com/ErinMcCarthyBooks
facebook.com/LoveAlwaysBooks
penguin.com

M1347T0713

HOT FINISH

"Sizzling hot, jam-packed with snappy dialogue, emotional intensity, and racing fun."
—Carly Phillips, *New York Times* bestselling author

"Hot and steamy." —*Smexy Books*

HARD AND FAST

"Hit me like a ton of bricks and didn't let up until I finished the last word." —*Romance Junkies*

"This book had my heart racing." —*A Romance Review*

FLAT-OUT SEXY

"Readers won't be able to resist McCarthy's sweetly sexy and sentimental tale of true love at the track." —*Booklist*

"A steamy romance . . . Fast-paced and red-hot."
—*Publishers Weekly*

PRAISE FOR ERIN MCCARTHY'S
OTHER NOVELS
HEIRESS FOR HIRE

"*Heiress for Hire* is a must-read." —*Romance Junkies*

"Characters you will care about, a story that will make you laugh and cry, and a book you won't soon forget."
—*The Romance Reader* (5 hearts)

"An alluring tale." —*A Romance Review* (5 roses)

"An enjoyable story about finding love in unexpected places, don't miss *Heiress for Hire*."
—*Romance Reviews Today*

"Priceless!" —*RT Book Reviews* (4½ stars, Top Pick)

continued . . .